Inferno's Shadow

THE ARTILLERYMEN SERIES

Purgatory's Shore
Hell's March
Devil's Battle
Inferno's Shadow

THE DESTROYERMEN SERIES

Into the Storm
Crusade
Maelstrom
Distant Thunders
Rising Tides
Firestorm
Iron Gray Sea
Storm Surge
Deadly Shores
Straits of Hell
Blood in the Water
Devil's Due
River of Bones
Pass of Fire
Winds of Wrath

INFERNO'S SHADOW

TAYLOR ANDERSON

ACE
NEW YORK

ACE
Published by Berkley
An imprint of Penguin Random House LLC
1745 Broadway, New York, NY 10019
penguinrandomhouse.com

Copyright © 2025 by Taylor Anderson

Penguin Random House values and supports copyright. Copyright fuels creativity, encourages diverse voices, promotes free speech, and creates a vibrant culture. Thank you for buying an authorized edition of this book and for complying with copyright laws by not reproducing, scanning, or distributing any part of it in any form without permission. You are supporting writers and allowing Penguin Random House to continue to publish books for every reader. Please note that no part of this book may be used or reproduced in any manner for the purpose of training artificial intelligence technologies or systems.

ACE is a registered trademark and the A colophon is a trademark of Penguin Random House LLC.

Book design by Daniel Brount
Interior art: Smoke background © swp23/Shutterstock.com

Library of Congress Cataloging-in-Publication Data
Names: Anderson, Taylor, 1963– author.
Title: Inferno's shadow / Taylor Anderson.
Description: New York: Ace, 2025. | Series: The artillerymen series
Identifiers: LCCN 2024045833 (print) | LCCN 2024045834 (ebook) |
ISBN 9780593641576 (hardcover) | ISBN 9780593641590 (ebook)
Subjects: LCGFT: Novels.
Classification: LCC PS3601.N5475 I48 2025 (print) |
LCC PS3601.N5475 (ebook) | DDC 813/.6—dc23/eng/20241004
LC record available at https://lccn.loc.gov/2024045833
LC ebook record available at https://lccn.loc.gov/2024045834

Printed in the United States of America
1st Printing

The authorized representative in the EU for product safety and compliance is
Penguin Random House Ireland, Morrison Chambers, 32 Nassau Street,
Dublin D02 YH68, Ireland, https://eu-contact.penguin.ie.

To Silvia

US M1841 6pdr Gun

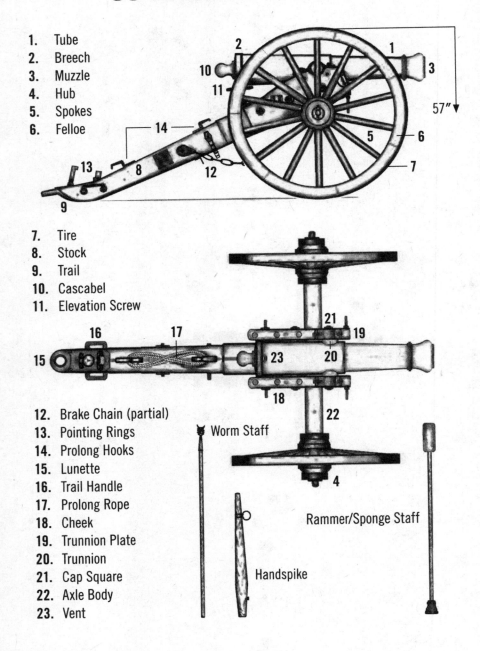

1. Tube
2. Breech
3. Muzzle
4. Hub
5. Spokes
6. Felloe
7. Tire
8. Stock
9. Trail
10. Cascabel
11. Elevation Screw
12. Brake Chain (partial)
13. Pointing Rings
14. Prolong Hooks
15. Lunette
16. Trail Handle
17. Prolong Rope
18. Cheek
19. Trunnion Plate
20. Trunnion
21. Cap Square
22. Axle Body
23. Vent

THE YUCATÁN, HOLY DOMINION, AND BEYOND

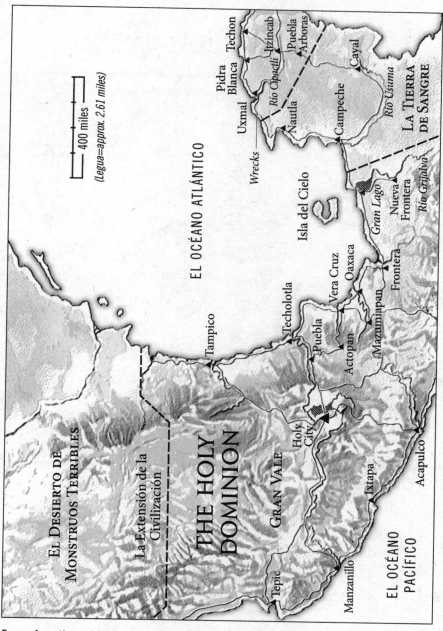

Drawn from the embroidered atlas in Uxmal. Important roads including the coastal "Camino Militar" are depicted, as far as their extent is known. Larger cities are symbolized thus: ▲

THE VALLEY CAMPAIGN

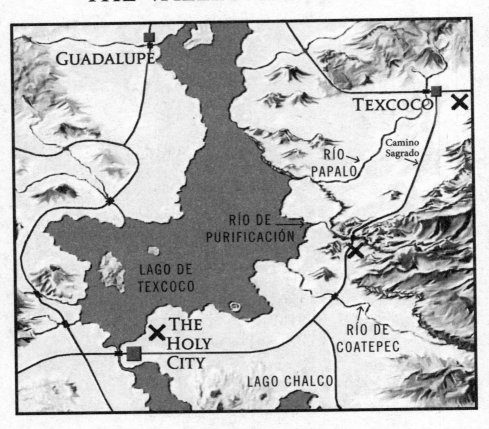

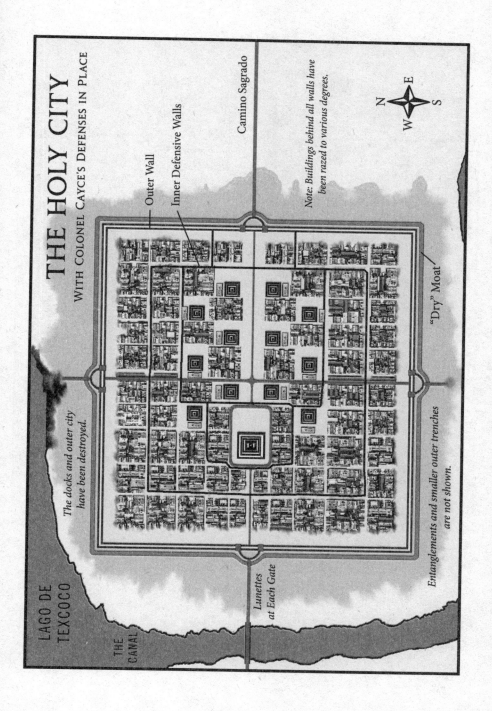

Still reeling from the traumatic "passage" from their Earth to this . . . very different one, the people we first referred to as "1847 Americans" (due to the year they arrived, since we knew little more about them) were even less prepared to comprehend their circumstances than we were when the decrepit US Asiatic Fleet destroyer USS Walker *was essentially chased to this world by the marauding Japanese in 1942. Still, in surprisingly short order, Lewis Cayce (formerly of the 3rd US Artillery) consolidated all the surviving artillerymen, infantrymen, dragoons, Mounted Rifles, and a handful of Texas Rangers—even a few Mexicans who'd been unluckily nearby onshore—from three appalling shipwrecks.*

Regardless of their confusion, the terrifying lethality of this world quickly convinced Cayce that they must all work together or die. Particularly after he discovered that the savage, unimaginable beasts all around them were the least of their concerns . . . and the savage Holcano Indians, their few but shockingly Grik-like allies, and of course, the vile, blood-drenched "Holy Dominion" became a constant, looming menace.

In less than a year, Lewis Cayce and his capable companions had united various city-states on the oddly shaped Yucatán Peninsula against the . . . Dominion and its Holcano proxies, built and trained an army, and repulsed a . . . "Dom" army at the "Battle of the Washboard." It was a stunning victory that convinced the locals they had a chance to live free from fear of the most significant, diabolical power known to dwell in the "Americas" of this world.

But Lewis Cayce knew that wasn't the case. The Dominion was obsessed with conquest (and blood sacrifice) and would never allow "his" new people to live in peace. Any example of successful defiance would erode Dominion tyranny over its own people and had to be exterminated. Moreover, a purely defensive stance was ultimately doomed to failure. The Dominion had to be beaten, and the only way to do that was to attack.

A bold campaign finally defeated the feared Holcanos, who . . . actually joined the Allied effort. A series of small battles against Dominion Blood Priests began to illustrate just how savage this war would be, and a final titanic battle against the already disillusioned Dominion army in the region under the command of General Agon not only opened the way to the heart of the Dominion, but earned the Army of the Yucatán even more unlikely allies.

As Lewis Cayce prepared his force for an unprecedented (in American military history) advance, rumors of a mysterious place far to the south called "El Paso del Fuego" began to arise, as did nagging concerns about just how secure the Allied rear would remain. . . . [Regardless], Lewis Cayce and his scratch-built army . . . churn[ed] up across half a continent to the virtual gates of the Holy City. Of course there had been mistakes, aching growing pains, but those had been impossible to avoid given the necessary haste of the campaign. It's a wonder he built such a competent force given the meager time and resources he had. And there was every reason to believe that victory was in his grasp in spite of the sudden and unexpected enemy presence in the Yucatán. But when gods use men to settle disputes and all the devils do battle, calamity always seems to chase triumph in Inferno's shadow. . . .

Some few historians in the NUS are still prone to criticize Lewis Cayce for his decision to press forward with his campaign against the rotten, wicked core of the Dominion in spite of the threat looming at home. Spoiled by the luxurious wonders of radio and fast steamships in our modern world, along with the omniscient gift of hindsight, they could even be right to do so. . . . [But given the distance,] the state of communications and the time it would take to cope with the threat . . . Cayce did the only thing he could. History may be written by the victors, the survivors at least, but it is then warped out of all recognition by their "intellectual" descendants, safe with their pipes in overstuffed chairs, intent on amassing fame for themselves at the expense of those who have earned it. . . .

Besides, Lewis had a plan. Numerous plans, in fact, not all of which were known or quickly guessed by his closest confidants. Nor might they all have approved if he openly discussed them.

Excerpt from the foreword to Courtney Bradford's
Lands and Peoples—Destiny of the Damned, Vol. I,
Library of Alex-aandra Press, 1959

Inferno's Shadow

PROLOGUE

Resplendent in his brilliant yellow coat with real gold embroidery on black velvet facings, cuffs, and collar, General Xacolotl would've stood out among any collection of subjects of the Holy Dominion, but he was also considerably taller. The correspondingly oversize coal-black stallion with only the slightest hint of native blood that he sat upon raised the peak of his elaborately decorated black tricorn hat more than a head above the tallest members of his gathered staff. All but a few of the unreasonably arrogant Blood Priests attending his supposed chief advisor and the newly appointed "Patriarcha de la Guerra," Don Thiago de Feliz Río, were also on horseback atop the rocky outcrop overlooking the Camino de los Californias, some distance below. None were gazing at the road, however, or the seemingly endless military encampment sprawling from near the base of the bluff they occupied, across a wide plain, and down to the Pacific seashore more than half a *legua* away. It was even longer than it was wide, and Xacolotl reckoned his army's camp occupied sufficient space to rival that within the walls of the Holy City itself, down in the Great Valley of Mexico.

At the moment, however, he and the rest were watching a colorful but otherwise hideous (in his view) messenger dragon vigorously flapping its wings to power its way off the ground near his command section at the center of camp. Slowly at first, then rapidly quickening, it spiraled up into the orange-tinted evening sky, brass rings and harness buckles securing the heavy leather message tube twinkling in the setting sun. The creature had no rider, of course. Even if it would tolerate one without eating him, it was much too small; barely larger than a man itself. Bigger dragons of all shapes and sizes were ubiquitous on this world, and a few of the purely terrestrial variety had even been domesticated to a degree. As far as Xacolotl knew, no one had ever been foolish enough to try to tame the larger flying sort. The smaller ones were hard enough to work with; vicious and capricious, always hungry and cunningly waiting for a chance to eat their handlers, they were otherwise far too stupid (or simply uncooperative) to learn the most basic verbal instructions. They apparently relied entirely on an uncanny memory for places they'd been and flew there based on colored pennants they were shown that somehow corresponded to their destination in their minds. Their motivation was simplicity itself. Once they arrived where they were supposed to go, they'd be fed to repletion.

Useful beasts, Xacolotl conceded, *though certainly unpleasant to associate with.* He snorted. Not that he, the overall commander of the Gran Cruzada, the greatest host ever assembled on this world, personally dealt with them. That was the job of the Dragon Monks, and just as well. He was afraid of no man, but dragons weren't men, were they? More properly demons, he suspected, disliking the very notion of the vicious-looking things swooping down, unannounced, in among his troops. It wasn't unknown for them to begin their arrival feast early, on those who couldn't get out of the way quick enough. If they weren't in the process of revolutionizing long-range communications, he'd never have allowed their presence or use.

Lowering his gaze from the diminishing, flying shape, he turned slightly right and took note of the flock of supply ships anchored offshore in the distance, a forest of masts silhouetted against the setting sun. Small boat traffic between the ships and beach was practically constant. Even so, supplies from home were only barely sufficient to provide for his massive army. Foraging was almost pointless here because there were no settlements or crops, and hunting parties sent to kill meat often wound up eaten themselves, by the terrifying beasts they pursued or couldn't avoid. He frowned before turning again to regard the huge force. It should've been hundreds of miles to the northwest by now, less than a month from its long-planned objective to expel heretical squatters subject to the Empire of the New Britain Isles from the almost-mythical Californias. (It remained remarkably mysterious because so few explorers from the Holy Dominion had ever been there, much less returned.) It was Dominion territory regardless, having been claimed as such for more than fifty years, and the Imperiales who'd established a colony there had to be powerfully chastised.

The commencement of the Gran Cruzada hadn't gone unnoticed by the empire, of course, and triggered a rather significant naval war off the Pacific coast. The tiny, distant, island-based empire could never compete with the Gran Cruzada on land, and its mainland colony certainly had no chance, but its navy was unquestionably better than the Dominion's and had been making a serious pest of itself, preying upon those precious supply ships in particular. Just stockpiling enough provisions for General Xacolotl's titanic force to proceed beyond the Dominion frontier in the first place had caused considerable delays. In addition, even before the recent... irregularities in the Holy City, including the passing of the former Supreme Holiness, the elevation of another (out of time-honored order), and the rise of the long-suppressed Blood Priests, there'd been warnings and rumblings that at least a portion of the Gran Cruzada might be diverted to deal with *another* heretical threat from the Yucatán.

Most had considered such rumors absurd. The Yucatán had remained an untamed haven for dissidents adhering to an older version of the True Faith, from before their ancestors came to this land aboard a Manila/Acapulco galleon and joined their culture to that of the vastly more numerous natives—themselves descendants of earlier, probably Mayan pilgrims. Their different beliefs had initially resulted in obligatory warfare, and the bloodletting was starkly one-sided in favor of those from the Spanish ship due to superior weapons and tactics. Native numbers were inexhaustible, however, and a stalemate ensued that no one would ever win—until visionary priests from both sides recognized that the near-identical nature of both groups' arrival—at sea in a storm, albeit centuries apart—could only have been arranged by God. The priests, perhaps in good faith or ever jealous of their own power and influence, took it upon themselves to "recognize" truths withheld from their respective cultures in that of their enemy. Why else would God bring them together? Thus was peace achieved and various forms and ceremonies unique to each faith gradually combined—along with a missionary fervor to convert the world to its adherence. Obviously, not everyone was happy with this, the Yucatános being one such group. But they were isolated and constantly under threat by debased descendants of other, even older faiths. Xacolotl could imagine no threat originating from that flat, impassably wooded, seabound peninsula.

Again, until recently, only whispered rumors had existed of yet another arrival from that "old world," one that brought soldiers with better weapons and tactics yet again. Much better tactics, apparently, and those soldiers had somehow raised a professional army in the Yucatán, destroyed a Dominion force sent to smash them, and now threatened the Great Valley itself! Hundreds of *leguas* away, the Gran Cruzada's march toward the Californias had been halted.

For months, the army had languished in the heart of the Desierto de los Monstruous Terribles with virtually no instructions but to "hold in place." It wasn't really a "desert" in the sense that usually comes to mind, the only sand being on the beach along the Pacific shore the army followed, always in sight of its shadowing flotillas of supply ships (and occasional damaging sea fights with marauding Imperial vessels). The term "desert" had likely been applied to the region more out of ignorance of its character or to discourage explorers. Xacolotl had decided it was really a rather pleasant land, at least as much as he'd seen, hilly and lush, with grass and forests, with glimpses of great mountains to the east. The strangest thing was that the water off the western coast, bound by the hazy presence of land far across it, was full of hazardous reefs composed entirely of the skeletons of momentous leviathans.

The creatures were sometimes called "Island Fish," or "Mountain Fish" because they were so immense. Enormous sun-bleached bones, cracked and chalky, were often visible jutting from the water near shore. Warship or supply ship captains knowledgeable about these waters and sometimes consulted by General Xacolotl said the bay—referred to as the "Sea of Bones" for obvious reasons—was very dangerous indeed. It was fabulously rich in fish, but few ventured in to seek them because legend had it that in all the world, this was where the great leviathans came to die. Though lethargic, the huge beasts were known to be even more irritable than usual at this somber time, and their corpses attracted other outrageously large and aggressive scavenging predators.

Though not a sandy desert, "*monstruous*" were certainly present on land and in larger concentrations than Xacolotl had ever seen. He hailed from Acapulco, far to the south, the most settled coastal city in the Dominion, but prided himself on his knowledge of dangerous fauna. As a soldier, he had to know how to defend against them. Few of the species they'd encountered on their trek beyond the last Dominion settlements were known to him, and many were far more dangerous, in unexpected ways, than he would've imagined. The planners of the Gran Cruzada had thought ahead in that respect; one of the reasons his army was so big was that they'd expected many more losses to monsters than the enemy.

In any event, the long delay in place had been harder on his army than combat. Soldiers will eventually grow bored, even with monsters all about, and the constant efforts to keep them occupied (and off impaling poles) were driving junior officers and NCOs to distraction. Just as bad, despite constant drilling and some truly imaginative punishments, the army had begun to lose its hard, sharp edge. Worst of all, perhaps, Patriarcha Don Thiago de Feliz Río had conjured the authority, straight from the Holy City, to skim off several significant detachments of troops and send them off by ship, refusing to say where they went. It seemed that was one of his new privileges. An increasingly frustrated General Xacolotl was curious how "privileged" the *patriarcha* would feel if he retired to his coastal villa and left Don Thiago to command the whole army, but he just couldn't do it. He frankly wasn't sure he'd be allowed.

The point was, he no longer really cared where the army went or who it was told to fight as long as it finally marched *somewhere*. Judging by the message the dragon brought, firmly refolded in his hand, he'd get his wish. The Gran Cruzada would never reach the fabled Californias after all and things must be serious indeed for a campaign over a decade in the making to be abandoned. It could take a generation to prepare it again.

Lost in contemplation, he felt someone tugging at the message and jerked it away before looking to the culprit. Don Thiago, beefy red visage covered by dark chin whiskers and mustache, eyes peering out from under the hood of the bloodred robe of his order, flashing with annoyance. "I have as much authority to see that as you," he snapped.

"I still rather doubt that, Don Thiago," Xacolotl replied evenly. The man he still saw as a jumped-up Blood Priest frowned dramatically.

"I can't remember how many times I've politely asked you to address me as 'Your Holiness.'"

"And I can't remember how many times I've refused," Xacolotl mildly replied. "That's the proper mode of address for Blood *Cardinals* only, as far as I know. On the other hand, I have sworn to support the new Supreme Holiness and have obeyed every command I've received from him." He arched a brow at Don Thiago. "I have even stood by and allowed you and your order extravagant latitude in regard to the authority you claim for yourself because I've been made aware that the head of your order, the Holy Patriarcha Tranquilo, wills it so." His expression turned dubious. "He enjoys the confidence of your chief benefactor, the Blood Cardinal Don Frutos, and His Supreme Holiness Himself." He paused. "The *particulars* of that authority, including what I should call you, have *not* been communicated to me, nor have you shared any of the numerous communications the messenger dragons have brought to *you*."

Aware he might one day regret overt rudeness to the touchy Don Thiago, he finally relented and offered the folded page. "As it happens, you may certainly read this one if you like, since I called you all here to tell you what it says. It's direct from His Supreme Holiness's spokesman and designated successor, the Primer Patriarcha Sachihiro. He confirms Tranquilo's order that the Gran Cruzada is to turn around and march for the Holy City at once." His tone had taken on an edge of disbelief, and there was murmuring among the staff. "It's true," he assured the men around him. "I fear that this . . . dubious threat from the Yucatán was not as insignificant as we were so . . . understandably sure. There's little new information concerning its composition, but it is now certain that it supports the pretender, the Blood Cardinal Don Hurac. Moreover, its commander is an imaginative and remarkably aggressive man named 'Lewis Cayce' who has *twice* defeated General Agon's Eastern Army of God, taken Gran Lago, Frontera, and Vera Cruz . . ." He paused. "Even Puebla is under threat, it seems. General Gomez has marched his Western Army of God to the Holy City and prepares to meet Cayce in battle short of Texcoco, but . . ." He sighed. "Gomez has a good reputation, and I know him well. He's competent and well prepared to face an enemy with similar training to his own—but so was General Agon, and *he* was always more imaginative and flexible. In all honesty, I must confess concern that General Gomez would find it difficult to fight his way out of an unfamiliarly and inventively constructed spiderweb." He shrugged. "If he's defeated, that will leave only us."

"But . . . what of the Imperiales?" demanded General Iforna, one of Xacolotl's senior commanders. "The only thing keeping them off our transports now is the Sea of Bones, but they savage our shipping coming and going. How will we be supplied? At least until we reach our own frontier again. And we had already exhausted the surplus of every settlement in the region as it was."

Xacolotl nodded at Don Thiago. "Actually, it would seem"—he raised the folded page that Thiago had resisted taking—"and is corroborated here, that a *truce* has been arranged with the Imperial heretics. As long as we no longer threaten their pitiful presence in the Californias, they'll stop attacking our ships. That they're willing to allow us to sort out our other . . . inconvenience is proof to me that they had no hand in instigating or supporting it. Rather shortsighted of them, in my opinion, especially since we'd have to abandon the Cruzada in any event, but I shall not complain." He looked rather bleakly at General Iforna. "As to the inhabitants of the frontier settlements, indeed anyplace the army must pass through on its way to the Holy City . . ." He took a long breath and slowly exhaled. "They'll not be troubled by our requisitioning all the supplies we need. You see"—he waved the folded page again—"some might infer that our return after so short a time might constitute a retreat. Others might imagine, correctly, that we go to meet another threat. Neither supposition is acceptable to His Supreme Holiness."

"What he means is that we may take what we want," Don Thiago said. "Those who possess it must be treated the same as anyone who has witnessed the result of opposition to Dominion rule, and they will not need it anymore."

"You're telling us . . ." Iforna began, but Xacolotl cut him off, tone uncompromising. "Yes. According to the Holy Patriarcha Tranquilo, they must be cleansed by Don Thiago's Blood Priests."

"That's . . . abominable," Iforna spat.

"But necessary," Don Thiago flared back.

"What of the army, then?" Iforna persisted. "The whole army will know we've been redirected to confront a threat to the Dominion even more urgent than the empire! Will we 'cleanse' it as well? Will you cleanse *us*?"

Don Thiago narrowed his eyes. "Have a care, General. No one is so pure—or necessary—that they could not benefit from a little cleansing. As for this great army, however, it has been created and sanctified to be God's sword of cleansing and retribution. Its duty and purpose is to do His will and destroy any who oppose Him. A . . . percentage of it will naturally accumulate much grace through suffering, and those who survive will have accomplished the task God gave them. Victory will assure the survivors an opportunity to earn more grace in the course of long lives." He hesitated, considering. "As to the people we meet, farmers in the region, villagers and townsfolk, I propose to conscript or enslave all we can feed. We'll give them the *opportunity* to cleanse their souls in service to God. The rest... the very young or old and infirm who can contribute nothing, it becomes our duty to help them accumulate the purifying grace of pain. And sadly, there will be others, those who will attempt to avoid our benevolence and flee to tell others what they saw, God's sword resheathed and redirected by necessity and not His will alone." He took a long breath of his own and peered intently at General Iforna, then gazed meaningfully around at the others. "That's the purpose of my order: to bring grace to those who won't accept it or cannot earn it themselves. Pray you earn your own in the months to come."

Even Xacolotl was chilled by that statement. The Blood Priests already took a tithe of men from his army for their sacrifices. Most had previously been slaves or excess daughters, gathered from surrounding settlements, but as the army left those behind, more and more support personnel went under their obsidian blades. Lately, they started using his troops, those guilty of grievous infractions at first, but there'd been a few whose misbehavior would normally be cured by a whipping with an NCO's vine staff. He'd objected, but as jealously as he guarded his military authority, the Blood Priests were equally adamant about their mandate when it came to matters of faith. He had no recourse. Ironically, though, as distasteful as he found the behavior of Blood Priests, even their very presence in his army, they did provide a strong inducement to unquestioning discipline. And just as he dreaded their "cleansing" of settlements they'd pass as the army marched back to the Holy City, perhaps they'd leave his soldiers alone for a time.

Gaining General Iforna's simmering attention, General Xacolotl asked, "How soon can the army move?"

Reverting to the contemplation of his profession, Iforna took on a thoughtful expression. "Most of the lancers and ready cohorts can march almost at once. As soon as they strike their tents, in fact." Each tenthousand-man division, called "legions" for the purposes of the Cruzada, contributed a cohort, called "regiments" of two to three thousand men in other armies, to a force that was theoretically always ready for anything.

"The rest will take longer, no doubt, having been encamped in one place for so long."

Xacolotl grimaced but nodded. "Very well. The ready cohorts will march tonight, with plenty of lancers leading the way." Night marches, particularly here, were vulnerable to nocturnal predators and could be exceptionally hazardous. "The rest of the army will follow as it makes ready, but I want every man, animal, gun, and vehicle of any sort on the road within two days. Anyone not ready by then will answer to Don Thiago's Blood Priests," he mercilessly added.

"It will be as you say, General," Iforna stated confidently. "Is that all, sir?"

Xacolotl shook his head, then glanced at the message once more before replying. "No, actually. One other thing was mentioned. The Blood Cardinal Don Frutos will be joining us somewhere along the march, escorted by a large mounted force of what are referred to as 'Reaper Monks.'" He looked questioningly at Don Thiago.

"A newly established force within the order of the Blood Priests," he explained. "Lancers are all very well in set piece battles, but the enemy employs mounted warriors that they call 'Rangers and dragoons,' who are more versatile and better equipped for scouting and harassing attacks. Though it wasn't intended at first—Reapers were originally meant only to serve as security for Blood Priests in remote postings—our newest ones have been raised and trained to counter such irregular threats. I think you'll find them quite useful, General Xacolotl. Obviously, as I'm sure you were about to mention, your scouts will want to be on the lookout for them."

"Obviously," Xacolotl agreed wryly, though the idea of the Blood Priests possessing their own militant arm was enough to give him gooseflesh. "That's what I was about to tell our men." He looked around, gaze now lingering on Don Thiago. "That, and the order of the Supreme Holiness that when Don Frutos does arrive, he's to be treated with the utmost respect due his position, but not allowed to command any force larger than his personal entourage. Apparently, it was his authority over General Agon that cost our forces a victory in their first encounter with our new opponent."

He pursed his lips, looking at the surrounding officers. "Whatever you may have thought or been told, the Empire of the New Britain Isles would never have presented a serious challenge to the Gran Cruzada in the Californias. It was expected they'd harry our supplies as we advanced—which they've done—but I find it more than likely sure that their colonies would've been abandoned before we ever got there. We would have experienced hardships, perhaps even significant losses due to interruptions of our supplies and natural threats along the way, but no Impie army of any size would've been waiting for us. This great host was assembled primarily to show we could do it, and we were willing to go to profound extremes to expel any nuisance to our land and faith."

He paused but continued. "Now, it seems, we shall face a true threat. An actual challenge. Condemn him if you will, but I knew General Agon. Not well, I admit. We moved in different circles. But to be entirely honest, he might've been the best of us. The best living general in the Holy Dominion. Regardless of Don Frutos's interference, for Agon to be beaten—and even I have heard the rumors that he has since joined our enemies—this... Lewis Cayce who leads them is a *most* serious threat indeed. Both in terms of his capability and his powers of persuasion." His eyes had continued scanning his staff as he spoke, but now returned to Don Thiago. "Trust me when I say this army will be *drenched* in 'grace' before this is decided."

Sitting up straighter in his saddle, General Xacolotl jerked a nod and then turned to look at the enormous force at his disposal. It was essentially sleeping now, but would soon uncoil and embark upon the real purpose, he was suddenly sure, for which God had caused its creation. "Return to your duties, prepare your men to move, and see that everyone understands what's expected of them. As to why we'll suddenly change our direction and objective..." He hesitated. "All they need to know is that the Imperials have been eliminated as a threat and we now answer His Supreme Holiness's call to duty elsewhere. No other explanation should be required. Carry on, gentlemen. That is all."

CHAPTER 1

DECEMBER 16, 1848
THE BATTLE OF TEXCOCO

"Hurry up, god damn ye. The bastards're strung out in column, an' if we get there quick enough, we'll catch 'em in the latrine with their breeches 'round their ankles!" rumbled Sergeant Major James McNabb, inexpertly urging his striped native horse past the mud-mired 6pdr guns of A Battery, now better known as "Barca's battery," struggling to obey the summons calling it to the front. "Sir," McNabb belatedly but sincerely amended, adding a hasty salute when he found his path blocked by an equally frustrated young officer. McNabb wasn't tall, built more like a rock-hard oaken barrel, reddish hair and side whiskers making a flyaway mane framing a cold-pinkened face between a faded blue wheel hat and high, red-trimmed collar. The dark blue of his shell jacket was faded as well, but the saber belt encircling his belly was as white as the snow atop the surrounding mountains, his brass beltplate and jacket buttons as bright as gold in the early morning sunlight.

The mounted officer couldn't have looked more different. He was whip-thin, ramrod straight in the saddle, and his dark blue frock coat showed less wear. The short but already curling side whiskers he'd begun to cultivate for fashion's sake were a glossy midnight black around a somewhat angular face just a few shades lighter than his hair. The rarest of men on this world of exotic people and beasts—even more so on the world he came from—he wasn't only a former slave, but now a respected artillery officer wearing the shoulder boards of a captain.

Returning the salute, Captain Barca simply said, "I'll thank you to stop berating my men. They're doing their best, as you can see." He gestured to encompass the mud-smeared men on the ground, heaving on the slippery spokes of the guns, pushing on axles, straining on horse harness. Even the men who usually rode atop the limbers, to which each gun and a half-dozen horses were hitched, had jumped down to help the rest of the crew. He noted without surprise the newly promoted Lieutenant Hannibal "Hanny" Cox right down there with his section, just as filthy, expression as indignant as the one Barca hid. Hanny had proven his courage many times, but no new lieutenant would answer back to a force of nature like McNabb. Hanny might officially outrank the sergeant major, but any superiority was somewhat . . . theoretical. Besides, Barca knew the two shared a history. McNabb had once been there for Hanny when few others would've dared.

"Apologies, Cap'n Barca. I know the damned mud is bad. So does Major Olayne." What made it particularly mucky was slow-melting snow that soaked the ground deep. "But the buggers nearly caught us with *our* britches down an' the major sent me tae hurry things on." Major Justinian Olayne was the army's chief of artillery. McNabb nodded at the infantry crowding the hard road, flowing by at double time. "Use some o' them tae help."

"I would without thinking, I assure you," Barca explained, "but as far as I know, Har-Kaaska's Second Division is all we have on line as yet, and First Division—that's the Third Pennsylvania alongside us at present—was called forward to deploy *before* us and has only now made it this far. God knows how things stand with Third and Fourth Divisions."

The army had split to advance on Texcoco along two briefly parallel roads precisely so it could arrive and deploy more quickly, hopefully overawing the inhabitants of the city a few miles ahead. From the forested track they remained confined in, Barca could see nothing yet, but judging by the rumble of guns and muffled staccato of skirmishers' musket fire—considerably closer than the city should be—it didn't sound like things were going as planned. The Allied Army of the Yucatán, the remains of General (now Colonel) Agon's Army of God, and the American "Detached Expeditionary Force" that had formed the rest or glued it all together, might well be the best, most professional military force on this earth, but it—and its revered overall commander, Colonel Cayce—was still occasionally surprised by the enemy's behavior.

It had been expected that the Dom general Gomez would defend Texcoco from its walls. Like other Dom cities, those walls weren't designed with defense against human threats in mind, only large marauding predators. Consequently, there were no ramparts behind the walls from which infantry could fight, nor were they pierced for artillery. But there'd been time for Gomez to prepare all those things if he'd been inclined. Instead, it seemed he'd chosen to meet the Allied force in the open and even Major Anson's Ranger scouts had missed his advance. Barca could hardly imagine that. The only possibility was that Gomez had brought out his whole force the very night before, under cover of darkness.

Well done, he mentally congratulated the enemy commander. As good as it had become, the various parts of the combined Allied army had rarely moved independently, nor had it often practiced doing so. The whole force together had usually been significantly outnumbered, after all. Large contingents often detached themselves to perform flanking movements or assemble in unexpected places once the general battlefield was defined, but the army as a whole had only ever split entirely once before, and never on the current campaign, with large numbers of newer troops who'd never done it at all. Confusion was the inevitable result.

"Well, we've got a grand total o' *one* battery in place—Dukane's howitzers, if ye can imagine," McNabb fumed, "an' whoever arranged the day's order o' march . . ." He shook his head and Barca nodded. All he heard from ahead was the duller boom of howitzers—and Dom guns, of course, that sounded very much like them. "But Colonel Cayce wants *all* the guns up right goddamn now—sir," McNabb continued, "an' I know there's at least two more batteries behind ye." He stood in his stirrups, gazing east. "Can't even see 'em 'round that bend in the road. If we don't hurry, them devils in the second column'll have their guns up before us an' take all the best places tae shoot!"

"Can't have that, can we?" came a shout from among the almost-jogging infantry. Anyone would've had to raise his voice to be heard amid the crashing rumble of hobnailed shoes, heavy breathing, and clanking muskets and accoutrements. Both men turned to see First Sergeant Visser fall out of line and salute Captain Barca. Gesturing toward the Number One and Two guns of Hanny's section, he continued, "I once assured Lieutenant

Cox that his guns'd never be overrun while the Third Pennsylvania was at hand—and here we're overrunnin' him ourselves! At least chasin' him off the road in the muddy ditch." Turning, he shouted at another officer on a horse, "Captain Cullin?"

"By all means, First Sergeant," Captain Cullin agreed without even looking, or indeed slowing his horse. He'd obviously been prepared for the request.

"C Comp'ny," Visser bellowed, "turn out an' clap onto these guns. The colonel wants 'em on the line, an' by God I expect we'll be wantin' 'em too!"

About sixty rough-looking men in dingy, sky-blue uniforms elbowed their way out of the column, breathing hard and shifting muskets off their shoulders so they could drop packs and bedrolls before re-slinging their muskets diagonally across their backs. This took a few moments while most retrieved their greatcoats from where they'd wadded them up in their knapsack straps and put them back on. Already sweating from their rapid march, they'd get badly chilled if they didn't. A few men were quickly delegated to take charge of the discarded packs, and the rest hurried to help the artillerymen without another word from Visser, who watched with a satisfied air. "You may recall, Cap'n Barca," he finally said, "that even before we fought so close with Hanny's section at Puebla, half his men started out in the Third as infantrymen alongside me. Good lads, most of 'em, an' they've made us mighty proud. Still think of 'em as ours, in a way."

Barca's whole six-gun battery started moving faster almost at once, and soon the straining horses were doing most of the work by themselves. Hanny was guiding his lead team a little farther from the road, where the ground was firmer closer to the trees. "That should do it, sir! Thanks, First Sergeant!" he called back, voice sounding absurdly youthful. He *was* young too, maybe the youngest man in his section—with the possible exception of one or two recent native recruits they'd picked up along the march. Barca, McNabb, and Visser continued to observe while the new commander of A Battery's 1st Section fell back from the lead and climbed up on the left-side horse directly in front of the splinter bar attached to the limber pulling "his" Number Two gun.

"He's an officer now," McNabb said lowly. "There might still be a few suitable horses in the artillery reserve," he added dubiously. They'd captured quite a few horses, former Dom officer and lancer mounts, but they generally made poor draft animals. Besides, the dragoons, the Rangers, and

Mr. Lara's lancers invariably snapped up the best ones. The artillery got the dregs; animals still strong enough to pull and which might be ridden—at least while constrained by their harness—but little more. Doms used large, plodding "armabueys"—basically a cross in appearance between giant horned toads and armadillos—to pull their own supply wagons and guns, so captured animals actually accustomed to that sort of labor were of no use to Colonel Cayce. Armabueys were simply too slow. A former artilleryman himself, Lewis Cayce was convinced the agility of horse-drawn artillery had tipped the scales in his favor more than once. Finally, and for that same reason, the artillery was in constant competition with the baggage train when it came to acquiring appropriate beasts. Officially, the artillery took precedence, but it didn't always work that way.

Barca just shook his head. "He'll never take a horse for his own. He still commands his section as the gunner on Number Two. I haven't changed that because both his guns are always together, and frankly, he's the best gunner in the battery. Maybe the whole army. No doubt he'll replace me when I fall—that's been my recommendation to Major Olayne—and he'll have to let someone take his place then," he related matter-of-factly as if his own death was inevitable. "Until then, however, I won't interfere with how he runs his section."

The sound of battle was growing in volume and intensity by the time Elijah Hudgens's battery finally appeared behind them, abruptly trapping itself in the same loblolly that captured Barca's guns. "Have your men give them a hand as well, if you would," Barca suggested to First Sergeant Visser, "then move on along. One of the new batteries armed with captured tubes on our carriages is still back there somewhere, but don't wait for it. It'll have to manage its own passage." He looked at McNabb. "Is that acceptable, Sergeant Major?"

"Aye," agreed McNabb. "The new lads try hard enough, but they aren't yet worth the powder they burn. Small use they'll be in *this* fight. I'll ride up with ye, if ye've no objection."

Barca nodded, and the two men urged their horses toward the front, quickly outpacing the rushing infantry and even Barca's freed battery. In just moments, it seemed, they emerged from the dense forest bordering the road and came to a vast stubbled plain. The ground was quite clearly cultivated, but there was no telling what grew there since it had been harvested down to the ground. The earth was very dark, rich and inconveniently soft, however, and already churned into a muddy quagmire where 2nd Division, Capitan Ramon Lara's lancers, Coryon Burton's dragoons, and Dukane's battery of howitzers had passed and deployed. At the moment, they had the whole field to themselves, opposite an equally rapidly deploying mass of Dom infantry wearing bright yellow coats with black cuffs and facings, as well as black leggings and tricorn hats.

The enemy had marched right up the road to meet them and had no cover, no advantageous terrain. The only such feature conveniently near was a strand of woods angling diagonally away a few hundred yards to the north, likely following the path of a large creek or small river tumbling down the mountains the Allied Army was descending. At any rate, it extended outward from the very forest the Allies were spilling from as well.

Beyond the quickening panorama of war in the immediate vicinity was a truly stunning sight. Huge tended fields, bordered by high walls of stones probably cleared and stacked by slaves over the centuries, paralleled the road and stretched as far down the long slope to the valley below as could be seen. Scattered fairly thickly along them, often incorporated into the walls, were countless stone huts surrounded by smaller enclosures, many confining livestock. There were goats and cattle and sheep, of course, but also larger bipedal creatures like Har-Kaaska's bizarre mount. These looked vaguely like giant feathery lizards with a duck's head—though the "bill" wasn't hard like a duck's. Other strange beasts were visible as well, many they'd already encountered, but some they never had. Most striking of all, except for the Dom army scrambling to oppose them, of course, not another human soul could be seen.

"They've been waiting for us," Barca observed, "and already cleared everyone out."

"I hope that's all they did tae 'em," McNabb somberly replied.

The land was dotted with armabueys, standing placid and apparently abandoned, still hitched to wooden-wheeled carts. Shaggy buffalo-size creatures with horns on their faces and colorful bony frills protecting their necks were still burdened by long trunks of trees or other heavy objects they'd been dragging, but they were less patient than armabueys and aimless ragged gouges marked the ground away from the road where they'd rampaged to get rid of their loads. Even a few walls had been knocked down. Most amazing of all were some stupendous woolly beasts with ridiculously long, whiplike tails and necks. These *"serpientosas"* had been encountered before, used by locals to move extraordinary loads, but none had been remotely as large, perhaps thirty-five paces from noses to the tips of their tails. Most were much farther away in the direction of Texcoco, standing in clusters around large clumps of trees. The high, bright white walls of Texcoco itself were recognizable ten miles or more farther down the long slope, but only because they contrasted so sharply with the dark earth all around. If there were any people still there, they were much too distant to see.

Past even that, the basin of the Great Valley of Mexico began. It was sunken much deeper than Barca had expected from his geographical studies of old-world maps. It remained somewhat greener than he would've thought as well, considering the time of year, and his immediate impression was of a momentous caldera rather than a valley. A haze lingered down low in the distance, and there was just the flickering hint of the two great lakes he'd been given to understand would flank the still-invisible "Camino Sagrado," or sacred road, which led to the Holy City. That city remained entirely obscured by distance or haze, but the horizon sharpened again up higher and farther, and great purple mountains ringed the huge valley, intensifying the impression of a caldera.

"Hard tae believe we're finally here," said McNabb, tone as hushed as the growing noise of battle permitted, as they located a cluster of mounted officers and steered their animals toward them.

"Yes," agreed Barca. "We've come a long, hard way." He snorted. "I only hope this doesn't turn into an example of the rabbit that chased and caught the wolf."

McNabb huffed. "Ye'll pardon me for pointin' out that *I'm* nae wee bunny, an' neither are you."

"Nor is Colonel Cayce—or anyone who's fought their way here," Barca agreed. "It was merely an exaggerated metaphor."

McNabb arched a brow at him.

Captain Felix Meder, commanding the mounted riflemen, threw them a jaunty salute as he and his regiment galloped past toward the gathering of officers, pausing only to exchange a few words before pounding on toward the guns in the center. Barca and McNabb brought up the rear of their column to join the officers themselves. Many were pointing and talking with animation. Barca raised his voice and saluted. "Major Olayne. Where would you like me to place my battery?"

"Good morning to you, Captain Barca," Olayne replied, returning the salute with a grin. "It seems we're to have a meeting engagement." He gestured toward the center as well. "Go into line directly to the left of the road, if you please. Except for a couple pair of guns they've pushed out to either side some distance back, the enemy is content to deploy as he arrives, leaving the rest of his force stacked in column. Dukane's howitzers are annoying it with canister and case, but solid shot will cut deeper and discourage more of the enemy."

Barca nodded. Clearly, the Dom commander had chosen to close as quickly as he could, but the soft, damp field to the side of the road had prevented him from deploying farther back and advancing in organized ranks. He was trying to do so now, as quickly as possible, just as this column of the Allied Army, equally constrained by the forest road and wet field, was doing the same. The differences were, Cayce's force remained concealed from view until it emerged from the trees, where the infantry regiments immediately went into line before advancing, and of course the artillery was light and quick enough to deploy wherever needed on the field. Likely still mixed with the enemy column, most of the Dom artillery was too heavy and cumbersome to leave the hard road without turning into something like armabuey-drawn plows, and those eight distant guns were the only ones in action yet. Barca saw one flash and heard the shot shriek by overhead about the time the report reached them.

"Trails're sinkin' in the mud an' they ain't adjustin' elevation between shots," McNabb surmised. Barca silently agreed. The 8pdr enemy shot wasn't shaped as uniformly as "American" shot, but flew straight enough and was equally deadly if properly directed. Fortunately, the enemy artillerymen were usually content to rely on the same tactic as their infantry: get close and keep as much metal in the air as they could. That wasn't as effective at distance. He realized then that if the Allied Army had already been ready and waiting, this would be a perfect time to close in on the sides and smash the enemy column. As things turned out, they were scrambling just as desperately to shake out into line as the Doms. At least this column was . . .

"What about lancers?" Barca suddenly asked with a glance at the wood-bordered river to their right. A lightning strike in their flank by hidden Dom lancers could end this whole thing before it truly started.

"No enemy horse has been seen," Olayne assured him in an understanding tone, then urged, "Do hurry, Mr. Barca. Disconcerting as it all appears, we do have an opportunity here."

"I'll send the Third Pennsylvania up to support you as soon as they clear the woods," promised Colonel Reed, florid face even redder than usual in the brisk morning air. "I know you work well with them."

"Thank you, Colonel. Should we leave room for more batteries as they arrive?"

Everyone turned to Lewis Cayce then, sitting atop his big chestnut mare, Arete, staring forward at the evolving scene. He wore his usual campaigning uniform: dark blue jacket with red herringbone trim, both worn and faded from long exposure. His white saber belt was slightly dingy from handling and wear, though the saber scabbard suspended from it gleamed almost magically bright. Still, about the only things setting him apart from any other officer were powerful shoulders broad enough to strain the seams under his shoulder boards, and a full dark brown beard instead of the otherwise nearly universal side whiskers.

His closest companions might've helped distinguish him as well. One was a tall, thin woman with straight, shoulder-length hair, almost blue-black like the feathers of a raven. Her eyes seemed black as well, as deep yet bright as a starry night sky, set in an almost delicate, golden olive-skinned face. Her sex aside, she was dressed just like Lewis except for a lack of colored trim on her jacket, and her belt supported a pair of holsters containing a brace of five-shot, .36 caliber Colt Paterson revolvers. Her name was Leonor Anson, and for a variety of complex reasons, she'd come to this world disguised as a man along with her father and two other Texas Mounted Rifles, or "Rangers." She remained a Ranger lieutenant here despite the abandonment of her masquerade because she was undoubtedly one of the most lethal fighters in the army, and frankly, because Lewis Cayce was in love with her and wouldn't try to change her. That's probably why she loved him too.

Mounted on the other side of Lewis was a different being altogether, not even human in fact. She was Varaa-Choon, a "Mi-Anakka," and one of only a handful of her species known to abide on this continent after a quite ordinary shipwreck on the Yucatán a score of years before. Mi-Anakka were shaped like humans except for long, expressive, very furry tails, and their faces had more . . . perhaps "feline" characteristics, though that wasn't a perfect description. Ears were lower down on the side of the head, and eyes were much larger in proportion to the rest of their faces than any cat's. Varaa's eyes were a bright pale blue. She was still considered "Warmaster" to the human Ocelomeh, or "Jaguar Warriors" from the Yucatán, even though they were now thoroughly integrated into the army. The Ocelomeh "king" (another Mi-Anakka named Har-Kaaska) had basically demoted himself to colonel in command of the combined 2nd Division.

After twenty years, less than half a dozen Mi-Anakka remained to govern the seminomadic woodland Ocelomeh, their authority originally based on a physical resemblance to ancient gods and since maintained by good leadership. Lewis counted Varaa and Har-Kaaska among his closest friends, but still had no idea where their homeland was. This secret was carefully guarded, not that they didn't trust Lewis—or many others within the Alliance—but out of fear that the Dominion might somehow discover where they came from.

Varaa wore the same dark blue jacket and light blue trousers as all the mounted troops in the army (foot soldiers wore sky blue all over, except for the same dark blue wheel hats) and carried a long, straight-bladed rapier with an ornate basket guard. She also always carried a musket slung across her back that, despite its markings, had always looked very . . . British to Lewis. It was distinctly like some of the earliest British muskets carried in the United States' war for independence, in fact. Varaa never spoke of that coincidence either.

Turning to face Barca, Lewis smiled and replied, "I don't think so, Mr. Barca. The opportunity in the center will be fleeting, and we'll need the rest of the guns on the flanks with the dragoons and lancers. We may even move those guns in action, and our mounted troops' horses can help with that." He gestured down at Arete's hooves, balled up with mud. "This ground is very clingy, and moving the guns around on the field will get more difficult than it already is."

Barca saluted once more and pulled his horse's head around, spurring it into a sloppy trot back toward his battery, just now emerging from the trees.

"I wish he wouldn't do that," Leonor growled. "Salutin' officers on the field . . . might as well hang targets on 'em."

"I doubt he would have if we were more visible," Varaa almost instinctively defended the young officer. She liked him a lot, knew exactly what it was like to be "unusual" in this land, and admired how Barca had managed to be so universally accepted by his peers and those he commanded by quiet but extraordinary accomplishment alone. In any event, nearly the whole of Har-Kaaska's division remained between them and the enemy in an elongated block, spreading out to the right for the most part, while the sporadic enemy volleys churned the mud short, as usual at this range. The armies were deploying roughly two hundred paces apart—very long range for any musket—but Dom infantry weapons were extra heavy and clunky, with ridiculously slow ignition. Offhand, they were amazingly fortunate to hit anything beyond fifty paces, and the few projectiles whizzing and fluttering around Lewis and his staff were mostly spent and flattened after striking the ground and bounding up.

Regiments of 1st Division were coming up now, led by the 1st US, extending the line to the left. Drums rattled, repeating and relaying shouted orders, and flags were uncased to stream in the slight, sharp breeze while men loaded weapons and brought them to the ready. The firing on both sides increased and a stuttering *poom-poom-ppoom-ppoom-poom!* of Dukane's howitzers, followed by bellowed commands and rising screams, was proof that things would shortly grow more violent.

"Prob'ly not," Leonor agreed with Varaa. "Still a bad habit."

"I doubt it is a habit either," Har-Kaaska maintained from atop his strange, stoic mount. The burly Mi-Anakka "king" of the Ocelomeh had finally discarded the last remnant of his traditional garb and dressed just like the other officers now. And his mount might be weird, but Lewis had repeatedly seen it absorb wounds that would've killed any horse. "Few of our soldiers have displayed bad habits throughout this campaign," Har-Kaaska continued, "and what mistakes they have made, large and small, reflect more on the training, discipline, and leadership we provided than on them." He was obviously referring to the way his own division broke ranks and engaged in a pell-mell chase of some shattered enemy infantry during the Battle of Puebla, and his weren't the only troops who did it. That could've ended in disaster and certainly delayed any organized pursuit of the enemy. Such a thing wouldn't happen again.

Barca's battery had regained the road and was clattering quickly along it, hooves thundering, iron tires crackling as the wheels threw kaleidoscopic sprays of damp soil in all directions, festooning everything including the men on the horses and limbers. Barca had galloped ahead and now turned to indicate the line his six 6pdrs would occupy, pointing with his saber just to the left and across the road from Dukane's battery. The 3rd

Pennsylvania was running up behind them, still in column, but with their state and national colors already uncased and flowing. A glance behind showed Lewis that Hudgens's battery of mixed 6pdrs and 12pdrs had appeared and set off across the mushy field toward the left flank. Colonel Reed nodded respectfully at Lewis. "It seems we'll soon have things in hand. We'll still be outnumbered, as is so often the case, but I remain in awe of your ability to adapt to the unexpected."

"You could've done it," Lewis deflected, "and it was the men far more than me."

"Nevertheless," Reed persisted, "if Anson and his Rangers had done their job and given sufficient warning . . ."

Leonor's face reddened and she was clearly preparing an angry retort in her father's defense when Lewis interrupted. "That's my fault. We knew the enemy—this time we face General Gomez himself, it seems—was preparing to move so as not to fight his battle on the very doorstep of Texcoco, and . . . well, in spite of everything, I rather hoped to meet him here." He shrugged. "I would've preferred to be better prepared, of course, and Gomez surprised me with how quickly he came, but it might be for the best after all. It came to me that he'd never be fool enough to fight from inside the city. I certainly didn't want to chase him around, and I'm not sure he would've come on as precipitously as he has if we were already arrayed to receive him. As for the Rangers, there *are* a few out there." He glanced reassuringly at Leonor. "A small squadron under the redoubtable Captain Hernandez and more than enough under normal circumstances. Something must've happened to prevent his report. I'm sure he's all right," he hastened to add. Sal Hernandez and Captain Bandy "Boogerbear" Beeryman had been like uncles to Leonor all of her life. Looking back at Reed, he continued, "But I sent Major Anson and the bulk of his Rangers to liaise with Colonel Agon and . . . perform another task."

Leonor arched a brow at him, and Varaa clapped her hands with anticipatory glee. Reed huffed annoyance, never happy when Lewis made last-minute adjustments to a plan without consulting him, and particularly when he was cryptic about it. Such things amused Varaa immensely, and she usually figured out what they were. Leonor trusted Lewis's instinctive ability to alter his tactics on the fly, but became just as exasperated as Reed when he could've informed her beforehand and didn't. No one could argue with him providing Colonel Agon with a strong mounted contingent, however, and not just to keep tabs on him. Not anymore.

The former Dom general Agon had proven his loyalty over and over and led both 3rd and 4th Divisions, at present. Each was almost entirely composed of former Doms and other native troops. That wouldn't have been a good mix before Puebla, where Colonel Itzam's 3rd had actually been given the secondary responsibility of keeping an eye on the 4th, but no such uncertainty about Agon remained. Besides, he was more tactful than the Uxmalo Itzam when it came to dealing with the Blood Cardinal Don Hurac, accompanying his force.

It had become a major part of the Allied strategy to install the "legitimate" successor to His Supreme Holiness on the throne—or whatever he sat on—so he could stop the war and call back the forces that had surprised them all by sailing through the wildly treacherous "Pass of Fire" far to the south from the Pacific. A large Dom army had landed in the Yucatán and laid siege to the seat of the Alliance in distant Uxmal. Other coastal cities might've already fallen, as far as they knew, but there was no way to maintain this campaign and relieve their friends at "home." Worse, even if they abandoned this campaign so close to success—and with the momentous Gran Cruzada certainly recalled to oppose them, that opportunity was fleeting—they could never move the army by ground or ship all the way back to the Yucatán in time to influence the outcome there. Even Sira Periz, *alcaldesa* of Uxmal and currently in command of 5th Division, much of which was scattered between Puebla, Techolotla, and Vera Cruz at present, understood that now. The only thing that could stop the enemy in the Yucatán was a messenger dragon sent from the Holy City by an uncontested Supreme Holiness. The Blood Cardinal Don Hurac was their only chance to accomplish that.

Lewis was convinced of Agon's conversion from the dark, twisted faith of the Dominion, and the diminutive Uxmalo Christian priest Father Orno was equally sure of Don Hurac. Lewis wasn't. Benign as he might truthfully be in comparison to other Blood Cardinals, Don Hurac had been one of only a dozen men considered apostles to His Supreme Holiness, the virtual human incarnation of God, and practically the brother of Jesus. As something of a Christian himself, that didn't sit well with Lewis and certainly not among his generally even more pious army. Worse, the Dom version of

Jesus didn't die for man's sins but was sacrificed by God in the most horrible way as an example, to demonstrate that blood and suffering was the only coin to buy the grace required for entry into some underworld heaven. The commingling of aspects of early Christianity with the blood-drenched pagan faiths of earlier arrivals in this land had resulted in a nightmare abomination, and the Blood Priests only sought to make it worse.

Blood Cardinals, like Don Hurac, ascended to their positions by virtue of actual blood relation to the founders of the Dominion. Blood Priests were a relatively recently established sect with no connection to this rarefied aristocracy and no traditional pathway to join it. A long campaign to supplant *obispos*, from which Blood Cardinals were chosen, and replace them with *patriarchas*—who might rise from any background through the priesthood—had finally come to fruition. Blood Priests earned God's favor (and renown among their peers) by soaking the earth with blood, *feeding* their underworld God the blood of those they sacrificed, coincidentally *arranging* for their victims to earn the grace they needed to join Him.

This belief wasn't entirely new, but Blood Priests had taken it to horrifying extremes, attracting new members in droves because even freedmen could join and gain power over others and exemption from sacrifice for themselves. Thus, a previously semi-outcast fringe group of radicals had grown exponentially and now controlled the Dominion.

Don Hurac, along with a few others, had rather passively opposed them for years, Don Hurac largely from the seat of his provincial capital at Vera Cruz. But he'd benefitted from the old regime, presided over his own sacrifices on appropriate occasions, and only fully "saw the light" when Captain Eric Holland accidentally captured Vera Cruz during a raid from the sea. Don Hurac and everyone else in the city had been doomed by that, simply for being there when it fell. Lewis couldn't read the man's heart, but was sure he was partially motivated by revenge for this, the murder of his many children and their mothers, as well as being kicked aside for ascension to the throne. He had no doubt that Don Hurac would help them crush the Blood Priests, might even do as he said in other respects, but often doubted the man would institute true reform in the Dominion.

The possibility existed that Zyon, his only remaining wife in all but name and coincidentally the firmer part of his backbone, would ensure that Don Hurac kept his full word. In the meantime, he traveled with Agon, as much because Colonel Itzam trusted him less than Lewis did and Agon absolutely hated the way Don Hurac occasionally referred to Agon's troops as "his." It might only be long acquaintance that kept Agon civil with him while feeling him out for hidden agendas.

"If you say so, Lewis," Colonel Reed said, kneeing his brown-and-black-striped horse closer and sticking out his hand. "In the meantime, I'll ride to the left to be with my division. You'll be here?"

"I'll be where I'm needed," Lewis replied, grasping Reed's hand and gripping it firmly. Reed hadn't always agreed with his strategy, or even been supportive, but he'd been a reliable friend and second-in-command. "If not here, messengers will know where." He smiled again. "Be safe. You won't need me, and the lads know what to do."

As it turned out, that wasn't necessarily true.

CHAPTER 2

"Load canister!" Captain Barca roared, riding sedately behind the gun line from one end of his battery to the other, between the three sections of two guns each and their horses and limbers behind them. He seemed utterly calm and oblivious to the hail of musket balls filling the air around him. None of his crews would've ordinarily countenanced a mounted man riding through such a busy space; Number Five and Seven men hurrying back and forth, bringing ammunition forward or returning for more, Number Three stepping back behind the protruding handspike at the rear of the trail to adjust a gun's windage at the gunner's direction, wounded being dragged or carried to the rear while replacements sprinted forward, but Barca had the innate sense and awareness to stay out of the way. His men were more worried he'd be hit than that he'd disrupt the fast-paced, intricate dance required to load their pieces.

Lieutenant Hanny Cox stopped his Number Five man, Billy Randall, from carrying the big leather haversack forward where Number Two, "Preacher Mac" McDonough, waited to fish another fixed round of solid shot out of the haversack, lift it over the wheel, and place it in the muzzle of the gun. Billy's hand was still heavily bandaged due to a wound he got at Puebla that took two of his fingers. "Take it back," Hanny urgently told him. "Load *canister*, damn it. Didn't you hear Captain Barca?"

"Hear the cap'n? Hell, Hanny, I can barely hear *you* over this racket, standin' right here!" He had a point. The noise had grown almost unbearably loud, here in the center of the battle line. The crashing volleys of musket fire, closest on the left from the 3rd Pennsylvania, and crackle of a dismounted detachment of Felix Meder's riflemen whose duty was to pick off enemy officers and NCOs with their supremely accurate M1817 rifles, had become noisy enough to compete with the cannon.

"Send the new Number Seven, Reco Sares, with it," Hanny called after Billy as he retreated past the horses to the limber. "You bring the next one."

"Should'hae shifted tae canister already," Preacher Mac yelled at him from the front, his Scots accent strong.

"Aye," agreed the Number One man, Daniel Hahessy, voice as staunchly Irish. It always struck Hanny, even in moments like this, how diverse this new "American" army had become, filled with people from so many strange lands and tribes, but the same had really been true of the "original" American force that wound up here from another world. Both men in front of his Number Two gun were the biggest in his crew, yet had somehow, miraculously, survived in those extremely short-lived positions through every battle he'd fought in the artillery. Their size and luck were the only things they shared. Brothers in action, they otherwise seemed to detest each other. Preacher Mac could be somewhat oppressively dour and devout at times, but was one of Hanny's best friends. Hahessy was . . . hard to describe.

Once a sergeant in the 1st US, he'd been a bully and tyrant, even picking on Hanny, who wasn't even close to a match for him. But Hanny, just a wispy young private at the time, may have been the first person who ever stood up to him and that made an impression. After Hahessy was later broken for brutality (nearly hanged for his part in a certain incident, in fact) and thrown out of every unit he was transferred to, he wound up in Hanny's section. To everyone's surprise, including his own, he'd found a home at last.

"Aye," Hahessy repeated. "Ducky's howitzers been bangin' away with canister from the start, buildin' a fine heap o' the heathen divils"—"Ducky" was Hahessy's name for Captain Dukane—"an' our roundshot was lovely at first, tearin' deep in the column, but haven't they shook outa column now? Aye, that they have, an' we're not killin' as many as we could. No, not by half." Hahessy might've grown cordial with most of the crew of Gun Number Two, but still cherished a seething hatred of Doms.

"Didnae ye hear Lieutenant Hanny, then?" Preacher Mac demanded over the powder-darkened bronze gun tube between them. "Which we're only waitin' fer the canister he ordered tae *come*, an' we'll get wi' it ourselves!"

"I heard him, same as you, ye long squirrel," Hahessy yelled back. "Commentin' on it is all, I was!"

Hanny looked in the haversack young Reco brought for his inspection and propelled the boy forward with a hand on his back. Preacher Mac pulled the canister out, a metal cylinder filled with ninety .69 caliber lead musket balls packed in sawdust, the whole strapped to a wooden sabot and powder bag. It was a deadly load and would turn their 6pdr cannon into a giant shotgun. Preacher Mac shoved it in the muzzle, powder bag first, and Hahessy immediately slammed it down the barrel with his rammer staff, giving it a brisk thump to seat it, before pulling the rammer back out.

"'Long squirrel,' is it?" snapped Preacher Mac indignantly, ignoring a cloud of blue fibers a musket ball snatched off his sleeve. "Why, you great, fat, howfin haggis! I'll . . ."

"You'll *both* step outside the wheels this instant," Hanny shouted, "so Hoziki can see to point the gun!" When firing canister at this range, careful aiming wasn't required. Hanny could judge elevation well enough by eye, had actually raised it more than usual by turning the elevation screw under the breech, because the soft earth would absorb too much of the cloud of projectiles that hit it. Hard ground sent them grazing up into the enemy. Hoziki, a young farmer recruit from Frontera, would heave on the handspike to shift the gun side to side to put the densest part of the pattern on the largest number of enemies.

"Spoilsport," Hahessy accused theatrically, but did as he was told, assuming his position outside the right axle hub of the fifty-seven-inch wheel that came up to his chest. "A bloody great battle is no reason ta stop fightin' with me mates, is it? Small excuse, says I."

"Yewd call this wee shindy a great bloody ba—"

"Gun Number Two, fire!" Hanny shouted. Hoziki, as the Number Three man, had hurried up to the right side of the breech as soon as he was satisfied with the lay of the gun. He'd then stabbed through the vent with his brass priming wire, or "vent prick," to pierce the charge Hahessy pushed down. Covering the vent with an explosive primer, larger but similar to the percussion caps Coryon Burton's dragoons used to ignite their Hall carbines, he held the heavy brass hammer on the Hidden's Patent lock to the side, while Tani Fik—the new Number Four man—took up the slack in his lanyard. That was all accomplished in an instant before Hoziki stepped outside the right wheel himself and raised a clenched fist to signal the gun was ready.

Still arguing or not, Hanny could see that all his crew had moved clear of the one-ton weapon's significant recoil before cutting off Preacher Mac's tirade. Tani briskly pulled the lanyard, the hammer struck the primer, and a jet of fire flashed down the vent into the bag of gunpowder. As always, Hanny was only partially prepared for the fierce blast of pressure that slapped him in the face, pounded his eardrums, and compressed his ribs when the gun fired, spewing orange flame and the yellowish white smoke curiously unique to canister. He'd learned long ago to keep his mouth open to equalize the pressure in his head. The muzzle dipped down until the tube slapped the carriage before the breech dropped back down with a clang on the elevation screw. At the same time, the whole thing jumped back about four feet—half as far as on hard ground—and the brake chain jangled and swayed under the trail. Hahessy, Preacher Mac, and Tani instantly sprang forward to push the gun back into battery with Hoziki guiding it with the handspike. He then rushed forward and stabbed a T-handled brush down the vent and yelled, "Clear!"

The other end of Hahessy's rammer staff was covered with a woollen sheepskin he'd already dipped in the heavy, practically bulletproof sponge bucket placed on the ground under the muzzle. Now he rammed the wet wool down the barrel while Hoziki pulled his brush and pressed hard on the vent with his thumb, covered by a thick leather thumbstall. This not only wet the barrel (only slightly cleaning it because the sponge was already black with fouling) but compressed the air inside and accelerated any sparks that might be feeding on fragments of the powder bag.

"Keep that thumb tight," Hahessy darkly warned Hoziki. "I hear a hiss, I'll snap all yer bones, one by one!" Hoziki only nodded. He understood. At least as much as water, the vacuum Hahessy pulled on the tube as he drew the rammer out with a satisfying *pong!* sound extinguished any lurking embers. All Number One men were justifiably picky about that. If a single spark remained, they'd be the ones with their arms blown off when they rammed the next charge.

"Reload canister!" Hanny roared back at the limber, even as Sergeant

Dodd, the other gunner in his section, shouted that his weapon was ready. Hanny nodded at him, raising his hand as a signal for Dodd to hold his fire. Standing behind the limber, his very best friend, Corporal Apo Tuin, had raised the lid of the ammunition chest, retrieved another round of canister, and placed it in Billy Randall's haversack. He hadn't stopped Dodd to watch that, however. Turning back to the front, he peered through the slowly dispersing smoke to evaluate the effect of their shot. It wasn't a pleasant sight.

A gap about five paces wide had been gouged out of the Dom front line, the ground covered with shredded and motionless or writhing, screaming bodies, yellow coats splashed with red. And for several paces on either side of the gap, the line had been thinned considerably. Doms were already moving to close the gap, however, heaving men aside—not all of whom were dead—or literally wading through them, NCOs screaming for them to make their muskets ready. One Dom sergeant seemed especially persuasive.

"Hammer that same spot, Sergeant Dodd!" Hanny cried. "Corporal Watkins," he called to one of Meder's riflemen, four or five of whom had stationed themselves in the spaces between the guns of Barca's battery. "There's a target for you. Do something about that man, if you please."

The 3rd Pennsylvania unleashed another crisp volley just as the enemy did, and figures fell all along the line. Too many of the 3rd also went down. Slightly closer now, the enemy fire was improving.

"Already marked 'im, sir," Corporal Watkins assured. He'd just reloaded and now sank to his right knee, supporting the long barrel of his 1817 rifle with his left hand, left elbow on his other knee. He pulled the cock all the way back.

"Fire!" Dodd bellowed, and another yellowish cloud gushed from the muzzle of the Number One gun, the high-pitched "shish" of canister flying through the air terminating with the clatter and drumming thudding of projectiles striking bodies and equipment. Dozens more Doms went down. Watkins cursed, his target obscured, but continued to focus on the area where the NCO had been. The other members of his squad were still shooting methodically at their own marks of opportunity.

"There the bugger is, still alive," Watkins said. "A lucky devil indeed." He squeezed the trigger and the lock flashed only the slightest instant before the rifle cracked. Hanny could barely see the enemy sergeant through the thick smoke but watched him pitch backward as if snatched by the hair from behind. Watkins stood to reload. "Not lucky anymore," he said simply.

"Gun Number Two is ready," shouted Hoziki, stepping to the right again. Hanny nodded. Hoziki might be relatively new at his position, but Blood Priests had murdered his mother and not even Hahessy could hate them as much as him. Hanny was confident he'd lay the gun for best effect.

"Fire!" Hanny yelled.

The Number Two gun roared and bucked once more. Captain Barca was charging up between Hanny's section and the one to its right. He whirled his horse to a stop. "Check fire, check fire!" he was shouting right and left.

"What the divil?" Hahessey indignantly cried. "We've just now set ta poundin' the buggers good!"

"Cease firing," Hanny yelled at his own crew and Dodd's. He didn't know what was happening, but Captain Barca wouldn't stop them without good reason. He noted the 3rd Pennsylvania, their muskets already loaded, had ceased firing as well, and the relative silence was beginning to spread.

"What's happening, Hanny?" Apo cried from behind.

"I don't *know*!" Hanny shouted back. "Can we at least load and hold?" he asked Captain Barca.

Barca hesitated. "Yes," he replied uncertainly. "Reload canister, but hold. I don't know what's happening any more than you, but they're sounding the cease-fire."

Hanny now heard the growing rattle of drums among the infantry and wavering notes of bugles. He shook his head. It didn't make sense. But the enemy fire was tapering off as well, and he saw the same ranks they'd struggled so desperately to fill just moments ago start to shift, men in the front ranks turning and scampering to the rear here and there, as if they were determined to re-form into numerous columns right in front of them. Wide gaps were reappearing. It was madness. Insane for the enemy to do, but also for Colonel Cayce not to exploit the opportunity.

Barca was staring hard to the front, standing in his stirrups. "Something's happening," he said, voice softer now that this utterly unexpected and . . . surrealistic silence had been imposed. "Oh my God!" he suddenly exclaimed, and Hanny was chilled by the horror in his tone.

"WHAT THE DEVIL? What are they doing?" Har-Kaaska demanded warily. Lewis Cayce raised his glass to see. Something was definitely happening, but what? He'd never liked this kind of fight, the traditional linear combat that seemed to rule the battlefield on this world just as thoroughly as it had "back home," considering it dreadfully wasteful of good men. He much preferred to fight battles of movement or localized defense *combined* with movement. But the enemy always *expected* this sort of fight and was prone to fully commit to it. When there were no landscape features Lewis could exploit to assail the enemy on his terms from the start, the easiest way to focus their attention away from something else was to give them the battle they wanted. At least for a while. In the past, they'd been doubly confounded when Lewis suddenly changed the rules.

Even so, and despite being heavily outnumbered, as usual, his column of two divisions had been more than holding its own, peeling off whole ranks of the enemy with the furious, terribly effective fire of his veteran troops. And the artillery had been reaping a vicious harvest indeed. He'd just about decided this General Gomez might be the stupidest enemy leader he'd met so far and believed this battle would be over in half an hour whether his "surprise" was sprung by then or not. Doms rarely retreated. The consequences meted out for that by their own leaders were grim. And they'd only actually *broken* Dom troops once before. Scouts had reported that units that broke at the Battle of Puebla had actually been decimated in the brutal historical sense, with one in ten of their number executed. Of course, these sad victims, chosen by chance, were not simply beaten to death by their mates, but were impaled on sharp stakes driven into the ground. A slow, utterly barbarous way to die.

They knew some of those they now faced had broken before and no one would bet whether that made them more liable to do it again, or the punishment they'd witnessed would make them fight to the end. Lewis was sure their morale had been crushed but knew which choice *he'd* make in their shoes. Yet now the enemy was doing something incomprehensible, clearly deliberate, and seemingly stupider than anything he'd seen.

"They're movin' back into column, right in front of us!" Leonor exclaimed. "What the hell?"

"It's a trap," Varaa declared. "They hope to draw us into a charge through those gaps. Break up our own lines, meet us with more troops, and defeat us in detail."

"They can't believe we'd fall for *that*," Leonor objected. "Maybe they're sendin' more Doms up the gaps in column, deepenin' their lines."

"A strange way to do it, but maybe you're right," Lewis mused, focusing his glass at the sight of movement in the gaps. "With this meager breeze and standing smoke we can't see much beyond their front ranks and there's no telling if they've brought more troops up the road behind them. Their army could've been bigger than Major Anson thought, or they might've been reinforced." He shrugged. "Either way, I wish we'd heard from Captain Hernandez, and I may have erred badly by not sending some of Coryon Burton's dragoons up to replace Anson's Rangers. I thought we'd need them all here." He glanced away from his glass long enough to smile apologetically at those around him. "And we shall, most likely. But I may have spent so much time planning how to appear predictable that I neglected to consider how they might've become less so."

He looked through the glass again and his smile suddenly vanished entirely. "No," he breathed aloud. Tearing the glass away from his eye, he regarded Leonor with an expression of fury and dread. "No," he repeated. "Not really unpredictable at all. They did this before, to the mounted brigade you and your father took north out of Gran Lago." He raised his voice. "They *are* herding people through the gaps, all *civilians*. The population of Texcoco, I'd guess."

Har-Kaaska blinked very rapidly before his fur-covered jaw firmed with decision. Mi-Anakka didn't have expressive faces, not in the human way, but their blinking, ear position, and various other things, not to mention their tails, expressed a lot of meaning and emotion to those who'd learned to read them. He'd clearly come to a distasteful decision.

"We gotta stop shooting," Leonor said, tone almost desperate.

"We must not," Har-Kaaska dissented forcefully at once.

Varaa was blinking rapidly as well. "I'm afraid Har-Kaaska is right, my dear," she told Leonor. "That's exactly what the enemy wants, and we won't have any choice but to withdraw—if we can."

"As soon as we stop shooting and start to pull back, the Doms will rush forward and overwhelm us," Har-Kaaska agreed, gesturing at the civilians. Those here at the center, at least, were now clearly visible. A few, probably more affluent, had fine fowling pieces in their hands, but more of them awkwardly carried obsolete Dom weapons such as matchlock muskets or pole arms. Some had swords. All of them, even women and children this time, were armed with something, often only farm implements. Regardless, they were also plainly terrified, advancing reluctantly out of fear, not zealotry or patriotism, and no battle cry rose from their lips. The only sounds they made were cries of fear, loud babbling begging, and an indistinguishable moan of dread.

Lewis's jaw firmed as well as he ground his teeth. *Of course* Har-Kaaska and Varaa were right, but for the first time in battle, he didn't know what to do. Even Leonor's objection was a snap reaction, and he knew she was only seconds away from changing her mind. He wasn't, and whatever happened next would be on him. It would be regardless. He was in command. But his next choice had the potential to lose the whole war. His confidence in his ability to cope with anything had taken a blow at Puebla. They'd won anyway, but it was ugly. There were far more casualties than he'd provided for, and chance might've influenced his victory more than planning. He didn't like that at all. Now chance might play a role again because he'd been *avoidably* surprised. As recently as the evening before, he'd been sure what General Gomez would do—and what he'd do in response—and sent Major Giles Anson to Agon, despite the Ranger's objection. He'd believed Sal Hernandez's Ranger platoon could keep the enemy covered and his secondary and tertiary plans (he always had several lined up) would be sufficient to deal with whatever Gomez did. That might still be the case, but his timing could've been drastically affected. Timing, often even more than the plans it regulated, could spell the difference between victory and defeat.

What it all boiled down to was that something had prevented Sal's report and Gomez was employing a loathsome tactic Lewis should've *known* he might use. Now the only thing he remained certain of was that he just couldn't let his army keep shooting at civilians. Some were falling even now, torn and bleeding from musket fire, tumbling to the earth while those stacked behind them tried to recoil in terror as they were propelled relentlessly forward.

"Oh, the terrible cowards!" Varaa bitterly cried when the enemy's full intent became plain. As each column of civilians reached the front line, bands of whip- and bludgeon-bearing Blood Priests swiftly herded their miserable captives to either side, deliberately masking the troops behind the shaking, sobbing bodies of old women, young children, and their impotently helpless sons and daughters, mothers and fathers. With no mercy forthcoming from their own, those unfortunates began screeching, desperately pleading with the "heretic" army not to kill them. It was more than Lewis could take. The Blood Priests might be the murderers, but they were making Lewis's troops their weapon. If it was just him, he might've taken it upon himself to continue, but he couldn't inflict a lifetime of horror, grief, and guilt on the troops he loved.

"Cease firing!" he shouted at his "personal" bugler, Corporal Hannity, who was sitting on his own horse just behind him. "Sound 'cease firing' at once, and keep it up until it spreads."

Varaa gasped. "Lewis, you *can't*!"

"She's right," Leonor grudgingly agreed, coming to the same conclusion even faster than usual.

"Do it," Lewis snarled at Hannity, who, wide-eyed, brought the bugle to his lips and blew. Lewis could almost see a ripple of disbelief flow outward from him, file by file, regiment by regiment, but the firing did abruptly ease. A pair of Barca's guns roared once more, but urgent shouting prevented others from firing as well. A last belch of canister far to the left, one of Hudgens's 12pdrs, churned the enemy—the civilian shield hadn't spread that far yet—but then even the most distant infantry stopped shooting and an eerie, unnatural, even perverted silence descended, broken only by the cries of wounded and the wet drumming of horse hooves as messengers converged on Lewis.

Not all were messengers. Leonor exclaimed and Lewis saw one rider was none other than Sal Hernandez. The tall Hispanic Ranger was spattered with mud and blood, and his lips were twisted into a ferocious scowl beneath his magnificent mustache. "*Lo siento*, Colonel," he said. "I tried to get back and tell you, but they spread their goddamn lancers like a net. The ground is too open and there was no way to evade 'em. We were spotted and they converged, chasing us farther an' farther south, while stayin' between us and you. We heard the first cannon, as did they, an' they just left us alone after that." He waved at the bizarre battlefield. "Guess they figured our news wouldn't matter by the time we got to you."

"They were right," Lewis told him. "We wondered why there were no lancers in evidence. Still, it's not your fault. I should've sent Burton's dragoons or Mr. Lara's lancers with you."

Sal was shaking his head. "Maybe all o' both would've made a difference, but there wound up bein' upward o' five hundred o' the devils. Peeled off to the east."

"I don't think they'll like what they find there," Varaa said, a note of satisfaction in her tone.

"No," Lewis agreed, but then looked back to the front when Leonor caught his attention.

"White flag," she said, shaking her head. "For folks who never negotiate, Doms're the talkinest bunch on a battlefield." She shrugged. "Might as well see what this Gomez fella has to say. Buys us time, anyway."

Lewis nodded. "Colonel Har-Kaaska? Send your reserve regiments back to the woods, if you please, and have them start digging entrenchments and throwing up breastworks. We'll need a place to fall back to when the enemy pushes again—and civilian shields or not, we *won't* be pushed back to Puebla! Let's see how they hide behind the unwilling in an assault on a defensive position, especially while Mr. Meder's riflemen kill every Blood Priest they see. Messengers," he added, that one word encompassing a number of other mounted men. He leaned forward and practically whispered to the lancer and dragoon messengers, then patted both on the arm and sent them away. He did the same with Major Olayne, who nodded emphatically before riding off. Lewis then raised his voice so the other messengers could hear. "Spread the word to move all the wounded back to the trees as well. Let's make the most of this time."

"What's with the secrets, Lewis?" Leonor asked, a little put out.

He waved her concerns away. "No secrets, just a few last-minute refinements to instructions you're already aware of."

Varaa *kakked* a chuckle and Leonor huffed in frustration.

A party of Dominion officers and escorts suddenly burst through the civilian front line of their army (the escorts battering those unfortunates back) and lingered a moment as if waiting to see if they'd be shot at before moving slowly forward.

Lewis absently scratched the whiskers on his chin. "Colonel Har-Kaaska, Varaa, Captain Hernandez, Corporal Hannity, come with me, if you'd be so good. I don't believe we'll need a larger escort." He didn't invite Leonor and would've preferred she stay behind, but he knew that wasn't going to happen. She'd appointed herself as his primary, ever-present protector, and he was resigned to the fact. "Let's go see what they have to say, shall we?"

"Lewis," Har-Kaaska began warningly, clearly about to object to his going himself, but then simply shook his head and urged his odd mount forward to follow because Lewis had already done the same with Arete and was moving up through the lines, Leonor cursing and rushing after him. Healers and their helpers, often natives of villages they'd liberated from the

Doms, had already been removing the wounded and dead, and there weren't many left on the ground to avoid. The same was true for the space between the armies since the enemy hadn't yet tried to come to grips. The civilians in front of them made a fairly bedraggled line, however, because the Doms had largely thrown their fallen out in front of them instead of removing them to the rear. Lewis continued forward, eyes straight ahead and fixed on a particularly ornately decorated officer with a long black goatee and impressively sculpted mustaches he assumed must be General Gomez. He didn't pause until he reached a point roughly halfway between the armies, stopping about ten yards short of the waiting enemy delegation.

CHAPTER 3

"Well," Lewis said at last, speaking the somewhat universally recognized Spanya. "General Gomez, I presume?"

The man bowed in his saddle, making ornate hand gestures as he did so. "Indeed," he replied in the same language, sitting upright again, before continuing in a tone touched with sarcasm. "And judging from descriptions I've had, you can only be the dreadful Coronel Cayce, commanding this violent rabble of Los Diablos, come to threaten the benign, peace-loving Holy Dominion that I have the honor to defend."

Leonor snorted incredulously.

"Ah!" Gomez exclaimed with a delighted expression. "And it is true what I have heard! You not only countenance the presence of lowly females in your army"—his narrow-eyed gaze slid to Varaa and Har-Kaaska—"not to mention animal demons, but their presence here with you implies you actually heed their counsel! Extraordinary! They will all turn on you in the end, you know. It is their very nature."

"We suspected you only requested this meeting to exchange insults," Har-Kaaska grumbled impatiently. "That has invariably been the case in the past. I suppose it's almost comforting to know that nothing has changed."

Gomez was peering intently at the Mi-Anakka. He smiled and shook his head. "I see its mouth moving, but hear no speech." He looked back at

Lewis and held his hands out to his sides. "The truly pious cannot hear the vile words demons spew."

"I bet you hear *me*," Leonor snapped.

Gomez rolled his eyes. "Of course. Females are such annoying creatures, little more intelligent than beasts," he confided conversationally to Lewis. "They *are* people, however, and their souls have value to God. That said, I do often wish their prattle was as silent to me as a demon's." He sighed. Lewis was prepared to reach over and grab Leonor's arm if her hand went to one of her pistols. He saw that Varaa was ready as well. Somewhat uncharacteristically, Leonor only sat in seething silence.

Lewis cleared his throat. "Now that the obligatory insults"—he nodded at the terrified civilians—"and your disdain for human life have established your consistency with what we've come to expect from your sort, whyever should I remain to converse with you further?"

Gomez blinked in surprise. "Why, I would've thought that to be obvious. Entirely aside from our mutual curiosity and desire to gauge our opponent, we both play for time. For my part, even now, my officers are . . . reconditioning regiments that you have admittedly handled harshly, while taking the opportunity to deploy our artillery where its fire will not be obscured. For your part, you seek to delay me for various reasons of your own. I can clearly see your efforts to establish defenses to your rear, you hope your Rangers off over there"—he waved at the trees bordering the river—"will arrive to sweep down on my flank, and you know that as soon as we recommence hostilities, you'll be forced to make a terrible choice: whether to fire on 'innocents' or not." Gomez smiled smugly. "I'm not foolish enough to grant you sufficient time to build adequate defenses; I've already sent all my lancers to counter your undeniably formidable Rangers, and you *will* have to kill what you deem to be innocent townsfolk in order to begin killing my soldiers again." He shook his head, seemingly perplexed. "I don't think you'll do it. By all accounts, you are far too sentimental about such things, even willing to preserve enemy civilians at the cost of your soldiers' lives. As you can clearly see, *I* entertain no such derisible inhibitions."

Lewis cocked his head slightly. "So, you think you have all the answers?"

"I do," Gomez confirmed, "and this battle is as good as won. We'll break you here and slaughter your survivors as they flee." He chuckled. "All because you cannot bring yourself to harm noncombatants. You are irresolute in that one respect, at least, because your weak, false God has made you so.

I will use that against you. There," he said triumphantly. "You see? Though we have never met, I know you already."

"If you think it'll be that easy, you do *not* know Colonel Cayce at all," Varaa said.

Gomez again pretended not to hear her, but it was obvious he did. Instead of pursuing that subject further, he abruptly changed it. "So where is the pretender, Don Hurac? It *is* he who leads this army, is it not? Doubtless, you command, but it is his cause you pursue. I would've thought he would appear alongside you to plead his case and try to win our support."

"Nope," Leonor snapped. "Colonel Cayce leads here. Don Hurac's just along for the ride."

"That's essentially true," Lewis confirmed. "I'm honored to command our entire combined force, and though we're sympathetic to and supportive of Don Hurac's purpose—he *is* the rightful claimant to the position of 'Supreme Holiness,' after all, and the man you serve is the true pretender—Don Hurac's motivation is somewhat coincidental to our own. The grievances that drive us to destroy you and your Blood Priest masters predate our acquaintance with Don Hurac and are more than sufficient, I assure you. As to where he is . . . it should suffice to say he accompanies the army and is safe from you. He isn't a soldier, you know." Lewis smiled wryly. "Besides, if I don't trust you not to attempt my assassination during this meeting, why should he?"

Gomez affected a hurt expression. "You wound me deeply, Coronel Cayce! I do assure you most emphatically that I would never stoop to such an outrage! To murder a colleague, even a heretic enemy, under a sacred flag of truce . . . what an appalling notion!"

"Not too appalling for the Blood Cardinal Don Frutos and his pet Blood Priest, Tranquilo. They made a rather elaborate effort to murder me and those with me the first time we met."

Lewis thought he finally detected genuine misgivings on the face of the opposing general. "Ah," he said. "Well, we are from the western Dominion, as you surely know by now, and the influence Blood Priests have acquired is a relatively new thing there. New things are never quickly embraced where I am from. As for our different customs concerning interaction with adversaries, our dealings with . . . other powers have accustomed us to this sort of thing. We understand there are rules. The same was not true for the army Don Frutos had at his disposal. And as for the Holy Patriarcha Tranquilo,

I've noted that he *is* rather zealous, perhaps even impetuous, and it seems that Don Frutos was more *his* pet than the reverse even then."

Leonor snorted again, a most unladylike sound that she probably made deliberately to annoy Gomez. "Holy Patriarcha? Who promoted him to that, himself?"

Gomez was annoyed, but perhaps just as much because Leonor guessed right. "He *has* become the right hand of His Supreme Holiness," he deflected.

"The hand holdin' the puppet strings, I bet," Leonor prodded.

Lewis cleared his throat again. "So, what shall we talk about? Are you seeking terms? Do you mean to surrender?"

Gomez barked a laugh. "Hardly. And I know it is pointless for me to ask the same of you since you are no doubt already aware that the only inducements I am at liberty to offer are slavery for your troops and a quick death for you and your officers. I've heard you do not believe in acquiring grace through suffering, and though it would grieve me to deny you salvation, I would give you my word that your deaths would be as free of pain as possible. Honestly," he confided, "I'd be terribly disappointed if you agreed. I have been a soldier all my life, but never have I enjoyed the opportunity to fight a proper battle. Events so far today have only roused my appetite for the . . . sport of the thing, if you will. You and your army are doomed. That is inevitable and ordained by God. My primary purpose in coming forward was to speak to a military peer opponent while I can. Have you any idea how rare that is? And I sadly doubt I will have the chance later."

Lewis urged Arete to take a few steps forward. "You truly crave the 'sport' of battle? If the outcome of this one is preordained by a cowardly God who hides his warriors behind those who can't fight, where's the sport in that?" He reached across and touched the engraved guard of his M1840 artillery saber. "On the other hand, I'll be most happy to give you all the sport you want, right now."

Gomez held up a finger and waved it back and forth with a grin. "Ah, but it is *not* guaranteed I will survive the battle."

Lewis shrugged. "Then let's fight, you and I. If our leadership is superfluous to the outcome, what difference could it make?"

The grin Gomez wore slipped away. "I suppose your logic is unassailable, but I believe I shall have to decline. I have fought men with blades before, and while I confess there's a measure of excitement to it, I don't really have a peer." He gestured at himself and the fine uniform he wore. "Besides, I am not dressed for it. The fabric of this coat is insanely expensive, rather tedious to acquire, and my body slave would never get your blood out of it. I'd personally much rather both of us live to enjoy at least part of the battle."

Lewis spun Arete around, deliberately showing his back to his enemy. "Then you're as much a coward as your evil God," he said contemptuously, "and we'll soon see what his promises are worth!"

Sal Hernandez surprised everyone by suddenly cupping his hands around his mouth and bellowing as loudly as he could, "People of Texcoco! We come to free you! Do not do the bidding of your oppressors and force us to slay you. Rise up against the Blood Priests and we will help!"

General Gomez's escorts surged forward, raising their musketoons, but Lewis was already spinning around, saber out, Varaa's sword was drawn, and Sal and Leonor both pointed revolvers at General Gomez's face. Gomez, wide-eyed, quickly shouted for his protectors to stand down.

"Have you changed your mind about a personal contest here, General?" Lewis asked lowly.

Gomez shook his head. "I have not."

As if disappointed, Lewis turned away again, saber still in hand. He nodded at his companions, and they all began trotting back to their lines. Leonor was the last to leave, revolver still pointed, rock solid, at Gomez. "No guarantee you'll survive," she reminded. "Fact, I reckon I can promise you won't." She grinned. "Not in one piece, anyway." With that, she spun and bolted after the others.

"I sure wanted to shoot the silly bastard," she said when she caught up with Lewis.

"Me too," Sal agreed. "I wonder what difference it would'a made?"

"Most likely, it would've only gotten us killed," Har-Kaaska said, barely moving in the saddle. The creature he rode had an incredibly smooth gait. "A lot of infantry had pushed through the civilians. Perhaps a hundred or more. The range was still long for an accurate volley, but with that much lead in the air, they were almost bound to hit us."

"Their own as well," Corporal Hannity said, adding a rare, unsolicited comment.

"I doubt they would've cared after Leonor already shot Gomez," Lewis said with a chuckle. A moment later, they'd returned to the lines and were pushing back through. "We've wasted enough time. Sound the call for the artillery to recommence firing, Corporal Hannity," Lewis ordered. Leonor looked at him in surprise, and Lewis confided, "I told Mr. Olayne to watch for their artillery to deploy while we were talking. Gomez told us it would. Now we can kill it—shooting over the civilians in front of the enemy." Hannity obligingly sounded the call and all the guns on the flanks immediately responded with earth-shattering battery fire—six guns each, all going off at once. The center guns took a few moments longer while their Number Two men hooked the ends of each canister load with their worm staffs and drew them out before reloading with spherical case. Even before the enemy guns got the word to commence firing themselves, dirty flags of gray-white smoke were bursting and unfurling above them, sheeting their crews with shell fragments and musket balls mixed with smoldering pitch.

"Now signal the dragoons and lancers to engage," Lewis said. Hannity quickly blew that call as well. It was answered and repeated, and the muffled thunder of hundreds of muddy hooves erupted on the left flank, two dense columns racing forward. The deep, thrumming horns of the Dominion were blowing as well, the signals seeming somewhat hurried. With a great deal of shouting and cursing, the dense line of terrified civilians, now completely masking the enemy infantry that had re-formed behind them, wailed even louder as they were pushed forward. The combined Allied infantry of 1st and 2nd Divisions stood fast, muskets forward with bayonets fixed, but there was nervous jostling and many significant looks at platoon leaders and regimental officers. Few of the soldiers in those dense lines would hesitate to fire if ordered, but even fewer would gladly carry out such a command, and Lewis was certain that many would deliberately miss. What mattered at the moment was that they look like they'd do it. His own officers and NCOs seemed to understand that, shouting at their men to stand firm, resolute, eyes forward.

The two columns of mounted troops were swinging wide, out of range of the musketry that had opened on that flank, and their objective should've become clear even to Gomez by now. The enemy artillery was being systematically smothered by an incessant hail of case shot, and only a few guns had even managed to fire. A single 8pdr shot smashed through the ranks of the 1st US, plowing a furrow through an entire file, shredding and throwing parts of men and their equipment at other troops standing by. It was terrible to see, but it could've been much worse. Other rounds either went long, shrieking by overhead, or struck short and bounded up amid a fountain of moist soil, usually falling harmlessly behind the army. Those short rounds would've done far worse if the ground were hard, so the muddy field had given them that advantage, at least.

What Gomez had failed to anticipate and now had no way to counter were Ramon Lara's lancers and Coryon Burton's dragoons, who'd suddenly gone from column into line almost instantly. The dragoons charged hard at the rear flank of the enemy force, Hall carbines and musketoons filled with drop shot blasting away as they fell on the Doms from behind. Lara's lancers swept down on the unsupported and hopelessly mired artillery line, which couldn't be turned quick enough to stop them. Lara rolled over each gun in turn. Lewis's artillery began to shift its fire to the right, toward the center rear of the enemy, as the mounted men entered their impact area. None of this had a bearing on what was happening right in front of Lewis, however.

"Do we start to fall back?" Har-Kaaska asked.

"Not yet," Lewis said, nodding at the oncoming mob. Torn between the Blood Priests pushing them from behind and the solid, triple-rank wall of gleaming bayonets leveled at them like a murderous steel hedge, the wild-eyed civilians were beginning to balk. Even while resolutely holding their ground, troops in those ranks were shouting in Spanya, urging the people to stop, begging them not to make them use their weapons—while assuring them they would if they had to. Many women, quite a few bearing infants, were simply collapsing, sobbing or wailing, while men tried to protect them from being trampled. Some finally started to fight with those pressing in behind, or desperately attempted to knock the bayonets aside with whatever weapon they carried and make a lane to pass. None Lewis saw were actively attacking his men, though some must have done. Screams arose here and there, out of view, likely when desperate soldiers were left no choice but to stab someone. The mass of people recoiled from such sounds, further compressing their numbers and inflaming their terror and growing hate toward those still crowding them forward. It was a horrible, heart-wrenching sight, but Lewis only watched, stone-faced and silent, hand held high beside him as if physically restraining his men, holding them in place, while prepared to motion them back—or forward.

Sal Hernandez remained near the front, still sitting on his horse and holding a revolver but yelling himself hoarse. "Now is the time, *mis ami-*

gos!" he roared, voice cracking. "Rise against the Blood Priests! It is *they* who are killing you, not us. Turn on them and we will help! They will only kill you in the end, after you do their bidding. We will protect you!" He visibly hesitated before continuing. "Don Hurac is with us! The rightful Supreme Holiness does *not* want your deaths! Rise up for him! Rise up for God! Strike your oppressors and clear the way for us to kill them all!"

Whether it was the unbearable pressure building in front of the wall of bayonets or Sal's harangue, taken up by others, that actually turned the tide was immaterial. What mattered was that more and more of those at the point of contact started shrieking their frustration and using their weapons to bash or slash a passage back the way they'd come. Taken by surprise, many died under these sudden frantic blows, but tragic as that was, it was the impetus others required to finally turn and fight as well. A growing fervor and purpose suffused the mob, radiating backward, and Lewis might've seen the first Dom civilian raise his weapon against a briefly glimpsed Blood Priest.

"That's done it, I think," he said sadly aside to Leonor.

"Maybe," she agreed. "I feel pretty . . . dirty, though."

"We'll feel even worse soon enough," he warned, "but better than if we'd killed them all ourselves, or lost the fight because we couldn't."

Leonor didn't have anything to say to that.

A tipping point had been reached, and the situation changed remarkably quickly. Still screaming threats and whipping and clubbing or stabbing their assailants with short swords they carried under red robes, Blood Priests were being mobbed under. Soon, except for the guns firing on the Dom artillery on the enemy left—those guns on the right had been overrun by Lara's lancers—the only real fighting here at the front (aside from some careful sniping by Meder's riflemen) was between the Doms themselves. A desperate Dom officer, seeing the nightmare in front of him, ordered his infantry to fire a volley into the civilian press. That fire was answered by agonized screams—and, incredibly, a return volley from the Dominion soldiers to the left of those who fired. Some officer over there had had enough of this. Lewis knew from Agon that many "*soldados profesionales*" held their personal honor close, and the wholesale murder of their own people, especially under circumstances like this, could turn them when nothing else would.

"I hope Mr. Meder restrains his riflemen from shooting *that* officer,"

Varaa said. Lewis hoped so as well, but it might make little difference. Even as the now-rampaging civilians vented their fury on the first regiment that shot them, a reserve regiment did the same, slaughtering hundreds. Shockingly, other troops then fired on *them*. Soon, a free-for-all pitched battle had erupted in front of the Allied Army.

"We should advance an' help those folks!" Leonor said. Har-Kaaska shook his head. "No. Not yet, at least. The civilians must do this on their own, at least long enough to clear our front. Our men still can't fire," he reminded, blinking significantly at Lewis, then added, "Besides, even those Dom soldiers already fighting their own . . . that doesn't mean they won't fight us. We remain their enemies."

On the enemy's rear right, Burton's dragoons were firing into them just as fast as they could reload their breechloading Hall carbines and Lara's lancers were re-forming to charge the Doms from behind, but there suddenly came a rapid, distinctly different stutter of gunfire on the enemy's far left—Lewis's right; the throaty thump of short-barreled musketoons, for the most part. Lewis raised his glass to see, then sighed with relieved satisfaction. "It seems the timing worked out well enough after all," he said, barely aloud. Major Anson's Rangers had poured out of the woods along the river and formed in a line just in time to deliver blistering fire into the charging Dom lancers. Yellow-coated forms tumbled to the ground, and squealing horses fell and rolled. Many other horses scattered and ran in all directions. The surviving Dom lancers pressed on, weapons lowered, but the Rangers leaped forward as well. The two forces quickly merged with a crash of shattering lances, horses colliding at crippling speeds, and more shooting heard even here. Lewis refocused his glass beyond the mounted fight, now just a swirl of motion and drifting gunsmoke, and grunted with more satisfaction when he saw the 3rd and 4th Divisions emerging from the trees.

"General Gomez may have stolen a march on us this morning, but his scouts clearly never probed deeply enough to catch Agon and Itzam doing the same to him, creeping up from the east."

"You knew they were there all along!" Leonor accused. Lewis shook his head. "I wasn't sure about Agon and Itzam, though I considered it likely." He smiled at her, his own relief still palpable. "I *was* sure about your father and his Rangers." He gestured at the distant trees. "I've been watching the progress of the lizardbirds erupting into the sky."

Varaa clapped her hands and *kakked* while Leonor stared north. "I should've seen that," she chided herself.

Colonel Reed came galloping up, his and his escort's horses blowing steaming breath that glowed gold under the sun, now standing high over the trees. "You did it again, Lewis," Reed said grudgingly, almost accusingly. "Even while preparing for the worst, you contrive to waste those arrangements. No wonder the men think you're a genius and would follow you anywhere!" He managed a grin. "By God, so would I!"

Lewis was shaking his head. "I could've just as easily lost it all today—and we're not finished yet. Our front's still blocked, and we can't fire effectively, or carefully enough to keep from hurting civilians, but they've opened a significant gap between us and the enemy. We'll advance into it. I'm not morally opposed to the locals doing their own fighting, mind, but they aren't armed and trained for it and there are too many women and children among them. The least we can do is have the men call out to them and pass them to the rear as we go. In addition, some of those Dom soldiers fighting their own may now be inclined to join us, or at least Don Hurac." He looked at Sal Hernandez, now drifting slightly back from the line. "That additional entreaty you shouted was well done, by the way. In any event, we'll try to give them that chance. Messenger," he called out to one of those who'd returned, "race to the right, as quick as you can, and apprise Colonel Agon of the situation. After the losses he suffered at Puebla, he might welcome more replacements, and his men are best suited to evaluate their sincerity, I believe."

"What about Father?" Leonor asked. Lewis raised his glass again before shaking his head. "I can't make him out at this distance, and no messenger will ever catch him. He isn't closing on the enemy infantry, at least, leaving that for Agon and Itzam, but the Dom lancers seem to be attempting to disengage, and he and his Rangers are hanging on their tail. No doubt they'll link up with Burton and Lara."

CHAPTER 4

"S hit," growled Major Giles Anson, slamming one of his two massive Walker Colt revolvers into its holster hanging under his armpit and along the side of his chest while reining his tall, powerful, old-world horse out of the yipping, shooting, thundering chase. The Dom lancers had broken, the second time for this bunch who'd done the same at Puebla, and the full Ranger regiment under Anson's direct command had been only too happy to chase them. Leaning forward, the iron-bearded officer explored a deep saber gash in the animal's shoulder with his fingers, eliciting an indignant, spuppering objection and attempted bite from the horse he'd—somewhat inappropriately in retrospect—named "Colonel Fannin" in its youth. The gelding had been full of potential but timid and flighty and with all the aggression and spirit of his unlamented namesake, yet had blossomed into a warhorse on a par with Lewis's Arete in the years since. Anson often regretted the animal was gelded, imagining the foals the two could've produced.

"Whoa there, you rock-headed bastard," he snapped as Colonel Fannin tried to rejoin the chase when Captain Bandy "Boogerbear" Beeryman peeled away from a cluster of pursuing Rangers—there was no cohesive force at the moment—and stopped his own rather impressive native animal, named "Dodger," to check on him.

"Poor fella's cut up," the giant, black-bearded Ranger mildly observed. "So're you," he pointed out, gesturing at a slash across Anson's thigh, blood soaking the sky-blue trousers.

"Same saber got us both," Anson agreed. "We've had worse an' kept on before," he seemed to decide.

Boogerbear nodded reasonably. It took more than a mere battle to get a rise out of the huge man. "Reckon so, but wounds add up an' yer neither one gettin' younger. Why don't you both just sit the rest o' this out? Throw a couple stitches in yerselves."

Anson looked angrily at his friend. "How the hell am I s'posed to do that? I ease off for a minute to check a couple o' scrapes, expectin' *you* to take charge while I do, an' you run off an' leave the whole regiment to straggle off an' fall apart!"

Boogerbear had known Giles Anson for close to twenty years, through both of their very worst times. If battles didn't faze him, his friend's irascible nature went entirely unheeded. He did respond, however. "Our boys're a little disordered, sure, but they were all wadded up with the Doms when they bolted. Hard to sort that out an' keep the scare hot too. You know that, an' you know *they* know what they're doin'. Most of 'em," he fairly amended. "An' tellin' the truth, I figgered I'd be back with 'em by now instead o' arguin' with you. Wasted breath on my part." He shrugged. "So go ahead an' come on back along. Ruin yer horse, bleed ta death. I don't care."

Anson just stared at his friend a moment; only a few Rangers were still galloping past, and Agon's and Itzam's divisions were nearly up to them now, the sound of battle a constant roar. Anson barked a laugh. "Point taken. Get back up with our boys. Keep the scare hot, as you say, but check with Major Burton when you see him before goin' off to take Texcoco by yourself. I'll get one o' Agon's healers to stitch me an' Colonel Fannin up, get another horse, an' try to catch up." He grinned. "*Then* we might take Texcoco together!"

"I'll swan," Boogerbear said, as close to an exclamation as he was usually capable of. "You must be half bled out ta see sense so easy." Turning Dodger, he kicked him forward and galloped after their men.

"C'mon, you ol' possum," Anson said to Colonel Fannin, pulling him around and heading for the advancing 4th Division, the predominantly green-and-black uniforms originally dyed that way from the yellow of its former Dom soldiers and now new-made. That had come about through replacement of campaign-ravaged garments, but also symbolized that, not only were many members recruits in the division, its veterans were "new" men as well. Anson noted that healers had already come out of the line with the skirmishers to check on his Ranger wounded.

"I do hope you are well," Colonel Agon greeted him when Anson angled through the ranks of his men, slogging laboriously through the damp, clingy soil.

"Scratched up a little, is all. Thought I'd get stitched an' borrow a horse."

"Of course." Agon raised his voice. "Messenger, a healer and a replacement mount for the major." He smiled. "And you might inform his wife, the *estimada* Senora Samantha, that her husband is here, in case she desires a quick visit."

Anson started to say, "I just saw her this morning," but a frowning Agon continued. "Discourage Don Hurac from coming as well." He looked apologetically at Anson. "I don't want him here when we join the action, which will happen quite soon, and your wife is much more sensible about staying back from the front. Don Hurac is less so. Unlike Senora Samantha, he feels he has something to prove."

"Could be he does," Anson tossed out, "but you're right. No sense riskin' him."

"You broke the lancers again," the diminutive Uxmalo priest Father Orno said warmly. As was his custom now, he was dressed in an entirely black version of the American uniform, complete with black wheel hat.

Anson waved off the praise. "Same ones we broke before. Gettin' to be a habit with 'em, I guess." He looked around. "Half expected to see Reverend Harkin up here with you."

Orno shook his head. "We all prevailed upon him to remain back with Don Hurac. I fear he is still too weak to spend any time on horseback." Harkin was a Presbyterian minister who'd lost an arm at the Battle of Puebla. The combination of Uxmalo, Ocelomeh, and American medicine had him healing surprisingly well. Like Dr. Newlin, he'd been directly engaged to administer to members of the 3rd Pennsylvania Volunteer regiment for its adventure in Mexico, but just as Dr. Newlin—and Samantha Anson, now—had found themselves better occupied by the army's logistical effort, Harkin's flock was vastly expanded.

"Too bad," Anson grunted as a harried-looking female Ocelomeh healer and Samantha herself arrived, both mounted, the messenger who'd gone for them towing a saddled horse. "Harkin always seems to get a kick out of a good fight." He smiled at Samantha's pretty, stormy face as the healer got down and approached while Anson gave Colonel Fannin a reassuring pat before switching horses without dismounting. The effort caused him to wince.

"Did I not tell you to be careful?" Samantha scolded. Her cultivated English accent and tone combined to make it sound like she was chastising a child.

"I *was* careful," Anson defended. "Bast . . . I mean the Dom lancer who done it would'a took my head off if I wasn't."

"Not careful enough, clearly," she huffed, maneuvering her own horse closer so she could lean over and plant a peck on his cheek before inserting a lit cigar between his lips.

The healer was trudging alongside them, trying to cut away the slashed trouser leg. She suddenly snapped up at him in Spanya. "If you don't want me to accidentally *amputate* this leg, you will stop long enough for me to do my job!"

Anson laughed and did as he was told, heaving back on the reins of his borrowed horse before waving at Agon and the others. "You'll be in the fight by the time this is done, so I'll say so long an' good luck. I'll ride around your right an' try to catch my boys in the Dom rear—if they're still there."

"Farewell, Major Anson," Agon replied seriously. "I look forward to seeing you in one piece when this is over."

"God be with you," added Father Orno, almost in benediction.

Shit, Anson thought. "Ah . . . You too, both of you," he answered somewhat awkwardly, surprised by the warm sentiments from a former enemy and a priest. He hissed in surprise at the pain when the healer plunged a needle into the lip of the open gash on his leg she'd been cleaning as best she could. "Damn it, woman! That hurt worse than the saber."

"My sympathies," the healer said offhand. "You might have hardly noticed if you would only hold that horse still. I nearly sewed you to the saddle!"

"My own horse, Colonel Fannin . . ." Anson said, looking around.

"Already removed to be tended," Samantha assured him primly, "and I must say that he showed considerably more sense about it than you. Now, Mr. Anson, as your wife, I have every right to insist that you pay more attention to your repairs, particularly if you mean to gallop off immediately and rejoin the fight," Samantha added in a scolding tone.

Anson bowed to the woman before turning to watch the advance of 3rd and 4th Divisions as the healer continued her work. The Doms seemed to be buckling in the center in front of Lewis, and in the rear where Lara's lancers, Burton's dragoons, and now his own Rangers had struck. Here on this flank, however, the enemy looked both intact and prepared. "I'll do my best, my dear. Just hurry it up, if you please," he urged the healer. A creditable volley crashed out from the Doms facing Agon's men, and a tragic number of them went down. Whizzing musket balls were loud all around them even here.

"Almost finished," the healer announced before he could rush her again.

"You need to get back," Anson told his wife.

"Nonsense," she said. "They'll never hit me here." She grinned. "Not without hitting you first," she added. "It's all about angles, you see."

Anson rolled his eyes. "Go! I'll find you when it's over."

Leaning forward and plucking the cigar from his mouth, Samantha gave her new husband a proper kiss before clamping down on the cigar herself and swatting her horse's rump. Skirt whipping in the breeze she created in her rush, she was shortly safe from all but the most cosmically lucky projectile.

"There," cried the healer. "Best I can do for now. Make sure you have it properly checked and redone when the fight is over."

"I will," Anson promised. "Thanks," he added grudgingly, then spurred his borrowed mount to the right.

The Doms in front of Lewis quickly went from "buckling" to "collapsing" as increasing numbers of them actively joined the captive civilians in their effort to overthrow their oppressors. Lewis hadn't seen anything like it before—no one had—and it came as such a surprise that, as soon as he realized the ones that turned wouldn't keep fighting his own men, he had to scramble to organize support.

"They're shooting at each other, not us," reported Captain Cullin of the 3rd Pennsylvania as Lewis stopped to consult with him as he, Leonor, Varaa, Sal Hernandez, and a cluster of messengers thundered to the left through the fighting.

"So I see," Lewis agreed. "I'll find Colonel Reed again. Should've told him just a few minutes ago when I had him, and I doubt he'll follow these orders unless they come straight from me. I want him—and you," he pointedly told Cullin, "to directly support the civilians and enemy soldiers fighting their own. Don't get mixed among them whatever you do, but help them all you can. It might be important later if we're remembered to have done so, to have 'been on their side,' so to speak."

Cullin stared doubtfully at the confusing fight ahead. "I'll do my best, sir." He hesitated. "You *will* square it with Colonel Reed?"

"That's where I'm heading now," Lewis confirmed, urging Arete forward once more.

"I figured out the difference," Leonor shouted at him as they pounded through the muddy battlefield just behind the front ranks of Pennsylvanians. The 1st US—and hopefully Reed—would be just ahead. "Aside from a buncha these Doms bein' from the west, where Blood Priests ain't so well established, an' a bunch more o' these in particular maybe licked by us once already, the rest, for the first time, might be troops *from* here. Born an' raised in Texcoco, they're less likely to kill their own people than soldiers from somewhere else."

"I think you're right," Varaa agreed. "They might have reluctantly done it at first, afraid not to. But with the civilians already rising, and whether they know what's happening behind them or not, the *feel* of the battle turning sour, I suspect some local officers have been given an opportunity to do what they feel is right instead of just what they're told. I hope we can save some of them."

"Colonel Reed!" Lewis greeted the man, who was apparently returning to meet them.

"A hell of a thing, Colonel Cayce," Reed said, waving to the front.

"Indeed. I already told Captain Cullin to advance to contact with a purpose, but do so as carefully as possible, not to engage potential allies."

"I agree, but that'll be difficult," Reed warned.

Lewis was nodding. "Risky as well, moving toward men in enemy uniforms and waiting to see who they shoot at—us or their own countrymen. We have to try," he added with a shrug. "Pass the word to our men to join those clearly protecting or fighting alongside civilians, but not to break ranks and mingle or advance beyond them. Can't leave them behind us. The only exceptions are women and children, who'll be passed through the lines. Detail reserve companies to take charge of them."

Refraining from saluting, Reed solemnly nodded. "Will you be remaining here?"

Lewis was clearly tempted, fascinated to see how this unprecedented situation would evolve, but he finally shook his head. "No. Colonel Agon has engaged on the right"—the sound of battle was furiously growing there—"where the same . . . complications aren't present. He'll be facing a fairly cohesive force. I'll see if I can confuse them a little. God bless," he called to Reed and all the nearby troops. A cheer was raised when he turned to leave. That gave him pause, as always, and he almost stopped his horse to look back.

"Don't wonder, don't ask why, just accept it," Varaa told him.

"Consider it a sign the men trust you to do what's right and leave it at that," Har-Kaaska agreed. He *kakked* a laugh. "Now what *are* we going to do?"

Lewis pointed. "One of your best regiments, Major Wagley's Second Uxmal, is virtually unemployed on your far right, as is the First Techon, backing it, as usual." The two regiments always fought well together. "Worse," he continued, "all their fire will soon be masked by Agon's push. Let's put them to better use." Lewis urged Arete ahead behind the battle line, which was even now beginning to tromp forward at a measured pace. Here, at least. Flags were streaming, drums thundering, and isolated, company-size volleys slashed at obvious enemies. Lewis's companions followed suit, and together they pounded down to the right where the more distant regiments had yet to move. Beyond them, 3rd and 4th Divisions were much closer now, firing dense volleys of their own while regiments on the Dom left attempted to peel away and face them.

"Now," Lewis cried triumphantly, pointing again. "Now, while the confusion is most severe! Messenger," he called behind. "Fetch me Major Suiz as quickly as you can—he now commands the First Techon, does he not? Major Wagley!" he shouted, catching sight of the young officer among a mounted cluster behind the 2nd Uxmal's line.

"Sir?" Wagley shouted back, turning to watch Cayce's party approach.

"My compliments, sir," Lewis said loudly. "Knowing you and your men as I do, I'm sure you're growing bored with your current role?"

"Indeed, sir," Wagley agreed, grinning. "I presume your presence here means our tedium will soon be relieved?"

"That's the idea. Do you see those Doms pulling away to face Agon?"

"I do, sir," Wagley agreed, nodding a greeting at Major Suiz as the 1st Techon's commander galloped up to join them. "Practically the only formation we had to shoot at," he lamented, "and poor Suiz hasn't had a chance to do anything yet."

"We're going to change that," Lewis said. "Please move your regiment up directly behind the Second Uxmal, Major Suiz. When your men are ready, as quick as they can, both regiments will push forward at the quick time, in good order, and smash into those people over there. We'll hit them like a bolt from the blue with as much sound and spectacle as we can manage. Colonel Agon will ensure that his troops don't fire on us, and I suspect he'll quickly grasp our purpose and join the charge as well."

Lewis had spoken loudly and more cheers erupted nearby, growing as word spread further. Everyone saw the signs of his growing enthusiasm and knew he expected this movement to utterly wreck the enemy. Moreover, it suddenly looked very much like it would. Their regiments would be the ones to take the glory for destroying the last Dom army standing between them and the Holy City itself.

Suiz was waving excitedly and rattling off commands to his own messengers, who darted back to his men. Almost at once, the 1st Techon started mowing up behind the 2nd Uxmal, creating a solid, nearly square block of nearly two thousand men. Nodding satisfaction, Lewis turned to Wagley, Har-Kaaska, Varaa, and Leonor. "Ready?" he asked, drawing his saber with a well-oiled *sheenk* sound. Only Wagley seemed surprised by his apparent intent to personally join the action.

"Sir," Wagley began a little hesitantly, "uh, shouldn't you remain back here? You're always telling us our place in battle is directing the action, not leading it."

"And how well has that worked?" Varaa asked in a light, if vaguely sarcastic tone, blinking something Wagley couldn't decipher as she and Har-Kaaska drew their swords as well. "For you in particular, Mr. Wagley?" she added pointedly.

There were no cowards in the Allied officer corps, and no matter what Lewis said, they simply wouldn't be stopped from leading from the front. The Americans had brought that tradition with them to this world, and it had taken firm root. It was costly, of course, and Wagley himself had once been grievously wounded. Defensively mumbling something about hypocrisy setting a poor example, thinly veiled within a sigh, he drew his own sword. "With the colonel issuing all the orders"—he nodded at Har-Kaaska—"I, at least, shall dismount." Stepping down from his horse, he handed the animal off to an aide before grinning up at his superiors. "Down here, I can fight right amongst my boys—and present a less tempting target."

"Most laudable," Har-Kaaska said, his own strange mount shifting beneath him, apparently anxiously anticipating what was next. No more so than Arete. Lewis's aggressive chestnut mare could sense the same moment approaching, and she blew impatiently and danced from side to side, slinging mud from her hooves.

Leonor missed her own battle-tested mare, "Sparky," killed beneath her at the Battle of Puebla. Her new horse seemed game enough, but she hadn't given him a name. Now she looked at Lewis, sorely tempted to add her own open admonition to Wagley's, but knew it would be pointless. Lewis was *in* the battle now, and despite his earlier misgivings, he'd seen this opportunity and simply had to pounce. She could no more attempt to suppress that part of him that awakened at moments like this than he could force her to stay back from him when they happened. It was part of what they were, part of what they loved about each other. Her duty now, as she saw it, to both the cause they fought for and the man she loved, was to protect the army commander as best she could when he seemed to instinctively lunge for the enemy's throat when it was exposed to him.

"First Techon! Second Uxmal!" Har-Kaaska bellowed loudly, a curious aspect of Mi-Anakka voices allowing his words to carry even over the roar of battle. "The enemy is in disarray before us, the battle in our grasp! Forward at the quick time in good order—let's dance to some music if you please—march!"

Drums thundered loudly and fifers broke into a lively rendition of "Come to the Bower" as both regiments surged forward as one with a yell. A ragged volley met them from the disorganized Doms, rushed and poorly aimed, but there were screams and shouts of pain from the front ranks regardless. Leonor saw Lewis give Arete her head so she could keep up with the jogging troops, only directing her slightly right while the narrow gap between the regiments still existed. "Varaa, this way," she called to her Mi-Anakka friend. Varaa nodded and followed. Corporal Hannity and several others noticed their commander's divergence as well, pursuing as best they could. Har-Kaaska remained where he was.

"He will want a straight shot at the enemy, no doubt, without our own infantry in the way," Varaa cried.

"I'm sure," Leonor shouted back. "Where the damn Doms have a straight shot at *him*."

Varaa was shaking her head. "Reckless as usual, but not mindlessly so. He'll want to be closer to Agon, be *seen* by Fourth Division and possibly signal it as well."

"Yeah. So? No easier on us watchin' out for him." Leonor caught a scandalized look from Corporal Hannity. "What?" Leonor snapped at him. "It's true, an' you know it."

Hannity's only response was to more vigorously urge his horse through the tightening, narrowing gap.

A roundshot, the first from the enemy guns not yet overrun in several moments, crashed down among the Uxmalos, smashing a whole file of men in a chorus of screams, spraying Leonor with mud and blood and other things. She ruthlessly applied her spurs. Nothing like the army style, her spurs had big silver rowels that raised a high-pitched, protesting snort from her horse, but quickly got him moving. Even so, it took time for her to follow Lewis almost two hundred more yards to 2nd Division's extreme right flank, and by that time, 4th Division's left was practically within pistol shot. The angle that formed as the Doms peeled their own left flank back against Agon's original assault was in terrible disarray, and despite a furious resumption of fire, it was clearly overripe for Har-Kaaska's and Wagley's charge crashing against it even now.

The first glance Leonor got of Lewis when she broke clear of the troops around her, he was somehow all alone in the tiny space between the divisions, roaring unheard at the 4th and slashing his saber diagonally toward the enemy as Arete cavorted in a circle and musket balls flailed all around him, snatching blue fuzz from his jacket and making a cloud of Arete's fur clippings. The noise was tremendous, and no one could possibly hear him, but someone—possibly Agon himself—grasped what he wanted. A growing tattoo of drums and a Dom horn, which Agon's division still used to blow American calls, sounded briskly. Almost at once, just before 4th Division smashed into the Doms in front of them, the whole block of troops with their bristling bayonets angled abruptly to their right, colliding with the enemy at an oblique. At virtually the same instant, a terrible crash heralded the savage contact between Wagley's men and the enemy.

Leonor, Varaa, and Hannity had only just joined Lewis when he spanked Arete's rump with his saber and hurled himself into the enemy as well.

"Damn it!" Leonor cried. "After him," she shouted at her companions, drawing one of her revolvers. Lewis—and his remarkable horse—had turned into wild things. Saber slashing, hooves stomping and kicking, they relentlessly rode men down with abandon, while those too far to even attempt a jab with a bayonet surged back and away as best they could. Those who were closer were less fortunate. Even through her fury, Leonor could only marvel. Never highly skilled or trained with a saber, Lewis made up for his lack of style with brutal power and aggression, creating a virtual fountain of blood all around him. And Arete! Leonor's father's horse, Colonel Fannin, could be relied on to do his part in a fight, slamming into enemy horses and bashing them down to crush their riders. He'd even been known to deliberately stomp or kick the occasional enemy. Leonor never saw any indication he actually enjoyed it, though.

Arete was different, a true warhorse. Normally placid, even thoughtful—much like her master, Leonor suddenly realized—she turned into something else in a fight. Teeth gaping, eyes wide and missing nothing, her hooves shot out and smashed heads, faces, chests. She even bit, traumatically so, crushing necks, shoulders, and arms, all while maintaining a steady platform for Lewis to use his saber, sometimes even positioning him where her peripheral vision told her he needed to be to cope with a threat to them both. That took extraordinary trust from an animal descended from prey. And if Arete possessed any prey instinct of her own, she'd either subverted it completely or channeled it into something else.

Leonor took all this in even as she fought at her lover's side, snapping off shots from first one, then her second Paterson Colt from mere feet away, shooting most enemy threats in the face. Varaa used her own sword with far greater skill than Lewis, slashing with the razor-sharp tip or lunging and stabbing men in the throat and upper chest. Corporal Hannity did the same, skillfully guiding his horse and using his dragoon saber with carefully honed precision. In spite of all that, they would've most likely been doomed, easy prey for massed musket fire, if the Doms they struck hadn't already affixed their plug bayonets in preparation for the infantry charge.

Dom bayonets were good, all-purpose weapons, actually excellent short swords with broad blades, wooden hilts, and brass guards. The problem was, their tapered, rounded hilts actually had to be driven into the muzzles of their muskets to be of use as bayonets, and those muskets couldn't be fired again until they were driven back out. A few of their foes were attempting to do just that, striking the guards with whatever came to hand, even rocks, trying to break the tight friction fit that held them in place. In most cases, by the time they succeeded and reloaded their weapons, they were dead.

Not all. A musket flashed and boomed very close, muzzle almost touching Varaa's horse in front of its left ear. The animal's legs retracted beneath it like a killed spider's, and it dropped and fell on its side. With an agility only a Mi-Anakka could possibly possess, Varaa was already off the horse before it hit the ground and had driven her long blade into the shooter's throat, under his jaw. Blood sprayed back at her as she ripped the sword clear and whirled to face another threat.

"Varaa's down, Lewis, an' my pistols are empty," Leonor shouted. "Time to quit playin' an' get outa here!"

Lewis slashed down at a final victim, slicing deep across his back, before he sat up straight in his saddle and seemed to take a deep breath. "Unnecessary," he said, voice strangely calm. "We've broken them here." He pointed forward with his bloody saber. "And Second and Third Divisions have joined in rolling the enemy up."

It was true. The greater fight was moving away, and the battle line was dominated by the backs of their own men, mostly the 1st Techon from this perspective. Doms around them were fleeing in whichever direction seemed safest, and that's when Leonor realized Lewis's charge hadn't been gratuitous or pointless at all. The block they'd shattered would've been left behind as the two divisions joined. It wouldn't have been large, but was plenty big enough to savage the joining flanks from behind. Lewis had seen at once that it needed to be distracted. She couldn't banish the suspicion he would've jumped in anyway, but felt a surge of guilt for simply assuming it was so.

Lewis quickly stepped down from Arete to check his horse for wounds while Corporal Hannity did the same. As Lewis looked up at Leonor, a small smile appeared on his blood-spattered face, as if he could read her thoughts. "Your horse is uninjured?"

"Not a scratch," Leonor replied.

"Can she carry you and Varaa both?"

"Sure, for a while. Not far in a run if we have to keep up with Arete."

"I will keep up if I have to run myself," Varaa pronounced, tail whipping fiercely.

"It shouldn't come to that," Lewis assured. "I expect we'll soon be able to replace your horse." Kneeling swiftly to wipe the blood off his saber with the tail of a dead Dom's coat, he returned the blade to his scabbard and swung back into his Ringgold saddle. The battle was moving away very quickly, leaving the damp field littered with wounded and dead. Most wore Dominion yellow and black, but there were too many sky-blue-clad men by far. Most surprising was the size of the group of civilians, mostly women and children, gathered off to the left. They were under guard, but not by a very large force, and there were many hundreds, perhaps thousands of them. A large percentage appeared to be weeping and wailing, either in grief, fear, or pain, but they didn't seem to present a threat. Colonel Reed must've thought not or he wouldn't have left them like that, or allowed some of the army's healers to go among them.

"We'll rest our animals a moment more," Lewis decided. "You might want to reload your revolvers," he said aside to Leonor, but saw she was already beginning to, driving one of the wedges out into her hand and pulling a barrel off.

"What then?" Varaa asked.

Lewis nodded forward. "Find you a horse and get back in the fight—though I expect it'll be mostly decided by then."

CHAPTER 5

Fighting flared and quickly died around the last active Dom gun position as mounted dragoons and Rangers swirled around it, firing their fast-loading musketoons and Hall carbines into a scratch formation of infantry that had gathered to defend it. Boogerbear himself galloped up and threw a loop around one of the gun's hubs and pulled the rope taut on the other side. Taking a dally around the fat horn of his Hope saddle, he tossed the rest of the line to another trooper and together, they simply pulled the gun over until it fell on its back. Recovering his rope, he shot a wounded Dom soldier who'd raised a weapon and then dashed back out to the expanding ring of riders.

"Re-form! Re-form!" came a familiar voice, echoed by a dragoon bugler sounding the call. "Make a line, god damn it. Where's Mr. Lara? We need his lancers here."

Boogerbear urged his horse over to join the new arrival as other troopers tried to sort themselves out. "Glad you caught up with us, Cap'n." He grinned. "I mean, 'Major Anson.' Sorry, you were 'Cap'n' so long, it was like your first name."

"I know what you mean," Anson replied, somewhat breathless after his long dash around the right side of the fight. His borrowed horse was even more blown. "Look," he continued, as Coryon Burton and more of his dragoons rode up, "we gotta hurry. The infantry's smashed the Doms in the front . . ." He sniffed. "Seems some o' the Doms themselves helped with that. Couldn't really tell what was goin' on. Either way, the rest might not've broke yet, but they're slidin' back pretty fast. Us in their way, I expect it'll get frisky, directly. We need to be ready. Where's Lara?"

Coryon Burton pointed. "He's been chewing hard on the enemy right rear, charging in and cutting it up before dashing back and re-forming for the next go. All very professional and a joy to see. I'm afraid my fellows have gotten so mixed with your Rangers, we haven't been able to remain as organized." He shrugged. "They fight so much alike, that hasn't really been a problem, but we should sort them out now."

Anson shrugged too, but nodded at the Doms. The sound of fighting on the far side of the enemy host was incredible, largely due to the fact there were so many fighting in what was, after all, a relatively compact space. But a great many Doms, still in reasonably good order, had turned to face them and the pressure was building behind them. They'd soon have to charge, to break through to the rear. The real wonder was that they'd maintained their discipline so long. "Well, we gotta reestablish contact with Lara to make a solid line. Pull back a ways to give us space to do it. Get a messenger to him if you please, Mr. Burton. He won't like takin' the pressure off," he mused. "Neither do I, but there's only about three thousand of us all together an' we won't get any help from the infantry here."

As soon as Lara acknowledged his orders, the pullback of the mounted forces began. It was quickly apparent things would be close. As soon as the menace of further charges was removed, Doms surged forward to fill the gap and they had to race to form up to oppose them again. That's when Anson, now in the center with his Rangers and consulting with Coryon Burton and Ramon Lara both, began to wonder again whether his friend and future son-in-law, Colonel Lewis Cayce, really could get into some kind of omniscient trance and see the whole battle as if from above.

"Look!" someone cried, pointing off to the left, and Anson shifted his gaze from the advancing Doms out beyond the enemy flank and the end of his own line. Closely spaced mounted men were surging through the muddy cropland, struggling to churn their way around the flank and come in behind what he was beginning to accept was his rather meager deterrent.

What's more, the blowing horses those men rode were heaving mud-festooned vehicles spraying clods of dark earth from spinning wheels.

"That's Captain Barca's battery, by God!" Coryon Burton exclaimed as the trundling blobs of mud resolved themselves into guns. "He's bringing them around to stiffen our line!"

"He ain't alone either," Anson confirmed. Felix Meder's mounted riflemen were coming, in column, and another battery, Dukane's 12pdr howitzers, was racing alongside Barca's as if engaged in some kind of grueling endurance race. More guns were coming up behind, some stopping to unlimber where they'd bear on the flank of the advancing Doms. These were probably Agon's guns, all captured 8pdrs mounted on new carriages.

"Look, sir." Burton pointed again, off to the right, beyond Lara's lancers. "That's Justy Olayne himself or I'm a blind man, leading Hudgens's battery and two others up to support us over there." He laughed out loud. "We're about to have more than *thirty* of the best-crewed, deadliest artillery on this whole godforsaken world!"

The Doms knew it too. Enough had faced American artillery before and knew precisely how lethal it was. They *might* come to grips with the mixed mounted line before the guns joined them in action, but it wasn't likely. Their mass advance began to falter. A clot of mounted enemy officers suddenly bolted out from amid the densely packed ranks, racing due west.

"Bugler!" Lara shouted. He paused and looked at Anson. "I was about to send some of my lancers in pursuit, but honestly, as blown as all our horses are, they'll never catch those villains."

Anson waved it away. "You're right. Nothin' for it. I'll send some Rangers after 'em on fresh horses later. Those fools'll wear their own horses out before long. We'll catch 'em."

The flying artillery batteries were swiftly reaching positions directly in front of the enemy, the mounted riflemen helping shift other troopers aside to make gaps. Captain Barca's battery, leading the rest, came closest to the center, and Anson heard Barca confidently shouting commands to the crews of his six guns as, exhausted, they practically fell off their limbers and gasping horses and struggled through the mud to unlimber their weapons and prepare for battle.

"Load canister!" came Hanny Cox's young, cracking voice, echoed by Barca's other two section officers.

"Glad young Hanny is well," Lara observed. "He will bear watching, if he lives. Captain Barca and many others also, of course." He addressed Coryon Burton. "My lancers still have a place as shock troops, but weren't materially different from the enemy's lancers until I started employing dragoon tactics as well. And your dragoons have learned much about . . . irregular warfare from Major Anson's Rangers. Even our infantry continues to improve, thank God, which can only be attributed to better training, exceptional and more . . . flexible leadership, and slightly better weapons, I suppose." He shook his head. "But our greatest advantage over the enemy from the start has been superior artillery tactics and design—and thankfully, the enemy's hesitation to learn the lessons we teach them!"

"That's about it," Anson agreed hurriedly. "Now you better get back to your regiments." The Dom charge had almost stalled at the sight of the deploying artillery, but was pushing forward again, closing within a hundred yards. The fierce fighting behind them the likely cause. "Dismount your men and send their horses to the rear. We won't be goin' anywhere while we support the guns with rapid carbine fire." He smirked. "I guess we'll finish this argument right here."

"All guns ready, Captain Barca!" came Hanny Cox's breathless voice, rising above the racket and sporadic enemy musket fire.

"Very well, Lieutenant. Battery, *by* the battery . . . *Fire!*"

All six of Barca's guns roared as one, scything out murderous swathes of projectiles, churning the mud and leading edge of the charging Doms, hacking great gaps in the front and second ranks. Dukane's battery fired next, followed by Hudgens's, then another and another. By the time that first ear-numbing salvo roared to an end, hundreds of Doms had been horribly savaged and Barca's guns were already reloaded. He was calling for independent fire. Carbine, rifle, and musketoon fire were erupting as well, and there was no single instant without the report of a weapon. Doms were firing back as best they could, some shooting wildly as they ran, and Anson saw occasional Rangers, dragoons, and artillerymen spin and fall to the earth, but the fire was generally ineffective.

Poom! Poom-poom! Pppoom! went Barca's guns, and the screams, closer now, seemed to rake the flesh off the back of Anson's neck. The other batteries fired. This was little more than murder now, but Anson couldn't stop it. Many Doms, confronted with certain death and the carnage in front of them, finally stopped and even went to earth, hunkering behind the heaped bodies of their comrades. Others, though, urged on by rabid-faced Blood Priests, charged right up to the line before falling to staccato carbine fire, joining ever-growing mounds of dead and flailing wounded. Anson himself, still mounted by Boogerbear, was firing his massive Walker Colt revolvers, aiming specifically for Blood Priests. Boogerbear wasn't shooting, more focused on protecting his friend, his double-barrel shotgun laid across his horse's neck, sling looped around the saddle horn. In his hands were his pair of Paterson Colts, held muzzle up in readiness. He couldn't do anything about all the musket balls whizzing about, but he'd be ready if anyone got too close or broke through the Rangers. It soon became apparent that wouldn't happen.

The last determined attack had been shot, even bludgeoned down, and the enemy was recoiling away. This caused even more fighting among themselves as Allied infantry kept squeezing from the front. A trickle of Doms started squirting out to the sides, turning into a flood. "Can't have that," Anson groused. "Bugler," he called to one of the dragoon musicians. "Sound 'cease-fire.'"

"Figured you'd do that pretty quick," Boogerbear said as the bugler sounded the call. He suddenly noticed a bloody furrow a musket ball had gouged across his left forearm. "Damn. That burns," he murmured mildly.

Slowly at first, then more quickly as other bugles passed the order, the carbines, rifles, musketoons, and artillery fell silent. There was still shooting in what looked like the center of the Dom army, but faint bugle calls and a rumbling of drums from beyond made it clear that Lewis Cayce was calling a halt as well. "Officer's call," Anson shouted at the bugler, who obliged by sounding a different sequence of notes. In moments, Burton, Lara, Meder, Barca, and other battery commanders collected.

"Would you enjoy the honor, Mr. Lara?" Anson asked.

Ramon Lara looked exhausted and now blinked in confusion. "Of course, sir," he said loyally, regardless. "May I ask which honor you mean?"

Anson grinned at the former Mexican officer. "Why, that of demanding the enemy's surrender. What else?"

A grin slowly grew on Lara's face. "I think I'd like that a lot." He frowned. "What if they refuse?"

Anson shrugged. "Then we start shootin' again. An' kill every damn one."

───

Unknown to Giles Anson and his command, Lewis Cayce had already delivered a similar ultimatum to the Doms in front of him. And despite having dispatched most of his artillery to aid Anson, he might've threatened the enemy with an even more terrible consequence. As soon as he, Leonor, Varaa, and Hannity rejoined Har-Kaaska and the battle line (Colonel Agon and Father Orno were now there as well, the left of 4th Division having intermingled with the 2nd's right), he'd been presented with a harried-looking, slightly wounded, and understandably frightened Dom colonel named Meza who'd declared his and his division's "pure-hearted" support for Don Hurac. He'd seemed confident at least half the army would swear the same, given the chance, and with all the enraged and armed civilians ruthlessly hunting anyone under Blood Priest control, those Doms still fighting for the current regime could expect no pity from their former comrades. He wanted the fighting to stop, however, and ended the brief meeting with an appeal for them to let him try to get the rest of the enemy to support Don Hurac as well.

Given their history with Dom fanaticism, Lewis was deeply skeptical. Not that some of the Doms would support Don Hurac—he *was* the rightful "Supreme Holiness," after all—but that they'd so easily abandon their worship of the vile Dominion God. That was incompatible with the greater cause of the Allied "American" Army, and anyone who wouldn't convert simply couldn't remain armed. That hadn't been addressed while the battle still raged. How could it be? And just as prickly, Lewis was reluctant to try to disarm the civilians after what they'd endured, no matter what they believed.

"We have no choice but to agree with Coronel Meza," Father Orno had urged. "Otherwise, the battle might rage on for hours and the bloodshed will be incalculable. Even with Meza and the oppressed civilians doing most of the up-close fighting, we could lose hundreds more of our troops." He sighed, looking to Agon for support. "I beg you to give mercy a chance. These people know *nothing* of mercy," he stressed, his argument growing in strength. "If we demonstrate it to them in the name of *our* God, what better inducement could we provide for an unreserved conversion?"

Agon had frowned at Lewis before speaking. "I am . . . sympathetic to Father Orno's plea, having been on the other side of a . . . similar situation. Yet it must be noted that these people are *not* like my army. They've had no contact with you or yours. Moreover, they are . . . closer to the lair of their evil God and He may have a firmer grip on their souls. I can't predict how the majority will react. My faith compels me to give them a chance because *some* will recognize mercy, and some of those may even convert." He'd shaken his head. "Others will see only weakness, I fear."

"I say we let *them* sort it out," said Leonor. Har-kaaska nodded in support. "Let them *fight* it out, if they want," she continued, "then sift through the ones that're left. Findin' out which ones we can trust ain't worth a single one o' our boys."

"You cannot mean that," Father Orno chastised her. "What would Reverend Harkin say?"

"He might surprise you an' agree with me, Father," Leonor had retorted.

Lewis had glanced at Varaa, but she made no sign at all what she thought, not a blink or twitch of an ear or her tail. He'd snorted and looked back at Agon. "I'll take full responsibility, but the choice must be yours, my friend. You're the only one with the experience to decide this. And you and your officers—and Father Orno—must be the ones to choose how we use any of the enemy in the future."

Agon's much taller aide, Major Arevalo, leaned over and whispered in his ear. After a moment, Agon had straightened and regarded Lewis with determination.

"No," he had said. "I propose we allow Coronel Meza to end the fighting however he must—and *I* shall accept all responsibility for the result."

"Who cares who takes the blame if we trust 'em an' they turn on us?" Leonor caustically snapped, but Lewis had finally nodded, regarding Colonel Meza.

"We're still in contact with your men?"

Major Wagley answered for the Dom officer. "They're in front of the Third Pennsylvania, soaking up fire for our boys as we speak."

"Very well," Lewis had said. "We'll give it a try." He'd looked at Father Orno. "I think it's time for Don Hurac to come up. I hope his speaking voice is ready for this today, because he's going to have his work cut out for him. Both of you will."

The battle wound down amazingly quickly after Colonel Agon, Major

Arevalo, and Sal Hernandez went among Coronel Meza's men (surrounded by a company of Wagley's troops with bayonets fixed) and started calling on the enemy to surrender and save themselves. Many pulled away, presumably to keep fighting, as Dom soldiers all around them promptly threw down their weapons and raised their hands above their heads. These were herded out of the line none too gently by the locals, and rushed to the rear under guard. Fighting flared occasionally as vengeful civilian mobs shoved through the ranks, slaughtering Blood Priests out of hand. There was little Lewis could say about that because he would've had them all hanged. In this way, over the next two hours, the once-proud Dom army opposing them that morning slowly ended all resistance and was broken up and sorted by "newly Allied," whom some of the army's healers also went among, and "prisoners of war." These two groups had to be separated, of course, but kept close enough that Don Hurac could address them all.

"We need to disarm every one of 'em," Anson harshly maintained. He'd ridden over with his Rangers and two batteries of guns as soon as a gap opened to him. "I still don't trust Don Hurac as far as I could throw one o' them big lizards with all the teeth, but we do need him. All it'll take is one silly bastard with a musket who still loves his wicked God an' we'll lose him. Religion drives people mad," he warned.

"I agree with you entirely," Colonel Agon said, "but we desperately need more troops. Even more so after today," he lamented. No one had casualty totals yet. They weren't expected to be crippling, but there'd been some close action and losses would be significant. Regardless, every casualty was a tragedy and made the army less capable. "Requiring those who just fought at our side to place themselves at our mercy will undermine the trust we hope to build."

Leonor was shaking her head. "It ain't like they fought *beside* us as much as they fought the same fellas probably murderin' their families. It ain't the same as your soldiers joinin' us—an' some o' *them* didn't either. You picked an' choosed pretty careful, I recall, an' some're still prisoners under guard at Gran Lago."

Father Orno held out his hands. "We will simply have to be vigilant. I believe Don Hurac will be ready for his moment, and I will do my best to support him. Still, perhaps we should keep Captain Meder's riflemen near. Just in case."

Lewis smiled. "Of course. Felix and his men are already here, in fact. They came over with Captain Barca and his battery." He looked at Anson. "Make sure his men are strategically placed when Don Hurac speaks, and have Mr. Barca place a couple of caissons close together for the speakers to stand on. He might emplace a section of guns nearby as well. An additional admonition for the audience to behave."

That seemed to mollify even Leonor. Meder's riflemen, armed with their excellent M1817 rifles, were likely the finest marksmen in the world. If they were mounted and able to see well enough, they could easily eliminate anyone posing a threat.

"By the way," Lewis continued, still addressing Anson, "I expect you already dispatched some Rangers to hunt the enemy officers that fled the field." It was a statement, not a question.

Anson nodded. "Boogerbear took half a company himself. I would'a sent more, but that's all we had fresh mounts for."

"I'm sure he'll make do." Lewis turned to Agon. "You may as well bring Don Hurac forward. I know we don't want him feeling like he has his 'own' troops, but in this instance, it may be appropriate if some of yours, 'ex Doms' themselves, constitute his close escort. A company surrounding the caissons should be sufficient. We'll have a whole battalion of the Third Pennsylvania backing them up."

That was the setting when the Blood Cardinal and rightful Supreme Holiness of all the Dominion, Don Hurac el Bendito, arrived, all smiles, accompanied by a frail, drawn, newly one-armed Reverend Harkin. They were helped up onto one of the muddy, weathered caissons by men in green uniforms still cut in the style of the Dominion and were quickly joined by Father Orno and Colonel Agon.

"You better get up there too," Leonor urged Lewis. He hesitated a moment, concerned his presence might make things more difficult for Don Hurac.

"She's right," Anson said grudgingly, more concerned about security than how it would look.

"Yes," Varaa adamantly agreed. "*You* command the army that beat them. That must be clear from the start." She *kakked* a chuckle. "I, on the other hand, a 'demon' in their eyes, should not make such a conspicuous appearance. That would surely complicate matters. The same goes for you," she said pointedly to a bristling Leonor. "Remember, Doms consider women to be property, for all intents and purposes. A female warrior might be just as jarring to them as I. Perhaps time to get used to us might help."

Leonor grumbled, but her father nodded. "I'll go with you, Lewis. We can stand on the other caisson. Maybe take a couple other fellas."

"Is the fightin' already over?" interrupted a rough, somewhat nasally voice behind them. The surprise in the tone obviously feigned.

Leonor rounded furiously on a scrawny soldier with corporal stripes, bushy side whiskers, and stubble on his chin and upper lip. "Willis," she sneered. "Of course it is, you nitwit. There ain't been a shot for an hour and a half. Can't you hear?"

Corporal Willis stuck a finger in his ear, twisting it as he shook his head. "What was that, Lieutenant Anson? Don't hear so well these days, after all my years in the artillery." He looked at Lewis and continued piously, "Which I been waitin' back with the baggage ta learn whether ta set up yer tent or come up an' pertect you with my meager life again, sir."

"*Malingerin'* with the baggage," Leonor hissed. Her relationship with Lewis's orderly was complicated at best, and she almost always seemed to despise him. Some suspected much of it was an act they both enjoyed. Willis was a poor artilleryman at best, but aside from once actually saving Lewis's life, he took surprisingly good care of the man she loved.

"Thankee, Lieutenant," Willis replied, still pretending not to hear her right. "Jus' doin' my dooty."

Leonor rolled her eyes.

"We won't camp here," Lewis said. "I hope to move on to Texcoco today if we can sort this situation out quickly enough."

"You gonna get up an' make a speech?" Willis asked, looking at the preparations.

"That's not my intention," Lewis replied. "Major Anson and I will make an appearance only."

Willis produced a thick-bristled brush as if by magic. "Which I guess it's a good thing I brung this, then. Stand still an' I'll brush yer wool soldier suit down." He shook his head. "Always toilin' away to whup off the mud an' blood you wallow in. An' yer saber—my God, did ye poke it back in the scabbard all bloody again? Takes *hours* ta get all that nasty dried gore out!"

Ultimately, after their brush-down, Lewis and Anson chose Justinian Olayne and Felix Meder (with his rifle) to join them and climbed up onto the ammunition chests still locked in place atop the second caisson. Both vehicles had been sturdily braced so they wouldn't shift or teeter under their weight.

The view was something to see. Much of the Great Valley in the distance still lay under a hazy shroud as the early afternoon sun cooked the moisture from the ground. The vast cropland and tree-lined streams separating them from Texcoco were better defined than before, as were the myriad strange animals standing between them and the white walls of the far-off city, now in sharper relief as well. The sky framing the hovering sun had remained almost perfectly clear, and it had grown warm enough to make Lewis sweat in his somewhat battered wool uniform. He was surprised that Anson hadn't removed his own dark blue jacket to go in his sky-blue vest and striped shirtsleeves as he often did for comfort. Perhaps he was sensible to the importance of the moment. Olayne, as always, looked surprisingly sharp, down to the fluffy black cravat exploding from within his stiff, red-trimmed collar under his scruffy blonde chin whiskers. Meder simply looked like his usual, businesslike self, comfortably cradling his deadly rifle in the crook of his left arm. It did look like he'd quickly brushed his uniform.

On the other caisson close beside them, Colonel Agon stood, hands clasped behind his back, dark green uniform with black cuffs and facings clearly groomed as well. Agon had never been tall, but he wasn't as... bulky as he'd once been. Father Orno was the shortest man there, in his black version of the American uniform. It was a relief that Reverend Harkin felt like appearing, but he still looked terrible. Once genuinely obese, he'd lost a great deal of weight since they came to this world. Losing his arm in battle had left him almost white-haired and virtually emaciated, his overlarge clothes hanging loose.

Unlike his own former "uniform" of bloodred tunic and cloak, Don Hurac now dressed all in white, with a simple white galero on his head instead of the bizarre contraption he used to wear. Once rather pear-shaped, he also looked slimmer, though not unhealthily so as in the case of Reverend Harkin. Most significant of all, a simple, large wooden cross now hung from a golden chain around his neck instead of the garish, spike-studded, twisted gold cross he'd worn all his life. Someone below passed up a large, ornately decorated speaking trumpet that he must've brought with him.

The enemy troops now gathered on the battlefield before him, both armed and the unarmed prisoners, had obviously noted his appearance with interest, and a babble of conversation erupted. Agon's escort, the mounted riflemen, and indeed the US troops close at hand, all appeared as if they expected to be needed. "Steady, lads," came the voices of various sergeants among the infantry. A Company's First Sergeant O'Toole's voice rose above the others. "No killin' now, unless we get the word." As if by magic, a hush descended over the gathered throng when Don Hurac raised the speaking trumpet in front of his lips. Not even the most die-hard holdout would interrupt when a Blood Cardinal spoke, regardless how outlandishly dressed.

"My children!" Don Hurac began, voice somewhat tinny through the trumpet, but somehow still deep and sonorous. "As many of you know, I am the Blood Cardinal Don Hurac el Bendito, next in line to succeed our beloved Supreme Holiness behind Don Datu el Humilde, who was cruelly murdered by the foul pretender Don Julio DeDivino Dicha. I am your *true* Supreme Holiness and I now address you as such."

Most of the enemy soldiers, even those who kept fighting the longest, promptly dropped to their knees. Some, perhaps several hundred, remained defiantly standing, and one even shouted, "*You* are the pretender! *No* Supreme Holiness can allow common folk to gaze upon his countenance!"

Don Hurac nodded sadly before speaking again. "That would have been true in the past, but as this is no ordinary situation—no ascension has ever been so wrongfully obstructed—I have determined it necessary that I be no ordinary Supreme Holiness. Much has changed, and much more *must* change. I am here for that purpose." He waved at Lewis and his officers standing on the caisson beside his, then to the army at his back. "I do not march on the Holy City merely to cast down the pretender and take my rightful place, but to *save* the Dominion from what it is becoming under the evil men who now rule it." Reaching out with his other hand, he took a large, obviously very old leather-bound book that was offered to him by Reverend Harkin after Father Orno reverently handed it to him. "I do not march on the Holy City with the aid of heretics to oppose God, but I come with the support of a righteous army in the name of the *one* God whose unaltered Word is written in the pages of this book for all to see"—he held the ancient Bible high—"the same word that was brought to this world by our founders, and has not been hidden, altered, or reimagined at the whim of those who lust for power through the suffering of those they rule!"

There was murmuring over that. A lot was said by the old priests and now Blood Priests about how their actions were supported by scripture, but no one had ever actually shown them any book or scroll that purported to contain any of it. Like His Supreme Holiness, those things were considered too holy for just anyone to look upon.

"God's true word is here, all of it!" Don Hurac shouted now, gently waving the aged book. "And many of the things we have been taught for generations are lies," he stated emphatically.

"Here it comes," Anson said tensely aside to Lewis, hand going to one of the Walker Colts suspended at his side.

"I guess we'll see," Lewis whispered back. No one had known just what Don Hurac would say, but most would've agreed the "religious angle" was likely to spark more violence, if anything did, and it might've been wise to wait a short time before it was brought up.

"Heresy!" someone cried. "Lies!" screamed another, and there was a lot of loud talking, even shouting, but amazingly, all went silent again when Don Hurac continued. "It is not heresy. It is not lies." Don Hurac smiled. "I will show you, right here in this book." He pointed at the civilians, almost silent now as well, only the injured still making noise. "And nowhere in them do these scriptures condone the atrocity committed today—men who call themselves soldiers hiding behind the very people it's their sacred duty to protect! I can think of no greater assault upon the true intent of God."

A number of the troops who'd wound up fighting to protect the civilians suddenly surged against those who hadn't, and there were a number of musket shots. Don Hurac quickly handed the precious old Bible back to Harkin and held up his hand. "No, my children! There will be no more fighting today, no more killing! Those of you who remained standing when I declared myself, please file out to the side. No harm will come to you. I will come among you soon and try to persuade you, but you won't be hurt, regardless what you decide." He paused. "Only the Blood Priests, the only real heretics here, will face retribution. I call on the rest of you to identify them all. As for the great majority, you'll be evaluated by General Agon and his officers, Father Orno, and myself. If you choose to aid us in our holy cause, you are free to do so. Your addition to our forces will be appreciated. Those who cannot hear the truth must be treated as prisoners of war. None will be mistreated, but you will be marched to the rear. For those who decide you want no more of war, you are also free to do so. You'll be disarmed and placed among the civilians, who will be returned to Texcoco once it is secure."

"Mighty generous terms," Anson grumbled. "He just make those up on the fly? God knows how we'll tell friend from foe, 'mongst those who join us."

Lewis was nodding slightly, watching the enemy troops noisily but voluntarily begin sorting themselves into whichever category they saw themselves in, as Don Hurac, the clergymen, and Colonel Agon were helped down from the caisson. "As was said earlier, those men will have their work cut out for them. One thing, though. Jumping right into the religious aspects of our struggle, Don Hurac made a pretty good start for the rest of us to cope with. Anybody who joins us knows where we stand. And I think I'm a little more confident about his own motives at last. It'll be damned hard to go back on what he told them today and put everything back the way it's always been."

Anson seemed to consider that while Olayne and Meder hopped down from the caisson. "Got a point," he said. "Mr. Olayne," he continued, raising his voice and patting his wounded leg. "A hand, if you please."

Lewis stepped over to the other group. "Well said, Your Excellency," he told Don Hurac. No matter how closely allied they might be, he'd never call him "Supreme Holiness" or "Highness" or "Majesty" or anything like that. It just wasn't in him.

"Thank you, Coronel Cayce," Don Hurac said with a bow. "I pray it was a sufficient start. We should know soon enough."

"Brief but to the point," Reverend Harkin agreed, indicating the precious, ancient book in Father Orno's hands, "if perhaps a little more papist than I would prefer, implying *that* book is the only source of God's word."

Lewis, now rejoined by Leonor, who was still looking at the milling Dom troops with suspicion, cocked his head to the side. "I honestly wouldn't know myself, but surely the differences between it and your protestant version can't be extreme enough to confuse these people with at this point."

Harkin frowned. "No. I suppose not . . . yet. As a Presbyterian, I find there is more than enough contention between the various Protestant viewpoints."

Lewis looked at Agon. "I want to move straight on to Texcoco. Isolate it with dragoon patrols and make camp just out of musket shot from the walls. I hope anyone left there will simply surrender, but I need a big enough force to break in if I have to." He cast a glance at Don Hurac. "In case they left any Blood Priests there—and civilians for them to play with."

"I understand completely. Leave this in my hands, perhaps with the aid of Third Division? They marched just as far and hard as we did. And pliable as Don Hurac seems to have made the enemy here, there are quite a lot of them."

Lewis was nodding. "I'll leave you Lara's lancers and a couple of batteries of guns as well." He looked at Don Hurac. "Do you feel comfortable accompanying me? I know there may still be some difficulties here, but your presence at the city might save more lives."

Don Hurac's . . . "wife" was probably the best way to describe Zyan, had approached in the company of Samantha Anson. Both women were nodding encouragement.

Don Hurac sighed. "Since my greatest purpose in life has become the preservation of life—perhaps in atonement for all the death I once presided over—how can I refuse?" He also looked at Agon. "The question is, can I be spared here?"

Major Arevalo barked an almost ironic laugh. "Most of those people would never have *seen* a Supreme Holiness in their entire lives, and you not only spoke to them, you showed them your face. I believe that will move most of them deeply and help us manage them well in your name. Any that would still cause trouble, well . . ." He shrugged. "If they aren't already Blood Priests or Reaper Monks in hiding—which we will have to be wary of," he warned, "they're probably so fanatical that they may as well be Blood Priests and we'll have to kill them anyway."

"Most unfortunate, but likely true," Father Orno concurred, watching an eruption of violent behavior among some of the unarmed Doms. "They may be handling that themselves. They'll know the most volatile dissidents in their midst better than anyone." He looked at Lewis. "I doubt you'll find many Blood Priests to hang hiding among these troops."

Lewis took a long breath before turning to Agon. "Very well," he said. "Do your best to wrap this up today, Colonel. Perhaps some of the more . . . energetic prisoners might tire themselves on burial details. That said, keep the more hardcore adherents to the Blood Priests' beliefs separate from the others and send them back to Puebla under guard, along with our wounded who can't march or wield a weapon. Use the empty supply wagons for them." He paused again. "I wish I could evacuate all who are hurt, but as close to the end as things may seem—if Don Hurac can stop the war—I can't help feeling we'll need every man before we're done." He cleared his throat. "Bring the rest of the civilians and, ah, more cooperative former enemies—take your pick from those who seem willing—up with you. I expect to see you at Texcoco tomorrow evening at the latest."

CHAPTER 6

Lewis Cayce didn't envy Agon the complicated task he'd set him, especially considering how difficult it was just to get his own portion of the army moving again. His divisions were disorganized and intermixed, the troops already tired after the brisk morning fight. NCOs ranted at dragging soldiers to fall in. Just as frustrating, all the artillery he meant to take had to be moved through the thickening mud back up onto the road, where the heavy, clingy soil could be scraped off gun carriages and limbers, not to mention the weary feet of animals that would have to keep pulling them. It took much longer than he'd hoped, and all he could do was patiently wait while his officers sorted things out.

"How's your section, Lieutenant Cox?" Captain Barca asked, riding up alongside Hanny and pulling back on his reins.

"A little tired, sir," Hanny replied diplomatically, "but we'll recover on the road."

"Casualties?"

"None serious, thank God, and those few we had have already been tended by a section of healers."

Barca suppressed a smile. A group of young lady healers from Uxmal seemed especially attentive to Barca's battery, and Hanny's section in particular. Small wonder. The one named Izel was Corporal Apo Tuin's sister and probably Hanny's fiancée. Other artillerymen in the battery had formed attachments to the ladies as well.

"I'm glad to hear it," Barca said. "Hot work for a while, and the whole battery was very fortunate. I've seen five horses hurt badly enough that they had to be destroyed, but only four men who'll require an ambulance wagon—and none of those fatally wounded. Almost a miracle, I'd say."

"Yes, sir."

"What's the material condition of your section?"

"Good, sir. No horses injured or debilitating damage to the guns and limbers, or even implements." He gestured. "The horses are worn, of course, but with a smooth road, and now we've lightened the horses and vehicles of several hundred pounds of mud, I think they'll manage." He paused to think. "Each gun expended eleven rounds of exploding case and twenty-one rounds of canister, for a total of twenty-two and forty-two. We've already replenished ammunition from our caissons, but those'll have to be refilled."

"Worrying about that is my job," Barca assured him before grinning. "Unless you'd care to be named my adjutant?"

Hanny's face heated and a horrified expression stole across it as he adamantly shook his head. "Uh . . . thank you, sir, but . . . not particularly, sir. No offense."

"I thought not, and none taken," Barca assured, laughing now. "In any event, you'll get your ammunition. All the, uh, martial baggage will follow our column and I'll see that a reserve caisson moves up when we stop for a rest."

"When do you think that'll be, sir?" Corporal Apo Tuin asked.

"We should cross a good stream in an hour or so, according to the Rangers. Have some men fall out upstream to fill canteens and fetch water for your animals. Rinse and refill your sponge buckets too. And eat your marching rations. Have to keep up your strength. Hopefully, we'll make a proper camp and have hot food tonight."

"Just how far is Texcoco?" Preacher Mac asked. "I can see it from here."

"Farther—and bigger, apparently—than it seems. About twelve miles, I'm told."

"Don't look that far," Hahessy said, squinting and shading his eyes.

"No. A feature of the long grade we're on, I believe." Barca smirked. "If it's any consolation, it *is* downhill from here." A bugle finally sounded from ahead. "We're about to get moving. Carry on, men. I'm proud of you all." With that, he urged his horse to the rear to confer with the next section back.

"Reckon he's proud o' me as well?" Hahessy asked.

"The captain's a rare, forgivin' sort. Seven times—or seventy-seven," Preacher Mac responded with an example from the Bible. "So I dinnae doubt he is, fer the now. As soon as ye wag yer Irish arse in the air again—as yer sure tae do—he'll have tae forgive ye again for his own sake, if not yers." The Number Two gun crew erupted in laughter.

"Why, you ill-favored divil," Hahessy began in a menacing tone, but Hanny and rumbling drums cut him off. "The Third Pennsylvania's starting to move," he said, nodding forward. "We're next."

———

"You finally gonna marry me after Texcoco's secure?" Leonor challenged Lewis out of the blue. They were riding together with Anson and Samantha, Varaa, Har-Kaaska, Major Olayne, and Colonel Reed at the front of the long column, and those others, including Leonor's father, practically sawed at their reins to let the couple move slightly ahead. None, not even Samantha (who strongly supported Leonor) or Varaa (simply for the amusement the controversy gave her), wanted in the middle of this. Leonor continued, loud enough for them to hear regardless. "A whole 'nother battle has come an' gone—which could'a killed either of us—an' I told you I'm tired o' waitin' on the damn war before we can enjoy livin' a little together." She jerked a thumb back at Giles Anson. "Bein' married to Mistress Samantha an' sharin' a tent ain't affected how my father fights, you might'a seen. Maybe even gave him somethin' extra ta fight an' live for than he had for a lot o' years. Might be a like arrangement could do the same for you."

"Hear, hear," Samantha said abruptly, unable to restrain herself. Lewis turned in his saddle to glare at her. Looking back at Leonor, his expression softened. No matter that she was essentially dressed as a man, they'd just fought a dangerous battle, and black gunpowder grains and flecks of blood had diffused in the sweat on her face before drying there, Lewis believed she was still the most beautiful woman he'd ever seen. Somehow, the war here, and perhaps her feelings for him, had made her bloom amazingly.

"It's not the same at all, and there remains a glaring difference: Mistress Samantha doesn't put herself at the forefront of the fight."

"Like you?" Leonor growled, gathering herself for more objections, but Lewis held up a hand.

"Please let me finish," he said gently. "We've already discussed that before, and I won't try to stop you from fighting beside me, or even use it as an excuse not to marry you." He shrugged. "I don't really *have* an excuse because I've actually come to agree with you. It's just . . ." He sighed. "I believe Reverend Harkin is with Don Hurac"—he grinned—"in an ordinary carriage instead of that bizarre monstrosity Don Hurac started with." The vehicle in question was absolutely huge, practically a land ship, full of luxurious accommodations. The biggest problem with it was that it was drawn by massive, plodding armabueys, like giant, spiky armadillos. To speed it up to match the pace of the baggage train, not to mention the infantry, would've taken half their reserve of horses.

"Even so," Lewis continued, "uncomfortable as he may find riding at the moment, I'm sure Reverend Harkin would happily come forward and marry us right now, without even stopping." He sighed again and glanced back at their audience. "My problem with that is . . . well, it just seems so self-serving. So . . . incidental to the pressing events of the day. I don't know about you, but I never expected to marry," he stated flatly. "Having found you, however"—he grinned—"a somewhat . . . volatile soulmate and true partner—even in battle—I find myself wanting our marriage to begin on a day of at least comparative peace, when the wedding is all I need concern myself with and I can devote all my attention to you." He shrugged. "Does that make any sense at all?"

"My goodness," Samatha gasped. "How romantic!" She reached over and slapped Anson on the shoulder with her ever-present folding fan. "Why do you not say things like that to me?"

"Honestly, my dear, I can't even *think* like that," Anson replied a little smugly. "What do you say to that, Leonor?" he asked his daughter.

"How fast can we get Reverend Harkin up here?" Leonor loudly inquired with a mischievous glint in her eye, and laughter erupted, extending surprisingly far among the 1st US infantry, marching directly behind. Leonor was holding up a hand of her own. "No, I get it . . . an' I guess it's kinda sweet." She arched a brow at Lewis. "But that still leaves 'when.'"

Lewis seemed to mull that as Arete plodded along, matching the brisk but frustrating (to her) pace of the infantry. Beyond the seemingly endless stone-wall-checkered cropland; tree-lined streams; massive, indifferent herbivores; and scattering of rock hovels, the last potential enemy stronghold between their army and its final objective loomed in the distance. "I don't mean to linger in Texcoco any longer than we must," Lewis said slowly, "and intend to march on the Holy City almost at once. We should find what awaits us there in a matter of days. Don Hurac assures us it's no better suited to defend against an army than any other Dominion city we've seen—no ramparts or artillery emplacements—so any troops or Blood Priests that mean to stand against us will either have to come out to do it or wait until we're inside. I don't need to tell any of you how messy and bloody the latter might be. If Gran Lago or Puebla are any guide, many civilians will have already left, but I can't imagine all of them can or will evacuate before we get there, so we need to be prepared for significant resistance. Still," he mused aloud, "with the fall of the Dominion capital, ascension of Don Hurac, and his command to end the war . . ." He smiled at Leonor. "I believe we might hold the first protestant wedding service—discreet, of course—behind the walls of the Holy City within a few short weeks."

Now Leonor was silent, considering. "I guess that'll have to do," she said at last. "Prob'ly be *another* war by then, though," she grumped.

Behind them, Major John Ulrich, still recovering from a terrible wound he got at Puebla but now able to ride a horse, suddenly called, "Let's have a tune!"

Drums thundered, fifes squealed, and the men started belting out "Blue Juniata," a favorite of the whole army. It wasn't lost on anyone that Leonor's name (as "Deadly Leonora") was laughingly substituted for "Bright Alfarata," and Leonor rolled her eyes and hunched slightly in her saddle, olive cheeks turning bright red.

"Now, now," Lewis told her lowly. "It only means they're proud of you—and love you, as do I. Embrace it."

She nodded and straightened, but asked, "How do you feel when they cheer you? They do that out of love and pride as well."

Lewis frowned. "Uncomfortable," he confessed. "Awkward and even something of a fraud," he added, "especially when it's my orders that send them to their deaths. And they only love me because we win," he added a little cynically. "That'll end quick if we lose."

Leonor shook her head and snorted impatiently. "If you really think that, you ain't as smart as I thought. Sure, they like winnin'. They're fightin' ta win because they believe in the cause you gave 'em. The troops that came to this world with us were more lost than they ever imagined they could be.

You kept 'em together an' kept 'em soldiers with a purpose. An' the Uxmalos, Ocelomeh, Itzincabos, an' the rest from the Yucatán, they were all just waitin' for the certain day when the Doms'd come for 'em. Their future was as bleak as anybody's already under the Doms. You gave 'em a chance ta change that, a future ta hope for. An' as for the ones who've joined us since, slaves, villagers an' refugees the Doms would'a killed, former enemies like Agon who were no more than slaves themselves—an' maybe even some o' those we fought today—now got a chance ta live free." She waved a hand. "Them in the army might not be 'free' to do what they want, but they can think an' feel an' say what's right an' wrong without bein' burned alive or impaled. They know they're fightin' so everybody can do that. Those're the things you've given *all* your soldiers, Lewis, just by bein' who you are. If, God forbid, you do ever lose, most'a your troops'll still love you for that, as I do"—she paused—"an' because nobody *else* could'a won." She grinned. "I bet even then they'll expect you'll come up with some other way to get it done." She looked at him significantly. "So 'embrace it,' Lewis," she quoted. "All you can do is your best."

It started clouding up by evening, getting colder again, and the half-hidden sun was touching the distant snowcapped mountaintops in the west when the head of the column entered the outer city surrounding the high, bright white walls of Texcoco. In the distance, right at the center of the city, loomed a towering pyramid, flaring a startlingly golden white under the setting sun, its stepped architecture lending it a jagged aspect reminiscent of the serrated obsidian knives the Blood Priests (and those preceding them) used in their gruesome ceremonies. As they'd also seen before, regardless how impressive the high wall enclosing the inner city, the sprawling suburb around it was a slum full of old, roughly made buildings, shack-like dwellings, even open-air shelters. If anything, these slums got even more squalid the closer they came to the heart of the Dominion, the lives of their inhabitants less valuable to the privileged on the other side of the wall. The only exceptions were a number of villas ensconced within smaller enclosures of their own, quite a few well-tended warehouses somewhat segregated beside a briskly running river tumbling down from the mountains to the north, and what looked like a comparatively reputable-looking outdoor market district paralleling the road as they neared the main gate of the city.

Animals ran loose everywhere, released or escaped livestock, no doubt. Most were pigs, goats, and the ubiquitous "gallinas" (basically fat, flightless, but still somewhat vicious versions of wild lizardbirds) that all natives kept for their eggs and meat. There were other things, more creatures like Har-Kaaska's bipedal mount, that fled their approach or lowed piteously in pens. Smaller versions of quadrupedal "wolf-lizards," like they'd encountered in the mountains, sometimes disrupted the marching column, but these creatures weren't necessarily aggressive.

"Act like dogs," Anson said, gesturing at a pair of the things they passed, nervously standing their ground and hissing, feathery fur standing up around their necks and down their backs. "I miss dogs," he confessed. "Maybe I could train one o' those."

"Don't look very pet-like, with all them teeth," Leonor noted.

"Might use 'em for huntin'," Anson speculated. "Varaa? You got dogs where you're from?"

"What are dogs?" the Mi-Anakka warmaster questioned, blinking.

"Damn," Anson muttered.

A few people were also seen, likely slaves or lowly *hombres libres*. Most lay dead in clusters with their throats cut, gallinas and hogs feeding on them. This darkened the mood of troops already angry with the tactics the enemy employed that morning. A few people must've somehow avoided the roundup that took most everyone else off to battle or left so many others dead by the road, and they peered fearfully out from their hiding places. Sadly, all this was much as expected based on prior experience, particularly the ghastly display of more than a dozen crosses erected in the center of the marketplace, each with a flayed, scorched, and crucified figure nailed up for all to see.

There was something curious ahead, however, but only an annoyingly unsatisfactory, cryptic message from Captain Sal Hernandez, scouting forward with some Rangers and dragoons, vaguely prepared Lewis and his officers for what they found as the main city gate came in view. Sal and his mounted troopers were arrayed in a semicircle in front of the wide-open gate, weapons at the ready, but none were raised or aimed. An open fire had been built right in the middle of the road, fueled by planks and timbers torn off and dragged up from what looked like produce racks. Several men in the deceptively festive local dress stood around the fire for warmth, as if waiting for them.

"Sal only told us things were 'weird' at the gate," Anson observed as the front of the column marched closer. "Now I see what he meant."

"Halt the column, Mr. Reed," Lewis said, peering ahead, then quickly in all directions before scanning the tops of the walls and the pair of gatehouses above them. The obvious concern was an ambush, but there wasn't another soul in sight. Reed called a halt, and drums rattled down the line. Lewis eased Arete forward, joined by Leonor, Anson, Varaa, and then Colonel Reed, Har-Kaaska, and Major Olayne. "What's going on here, Mr. Hernandez?" Lewis brusquely asked Sal as he came up beside him.

Sal just shrugged and waved. "Haven't got a peep out of 'em yet, aside from 'em askin' not to get shot. Oh yeah, they specifically asked to talk to you an' Don Hurac."

"I assume you've got scouts out?"

"Sure, all over," Sal replied. "Went a ways an' looked myself. Saw a couple scared folks, but no soldiers. No ambush."

"Any sign of Blood Priests causing the usual . . . unpleasantness in the city?"

"No, sir. Course, it's a big place. They could be peelin' people alive in there an' we'd never hear it."

"All the more reason to get inside quickly."

"Yes, sir."

Lewis urged Arete ahead, stopping just short of the gathered locals. "I'm Colonel Lewis Cayce. I understand you've been waiting for me?"

"And Don Hurac," the tallest man in a plain blue tunic agreed in Spanya. He had long black hair and a salt-and-pepper goatee.

"I'll have him brought forward," Lewis said, "but in the meantime, my troops will be entering your city."

The locals looked at each other in concern. "We would prefer that you wait until we can speak to you and Don Hurac together."

"So the god damned Blood Priests can finish murderin' innocent people?" Anson accused, and the men recoiled in horror.

"No . . . No!" the blue-clad man stated adamantly. "There *are* no Blood Priests here! They all marched with the army—and whatever civilians they could find—or departed for the Holy City. None have returned."

"You'll have to forgive my skepticism," Lewis said darkly. "They've engaged in unspeakable atrocities in every city we've . . . liberated." He looked at Sal. "Who's that with you, Lieutenant Buisine?" It was quickly getting dark. "Yes, Buisine," he said without awaiting a response. "Take the Rangers and dragoons into the city. Scout it as quickly and carefully as you can in an hour, then return. I know you can't see everything in that time, but you should get an inkling of what we can expect. Mr. Reed? I believe a couple of regiments of First Division as well. Not the First US, though. I want them here."

Reed started barking orders even as Sal's mounted troopers simply went around the men by the fire and entered the city. The locals appeared put out, but there was nothing they could do. "My apologies," Lewis said down to them, still on his horse, "but I'm not prepared to risk any lives for the sake of courtesy. You can say whatever you want to Don Hurac and myself at your leisure while we assure ourselves no one's suffering needlessly—or preparing to attack us. You have nothing to fear"—he paused, gesturing behind at the crucified men and women—"unless you had something to do with that, and the other victims we've passed."

"Oh no! Nothing!" blurted a shorter man in an embroidered green tunic, eyes bulging in true horror. "That was the Blood Priests entirely, just last night. Even the army commander objected."

"Really?" asked Lewis, surprised. "Gomez didn't strike me as a humanitarian."

Tired but determined-looking infantrymen were streaming by on either side, passing through the gate. Most cast curious glances at the four locals, though some looked genuinely hostile. All, even the most recent enlistees, were veterans now, of at least one battle and a long march after. They looked very rough and tired, faces and hands smeared with black gunpowder stains from tearing musket cartridges with their teeth and handling fouled locks and ramrods. Weary or not, they looked fully prepared for more violence. The four locals clustered more tightly together.

"Messenger," Lewis called. "Please be good enough to ride back and present my respects to Don Hurac and Reverend Harkin and ask if they're at liberty to join us. Clear the road for the coach as you go."

A mounted dragoon hastily saluted and turned his horse for the rear before kicking it into a trot.

"Idiot," Leonor grumbled. Not that it mattered that much just now, with

Lewis so prominent at the moment, but her crusade to prevent men from saluting him in the presence of the enemy was never-ending.

"They just won't be stopped," Willis agreed with her. He'd ridden forward on his horse (which he fervently loathed) to join them at some point. "Won't catch *me* doin' such a thing!" he added piously.

Regarding the orderly with a frown, Leonor couldn't remember Willis *ever* saluting the army commander, or anyone else, for that matter.

The tall local in blue cleared his throat. "Allow me to introduce—"

Lewis raised his hand to stop him. "Hearing the same thing over and over is the worst waste of time I can think of. You may as well wait until Don Hurac is here," he told him, before devoting his attention to Felix Meder, who'd ridden up with a cluster of riflemen. "Take half your men inside the gate and secure it. Put some in those gatehouses too, where they'll have a good view all around."

"What are their orders?" Meder asked.

"Keep an eye out—and shoot anyone who looks like they're sneaking around."

"Yes, sir," Meder said, refraining from saluting after a quick glance at Leonor.

Lewis continued issuing orders or receiving reports from messengers while they waited for Don Hurac and Reverend Harkin to arrive. When the carriage finally approached and drew to a stop, men in green uniforms hopped down to open the doors and help the occupants out. The locals all fell to a knee and bowed.

"Do stand up," Don Hurac said, tone jovial. Reverend Harkin said nothing, but his pain-pinched expression was suspicious. "Who do I have the honor of addressing?" Don Hurac asked, peering into the gloom. "Is one of you the *alcalde* of Texcoco?"

The men stood as directed, but appeared to bow even lower while the man in blue replied. "Ah . . . no, your . . . Supreme Holiness. I fear the *alcalde* is one of those unfortunates . . . displayed on a cross over there."

Frowning, Don Hurac turned to view the atrocity once more. "Most unfortunate indeed. I have made the man's acquaintance during my infrequent visits, and my impression of him was positive. Sadly, I did not recognize him."

"Understandable, as he is now," another of the locals in a light brown tunic declared bitterly.

"Of course," Don Hurac said sympathetically. "And you are?"

"I am Vice Alcalde Don Amil," the man in the blue tunic interrupted, stealing Don Hurac's attention. He seemed intent on being the group's spokesman. "And that is Magistrado Don Renaud. The others are Don Radarado and Don Xoteca," he said, pointing at each in turn. "Together, we are likely the most prominent citizens left alive in Texcoco. I can speak for us all, and the city in general in most respects, but can only relate my own survival experience. To my everlasting shame, I evaded the attention of the Blood Priests by ignominiously concealing myself while better men were murdered or whipped off to face you in battle."

"You did what you had to, as did we all," consoled the one named Don Renaud.

"Nevertheless..." Don Amil stood straighter. "As I attempted to convey to Coronel Cayce—indeed, sir, we all know who you are and why you are here," he said aside to Lewis, "in the name of the—hopefully—many hundreds of others in the city who survived as we did, it is my pleasure to surrender Texcoco to you and Don Hurac, and declare our profound appreciation and support for your divine undertaking, Don Hurac's ascension, and the restoration of the Holy Dominion to the form we all hold dear."

"There is more to our mission than that," Don Hurac responded wryly, with an arched-brow glance at Lewis, "but I am honored by your support. You will be overjoyed to hear that a great many of your people, 'whipped off' to fight us, have been saved—largely through their own efforts—and indeed, a large percentage of the army they accompanied is now in our custody. Tomorrow, most of your people will return to their homes and your benevolent care."

Don Amil could only stare and blink. He finally managed to say, "There are no words." He shook his head and smiled broadly. "Delightful news indeed!"

"In the meantime," Lewis said through a tight smile of his own, "now is the time to tell us if we're liable to encounter resistance in your city and where we'll find it. Surely you know, if you managed to avoid it yourself. If we discover it on our own, or any of my men are killed because you failed to warn us, all those poor people will remain homeless because we'll raze Texcoco to the ground." He gestured at the other locals. "Nor will you and your friends be forgiven."

Leonor leaned over and whispered in his ear, "You don't trust 'em?"

"No," he whispered back.

"Good."

Don Amil did manage to remember where some Blood Priest holdouts might be, and Anson and Sal took more Rangers and Hanny Cox's section of Barca's battery to deal with them. There were sporadic, ferocious outbursts of shooting, and Hanny's guns roared a few times as the darkness wore on, blasting surprised ambushers out of their lairs. The rest of Lewis's detachment of the army marched into the city and established a defensive marching camp in the broad plaza surrounding the central pyramid, set sentries, and generally got some well-earned rest.

There were other exceptions to this besides Anson's Rangers and a section of artillery. Lewis and many of his officers, along with Don Hurac and Reverend Harkin, spent most of the long night interrogating Don Amil and gathering information from a constant stream of frightened civilian survivors who tentatively approached the camp and were passed inside, under guard. Much of the intelligence they brought was the same, but occasional new tidbits were gleaned. It was interesting to note, for example, that few had any idea who Don Amil was, but even Don Hurac assured everyone that vice *alcaldes* had extremely limited public duties and it wasn't unusual that Don Amil wasn't well-known. He did seem genuinely relieved by their presence and excited to tell them whatever he could about how things stood in the Holy City. He was adamant, for example, they had crushed the last large force the Dominion could muster in the region and, aside from more Blood Priest holdouts, the Holy City stood practically bare. He was less helpful when it came to his knowledge of the status of the Gran Cruzada.

"The *alcalde* and I discussed it," he admitted, "after he collected a few details from General Gomez and some unguarded talk among Blood Priests. It was his understanding that a cautionary command had been sent to General Xacolotl—it is he who commands the Gran Cruzada—that the army halt its advance and await further developments. Even if General Xacolotl has since received orders to come to the rescue of the pretender in the Holy City, he's almost certainly still almost a thousand *leguas* distant."

"We've heard that as well. For too long, I am thinking," Varaa said.

Lewis was nodding wearily as he gazed at the last of a handful of cigars that Anson had given him the day before. He decided not to light it. The cigars were improving in quality, and he enjoyed them. Six in a row over just a few hours, however, had left his mouth tasting awful. "True or not, I don't believe this 'Xacolotl' is just sitting and waiting," he finally said. "We need to move quickly."

Colonel Reed yawned tremendously. Few senior officers had slept, not only due to the marathon questioning and planning session, but because reports were still coming in from Major Anson. There hadn't been any real fighting for hours, but Texcoco was a big city, the largest they'd liberated so far. It would take days just to explore it. A proper search for every hostile element was practically impossible. They'd have to rely on the actual inhabitants, when they returned, to do the job right. Reed covered his mouth and clamped his jaw shut. "It's already morning and will soon be dawn," he declared. "We must get some rest or we'll be no use to anyone." He looked at Lewis. "How long do you mean to stay here?"

Reed's yawn was contagious, and Lewis endured one of his own that loosed a cramp in his neck. Tilting his head back until it passed, he then regarded his second-in-command. "As few days as possible. Third and Fourth Divisions should arrive today with the civilian survivors of the fight. Hopefully, Agon will have sorted out whatever Dom troops he considers likely recruits. Otherwise, we'll have to wait a little longer for supply to catch up." He got Vice Alcalde Don Amil's attention. "We'll be requisitioning more supplies here, of course, and I want someplace safe to assemble them. I thought about the warehouses we saw by the river, but I'd prefer something more secure."

Don Amil was stifling a yawn as well. "There are any number of places in the city."

Lewis frowned. "Not yet, I think."

Leonor, who'd seemed to be dozing, perked up. "Why not use one o' those big villas in the outer city? They got their own walls like a fort an' some look plenty big for a supply depot—with a regiment of troops for security to boot."

Don Amil seemed about to object, but Reed nodded. "An excellent idea, though I think we should leave a light brigade, at least, to occupy Texcoco. Perhaps a regiment to guard the supplies and another, possibly one of Agon's, inside the city. They may be needed to protect the citizens from intimidation by lurking hostiles."

Varaa *kakked* a laugh. "Might wind up the other way around, but I agree with Colonel Reed."

"Very well," Lewis said, "and that's enough for now. We'll reconvene when Agon and Itzam arrive with their divisions—and whoever else they bring. We'll complete our planning then. Either way, I don't want to stay here more than three days."

The gathering quickly broke up after that, the exhausted officers seeking their tents. Leonor accompanied Lewis to his under a reddish, predawn sky, and he embraced her. Self-conscious about his cigar breath, he kissed her lightly on her forehead. Instead of continuing on to her own tent, she just stood there, leaning against him. Loud snores came from Corporal Willis's tent, erected a short distance away.

"I'm pretty tired," he said, a little nervously. Once before, they'd shared his tent, right after the Battle of Puebla. It was something they'd both needed badly, but Lewis still felt conflicted by the encounter, torn between his love and genuine desire for her and the awkward example it set for the men.

"Me too," Leonor said, "an' we both smell like dead goats. But it's been a *damned* long day, I'm cold, an' . . . " She exhaled and her breath steamed. "That rope bed contraption the fellas built you is bigger than my cot, an . . . I just want your arms around me, all right? I won't even take off my pistol belt or boots."

Smiling faintly and nodding, Lewis stepped under the fly and lifted the flap to his tent. Willis had left a single candle burning inside. "Corporal Willis will be scandalized when he comes to wake me." Lewis chuckled.

"Yeah," Leonor also laughed lowly, "but who knows which'll shock the scrawny ol' lizard more: findin' us together—or that we're still dressed."

"That is the question," Lewis agreed seriously, then paused, waving a finger at her. "Weapons are one thing, but no boots in the bed, if you please."

CHAPTER 7

"What news, General Gomez?" demanded Primer Patriarcha Sachihiro, standing on the exquisitely fitted stone floor of the underground sanctum beneath the great central temple in the Holy City. For what was, after all, essentially an ancient cave, long ago architecturally adapted to resemble a palatial chamber in the heavenly underworld, with sound-deadening tapestries and huge, ornate columns seemingly supporting the massive temple above, the whole thing was somehow executed with equal precision. Nothing could eliminate the dank atmosphere, however, and even the well-fed braziers located strategically around the sanctum left it gloomy and chilly. Somewhat menacingly attended by a pair of brown-robed Reaper Monks holding naked swords, the rumpled, mud-spattered General Gomez and his sole companion, Teniente Juaris, were distinctly uncomfortable lying face down, arms extended, on the cold, damp floor.

Primer Patriarcha Sachihiro, former *obispo* to the murdered Don Datu and chosen successor to the reigning Supreme Holiness, had advanced to loom directly over Gomez. He was a young man; tall, thin, with predatory eyes under a heavy brow, wrapped in a light gray robe the same color as the naked stone of not only the temple they met beneath, but also the smaller replica once inhabited by his deceased lord. His current master, previously the Blood Cardinal Don Julio DeDivino Dicha and now His Supreme Holiness, messiah of Mexico, and by the grace of God, emperor of the world, was also present, but not clearly visible. Sachihiro, and now it seemed the Holy Patriarcha Tranquilo alone, were allowed to bask in the radiance of the Supreme Holiness's direct gaze and look upon his naked face. Backlit and projected upon sheer, red drapes by more flaming braziers, only his enlarged and sharply contrasting form could be seen, reclining on cushions and attended by lithe, naked young women chosen for their beauty and purity in faith and behavior. They lived better than most women in the Dominion and would want for nothing during their time with His Supreme Holiness. That came with a cost, of course. There could only be so many, and they only lasted as long as they were pleasing to the eye, capable servants, and . . . talented entertainers. Being in direct contact with the representative of God on Earth also required that they be blinded and have their tongues removed.

The other men present, moving to form a semicircle around the prostrate officers, were arguably the most powerful figures in the Dominion. The dingy-red-robed Holy Patriarcha Tranquilo wore a predatory expression as well, very like a weasel's. He was old and scrawny, with just a wisp of tousled white hair remaining on his age-spotted skull, his small, black eyes narrowly spaced on either side of a long bony beak of a nose. Hairy, skeletal legs ended in gnarled, sandaled feet, and he looked as much like a vulture as it was possible for a man to approximate. He had, however, practically founded the long-suppressed Blood Priests many years ago, and since their recent rise in prominence, and after having engineered the elevation of the current Supreme Holiness, Tranquilo probably exercised more raw power than anyone in the Dominion.

Beside him stood a mountain of a man called "Brother Escorpion" in a shabby gray tunic with a jagged golden cross that was stitched on the breast. He was one of the very first (and longest-surviving) Reaper Monks. Many others had been recruited into his order of late, their dress and even purpose—to counter the Demon Rangers—now revised, but none could be as selfless and capable as Escorpion. He was dark-haired and massively muscled, his countenance surprisingly pleasant. Utterly devoted to Tranquilo, however, even carrying the old man when he must, his primary role remained to serve as the intimidating physicality Tranquilo lacked. A mere word or look from his master was all it took to unleash the remorseless brutality lurking within him.

Father Armonia was yet another Blood Priest who actually often impersonated the Supreme Holiness (wearing a ceremonial mask) for public ceremonies. The former Don Julio despised such activities, anything requiring physical exertion, in fact, and preferred lounging down here and enjoying the perquisites of his lofty status in a drug-induced haze over donning his heavy mask and regalia and appearing in front of the masses. He'd gained enough weight that it might be awkward if he did, at this point, since he wasn't shaped at all like Father Armonia anymore.

Despite being a Blood Priest himself, Armonia was a quiet supporter of the more secular Sachihiro. He was no coward, but Tranquilo frankly frightened him and the more time he spent around the founder of his order, the more concerned he grew about the increasing subversion of virtually every tradition in the Holy Dominion. His confidence that was done solely to advance causes the Blood Priests were originally raised to address was diminishing and that pushed him closer to Sachihiro—dangerous indeed, if Tranquilo ever guessed.

Sachihiro leaned lower over Gomez. "I take it, by your presence here, that you were victorious over the pretender and this . . . Coronel Cayce's army of heretics. You came here in such haste to report this, did you not?" he urged.

Gomez hesitated, not looking up. "I, ah, came as quickly as I could to inform Your Holiness that we met the heretics in battle yesterday morning and . . ."

"Excellent!" Sachihiro proclaimed, straightening. "I have been perhaps too preoccupied with the threat they posed of late. I will be pleased to direct all my focus elsewhere." He looked back down at Gomez, who hadn't stirred. "Did you take many slaves? Perhaps you even caught the pretender himself!" He smiled at Tranquilo. "What a spectacle his sacrifice will make!"

Gomez cleared his throat. "We took no slaves, Your Holiness, nor was Don Hurac captured. I fear"—he took a long breath—"we were unable to stop the enemy and they now almost certainly hold Texcoco. To provide the . . . incentives the Holy Patriarcha commanded, we recruited all the locals we could find to the cause, but not only did the prospect of firing into civilians not break the enemy's resolve, as predicted"—his tone practically accused and he began speaking faster—"they . . . the *civilians* of Texcoco actually *turned* on us, attacking their very defenders, anointed by God!" He sounded amazed and scandalized by that. "It was a dreadful surprise and badly disordered my soldiers in the face of the enemy. It left them vulnerable to unexpected maneuvers that flanked us on every hand." He hesitated again, then almost mumbled, "Perhaps worst of all, some of the locally raised troops fired on my soldiers as well, doubtless in response to how we were using their families and neighbors. I . . . respectfully and worshipfully submit that tactic may have been ill-conceived."

"Defeat!" came a dreamy gasp from behind the red curtain. Drugged or no, His Supreme Holiness was listening.

"If not to Texcoco, where did your beaten army retire?" asked Father Armonia. "You must throw it at the enemy again!"

It took longer than before for Gomez to answer. His tone was full of misery. "To the best of my knowledge, since I didn't see the very end, there was little left of the army to withdraw."

"So . . ." Tranquilo began flatly, croaky voice rising as he spoke, "after presiding over a disaster, you fled. You did not even stay to fight to the last and die for your God!"

"I did *not* flee in fear," Gomez responded. "Duty alone compelled me to escape and bring you this news . . . this warning. I know well what fate may await me and would rather have died on the battlefield." There could be little question he was sincere about that. He might face impalement, at least. "My lancers were shattered and beyond my control," Gomez defended, "and other than them, only my officers and myself were mounted. Defeat was inevitable, and happening very quickly. I believed it essential that you be aware the Holy City is no longer defended, so preparations could be made."

"You and *all* your officers fled?" Sachihiro accused in a dangerous tone.

"Not all—of course not. But as you know, the enemy has a large mounted contingent—their Rangers and dragoons, aside from their own lancers—and I needed to take enough so we could split up and divide our pursuers." His face couldn't be seen, but a frown entered his voice. "It worked. But the last ones on our trail were a group of Rangers—the very devils of the enemy—under one of their finest trackers. Our spies call him 'Beeryman,' or 'Boogerbear,' I believe. I don't know which is correct, but he's a true demon. I was obliged to split my dwindling force twice more, and only God

Himself could have influenced the devils to pursue the others instead of Teniente Juaris and myself."

"You dare imply that God has blessed your cowardice?" Tranquilo demanded.

"Never, Your Holiness." Gomez had no idea how Tranquilo preferred to be addressed since he'd anointed himself "Holy Patriarcha" of the Dominion and didn't intend to err on the conservative side. The same honorific as Sachihiro seemed likely. At least it didn't result in a rib-shattering kick from Tranquilo's pet monster, Brother Escorpion. "I do believe God aided my escape from the devil Rangers so I could perform one final duty—to tell you directly what happened. The shame of that should be mine alone to bear."

"Indeed," Sachihiro reflected grimly. He looked up at the others. "So. What now? It seems, in spite of everything, there's simply no way to stop them short of the Holy City itself." He sighed. "You all know what this means. With the heretics barely a dozen *leguas* distant and no appreciable force to place in their path, a determined march could have them here in as few as two or three days."

"A little more, most likely," Gomez proposed. "The enemy *was* damaged and disorganized. And they may feel compelled to secure Texcoco first. I cannot imagine them taking more than a few days longer, however. They are a formidable force and seem quite driven."

"Still," Sachihiro fumed bitterly. "Now *we* must flee. The Gran Cruzada is closer than the enemy can possibly know, but simply can't arrive in time."

Armonia frowned. "By ancient tradition . . . I believe we have two choices." His expression turned dark. "We can cleanse the city—kill everyone, burn everything—"

"You will *not* burn my city!" exclaimed the man behind the curtain, voice surprisingly forceful.

Armonia shrugged. "Then we should begin the evacuation of all the quality citizens at once. Tell them they flee from the Vomito Rojo they already believe has infested Vera Cruz. They won't have seen the enemy nor fled in the face of a heretic horde. They can be salvaged. The rest of the people will eventually learn the truth and must fight for their salvation. Perhaps, fighting house to house, they can hold until the Gran Cruzada comes. Once the enemy has been thrown back and utterly crushed, we can decide whether to cleanse the city or not."

"In that kind of fight, the city will still burn regardless," Sachihiro brooded.

"And you cannot count on the people," Gomez said to the floor.

"Shut your cowardly mouth!" Sachihiro flared, almost screaming, a measure of his fear finally breaking through. He'd never be in direct personal peril because he wouldn't be here, but he'd worked too long to win his position, and all that was threatened.

"No, he's right," Tranquilo said, voice as mild as it was capable of being. "*Most* of the people will be of no use, but some . . ." He nodded to himself. "There's a third choice," he said to Armonia. "We let the enemy in."

"You can't be serious!" Sachihiro exclaimed.

"Quite serious. The enemy comes, conquers the city, even elevates Don Hurac." He nodded at the curtain. "The true Supreme Holiness will be elsewhere, of course." He turned back to the others. "And they will think they have won." He sneered. "Their guard will drop and loyal elements in the city"—he smiled at Armonia—"under *your* direction, I think, will begin to strike, sow discord, distrust, and fear, destroy their confidence and any sense of accomplishment, murder their soldiers, assassinate their leaders . . ." He cackled, and the sound was like a lizardbird's hunting cry. "With what seems like half the city rising against them and their vaunted discipline in tatters because most would just as soon leave, *then* the Gran Cruzada comes! They will surely surrender then—the mere chance of life preferable to the alternatives we will allow them—or they will die." He looked at Armonia. "Then, as you say, we cleanse the city."

"That sounds . . . most regrettable, that heretics will be free to defile the Holy City, but also a possible answer," Sachihiro allowed, with a glance at Armonia. "Yet what of the pronouncements Don Hurac will have issued? He will stop the war, outlaw us . . . who knows what else?"

"Let him," said Brother Escorpion, speaking for the first time. "Those proclamations will have to reach their destinations, will they not?" He shrugged. "We can stop many and preempt the rest. We'll have the vast majority of the messenger dragons, taking them with us when we leave. Don Hurac will have only those in transit at the time, and ours will already have been dispatched with messages to those he would send his own to."

"An excellent point, Brother Escorpion," Tranquilo said, looking to the others. "Do not concern yourselves. All is under control. I know Don Hurac quite well, and have even met the demon Colonel Cayce on two occasions.

Neither is ruthless enough to cope with a civilian insurgency on the scale I envision." He sighed. "Ever since that first battle near Uxmal when Coronel Cayce defeated General Agon and Don Frutos, I have feared this day may come. I have been planning for it." He wagged a bony finger. "There's a great deal more than you know going on, here in this city, with the Gran Cruzada, and even in the Yucatán, the very home of many of our enemies. In spite of their victories on the battlefield, they'll soon face calamities in so many quarters, they won't know which way to turn."

He glanced down at Gomez and Juaris. "Oh, do get up. We're all . . . disappointed by your failure, but I, at least, was not surprised. As I said, I've been making ready for it." He seemed to decide something. "I don't believe I shall have either of you impaled today. Don't leave the city or make any long-term plans." He actually giggled at his own wit, and it sounded like gravel crunching under a boot. "But I shall give you the same chance to redeem yourselves that I allowed the Blood Cardinal Don Frutos, who should soon join the Gran Cruzada. Perhaps he'll make use of himself there, though I honestly can't imagine how. In your case, at Father Armonia's disposal, I have higher hopes. Your rank will mean nothing and you'll answer to him, but he might need a military mind to advise him or provide rudimentary training to operatives he will lead."

Groaning slightly as he stood, Gomez asked, "Who will these 'operatives' be?"

Tranquilo waved the question away, gesturing at Armonia. "I will tell him first, a little later. He can share it with you if he likes."

"I take it this course of action is decided, then?" Sachihiro asked with a glance at the curtain. There was no objection. "Very well. We have much to do. At the very least, as earlier mentioned, our quality supporters must be preserved. Any others who choose to flee . . ." He shrugged. "No one can be blamed for attempting to escape what they believe is a looming plague of the Vomito Rojo. They'll receive no support or transportation, but why not let them go?"

"It may even be helpful to do so," Brother Escorpion mused thoughtfully. Looking around, he explained. "Once it has been decided that the time has come to launch our . . . 'spontaneous' acts of violence and disobedience in the city, their absence will increase the perceived percentage of those who are dissatisfied. And some who remain may even join our activists. Many will not, of course, and they cannot be allowed to live." He smiled tentatively. "An imaginative use of their deaths might inflame the resistance of others."

"You see?" Tranquilo chortled gleefully. "I don't only keep him for his muscles! I may even leave him with you," he told Armonia. "At present, Brother Escorpion, would you please speak to the guards outside the temple and have the *alcalde* of the city brought to us here?" He looked at the others. "I honestly don't know his position on how we rose to power, but it really doesn't matter. He must be involved in the evacuation, but no one will speak a word of the true cause. Or our other plans, of course."

CHAPTER 8

DECEMBER 19, 1848

Just after dawn, three days after the occupation of Texcoco, the recombined Allied Army, its own members increasingly identifying themselves simply as "Americans" in the American army, regardless of whether their home cities had entered into a proper union or not, paraded its regiments and divisions on the plain southwest of Texcoco between the river and the Camino Sagrado. One road continued westward, then northwest, it was said (they now had a wealth of local guides to lead them), and a company of dragoons under their bright, fluttering guidon pounded across a stone bridge spanning the river to scout that direction, replacing some returning Rangers. But the "Sacred Road" they'd long been following, which led to the Holy City itself, had turned abruptly southward. That was the direction most of the army would resume its march.

Lewis Cayce sat astride Arete, accompanied by Leonor and Varaa (of course), as well as Har-Kaaska, a slightly less haggard-looking Reverend Harkin, Colonel Agon and Major Arevalo, Major Olayne and Sergeant Major McNabb, reviewing the force as Agon's 4th Division in their green-and-black uniforms filed out by regiments in columns eight abreast to take the place of honor at the head of the host. The fine road had widened sufficiently to double the line of march, thus shortening it, and Lewis would take full advantage. What he now beheld under a clear golden sky with the sun just cresting the mountains was a magnificent, soul-stirring sight. His commanders had used the short time of "rest" to not only re-equip their soldiers from the baggage train, but also mercilessly drill them in the firm fields surrounding the city.

Drill had fallen by the wayside on the long march and, especially considering how many new recruits they had, relearning how to properly maneuver large formations in a fight had been a dire necessity. The result was a near-flawless evolution as nearly thirty thousand men in new or carefully groomed kit still stood at rest or heeded the drums and peeled out of parade formations under fluttering flags and followed their leaders to the road. The gold-tinged tops of the walls around Texcoco were lined with liberated citizens who cheered as the army commenced what many must hope was the final campaign to end their oppression. After what those people had been through, that final horrific abuse by their own countrymen using them as they had still fresh, Lewis believed most of their enthusiasm was genuine.

Gazing out at the valley below, Lewis was granted his first clear view of this place they'd come so far to find. The larger, northernmost lake at the bottom of the valley, El Lago de Texcoco, gleamed serenely perhaps thirty miles away under the rising sun. He understood from maps provided by Vice Alcalde Don Amil that they'd get generally closer to the lake as they advanced but would rarely have a better view of it. It was surrounded by rich cropland, perhaps the most fertile in all the Dominion, but also towering mountains ringed by thick forests and crowned by perpetual snow. At least some of those mountains were volcanoes topped by sullen wisps of steam or gray smoke. Their ultimate objective, the Holy City, was still sixty miles away. Despite its reputed size, he'd been a fool to think he might glimpse it from here. He'd have even less chance the closer they got, crossing the lower, rougher, and more wooded terrain. He'd somehow come to expect it to appear as a distant, dark blot of evil, but all he could see at the moment was a beautiful, peaceful, almost storybook land, the bizarre beasts adding credibility to that impression.

He took a deep breath. Here, upwind of the city, which still reeked of death, all he could smell were the wholesome scents of the land and his horse, along with the constants of sweaty wool and leather, of course. But even the tang of animal dung was normal and relaxing, no matter the outlandish bottoms some of it dropped from. He turned to Colonel Agon and smiled.

"Your men look very fine, Colonel," Lewis told his former enemy, bowing slightly in his saddle. "Especially impressive since... How many locals and former Doms have you integrated?"

"More than two thousand," Agon replied, bowing in return.

"Two whole regiments' worth," Leonor reminded, darkly untrusting.

"But not two *new* regiments," Agon countered. "Much like you initially did with the Third Pennsylvania—and still do throughout your longer established divisions—the new men brought existing regiments up to strength. Believe me, Teniente Anson," he assured Leonor, "the veterans in those units will quickly discover and pull any, ah, 'weeds in their garden,' as Coronel Tun assures me."

"I hope so," Leonor grumped.

"I've seen it," Varaa confirmed. "It seems the true zealots can't help but give themselves away. Some even actively agitate. Fools. Those who declared their devotion to the Blood Priests, or even the traditional Dominion, were sent away." She blinked something no one but Har-Kaaska could fathom. "Those who tried to join our army and took the oath while fully intending to subvert it were treated like traitors in the ranks. Those who were reported were shot, but most by far have met with tragic—sometimes unlikely—fatal accidents."

Nodding, Lewis said, "I'm not in favor of that. I might argue it indicates an erosion of discipline."

"Good fer the army, though, if ye'll pardon me sayin'," growled Sergeant Major McNabb. "Comp'ny er regimental punishment's bad for morale; makes everyone feel kinda low. Take it from me; the lads'd rather sort it themselves."

Lewis nodded, and so did Olayne. "Far be it from me to disagree with the wisdom of such a venerable NCO," Olayne proclaimed, and McNabb gave a snort.

"He's right, though," Lewis said, earning a respectful glance from the grizzled artilleryman.

The last of Agon's division was passing, followed by Hudgens's battery of 6pdr and 12pdr guns, along with one of the batteries composed of captured Dom 8pdrs on new carriages. Squads of Felix Meder's mounted riflemen rode between each gun and among the auxiliary vehicles. Lewis saw young Felix himself riding alongside his friend Elijah Hudgens. If 4th Division ran into anything, it would have plenty of artillery support. Agon turned to Lewis and, along with Arevalo, saluted. "With your permission, I shall rejoin my division."

Lewis returned the salute. "Of course. I'll see you on the march." He grinned, gesturing back at the rest of the army, still immobile. "That might be a while. Keep an eye out. Major Anson and a full battalion of Rangers are scouting ahead, and I'm expecting frequent messengers. Don't let them just gallop past you looking for me. They have orders to share what they see with you first."

Agon bowed his head. "Thank you, Coronel. I look forward to seeing you later." With that, he and Arevalo turned their horses' heads and trotted away to catch the front of their infantry, now quite a long way down the road.

"May as well go and join Mr. Hudgens," Olayne told McNabb. They also saluted Lewis and departed, just as Colonel Itzam, commanding 3rd Division, and Reed from 1st Division cantered up with their small staffs, incidentally escorting Don Hurac and Father Orno. Lewis was vaguely disconcerted to see Mistress Samantha and Don Hurac's lady, who everyone called "Mistress Zyan," with them, both riding sidesaddle. Another surprise was the presence of Don Amil, the vice *alcalde* of Texcoco.

"Gentlemen . . . and ladies," Lewis greeted, returning the officers' salutes.

"Good day to you, Coronel Cayce," Don Hurac enthused, arms stretched wide to encompass the army. "What a magnificent sight! No one could view this glorious spectacle and doubt the success of our cause." He paused. "And they look so much more . . . purposeful than they did when we departed Vera Cruz."

"Leaving like this will facilitate organization and supply on the march," Varaa said after further greetings were exchanged. "And I'm sure it will swell the hearts of our troops as much as it reinforces the confidence of our new allies." She blinked meaningfully at Don Amil. "We're leaving a great hoard of supplies here, relatively lightly guarded, and it's important the locals expect us to return." Never burdened with social superfluities, she immediately proceeded to voice the question on many minds. "Which leads me to ask why *you* are here, Don Amil. Just to watch our departure from amid it, I hope. You can't be contemplating accompanying us. Your city still needs your leadership to recover from the trauma it suffered."

Don Amil gave a tentative smile and cleared his throat. "Magistrado Don Renaud, Don Radarado, and Don Xoteca are much closer to the people than I, more directly involved in day-to-day matters in the city. My people are in excellent hands."

"I asked him to come," Don Hurac interjected. "He has been in the Holy City more recently than I. Not only does he have more contacts there (most of mine have met with misfortune, no doubt), but he has watched the city's descent into hell firsthand. His advice might prove invaluable."

Leonor and Varaa exchanged skeptical looks, and both were surprised to see similar expressions on Samantha's and Zyan's faces. But if Don Hurac wouldn't listen to Zyan, he wouldn't listen to anyone.

"Have you anything to report?" Lewis asked Reed and Itzam. Colonel Reed smiled and shook his head. "No, sir. Not me, anyway. Just thought I'd stop and wave. First Division's next in line of march." They all turned to look. The 1st US Infantry Regiment was leading the division, and the musicians had been joined by two regular infantrymen with their own fiddle and banjo. They and a couple of others were extremely popular among the natives, enough so that replicas of their instruments had been made and quite a few Yucatános were learning to play. Grinning hugely, the men struck up the rapid, jaunty notes of "Natchez Under the Hill" as they passed. A cheer sounded, and drummers and fifers eased into the tune.

Lewis matched the musician's grin. "Now *that's* what I call marching music."

"Makes it difficult to keep your feet still, doesn't it?" Reed asked. "The lads discovered you liked the tune," he explained.

"I do, and thank them for me. I hope to hear it often."

Reed nodded. "I expect you will."

After a while, Lewis found himself reviewing the passage of the army virtually surrounded by females, for, aside from Father Orno and Reverend Harkin, the only others close to him were Leonor, Samantha, Zyan, and Varaa. Don Hurac and Don Amil had gone with Colonel Reed to join 1st Division, and Har-Kaaska and Itzam went to personally lead the 2nd and 3rd Divisions before they even began to move.

"I don't like that Don Amil. Don't trust him," Leonor suddenly announced. Lewis smiled at her. "You never trust anyone at first," he reminded, which was true enough.

"I find myself in agreement with Leonor," Varaa said.

Brows rising, Lewis looked at the other females. Samantha frowned and touched her fan to her chin, and Zyan pursed her lips. Lewis couldn't remember ever hearing her speak without Don Hurac present, and she surprised him by doing so now, in Spanya. "His Holiness Don Hurac is perhaps somewhat overtrusting at times. After all that has happened, including the murder of all his children, I'm somewhat mystified by that." Her voice was darkened by uncharacteristic bitterness, entirely understandable since some of those children had been hers. "Yet he has always been . . . different from other Blood Cardinals. Even constrained by the traditions he now opposes, he genuinely cared about the people in his province, even the slaves, and I always admired his capacity for seeking and perhaps occasionally inspiring the best in others."

"Don Amil's explanation for joining us makes sense," Samantha guardedly confessed. "Especially if Don Hurac asked him to. Remember, if all goes well, he'll soon be the closest thing to God on Earth as far as Don Amil is concerned. Difficult indeed not to consider such a request a command."

Leonor frowned, then nodded. "Maybe. I'll be keepin' a eye on him, though."

"As you should," Varaa agreed. "As will I."

Reverend Harkin cleared his throat. "Not to change the subject, but some of you may recall that, despite being a man devoted to the literal word of God as recorded in His scriptures, the study of natural history, the story of His creation, has long been a passion of mine." He puffed out his once-voluminous, now-somewhat-meager chest. "Our adventures here have, in fact, allowed me to lay all those subversive theories of extinction that ran rampant where we came from to rest. Much like He did to us, God simply transported various disappeared creatures from our old world to this one," he pronounced triumphantly.

Lewis remembered Harkin's excitement when he came up with that notion—and it even made a measure of sense—but Lewis remained skeptical, even leery of such inflexible beliefs. His own faith wasn't cast in any denominational stone, but especially after the adventures Harkin referenced, he considered it rank hubris to limit God's power in any way. He could certainly change His own creations over time, or even clear the slate if He chose.

"In any event," Harkin continued, "now that we're able to examine more maps than the admitted artistic masterpiece in the great hall in Uxmal, my fascination with the similarities—and vast differences—between this world and our old one has increased." He peered about. "We had our own maps of this region when we came here; this very valley was our ultimate objective then as well. No doubt those maps were incomplete, but most were contextualized by books with exhaustive descriptions." He sighed. "Yet all the way here from Vera Cruz, we've found those descriptions either inadequate or wildly inaccurate. Now that we behold the Great Valley of Mexico itself, it seems clear that its center lies at a much lower elevation than it should, the mountains all around considerably taller and more extreme, perhaps even more volcanically active, as are other places we've heard of, such as Captain Holland's 'Pass of Fire.'"

"Do please make your point," Varaa said good-naturedly, blinking and rolling her eyes. Lewis refocused on his passing army to return the salute of Captain Barca, riding at the head of his battery. Dukane's battery was next in line, then would come Colonel Itzam's 3rd Division.

"Very well." Harkin sniffed at Varaa with a glare. "You can't be familiar with a German geologist named von Buch, but I was gifted a translated volume that included some of his proposals, along with those of various others—mostly Frenchmen," he inserted darkly. "But von Buch applied the term 'caldera' to describe what is essentially a deep pit or crater into which the land has collapsed after the supporting magma chamber beneath a volcano has emptied, presumably vented by an eruption." He waved grandly down at the valley.

"I don't know any 'von Buch,' but my people have similar theories." Varaa blinked. "Oddly, we call such depressions '*caldarias*.' An interesting coincidence, is it not?"

"Indeed," Harkin agreed.

Wide-eyed, Samantha gazed at their destination anew. "Surely you're not suggesting that this entire region fell into a great, monstrous hole after a volcano erupted?" She squinted at one of the distant smoking mountains. "Why, it must've been the biggest mountain in the world!"

"Not necessarily," Harkin denied, "and it needn't have resulted from one gigantic event." He frowned. "Though it might have, I suppose." He shook his head. "My understanding is that it could have happened gradually, the floor of the valley dropping only a step at a time."

"Just as long as it doesn't keep 'steppin'' while we're here," Leonor declared. She tilted her head to the side. "You reckon the valley we were aimin' for 'back home' was in the same fix? Just hadn't dropped in its own big hole yet?"

Harkin shook his head. "I have no idea, my dear. I can't even be certain I'm right, or that the same conditions exist beneath this earth. Not all geologic and geographic differences we've encountered can be explained by volcanism."

"But there *are* still volcanoes here, so if this valley is a caldera, not all the underground magma has been exhausted," Lewis speculated aside, returning Dukane's salute.

"Or the source remains," Harkin agreed, then raised his only hand and waved it. "I don't *know* any of this, and my theory is based solely on a whimsical effort to explain the depth of this valley. It might as easily be that all the land around it is higher. The more I compare our old world to this one, the more they seem mere . . . caricatures of each other."

Varaa *kakked* in amusement. "As good a description as my comparison of all the small differences between two musket balls!"

Lewis turned back to look at Harkin, and Father Orno beside him. The short Uxmalo priest seemed to have an opinion of his own, but didn't express it. "This is all very interesting, but none of it matters at present. And true or not, I'd just as soon you don't spread such speculations about. None of our troops, from our old world or native, need more reminders of the strangeness of this world. They certainly don't need to worry about calderas under their feet. We have other business to attend to, and nature, of any sort, is beyond our power to affect." He scratched his bearded cheek and sighed.

"The two of you . . . sanctified gentlemen . . . have done as much or more than anyone to make our presence here possible. In spite of your many . . . canonical differences that might've wrecked our combined efforts, you became fast friends, and I consider that nothing less than a miracle itself. Together, you've brought our disparate peoples closer than any political settlement in the Yucatán might've done and more than half convinced even me that God is behind all this, from fetching my 'old soldiers' to this different world, to the very cause we pursue. I refuse to worry that, after all the trouble He must've gone to in order to bring us to this point, He'd immolate us and drop us in a hole." He grinned somewhat warningly. "So let's make sure the only thing our troops are worried about is beating the enemy, shall we?"

"Damn right," Leonor agreed.

"Well, there *are* still pesky monsters, of course," Varaa said cheerfully. "It won't hurt to remind the men about them from time to time. It's likely the same here as anywhere—dangerous predators are fewer the closer we come to a large city. I suppose the availability of plentiful, easier, even somewhat domesticated prey is offset by the fact that the predators are hunted in turn, but as we've consistently seen, those that linger tend to be bolder." She blinked at Harkin and Orno, tail whipping behind her. "Please do help ensure the men remain mindful of that."

CHAPTER 9

DECEMBER 20, 1848

It was a bright, sunny morning, the warmest in many days, and Major Giles Anson was leading a troop of Rangers himself, scouting down the Camino Sagrado some thirty-five miles ahead of the army. The land close to the road was still relatively clear and given to extensive agriculture, but the near-geometric precision of the fields near Texcoco had given way to a more disorganized effort necessitated by the rolling mountain foothills they'd entered. Most were relatively small, basically large bumps with gentle grades that were cultivated themselves to an extent. Others were more extreme, topped by wooded crowns and great boulders.

"Bet that's what they use all those giant, fat snake-lizards for," Boogerbear had speculated the night before as they smoked cigars around the small fire they'd built within a cluster of the stones atop a respectable rise. Anson had waited for the big Ranger's wisdom. Boogerbear didn't often speculate on the nature of the world; he just observed, recognized, and used or avoided what *was*, little caring how or why it got that way. When he did voice an opinion, he'd usually thought a lot about it.

"We've been told the locals use the big devils for heavy construction work," Anson commented.

"Sure," Boogerbear had agreed. "But how much o' that is there? All the time, I mean. Their big cities are built already—walls, tall pyramids, big buildin's an' such—like them ... agua doodles we seen, stretchin' for miles an' miles, as far as you can see."

"Aqueducts," Anson had corrected with a grin.

"Whatever." Boogerbear had waved it away. "An' it ain't like they do a lot o' big construction in the small villages we've seen along the way." His voice had darkened somewhat. They'd met no enemy resistance yet, but all the little communities they'd passed had received the same treatment they'd come to expect from the enemy. Especially the roughly two hundred Reaper Monks the very few survivors with the courage to approach them had identified as the ones to blame. Essentially, anyone not deemed "important" in some way hadn't even been warned to flee the approaching American army. They'd simply been murdered. At least the Reapers hadn't believed they had time to do it "right," as they reckoned such things, and merely lined the locals up along the road and slashed their throats. The fifty-odd Rangers in Anson's troop had been furious and disgusted, as always, and the pervading sentiment seemed to be, "If they'll take the time and effort to do this to their own, why won't they fight us?" Rangers hated Reapers with a passion, and regardless of the reported disparity in numbers, everyone wanted to catch them.

"Anyway," Boogerbear had continued, "you remember all them walls between the fields near Texcoco, the armabueys an' horny oxes"—that's what he called the large beasts with frills and horns on their faces—"draggin' the bigger rocks ta throw on the boundaries? No different from farmers back home, clearin' fields." He'd gestured at the massive stones nearby. "But these big ol' gray boulders, all heaped on hilltops an' along the creeks an' such, or gathered in piles like a hill o' their own, didn't get there by theirselves. What's more, I figger it'd take a dozen armabueys ta shift some of 'em. 'Magine that. I reckon it'd work, but why not use just a single big snake-lizard, if you got one?"

Considering what they'd heard from Don Hurac and others, there wasn't much large-scale manufacturing in the Great Valley. Yet the whole thing seemed to be under intense cultivation, possibly feeding much of the Dom empire by itself. Boogerbear made sense, as usual.

Anson considered that anew as the increasingly forested rolling hills, even mountains they'd entered seemed to suddenly drop off a cliff and the road plunged down through a broad, wooded cut in what could only be a dramatic escarpment. He'd been expecting it. Boogerbear had taken a five-man scout ahead and sent word. Other outriders on the flanks would have to close in on the road once again because the Río de Purification was reported to lie just ahead, winding through a chasm far below a massive stone bridge that even Don Hurac spoke of in a tone of awe.

"Boogerbear's snake-lizards probably helped build that, I bet," Anson said to himself, actually looking forward to viewing the wonder. Trees quickly thickened alongside the road in the cut, making a pleasantly shady forest that hung over the road in places. It was, of course, a perfect place for an ambush, and Anson's senses sharpened. But Boogerbear would've come through here less than two hours before, his messenger more recently, and Anson couldn't imagine anyone avoiding the big Ranger's detection or getting past him without notice. Still . . .

"Sergeant Nares, take two men a couple hundred yards ahead an' have an extra look as we go."

"Sir." Nares nodded. Rangers rarely saluted, and never at times like this. Calling a pair of names Anson recognized as Ocelomeh "Jaguar Warriors" that made up the backbone of his Ranger force, Nares urged his dark-striped horse forward with his companions. Anson plodded on, Lieutenant Riss by his side. With Boogerbear ahead and Sal Hernandez probably far to the northwest by now, Riss was the deadliest Ranger with him. As a sergeant, he'd been Leonor's "favorite" platoon leader on her various outings. Even though Riss had been recently elected lieutenant, Leonor would probably still pick him for anything particularly dangerous. He clearly approved of Anson sending extra men ahead.

"Only t'ing Boogerbear report before the bridge was a 'bad stink' along the road," Riss now said. "Like at the towns," he added darkly, "but from a dead critter." They could already see a cloud of lizardbirds swirling over the trees in the distance ahead, raucously contending for whatever carrion constituted the smell. Regardless of how unpleasant it might be, Boogerbear would've investigated more carefully if he'd discovered another mass murder site. Animals died for all sorts of natural reasons, and he wouldn't have wasted time determining the cause.

"Let's pick up the pace," Anson said. "We'll look the bridge over when we get there, wait for our flankers, then push on." He quickened Colonel

Fannin's gait to a trot. The cut apparently widened as they went, and the wood on either side of the road grew deep enough to impress him with a sense of gloom. Sergeant Nares's detachment was still visible ahead, cantering lightly along, men's heads swiveling from side to side. Occasional lizard-birds swooped belligerently as if trying to chase them off. They didn't get too close because most things the size of a horse and rider could jump and snatch them from the sky. There were a lot of them, however, more than something the size of a dead pig or goat would draw. Whatever they were feeding on was big.

"I wish Boogerbear could've caught every officer that ran off at Texcoco," Anson thought aloud. "Not his fault," he quickly defended, "only a pair got away, but word must've spread pretty quick. Fast enough for them damn Reapers to run a'murderin' up the road."

"Wasn't just officers," Lieutenant Riss consoled. "A buncha their lancers scattered too. Too many to chase. No way to stop what we seen on this trip."

"I guess," Anson agreed with a grunt. "Just can't get used to it. Where I come from . . ." He hesitated. "There's always been brutal fightin' an' savage killin'. Hard, like, an' mean. Kinda like it was with you Ocelomeh an' the Holcanos—before we whipped 'em an' got 'em on our side." He thought briefly about the Holcano war leader Kisin, off with Sal at the moment, and caught himself missing the big, uncouth ex-cannibal. "I can't ever imagine bein' on the same side as Comanches, though." He pondered that, and Ramon Lara sprang to mind. He snorted. "Course, I never would'a thought that about Mexicans either. I mean *Mexican* Mexicans, not like Sal . . ." He saw Riss looking strangely at him and realized how weird that must sound. "The point is, ugly as the fightin' where I come from could get, *nobody* killed their own people just to keep 'em from knowin' different kinds of folks, folks who *thought* different, even existed. The only reason we fought one another, even us an' Comanches, was the same reason we fight here: to *protect* our people, see? What the Doms do is just . . . insane."

"Is evil," Riss stated flatly. "Wrong, evil faith. An' that's why they do it," he pointed out. "Lots o' their people, when they find out, even they think it's evil. They join us, no?"

"Yeah, some do," Anson conceded, then frowned. "But some don't. I guess they're the real crazy ones—an' they're in charge."

"Can't all be crazy," Riss disagreed. "Some're just hungry for power.

All-over control o' everybody from their evil faith to do whatever they want. So even more evil," he concluded.

Anson was nodding, but he'd noted the trio of riders, including Sergeant Nares, had stopped in the road, hurriedly bringing weapons to bear while hundreds of lizardbirds exploded from the trees. "Trouble," he said grimly.

They'd eaten up about half the distance to Nares and his men before Anson realized they'd stopped while the column continued to advance. His first instinct was to charge forward to their aid, but that negated the point of their presence out front. "Column, halt! Arm yourselves!" he shouted, raising a hand. The sudden command, without any warning, might've thrown less-experienced troopers into chaos. As it was, it wasn't exactly pretty, and there was minor confusion as thirty-odd riders quickly stopped their animals and readied their weapons, but these men were veterans and used to such things. In seconds, they were ready to fight. Barely a hundred paces away, the lizardbirds were erupting from the trees on both sides of the road, perhaps thicker on the right, but Nares and his men were all facing left, horses capering nervously. "What is it, Sergeant?" Anson shouted loudly.

"Dunno, sir," came the reply, distorted by distance and incessant squawking, both deadened by the forest and echoing off the road. Nares barely sounded like himself. "Somethin' big comin' through the trees downwind."

"Fall back on us," Anson directed.

"With pleasure, sir," Nares yelled, spinning his mount and ordering his companions to follow. There was a loud, deep, crackling sound now, as something smashed through limbs and small trees. A great forest giant, like a ferny-leafed pine almost a hundred and fifty feet tall, actually juddered from an impact.

"Move yourselves!" Anson bellowed at the three men. They needed no encouragement. Unfortunately, one of the terrified horses balked. Native animals were generally instinctively wiser to the perils of this world, and a rider might safely defer to their judgment in certain situations, but, torn between its master's command and its own sense that safety lay in a different direction, the frightened beast simply stopped and reared. A fatal mistake.

A gigantic reddish, gray-brown head, gaping jaws bristling with bayonet-length teeth, darted from the trees alongside the road and clamped down on the distressed Ranger—and the top half of his squealing horse. If the Ranger screamed, they never heard it as the jaws snapped closed and the head jerked upward in a shower of blood. The horse rose as well, for just a short distance. Already limp, it crashed to the road when its spine finally parted.

"Good God a'mighty!" Anson snapped, instinctively drawing one of his Walker Colts even as he knew it was futile. His big revolvers might be the most powerful handguns on this world, but they'd likely only aggravate a creature like this. His Rangers were pouring out of their column and forming a line, raising their weapons.

"Hold your fire, god damn you!" Anson roared. Nares and the surviving Ranger, pounding toward them at a sprint, were still between them and the monster that now strode fully out on the road. The thing was immense, the biggest of its sort any of them had ever seen, standing twenty feet tall and supported by hams nearly as large as its barrel-shaped torso, which tapered into tree-trunk-thick legs and enormous three-toed feet. There were something like giant turkey spurs between them. Anson hadn't seen that before. Bent over like it was, its back parallel with the ground, its height didn't give justice to its perhaps fifty-foot length, from the upended tip of its chomping jaws, working to swallow its mighty mouthful, to the end of its spastically whipping tail. As far as Anson could see, the thing had no arms or forelegs at all. Swallowing its bite practically whole, it trod on the front half of the very dead horse and bit down on the back half, effortlessly tearing it away and spilling gray intestines and bloody-white stomach as it prepared to upend and swallow that as well.

"Where did d'at t'ing come from?" Riss practically whispered at Anson. "Boogerbear never miss *d'at*!"

"Easy," Anson whispered back, despite the absurdity of it. They'd never be heard over the noises the monster was making. "It wasn't here when he passed. It came to the smell of the dead critter he reported."

"But . . . our flankers not see it either!"

"They're behind us now. An' the wind's blowin' across us, right to left. I bet we'll find it blowin' down toward the river just a short way ahead. Boogerbear did say there was a well-used trail, followin' the river up high on this side. Damn thing might've been miles away when he passed."

"Funny it come up jus' now," Riss observed.

"Yeah," Anson agreed. "Funny."

"What we do? Is blockin' the road. An' one d'at big . . . it be faster than a horse in a sprint."

That was hard to believe, but true. Anson had seen it before. With the stride the thing had, it could outpace a horse for a short distance. At least from a standing start.

"Yeah," Anson reluctantly agreed. "The first time I go off without a section of Barca's battery, we run into somethin' too big to shoot. I won't make that mistake again," he vowed.

"We all shoot at once?" Riss suggested.

"Not sure," Anson confessed. "We've taken down smaller ones that way. A *lot* smaller," he qualified. "Even chased a few off. I figure we'll just make this one mad." It was finishing the horse as they watched and Nares and his companion joined them.

"I'm sorry, sir," Nares said at once. "I should've got out quicker."

"Not your fault. On this world, the same could've happened to your trooper just steppin' off from camp for a shit."

Nares reluctantly nodded. "That's why we use latrines, with sentries near, but I get your point. What do we do now?"

"We could just let it finish, go off to eat the stinky thing, then ride on past," Riss suggested.

Anson considered, then shook his head. "I have a sneaky feelin' the 'bait' ain't far enough from the road to make that safe."

"Bait?" Nares repeated. "You think it was *baited* here?"

Anson just nodded, peering at the great beast as it nosed around on the ground, looking for another morsel and apparently oblivious to their presence. Pulling at the beard on his chin, he spoke, "Won't have any choice if we wait too long, though, an' I bet somebody out there *expects* us to shoot at it too. Might be the only way to sort 'em out." Ten more Rangers had joined them from behind, the flankers coming in and finding them on the road.

"What do you mean?" Nares asked. Anson looked at him. "If somebody was layin' for Boogerbear an' his boys, somewhere ahead—he'll prob'ly be waitin' for us just past the bridge on the other side of the river by now. That's what he said he'd do—how would they know we were too busy to help 'em?"

"They hear shootin'," Riss said, nodding.

"Right," Anson said. "Question is, how do we raise a ruckus without gettin' tangled up with that booger—doin' just what the enemy wants? An' without gettin' ate, o' course."

"We split up," Nares suggested. "Maybe a little more than half of us fade into the trees on the downwind side of the road, and the others get it to chase 'em. A hundred-pace head start should be safe enough to avoid gettin' caught."

"That's what we'll do," Anson decided, nodding. "Your detail, Lieutenant Riss. Shoot the hungry bastard up and then run like the devil. The rest of us'll slip past behind it and go down to help Boogerbear. You come a'runnin' as well, as soon as you shake that big bastard."

Anson doubted the monster could count, but was subtle about how the detachment he and Sergeant Nares led left the road. They managed it quickly, but without changing the apparent size of the line they'd formed when the column spread out. They needn't have rushed, however, since the huge creature no longer seemed as interested in whatever festering carrion lay in the woods and had thrown its gurgling, drooling attention to the Rangers. Appetite whetted, perhaps in the mood for more fresh horse, it began striding slowly toward them as if attempting to get closer before they spooked. Already a dozen yards in among the trees, Anson called out for Riss to make his move.

"Rangers, take aim!" Riss roared. All his men raised musketoons, but many made sure the bows over their shoulders were ready for use. There was good evidence their heavy arrows with long, razor-sharp obsidian points penetrated deeper through the thick hide and dense muscle of monsters like this, and they wanted the weapons handy.

"Fire!"

Musketoons *foomp*ed loudly in the cut, shrouded in stabbing yellow flashes and billowing white smoke. Even at nearly a hundred paces, it was inconceivable that any of the large musket balls missed the mark. Rangers were steady marksmen, and despite the inherent inaccuracy of their cutoff musketoons, the beast was a very big target. Clearly furious and pouring blood from twenty-odd wounds all over its body, the monster bellowed a high-pitched whistling, squealing roar and charged.

"Fall back!" Riss roared. "No, you silly buggers, don' touch them bows! Not yet."

Anson saw the Rangers on the road turn away, becoming flitting shapes through the trees. Remarkably quickly, the gigantic monster swept by as well, rumbling deep in its throat as it heaved in great gusts of air, blood pattering the hard top of the road as it passed. As always, Anson was struck by how remarkably graceful something so big could be, huge muscles clearly visible, rippling beneath the short fur on the skin. Head down, tail up, it practically flowed by their position. He supposed it was actually beautiful in its purpose-built way, perfectly suited for what it was created to do. He feared it but respected it, and certainly couldn't hate it. *Not like Doms*, he realized darkly. *It does stink, though*, he conceded to himself, starting to count out loud. At fifteen, he already heard a few popping shots from the way they'd come, and pride surged up in him. Even bounding away on horses, chased by something like that, at least a few of his Rangers had managed to reload and shoot again.

"Let's go," he called, urging Colonel Fannin into a weaving trot, then a full-out gallop as soon as he cleared the trees. A glance over his shoulder assured him that the monster had no interest in them, probably never noticed the twenty-four horses and riders, including himself and Sergeant Nares, thundering down the road behind it. Almost immediately, they passed through the place where a trooper and horse had died, obvious by the wide spatter of blood. At the same time, they began to smell the stench of whatever summoned their killer. "If this *was* a trap, whoever set it's gonna pay," Anson said aloud to himself.

It wasn't far before the road came up a little ahead and the trees began to thin. Quickly, they could see much deeper in the woods and saw the steep face of the cut fall away into an easier grade like one might find at the base of an ordinary hill. Anson saw the trail the monster must've approached by then; a rough cart path, in fact. Still shrouded by woods and veering southeast, it meandered along close to the edge of a cliff. Cresting the rise, they finally reached the river—although they could see no water. It was down there, no doubt, at the bottom of what looked like a gorge, but Anson doubted they'd see it until they reached the great stone bridge, also now in view, spanning the deeply eroded landscape like a crack in the world. For the first time in a while, they could see a good distance. The area remained fairly hilly, almost mountainous, but there was space between each feature.

Much like here, there was a wood along the far side of the gorge, and it must've been from there that the fifty or so brown-clad Reapers had emerged to attack Boogerbear's party. The firing was audible now, even over the beat of their hooves, and smoke drifted away to the left from a line of timber beyond a stone shack just past the far side of the bridge. *Maybe it's a toll booth or somethin'?* Anson mused. *Can't say much for the amenities, if so.* It truly was a shack, like so many they'd seen near Texcoco, and it couldn't have been more unlike the bridge.

Solidly built on massive, graceful arches, the bridge looked as sound and well-engineered as anything the Romans could've managed. "Looks like the aqueducts we've seen in the distance, only heavier built," he observed aloud before refocusing on the situation. Puffs of smoke emerged from the shack, so shoddy in comparison or not, at least it provided some cover for their friends. As they drew closer, he thought he saw a body lying outside on the ground. There were certainly the carcasses of two horses there, and as they swept down the road and prepared to cross the bridge, they met three riderless horses running to them. One was Boogerbear's "Dodger."

"Hope that doesn't mean they got him," Nares observed, recognizing the horse as well. "Somebody catch these animals!" he added over his shoulder.

"I doubt it," Anson replied. *I sure hope not*, he told himself. "No, Boogerbear would have known we'd come, one way or another, and forted up to defend the far side of the bridge. He ran off the horses to spare 'em."

"Courageous to send your only chance of escape away," Nares commented.

"No, just Boogerbear bein' himself," Anson countered. "He'll do what's needed. Always." He paused. "Dang, this bridge is somethin'." Now that they were on it and the sound of their thundering hooves didn't change at all, he knew how solid it was. Fairly long as well, almost eighty or a hundred paces. He'd love to inspect it more closely later.

"Reapers, sure enough," Anson growled, seeing the gray-brown tunics on figures taking better cover at the edge of the far woods. "Remember what them locals told us. Could be two hundred of the devils. We won't go right at 'em, like it looks like they're gettin' ready for; we'll swing wide around 'em. As soon as we're across, cut right with half the men," Anson directed. "I'll take the other half left."

Reaching the end of the bridge, Anson hooked hard left, just behind the stone structure his friend was defending, and then kicked Colonel Fannin into a sprint, his men following his example. Nares was already doing the same in the opposite direction. A fusillade of fire erupted from the trees and musket balls *vipp*ed and moaned around them, kicking up dusty gravel, even tearing at clothes, but the range was too long for the enemy's indifferently bored weapons, and only sheer luck could be relied on to hit the wildly charging horses and riders. No one was noticeably harmed.

"Why not go right at them now, Major?" a Ranger with an Uxmalo accent called from behind. "I bet they just shot themselves empty."

"They'll just run away," another Ranger answered. "We'd get some, but Major Anson wants 'em all."

That one knows me pretty well, Anson mused, pushing Colonel Fannin around some large boulders and across a treacherous spread of loose shale. The noise he and his troopers made, echoing back from the cliffs across the river, was stupendous and all out of proportion to their numbers. *If they hadn't seen us, that'd be enough to scare the Doms away by itself,* he fretted. *The first fellow might've called it right.* There was nothing for it now but to press on, however. "Tree line ahead," he called back. "A fair-size game trail, I reckon. Maybe another cart path. Watch for low limbs," he warned, vaguely encouraged to hear the shooting at Boogerbear resume. That meant at least some of the enemy stayed where they were.

Dashing in under the stunted, peripheral trees, he slowed Colonel Fannin a little. Low-hanging, brushy limbs were indeed a hazard, and these were like hackberry trees, lined with vicious, serrated thorns that tore his skin and uniform. Once again he was glad for his thick woollen jacket. The thorny foliage lay only at the border of the tall forest trees, however, like those on the other side of the gorge. The ground soon opened beneath them, covered by a thick layer of dead, fernlike leaves, and as the stony ground had amplified their passage before, this yielding carpet practically silenced them. "This way," Anson said lowly, veering right. He still didn't know if they'd been on an actual road, but lesser trails, marked by wandering depressions, led every which direction. The sun was obscured by the canopy above, and without a good sense of direction and the muffled booming of the ongoing fight it would've been easy to get turned around. *Maybe that's what they're countin' on,* he thought. *This is their land an' they might not think we can find our way through. Even the gunfire could get confusin' to a novice, the way it echoes around. Prob'ly still ain't used to copin' with Rangers.* He managed a small smile. *Course, most Reapers who learn enough about us to teach others our ways don't live to do it.*

The firing was much closer now and he reined Colonel Fannin to a stop, raised his hand (still gripping a Walker Colt), and peered ahead. He'd merely galloped to the sound of the guns, as it were, and there was the enemy, about fifty, he thought, still shooting at the stone shack and arrayed much as he'd seen from the start. Some on the far side seemed to have shifted to defend against Nares's approach—Anson could actually see the other Rangers closing through a patch of thinner trees—but no one seemed to even be looking this way. There was a loud, ongoing argument however, among a trio of Reapers standing back from their firing line. From what Anson picked out, one man with his hands on his hips was advocating simply charging Boogerbear and his men and swarming them under. There were only four of them, after all. The Reapers could quickly kill them, then race back across the bridge and array themselves near the monster bait they'd left. That mystery was solved with certainty, at least, though the one proposing they do that seemed to assume their trap hadn't yet worked. He sounded certain the huge beast they'd baited would arrive by the time the mounted Diablos pursued the Reapers there. They could then kill more of their enemy in the confusion of the monster's attack.

A Reaper leader, standing with arms folded over his chest, was shaking his head and arguing, voice carrying well enough that Anson heard every word.

"You are a fool, Domingo. Despite our best efforts, we did not surprise those four Diablos in the hut. They were prepared for us and killed twice their number before we crept close enough to slay more than one." He snorted. "And he was killed only because he was closest. Every one of our men probably shot at him. No, your initial scheme was intriguing, and I supported it, but I won't heap more corpses upon your madness. After cleansing the countryside, ours is the last full company of Reapers remaining between the enemy horde and the Holy City. I've been commanded to preserve it intact. We will repel the riders approaching from the left, and when they are in disarray, we shall retire to our own horses."

"Flee?" spat the man with his hands on his hips.

"Retreat and live to keep stinging the heretics as I was *ordered* to do. We will strike again elsewhere."

"What of the other horsemen?" asked the third man. Crossed Arms shook his head, turning toward Anson. "They are surely los..." His mouth hung open in an O of shock, eyes bulging as his words tapered off.

"At 'em!" Anson roared, ferociously kicking Colonel Fannin forward. His horse needed little encouragement, fully aware of what was coming. Twelve Rangers swarmed out of the trees, spreading out, charging straight in against fifty-odd Reapers. It would've been insane, but no one was even remotely ready for them, and Anson's hard-bitten veterans literally rode them down, trampling them into broken heaps or firing their weapons from a range of feet or inches as they thundered past, whooping and yelling like Comanches. A stutter of shots replied, crashing a couple of squealing horses and blowing a man from his saddle in a spray of blood. Another was stabbed off his horse with a pike, Reapers converging to stab and beat and shoot the dying man. Colonel Fannin scattered them, trampling the poor Ranger as well, but he was beyond caring. Anson started shooting, his big revolver booming loudly, practically flinging Doms to the ground. Most of the remaining Reapers began to waver, some already sprinting away. All the men who'd been preparing to counter Sergeant Nares were distracted by the chaos behind them—and died just as quickly when Nares charged without the slightest hesitation, blasting and tramping through them.

Anson and Colonel Fannin kept moving, bashing and shooting their way directly through to the leaders. One raised an ornate, brass-barreled pistol and fired, the ball actually shooting a hole through Colonel Fannin's ear and cutting Anson's also, but the Ranger commander simply re-cocked his heavy revolver, already five rounds down, then pointed and shot back. A black-red hole appeared in the Reaper's face, right under his cheekbone, the eye above it bulging from its socket as a gory spray erupted from the back of his head. He dropped like a sack of rocks. Another of the leaders turned as if to run, but Anson shot him in the back with his second Walker Colt, now in his left hand. Colonel Fannin didn't need the direction of reins in a fight. The Reaper went down, shot through a lung and spewing blood. "Sorry," Anson said, offhand. "Not as good a shot with my left." Holstering his empty revolver, he now took the smoking weapon in his right before aiming it at the final apparent leader, the one who'd stood so long with crossed arms. An expression of triumph on his face, the man was reaching for his own pistol now, another well-made example of the gunmaker's art.

"No point in even makin' the effort," Anson said brusquely. "You'll be dead before you touch that fancy piece. Good thing your whole army ain't as well armed. Still, it only shoots once. *Mine* shoots *six* times. See all them extra holes in the cylinder behind the barrel? Most of 'em are still loaded." He flicked his eyes at the officer drowning in his own blood. "Said I was sorry to him because, unlike you bastards, I hate to see a man suffer. He'll have to, a little, 'cause I won't waste another bullet to finish him until things settle down." He glanced quickly around. Not a single other Reaper still stood nearby, but shots sounded in the woods as those who'd fled were hunted. The ground all around was strewn with bodies and several of them were Rangers. He grimaced at that. "Won't be long now," he told the dying man.

"He earns much grace," the Reaper said piously.

"That's a bunch a shit," Anson retorted. "He's just hurtin', is all, an' I *am* sorry for it."

The Reaper leader worked his jaw, grinding his teeth, then shook his head stiffly. "I suppose I am your prisoner, but I will tell you nothing other than my name. I am—"

"I don't care who you are," Anson interrupted. "An' you already told me what I do care to know while you fellas was bickerin'." He curled his lip. "I figured it was you Reapers who baited that big lizard, or whatever he is, an' he *did* get one of my boys. So that wild-ass plan actually sorta worked. Besides that, all I would'a asked was how many o' you bastards were still hereabouts. You told me that too, an' now you're done."

He looked around again, to ensure no Reapers were faking death. They'd done that before. He also noted the approach of Boogerbear and the three other men with relief. All seemed hale and uninjured, if a little out of sorts over having had to walk over to join him. Frowning slightly, he altered his aim and shot the gasping, choking Dom on the ground in the back of the head. The extremely loud report and chest-thumping pressure of the powerful weapon was startling in the relative quiet, all the other shooting having moved farther away. The wounded man lay still. "See? Told you it wouldn't be long."

Glancing at the other Rangers, the remaining Reaper looked as if he might reach for his pistol again. Anson re-cocked and re-pointed his, shaking his head. "I'm still loaded. Oh, an' see there? That really big fella who looks like he's wearin' a dead critter on his face is already pointin' a smaller repeatin' pistol at you too. Again, no point in even makin' the effort."

The Dom took a long, deep breath. "What will you do with me?"

Anson scratched his chin under his beard. "We treat prisoners o' war pretty good. Hell, a bunch have joined us. At worst, they get carted off to Puebla or Vera Cruz, maybe Gran Lago, an' put to work. They eat good, though." He looked pointedly at the Reaper as Boogerbear stepped up and took the pistol from where it was hooked on the man's belt.

In a mild, even gentle voice entirely at odds with his frightening appearance, Boogerbear said, "Your sort, an' Blood Priests, we usually hang. You hadn't heard that?"

The Reaper's eyes widened in alarm.

"Ha!" Anson barked. "You just told me somethin' else. We can't've killed every one o' you devils that's seen us, or even fought us, but you not knowin' what's happened to those we catch, an' your stupid tactics today, prove that little *about* us is gettin' spread around. Too bad for you, but good for us. Thank you, sir." With that, Anson urged Colonel Fannin a step closer, and a final thunderous blast shook the air when he shot the Reaper in the forehead. As soon as the man hit the ground, he leisurely began the complicated process of reloading his empty chambers.

"No hangin's today?" Boogerbear asked, staring at the last fallen Reaper, whose head now resembled a hollowed-out melon. His tone was void of inflection.

"No. Between the fellas still chasin' Reapers an' Lieutenant Riss maybe still playin' tag with a huge man-eatin' lizard, we're scattered all to hell an' gone." He tilted his head to the side. "I know the boys enjoy watchin' Reapers an' Blood Priests swing, an' I can't hardly blame 'em. Today in particular, after one of us got ate. But we've suffered more losses than just him, poor bastard, an' we need to get 'em buried deep an' fast." He looked around again. "Hell, I don't even know how many we lost." He breathed an angry sigh. "Anyway, we gotta send a dispatch to the column an' push on ahead ourselves. If it really is practically clear all the way to the Holy City, Lewis'll want to know, an' he'll want to move quick."

"What about the Reaper bodies?" one of the Rangers with Boogerbear asked. Others had begun filtering back, some dragging enemy corpses behind their horses. Nares had three of them bumping and sliding along, plowing up the carpet of leaves. "Will we hang them up as a warning to others, as usual?" Native Rangers, and Ocelomeh more than others, used to take heads after battle. Allied Holcanos, once mortal foes, had engaged in somewhat more than just ritualistic cannibalism. Hanging their most hated enemies up in trees was a comparatively benign abuse of the dead.

Anson shook his head. "Leave 'em. I don't mean to let anybody ahead of us live to see 'em, an' that booger that jumped us on the road, or somethin' else, will just pluck 'em from the trees like pears. Waste of time an' trouble."

CHAPTER 10

DECEMBER 25, 1848

It was doubly ironic considering the vastly different emphasis placed on the life of Jesus Christ by the faith of the Allied "American" army and that of their enemy that Lewis Cayce's force finally reached the Holy City on Christmas Day. Armed with Anson's reports on enemy activity, both in regard to what that meant to the poor locals as well as the ongoing campaign, almost thirty thousand men, six batteries (forty-two guns), all the associated baggage and support vehicles, and countless animals had swept down the Camino Sagrado at a rapid, irresistible pace. All was now sedately, almost ponderously gathering with much pomp amid thundering drums, streaming flags, and far more bugle calls than strictly necessary on the plain east of the expected shantytown built right up to the high, white walls of the inner city.

A pair of large marching camps were being constructed under the bright, pleasantly warm—if somewhat humid—late-morning sun smiling down from a perfect blue sky. Weatherworn but well-drilled and triumphant regiments, standards flapping bravely in a haze-clearing breeze, went straight from column into line at the edge of the slaves' and freedmens' slum roughly half a mile from the eastern gate. Battery after battery of artillery crunched and trundled across gravelly earth through to the front and unlimbered with menacing, near-mechanical efficiency. Mounted troops, mostly polished lancers and dragoons, put on a show as well, extending the line as if on parade until more infantry moved up to go into line behind them. They then galloped elsewhere to do the same—as they had for hours now—while more of Lewis's army kept coming. With the exception of the slum and what it implied, of course, the combination of the deploying army and marvelous city—league-long walls enclosing epic pyramidal structures on four sides—the even more epic setting like a gilded frame for the dramatic scene; a ring of distant, snowcapped, impossibly high mountains, the bright blue Lago de Texcoco to the north and Lago Chalco to the south. The whole made for a thrilling, fantastic sight.

Lewis Cayce had accomplished what no one ever had; he'd built and brought a powerful army through battles and hardships across vast, unknown reaches, to the very dark heart of the Dominion, and it was a heady moment for most. Even from Texcoco the journey hadn't been without difficulty, but aside from Anson's encounter with Reapers, there'd been no fighting, and the only problem they had with monster attacks had focused on the baggage train draft animals at night. It had warmed quite a bit as they descended sharply into the valley, however, and a heavy rain mixed with skull-smashing hail had assailed one of their great marching camps, resulting in one man killed outright and a surprising number of serious injuries. More costly was a flood that accompanied the storm, overwhelming part of the camp at the bottom of a slope near what had seemed a very modest stream. Two score tents full of soldiers sheltering from the sudden rain and hail were unexpectedly scoured away without warning, and nine men were sluiced to oblivion.

That was three nights before, and the army had since surged farther down the valley, over the fascinating bridge spanning the Río de Purificacion (like other amazing structures, including one of the aqueducts now paralleling the road, Don Hurac insisted it was older than the Dominion), and then across a similar if smaller and much less lofty structure in the mountains through which the Río de Coatepec flowed. Ramon Lara was the only man with them who'd been to the city of Mexico on the world they came from. Even his Lieutenant Espinosa, a friend from there, never visited the Mexican capital. Lara swore that, of all the places they'd seen, this land diverged most from what he remembered. At least in terms of elevation.

That was saying something and tended to support Reverend Harkin's theory.

In spite of everything, however, they'd made it at last and their final objective lay before them. At least they all hoped it was the last. A number of uncertainties remained, of course, even if everything continued as planned. No one knew where the Gran Cruzada was, and they only had Don Hurac's assurance that he'd be welcomed as the rightful Supreme Holiness. That was an essential precondition to ending the war and not only halting the Gran Cruzada, but taking the pressure off the Yucatán, where another formidable enemy force still threatened their "home." An awful lot depended on what happened next: how they were received, how much resistance Don Hurac would face to his elevation, whether he actually *could* stop the war, and if he was truly sincere about . . . pretty much everything he'd promised. Lewis finally believed he most likely was, but feared it might take a great deal more than his just showing up and commanding it.

Riding forward of the lines with his entourage that included those usually with him and now Major Giles Anson and Boogerbear, both Reverend Harkin and Father Orno, as well as Don Hurac himself and his new "pet" vice *alcalde*, Don Amil, Lewis joined Olayne and First Sergeant McNabb where they sat on their horses behind Barca's and Dukane's batteries. For a moment, he appraised both battery commanders. Emmel Dukane was one of the few "professional" artillery officers from the old world still in direct command of a battery and was somewhat fidgety, as usual, as if tempted to abandon his place and rush forward to correct one of his men's drills or someone's position around the guns—who knew what—to perfect his battery's parade appearance. In contrast, though it was clear they'd made an effort with their harder-used kit, Captain Barca's artillerymen were talking quietly among themselves as they observed the objective before them and young Barca himself seemed entirely at ease, sitting on his horse and smoking a cigar.

"Just goes to show it don't take spit an' polish to maintain competence an' confidence," Anson observed to Olayne, selecting cigars for himself and Varaa from the slash pocket in his jacket. Mistress Samantha, sitting on her own horse beside him, frowned disapprovingly, but Varaa grinned hugely and accepted the offering. She adored cigars and had practically abandoned her pipe.

"It doesn't hurt," defended Lewis's chief of artillery a little sharply, but then he relented, "yet on the whole, I can find no reason to fault Captain Barca. No other battery in our army *performs* more reliably and professionally."

"I can bear witness to that," Anson said, nodding, borrowing a light from Reverend Harkin's smoldering pipe.

Olayne raised a brow at him. "Indeed, sir. You do seem to have Barca's battery at your disposal more often than I. Has it occurred to you that other batteries could use some detached experience, or even that the rest of my artillery train might benefit from Captain Barca's example?"

"Sure," Anson agreed through a stream of smoke. "I expect they would—if we were just on maneuvers or practicin' for a fight. As it is, lives're at stake. My mounted boys need gunners they can count on—an' not knowin' what to do will just get otherwise good gunners dead."

"All the same, Major Olayne has a point," Lewis inserted himself. "It's past time that all our mounted components, including lancers and dragoons, were able to call on full batteries for support instead of just scattered sections of Barca's battery. Others have done it in the past, but now that we have sufficient guns and crews, every battery needs to know what's expected of them in isolated situations. We'll always try to mass the bulk of our guns in the face of large enemy concentrations, but long-distance scouting might be more important than ever, and we aren't dealing with that at the moment. It's time to give Barca a break and spread the duty around."

Anson made a face. "Fine, for now," he allowed. "If things start gettin' serious, though..."

"You can choose whichever battery you want," Lewis assured. Looking at Barca again, taking in his fine gun's crews, he smiled a little wistfully.

"You miss it, don't you?" Leonor guessed. "Just commandin' a battery, even one gun."

Lewis had to nod. "I really enjoyed it. Even the chief of a single piece has considerable responsibility. A section or battery commander has more, but you're still right there with your brothers on the guns—the bonds formed there can be quite close—and it's all very personal and ... tactical, if you know what I mean. Nothing's more important than your comrades except your primary collective weapons—your guns—and you'll do anything to use them well. And protect them, of course. Sometimes, rarely, you see the effect your execution has on the overall strategy, but more often all you're aware of is your own small part of the action." He chuckled self-consciously. "Perhaps I miss that most of all."

"You'd be wasted in that role," Colonel Reed exclaimed dismissively. "*Were* wasted, even when it was yours," he added. "No one sees the 'big picture' in their head better than you." He waved at the shantytown and massive walled city before them. "After all, here we are."

"Perhaps," Lewis grudgingly allowed. "But I never expected to be in this position. I don't mean here, now, but in command of an army at all." He lowered his voice. "I had no ambition for that. It may be that I'm suited to command more than a single battery of guns, but I honestly often doubt I'm cut out for anything like the scope of . . . my current duty." He sighed. "I've made mistakes and cost many lives." He frowned. "And it seems the bigger the army gets, the bigger my mistakes. Maybe it's just too big for me."

"Nonsense," growled Reed, rolling his eyes in frustration.

"Indeed," interrupted Father Orno. "Reverend Harkin and I have long agreed your 'current duty' is your destiny on this world."

"I don't know about that, though it does make sense," Colonel Reed continued cautiously. "But one thing is sure: the bigger our force, the *smaller* our proportionate losses have been. If you mean to measure your competence to lead in such a ludicrous way, then 'statistically,' you do *better* with a bigger army!"

"Of course you make mistakes. Everyone does," Reverend Harkin scoffed. "Every general in history has! Would you put yourself above them all? Alexander, Caesar, Napoleon? Even Saul? Joshua?" He paused, considering. "And with their examples to guide you, you should easily avoid most of their blunders."

Anson chuckled. "The first two o' those examples thought *they* were gods. Napoleon swapped his faith like socks, dependin' on where he was. Seems I recall Saul an' Joshua paid for not heedin' God enough, right? Well, Lewis's personal faith is his own, an' I won't poke at it, but I know he don't think *he's* a god, an' he ain't fixin' to take up the Dom faith."

"I think I'm safe from the fate of Saul and Joshua." Lewis chuckled grimly. "I've been praying a *lot*." He tilted his head toward the Holy City. "But Napoleon's experiences in Russia, even Egypt, might serve as relevant lessons. He took Moscow, for example, but didn't win the war. I've always thought in terms of 'take the enemy capital and you win.'" He glanced at Leonor, then Anson. "My conviction that will be the case in this instance is fading."

Varaa coughed. "King Har-Kaaska never believed, at the beginning, anything like this was possible." She looked at Lewis and blinked rapidly. "Even I, despite my esteem for you, suspected the best we might achieve was to beat back the Holcanos and bloody the Dominion enough for them to leave us alone on the Yucatán awhile longer. Never did I dream we would one day stand at the gates of their capital city." She waved a hand. "Now even Har-Kaaska feels as if the war is virtually won, and I believe . . ." Varaa paused thoughtfully. "Even if, despite our best efforts, the whole of the Yucatán falls to the invading force infesting it and this army was somehow destroyed tomorrow, the Dominion will be forever changed, more timid about expansion, and any such effort might be delayed for generations. There will be *someone* by then to face them again."

"How gloomy you are, just as we stand at the threshold of victory!" Don Hurac grandly proclaimed. "Do not forget, those are *my* people beyond those walls, and any who remain will welcome me."

"That, sir, remains to be seen," cautioned Don Amil. Most had thought, if anything, the vice *alcalde* from Texcoco had won a place advising Don Hurac through sycophancy, and they regarded him now with surprise.

"Very true," pronounced Father Orno. "With respect, you must be wary—all of us must—and test every declaration of devotion." Glancing at the Holy City, his face turned grim. "This is the dark cradle of evil in the Dominion. The very putrid nest in which its poisonous faith was nurtured. Do not think for an instant it will meekly surrender to the light."

Slightly chastened, Don Hurac's smile shrank a little, but his excitement was undiminished.

Standing in his stirrups, Anson looked around at the army, the guns emplaced before it, and the seemingly endless lines of infantry radiating to either side. Turning to look behind, he saw other units still coming up. Shaking his head in something like awe at the force they were assembling in this strange and captivating, yet ominous and unsettling place, he sat again with a creak of dry leather and looked at Lewis. "So, what now? I've glimpsed scared folks runnin' here an' there through the hovels, but no sign of a white flag or anybody comin' to talk. The day's movin' along. We gonna just sit here till dark or start shootin'?"

"We could send a delegation forward. I will lead it," Father Orno offered.

Scratching his chin whiskers, Lewis looked at Don Hurac. "What do you know of that gate? You must've passed through it before."

Don Hurac blinked. "Why, I never paid much attention. Two heavy wooden leaves, I believe, strapped with iron. Like the walls themselves, they were built to keep large predators out, so I assume they are rather robust."

Without consulting Don Hurac further, Lewis shook his head at Father Orno. "Thank you for your offer, but no. First, I won't risk you or anyone within range of enemy weapons until we know their intentions. Second, as Major Anson says, the day is passing. Whoever remains behind those walls to speak for the people has had plenty of time to take our measure and do it. We may as well demonstrate that any relations we have with them moving forward will be at our convenience, not theirs. Mr. Olayne," he said aside to his chief of artillery, "I believe we can shoot over most of the . . . dwellings lying between us and the main gate without harming anyone, can't we? Anyone outside it, at any rate. Why don't we knock on that gate."

"Sir," Olayne replied briskly. "Mr. Barca," he called, gaining the Black officer's attention. "Commence firing solid shot against the main western entrance to the city, if you please. Make it sharp and brisk. No short rounds or long, and not a strike on the wall itself. I believe Colonel Cayce desires to make an impression."

An expression of surprise crossed Barca's face. "Just my battery, sir?"

Olayne frowned, but humor glinted in his eyes. "Just yours, sir. The leaves of that gate look quite large, even from here. Surely you can't miss them at less than nine hundred yards. Or don't you believe six guns will be sufficient to open them? I can certainly offer the privilege of being the first to fire on that dreaded edifice to someone else." He smiled at Captain Dukane, now watching the exchange. "My apologies, Mr. Dukane, but this is a job for solid shot, and I fear your howitzers won't do."

Dukane's 12pdr field howitzers were excellent weapons for firing exploding case shot or canister, but too lightly built to throw solid shot with a full-power charge, which couldn't even be loaded because of their chambered breeches. Captain Hudgens had their only proper 12pdr guns, and he wasn't close by. Besides, that wasn't the point.

Dukane graciously bowed his head, then grinned at Barca.

Recognizing his commander's teasingly sarcastic tone, as well as the singular honor being offered him, Barca finally grinned as well and snapped a sharp salute. "I will be most happy to open those gates directly, sir."

"I got a dollar that says he doesn't get more than one hit in six," Anson said lowly to Lewis. It was a fairly long shot. Then again, the gate looked as big as a small barn from here.

"I'll take that bet"—Lewis smiled wryly—"and another dollar for each shot that strikes."

Barca heard. "I'll take that wager as well, Major."

Anson nodded. "You're both on." He shrugged. "Not much to spend our pay on anyway. Crap we don't need at the sutler's."

Whipping his horse around, Captain Barca trotted forward and stopped between the limbers behind his Number Three and Four guns. "Battery!" he shouted, voice harsh but excited, "Action front! Target that big bloody gate to the city—and the crew of any gun that misses will be on latrine duty for the whole battery for the rest of the war! Load solid shot and hold!"

"Oh, an' a bloody-minded policy *that* is," groused the familiar voice of Daniel Hahessy on Gun Number Two. It was clear he was only pretending to stifle it. "Why, the finest crew alive, on the newest, tightest gun in creation, can't *guarantee* a hit at such a distance!"

"Hush yer shite-spewin' mouth!" Preacher Mac hissed rather loudly, provoking scattered chuckles. "An' it'll never be us that's punished so, not with Lieutenant Hanny doin' the aimin'."

"Aye, even then, an' it ain't *justice*, is it? Ye know it as well as I!" Hahessy persisted. "Sweet as she is, our gun ain't new enow, an' she was never a *rifle*. No such thing that I know of. Aye, even with Lieutenant Hanny aimin', that gawpy Hoziki might smack the handspike an' shift the trail, or a sabot might fail an' throw the shot wild . . . a *hunnerd* different things might have us diggin' shite trenches the rest o' our lives!"

"Never." Hoziki glowered. "Clear," he added as he cleared the vent and pulled the pick back out before mashing down on the vent with his thumbstall while Preacher Mac pulled the fixed charge out of the leather haversack the Number Five man brought.

"Shut up, all of you. You'll ruin the moment," Hanny angrily snapped, which caused genuine laughter to erupt.

"Silence on the gun line!" Barca called harshly, but then softened his tone. "Just do your duty, gentlemen. I doubt *anything* could ruin this moment."

Leonor was chuckling, and Lewis joined her. Don Hurac and Father Orno, even Reverend Harkin, seemed annoyed. "He's right, you know," Leonor told them. "Whether the city surrenders right off or we have to fight through it street by street, this is a moment to celebrate, an' we'll remember it too."

"Perhaps," Reverend Harkin huffed, "but I would have imagined a little more . . . solemnity might be in order." He glanced down at his empty sleeve. "I gave an arm to be here."

"I would have thought so as well," Don Hurac agreed. "Are we not here to be the rational, pious, adult leaders these people need?"

Leonor shook her head. "That's *your* job, if you can pull it off." She looked at Harkin. "An' a lot of fellas gave more than you. All of us, everybody in the army, has lost friends. Even family. A hell of a lot lost their lives. I figure it's up to the men in the ranks how they *feel* about all that. Can't say, 'Now all you fellas stand there an' look gloomy like Reverend Harkin while we crack the Dom capital.'"

Lewis laughed out loud and so did most of those around him. Even Harkin finally snorted amusement.

The guns had finished loading while they debated, and Barca's three section chiefs stood with their right hands raised, looking back at him. Barca nodded. "Battery!" he shouted. "*By* the battery . . . Fire!"

With a thunderclap crash, all six guns roared at once, leaping back from the fiery white cloud they vomited into the shantytown before them. The ripping canvas sound of roundshot arcing up and tearing downrange was mixed with the clunking, clattering, jangling noise of the recoiling guns. Just as the breeze cleared the smoke, the distant gate was seen to shiver dramatically under multiple impacts, spewing blasts of splinters. One round—it was impossible to tell whose—did strike the wall very close by, and bright white dust exploded, drifting across to obscure the gate.

A hushed, expectant silence ensued until the dust cleared away. Then a tentative cheer rose up that soon mounted to a great, feral roar. Both wooden leaves lay in shattered heaps, and the gate to the Holy City was open.

"Well done, Captain Barca," Major Olayne yelled over the tumult. "Cease firing and await further orders but don't secure your pieces yet."

"Yes, sir." Barca repeated the command and his section chiefs did as well.

"It looks like I owe you both six dollars," Anson said loud enough to be heard. "Pay the gentlemen for me, my dear," he called loudly to Samantha. "My wife carries all our money," he confessed with a laugh. More laughter erupted.

Strangely, the first reaction from the locals was wholly unexpected. Poorly dressed people, free but destitute men and women as well as abandoned slaves, began filtering out from hiding. Yet instead of fleeing in terror, which one would reasonably expect, they moved toward the invaders. Even more unexpected, many were openly weeping or crying out with what sounded like relief, even joy.

"This is new," Anson exclaimed, taken aback.

"You see?" Don Hurac gushed. "My people welcome me!"

"With respect, sir, those are *not* your people. Not yet. The poor and subjugated have never been claimed by the elite in this land," Father Orno pointed out.

"Then I'll make them mine," Don Hurac countered with determination as the crowd before them grew. "Through rumor if nothing more, they will know who I am and that I am with you . . . and they wouldn't be coming to greet us if they didn't at least hope I'll be better for them than what they've known."

"Maybe," Leonor conceded without much conviction, watching the assembling mob with care, right hand resting on the butt of one of her revolvers. "Even if that's so, there could be Blood Priest killers amongst 'em."

"She's right," Varaa urged Lewis. "Treat them as you did the Texcoco civilians. Gently but firmly herd them through your lines and have them gathered and watched while we proceed with the business at hand."

Lewis nodded, and Colonel Reed and Major Anson seemed to have been waiting for that. Reed passed instructions for the 1st US Infantry and Captain Meder's riflemen to move up and guard the artillery while leaving gaps for people to stream through—many pulling reluctant animals, which were probably their only possessions of note. Anson called for Lieutenant Riss to bring his company of Rangers to add to the command party's security. It was as if someone pulled the drain plug in a tub. Seeing they were welcome and no harm was offered, hundreds of the denizens of the outer city happily started gushing through the lines.

Though mostly "Indios" of some kind, generally fairly dark-skinned, quite a few people clambering to join them were jet-black, darker than

Barca, and every shade in between. Some were even lighter-skinned than Lewis under his tan, and there seemed to be no distinction between them based on color. Any of them were just as likely to be somewhat better dressed in colorful, better-quality fabrics (probably hidalgo merchants, Lewis thought) as they were to be draped in rags. That appeared to be the only real difference in status in the outer city: those with a little money and those with none. The rest might all be slaves or "free men"—virtually indistinguishable—who'd been laborers in fields the army already crossed and only fled this far. Lewis noted another "class" of folk who were uniformly destitute. Women. Slaves themselves or not, women had no rights at all and might even be "owned" by male slaves. He'd seen that throughout the Dominion, but never as bad as this. In most other places, particularly on the frontier, women had earned a measure of status, even affection and respect. Here, they were treated no better than livestock and might be selected as "sacrifices" in the city on a whim.

Everyone was disgusted by this, perhaps especially Don Hurac, Lewis was intrigued to see. He, and apparently his murdered friend, Don Datu, who should've "ascended" before him, were known to appreciate women. Don Hurac in particular was devoted to his wife, Zyan. Better treatment for women was one of the reforms he sought to institute. Lewis glanced at Leonor. She and Mistress Samantha looked furious enough to kill anyone they could blame while equally frustrated no such individual was at hand.

"Shit," Anson grumbled a little nervously as the tide of humanity surged beyond what Reed's instructions could cope with. Lewis's second-in-command had to shout further orders to quell the rising disorder. Anson's choice of words was immediately and pungently proven appropriate as well. Until now, the breeze had carried the stench they'd encountered at all such outer city slums away, but now the reek of human and animal waste arrived on the shoes and bare feet of the people.

"Goddamn!" Anson wheezed as another gust hit him, earning a sharp glare from Reverend Harkin. Anson waved reassuringly at him.

"I *ain't* takin' His name in vain, parson. I honestly wish He'd damn this *stink*! It's worse than a two-week latrine."

"It's pretty rough," Lewis agreed, eyes watering. "We'd dig new latrines or move on long before it got this bad."

"People here don't have that choice," Father Orno scolded. "It's not their fault. Just imagine if you had to stay in one of your big marching camps forever. Eventually, you'd run out of ground for new latrines."

"We'd never just let it pile up in the company streets," Lewis countered, "but I take your meaning. And there's always a stink from somewhere when the wind is wrong. Even at Uxmal, where covered sewers take the waste from public and private toilets to the sea." He considered that. "And you're almost always downwind from somebody's outhouse." He frowned. "But why not do that here as well? There are the lakes."

"Which many likely use for drinking water," Varaa pointed out. "Though I doubt that stops those in the inner city from dumping their waste there." She pointed. "*They* get fresh water from the aqueduct."

"There are many cisterns and fountains as well," Don Hurac agreed. "Texcoco used the running river, taking drinking water from upstream of the city, even piping it to fountains outside the wall. Waste was discharged downstream, and the smell in the outer city wasn't quite as bad because people there used public toilet houses built out along the river.

"There's no such accommodation here," Don Hurac admitted. "I understand that merchants who do business in the outer city sometimes clear waste from the nearby streets at their own expense, and even sell 'clean' water—though there are few who can afford it and I expect they just take their 'merchandise' from the lake themselves."

"Sounds like if you get the job of king, or whatever, you'll have your work cut out," Anson pointed out.

"I will," Don Hurac agreed, frowning as he watched the poor people he'd come to care for continue passing through the ranks. The tide was ebbing now, however, and he returned his gaze to the shattered gate in the distance.

"Well, Lewis, what now?" Anson deliberately repeated his earlier question.

Lewis regarded him thoughtfully. "Now," he practically drawled, "you and your Rangers will scout forward through the outer town and ensure there's no ambushing force, particularly hidden artillery, while Colonel Reed re-forms First Division into column and advances to the gate—"

"Look," Don Hurac interrupted, pointing. The tops of the walls were still barren, no surprise since there were no fighting platforms behind them, but now a number of figures were gathering somewhat tentatively in the missing-tooth aperture where the demolished gate had been. Some looked like soldiers, dressed in yellow and black, dragging debris and the larger remains of the gate leaves aside. Once a lane was cleared, a single horse appeared, briskly drawing a decoratively painted carriage with several equally colorful passengers grouped within. Passing under the empty arch, it hastily advanced. There was no escort.

"It seems that someone inside the city has finally taken notice of our presence—and modest demonstration," Varaa dryly remarked.

CHAPTER 11

"I know those men," Don Hurac exclaimed with surprise as the carriage containing the representatives of the Holy City drew near. His eyes narrowed. "One of them, at least."

"I as well," agreed Vice Alcalde Don Amil. "One of them, certainly. Perhaps one or two others. My visits here were never frequent," he said apologetically to Lewis.

"More so than mine in recent years," Don Hurac reminded. "One of the reasons I asked you to accompany me here is that you were closer to the ... changes in the capital under the Blood Priests and their creatures."

Don Amil humbly bowed his head. "Fortunately for me, I was not sufficiently close—or influential—to arouse much notice. But that does limit my usefulness to you," he pointed out.

The carriage veered slightly and came to a halt with its occupants about ten paces from Lewis and his companions. Four men, all obviously *patricios* by their dress, quality tailored tunics woven in bright colors from thread as fine and shiny as silk with painstakingly embroidered designs at cuffs and hems, were seated on benches covered with soft, deep cushions. A single unarmed soldier sat on a higher hard, bare bench, controlling the horse. He and perhaps a single occupant were the only ones not openly terrified, eyes wide and darting at the sight of them, but none would look directly at Don Hurac. Oddly, as Lewis understood such things, that was a good sign. One man, smaller and slighter than the others and wearing chin whiskers and mustache dyed a deep blue-black in contrast to the graying brown hair on his uncovered head, rose to stand unsteadily on the carriage deck. Managing to bow very low with the supporting hands of one of his companions, he spoke.

"I—I greet you, Your Holiness!" he blurted, voice high-pitched and quavering. Suddenly glancing up with wide, desperate eyes before diverting his gaze, he cried, "I mean, Your *Supreme* Holiness! I beg you to forgive my use of the former title I knew you by—and m-my having just gazed upon you!" he stuttered, voice almost squeaking now.

Don Hurac cleared his throat and responded in his usual sonorous, even gentle, tone. "Greetings and well met, Don Estilio. He is the *alcalde* of the Holy City," he said aside to Lewis, making no effort to lower his voice, "though, as you might imagine, his duties were largely ceremonial even before the usurper rose to power. I'm honestly surprised to find him alive." He turned his attention back to Estilio. "Kindly identify your companions. I may have met them before, but do not know them by sight."

Still stuttering, the *alcalde* gave the names of the others. All somewhat comically stood and shakily bowed atop the unsteady platform as he did so. Each name except that of the sole, apparently unafraid and hard-eyed noble called Don Armonia, identified as Estilio's new "Voz de El Gente," or, roughly, voice of the people—a post Lewis never heard of—flitted past him. Not Don Armonia's. The man wore a distinctly belligerent, challenging expression, and in addition to his bearing, very different from the others, he might as well have been screaming, "I'm a threat to you." Leonor, as usual, caught it too, leaning close in her saddle and whispering in Lewis's ear, "Have to watch that one."

When Don Estilio finished, Don Hurac addressed him and the others. "I'm pleased to make your acquaintance." His countenance darkened. "Now tell me, where is the vile usurper and his minions? Do they hide in the city even now?"

"G-gone, Supreme Holiness. All gone, along with as much as half the population of the city. The wealthiest, certainly," Estilio said quickly. "None of them told me, of course," he hastened to add, "and I never spoke directly to His—I mean, Don Julio, since his unseemly elevation. Nor did I ever speak to the new 'Holy Patriarcha Tranquilo.'" The man actually shuddered as he uttered that name.

"The monster Tranquilo was here?" Don Hurac asked, sliding a glance at Lewis.

"Indeed," Estilio confirmed, still shuddering. "A most . . . disconcerting figure. It was rumored that they left to seek sanctuary with the Gran Cruzada and perhaps attempt to contest your presence here. That, and the sheer numbers involved, might be the only reasons the remaining populace wasn't cleansed and the city razed to the ground when they fled." He puffed out his chest. "That, and the fact they knew we were prepared to defend the people." He hesitated. "Though I rather expect they may have mistakenly believed we'd defend them from *you* as well," he conceded.

"Then I take it you have no such intention and are here to formally acknowledge my ascendancy, placing the Holy City and the entire Dominion in my care?"

"Of course, Your Supreme Holiness," Estilio gushed. "All that is yours by right!" He hesitated. "A proper elevation must still be performed, though there will have to be . . . deviations from tradition since you were unable to bathe in the blood of your predecessor. Even his mortal husk was disposed of in fire instead of being preserved for display in the Holy Sanctum!" Don Estilio seemed incensed by that. "The usurper presided over *numerous* irregularities and was not himself even elevated in an open, traditional manner."

"Very well," Don Hurac said. "Then I shall begin my rule by casting away various other abuses that have come into 'traditional' use over time. The first of these is my own place in the world. I am *not* a kind of God in my own right as my predecessors pretended, only the representative of the *one* God—whose laws and requirements have been warped out of all sanity. Look upon me now, all of you," he commanded.

"But . . ." one of the men in the carriage began fearfully.

"Do it," Don Hurac insisted. "See me as I am, as all my predecessors—worthy or not—have been: just a man."

Hesitantly, as if fearing they'd be struck down, they raised their gaze to behold him, and all except the one named Armonia seemed to glow with the honor. Armonia appeared to seethe, aching to object, but he didn't.

"Definitely have to watch that one," Anson agreed with his daughter, obviously having heard her whisper. "Doesn't make sense, though. If he means to make a pest of himself, you'd think he'd be more subtle."

"Good," Don Hurac said with satisfaction. "You see? Just a man"—his voice turned hard—"but a man whose duty it is to rule the Holy Dominion and its people. Never doubt I shall do so as lovingly and benignly as possible"—he gestured at the great army around him—"yet forcefully, if necessary. I believe it's time you met my friends and allies. Contrary to what you've doubtless been told, they're not 'demons' or 'devils,' and might only be perceived as 'heretics' by those who have tortured the faith of our founders beyond recognition. It is *they* who are the true heretics. Together, we shall begin a process of eliminating their foul influence forever!"

All the men in the carriage looked a little uncomfortable about that and glanced nervously at one another. Lewis was impressed by what he heard. Apparently, Don Hurac had been sincere all along. Father Orno and Reverend Harkin both beamed. Observing the reaction of the men who'd come to them, Lewis wondered if the new "Supreme Holiness" might've shown his hand too soon, but that horse was out of the barn. He was even more convinced there'd be trouble.

"We might have to use your Rangers to keep peace in the city for a while, until things sort out," he murmured to Anson, who glared back, aghast.

"No way! Rangers *ain't* police. Never will be! The only way we deal with problems is killin' 'em."

"If things go like I fear they might, that won't change," Lewis predicted. Don Hurac had begun introducing them, and he nodded a little angrily when the Supreme Holiness called him *his* supreme army commander. *Probably just as well they think that at the moment*, he grudged.

"When it comes to military matters or anything concerning the defense of the city or behavior of the populace, Coronel Cayce will speak with my voice. Is that understood?" Don Hurac firmly decreed.

Again, everyone but Armonia apprehensively nodded. Armonia himself seemed to regard Lewis with a kind of appraising interest. The rest of Lewis's officers and companions were named, including Varaa-Choon. It was obvious the delegation was deeply troubled by her presence, and they tried not to even look at her. *Then again, even if she isn't a "demon," they still think she's just an animal*, Lewis decided. "What's the latest information on the position of the Gran Cruzada?" he demanded at once.

Don Estilio looked at him, mouth opening and shutting in something like panic as if one of those huge two-legged monsters had spoken. "Uh, we, ah... It is far, Your... Excellency. Very far, still. We don't know where precisely, but hundreds of *leguas*, certainly."

Looking at Anson, Lewis said, "I hope that's true, but we need to check on it immediately. A strong scout by Coryon Burton's dragoons, perhaps accompanied by some of your Rangers, can set out in the general direction we believe it to be."

"I'll go myself," Anson quickly suggested, brazenly attempting to avoid the duty Lewis had proposed in the city.

"Absolutely not!" Samantha declared. It was just as well they were speaking English among themselves instead of Spanya. There was no telling how the Doms would react to a female giving any man an order. "Not only is your duty here, protecting Lewis and your daughter from potential unrest, but in case you"—she glared at Lewis—"and Colonel Cayce have forgotten, they will soon be wed. You wouldn't want to miss it, would you?"

Lewis flushed, and Anson grumbled, but no one objected to what Mistress Samantha said. Lewis had given his word. He cleared his throat. "Whether the Gran Cruzada is distant or close, we have to start preparing the city for its approach. I'll make my needs known in terms of material and manpower as soon as I can after we go inside. Where's that damn Corporal Willis now? He can make a list."

"Which I'm duty-fully sittin' on this vicious nag right behind you," came Willis's reedy, indignant voice.

"Good. Fetch something to write with and on. And don't take the rest of the day doing it," Lewis warned.

"Which I already got somethin', ain't I?" Willis retorted in a surly tone. Varaa *kakked* a laugh, and Leonor turned and hissed at the man.

"Very well. First thing on the list." He looked at Estilio and continued in Spanya. "I want barracks for my soldiers within the walls." He considered. "For that matter, we'll need to find space for the people living outside the walls as well."

The *alcalde* stared with alarm and distaste. "Ah... your soldiers, yes. Of course." He motioned to where the civilians had been gathered behind the lines of infantry. "B-but *those*... creatures? What on earth for? They are the lowest specimens of humanity, and most would never even be allowed inside the walls long enough to deliver a burden!"

Don Hurac didn't know where Lewis was going with this, but asked,

"Why not? There are many lowly free men—even women—in the city, and a great number of slaves."

"Yes, of course," Estilio granted, "but they *belong* there, performing essential tasks, or at least they belong to someone who will take responsibility for them." His lip curled. "Someone who will clothe them . . . and ensure they bathe."

Lewis was nodding. "Your city is half-empty, you said? The abandoned property now belongs to my army, by right of conquest, as do all the slaves we liberated outside your wall. As of this moment, they are all free men and women. *I'll* clothe them and give them somewhere to bathe and live, as well as make sure they have plenty of 'essential tasks'—along with many of those already behind the walls."

Lewis had spoken loud enough for many of the outer city folk to hear, and his words quickly spread. Voices began rising in shocked appreciation.

Estilio was shaking his head and wringing his hands. "But . . . why?"

"Simple," Lewis replied, gesturing to encompass the entire shantytown surrounding the gleaming white walls. "Because all this must come down. Even while we reinforce the walls and build fighting platforms, gun emplacements, watchtowers—everything we need to properly fortify your Holy City—we need clear fields of fire and to deny the enemy cover and shelter, not to mention ready building materials they can use to make ladders to scale your wall." He waved again. "All this will be demolished. What materials we don't use ourselves will be burned." He removed his somewhat misshapen wool wheel hat and raked sweaty hair back with his fingers. "If there are any crops ready for harvest, we'll get on that as well. Anything we can't get in will be burned as well, for a considerable distance all around."

Lewis looked at Don Hurac. "Now, sir, I recommend we occupy your capital. And the first thing I hope you'll see to is the dispatch of messages to every corner of your country to the effect that the war is over. Hopefully, all the work and sacrifice I've described will be a waste of effort, but knowing our common enemy, I won't rely on it."

The Rangers and 1st US deployed as Lewis had ordered, the 1st Uxmal filing past them through the demolished gate and into the city itself to assume a protective stance before Lewis and his party made their way in. Colonel Reed directed the 3rd Pennsylvania to enter behind them, allowing half the Rangers and the 1st Uxmal to probe onward once Barca's and Dukane's batteries were available for support. As soon as the entirety of 1st

Division was spreading out through the Holy City, Lewis would bring Colonel Agon's 4th Division in. He didn't believe there'd be no resistance at all, especially here, and was determined that his people have sufficient force to ruthlessly crush any they met.

"Be careful, but do it right," Lewis told Anson, who'd personally join his Rangers. "Do your best to minimize harm to innocent lives and property. On the other hand, if you're challenged or take any fire, don't try to sort it out gently. Pin whoever's responsible in place, then call up whatever reinforcements you need to eliminate them entirely."

"Understood," Anson said with a satisfied tone that seemed to alarm Alcalde Estilio and even Don Hurac to some extent. "No tappin' hammer today. We'll take the top maul to 'em."

Lewis nodded. "I want no reprisals on innocents, and it seems to me the best way to avoid that is to make a harsh example of the guilty from the start." Anson saluted ironically and urged Colonel Fannin forward to fall in beside Lieutenant Riss. Together, they led about three hundred Rangers through the gate alongside the Uxmalo infantry.

"I should be in there," Estilio said, wringing his hands again.

"No," Don Hurac denied. "We shall need you, my friend. Some in the city will see you as a traitor, and you will make just as tempting a target as I. Best we all wait until sufficient space has been secured around us."

"I do wish you could've waited for Boogerbear to lead the Rangers in, instead of sending Giles," Mistress Samantha groused. "To embrace his distasteful metaphor, Giles does tend to, ah, wield the hammer harder, but doing so seems to take a harsher toll on him. Mr. Beeryman can be just as ruthless when required, but I don't believe it much bothers him afterward."

"Father's counting on Boogerbear to cope with the enemy in this," Leonor said, gesturing at the shantytown. "Already sent him to do it. With Sal up north, that left him"—she shrugged—"or me, I guess, to lead the Rangers past the gate." She rolled her eyes at Lewis. "No arguin' today, I promised. Father'll be fine," she assured Samantha.

They watched while the 3rd Pennsylvania almost seamlessly relieved the 1st US in front of the gate and Colonel Reed took his leave to lead the 1st US into the city. A few muffled shots were heard beyond the wall, but not as many as most expected, and soon the 1st Ocelomeh was streaming forward to replace the 3rd Pennsylvania as a thin, drawn Major John Ulrich triumphantly led his own regiment through the gate at the double. Small talk ensued for quite a while, interrupted by occasional messengers. Lewis sent his compliments to Colonel "King" Har-Kaaska and Colonel Itzam and told them to occupy the big marching camp and supply a couple of regiments to secure all four city gates after 1st and 4th Divisions were entirely inside.

"Ah, Colonel Agon! Good day!" Don Hurac greeted as the former Dom general rode up. "Have you met the Alcalde Estilio?"

Agon saluted Lewis—there was far too much of that going on, in Leonor's opinion—then regarded their reluctant host and his associates. "I have not had that honor," he said neutrally.

"Certainly you've heard of the commander of our Fourth Division?" Don Hurac asked Estilio and the others somewhat goadingly. The *alcalde* nodded nervously, and Don Armonia appeared to seethe. "The ultimate traitor," Armonia practically hissed before remembering himself. "Or so he may be perceived by some."

Agon shook his head. "That may be, and I have happily turned against the malicious vision of God the degraded Dominion created, but I'm no traitor to the one *true* God, my soldiers, or my honor. After honest reflection, can you say the same?" Proceeding to ignore the representatives of the city, he turned back to Lewis. "You have a chore for my division?"

Lewis told him what he wanted and essentially repeated what he'd said to Anson, before nodding forward. "That's Major Don Roderigo's First Vera Cruz double-timing through the gate now, the last of First Division. We'll follow them in"—he obviously meant the party around him—"and you're next. Time for us all to see what this long campaign has been about."

The Holy City inside the brilliant white walls (Lewis estimated them at roughly thirty feet high, perhaps twenty feet thick at the bases, and made of stone that was smoothed and brightened with thick lime plaster) couldn't have been more different from the ramshackle slum outside. The first things that seized his attention were the twelve great pyramidal structures lining the central avenue but set somewhat back. Most, though strangely not all, were washed with different bright colors and other embellishments. Don Hurac had told them what (he thought) the different colors meant, but Lewis didn't remember and really couldn't care less. Father Orno seemed interested and was discussing it with Don Hurac as they advanced. Most stunning, of course, was the great central pyramid some distance away, looming exactly twice as tall and broad as every similar structure. Its natural stone composition was unstained except by the dried rivers of black-red blood that had poured down the steps from the top over time. Lewis felt deeply oppressed by the sight.

"A dreadful thing to view," Varaa told him, guessing what he was thinking. "No doubt intended to strike awe and fear into visitors, in equal measure. I don't think it's as big as the ruined temple at the heart of Acapulco, but it's the biggest such structure known that isn't falling down and covered with vines and trees. It might even be just as old. Nobody really knows."

Lewis's attention was drawn to the jagged gold cross on a bloodred field of a large Dominion flag fluttering at the top of the golden chamber at the peak of the pyramid. All other such flags had been discreetly removed. "Colonel Agon," he said to the former Dom officer moving up behind them. "At your convenience, please send a detail to tear down that filthy rag, but you're not to go yourself, understand?" Lewis was suddenly concerned by the singularity and prominence of the symbol and feared a trap or an ambush.

"With pleasure," Agon said, noting Lewis's tone and recognizing an argument would avail him nothing. "Do you want them to put our own flag there?" After some experimentation, 4th Division had settled on a bright yellow, almost golden flag, with a simple white cross upon it. But even they revered the Stars and Stripes as the flag of their combined army, and each regiment carried it alongside their own as a "national" emblem. Even while recognizing how appropriate it might be, since the flag he was so personally devoted to truly was the ultimate uniting symbol of the army, he was still deeply touched by that. In this case, however...

"No," Lewis almost spat. "*Our* flag will *never* fly over such an abomination."

"The building is not to blame for what people do there," Father Orno said, moving closer. "We've made a temple to Jesuchristo out of the similar structure in Uxmal, and then in Gran Lago."

Lewis looked at him. "When you've scrubbed the evil from the place, if you ever can, you can fly whatever flag you choose atop it. But not until then."

Father Orno nodded seriously. "Perhaps you're right," he agreed, "and I think the first cleansing touch should come from a simple, proper cross, in any event."

Lewis shortened his gaze to regard his nearest surroundings. There was an open market here as well, though its neat appearance and the quality of goods and produce on display were markedly different from those of the one outside the gate. The same could be said for the few inhabitants who'd been watching them from the start, and more who'd begun to venture into view. Most were still probably slaves or free men, though they dressed like royalty in comparison to the people outside. Even so, though some seemed suffused with abject terror, many wore expressions of hope on their faces.

Gesturing behind him for members of his entourage to approach, Don Hurac said, "I shall sound the horns to call forth the masses so we might be properly met! This is a glorious occasion and should be marked as such!"

Some musketry erupted down the main thoroughfare closer to the central pyramid and a howitzer coughed a case shot that exploded loudly, vomiting smoke and twirling debris from the second-story window of a large, ornate structure. One of the "office villas" for a Blood Cardinal associated with a lesser pyramid, Lewis assumed. He held up a hand. "Let's wait awhile longer. There might still be a fight, and there's no sense drawing more people into it." He paused, looking back at the gateway arch and the walls extending away from it. "Who's the best engineer we have?" he asked, almost to himself.

"Besides you?" Leonor questioned with a grin. All artillerymen who'd graduated from West Point had at least some engineering training.

"Mr. Olayne, I suspect." Lewis answered his own question. "Has he joined us yet?"

"Not yet, Coronel Cayce," Agon said.

"Could you send a runner to fetch him?"

"Of course."

"Wh-what are you going to do?" Alcalde Estilio asked.

"I already told you," Lewis replied impatiently. "Holdouts or not, this city is ours. Hopefully, your new Supreme Holiness will stop the Gran Cruzada in its tracks, wherever it is. But I've met Tranquilo and learned enough about your evil God to know he—Tranquilo, at least—won't just roll over and quit. So I don't place much stock in 'hopefully' either. Therefore, even as we secure the city from within, we'll start fortifying it against external threats. Today. How many cannon are in the city?"

Don Estilio blinked, glanced nervously at Armonia—a gesture no one missed—then looked back at Lewis. "I haven't the faintest idea. There must be some, I suppose."

Leonor frowned at him. "You're the leader here?" she asked with equal parts sarcasm and disbelief.

Flaring slightly, for the first time, probably at being so questioned by a woman, Don Estilio said, "The civic leader, not military."

"There must be a couple dozen pieces, surely. In military armories," Vice Alcalde Don Amil supplied. "We had that many stored in Texcoco, and possessed one of the few foundries in the region capable of casting tubes."

"I'd understood that was the case," Lewis agreed, "and I wish I'd had the opportunity to inspect your foundry. As for the finished guns, I saw them brought out of storage and we left them to defend your city. We shouldn't need them here because, combined with the captured guns we're bringing forward, whatever we find here should provide Mr. Olayne with sufficient guns to fill a hundred emplacements on these walls. I won't permanently emplace any of our flying artillery in fixed positions." He looked at Alcalde Estilio. "That's what we'll need so much willing labor for. To build those emplacements and the equally high fighting platform and other improvements behind the wall all around the city."

Estilio was wringing his hands again. "But . . . the *beauty* of the Holy City shall be ruined! And what of all the villas built up against the walls?"

"If they can't be incorporated into the defenses, they'll be pulled down," Lewis stated simply. "As for preserving the 'beauty,' what do you think the whole place will look like if it falls to the usurper?"

"He's right," Don Hurac confirmed. "If you wish to remain in your position, you must recognize that every aspect of your 'civic' leadership must now be devoted to organizing support for Coronel Cayce's projects. For everyone's sake. Always remember, you didn't just turn the city over to me—its rightful ruler—you surrendered it to an invading army. If we fail to hold it . . . well, you *must* know the city and all within it are doomed."

CHAPTER 12

DECEMBER 31, 1848

"We shall stop here. I am cold and I tire of this endless wandering," proclaimed the Holy Patriarcha Tranquilo, stopping his horse and shifting his bony frame uncomfortably in the saddle. The farther, generally northwestward, and consequently higher they came from the Holy City, the more winter-like the weather grew. Besides having spent most of his life in the south and possessing virtually no natural insulation, Tranquilo never had any patience for discomfort and certainly wasn't young anymore. What finally prompted his declaration was that he and "his" entourage, consisting of hundreds of Blood Priests, devoted *patricios*, a large number of hidalgos, and uncounted hangers-on, had reached the inviting outskirts of a thickly forested mountain town called Teocaltiche.

No one remembered the reason for the name. Situated on the Camino de la Plata and only recently gaining in population and importance as an early supply hub for the Gran Cruzada, the name had probably been one of countless others bestowed by the founders to make geographical references more familiar to them. The entire "Holy Party" had been assembled around His Supreme Holiness, the former Don Julio DeDivino Dicha, who remained out of sight in his own sumptuous carriage. He might be the personal representative of God to the faithful in this world, but there was no question the Holy Patriarcha Tranquilo was in charge of their day-to-day movements, never consulting or even visiting His Supreme Holiness. He certainly hadn't done so before making his recent announcement.

"It's only midday, Lord," objected Teniente Juaris, with the utmost respect in his voice. "We can make another three *leguas* today, even with the baggage train. There's another small town I had thought you—and His Supreme Holiness, of course—should find considerably more comfortable." Despite his lowly rank, Juaris was in nominal command of the Holy Party's military escort, a mix of perhaps four hundred demoralized and dejected lancers who were increasingly bolstered by a growing number of fanatical but inexperienced mounted Reaper Monks. Those seemed to be drawn to the Holy Party like iron filings to a magnet, and there were more than six hundred so far. "Is it not too early to stop for the day?" Juaris questioned.

Tranquilo gave him a narrow, beady-eyed glare. "I do not mean to merely stop and camp. I mean to stay." He waved at the town in the large, sloping, clear-cut area ahead. Aside from new warehouses set on terraces descending from a mountain and other recent construction, the town itself was rather small, and most of the older buildings were either timber or adobe with thatch or shake-shingle roofs. A number of people were assembling to view the visitors that had paused at the edge of town, but most looked rather poor in dress, or somewhat "frontierish" at best.

"I am tired. His Supreme Holiness is tired, and we have put more than a hundred *leguas* between the marauding heretics and ourselves. Not only am I spiritually and physically sick of *fleeing* such creatures," he practically spat, "but the farther we move toward the Gran Cruzada, the longer our return journey shall be. The stockpiles of supplies gathered here for the Gran Cruzada are no doubt depleted, long since sent to support it, but anyplace gifted with such largesse will have found ways to set some aside. More than sufficient for us."

"Yet . . ." Juaris began, then plunged on. "We know the enemy has occupied the Holy City" (a runner had arrived the day before with that devastating news), "and we also know their scouts—those under the Devil Anson in particular—have been known to press a hundred *leguas* and more to observe their surroundings. They could discover us here."

"In which case, *you* will discover them first and destroy them, Teniente Juaris," Tranquilo said firmly, as if there was no doubt in his mind. Juaris actually felt the skin crawl on his back. He knew what the penalty would be if he didn't satisfy Tranquilo's expectations.

"Yes, Lord."

Tranquilo called back beyond Juaris to his senior, most devoted Reaper officer. The man wore no rank on his thick, roughly woven, gray-brown, calf-length tunic, its only device a jagged red cross sewn on the breast. There was no doubting his status, however. *Much higher than mine, in reality*, Juaris knew. *How am I to command such people?* "Take a detachment into town and seize all the food," Tranquilo told the Reaper. "There will be no exceptions, and no entreaties will be entertained. Kill any who object and make sure the rest understand that if they do not amass *more* food supplies—I don't care from where—similar in quantity to what they last sent the Gran Cruzada, all will be sacrificed." He chuckled. "Tell them we shall eat *them*, if we must."

Juaris shivered again. There'd been rumors about Tranquilo and some of his . . . ceremonial practices. He wondered whether the ancient Blood Priest was merely playing on that reputation or truly meant what he said.

"At once, Your Holiness," the Reaper replied and whirled his horse before barking orders.

"Of course, they'll all have to be sacrificed anyway, once the Gran Cruzada arrives," Tranquilo casually continued to Juaris. "Most regrettable, even wasteful, but that is something they cannot see and live to tell about." He sighed. "The Patriarcha de la Guerra, Don Thiago de Feliz Río, is already employing a similar policy in the Gran Cruzada's wake. I'm sure he finds the work as distasteful as I, but God will feed well on the innocent blood we spill on the ground and into his very mouth!"

Utterly horrified, Juaris could only nod. "But . . ." he began, terrified to continue. He had no choice. "I beg you to forgive my ignorance. Surely you and His Supreme Holiness have already deeply contemplated these things, but . . . General Gomez is a professional soldier if nothing else"—he had to walk a fine line since Gomez had been left in the Holy City in disgrace—"and he taught me always that constantly insuring the supply of all things an army might need is an essential requirement for its proper performance on the battlefield."

Tranquilo was nodding. "Yes, indeed. As you say, in *that* at least he was correct." Tranquilo's expression hardened. "Yet what good did it do *him* when he was tested?"

Juaris started to point out that Gomez hadn't had half of what he would've liked but chose not to pursue that. Instead, he merely asked as if pondering aloud, "If all of our ... all the Gran Cruzada's means of support has been destroyed behind it, how will it sustain itself once it reaches the Holy City?"

Tranquilo looked at him in surprise, blinking his beady, wrinkled eyes. Unnervingly, Juaris was reminded of a vicious black spider peering up from a hole in dry ground. "Don't be ridiculous," Tranquilo scolded, rather gently, Juaris thought. "The Holy City is fairly bursting with supplies of every imaginable sort. It was a fruitful harvest year, you'll recall, and more crops will be ripening as we arrive. All who currently inhabit the place will be destroyed or sacrificed as soon as we have it back. Tragically, it will also be necessary to sacrifice a large portion of the Gran Cruzada as well. Common *soldados*," he quickly assured, then took on a pained expression. "It will be years, I fear, before we sufficiently recover to take up our original crusade against the Empire of the New Britain Isles in the Californias once more." He sighed. "There's nothing for it, I fear, and I won't live to see it, but our bigger business at home must take precedence over such distant adventures." He paused a long moment while something like wistfulness contorted his leathery face.

"Ultimately," he finally continued, "the 'privileged elites' evacuated before we were, largely to Acapulco or Manzanilla, as you know, never saw our enemy and will never see the Gran Cruzada. They'll believe the dreaded Vomito Rojo has finally run its course when they are invited to return. They will bring hordes of new slaves from where they have been, and the city will quickly begin functioning normally again. There will be plenty to sustain our ... diminished numbers in the meantime."

Juaris translated "our" to mean the clergy, the elites, and well-born officers in the army, stunned that anyone could so casually contemplate the death of so many hundreds of thousands of civilians and soldiers simply to maintain the secret that a deadly enemy dared to oppose them. It was madness. *Wouldn't it be easier—and far more humane, even beneficial—to arouse the nation against the invasion?* He was astounded at the sheer bloodthirsty expediency of the entire strategy and, for the very first time, began having doubts that he could possibly be on the side of God in this struggle.

There was another small detail Tranquilo had avoided as well. Juaris had seen the enemy himself and fought them twice. He couldn't even imagine the scope of the Gran Cruzada, but overwhelming numbers or not, he didn't think the army led by the ruthless "Coronel Cayce" would be as easily or quickly smashed as Tranquilo seemed to believe.

He bowed in the saddle. "Thank you for enlightening me, Lord. Much is now clear that was not, before. With your permission, I'll begin acquainting myself and my men with the roads and trails we must defend against a probing enemy." *And demoralized and beaten or not, I must make it clear to my lancers in particular that they dare not fail in this. They must take their defeat as a guide and learn from it instead of being disheartened. Only then can they hope to survive. In the meantime, I'll try to imagine how to save them from the culling that will reward their success.*

CHAPTER 13

JANUARY 27, 1849

"Gives me the creeps, the way they look at us," proclaimed Corporal Apo Tuin in English, looking around in the predawn light at people pausing their work to lean on spades and mattocks and watch them pass. As usual, Apo rode the ammunition chest atop the limber with Billy Randall behind the six-horse team pulling "his" Number Two gun. Apo was "Chief of the Piece" and still gunner in action or not; Lieutenant "Hanny" couldn't focus on a single gun while the section was on the move any more than Captain Barca could. He'd even been ordered to take a horse of his own. His former place on the lead horse right in front of Apo had fallen to Private Hoziki. And Hoziki was turning into a tolerable gunner himself and could do the job if needed. At present, though, Hanny was pacing the grumbling limber on his willful, nameless "local" horse and talking to Apo (his probable future brother-in-law) while the section clattered and jangled through the city behind a company of Coryon Burton's dragoons.

"'Creeps' is the right word, yeah?" Apo asked. "When the skin on your back moves by itself?"

"Aye," growled the hulking Private Hahessy up ahead, who proceeded to blow his nose with his fingers and shake the snot off. His size made the striped horse he was riding look like a donkey.

"Charmin' as always this mornin', I see," Preacher Mac groused at him from the back of the horse hitched beside him.

"An' a mighty suitable word is it too. 'Creeps,'" Hahessy continued. "Like that feelin' ye git 'tween yer shoulders when yer expectin' a ball er arrow strike any instant."

"Ach! Shut yer fool mouth, ye damned hoodlum!" Preacher Mac objected, unconsciously tapping the wood stock of the musket slung over his shoulder. Nearly all the crew that had once been infantry had taken to carrying their "borrowed" former weapons, on duty and off. Captain Barca didn't object as long as it was understood they'd be stacked to the rear if the section went into action. A musket would get in the way, and their 6pdr gun was the only weapon to focus on at times like that. "Puir, heathen lads're superstitious enough wi'out yer thoughtless, jinxin' blather," Preacher Mac elaborated. "'Specially the local lads wi' only what wee exposure tae *proper* scriptures I've been at liberty tae share!"

Hahessy glared at him. "Reverend Harkin comes a'preachin' often enough, ta all the lads. As does Father Orno. Yew needn't strain yerself. Lucky's the divil that'll find salvation followin' a grumpy dour Scot such as *yew* in search o' it!"

"Why, ye damned, idol-fondlin' papist!"

"Enough!" Hanny snapped. "None of that. Ever. We all agreed," he reminded. He personally leaned more toward Preacher Mac's path, but had made it clear the men in his section could profess whatever they liked—except Dom beliefs, of course—as long as they kept it civil. He wouldn't allow heated theological arguments that turned personal. He looked back at Apo. "What's got you on edge?" He waved at the people they were passing. Aside from those working on Mr. Olayne's projects, some were opening their open-air stalls, preparing to sell everything from produce (including liquor) to finely woven bolts of cloth. Strikingly well-crafted personal grooming items like intricately carved bone or horn combs were popular as well. Finely made wood and clay pipes, and what might be genuine tobacco, were favorites. Much to the annoyance of long-bought-out sutlers following the army, now virtually out of business pending resupply, many off-duty soldiers with unspent or un-gambled pay made enthusiastic customers for local goods. Especially booze. The sutlers even tried to buy it all up, to corner the market, but the locals were too savvy to let them.

After almost a month in the Holy City, a few people still sent them resentful, hateful looks. There were even occasional protests and efforts to subvert or sabotage ongoing work, but these were broken up or swiftly punished by squads of Colonel Agon's infantry. Though they still "scouted" the city as well as the environs around it, Anson had maintained his refusal to allow his Rangers to serve as "police" for anything short of a riot. "You do *not* want to turn my boys loose on anything that doesn't need killin'," he insisted.

Most locals regarded them with smiles and grateful nods, however, despite the heavy labor the majority were required to perform each day. Inside the city, this primarily involved tearing down buildings behind the great wall and heaping cartload after wagonload of soil on top of the piled-up debris behind it, tamping it down as they went. The dirt came from work outside the wall, which was even more exhausting, and a lot was being performed by surprisingly willing Dom army prisoners marched down from Texcoco, where they'd been similarly employed.

First, the whole outer city had literally been swept away by giant, long-necked *serpientosas* with heavy chains stretched between them. Hordes of armabueys and other creatures did the same on a smaller scale, or dragged potentially useful materials into the city to shore up the new parapet. The rest of the debris was scraped into piles and burned. Dark smoke had towered over the city for days. The prisoners, townsfolk, and eventually even soldiers worked somewhat companionably digging what had been envisioned as a deep, wide, dry moat, to create a terrible, impassable killing field. The proximity of the two great lakes and how low the city stood made a dry moat impossible, however, and it began to fill even as they dug it out. That was a little disappointing, if rather expected, but any enemy would most likely focus on the four main gates in any event. At least they wouldn't have to worry about sappers undermining the wall since tunnels would fill as well.

Yet despite all the work, after the first couple of weeks, there'd been strikingly little overt resistance to their presence. Men had been knifed or badly beaten in alleys, largely near drinking establishments, and the order that off-duty troops go nowhere by themselves was reinforced, but things hadn't generally been all that bad. Hanny was surprised to find Apo, or any of his men, so anxious. "Have you seen more ugly looks than I have? Maybe heard rumors I should pass on?"

Apo shook his head. "I ain't the only one who figures there's a bunch of them damned Blood Priests lurking among ordinary folk, just waiting for their chance. Word is, even Colonel Cayce fears it." He pursed his lips. "But nah, no rumors. Nothing like that. I don't *trust* these people, mind." He waved at some more affluent-looking men plying their spades, probably upper-class hidalgos. Aside from the *alcalde* and some of his people, virtually no *patricios* had been found by the occupying force. "Don't even trust the former slaves," Apo continued, "the women neither, which is crazy. Hard to credit how upset they were when Don Hurac proclaimed an end to their bloody sacrifices. It was like he took their only entertainment. Probably did," he reflected, then snorted. "Imagine that. And women the most likely to get picked to be gutted. Father Orno's got his work cut out!"

He tilted his head at another cluster of watchers. "Agon's troops ain't that different from us, underneath, but they were more, I don't know, like, frontier troops. A bunch came from Vera Cruz too, which was under Don Hurac and kind of on the 'frontier' itself, in a way. Their 'crazy' laid on 'em in a thinner layer, I guess." He shook his head. "Folks here . . . they ain't like us at all. Maybe never will be."

"They all seem tae know, like us or not, they'll be for the chop if we lose," Preacher Mac interjected.

Apo was nodding. "Yes, but that means our only common cause is survival. And if not for Don Hurac, I'm not sure they'd even join us in that." He sighed. "So worse than the ones who look at us ugly, I guess, are the ones who look at us like saviors."

Hanny thought about that in silence for a moment as his section passed out of the western gate and increased its pace as the dragoons spurred into a trot. Since Major Anson's fight for the Río de Purification bridge, Colonel Cayce had ordered all large scouts should have at least a section of guns. This was Hanny's section's first "turn" since they got here. "Yeah," he finally said. "'Saviors' only here to put things back the way they were before the Blood Priests took over. I know what you mean, and it feels . . . weird."

"Yer *other* left, bless ye!" came an incredulous bellow in strongly Irish-accented Spanya, and they all looked to where a corporal was trying to teach close-order drill to roughly a hundred civilians, mostly former slaves by their dress. An impressive stone bridge crossed a canal connecting the Lago de Texcoco to Lago Chalco about half a mile from the western gate and the obliteration of the outer city had left the ground a dusty, dry, fire-scorched plain. It wasn't a perfect parade ground to train the hundreds of locals conscripted into the guard, but at least there was plenty of room. Training started early.

Corporal . . . Flynn, Hanny thought it was, late of the 1st US, wasn't the only junior NCO with his hands full at the moment. The City Guard worked on the defenses like everyone, but also had to learn to be soldiers. Regardless of their beliefs, if the Gran Cruzada came, they'd all be fighting for their lives. Company-size groups rotated in and out for a few hours each day, and there were currently six other formations (and their appointed trainers) undergoing the same ordeal. None had been given proper weapons yet, though a sufficient number of current-issue and obsolete Dom muskets had been found in city armories to equip nearly five thousand troops. The trainees carried boards, for now. Teaching them the complicated procedure for using real weapons would come after they started to move and think like soldiers. Unfortunately, the shouted commands of the various instructors were intermingled, and the resulting confusion was predictable.

"Don't ye know which foot is yer left, boyo?" Flynn was raging, his furious face mere inches from an unlucky recruit's. "Aye, that one indeed. Ye'd only two choices, an' yer first was wrong. Now, which *arm* is yer left?" The poor lad hesitated, and Flynn punched him hard in the appropriate bicep. "*All* yer lefts're on the same bloody side! Tell me now which *direction* is left? No, that's *my* left, goddamn yer leakin' bowels! There, aye, ye've got it at last!"

"*Right* face means turn to your *right!*" screamed an Ocelomeh sergeant at his own charges, who'd probably been distracted and confused by the nearby drama. "It's a wonder how you manage to feed yourselves, or take two breaths in a row."

"Column into line, into *line*, god damn you! Not a gaggle. And none of you even facing the front!" roared another Uxmalo NCO.

"Is that a *tear* I see on yer womanish face?" Corporal Flynn now screeched incredulously. "A *tear*? P'raps prompted by me sweet, tender tone?"

"N-no, ah, Corporal."

Flynn blinked and took a step back. "That's what I thought," he said loudly. "I can tell young Lefty'll be a rare, fierce soldier, an' either I sprayed a drop o' me spittle on 'is cheek or 'e's 'avin' a piss from 'is eyes." He raised his voice to a yell. "*Real* soldiers don't cry at *words*, by God. It ain't like they're musket balls er blades. Words can't really hurt ye." He glared back at "Lefty," which would likely be his name forever more. "But yer left is yer *left* an' yer right is yer *right* an' we won't be confusin' 'em again, will we now?"

Apo's gloomy expression had been replaced by a grin. "Poor devils," he said. "I think we were even worse when we started."

"Aye, that's a fact," gruffed Hahessy.

"So I think they'll be all right, some of them," Apo qualified. "I cried like a girl when Sergeant Visser got in my face like that. I didn't know why he was being so mean. But I got tough, and only later did I realize that the way he did it . . . it was certainly memorable and actually rather funny. Not only did his teaching stick with me, he . . . *trivialized* that kind of meanness so I'd be stronger in the face of the real thing. In battle."

"It has that effect," Hanny agreed, "whether the one doing the chewing even means it to or not." He sent Hahessy's back a strange look. Hahessy had been a sergeant, a bad one, broken for truly wicked behavior. He probably wasn't completely reformed, but was loyal to his gun and an asset as a private. And though certainly not intended to strengthen him at the time, Hahessy's long-ago bullying of Hanny himself had helped to make him a man. *That's what Apo means*, he thought. *Those instructors are turning slaves into men—and all these people are slaves of a sort, whether they know it or not. Men will seek freedom, to win liberty, to protect their comrades . . . and preserve what they've become. All of which are causes beyond simple survival.*

He contemplated that for a while as they came to the bridge, rumbled over it, and set off once again into the unknown.

"When are we gonna get married?" Leonor asked quietly, almost hissing, poking Lewis in the ribs. Rather savagely, in fact. He turned to look at her, managing a pained smile at the daily, only half-serious question. They were standing near the east gate of the city with the rest of the command staff, including "His Supreme Holiness" Don Hurac, present for another of his shockingly frequent public appearances that both delighted and scandalized his new subjects. Alcalde Estilio, Vice Alcalde Don Amil, and the enigmatic Don Armonia attended him. As usual, Armonia wore a disapproving frown.

Varaa *kakked* a chuckle, and Giles Anson rolled his eyes. In the glare of the sun, only now rising above the distant mountains and washing through the open gate, Leonor's blue-black hair practically glowed, and her dark eyes seemed to glitter with humor. Lewis was nearly overwhelmed by both the inner, and increasingly outer, beauty the woman reflected, but her emerging humor was probably most attractive of all.

"Hear, hear," Samantha said lowly, and even Colonel Agon seemed to have difficulty stifling a laugh. Everyone else managed to remain silent, as did the rather large number of locals who couldn't have heard the exchange, but had either paused in their labor or specifically come to see Don Hurac as word of his presence spread. His unorthodox behavior and unprecedented availability might confuse them, but since the strangely brief and informal elevation ceremony he presided over himself, most still believed he represented their God here among them. Beyond the great, arched entryway through the thickening wall, the groping rays of sunlight promised another warm day as they lit the top of a dust cloud, stirred by an approaching mounted force.

Despite the humor, Lewis uncomfortably recognized there *was* an element of seriousness in Leonor's question, and he was running out of reasons to delay. He wasn't even sure why he did anymore. Things certainly *seemed* under control. Don Hurac had declared the war over and sent the few messenger dragons that came to the city to carry his command far and wide. Few had returned, even fewer with an acknowledgment, but that wasn't too concerning just yet. Don Hurac *was* the legitimate Supreme Holiness now, ensconced in the Holy City. Some might still consider him a usurper—the ousted Supreme Holiness and Tranquilo in particular most certainly would—but absent a visible effort to depose him, people would get used to it in time. Conservative Blood Cardinals and *alcaldes* on the west coast, still uncomfortable with the rise of the Blood Priests, might even greet his elevation with relief.

Not all was going well. The whereabouts of the Gran Cruzada were still unknown, as were General Xacolotl's intentions. On some level, everyone remained worried about them both, especially since there'd pointedly been no response from Xacolotl at all. Perhaps more concerning, there were hints of more unrest in the city than was generally acknowledged, likely fueled by Blood Priests hiding among the people. A few had been turned over to Don Hurac's guards, but contrary to Lewis's wishes, they were being held instead of hanged. Almost predictably, a lot of informers had been swiftly and brutally murdered. All that aside, the vast majority of the civilian population continued obeying Don Hurac's orders to help build defenses and learn to fight.

At present, there was a kind of peace, and even with all the upheavals some of Don Hurac's immediate social reforms were causing, a growing sense of acceptance, perhaps even guarded optimism, was beginning to prevail. Lewis examined his feelings and came to the conclusion that his hesitancy to fulfill his promise to Leonor was based on his own fear of hope, and an almost overwhelming superstitious dread that if he trusted the situation to the extent of finally pursuing his own happiness, everything would fall apart. Taking her hand in his, he said, "Perhaps sooner than you expect, though I don't half deserve you."

"Hear, hear," Samantha repeated, louder and more adamantly.

"Hush, woman," Anson scolded, and Samantha turned astonished, flaring eyes on him. "How dare—" she began, but Varaa interrupted her.

"Perhaps we can save this, ah, 'discussion' until after we greet our guests," she said, blinking at the approaching column, tail flicking with amusement.

The great gate, newly repaired and strengthened, stood open, but a company of the 1st US lined the avenue on either side for security. Anticipating a pleasant day, none of the troops wore greatcoats, and the muskets on their shoulders and all their brass buttons and beltplates had been polished to a gleaming luster. Their sky-blue uniforms and white trim remained somewhat dingy from the campaign despite careful brushing, but they still looked very fine. A gust of wind off Lake Chalco carried away the ashy dust, all that remained of the outer city, and a clump of officers leading a column of Rangers alongside a column of dragoons clopped in under the archway, horses shying slightly at the unexpected echo resounding in the twenty-foot passage.

"Atten-shun!" Colonel Reed barked. The troops stomped a foot as they'd been instructed and stood slightly straighter. All the officers around Lewis rendered a salute. So did Lewis, though Don Hurac and his entourage merely bowed respectfully. There was no question that Lewis outranked their principal visitor from a military perspective, but Colonel Sira Periz, commanding 5th Division, was also the *alcaldesa* of Uxmal and the closest thing to a head of state over the Allied cities on the Yucatán. Lewis wanted her first visit to the enemy capital to be memorable. She'd earned it.

Sira smiled brightly under the light layer of dust that did nothing to diminish her dark, almost elfin beauty. She was barely five feet tall, if that, and the magnificent captured Dom stallion she rode with a confidence Lewis wouldn't have expected made her look even smaller. Returning the salute with evident pleasure, she promptly pulled the white leather gauntlets from her hands and proceeded to raise a cloud of dust around herself as she whipped it from her uniform. "The mud is still deep in the high country," she said. "I hadn't expected it so dry."

"All the moisture is in the air today, my dear," Reverend Harkin warmly replied. "It may even become uncomfortable as the day progresses." He gestured at Don Hurac. "The locals predict rain in the next few days."

"A *warm* rain, I trust," Sira replied, sliding gracefully down from her horse. "I've had quite enough cold rain, and certainly snow, for a while." Before she left the Yucatán, she'd never seen snow in her life. Three of her companions, Captains Sal Hernandez of the Rangers and Thomas Hayne leading the dragoons, as well as the big Holcano warrior named Kisin, quickly joined her on the ground. Sal had been a Ranger as long as Anson, and Leonor loved him like an uncle. Tall, dark, and lanky, he'd allowed his mustache to reach outrageous proportions in the weeks since she'd seen him last. Tom Hayne, a former sergeant in the 3rd Dragoons, looked as different from Sal as could be. His broad-shouldered, barrel-chested, bull-necked physique was the very caricature of the Irish-born NCO he'd been, and his tanned but still paler freckled face had been consumed by light brown whiskers *except* on his upper lip. Kisin had been a war leader of Holcano Indians, the oldest enemy of the Ocelomeh, but joined the Alliance after his people's defeat in the Yucatán. They'd also finally come to the realization that the Doms, who'd very scantily supported them, were far worse enemies than the Ocelomeh.

"Where is food?" Kisin demanded in Spanya. "We didn't eat yet today."

Ignoring Kisin, who attracted a number of disapproving looks, Don Hurac stepped forward and bowed very low to Sira. "You should not be inconvenienced by snow in this place. Even now, in deepest winter, it only rarely freezes and numerous crops can grow year-round. Proof that this valley truly is blessed by God." He straightened. "Your presence here does me great honor, and you are most welcome. Zyan will be happy to greet you as well."

The men standing with him, even Don Amil, seemed horrified that he'd show such deference to a woman. *Any* woman. A gust of whispers arose from the local onlookers, and Don Armonia visibly seethed. Lewis inwardly cringed himself as Don Hurac gallantly introduced the *alcaldesa* to his followers. All the Allied leaders had wanted the new Supreme Holiness to make changes to the Dominion, but there was growing concern that he might be moving quicker than his people could—or would—accept. Even slaves had higher status than women in this twisted society, often owning women themselves. That kind of thinking, that even the lowliest was "better" than someone, could take a while to change. The only thing lower, as these folk reckoned, with less right to live than a bug, was a heretic. Only fear of what their own people would do to them, respect for the army's power, and Don Hurac's assurance the invaders were *not* heretics had ensured the level of civilian cooperation they enjoyed. They couldn't afford to let Don Hurac's credibility slip.

Lewis stepped forward with Leonor, Varaa, Anson, and Samantha, but held Leonor back from embracing Sal. "Let's all observe the *local* proprieties at the moment," he suggested with a smile, indicating their audience by shaking his head slightly from side to side.

"Ah. Indeed," Samantha agreed.

"Your . . . Supreme Holiness?" Lewis pointedly asked, tripping on the title as always in spite of himself.

A light seemed to flash behind Don Hurac's eyes. "Yes. Of course. Let us make our way to your command post, Coronel Cayce," he added loudly, "where we may hear the report of *all* your esteemed officers."

Catching on at once and nodding slightly, Sira Periz stepped behind Sal and Tom Hayne, who shook Anson's hand when he offered it. "Good to see you fellas. Anxious to hear what you've seen." Both had been doing a lot of scouting to the north. "Get your boys settled an' meet us at the command post. Can't miss it. Tents're in the plaza surroundin' the biggest pyramid in the city." He frowned and lowered his voice. "Personally, I'd just as soon not even look at the blood-smeared thing, if you know what I mean. Been down inside a kind of dungeon part a couple times, an' it's creepy as hell. Don Hurac stays in a fancy apartment about halfway up, in the middle. He's *supposed* to stay there, an' I guess that part ain't so bad. We all could'a had quarters in some real fancy villas. Officers, at least. Hell, they're full o' freed slaves, now. But you know Lewis. He decided we better stick close together—an' close to Don Hurac—so it's tents."

A proper reception, complete with orderlies distributing refreshments, was held in the large command tent at the base of the central pyramid. As Lewis's personal orderly, Corporal Willis enjoyed his status as "first among equals" far too much, and his tyranny would've been oppressive if anyone paid it any mind. Leonor finally got to give Sal a big hug, and one to Boogerbear as well, who was just in from a scout to the south that morning. Every Ranger who'd originally come to this world together was in the same place for once. Don Hurac had been joined by Zyan, who affectionately greeted Sira Periz. The two, along with Samantha, had become close friends. Don Hurac himself had retreated somewhat back in among his local advisors, who continued to whisper gravely among themselves.

"Don't take this wrong, I'm glad you're here," Lewis finally told Sira, "but the messenger with news you were coming only arrived last night. In the *middle* of the night," he added. "That was a little worrisome. So I suppose the question foremost in my mind is *why* are you here?"

Grinning a little, Sira waved his concerns away. "I apologize for any drama." Her eyes twinkled at Leonor. "But it came to my understanding there would be a wedding very soon after we achieved control over the Holy City, and I was determined to attend."

Lewis very nearly sprayed the sweet juice he'd just sipped out his nose. Turning as red as the juice, something that looked and tasted like a mix of grapes and cranberries, he shifted his attention to Leonor. Her expression was one of pure innocence. "Has that commitment been made public to the entire Allied army?"

"Apparently," Sira laughed. "As I've recently discovered and you're no doubt aware, no order moves as fast—or far—in an army as a rumor. I imagine many of the, ah . . . particulars . . . have evolved as the gossip spread, but based on your reaction, I take it the central truth has not."

"It has not," Leonor confirmed with a challenging look at Lewis.

"No. I suppose it hasn't," Lewis agreed quietly.

"Excellent!" Sira exclaimed, clapping her hands together in emphasis like Varaa so often did, then let Lewis stew under the scrutiny of all his friends and officers for a moment. "That is, however, only one reason I'm here," she finally confessed.

"Do tell," Anson said.

Sira nodded, her expression suddenly touched by annoyance. "After my division was spread so widely about, with detachments hither and yon, I was obliged to remain in Puebla." She sighed. "In retrospect, I imagine that was for the best."

Lewis nodded gently. It had been essential, in fact. As soon as she'd learned another Dom army was on the Yucatán and the cities there under siege, her first impulse had been to march back to Techolotla, seize every ship they'd captured, and sail to the rescue of Uxmal. Entirely understandable—and pointless. First, Colonel Ruberdeau De Russy, entrusted with the defenses there, had sent word that he believed he could hold and the crisis on the Yucatán would be over, one way or another, before she could even get there, much less affect it with her force. More important, however, her movement would've destroyed Lewis's ability to continue his campaign to the Holy City, and a successful outcome there had been the quickest way to relieve Uxmal, by Don Hurac's command. That command had been sent at once. They could only hope it was heeded or, at the very least, De Russy continued to hold.

In any event, Sira Periz had been reminded of the bigger picture. Uxmal had been evacuated of noncombatants, and the fate of the city itself, beloved to her as it was, must remain secondary to the overall cause. Only true victory, what Lewis *seemed* to have achieved, could win any long-term security.

"Any news from Uxmal?" Father Orno asked somberly.

"Nothing new, I'm afraid," Sira replied. "Captain Holland was going to sail down and investigate again, with a larger force this time. He may have already left. But no, nothing new."

"So," Varaa observed, "as soon as the brigade you were left with at Puebla received enough reinforcements from Techolotla to keep Puebla secure, you moved forward to Texcoco. We knew this, and Lewis approved. His question remains."

Sira looked around and turned her nod into a bow of the head to "King" Colonel Har-Kaaska as the big Mi-Anakka Ocelomeh swept in under the tent flap to welcome her as well. He'd been with his 2nd Division on the far side of the city when she arrived. "My second reason was also personal." She gestured around. "This . . . city has been the seat of all evil my entire life, the *real* monster to frighten young children into doing their chores. The monsters of the wilderness were as nothing compared to it. They were a natural thing. The Dominion is not. It has long been an artificial construct of evil by a devil posing as a god and has haunted my every waking action, indeed, every dream in my sleep for as long as I can remember." She stood straighter and looked at Lewis before casting a sharp glance at the men around Don Hurac. "I . . . I simply had to come and see it for myself." She shrugged.

"Well said," granted Har-Kaaska. "Well said indeed. The aura of evil remains, its stench still strong, but it's just a place, after all. Another place where evil has been and we chased it out."

Giles Anson remained strongly unconvinced of that, as did Leonor, for that matter, and both made sure Lewis never became complacent about the possibility. He *wanted* to be as positive as Har-Kaaska seemed, that their only remaining threat was the Gran Cruzada. With the defenses they were building, Har-Kaaska was becoming beguiled by the notion they could hold the city against it. But even as their defenses grew stronger and the panic of those who worked on them waned, Lewis almost tasted a growing evil inside the walls, as if they'd trapped it in there with them. Now it was feeding on confined souls around it, slowly growing stronger.

He shook his head. "You have another reason, Alcaldesa?" he asked.

"Yes." Sira indicated Lieutenant Hernandez and Lieutenant Hayne. Kisin had stationed himself by a table laden with meats wrapped in tortillas and various treats and was gorging himself. "Behind us to the east is secure. These men have thoroughly scouted north and detected no threat there either." She paused. "A medium-size city lies on the north coast of Lago de Texcoco, called Guadalupe, and it alone of those we've encountered hasn't been razed by the enemy." She blinked in confusion, like Varaa would've done. "It's like they have no concept a war even rages. Their young men were taken into the Gran Cruzada some time ago and they have no real armed force."

"How could they not know . . . anything?" Colonel Reed inquired.

"The plague explanation again," Colonel Agon guessed, speaking for the first time. "That was how they stopped commerce and questions here so long. How they explained why there could be no travel to Vera Cruz. I presume Guadalupe has been told, and now believes, it's the sole uninfected city in the Dominion."

"Which is true in a way, I reckon. Least around here," Boogerbear grumbled.

"Uninfected by fear of an invading force, and therefore not subject to extermination—yet." Lewis nodded.

"That's what we figured," Sal explained. "We only scouted to the outskirts an' folks ran from us. But not like we was demons er somethin'. More like they didn't want to catch what we had. We left 'em alone."

"Probably right that you did," mused Colonel Reed. "For now. If the Gran Cruzada comes, however, it might be a good idea to warn them. I don't imagine they'll fare much better if they learn the greatest army ever put together has been recalled to cope with a domestic threat."

Don Hurac's eyes were widening.

"God save us all!" Reverend Harkin exclaimed in horror.

Don Hurac was briskly nodding. "Yes indeed. Learning that might be as bad as seeing your army," he said. "Oh, when I contemplate how many cities the Gran Cruzada must pass through to here . . ." He looked like he might vomit. Even Armonia looked vaguely conflicted, though Lewis didn't know if it was inspired by empathy or concern over how difficult such a task would be. Lewis frankly didn't know what to think about the man. Everyone was suspicious of him, thankfully including Don Hurac. Lewis often thought the new Supreme Holiness could be painfully naive at times, but he wasn't a fool. Armonia was confusing, though. The sense of him was that no enemy spy or saboteur would deliberately draw so much scrutiny upon his rather blatant hostility. On the other hand, that might be the perfect cover. Reverend Harkin had openly wondered if Armonia was simply playing devil's advocate or was a true advocate for a very real devil. He'd strongly recommended arresting him. Ironically, Father Orno and Colonel Agon feared the example that would set. The man was unpleasant but, as far as they knew, hadn't been spreading sedition. It couldn't be proved he'd actually *done* anything but privately express his opinions, and everyone rebelled at the thought of punishing that. Lewis and Don Hurac both felt it was better to keep him close and easier to watch.

"Very well," Lewis said, clearing his throat and refocusing on the question at hand. "We'll stand prepared to warn the people of Guadalupe." He looked at Sira. "You weren't contemplating taking your brigade there to *protect* them, were you?"

"No," Sira said. "But proceeding with my argument, I actually thought to bring it here. My full division, in fact. Between the troops you left in Texcoco and more I can leave as well—reinforcements are still coming up, you know . . ."

"All as green as grass, I believe the phrase is," Colonel Agon pointed out.

"Granted," Sira replied. "But well trained." She looked at Lewis. "I saw the training of local . . . troops . . . under way outside the wall. Very rudimentary at present, and we have no idea how well they'll hold. I thought you might want my troops here."

"With the greatest respect, Sira," Varaa interjected, "most of *your* troops are 'locals' as well, from Vera Cruz and Techolotl. How will *they* fight, do you think?"

"Better," Sira almost snapped, eyes flaring. "Most assuredly."

"All the more reason for them to remain in Puebla, for now," Lewis assured her, and she looked at him in surprise. Lewis elaborated. "*If* the Gran Cruzada comes, we'll largely be forced into a purely defensive fight." He looked at Don Hurac. "To defend the people here. I don't like it, but—as you say—we can't make enough professional soldiers from the population of the, ah, Holy City, to give us a chance in a battle of maneuver against a force the size we expect." He held up his hand. "Nor would your fine division make a difference. We'll have to defend the walls"—he looked around—"and despite the improvements, they're *very* long walls indeed. We'll need every man."

"Arm the women too," Leonor urged. "A bunch have told me they'll fight if they can."

Lewis looked at Don Hurac. Aside from Sira herself, Leonor, and Varaa—the most notable examples—the Allied Army did have some women in its ranks. These were mostly Ocelomeh, but a few Uxmalo, Itzincabo, even Holcano women were under arms. The vast majority of the army's healers, its "medical corps," was female as well. Unfortunately, even though Don Hurac accepted the role of those specific women, even he seemed horrified by the thought of large-scale female participation in combat—if probably not for the same reason as the locals around him. They were positively apoplectic over the notion. In point of fact, so was most of the Allied Army, but that was cultural protectiveness, not bigotry.

"I . . . don't think that will work just now," Lewis said. "The point is"—he looked back at Sira—"if we find ourselves trapped in the city, only your division . . . and a few other detachments," he added vaguely, "will be on the loose to harass the enemy encircling us. A lot will depend on that."

He smiled a little sickly and took a long, deep breath as he regarded everyone present before settling his eyes on Leonor. "As to your first 'personal' reason for coming, well, I think that if you can spare a few days, we might be able to accommodate you."

Leonor's eyes grew wide, and her pretty face darkened, her olive complexion taking a reddish hue. "Really?" she said at last. "After all this war talk, now? Finally?"

"Yes," Lewis said. "If you'll have me."

Word spread quickly, and the reception almost turned into a planning session for the wedding before Lewis broke it up, reminding everyone they had duties. He took Anson aside for a moment before he and Leonor, with Varaa and Har-Kaaska, left the big tent. Anson had nodded at what Lewis told him and then stood there watching Don Hurac and his advisors preparing to leave as well, waiting for their escort to assemble. He snapped his fingers at Boogerbear, who drew Sal and Kisin along. "Olayne's dragoons headed out on a scout in the direction we think the bigwigs here took off," Anson told Boogerbear, "which is probably the same direction we'll find the Gran Cruzada. The dragoons are better on their own than they were, but I want you an' half our Rangers out scoutin' for *them*." He eyed Kisin. "Take half the Holcanos too, an' all General Soor's Grik—not that there's many of 'em, but the last thing we need in the city is a buncha lizardy-lookin' 'demons' runnin' around."

Boogerbear just nodded.

"What about us?" Sal asked. "My Rangers an' the rest of Kisin's Holcanos?"

Deliberately gazing only at Sal, Anson replied. "See that rough, grumpy-lookin' fella with Don Hurac?" he asked softly. Kisin turned to look.

"No, you idiot! What's the matter with you?"

"You asked if I see him. Now I did," Kisin replied reasonably.

Anson sighed. "Okay. His name's 'Armonia.' Claims to be 'the voice o' the people,' or some such. Thing is, I think that's a load o' shit, an' we need to detail some Rangers—good ones—to keep an eye on him, careful like. See who he talks to or meets with."

"I thought you tole Colonel Cayce we ain't police," Sal accused.

"I did. We ain't," Anson whispered back. "Ain't gonna be either. Our boys're trained up like bear dogs: to chase, latch on, an' kill. You can't turn that on an' off on a whim. But they're good at sneakin' an' scoutin' too, so they can bring in the rest o' the pack. They can do that as easy in the city as the woods. Just don't get caught or we'll likely have one o' two things happen—either we'll never find out if he's up to somethin' he shouldn't be, or we'll have a wild-ass bear killin' right here in the city. Might be hard to smooth that over."

CHAPTER 14

FEBRUARY 1, 1849
UXMAL

"No thank you," Colonel Ruberdeau De Russy tiredly but graciously told the orderly who'd brought him a heaping plate of ham, gallina eggs, and something that tasted like buttered grits. It might've been grits, for all he knew. Uxmalos had corn. Taking a sip of strong, unsweetened chocolate, he straightened his freshly pressed mess-dress uniform, leaned back in his chair away from the oil lamp–illuminated breakfast table, and sighed somewhat wistfully. It was already warmer than he would've liked, even before the sun was up, and the mess dress was slightly cooler with the front open, even with a vest, than the "undress" uniform he usually wore. Besides, De Russy was certain there'd be a battle that day and was determined to look his best.

Gray light sneaked around the minimal shutters into the chamber within the squat, thick-walled tower at the center of the north harbor defenses. The air was close, but the shutters were kept closed at night so the lamplight wouldn't provide a mark for the Doms to shoot at. Their gunnery was improving, and they'd increasingly taken to firing in the dark. That still always resulted in even better return fire, however, and the ending night had passed peacefully. Another reason De Russy was sure the calm would soon break. No doubt it would start when the ships in the bay swept down into range of their guns and let loose once again.

Even 18pdrs, the heaviest weapons they'd noted on these Dom ships, had little effect on the stout seaward walls from what the enemy considered a "safe" distance, but they did it nearly every day to remind the defenders they *could* launch a seaborne assault. They probably wouldn't; there were a lot more Dom soldiers encircling the city on land than their ships could quickly put ashore, but the seaward approach had to be defended regardless. That left other walls weaker than they might be. The coastal demonstrations were risky too, since the four 36pdrs mounted on the wall had proven quite effective and the water closer in was littered with snags, sunken wrecks of previous, less cautious approaches.

De Russy reconsidered and caught the orderly's eye before the young Uxmalo turned away. "Perhaps . . . just a piece of toast, if you please. Something in my stomach to accompany the chocolate."

"You can't survive on a piece of toast!" scolded his nominal second-in-command, the Vice Alcaldesa Concejala Urita Xa. She was dressed as she always was now, in an ordinary, unadorned, sky-blue infantry uniform. She was also quite thin and somewhat elderly, considerably older than De Russy himself, but possessed immeasurably more energy than the borderline-corpulent former politician from Pennsylvania. "You need your strength, and it's not as if we are short of food," she stated flatly, motioning the orderly to return.

De Russy managed a fond smile at the motherly figure sitting across from him, her own generous plate set before her. "No," he agreed. "We have sufficient provisions to last many months." He sighed again. "Sadly, I fear we won't need them and they'll have to be destroyed." He nodded at the plate the now-hesitant orderly held. "I don't believe a hearty breakfast will have any bearing upon my survival."

"Nonsense," snapped Urita Xa, gesturing for the orderly to put the plate down while rolling her eyes at the youngster as if to say, "You know how he gets." The orderly quickly obeyed her and fled. Official rank aside, hers was the stronger personality by far. "It certainly won't hurt you, and it might improve your disposition."

"Well, perhaps just a bite," De Russy relented, seizing a fork and briefly toying with his food before diving in.

"Why so gloomy today?" Urita Xa asked, nodding toward the departed soldier. "I would worry you undermine our people's morale—if you weren't already like this so often. They are used to it. I know you miss your wife,"

Urita Xa tentatively consoled. The stunning young Frenchwoman Angelique Mercure had been safely evacuated inland to Itzincab with the rest of the city's noncombatants, and De Russy had figuratively but noticeably deflated soon after. He cherished no illusions that Angelique loved him—he wasn't particularly handsome and was twice her age—but he was confident she was genuinely fond of him, and he *tried* to be dashing and appear self-assured for her. With her gone... "You must take comfort in her safety, and in that of all of those whom we remain to protect," Urita Xa continued. "Itzincab is not only more defensible than Uxmal—it saw off the Holcano hordes even before being so liberally festooned with cannon—and the enemy doesn't even know it exists. Not yet, at any rate. By the time they do, if ever, the Doms won't have nearly as many men to throw against it and those same Holcanos, now on our side, will harry them from the forest. Itzincab, and those within its walls, will be quite safe." She snorted. "Yet still you insist on grumping about, bemoaning our lot. Contrary to what you clearly believe, Angelique is *not* the sole inspiration for your courage or ability as a leader. You have given the Doms a thrashing every time they have attacked."

De Russy almost choked on a piece of ham. "*I* gave them thrashings? I think not. I just stand there and look pretty—as you so often imply is my primary duty—while you and others command our defense in most respects." He shook his head. "No, and before you chastise me again, I'm not whining. Believe me when I say I'm quite aware of my martial deficiencies."

Appointed by the governor of Pennsylvania to command the 3rd Pennsylvania Volunteers, De Russy had never even pretended to be a soldier. On top of that, his first taste of combat had been on this world against a horde of terrifying semireptilian Grik warriors, then allied with the Holcanos. That fight came almost immediately after they were so traumatically marooned on a beach where their ship literally crashed down from the sky in the surf. He was still in shock over that and had been petrified, utterly useless, and promptly delegated overall military command to the man who'd ultimately saved them all, Colonel Cayce. His second attempt to lead men in battle had not been planned, but he'd been forced to step forward and command what amounted to a regiment in their first major action against the Dominion. That episode was marked by a compensatory aggressive abandon just as dangerous and costly as his prior inaction.

He simply wasn't cut out for warfare, and unlike Lewis, had no training or talent for it. He was an excellent politician, however, able to bring wildly disparate groups to consensus by focusing them on commonalities that trivialized their differences. He'd been perfect for his role as manager of the Council of Alcaldes, the neutral chairman of their alliance on the Yucatán, while still looking the part of a military commander of their garrison at Uxmal—a place they'd never expected to be threatened again.

"El Paso del Fuego," or the "Pass of Fire," had been entirely unknown to anyone here before the war brought them Dom prisoners and . . . associates . . . who were at least vaguely aware of a wildly dangerous natural sea route between the Atlantic and Pacific Oceans, about where Costa Rica should be. Captain Holland promptly investigated in HMS *Tiger* and discovered that a transit *was* possible when he rescued a "privateer" from the Empire of the New Britain Isles, named *Nemesis*, that had been chased right through it by a pair of Dom warships. The pass was so treacherous, however, narrow and winding and assailed by impossible currents, that not only had twice as many Dom warships been wrecked in the pursuit, *Nemesis*'s captain, Stanley Jenks, refused to try it again and had joined their cause. He and Holland firmly agreed only a madman would risk ships full of *troops* in a passage. They'd all been fools to believe that concern for the lives of mere soldiers would discourage those in power in the Dominion. Especially anyone influenced by Blood Priests.

Urita Xa toyed with her own food while gazing intently at him. "Even without the guards for our people and reinforcements we sent to Itzincab, we still have more than seven thousand men defending our walls. Granted, few are 'proper soldiers' as Coronel Cayce would define them, and perhaps half are only armed with bows or pikes. There are far too many who were too old or too young to accompany his army as well. But those who are 'properly' armed with muskets have much better weapons than the enemy. They may have started as Dom muskets themselves, but all have been reworked and are a great deal more lethal." She paused. "And that hardly matters since we have so many cannon, sent back from the army's victorious campaigns. Even unmodified, those guns have broken every Dom attack almost by themselves." Her eyes gleamed. "I do so love your 'canister,' and we have a lot of it."

She shrugged and took a bite of egg. "Like you, I expect another attack today, but I do not understand why you think it will fare any better than others. Why will today be different?"

De Russy set his fork down, appetite lost once more. "I may be too gloomy, but I fear our small successes—and they *were* small, against mere probing attacks—may have left you a little overconfident. Yesterday morning, our best estimate of the enemy's strength on land placed their numbers at roughly nineteen thousand. With our strong position, we retained the advantage. Since then, at least ten thousand more enemy soldiers have arrived from the east, marching up the road from Pidra Blanca." Without any defensive walls, they'd long feared that nearest city would fall. Apparently it had, and its conquerors were here.

"Even worse," De Russy continued, "was the arrival last evening of perhaps a like number of Doms from the *west*, up the Nautla Road. They continued streaming in long after dark, so we can't know for sure how many they are. Say another ten thousand, probably landed by sea between here and Nautla. That means a larger Dom fleet and actual reinforcements have come from the Gran Cruzada through the Pass of Fire." He shook his head. "I think it's now clear that the enemy has ignored Don Hurac's command to cease all hostilities!"

They'd been aware of Don Hurac's proclamation for over a week. The Allied Army possessed a single, captured "messenger dragon" independent of those controlled by Don Hurac, but they'd had to physically bring it all the way down here before it could be of use. Messenger dragons could only fly to places they'd been before. That had apparently been an interesting voyage, and Captain Razine of the *Roble Fuerte* swore he'd never carry one of the damned things on his ship again. That was before Captain Holland's final voyage here, of course, after the Doms arrived, and they'd only been able to signal him from shore since their dragon had already been winging to Vera Cruz with the news. In any event, it had since returned and they were aware of the expeditionary force's accomplishments. The question was, did the enemy know, and if so, would it make any difference?

"That may not be," countered Urita Xa. "The enemy would have had to bring their own dragon as well."

De Russy was shaking his head. "That damned Blood Priest, Tranquilo, had one hidden near here. Apparently for quite some time. They could send it."

"Perhaps," Urita Xa conceded. "Or maybe it died, or is busy elsewhere—who knows? The point is, I doubt even twice as many Doms as we've faced can take this city."

"They can!" De Russy insisted. "Don't you see? We're entirely surrounded now and can't be strong everywhere at once. As I said before, all their attacks have been mere probes. Bloody ones, I grant you, but if they're willing to pay the price their twisted faith insists on, they can indeed take Uxmal. Today," he stressed.

Urita Xa's silence was interrupted by a crashing rumble of heavy solid shot striking the walls beneath them, followed by the rolling booming of many guns on the water. Not requiring permission to return fire, there being plenty of powder and shot in the city as well, much louder roars sounded quite close as their 36pdrs replied.

"Well," she said, expression unchanged as she dropped her fork and stood in the fine dust cloud filtering down from the heavy timbers supporting the floor of the watchtower and fighting platform above, "if that is the case, then so be it. We will *choke* their vicious God on the blood we spill."

De Russy finally managed a smile at Urita Xa as aides opened the door and they stepped out into a day of battle. Cannon fire had erupted all around the city. Mingled with the crackle of musketry, an almighty din assaulted their ears. The crew of one of the 36pdrs could be seen, heaving mightily on thick cables to run the multi-ton monster back out, into battery, so it could fire again. A similar great gun a few dozen paces beyond it jetted red-yellow flame into a roiling, thunderous plume of smoke as it recoiled against its restraints. A loud, shrieking, tearing-sheet sound ended in a hollow, splintering *crack*, and cheers went up around the gun that had clearly achieved a solid hit on a ship.

A gasping messenger who looked like a uniformed boy of ten or twelve came to a halt in front of them and attempted a self-conscious salute. Very seriously, De Russy returned the gesture as the wall beneath his feet shook from the impact of another broadside in the bay. They were protected from the shot, but gravel and dust rained thickly down, inducing a reflexive crouch. Occasional larger shards of stone fell on the roof of the barracks building, originally constructed to house the American soldiers when they first arrived.

"Beg to report," the boy said in anxious Spanya.

"Please do, young man," De Russy shouted back over the racket as calmly and cordially as he could.

"Coronel Shais's respects, sir." The boy bowed his head to Urita Xa. "My lady," he added. "He says 'the damned-to-hell Doms are attacking in force, coming in under their own artillery.'"

"Where?" Urita Xa asked.

The boy blinked at her. "Coronel Shais has his 'aich kyoo' on top of the grand audience hall, next to the great temple. He can see the whole city from there." The youngster hesitated. "He says 'everywhere.' They are attacking around the entire perimeter of the city." He gestured at the wall separating them from the sea. "Maybe even from the water too. Our guns're smashing their ships, but they still come, this time."

De Russy actually barked a laugh. "By God—*our* God—I was right! Come with me." He rushed back into the chamber they'd just left and snatched a quivering quill from an inkwell that had sloshed onto the table, furiously applying it to a sheet of thick paper beside it that had barely survived the spill. "Imagine that. Me, right about a battle. First time for everything, I suppose," he mumbled aside as he wrote. "You were right as well, my dear," he told Urita Xa. "We shall choke their God with blood this day if it is the last thing we do." Quickly dropping the quill and folding the page, he handed it to the boy. "Take this to the dragon keepers at once. Make absolutely certain it goes in the beast's message tube."

Wide-eyed, the boy asked, "Should they release the beast now?"

De Russy shook his head. "No. I hope to add to what I have written as the day progresses. If I cannot, the keepers *must* release it if it's the last thing *they* do, understood?"

The boy saluted even as he nodded.

"Good, now off with you, lad." De Russy gestured away, then followed him back outside, still accompanied by Urita Xa.

"You think, already, that things will become that . . . that desperate? You have not even seen the whole battle yet." Urita Xa had to yell to be heard.

"We shall go and do that directly," he replied, eyes narrowing as he peered as far around the perimeter as he could from here. Uxmal was a fair-size city, the largest still inhabited on the Yucatán. The only one larger was the long-abandoned ruins of Campeche. Along with Itzincab, it had been blessed with stout walls to protect it from large marauding monsters, and those walls had been strengthened and pierced for cannon. The problem was, most of that work had been done with a great many more defenders in mind to protect against the first Dom army that came for them—which was actually surprised and defeated in the open. With the "regular" army and all noncombatants gone, who'd originally been envisioned contributing to the defense, the perimeter was simply too big.

Smoke was rising everywhere, mostly from their own cannon and musket fire, but the enemy had been landing their own heavy naval guns for weeks and probably had just as many or more of them. Some were clearly directed at the walls, occasionally striking the top edges and sending shards of stone scything into defenders. Many more were landing in the city itself, and buildings were starting to burn.

"Colonel Sais may have only been a lieutenant at the Washboard, but he's an experienced and courageous soldier. I trust his observations and fear he has pronounced our doom. *All* the Doms are coming, from every direction, and they'll not stop. Our people will fight them to the last, but most aren't really soldiers, and they're simply too few. Still, even as we die, we shall *wreck* this Dom army, and our families at Itzincab and elsewhere in the interior shall be safe for some time to come." He laughed again. "Damn you, Lewis Cayce, wherever you are—and God bless you as well, for leaving me in this predicament . . . with this opportunity."

"Opportunity?" Urita Xa asked, but she smiled somewhat resignedly as well, rather sure she knew what he meant.

"Of course," De Russy replied, straightening his coat and sword belt before heading for the stone stairs. A carriage awaited on the parade ground below, and he meant to join Colonel Sais for a while—before choosing his own place on the wall. He grinned ironically. "I just hope Lewis can conjure us as stirring an epitaph as Simonides did for those Spartan fellows."

Urita Xa looked at him strangely. "I take it the 'Spartan fellows' faced similarly gloomy circumstances," she guessed, "yet are well regarded where you are from."

"Quite well. Even after a very, very long time."

"Being remembered—honored—is important to you?"

Now down on the parade ground, De Russy continued briskly forward. "Suddenly . . . yes. More important than anything in the world. Not just for me, but for our people. It's the last thing we can give them, is it not?"

Those had been brave words indeed, especially coming from him. Two hours later, smoke-stained, blood-spattered, and hungrier than he thought he'd ever been, he was pacing slowly among the tired and horrifically thinned defenders on the east wall, sword drawn and lying on his shoulder. Stepping over the bodies that littered the fighting platform, De Russy remained just as committed to his earlier words, but wasn't feeling them as strongly. Even so, he remained perfectly capable of patting the occasional soldier's shoulder and passing a little encouragement or handing cigars to exhausted, frightened, often bandaged youngsters, whose faces were smeared black with powder mixed with sweat after biting open countless musket cartridges. De Russy had more cigars in his coat pocket than he would ever smoke.

They'd just repulsed another attack on the wall he'd chosen for himself, and he felt vaguely cheated by that, having picked it—he thought—as the most vulnerable. That was entirely due to the numbers arrayed against it, not for any lack of defensive design or courage on the part of those holding it. Absolutely not. No, having made his peace with death, he just supposed he'd wanted it all over with as quickly as possible. That wasn't to say he welcomed it or he wasn't afraid. He rather cherished the life he lived on this world, not to mention the role and wife he'd found. And he was terribly afraid of the pain of death, or worse, not being killed outright and becoming a plaything for the Doms. But he'd spiritually and philosophically prepared himself. It wasn't their fault that the fine soldiers here weren't as ready to end it as he was—and if it took too much longer, he was simply going to *have* to find something to eat. "Urita Xa was right again, bless her," he said.

"What was that, sir?" asked an older man with sparse white whiskers on his weathered, dark brown face.

"What? Oh." De Russy smiled. "You're all doing splendidly." He raised his voice and waved his sword. "Spendidly! I haven't once been even slightly tempted to dirty this lovely blade. Though to be entirely honest, I'd likely only get in the way." This truth was met by tired, knowing, but affectionate chuckles. "Why, just *look* down there." He gestured over the wall at the heaped carpet of bodies and ladders knocked askew. "You men have easily destroyed twice the numbers you started here with yourselves." Of course, there were less than half as many left, and the enemy artillery was starting to pound the wall again. They'd probably never make a real breach, but they'd piled enough rubble in places that the climb wouldn't be quite as far. Then again, De Russy didn't think climbing through loose debris would be very easy either.

"They're forming for another attempt," called a young guard lieutenant most recently employed in one of the military factories established in the city. The majority of the able-bodied men had been similarly engaged. That was something else De Russy had to consider. In addition to knowing just when it was time to release the messenger dragon, all the food and military stores, major industries, and the powder works in particular had to be denied to the enemy. They'd been mined, with fuses laid, but knowing when to light them was the thing. At the moment, he was probably more worried about doing that right than dying.

He needn't have been. Even considering the relative peace on the east wall at the moment, at least two of the other walls were under assault, and the noise remained cacophonous. De Russy couldn't even tell exactly *which* walls were fighting because of the all-consuming column of smoke towering over the intervening city. A rising roar, like predatory beasts unleashed on their prey at last, began to mount in the distance, perhaps along the coastal or eastern wall. The wind had quickened with the day and moved the noise around. He couldn't tell exactly where it was coming from, but was suddenly sure that somewhere, the enemy had finally broken Uxmal's defense.

"Runners!" he shouted, motioning several boys near. "Count off! As quick as you can, acquaint yourselves with the source of that commotion. If it's what we fear, even numbers come find me and odd numbers go to the grand audience hall and have them prepare to release the dragon and fire all the fuses."

"Prepare to, or do it?" one boy asked anxiously.

De Russy shook his head. "If it is a breakthrough, it may yet be manageable. I'd rather see for myself." He looked over the wall at the next enemy assault wave, still forming. "A squad of quick men on me, Lieutenant. If you please."

He looked back at the boys. "That said, if you see a great many Doms running loose unopposed and heading that direction, be prepared to fire the fuses yourselves, if you must. Likewise, if the order has already been issued from sufficient authority, do not interfere. Is that understood?"

Several of the boys gulped, but all nodded and rendered various forms of salute. Heart pounding, De Russy returned the attempted gesture with due solemnity. "Now go! I shall be behind you directly, right up the main road to the temple grounds. You'll find me on the way and report."

The lieutenant had directed seven or eight men to go with him. De Russy never counted them as he rushed down the stairs behind the parapet and began to jog, already wheezing. Each man with him was precious and could scarcely be spared from the wall, but if the enemy was in the city in force, holding the wall was pointless. In that event, every defender was to fall back and rally behind the waist-high stone wall surrounding the temple grounds anyway. De Russy supposed it was likely that the men he was leaving would come to him before he returned to them.

Working his way along the road behind the wall before he reached the gate, De Russy was stunned to see that virtually every building they passed was afire. Higher up and a little farther away, actually on the wall, it hadn't been as apparent and he honestly hadn't expected it. Many of the buildings were made of stone or adobe brick, and the roofs were mostly tile instead of thatch these days. That hadn't protected them like he'd thought it would. There was plenty of fuel inside them to burn, mostly heavy timber framing, and they were built closely enough that heat alone could ignite them. And it wasn't like there'd been enough men to spare for fire brigades. Most who would've performed that duty were on the walls with weapons. Besides, he supposed that once the great fire got enough of a start, it had become impossible to put it out anyway. He was just glad they'd cleared a wide space between the buildings and walls, or the defenders would've been forced off or burned long before.

Coughing and gasping, and falling somewhat behind his escort, he turned onto the *camino principal*, which ran straight from the west gate to the temple grounds about a mile or so ahead. *I can't possibly run or even trot a mile*, he confessed to himself. He'd never been the most active person, especially in recent years. "Someone . . . find . . . me . . . a horse," he called. That shouldn't be hard. Men were galloping to and fro, up and down the main street ahead. One dressed as a dragoon stopped of his own accord, saluting.

"I was just coming to find you, Coronel! The enemy . . ."

The young man didn't finish, interrupted by a terrible blast and towering mushroom of smoke about halfway to their destination.

"The tent an' uniform factory!" one of the escorts exclaimed.

De Russy steadied himself. "Perhaps the fire—"

"No, Coronel," the rider denied. "The city is not burning in the very middle yet, but the order has been given to fire the fuses. Look!" Even as they stood watching, the lithe, vaguely serpentine shape of the green, brown, and yellow messenger dragon, small in the distance, was flapping furiously to claw for altitude, doubtless as happy to flee all the unpleasantness around it as it was to be released. The creatures always resented confinement, no matter how well they were fed. "The east wall has fallen," the rider now continued. "Nothing stands against the enemy there, and they're pouring into the city. Vice Alcaldesa Urita Xa is presumed to be dead."

De Russy had been expecting it, but the news still struck him hard, and his pounding heart broke when he heard the words. Another terrific blast from the direction of the seawall shook the ground, followed by what seemed an unending rumble of secondary explosions, large and small. "The magazine under the barracks block," De Russy presumed.

"Yes, sir," the rider agreed. "That means the main magazine and powder works by the river will go up in ten to twelve minutes." They'd watched the enemy finally occupy the powder works the day before. Understandably hesitant to fire on it, they'd been kept at bay by a handful of bold defenders who finally pulled back to the city. There was a great deal of gunpowder inside the facility that the Doms would be happy to have. They'd be less happy when more barrels of gunpowder buried underneath the place went off.

"Then you'd best be about your business," De Russy said briskly. "Continue on and clear the west wall, then make sure the withdrawal order has reached the rest of our people. God be with you, young man." He looked at his small security detail. "We shall wait here until our comrades join us."

Large numbers of Dom soldiers were already arriving at the temple ground square, spreading out to encircle the defenders when De Russy and his command from the western wall charged the disorganized troops and smashed their way through.

"Well done, lads!" De Russy cried, a rather puzzled expression on his sweaty face as he wiped blood from his sword with a rag. "Now find yourselves a place to reinforce the fellows already here. Lieutenant! Make sure they stay close enough together to supply with ammunition—and find whoever is distributing it." There was a respectable magazine within the temple itself. Colonel Sais sought De Russy out at once, the sound of musketry swelling all around, accompanied by a couple of field pieces that were dragged here by enterprising crews coughing canister.

"Coronel!" Sais greeted him. "What do you recommend we do? Perhaps five minutes remain before the grand magazine and powder works explode. There will inevitably be a distraction. Perhaps we can take that opportunity to attempt a breakout? Make our way upriver to Itzincab?"

De Russy was still breathing hard and held up a hand for Sais to wait a moment. Finally, he said, "It is a fine, noble goal to attempt to save as many of our men as we can. That it was your first thought does you credit. But which is more useful to the safety of our people? A possible escape, during which a great many or most of us will be cut to pieces by the enemy or ridden down by their lancers—all without inflicting significant harm on them—or continued organized resistance to the last, killing as many of the enemy as we can?"

Colonel Sais was taken aback by De Russy's apparent determination and took a moment of his own to consider that. "Put in such a way . . . I think the answer is fairly straightforward, don't you?"

Ruberdeau De Russy nodded his agreement and stuck out his hand to shake. "Welcome to the 'Spartan Contingent,' Colonel." Taking note of the much smaller and lower wall perimeter, he added somewhat ironically, "Or perhaps the 'Alamo,' I suppose, and may God have mercy on us all." Noting the confusion spreading on Sais's face, De Russy smiled at him. "Those are references to similar circumstances that others experienced on my world. One in antiquity, the other quite recently. If we had more time, I'd love to describe them. Both are quite inspiring."

"Inspiring or not, I take it the outcome was somewhat . . . unfortunate for the participants, however?" Sais asked dryly as the musketry increased and balls *vipp*ed or warbled past in increasing numbers.

"Sadly true," De Russy conceded, "but both served a higher purpose and shall be remembered forever—as shall we—and I am honored to have you with me, sir."

CHAPTER 15

FEBRUARY 15, 1849

"Comin' in!" came a shout from a sentry in the woods. Moments later, Captain Boogerbear loped in from the forest atop his horse, Dodger, ahead of a half-dozen Rangers. Looking quickly around the camp clearing and immediately noting the absence of more than half the dragoons, Boogerbear growled, rather loudly for him, "What's that idiot Hayne up to now?"

Lieutenant Hanny Cox jumped up from where he'd been sitting with some other officers and NCOs about equidistant between the two guns of his section. Each was in battery pointing outward on opposite sides of the clearing, loaded with canister and half-manned. A sour-faced dragoon, Lieutenant Buisine, only recently raised from sergeant, and Lieutenant Riss of the Rangers, stood up beside him. Riss had just returned from a night scout up the Camino de la Plata and its environs, generally westward, and looked worn-out. Most of his squad was laid out near their horses on the picket line, already asleep. Other Rangers stood and drifted over, as did some of the dragoons. More were on watch in the woods.

"Does anybody even know where he is?" Boogerbear pressed, voice closer to his normal, low rumble. Hanny bit his lip and looked at Buisine, who cleared his throat.

"He, ah . . . left, sir," Buisine finally mumbled and cringed.

Boogerbear blinked before sliding to the ground and relieving his horse of his giant frame. Still holding the reins, he regarded the young dragoon. "Did he, now? Mr. Buisine," he began in his usual, reasonable way, "I recollect back when we first got here, crashed down from the god . . . derned *sky* in the old *Mary Riggs*, right in a forest a lot like this."

Boogerbear rarely really cursed, and, despite his tone, his near slip was a clear indication of his fury. He seemed to contemplate their surroundings a moment, calming himself. "It was a mite warmer on the Yucatán, I'll allow." As they had ascended out of the Great Valley, it had grown colder again, especially at night. "But you was just a private then," he continued, "not scared o' nothin'. Why, I saw you scamper straight up a tree a hunnerd feet tall without a thought, just ta have a look around. I'd'a shivered my insides out ta do such a thing." He grunted. "Now here you're actin' like you think I'll eat you for answerin' a simple question about some *other* idiot."

"Cap'n," Riss interjected, "the 'idiot' we're talkin' about is *his* commandin' officer."

Boogerbear ruffled his huge black beard, then stroked it flat with his fingers, blowing out a frustrated breath. "So? *Somebody's* gonna tell me, an' they best do it quick. Look, son," he said back at Buisine, "nobody's questionin' Hayne's courage. Ain't a braver Irishman alive, I reckon. Why, he helped take Vera Cruz with just a handful o' troops. My pal Sal Hernandez thinks the world o' him." His tone darkened. "But whatever he did before, he's acted a idiot this whole trip, always tryin' to run off an' kill Doms at the slightest whiff of 'em, before we even know what's what. How many there is, if they know we're lookin', or if they're already waitin' for *us*." He slammed the last down hard. "I don't know about Doms, but you try that with Comanches or even Holcanos, they'd lift your hair or eat your head."

That wasn't entirely fair. Few of those present knew what a Comanche was, though the farther the army had advanced, the more they heard strange references to savage, implacable enemies of the Dominion residing in the far north. About where Comanches would be . . . It wasn't fair to the scattering of Holcanos among the Rangers and dragoons either. None would admit to eating their enemies anymore—they'd sworn not to—and there was no absolute proof they had.

Riss interjected. "We put the sneak on some Doms up ahead a few miles, mostly raggedy-assed lancers by the look of 'em, maybe run off from the fightin'." Riss was speaking English instead of Spanya, and it was amusing that his accent so closely resembled those he'd learned most of the language from. "Anyway, there was about thirty of 'em camped about like us, but careless like, an' right by the road."

Buisine cleared his throat again. "Captain Hayne thought he'd catch some prisoners to question."

Boogerbear looked around. "Took about forty men?"

Buisine nodded. "Yes, sir."

"Well," Boogerbear continued, "by the look of it, at least he left the better-armed fellas behind. The ones with Hall carbines an' such. That's somethin', I guess."

There was no doubt that a few breechloading Halls had fallen into enemy hands, but most had ultimately been recovered. Some still couldn't be accounted for, but even if they'd made it to someone among the Doms who might try to re-create them, it wasn't believed they could. Not quickly, anyway. It had been hard enough for the Allied force to make the percussion caps they required, and quite a few people knew how. The machines necessary to achieve the absolutely essential tight tolerances of the weapons themselves, or even revolvers for that matter, didn't yet exist within the Alliance. No one believed the Doms could do better in that respect.

All the same, it was known the Doms had made a careful study of *Isidra*'s steam engine before she was recovered at Vera Cruz and standing orders were to prevent them from obtaining more examples of the few technological advantages the Allies enjoyed, if possible. Most critical of these were the rare revolvers in the possession of the "original" Rangers, for the most part, the excellent M1817 rifles belonging to Felix Meder's command (it wasn't believed that Doms yet understood rifling); the far superior field artillery carriages and limbers, even more than the gun tubes themselves; and Hall carbines, of course.

With an irritated sigh, Boogerbear climbed back on his horse and the watching Rangers quickly trotted to get their own animals. "I reckon it's possible Hayne did right, but there wasn't no rush, sounds like." Boogerbear grumbled, "He should'a waited on a more careful scoutin' job an' I would'a told him a handful o' deserted lancers wouldn't know much o' interest. I've a mind they was bait."

He raised his voice. "Everybody, mount up." He looked at Hanny. "Your boys too. I got a bad feelin' we're gonna need the whole works, ta keep the Doms from gettin' pris'ners o' their own ta question—an' worse. Just as bad, they'll learn we was around here in the first place, an' that'll make 'em harder to put the sneak on. *Idiot* Irishman!" he snapped, whirling Dodger around, as Hanny called to his men to hitch the horses to the limbers and Riss and Buisine started yelling for their riders to break camp and get in the saddle.

They'd only advanced a couple of miles up the road before the muffled, booming clatter of muskets and the shorter musketoons erupted ahead, and there was considerably more of it than Hayne's detachment could maintain.

"Sometimes I hate bein' right," Boogerbear groused. "Don't sound like Hayne got the drop on anybody, does it now? Forward at the trot!" he called louder.

"Pick up the pace, Sergeant Dodd. You're starting to lag," Hanny advised his chief of the piece for Gun Number One. Hanny was riding alongside his section about halfway back from the front. Dodd merely nodded and gave the order. The older man, a professional artilleryman, might still resent Hanny being promoted over him, but he was a professional and would do his job regardless. Besides, Daniel Hahessy, who'd started on his crew and genuinely frightened him, had made it clear that no other behavior would be acceptable to him, personally. The Number One gun closed the gap that had been forming between it and Number Two, the whole section clattering and jingling forward, close behind the Rangers.

The sound of firing intensified, the distinctive *foomp* sound of Dom weapons, due to inferior powder and less uniform bores, rapidly rising much farther beyond the number of enemies they'd been given to expect. Boogerbear peeled off to the side and waited for Hanny. "Hold yer section here, Mr. Cox," he said.

"Section, halt!" Hanny obediently cried. Horses whinnied as their riders pulled them up, slowing the guns and limbers to a stop.

"Don't know what kinda hornet's nest Hayne kicked, so you fellas stay back, set up on the road. I'll leave half the dragoons for your support. You hear that, Mr. Buisine?"

"Yes, sir," the young dragoon officer called, riding up. Boogerbear looked back at Hanny. "I might call you up, or we may come gallopin' back, hell for leather. Either way, be ready."

"Yes, sir," Hanny replied. "You can count on us."

"I know, son. I'll see you soon. One way or t'other."

Boogerbear kicked Dodger forward and dashed back toward the front of his small column. Hanny ordered his crews to unlimber their pieces right on the road while half the remaining dragoons thundered past and seventeen or eighteen of them ranged out on his flanks.

"Aye, an' there 'e goes again, then. The great hulkin' Ranger chargin' off tae lure the heathen Doms down on our hungry guns!" Preacher Mac griped, helping shift the gleaming Number Two 6pdr over to the left side of the road.

"Aye." Hahessy grumped agreement instead of instinctively taking the opposite position as usual, regardless of what he actually thought. "Somebody's always startin' a fight fer us ta finish." His expression turned uncharacteristically thoughtful as he took the sloshing sponge bucket Billy Randall had topped off from a stream in a gully alongside the road and set it on the ground just forward of the gun's axle. "That Boogerbear, though, he's a rare fighter 'isself, at least." He was also probably the only man in the world who physically intimidated Hahessy. "An' if he brings them heathen bastards down on us, he'll stay an' fight 'em as well." He turned to look back at Hanny. "Ye want we should reload that charge o' canister we drew?" Preacher Mac had hooked it with the worm and pulled it out before they moved.

Hanny considered that. The road ahead, already almost empty as the mounted troops swept forward toward the growing fight, would only leave a couple hundred paces of visibility to the front. At such short range, canister was their best choice. "Yes," he said. "Section, load canister."

Boogerbear halted his troopers and waited for the two riders racing back to them from beyond a densely wooded bend. One was a Ranger he'd sent ahead; the other was a young Uxmalo dragoon whose blowing horse almost went down as the lad pulled back on the reins. "Ambush, sir!" the boy almost yelped. "Captain Hayne's holding for the moment, but needs assistance!"

"That's why we're here, son. We won't just gaggle in like a buncha ducks, though. What's up ahead?"

"But sir! My *friends* are up there, outnumbered and surrounded!"

"That may be," Boogerbear agreed more harshly, "but only because *somebody* forgot our mission was scoutin', not destroyin' every Dom we find. What good'll it do your friends if we *all* wind up surrounded an' outnumbered?

Now take a breath an' describe the ground, numbers, an' what the enemy did. The sooner you do, the sooner we'll try to fix this mess."

"I was a fool," Thomas Hayne confessed, pressing hard on a wound low on his left side where a Dom musket ball might've taken off the top of his hip bone. At the very least, it had grazed the bone hard enough to distort the soft lead into a truly wicked gash-slashing shape. "An' that damned bloody Ranger'll never let me forget it either." That wouldn't matter much longer, of course, if that same Ranger didn't come to their aid.

Hayne and his men had dismounted and snuck up on the apparent deserters easily enough, or so they thought, but even before they could shoot, they'd been taken under heavy fire by perhaps as many as two hundred men they'd never known were already in position around the wide, shallow, rocky bowl just off the road. A third of Hayne's dragoons went down under the very first volley, screaming or dropping without a sound, a cloud of blood spray and blue uniform fuzz erupting from their midst. That was when Hayne himself was hit. The rest of his men quickly returned fire, hitting several Doms with heavy charges of drop shot loaded in their musketoons, but Hayne had been stunned into helplessness. The "bait" ran to take cover on the other side of the road, and suddenly, there weren't any easy targets left.

The horse holders probably saved them, tying off the animals and charging forward to shoot some of the encircling Doms from behind, but they were driven back, a couple falling. Hayne heard at least one man gain his horse and gallop away chased by musket balls. That short distraction was the only reason anyone still clustered around him, shooting back as often as they could. Even without an order, Hayne's surviving troopers, one dragging him along, dove back into the cluster of deadfall they'd used to creep forward in the first place.

"Looks like they're mostly lancers," Corporal Xalt said urgently in Spanya. "Some of those damned Reapers too, but how did we never see all those yellow coats an' brass they wear?"

"They covered up!" cried a private, rising to fire over a barkless white trunk. Dropping down as chunks of wood rained on him, he started reloading. "Looked like a gust of yellow wind raising a cloud of leaves—and then they were shooting!"

Hayne had recovered enough of his wits to nod at the good description. "Of course, we weren't really *looking* for them, were we? My fault, and I'm sorry, lads."

No one said anything, but all must know he was right. They'd been too focused on their prey—exactly as the enemy had hoped. Corporal Xalt eased his musketoon up over the tree trunk and waited for the expected explosion of splinters to pass. He then quickly rose, put the weapon to his shoulder, and pointed it at a Reaper standing by a tree, reloading, just thirty paces away. Pulling the trigger, he held his rough aim while the cock leaped forward, the flint in its jaws scraping a shower of sparks off the frizzen as it knocked it forward. Powder flashed in the pan, and the weapon fired, recoiling heavily back. Xalt had just enough time to grunt with satisfaction before the left side of his head exploded in a red-and-tan shower of blood and brains. Tipping back, he collapsed like a wet rag doll.

"Corporal!" the private cried, starting to lunge toward the dead man. "Stay down," Hayne snapped. "You can't help him!"

"We all gonna die," a Holcano dragoon grimly muttered. He didn't seem the least bit afraid, but others sent him nervous glances.

"No, we're not," Hayne insisted. "Captain Beeryman will come." He tried to keep believing that for the next half hour while Doms and his survivors picked one another off. The Doms had the numbers, though, and Hayne couldn't understand why they didn't just charge and hack them apart with their sabers. Dragoons carried sabers as well, however, and the end would be brief but bloody. The only explanations he came up with were: either whoever commanded this enemy was intent on minimizing his casualties, or he knew Hayne's men were hoping for relief and meant to use *them* as bait. It seemed he'd succeeded when a bugle sounded back up the road and many of the Doms turned their attention that way.

"No, Beeryman, you fool. Don't just charge up the road!" Hayne hissed, the pain of his wound getting bad. But "Boogerbear" Beeryman wasn't a fool. Particularly in situations like this. He did suddenly appear, galloping straight up the road with Lieutenant Buisine and a cluster of dragoons, but at the same instant, signaled by the bugle, Rangers opened fire from the woods. They'd taken the time to surround the surrounding enemy, at least on the eastern side of the ambush, and attacked with bloodcurdling cries and a stunning ferocity that took all the Doms' attention and sent them milling into the open, looking behind them. That's when Boogerbear and his small party smashed into them, sabers slashing and the big Ranger firing his revolver at enemies from mere feet away. In the midst of this whiplash attack, Boogerbear's eyes unerringly found Hayne's. "Get out," he shouted. "Your horses are still where you left 'em. Pull back down the road. We'll poke the badger a bit more. Get 'em to chase us."

Mystified, Hayne could only nod. The private sheltering closest to him pulled him to his feet and the pain was like nothing he'd ever experienced. Still, he was determined not to slow the brave trooper down. "I can manage, lad," he said, before starting to run back through the woods. Tears burst out and ran as freely as the blood down his leg. He gasped and slowed. He simply couldn't keep up. The private hesitated, looking back, but Hayne waved him on. "Go. That's an order," he wheezed. "I'll be along." He drew his pistol from the sash around his waist, under his saber belt, and held it up. "I'll be fine. Now go, will ye?"

As soon as the youngster, the last of his surviving men, disappeared from sight, Hayne gasped and sank to a knee. "God," he almost whimpered. A crashing sound drew his attention to a Reaper Monk running toward him with a Dom infantry musket, bayonet stuck in the muzzle. The man seemed to notice him at about the same instant and veered just a little, a triumphant, rabid snarl twisting his face.

Hayne had to cock his pistol and the time that took cost his life. Even as he thumbed the cock all the way back and raised the weapon, the bayonet slammed into his chest and threw him down on his back. It was the breath-stealing blow that actually hurt, like he'd been kicked in the breastbone by a horse. He had a brief instant of consciousness, however, before his heart—which he knew had been pierced—failed him completely. "Very well," he whispered at the man standing over him, trying to jerk the bayonet clear. He didn't know if his words were even audible and didn't care. The Dom Reaper wouldn't understand English anyway. "At least I'll have someone to ride into hell," Hayne said as his vision quickly darkened. The last thing he saw was the flash of his pistol right in his killer's face.

"Here they come a'runnin'!" cried Billy Randall. He'd climbed up on the footboards of the limber in front of the ammunition chest for a better view forward. The horses were still hitched and shifting nervously in the traces, which made the limber an unstable perch.

"*Idiota!* Get down from there before you fall. We *all* see 'em!" shouted Apo Tuin.

"Bound tae have the devil snatchin' at their arses as well," Preacher Mac predicted.

Hanny, pacing between the limbers and guns, almost shouted the "post" command, but everyone was already in position and had their implements as well. He settled for calling, "Stand ready, men, but don't prime." It was still just a nervous order, entirely forgivable as a reminder. Both guns were pointed straight down the road, loaded with canister. All that remained was to pierce the charges with vent pricks and prime the weapons. Hanny wouldn't call for that with Boogerbear's galloping gaggle of horsemen in the line of fire. "Let them through on the flanks, Sergeant Nares," Hanny told the only Ranger who'd stayed behind, in charge of the detachment of dragoons.

"I'll keep 'em from squirtin' 'tween the guns, Lieutenant Hanny," Hahessy assured, raising his rammer staff to menace any horseman who tried to shoot the gap. Even in these circumstances, no gun crew appreciated that sort of behavior. Infantry was allowed to pass between guns, preferably after some warning, but horses, particularly fearful ones, acted unpredictably within the confines of a gun line, endangering the weapons' crews and disturbing the teams hitched to limbers. They needn't have been concerned. Boogerbear was well aware of what he was riding into and already calling for his men to spread out around the guns.

Fifty-two men made it through, quite a few wounded, including several who'd simply been thrown over the saddle and lashed in place. Those animals were led by other troopers. The dragoons to the side of the road made way as they crashed through, clods of mud and splashing droplets from the ditch and stream arcing in the air.

"Get turned around an' back on line," Boogerbear rumbled loud. "They ain't far behind us an' I want a volley as soon as we see 'em." He looked at Hanny. "Lancers, mostly, two hunnerd or so. Us towin' our wounded, they would'a already been on us, I reckon, but was fightin' on foot an' had to fetch their own horses. We'll shoot when they show an' it don't matter if we hit any or not. Our smoke might screen yer guns, help suck 'em in." He grinned. "*You'll* give 'em second thoughts, I expect!"

Hanny nodded. "Section! Prime your pieces and come to the ready!"

"Riders, commence firin'!" Boogerbear unexpectedly shouted almost at once and his Rangers and dragoons unleashed a ragged, clattering volley at the enemy that suddenly appeared. As Boogerbear predicted, Hanny doubted it inflicted much damage. The range was too long for the drop shot most of the Rangers' musketoons were loaded with and a stretch for a Hall, even from a rest. Shooting offhand from shifting, huffing horses made careful marksmanship virtually impossible. The volley did make a lot of smoke, however, and Hanny just caught a glimpse of a dense clot of yellow-clad horsemen charging around the bend.

"Gun Number One . . . fire!" he cried. Dodd's gun roared and leaped back from the swarm of musket balls it unleashed like a gigantic shotgun, smoke roiling down the road. "Gun Number Two, fire," Hanny yelled and Tani Fik gave the lanyard a brisk yank, moving only his hand at the wrist. The odd-shaped hammer of the Hidden's lock snapped down on the primer, igniting the second gun. Another cloud of canister sheeted downrange. "Reload canister!" Hanny immediately yelled.

In the brief relative silence that followed while everyone reloaded carbines, musketoons, and cannon, Hanny could hear screeching horses and wailing men. He also heard thundering hooves and knew, whatever havoc they'd wrought, the Doms were coming on.

"Run, Billy!" Apo told Billy Randall after dropping a fixed load of canister in the young man's leather gunner's haversack. Billy scampered forward, pausing only to raise the flap so Hanny could see he was indeed carrying what had been called for. Hanny waved him on. Stopping outside the left wheel of the gun, Billy raised the flap again so Preacher Mac could pull the charge out, raise it over the wheel, and turn to insert it in the muzzle. Hahessy was waiting, rammer head poised, and swiftly, firmly seated the load down the barrel to the breech. Hoziki took his thumb off the vent. He'd already guided the gun onto the target with the handspike when it was rolled back into battery. As always, careful aiming wasn't crucial when shooting canister. Now he pricked the charge through the vent and tended the hammer while Tani stretched the lanyard once more. When Tani was in position, he nodded, and Hoziki primed the gun. Stepping quickly outside the right wheel, he raised his hand.

"Gun Number Two's ready, sir!"

Hanny hesitated an instant, waiting while the meager breeze stealing through the woods cleared a little more smoke. Hall carbines were firing again. Dark animals and bright uniforms were bearing down quickly; flashes came from polished lance heads coming down.

"Number Two, *fire!*"

The enemy was coming fast, already within fifty to a hundred paces. This time, Hanny saw the dreadful effect of what his guns did. As always, even standing behind the gun, the overpressure of the blast compressed his chest and slapped his face. He was used to it now, even vaguely welcomed it. It was considerably harder on Hahessy and Preacher Mac. Standing just outside the axles, they'd actually be slightly in *front* of the muzzle by the time the piece finished recoiling on a smooth surface like this. Yet the pressure crashing forward was sufficient by itself to smash the very closest men and horses like overripe melons. That was only incidental to its even deadlier purpose of spewing ninety .69 caliber musket balls at a much higher velocity in a denser pattern than the previous shot achieved at greater distance.

Squalling horses and shrieking men went down in a blood-spraying heap. Other animals, only lightly or not hit themselves, snapped legs and other bones crashing headlong into those already down, squashing screaming riders they rolled on. Intermingled with the prolonged *thwopp*ing of balls tearing flesh was the gruesome crackle of those breaking bones.

Raised by loving parents and in a church deeply concerned for his soul, Hanny had always done his best to guard it himself. At the moment, and previously more often than he could recall, he'd almost thought he actually felt his soul falling to pieces and drifting away, like crumbs of dry bread in the crashing sea that brought him here. He mourned his soul and feared how he'd manage, what he'd become, without it. That didn't stop him from roaring, "Gun Number One, fire!"

Sergeant Dodd's 6pdr coughed its own canister and leaped back on the road, brake chain jangling and breech clanging loud on the elevation screw. Carbines and musketoons thumped and clattered, men yelled and screamed, and incoming fire was growing as well. The lancers had abandoned their charge. It simply wasn't possible to drive it home on a road so choked with fallen men and animals. Those behind the ones who'd tried now split off to either side of the road and dismounted to fight on foot, from cover once more. A musket ball whizzed close enough by Hanny's head that he felt it pass. Rangers and dragoons were falling or jumping off their rearing, wounded horses.

"Get down," Boogerbear bellowed. "Horses to the rear an' take cover!" Casually, he walked over to Hanny, oblivious to the warbling death that followed. "What can you do for us now?" he asked Hanny, who was wondering that himself. He could see individual Doms here and there, rising up behind fallen trees to shoot, but there wasn't much of a target left for artillery. Unless . . .

"Section, load solid shot," he called. "We'll put fire on the deadfall and smash it up. The enemy won't enjoy the splinters we throw, at the least."

Boogerbear nodded. "Try that," he said, "but have your boys hunker down, best they can, when they ain't doin' their duties."

"I was about to move my limbers back, make it harder for them to hit our horses," Hanny replied. "Farther to run for our ammunition bearers, but they're smaller targets."

"Fine," Boogerbear said, "but take a couple shots first. I'll leave it up to you. If yer helpin', stay put an' keep at it. I'll send Rangers in the woods to flank the devils while you an' the dragoons keep 'em pinned. If you ain't doin' any good, though, just pull yer guns back. No sense gettin' chewed up for nothin'."

"We got our own muskets," Hahessy pointed out.

"Sure you do, an' I know you boys can use 'em," Boogerbear answered mildly. "But I don't know many fellas with muskets who can jump up an' do what *you* fellas can. This ain't a 'do or die' day, not yet. Save yer 'last stand' fightin' for one o' those."

It wasn't much of a battle compared to others Hanny had experienced, but in terms of concentrated slaughter and sheer determined ferocity, it was certainly a memorable fight. The marksmanship of these Doms was better than average as well. Even armed only with their own musketoons, they took a steady toll on Buisine's dragoons. Hanny had his men hunker down out of sight or take cover behind the gun itself whenever they didn't simply have to expose themselves. His roundshot started smashing the enemy cover to bits, spraying lethal splinters into Doms. In spite of a couple of horses wounded in the traces before Hanny ordered the limbers back, some superficial but growing damage to his gun carriages, and several wounds sustained by his crews, Hanny judged that his section's presence remained worth the risk.

Still, as the day wore on, neither side seemed to gain an advantage. The

Doms couldn't displace them and certainly couldn't overrun them, but there were still more Doms than they could cope with as well. More worrying; the longer the fight lasted, the more likely it was the enemy would be reinforced. Of course, the Doms might be thinking that too. Apparently, they were.

"*Basta!*" came a harsh, frustrated shout, closer in the woods than Hanny would've thought. "*Basta! Haya paz! Deja de disparar!*"

"Who's that, then?" Hahessy asked, crouching by the muzzle, waiting to ram the next round.

"One o' them Doms, I ken," replied Preacher Mac, face screwed up in confusion. "Sounds like he's callin' tae stop the shootin'. His own men, an' us as well!"

"Yer soul ta the divil!" Hahessy exclaimed. "That's a black, festerin' lie!"

"Call *me* a liar, will ye?" Preacher Mac flared.

"Enough!" Hanny snapped. "It's true, Hahessy. Mac's right."

The shooting was already tapering off, likely as much from surprise as anything.

"Stop shootin'," Boogerbear called out. "Reload an' stay ready, but hold yer fire." He stood from where he'd been kneeling in the left-side ditch with some of his Rangers, an unfired Colt revolver in hand, and walked to the middle of the road. Only a couple shots followed him, missing by a considerable distance, and the same Dom voice, furious now, berated the men who fired.

Hanny, also crouching, slowly stood to join Boogerbear. "What do you think, sir?" he asked.

Boogerbear slightly lifted his big shoulders and shook his head. "Can't think o' nothin' but how weird this is."

With no shooting at all, a youngish-looking Dom officer, clearly hesitant, revealed himself in the trees. Forcibly standing as erect as he was able, he marched into view and advanced toward the road, directly in front of Hanny's guns. Another, even more hesitant-looking Dom soldier followed.

"Looks like they want tae talk," Preacher Mac observed.

"I'll be . . . So it does," Boogerbear agreed.

"A foul, treacherous trick it is," Hahessy warned, deliberately, even malevolently ramming a fixed roundshot down the barrel of the Number Two gun while glaring at the Doms who stopped right in front of it, perhaps thirty paces away.

"Could be"—Boogerbear nodded—"but I've always had a curious streak. Stay where you are, Mr. Buisine. You too, Mr. Riss," he called out louder, then glanced at Hanny. "I'll take Mr. Cox along." Immediately stepping forward, he passed between the guns. Hanny hurried after him.

Picking their way past the mangled bodies of horses and men, they stopped about three steps from the enemy, both of whom had been looking solemnly around them, but now eyed the revolver still in Boogerbear's hand with what looked like a mix of interest and fear. Noting that, Boogerbear frowned and holstered the weapon.

"Reckon I'm a touch distracted," he allowed in Spanya. Hanny was examining the young officer—*very* young, the black mustache and chin whiskers barely coloring his face—and Hanny suspected they were close to the same age. *Somewhere past sixteen. Twenty at most*, he thought. Apparently remembering how the officer had spoken, Boogerbear offered, "I can manage regular Spanish."

"Spanya is entirely satisfactory," the young Dom stated, then continued, "I am Teniente Yatsh Juaris, originally of the Third Lancero Ala, Army of God in the west, currently commanding the three *turmae* engaged with you here." He gestured to his companion. "This is Senior Decurion Yulis." He waited expectantly a moment before asking, "Who do I have the honor of fighting today?"

Boogerbear tilted his head to the side as if to say, "Why the hell not?" then answered, "I'm Cap'n Bandy Beeryman, in charge o' whatever Rangers an' other mounted fellas Major Anson gives me." He waved around. "These fellas, right now." He gestured at Hanny. "An' this is Lieutenant Hannibal Cox, First Section . . ." Boogerbear grinned. "You don't need to know which battery."

Juaris looked impressed. "You are the one they call 'Boogerbear'!" he exclaimed. "Chief minion of the Devil Anson himself!" He pointed at Hanny. "And you are part of the Black devil Barca's battery!" He quickly looked at the decurion. "We have been fighting their best!"

"I won't even ask how you know all that. Figger *I* already know," Boogerbear said, certain that spies in the Holy City were still, somehow, getting word out. "But here we are talkin'. What's on your mind? You bushwacked some o' my dragoons—well done, by the way—but I reckon that means you never got the word from 'His Super Holiness' that the war's s'posed to be over."

It was Juaris's turn to frown. "I did . . . hear that the usurper, the Blood Cardinal Don Hurac, presumed to make such a declaration," he began cautiously. "Unfortunately, your . . . new Supreme Holiness and the one whose orders I am bound to obey do not agree about that. Nor, I assure you, will General Xacolotl, commanding the Gran Cruzada." He paused a long moment as if considering how much more he should say. Finally, he took in a long breath of his own. "General Xacolotl and his army are very close. Much closer than you might imagine," he warned significantly.

"So what? For all you know, I can whistle up another regiment or two of dragoons. Might've even done it already."

Juaris nodded. "That is the point of this meeting. At present, I have more men"—he gave Hanny's pair of 6pdrs a respectful look—"but you have done much to equalize that disparity. All that can result from prolonging our engagement is a wasteful effusion of blood, perhaps even mutual annihilation, to no real effect. At least until one or both of us is reinforced," he hastened to add. "How strange it would be if we precipitated a major battle here today." He glanced down at the blood-smeared road. "While that might be pleasing to God," he mused aloud with an expression of distaste, "it will be most unpleasant for our respective commands." He looked up. "I would like to propose an alternative."

Boogerbear blinked, eyes betraying confusion and curiosity. After a moment, he motioned for Juaris to continue. Juaris did so. "Essentially, I propose that we both disengage and withdraw from this place, and at least for a brief time, neither of us should scout this far and risk further contact. For my part, I can promise this because I currently command *all* the mounted forces nearby and . . . I would like to see some of them survive the coming holocaust. I do *not* want to fight you again to no purpose."

"A brief time?" Boogerbear asked pointedly. "How long's that?"

"Sadly, not long. I told you the Gran Cruzada draws near. When its mounted elements begin to arrive, within days, I suspect, I'll no longer be in a position to direct our activities. In the meantime, however, if you remain back as well, I shall not fight you—until superior officers among the Gran Cruzada draw my men forward once more." He paused. "If you agree, I shall require . . . concessions, however. For me to return with half my men killed or wounded and report to Holy Patriarcha Tranquilo—"

"Wait," Boogerbear snapped. "That slimy bastard's with *you*?"

Obviously realizing his mistake, Juaris could only nod. "Yes," he confirmed.

"We are encamped with a very *large* force rather nearby." He glanced at the decurion again. "And regardless of my own opinion of Tranquilo, you cannot have him. As I said, he is sufficiently well protected that he feels safe and content to await the arrival of the Gran Cruzada as well. My condition," he went on, "is that you allow me to take the bodies of the men you have lost back with me as proof we 'destroyed' you. We *did* ambush you, as you say, and our losses were significantly greater than yours," he added bitterly, "but the fact we 'held the field' and recovered your fallen should allow me to keep breathing and honor my word to you."

Boogerbear pulled on his huge black beard. "We'd sure rather not leave our dead to be hacked up or put up on poles. Or eaten, for all we know. An' you haven't said what's in it for me. Seems I'm still better off to just kill you an' bring up more forces to kill Tranquilo."

Juaris straightened. "First, though I am sure that Tranquilo will wish to . . . despoil your dead in some outrageous way, I give you my word they will ultimately be cremated and honorably interred. I believe that is your way?"

Boogerbear grunted but nodded. "On campaign on *this* world it is, most often. Keeps the boogers from diggin' 'em up an' eatin' 'em. But again, what's in it for me an' mine? You're askin' a awful lot, an' why should I care what Tranquilo does to you?"

Juaris nodded slowly. "Would you believe me if I told you that even now there are plans to . . . exterminate a large percentage of the Gran Cruzada—any large standing force at all—after your invasion is destroyed? Entire towns behind the Gran Cruzada have already been pillaged and eradicated of life simply to *feed* Xacolotl's army and prevent word it has returned to confront another threat from spreading? Oh, I am sure some forces will be sent back down your line of advance to destroy whatever troops you left behind and reoccupy cities, but only those who think like Tranquilo and his Blood Priests will be allowed to live, in the end."

Hanny was intrigued by the expression of outraged horror that appeared on the decurion's face. This might be the first he'd heard of it.

Juaris sighed. "Personally, having had these outrages related to me from the lips of Tranquilo himself, I would much rather follow the command of *your* Supreme Holiness and end the war here and now. I would gleefully *join* you—if the bulk of my men were not still in Tranquilo's power. I have sworn to save them, you see." He gestured at the heap of bodies in the road, practically at their feet. "This does not help me do that.

"But you asked what you would get in return. First, no attack from me until the Gran Cruzada advances on the Holy City. Even then, I and my men will not personally attack if it is in our power to avoid it. I give you my word." He hesitated. "Of course, if that . . . situation is ever reversed, I would appreciate the same consideration in return.

"Second, you will have no need to scout dangerously further to discover your enemy's disposition for yourself. I will supply you with all the information I obtain and will continue to do so if we arrange a suitable place for small parties to meet." He paused to consider. "Perhaps for that, this place might suit well enough. I am sure we will all remember it," he added bleakly.

"There's one problem, I think," Hanny pointed out. "The Reaper Monks among you. I caught glimpses of a few, at least. There are more," he added, pointing at the heap of dead in the road. Several Reaper corpses were among them.

"Yes," Juaris agreed. "There are quite a number of them among my men back at Teocaltiche. That is the unfortunate town where the Gran Cruzada shall join us. In any event, I am actually outnumbered by Reapers and am bound to allow them to accompany my patrols. Another reason this shall be dangerous for us all. Sadly," he said in an ironic tone, "it would seem that all those with me today have fallen in battle." He shook his head with more irony. "You heretics *do* so hate the Reapers and clearly specifically targeted them, especially when they attempted to flee. It is truly shocking how many of them were shot or stabbed in the back."

Boogerbear's eyebrows rose in surprise. "Tragic, ain't it?" He almost laughed.

"Is it not?" Juaris agreed. "There are many more of the . . . depraved creatures, however, and I shall just have to be extra careful. Particularly if we continue to meet."

Boogerbear was tugging at his beard. "Gotta think about this. Huh. You say 'days' before more o' your horse gets here. Our little truce can't last long an' there won't be *many* meetin's. When'll the rest o' the Gran Cruzada get to . . . what did you say? Teocaltiche?"

Juaris looked down again. "Holy Patriarcha Tranquilo is confident that advance legions will arrive within the month."

"Huh," Boogerbear grunted again. "Might be easier just to finish our little fight. Wouldn't have to *trust* you, then. Weird thing is, if you'd up an' volunteered to run off with us, I'd'a just shot you dead, right here. Too damn convenient to lie an' then jump us when we was outnumbered an' all ridin' together. Don't make sense for you to quit fightin' at all, to be honest—Doms don't do that—unless you're tellin' the truth." He tugged even harder on his beard. "Lemme think. You say our poor dead boys—no wounded, mind, an' I'll have to check 'em, hear? But they'll get treated right"—he scowled—"after Tranquilo's through playin' with 'em?"

"Again, you have my word. I will see to it myself, somehow."

"Hmm."

"DO YOU THINK we did right?" Hanny asked Boogerbear later as the reduced column moved east. They wouldn't go far before they left the road and made a new camp, but they'd secure it more carefully than ever, just in case.

"Don't rightly know," Boogerbear grumped. "Just a feelin', I reckon."

"I hated to leave Captain Hayne with them, or *any* of our men," Lieutenant Buisine quietly murmured. They'd all seen Hayne and knew he died well, for what it was worth. More than half his men had died well with him.

"Me neither," Riss agreed. "But worst case, we would'a lost a lot more men in a no-point fight. That was Hayne's fault," he reminded Buisine. "An' there just wasn't any disengagin' from that many of 'em."

"He couldn't know it was an ambush," Buisine defended.

"Yeah he could. Us Rangers could'a *told* him if he wasn't in such a rush."

Buisine seemed prepared to argue, so Hanny spoke up.

"Captain Hayne was a good officer. A good man," he said, also quiet. "Probably a better lieutenant than captain, though. Like me. And aside from our casualties, it might've all turned out for the best," he continued. "We got a lot of information for Colonel Cayce. We know roughly where the closest enemy concentration is, and about how long we have left to get ready for the biggest army they've got. A month," he said, massaging his brow, wondering how long it would take the pair of Rangers they'd dispatched with that news to carry it.

"Longer than that to get to the Holy City," Buisine pointed out. "Not much, though, I guess."

"*If* that Juaris fella told the truth," Boogerbear rumbled. "Which maybe we'll know tomorrow, when Riss makes the first meetin' we set up." He glanced at the Ocelomeh Ranger. No one would sniff out treachery quicker than Riss. He made a growling noise deep in his throat. "I ain't never been paid for strategyzin', just fightin'. My feelin', my sense o' things—my gut, I reckon—has always been part o' my fightin' . . . so . . . I guess we'll see, won't we?"

CHAPTER 16

FEBRUARY 20, 1849

Helm hard over, HMS *Tiger* swung into the wind and wallowed to a pitching stop as sailors shoved their way roughly through the smelly, huddled mass of people choking the ship's deck. Finally reaching the shrouds, they raced up the ratlines to furl the foretop'sl. "Let fall!" hollered Captain Eric Holland through a speaking trumpet at waiting men on the fo'c'sle. He was just too tired to conjure his normal, powerful, quarterdeck voice. The starboard anchor splashed down in the brown, tumultuous water between the island fort and coastal city of Vera Cruz.

Just as Holland's natural vigor ordinarily belied his probable eighty-odd years (the true total eluded even him), the waters here were normally a clear blue topaz. A storm had taken its toll on both, pounding the elderly *Tiger*, roughly the same age as Holland, all the way up from Gran Lago City, far to the south-southeast, before rushing ahead to scour Vera Cruz the previous day. The sea in the anchorage was still stirred up. This morning had dawned bright and warm under a cloudless sky, however, and the sun raised steam from *Tiger*'s damp timbers.

Ship's too old for this much work, Holland thought to himself. *So am I*, he had to concede. *Tiger* had been built as a heavy fifty-gun frigate and served for decades in the British Navy without a truly appropriate role. Too heavy and slow to catch other frigates, she was also too fragile and lightly armed for a place in the line of battle, where first and second raters could pound her to splinters. She'd still had a long, relatively undistinguished career before being retired, largely disarmed, and sold into the merchant service. That's how she wound up on this world, carrying European passengers away from the inconvenience of war in another Vera Cruz after the American amphibious landing. The same . . . indescribable phenomenon that brought Colonel Cayce and his soldiers to this different earth swept *Tiger* along as well. Unfortunately, most of her passengers, minus Samantha Wilde and Angelique Mercure, wound up in the merciless hands of the Doms. Even now, little was known of their fates.

Tiger had been repaired and rearmed to a degree, her gundeck reinforced to bear a handful of very heavy 36pdr siege guns captured from the Dominion and provided with new carriages. She may not carry as many guns as she once had, but was arguably more powerful now. No enemy warships they'd seen could bear such massive guns, nor could they survive even a single shrewd strike at the waterline. Still, *Tiger* had been very busy, almost constantly at sea, even fighting the occasional action. The most damaging battle she'd endured had been during her last visit to the besieged city of Uxmal, where she fought both sides to smash through a far superior force. Since then, with only what repairs her crew could make under way or during brief stays in Allied-occupied ports, she, along with the steamship *Isidra*, the Imperial ship-sloop *Nemesis*, and a large number of captured Dom vessels, had been transporting garrisons and "liberated" civilians from those suddenly vulnerable ports to Vera Cruz and Techolotla.

Striding past a number of those milling, miserable, but increasingly excited refugees, even here on his quarterdeck, Holland leaned on the larboard quarter rail and gazed out in the direction of Vera Cruz.

"Looks a little disheveled," observed First Lieutenant William Semmes, stepping up beside him. Semmes was one of *Tiger*'s original British crew. Holland liked him anyway, and that would've shocked anyone who knew him long or well. He'd been aboard USS *Essex* during her fight with HMS *Phoebe* and HMS *Cherub* at Valparaiso back in 1814 and had hated the British ever since—almost as much as he hated carronades.

"Aye, a bit," Holland conceded. "A few roofs knocked ahoo an' some damage to the docks an' nearby warehouses. Anchored ships don't look too bad, but some that was tied ta the docks've been banged about. Defenses stood up well enough, both ta seaward an' what I can see of the landward works from here." He shook his head slowly. "I wouldn't worry near as much about Uxmal if we'd lavished as much labor on protectin' it as we have Vera Cruz. Nobody could take this place from land or sea."

"We never thought Uxmal would be endangered. How could we? Colonel Cayce's army stood between it and any threat we were aware of," Semmes consoled. "And Vera Cruz is our most important port in this ocean. Anyone would've thought the enemy would focus his attention here." He pointed to redirect Holland's gaze. "I wasn't speaking of the city, however. I was thinking of her."

Holland grunted. The private ship of war *Nemesis* was herding a pack of stubby, galleon-shaped vessels into the inner harbor. Sleek and trim, the swift but lightly armed vessel under the command of Captain Stanley Jenks looked shipshape enough. Semmes was talking about their steamer, USS *Isidra*, probably the only thing like her on this world. Even as they watched, she was taking in sail and raising steam so she could steer straight for the docks. *Well, she can do it too,* Holland grumbled to himself. *Move an' maneuver right into the wind, wherever she likes. An' that ol' pirate Randy Sessions crows about it enough.* The ship had taken its own beating, though, and had probably steamed continuously for longer periods of time in the last few months than since she was built. Her new masts looked weathered and gray, and the recent new coat of black-and-white paint on her hull was dingy and streaked. Gusts of escaping steam mixed with her boiler smoke, a clear sign her pistons needed new seals.

Despite her engine, *Isidra* had been built to rely on the wind for primary propulsion just like everything else afloat. Sadly, even though she had a nice, sleek hull, her own propellor acted like a sea anchor when she was under sail alone, and that made her dreadfully slow. Now, not very large to begin with, she was further handicapped by first a pair, then a trio of 36pdrs mounted on pivoting carriages. That was a considerable burden even before the tons of wood fuel for her boiler and far too many more refugees.

"I'm told those piston seals're easy ta replace. They're just leather, ain't they? Lots o' leather hereabouts. All the same, considerin' the trouble we took ta get her back, I hate ta wear her out. With her heavy guns that can shoot to either side, an' bein' able ta keep 'em on target an' outa the enemy's field o' fire, she could chew up a whole fleet like we ran into at Uxmal, all by herself."

That was unlikely, but truth be told, Holland vaguely envied his old, half-Black, former shipmate friend who had command of her. He could've had the ship himself, of course, but was devoted to *Tiger* and too set in his ways to "learn" steam. He snorted. They'd only started with a very few men who knew anything about steam at all, and every one was black. A few of *Isidra*'s engine and boilermen had barely survived starvation by the Doms long enough to be rescued with the ship. The rest of the crew and all the passengers were sold as slaves or sacrifices, and these had only been preserved to provide technical assistance and were very keen for revenge. Daney Reese, a miraculous survivor of the transport *Xenophon*'s literally upside-down crash on this world, had spent several years as an engineman on a Mississippi riverboat and was now *Isidra*'s chief engineer.

"An' she does look a little ragged," Holland agreed with Semmes, tone a little more cheerful.

Semmes looked at him strangely. "I thought you and Captain Sessions were friends."

Holland shrugged. "Sure. But what's that got to do with whose ship looks smarter? *Tiger*'s older'n Noah an' been through worse. *Isidra* ain't even been in a fight. But thanks mainly ta yer tireless efforts, an' the lads, o' course, I'll lay that ol' Randy Sessions is wipin' his eye over how much better our ship looks than his!"

Semmes chuckled, then nodded toward shore. "Look there. A vast shoal of longboats heading this way, to take our passengers off."

"Thank God," Holland sighed. "I hate ta keep the lads any longer than I must, but soon as we're clear o' 'cargo'"—he drew his lips back from a surprisingly complete set of teeth—"men an' women pukin' wherever the notion takes 'em, babies shittin' in *amazin'* directions, at lethal velocities . . ." He shook his head. "We'll pump the decks clean above an' below an' scour 'em down. The ship reeks like a slop bucket on a whaler, by God. Then it's liberty fer all, except an anchor watch." He grinned wickedly. "Defaulters fer that. Pass the word there'll be pardons tomorrow fer them that do their duty—an' a rope fer them that don't."

Isidra had passed to landward of the anchoring ships and was wheezing her way right up to the dock. Quite a few of the approaching boats had gathered near other vessels, but nearly a dozen were rowing on over to *Tiger*. Holland recognized one man in particular standing in the bow of the closest.

"Why, it's that old villain Finlay down there!" Holland exclaimed in surprise at the sight of an old shipmate from *Mary Riggs*. Mr. Finlay had been the ship's purser and had, along with an Uxmalo named Samarez, initiated the creation of an "Allied Quartermaster Corps." Despite Holland's opinion that Finlay—all pursers, in his experience—was a thief, the rather scruffy-looking man in old-world civilian attire, along with his partner, had worked wonders establishing entire industries in various cities where nothing like them existed before in order to supply the needs of the army. Not to mention Holland's growing fleet of ships. Finlay and Samarez had been lacking in terms of organizational and logistical expertise on the necessary scale, however, and somewhat to the surprise of many, Dr. Newlin and the former Samantha Wilde had helped sort that out, putting enough equally talented people in place to relieve Finlay and Samarez of a task wholly beyond them. That left them free to work on what they did best. Holland hadn't seen them, but remembered the two men had brought shiploads of tools and workers to Vera Cruz to re-create many of the same industries they'd previously established farther away. Possibly chief among these was another gunpowder mill and ammunition works.

"An' young Cap'n Orno's with him, it seems. You remember him: Father Orno's son." Holland chuckled. "One of 'em, anyway. Don't remember how many there are all together. Orno's not yet forty, but that little priest's wife must've been continuously pregnant since they met, poor woman."

"Which one is he?" Semmes asked. There were several uniformed men in the boat.

"The *tall* one by Finlay." Holland grinned. "I know, it's a curiosity ta be sure. Father Orno barely tops five feet, an' his wife's shorter yet."

The boat hooked on, and Finlay and the soldiers scrambled up the side. Holland was touched to see them all salute both the Stars and Stripes streaming above the quarterdeck and the Union Jack at the masthead. Semmes practically radiated pleasure.

"Good day, Captain Holland," Finlay said stiffly. "I had rather hoped my days in an open boat were over, but it was believed by some"—he frowned—"that the news I bear might be better received from an . . . acquaintance. No others besides Captain Orno and myself being readily available . . ." He gestured vaguely.

"What's everyone else up to today?" Holland asked. "Some" obviously meant "people he liked better than Finlay," and his understanding of that was clear in his voice.

"The same thing we do every day, Captain," Finlay sourly replied. "Either fighting a war, preparing to defend Vera Cruz if necessary, or providing the means to do those things."

"Good day, Capitan Holland," Captain Orno said. "I volunteered to come," he added.

"Very well. You must have bad news, then." Holland waved around. "Can we at least get started transferrin' all these people while I hear it?"

"By all means," Finlay agreed. "We must clear all the ships as quickly as possible."

Holland had a sinking feeling when he heard that. "I take it we won't be here long."

Finlay shook his head. "Just until you've watered and victualed. Those things will be brought out to you." He looked around, taking in the condition of the ship. "Have you need of any sailcloth? Cordage?"

Holland shook his head, fuming. "Not *Tiger*. Not yet. I can't speak for the other ships." He paused, considering. "Captain Razine's *Roble Fuerte* blew out a top'sl in the storm—and *Isidra* ain't goin' anywhere without repairs."

"We need every—"

Holland held up a hand. "We need *Isidra* ready ta fight. Is that what ya need us ta do?"

"Perhaps not at once," Finlay hedged.

"Fine. Then she stays here an' gets ready to. The shape she's in, she's too slow an' can't carry enough people ta justify delayin' repairs." He looked at Finlay and Orno. The other officers had begun helping *Tiger*'s crew organize their passengers into boatloads, counting them off and positioning them into groups so they'd know how many boats would be needed and the refugees would be ready to board them quickly. Finally, Holland scratched the white stubble on his chin. "If there ain't a fight in the offin', I take it an emergency's arisen that requires us ta redouble our passenger service?"

"I'm afraid so," Captain Orno answered heavily. "The commanders of some of the other ships, Mr. Sessions, Mr. Razine, Mr. Jenks, for example, have been alerted to join us here. It seems that . . ." Orno took a deep breath. "Something dreadful has happened."

―――――

"Uxmal has fallen, then?" asked Captain Stanley Jenks of *Nemesis*. Tall and somewhat portly, Jenks had a long, dark, braided beard, and though he was much younger, his face was even darker than the lifelong tan Holland wore. He'd explained that nearly everyone in the Empire of the New Britain Isles, far across the Pacific Ocean, was descended from a variety of races: white Europeans, Indians, Malays, Black Africans, even Chinese. Most recently, they'd added quite a number of Doms to the mix, first trading for, then abducting—possibly saving from sacrifice, they rationalized—female slaves. Their forebears had crewed and been passengers aboard a trio (then a pair) of Honorable East India Company ships that found themselves on this world a century before. Jenks's particular friend and second-in-command, Mr. Blakeslee, had accompanied him. Just about every ship had sent more than one representative, and even while *Tiger* swiftly disembarked her human cargo, her crew attempting to hoist up water and salt pork casks, lowering the empties at the same time, the quarterdeck had grown more crowded.

"That is more than likely true," Finlay conceded. "Colonel De Russy was quite specific about the odds he faced and implied in his note that the . . . uh . . . dragon wouldn't be released to fly to Vera Cruz unless it seemed all was lost. There was more information and a few personal sentiments intended for Alcaldesa Periz and Colonel Cayce, but it was clear De Russy hoped they'd remain as confidential as possible." He worriedly ran a hand across his sweaty forehead. "I can only imagine how the *alcaldesa* will receive this news. I expect she'll demand to return the army to the Yucatán at once."

Holland shook his head. "You misjudge her, I think. At one time, she might've, but with her people largely safe—the note said that too—I'll wager she focuses on winnin' the war. Can't do that by backin' up." He shrugged. "Uxmal—anywhere—is just a place, now. Home is where your people are. Sailors an' soldiers know that as well as anyone. I reckon she's been in charge o' Fifth Division long enough ta know it too. We'll get Uxmal back after we whip the Doms," he ended confidently.

"That may be. I hope you're right," Finlay responded doubtfully. "But the fact remains that Don Hurac's command to his various forces in the field that the war be ended has been ignored. At least on the Yucatán. We must assume the Gran Cruzada, wherever it is, will do the same. I hope Colonel Cayce has made sufficient preparations to defend the Holy City."

"How long will it take this terrible news to reach there?" asked Captain Razine.

"A few more days. We sent the entire message from De Russy by semaphore, but the towers only extend as far as Puebla, as yet. Couriers must take it the rest of the way."

"Why not just send the beastie that brought it here wingin' off tae the 'Holy City,' then?" asked Blakeslee. "Let the dragon carry the news tae Colonel Cayce."

Captain Orno frowned and spread his hands. "Unfortunately, we don't know if the creature has ever been there. You're all aware dragons can only be relied upon to carry messages to places they are familiar with, correct?" His question was met with nods.

"So," Stanley Jenks continued that line of thought, "the bugger is just as likely to take the news—along with whatever you included about what you mean for us to do, for example—straight to the enemy."

"Very astute, Captain Jenks," Finlay complimented.

"Which is what?" Holland demanded, growing impatient. "You rowed out here all in a rush for us ta get back under way, an' now we're wastin' time."

Finlay rolled his eyes. "Are you *already* quite prepared to sail, Captain Holland?"

Holland frowned, watching the last civilians from Gran Lago disappearing over the side at last, but casks were still coming aboard while pumps splashed water on the deck and crewmen swept it around with brooms, pushing it toward the scuppers. "Not *quite* yet," he admitted.

"So it's back to Gran Lago for us, then, to carry off the last people there?" Captain Jenks asked.

Finlay nodded. "Gran Lago, Frontera, anywhere we left people behind. I will remind you that De Russy also reported more troops approaching Uxmal from the west. No ships were seen to leave the enemy fleet in the bay, so they had to have been landed by another, unknown force that joined the first through the Pass of Fire. That, or it came from Pidra Blanca after *it* fell.

Either way, it represents even more enemy ships than we were aware of that might be on their way to threaten already diminished outposts." He paused and blinked. "Or possibly even heading here."

Captain Orno continued, "In any event, that's the reason for the rush. To save the rest of our scattered people—and any more locals who want to come, of course—and return as fast as you can to defend Vera Cruz." He sighed. "Colonel Cayce, Alcaldesa Periz, and the entire expeditionary force of Allied cities are on their own in the Holy City. I do not diminish what they do to gain the ultimate victory there, but if Vera Cruz falls, there'll be no more supplies for them and nowhere to fall back on, at need. They will be doomed and everything lost. We must hold this place no matter what."

CHAPTER 17

FEBRUARY 23, 1849

"Even now, I don't really believe it," Leonor confessed to Samantha, her tone still hopeful, but deeply skeptical. "Somethin'll come up. Somethin'll happen." The two of them, along with Varaa-Choon and perhaps a dozen young Uxmalo and Ocelomeh women from the hospital train (Hanny's unofficial fiancé, Izel Tuin, was one), were gathered in a chamber of the huge abandoned villa barely two blocks from the central pyramid that Don Hurac had "given" the army as a more comfortable, and in his mind appropriate, headquarters compound. The place was fairly secure, surrounded by eight-foot walls and taking up an entire city block, but Lewis remained hesitant to actually use it as an HQ, concerned the apparently willing and grateful local staff that came with it would be infiltrated by an ever bolder and more vocal minority in the city that was opposed to his army's presence there. The virtual palace served quite well as an officer's dining hall, however, as well as a social center for diplomatic or less purely martial gatherings. Lewis had made it plain that open, operational discussions were to be avoided in there.

The ladies had appropriated the elaborate, well-furnished chamber as a dressing room, where all but Varaa were busily, cheerfully fussing around a nervous and excited, but extremely uncomfortable Leonor. Their constant motion and frequent touching, experimenting with her hair and makeup or insistently performing final alterations to her dress, was beginning to remind her more of flies buzzing around a corpse than bridesmaids and a few helpers doing a "fitting out," as Samantha called it.

The dress was utterly stunning, with a formfitting bodice practically *smeared* with silver embroidery. The lacy, low-cut collar sort of thing was just as fancy. Leonor was watching the proceedings in a tall silver mirror and had to admit the whole thing looked nice in contrast to her dark skin and hair. When she asked Samantha where she got it, the Englishwoman simply said, "So little faith in my powers of preparation. I have been working on logistics, you know! I had it made in Vera Cruz before we even began this campaign!"

Leonor didn't need a corset, thank God, though Samantha had tried to inflict one on her anyway. The one time she'd worn one, she almost died. Not for lack of oxygen, but because it made her feel too constrained to fight if she had to. The lower part—she thought of it as a skirt, but that seemed too small a name for something so voluminous—flared out over the petticoat and hoops underneath. She actually liked that. Since the flare started just under her ribs, she could still wear both her revolvers down low on her hips, perfectly concealed. She was somewhat concerned that she couldn't remove the getup prior to her own final preparations, a bath for example, because it felt more and more like the thing was being stitched directly to her. Honestly, though, her deepest concern remained that she wouldn't be putting it back on at all. Some calamity would *certainly* arise to make it necessary to postpone the event, and she would, of course, understand. There was a war, after all. Just as worrisome, in a different way of course, was the small possibility she was wrong and she and Lewis Cayce really would finally get married that evening.

Two days after Sira Periz's arrival, Lewis had joined Leonor for breakfast in the lavish, sprawling dining room of the unknown *patricio*'s villa, and during that breakfast, between bites of gallina eggs and something very much like bacon, Lewis proposed to Leonor that they "go ahead and get married" at that very place, two days hence. Leonor had been flabbergasted, elated, furious, and suspicious all at once, but despite the pragmatic and wholly unromantic nature of the suggestion, she could tell by the desperate, sweat-beaded, red-faced expression Lewis wore that the fearless army commander was not only quite sincere, he was horrified by his delivery of the question and utterly terrified of her response.

She blinked, much like Varaa-Choon, who'd been sitting beside her.

"Okay," said Leonor, still blinking. "Two days. Evenin' of the day after tomorrow, ta be precise," she insisted, trying to gain a little control. "Here, as you say, but just family an' friends. Don Hurac too, I guess," she conceded. "He might be put off if we don't invite him. But no big production, no parade through the city or mile-long saber arch. Just a little music, maybe." She thought about it. "Gotta let Reverend Harkin and Father Orno be involved... Damn." She glowered. "Still gonna be a spectacle."

"Of course it will!" Varaa had gleefully proclaimed. "The whole army will want to be here. Obviously, that is impossible, and we must keep it as small as we can for security reasons." Her tail swished as she eyed Lewis. "And whatever service is performed, it will still shock the locals. Remember, Dom 'weddings,' such as they are, though still with a religious aspect for the legitimacy of the thing, more closely resemble the purchase of a slave. The legalities are more for the benefit of the families being joined, to improve their social and financial standing."

"I guess they're in for a shock, then." Leonor chuckled.

"They are," Varaa agreed, tone serious. "Perhaps yet another unpleasant one, for some. Certainly confusing for all." She looked at Lewis again. "I do hate to say this, but especially after the rather painful points you made to Don Hurac, it might not be the best time."

Lewis nodded slowly, looking at Leonor. She was nodding too, in resignation.

"Possibly," Lewis finally said, standing from the overstuffed chair by the long table, "but that's too bad. I finally got the nerve to go ahead with this, and there may not be . . ." He stopped and forced a smile at Leonor. "If you're willing, we'll do it. No matter what."

Leonor stood as well. Then, right in front of many of the army's officers, she embraced its commander.

"Yes," she said. "Finally."

Varaa looked around. "The whole army will know within hours. So will the city. I hope that doesn't stir things up any worse than they already are." She grinned. "Too bad if it does. Whatever is going on below the surface, something like this might bring it into the open, where it can be stepped on. At the very least"—she pointed at Leonor—"your father and his Rangers might sniff out the source."

The rationale and motivation of the objectors was still somewhat vague and by no means monolithic. Some might've been supporters of the previous regime, though they weren't too open about that. Enough "ordinary" Dom priests had resurfaced to make denunciations of Don Hurac hazardous. Then again, despite having benefitted from them, many of those same priests had to be uncomfortable with Don Hurac's quick reforms. Particularly his proscriptions against human sacrifice and attempts to eliminate the strict caste system in the Dominion. His immediate emancipation of all slaves had stirred particular animus, especially among the classes just above them. Free men and hidalgos had staged actual demonstrations, not all of which seemed spontaneous. That made Lewis and Anson even more suspicious of Don Armonia and various of his frequent companions. There'd been no violence aimed directly at Don Hurac's regime or the occupying army as a whole, as yet, though unwary troops caught off by themselves were still being murdered. Some, possibly understandably, did a little killing back, and that seemed to feed the overall resentment. So far, however, most of the violence was confined to the various brawling factions.

As Varaa had intimated earlier, Lewis had very tactfully blamed a confused Don Hurac.

"You wanted these reforms as much as I did!" the new Supreme Holiness accused when the subject came up at a meeting.

"Of course I did," Lewis agreed. "And most of your people will eventually appreciate them. On the other hand, right now, many are baffled by the speed and extent of the change and could mistake your benevolence for weakness. It might've worked better to move a little slower."

Lewis couldn't help feeling a little hypocritical as Corporal Willis and a small escort had fallen in with him as he left the central city villa with Leonor, Varaa, and a beaming Colonel Reed, headed for the "proper" HQ by Don Hurac's pyramid. *Besides*, he'd thought, *Varaa's probably right. She usually is.*

Back in the present, Samantha spoke with certainty. "Colonel Cayce would not *dare* let anything stop this now. If he did, you would be entirely justified in shooting him. Perhaps somewhere nonfatal, but quite excruciating," she equivocated. "We do still need him, I fear. Shoot him in the top of the foot," she decided. "He needn't be able to walk to lead."

Leonor snorted, then frowned. "The more I think about it, the surer I am Lewis'll actually go through with it. 'No matter what,' like he said. That worries me a little too."

"Whatever for, my dear?" Samantha asked, brows arching in surprise.

Leonor shrugged very slightly. "I don't know, an' that's what bothers me most. I . . ." She paused, then restarted. "It's just that he's always been so sure of things. So damn confident." She managed a smile. "Even about me. Course, I gave him plenty of reason. Here lately, though . . ."

Varaa broke in. "I have seen this too," she said lowly, so no one else would hear. "Even as we have been more successful, all our goals at last in our grasp, I have seen him . . . not indecisive or afraid, or anything like that"—she blinked as if annoyed that she couldn't define what she meant—"just less . . . sure, somehow," she finally made do.

Leonor was nodding. "Maybe that's it," she agreed. "A feelin', nothin' more, that all of a sudden *he's* startin' to feel like we're outa time."

Shaking that off, she raised her voice and anxiously asked Samantha, "What does Father have to say about this?" She'd yearned to see her father, to speak to him about this momentous step, but he'd been "busy," off "doing something," and she hadn't seen him in days. Barely half a decade apart in age or not, Samantha was her stepmother, after all. If anyone would know, she should.

But Samantha shrugged. "I don't actually know, dear. I haven't seen him either. I *hear* he has been creeping about, spying on . . ." She glanced around. ". . . certain suspected subversives. He and Captain Hernandez, among others."

Leonor looked alarmed. Not out of concern for her father, necessarily. Giles Anson was too skillful and ruthless a fighter for either woman to seriously fear for his safety in anything less dangerous than a full-blown battle. Death was random enough to take anyone, then. "He *does* know, doesn't he? He'll be there, right?" she asked.

"Of course he does. He will. I've sent several messengers to find him, and regardless how . . . private the ceremony was supposed to be, that has gotten quite away from us. We all knew it would. It is the talk of the army, and whether or not any of my messages have reached him, Giles will know."

———

"Gonna hafta leave off our sneakin' pretty soon," Sal Hernandez said, glancing at the watch he'd taken from his vest pocket. "Don't think that *extremely violent* chica of yours'll ever forgive you if you ain't there to throw her at Colonel Cayce."

"Plenty of time," Anson assured, leaning over a table covered with extremely handsome handmade pipes. He pretended to examine several of them, but his eyes were on a group of men gathered in the shade of some trees just off the square avenue surrounding the great temple. There were no permanent barriers, just the occasional squad of sentries, but the road separated that part of the army encamped at the base of the pyramid from the people of the city. A line they'd been commanded not to cross. That included literally hundreds of small merchants set up to sell their wares to soldiers. They were open to townsfolk as well, of course, accessible from inside or out, but their generally hollow rectangular stalls actually formed a better physical barrier than many other things would have.

The pipe merchant, probably the maker, was leaning hopefully over the table as well, hands clasped together. "An' we ain't sneakin' a'tall," Anson continued in English. "We're both in uniform." He glanced at Sal, a wide-brimmed straw hat on his head. "Mostly. We're right out in the open where anyone can see us, lookin' at pipes."

"For maybe too long," Sal accused.

Anson frowned. "Could be. Guess we can leave the real sneakin' to the other fellas you've got scattered around. Only spotted one of 'em myself, but that's because I recognized the boy. The rest blend in pretty well."

"What was it that you wanted to see for yourself?" Sal asked, selecting a pipe to look at as well.

"Your boys said Armonia's been meetin' with a tall, soldierly-lookin' fella that might be General Gomez himself. Somebody told 'em it was. I can think of all sorts o' reasons Gomez'd be decoratin' a cross or impalin' pole when we got here, or if he escaped that, makin' himself known to us, swearin' ta help." He shook his head and put a pipe down before picking up another, holding it to the light. "Can't figger why he'd be slinkin' around, talkin' ta fellas in secret, if he wasn't up to no good. An' that bastard Armonia's talkin' to him right now, if it *is* him. Next time you get a chance, take a look an' see for yourself. *I* just wanted a face for the name. Now I've got it, I'll get me one o' these pipes for a weddin' present for Lewis."

He paused and almost raised his head to stare full on. "Wait a second. Look as quick as you can. See that great big bastard standin' back a ways in the crowd gathered up around 'em? Look familiar?"

A few moments later, Sal waved the pipe as if showing it to Anson.

"Yeah. Took me a bit, but I seen him before, for sure. Big *bastardo feo* like him is hard to forget, but I had to put him where he was in my mind."

"Which was?" Anson asked.

"With that damned Tranquilo when we first showed up at Uxmal. One o' them Reaper Monks."

"That's what I thought," Anson said, shaking his head as if at the pipe Sal held.

"Let's go kill 'em," Sal suggested, pointing at another. "Strikes me, he's reason enough by himself for us ta kill all of 'em."

Anson picked up the finely carved pipe Sal had indicated. It really was very beautiful. Nodding, he handed it to the proprietor of the stall. "Can you wrap this up with somethin' nice?" he asked in Spanya.

"*Sí*. All my pipes are unique works of art and come with fitted, ah, boxes." The man hesitated. "We have yet to agree on a price."

"What do you want for it?"

After an even longer hesitation, the man blurted out, "Three of your *dolares*."

Sal immediately intervened. Acting astounded by the price, he started vigorously haggling. To give the craftsman his due, he held his own. Of course, he'd probably practiced on a lot of soldiers already. The pipe *would* eventually sell for what he asked. Anson felt lucky that Sal got him down to two, which he paid. When the "box" came out, he was surprised to see that it was at least as well crafted as the pipe. Turning with his purchase, he said aside to Sal, "I may regret it, but we won't kill 'em now."

"How come?"

"A few reasons. First, it'll stir up a hellova ruckus, probl'y get a bunch of innocent folk killed too"—he shrugged—"an' start a big fuss right before Leonor's weddin'. Might have to postpone it an' I'd be in for it then. Another reason is that your boys'll stay on 'em an' might follow 'em to even more o' the devils. The whole First US regiment's on standby for a notice like that. Don't even have ta tell 'em ta 'go' if they get word of a big heap o' seditionists." He paused. "An' the weird thing is, that Armonia looked like he was arguin' with the one that might be Gomez. Ain't likely, but could be he really is on Don Hurac's side, or at least wants to make himself valuable enough to keep alive. Keeps a foot in both camps so he can warn us of somethin' big about ta happen so we'll let him live." He scratched his bearded chin. "Who knows. 'Sides, we can't just kill Armonia anyway. That'd surely aggravate Don Hurac. Think I'll report that I saw him with a known confidant o' Tranquilo's, though. Confront him with it. If he's sittin' on the fence, that'll push him off. One way or the other. If he denies it, we can kill him in the clear. If he don't, we might just roll the whole bunch up."

"What now, then?" Sal asked.

Anson slapped his old friend on the back and handed him a cigar. "Now we go get soaked down, spruced up, an' put on our least stinky clothes." He chuckled. "Then we'll go 'throw' my troublesome daughter at Lewis Cayce."

"I've never seen anything like it," Lewis admitted, gazing at a kind of wedge-shaped contraption about the size of a small wagon. "Yes, I have," he remembered. "It's like a giant quoin. A crude elevation device like the Doms use on their artillery."

"Yes, sir," acknowledged Major Justinian Olayne, chief of artillery, "but this is intended to *depress* elevation." Lewis, Sira Periz, Har-Kaaska, and Felix Meder had joined Olayne and Sergeant Major McNabb atop the new, reinforced, and impressively deep fighting platform above and around the western gate. That area, and a considerable distance radiating outward from all four main gates into the city, were the only ones "finished," as yet, but the thick, wide, earth-and-stone berm was still rising to connect them all behind the entire four-*legua* (twelve-mile) radius of the great wall. They didn't, and wouldn't ever, have nearly enough soldiers to adequately man such an extensive defense, but the top of the platform and the newly created space behind it would facilitate the rapid relocation of troops to where they were needed most. Various avenues within the city had been widened as well, not only to quicken movement, but to make broader killing fields in front of numerous interior positions also being built for Cayce's troops to fall back to at need. Hopefully, they'd never be required.

At the moment, however, Lewis and his party—each (aside from Lewis himself) already dressed in their best for the upcoming ceremony—were inspecting one of Olayne's numerous artillery positions, primarily intended to accommodate pieces the army had captured throughout its long campaign. Even aside from those guns given to Captain Holland to arm his growing navy of armed merchant ships and more that had been emplaced, unmodified, to defend Vera Cruz, Puebla, and Texcoco, almost two hundred more "standard" Dom 8pdrs had either been captured in the numerous engagements on the way here, or taken from storage in the various cities. And this number didn't include the nearly fifty weapons taken and modified early on that already served in established, increasingly professional batteries in the army. Some of these batteries were just as well served and capable as the very first ones they'd created around the American weapons they'd brought to this world.

In any event, Olayne was building enough embrasures in each long wall to accommodate half of the three-hundred-odd guns on hand. Reliable sources placed the strength of the Gran Cruzada at a quarter million men, and Lewis would be lucky to augment his roughly thirty thousand with another ten thousand local militia. But even a quarter million would have to focus their attack *somewhere*, perhaps more than one somewhere at a time, true, but they couldn't attack *everywhere* all at once with any hope of overwhelming such a formidable defense. And such a massive force would be a ponderous thing at best, necessarily preparing an attack in full view (even nighttime observation) of the defenders. True surprise would be difficult to achieve, and guns and troops could be moved from elsewhere to meet the attacks. At least that was the idea.

"Their purpose should be clear enough," Olayne defended, glancing at Sergeant Major McNabb a little anxiously.

"Very clear," Har-Kaaska agreed, blinking a little skeptically. "They will be moved up under the trails of the guns so they can fire downward at the enemy near the base of the walls."

"Exactly." Olayne nodded. "And their shape will allow a measure of the recoil energy to be dispersed and spare excessive wear on carriages and trunnions."

"We thought about constructin' a descendin' ramp alongside each gun," McNabb supplied, "but that'd not only require a deeper, wider piercin' in the wall, but'd pose a hazard tae the crew while loadin'."

"You're assuming an attacker will get that close no matter what we do," Lewis observed.

"Aye, sir," McNabb confirmed. Olayne nodded.

"Good," Lewis said. "Always prepare for the worst. I hope, if these defenses are actually needed—I do hate to plan for a purely defensive battle," he inserted almost wistfully, "but we should have other things ready to help cope with that." He bowed his head to Sira Periz. "Our near-continuous baggage train from Vera Cruz and Techolotla, via Puebla and Texcoco, should have us sufficiently supplied with ammunition. And there were large stores of local manufacture ammunition here and in Texcoco as well. Much is being brought forward. Dom gunpowder is poor compared to ours, and we've no need of it for our cannon and small arms, but we'll use it to spring other surprises."

"We've been sending surplus grain and other staples from Texcoco as well," said Sira Periz. "I'm told that there was a fine harvest this year."

"More is still coming in," Lewis agreed. "We aren't even reliant on the aqueduct for water." Like the bridges over the rivers, even the pyramids, it was believed the aqueduct was an artifact from an earlier civilization. "There are plenty of water wells in the city, both here and at Texcoco," Lewis continued, "and there's enough food to carry us through a more protracted siege than I think the enemy's quarter million can maintain." He nodded at the awkward-looking ramp. "That, and other imaginative things, will be a help as well." He cocked his head to the side, then observed, "It has to be heavy to be stout enough to do what you want, though. How will you move it, or I assume 'them,' since I doubt you want to build just one"—he grinned—"and carry it wherever it's needed? Even with one for each gun emplacement, they'll be difficult to shift into position in action."

Smiling, Felix Meder spoke up. "I bet if it comes to that, there'll be plenty of infantry around to help."

Kakking a kind of laugh, the Mi-Anakka Har-Kaaska said, "Of course there will. And they *will* help too."

Meder was shaking his head. "Not my riflemen. Unlike regular infantry who blast their musket balls willy-nilly all about, my riflemen fire slower and much more lethally." He grinned. "They need to control their breathing."

Everyone, even Lewis, laughed at that. "We'll see," Lewis finally said. "Or, hopefully, we won't. I can't say I'm optimistic, but it would be nice if the enemy obeys Don Hurac's command and we never even see the Gran Cruzada."

That was a wonderful thought, of course, but there wasn't a single person present who was ready to count on that. Olayne cleared his throat. "I do have one other thing I'd like to run past you, sir."

"Of course," Lewis said.

"Lunettes, sir. Preferably one every few hundred yards. Despite its increasingly impressive walls, the city isn't shaped like a proper fortress. We can alleviate that to a degree with lunettes." Glancing at Sira Periz and Har-Kaaska, he explained, "Semicircular fortified positions outside the walls, each with several guns and supporting infantry. They can provide enfilading fire as the enemy closes on the walls." He gestured around. "None of these guns up here can do that."

Lewis massaged his whiskery cheeks, thinking. "Very well, but only outside and encompassing the main gates." He held off Olayne's objection. "They must be at gates if we're to keep them manned and supplied, and we have to be able to evacuate them as well. I won't gift the enemy any more potential openings in the walls either."

Felix Meder was examining his watch. "The day is getting along, sir," he hinted gently.

"Your point, Mr. Meder?"

Sira Periz laughed at Lewis. "Colonel De Russy once attempted to explain your personality to me and described it as 'stoic.' Personally, if I understand the notion, you seem slightly more prone to certain passions of the moment than would ordinarily be ideal for a stoic. Fury is one, though you rarely show it. But when you do, you *really* do. And you simply will not 'patiently endure' what your conscience perceives as 'persistent evil,' and your tireless opposition to it makes it clear you will not bow to the dictates of 'fate.'" She grinned.

"There are different interpretations of stoicism," Felix Meder advised, also grinning. "Not all admonish us not to keep trying to fight what may only *seem* to be too big for us. I'd say Colonel Cayce is only 'stoic' in the way Cicero described *summum bonum*, the pursuit of the 'highest good.' He just needs the four virtues for that: wisdom, courage, temperance, and justice. He already has all of those."

"You know Cicero?" Olayne asked, obviously surprised that a young man who'd started as a private soldier would.

"My father made all us kids read him," Meder replied. "Even my sisters."

"Regardless," Sira continued, addressing them all. "'Stoic' as I understand it or not, Colonel Cayce's pretended indifference to his momentous appointment rings rather false, to me." She regarded Lewis once more. "I believe Captain Meder's intention was simply to remind you of it." She looked him over and sniffed. "And you are not even remotely prepared."

Nodding vaguely, Lewis looked down at his dingy everyday uniform and grinned a little sheepishly himself. "I suppose not," he allowed. "Gentlemen." He nodded at Olayne, McNabb, Meder, and Har-Kaaska, then bowed to Sira. "My lady. If you'll excuse me, I'll go place myself in my orderly's surly but capable charge."

Meder chuckled again. "Being married to Miss Lieutenant Leonor Anson is bound to be . . . an adventure, but I doubt it will compare in any way to putting up with Corporal Willis's strident nagging all this time." Hesitantly, he stuck out his hand to shake. When Lewis took it, Justinian Olayne moved to offer his as well, saying, "I think it's fair to report that every young officer in this army has been attracted to Miss Leonor at some point. Much of that has been due to her beauty, of course, which you had more to do with her revealing than anyone. Partly too was the . . . challenge she represented, some innate urge to 'tame the *bon sauvage*,' if you will." He shook his head. "But there's no taming her, nor should anyone try. I think you alone have the courage and confidence to cope with her as she is. No doubt you'll always try to protect her, yet won't insist she accept that protection. A man with such strength is the only possible match for her."

Nodding in agreement, Felix Meder said, "You have my deepest and most profound congratulations, sir, and my most fervent wishes for a long and happy marriage."

CHAPTER 18

"Awful lot o' folks turnin' out," Giles Anson observed as he, Sal, and half a dozen Rangers left their tents and gathered at the edge of the army's true headquarters area surrounding the base of the central pyramid. Most available Rangers and dragoons were serving as roving, mounted security, while an entire regiment of Colonel Agon's 4th Division, in their green uniforms, had formed a tight cordon to and around the lavish villa HQ. Anson was surprised by how many locals had turned out to see what they could, more than usually gathered in the open-air market of late, not all of whom looked simply curious. A fair percentage of what Anson considered fighting-age men wore grim, purposeful expressions.

"I don't like it," Sal concurred. "Sure, it's dusk, an' most of the work for the day has stopped, but if I'd sooner just drop on my cot for the night, how come all these folks, who likely worked a heap harder, would rather come here an' . . . glare?" He shook his head, pulling his tight-fitting blue jacket down to just above his pistol belt. "Don't all of 'em look offended. Some're surely just curious—an' Don Hurac's s'posed to be here. They always like seein' him. But some don't look too happy."

"Don't care if they're happy," Anson growled. "Long as they behave. Sing out if you catch sight o' that Armonia fella, or any others that could be trouble." A Ranger had brought news that, like Don Hurac, Alcalde Estilio, and Don Amil, Don Armonia was also planning to attend. Only Don Hurac was specifically invited, but it wasn't like they could turn the others away. Besides...

"You figure Colonel Cayce *knew* his weddin' would stir up a stink?" Sal suddenly asked.

Anson looked at him, surprised. "I *know* you ain't stupid, *hermano*. Course he did." He shook his head. "You an' me, we're blunt instruments. We can be subtle when we're scoutin', but we're hammers in a fight. In spite o' bein' an artilleryman, Lewis can be subtle all the time—right before he takes up a hammer. I figure, aside from decidin' it's time ta keep his promise to my girl, he thought this spell o' sorta peace we have was the best time ta smoke out the rats. Rats we won't want slinkin' around amongst us when it ain't so peaceful no more." He tilted his head at the still-growing crowd and the approach of what they'd identified as Don Armonia's personal coach. It was a small but ornate vehicle, entirely closed, drawn by a team of white Dom horses. Straightening his own jacket under hand-tooled holsters and braces supporting his Walker Colts, as well as his pistol belt and pair of Paterson Colts, he started walking forward. "Let's go do this, an' keep our eyes peeled," he said, then added, "Never expected to go to my daughter's weddin' this heavily armed. Don't know why. Prob'ly should'a."

"Just one more damn minute," Corporal Willis wheedled, quickly brushing the back of Lewis's only "dress" frock coat, practically hopping after him as he tried to whip the last dust and horsehair off the garment. "If ya please," he added in a surly tone for propriety's sake. "Would'ya just *stop movin'* for the love o' God?" he finally pleaded. "Yer sash is all bunched up back here, under yer saber belt! You want ever'body pointin' an' snickerin'?"

Lewis stopped and sighed, watching Colonel Reed, Har-Kaaska, Sira Periz, Colonel Itzam, and Colonel Agon approach. "Less than a minute ago you were insisting that I 'hurry, hurry, hurry,' or they'd start the ceremony without me. I personally rather doubt that," he continued with a gentle note of sarcasm, "but I know how stressful it is for you to help me look my best. Now it seems you're determined that I miss the whole thing."

"Which I'm just tryin' ta help," Willis objected. "Strange enough for me, since as soon as you marry that wicked woman, my lifespan'll likely shorten to days. Maybe hours."

"Nonsense," Lewis objected as Willis tugged at his sash. "Why would she harm you?"

"She hates me," Willis simply said.

"Oh, good God. She doesn't *hate* you." He chuckled. "She just enjoys tormenting you. She'll tire of it, eventually."

"*Then* she'll shoot me, for one last lark," Willis warned darkly.

Lewis rolled his eyes. "Good evening, gentlemen," he greeted his division commanders. "My lady," he added, smiling at Sira Periz. "I appreciate you all agreeing to be my wedding party."

Colonel Reed also looked at Sira, then Har-Kaaska. "However eminent and . . . singular it might be," he replied wryly, though he didn't seem scandalized in the least. Only amused. Lewis would've probably asked Giles Anson to be his best man, but he had other duties. Not least of which was to give the bride away. Lewis requested instead that all his senior commanders stand—and be seen—with him. The fact that one was a woman and another a "demon"—and that Leonor would have another "demon" in her bridal party—should bring any major opposition to their occupation out in the open. It was risky, of course, putting all their command eggs in one basket, but everyone believed their security preparations, much deeper than they appeared, should be sufficient.

"Yes," Lewis agreed. "Distinguished and extraordinary to all our cultures." He motioned forward. "Shall we proceed?"

Seeing them start out, drummers that were mingled with the security cordon opened a thunderous fanfare.

"My God, I'm going to the altar, not the gallows," Lewis objected.

Colonel Agon looked accusingly at Reed, who shrugged. Lewis knew who was responsible at once.

"Are you, Lewis? Are you really?" Reed asked with a grin.

Preceding Lewis and his division commanders by some distance, Anson, Sal, and their own Ranger escorts might've been mistaken for the principal honorees, especially when the drums began, just ahead of the fifes. Anson didn't know the tune, but wasn't very musical anyway. "Sounds a little doleful," he remarked.

"Look, up by Armonia's carriage," Sal said, voice suddenly urgent.

Anson's eyes skimmed the crowd, then stopped. "That's that same fella, that Gomez," he snapped. The tall man in civilian clothes was arguing with Armonia again, but his eyes swept over the approaching Rangers. Without another word, he attempted to fall back into the milling civilians. "Well, he's seen us, now," Anson said. "Take two men an' get after him," he told Sal, who acted as if Anson just dropped his leash when he gestured at two Rangers, and bolted.

"Shit," Anson muttered. "I wonder if Don Hurac's already here. Not even sure how he meant to *get* here. I hope Lewis knows what he's doin'. Hold up," he said louder, to the Rangers remaining with him. "We'll wait for Lewis an' his colonels. Go in together." *Then I have to find Leonor an' Samantha*, he told himself. *Try to just be a father for a while. If I can.*

Standing still for a moment, Anson saw the movement around him even better than before. There was a lot of it too. The crowd of hundreds had grown to thousands and for each of Agon's infantrymen facing inward toward the procession, another had turned to face the crowd, musket off his shoulder, held at port arms. No bayonets had been fixed and no one was pressing forward at the moment, but if the mob chose to do so, things could quickly get dangerous. Anson rested a hand on the grip of one of his powerful Walker Colts.

Then, when Lewis and his party finally joined him, something utterly unexpected happened. A loud, spontaneous cheer erupted from Colonel Agon's troops, former enemies who'd fought them hard and skillfully, yet become as loyal to the cause as any. Certainly when it came to the Allied interpretation of God, as opposed to the capricious, bloodthirsty God the Doms still worshipped. What turned them more than anything was the scriptural "proof" in Father Orno's and Reverend Harkin's Bibles that had been warped, edited, and even withheld for generations. Many had gone among the people in all the cities they'd taken, engaging in their own evangelical campaign. Though their message was demonstrably appealing to freed slaves and *hombres libres*, Lewis hadn't been hopeful for the upper classes. In that moment, he knew different. Few *patricios* remained in the city, but quite a few hidalgos did. Many of those present now were hidalgos, and despite the hard work most had been engaged in, the unprecedented changes impacting their lives, and the dire threat of extermination brooding over them all—perhaps as much *because* of that threat—the swelling mob began to clap and cheer as well.

"I'll be damned," said Colonel Reed, genuine wonder in his voice. "I've seen them behave this way when Don Hurac was with us, but not when he wasn't." He looked at Lewis. "They're cheering us. More specifically *you*."

"They are," Har-Kaaska agreed. "I sincerely doubt that they are cheering me"—he *kakked*—"but that I am with you does not stop them." He blinked with what Lewis had learned meant something like curiosity. "Granted, not all appear as supportive as others, but they are a distinct minority. A most surprising development."

Tentatively, Lewis raised a hand to wave back at the spectators, and the cheering grew louder, echoing thunderously against the façades of buildings down the spectator-lined street. "I'll be. I think you're right," he said, face reddening slightly. He cleared his throat. "Let's move along. This is a wedding procession, after all, not a triumph. It won't do to keep my dangerous bride waiting long enough to grow annoyed."

The large common room in the villa they'd dedicated to an officer's mess looked nothing like it had that morning. Previously somewhat stripped and austere, it had since been festively decorated with ivies, flowers, and colorful tapestries, all surprisingly well lit with hundreds of reflective oil lamps. It was also packed. *So much for the small, intimate service Leonor imagined*, Lewis thought. Granted, the majority of "guests" were in uniform, about an even mix of officers from the United Cities and men who'd known Lewis—and Leonor—since they came here. The rest were high-status locals, dressed in colorful, formfitting coats encasing equally gaudy but blowsy tunics. Breeches were relatively blowsy as well, ballooning around thighs above black, mirror-polished knee boots. The style struck Lewis as vaguely absurd, a mixture of fashions from his own fifteenth through eighteenth centuries. De Russy would make an impression here, in his formal mess-dress uniform. Neither Lewis nor any of his officers had anything remotely like it, the only decorations on anything they wore being shoulder boards, brightly polished buttons, sashes, and white saber belts. He thought they looked sharp, but there was no comparison to the locals, particularly Don Hurac himself, whose white coat, weskit, and breeches somehow shimmered in the lamplight as if someone had poured molten silver on him. As Lewis guessed, Don Hurac was already here and had nodded from within his circle of advisors with a smile of greeting.

The only women present as yet were some camp followers or locals from other cities who'd formed attachments to some of Lewis's officers. They'd adorned themselves in nice, simple dresses like Lewis remembered from home. Designed by Mistress Samantha and Angelique Mercure, these were carried and sold by sutlers now. There were female servants bearing trays of drinks and unknown dainty tidbits as well. None were naked, as had apparently once been the norm, and all wore nice, modest tunics belted around the waist. *No doubt, given time, Samantha will explode another fashion revolution here, just as she did at Uxmal,* Lewis thought. *Might take a while longer, though.* Women in Uxmal were considered equal to men in most every respect. Here, they'd been the lowest of slaves. Those working the room now seemed on edge, but none were treated with open disdain or disrespect. At worst, they were simply ignored by men wearing annoyed expressions. He didn't know whether to be amused or annoyed himself, by the scope the event had achieved.

"Hot in here, with all these lamps an' smelly bodies," Anson observed.

"Yes," Lewis agreed, a little sourly. "A lot bigger turnout than Leonor and I expected."

Colonel Reed shrugged. "The army has been anticipating this almost as much as a final victory. Watching you and Leonor pretend to be only professional associates so long has been quite excruciating." He grinned. "To me as much as anyone. I believe the betting is even money that that will continue. In public, at least. In any event, the lads are all hopeless romantics, you know, and I believe it's important they get a good description of the festivities from a number of viewpoints as soon as they can. It'll be good for morale."

He gestured around. "As for the bloody Doms . . . call it curiosity, I suppose. Their weddings are very different, or have been, and at least this'll show them we value our women quite highly. Most of those who didn't flee our approach will unconsciously equate that behavior with our ability to beat them. Perhaps some of our better practices will catch on."

"I can think of a few I hope they don't adopt," grumbled Anson, then he looked at Reed. "Never figured you for such a philosopher."

Reed waved around. "With our thoughtful clerics Reverend Harkin and Father Orno otherwise occupied at the moment, and Dr. Newlin still in Texcoco organizing the forward movement of munitions, someone must take up the slack."

"Dr. Newlin will be distressed that he missed this," said Sira Periz, "but I don't suppose it would do to delay it solely for his benefit."

Lewis shook his head, then managed a small laugh. "No. I've prepared myself as best I can, but I doubt I'd go through with it if I put it off."

"Gettin' the nerves?" Anson asked. "Good. You should." He grinned wickedly. "Just think of it as a battle. You deal with those well enough. An' bein' married to my daughter, you'll likely have a battle every day."

Har-Kaaska and Colonel Agon had been studying the crowd as they talked, no one coming near as they did so. "The number of 'locals' is increasing," Agon suddenly pointed out. A group of half a dozen ostentatiously dressed hidalgos were coming in just then. As everyone from the city whom Don Hurac or his entourage invited, they were given a cursory inspection for weapons, but no one patted them down. Unwonted touching was a grave insult to Doms and would've sparked invitations to duels with each and every one thus "mistreated." No one had expected it to be a problem since Samantha, who was "in charge" of the event, hadn't thought so many locals would attend.

Hopefully, it still won't be a problem, Lewis thought. Anson was eyeing the new arrivals and every other local in view while idly fingering the plowshare grip of one of his Paterson Colts. *With him on alert, and so many others, it shouldn't be.*

Drums near the rear of the room suddenly thundered, extraordinarily loud in such a space, and Lewis saw Father Orno and Reverend Harkin emerge somberly from a chamber to the side, marching together to an altar in the far center of the room. The altar might've been there all along, blocked by bodies that quickly withdrew to either side. Lewis was surprised to see Don Hurac, Don Armonia, Alcalde Estilio, and Vice Alcalde Don Amil lead a small procession of their personal guards up and around behind the two clergymen, as if to preside over the proceedings.

Despite Armonia's habitual expression of disapproval, it was clear they meant to demonstrate the opposite. The altar was a humble thing, about four feet high, likely built by a carpenter in the ranks. A platform was at the top, on which was laid Harkin's own battered Bible, and the whole thing was supported by a pedestal in the shape of a naked wood Christian cross. That was entirely different from the gold lightning bolt cross of the Doms. Even over the still thundering drums, Lewis heard a few exclamations. Most sounded pleased, he noted. Only a few seemed to object. Harkin and Orno arranged themselves welcomingly on either side of the altar, facing Lewis and his senior officers. Harkin smiled and discreetly motioned him forward with a single finger on his only hand.

"Damned drums," Lewis murmured aside to Anson as they parted and the Ranger turned to seek his daughter. Something he suddenly figured he should've done as soon as he arrived.

"Adios, Lewis," he said over his shoulder. "Back in a minute."

"I better go after him," said Sira Periz. "I know little of your customs, but in cases like this, ours do not seem entirely dissimilar." With that, she gave a grinning, ironic salute and turned to try and make use of Anson's wake through the crowd.

CHAPTER 19

Squirming through the crush toward the hall down which Samantha had left word Anson would find them was hot, difficult work. It had been relatively cool, if humid outside, but the number of lamps and people inside made it almost unbearable, especially to a wool-clad, increasingly irritated Ranger exerting himself. "Father of the bride, father of the bride," Anson rumbled as he went. "Stand aside, if you please. Father of the bride—move, god damn you! Move. S'cuse me, Captain. Hope that don't bruise. Out of the way, out of the way. Who the devil are you? A duel, you say? Sure, say when, now git."

By the time he finally broke through, it was possible he'd have to meet several of the "new" upper class in the Holy City on the field of honor, but he doubted it. He didn't care if he did. "Puffed-up buncha toads," he griped aloud to himself. "Tip the rock off the top of 'em an' watch 'em all scamper to be the new rock. An extra hole in a few'll do the rest a world of good."

"I am afraid you may be right," Sira Periz confirmed, surprising him by her sudden proximity behind him.

"Why, Alcaldesa . . . Colonel . . ."

She waved a small hand at him. "Tonight it is just 'Sira,' if you please."

"Sure," he reluctantly agreed. "Stay tucked in behind me as I press on. There's still a fair clump to get through."

"That is what I have been doing."

They finally reached the door to the chamber Anson had been directed to and returned the salutes of a pair of 3rd Pennsylvania guards who gently opened the door and let them in.

Several women—and Varaa-Choon—were gathered at the far side of the room. All except the Mi-Anakka were in fine dresses, either provided by or designed by Samantha. Varaa herself—Anson assumed she'd be part of Leonor's wedding party—was the only one in uniform, hand resting on the pommel of her long-bladed, basket-hilt backsword. She blinked and nodded at him as the women parted, revealing his wife and daughter. He uttered an audible gasp when he saw Leonor. "My God, girl. You're beautiful."

Leonor stood and turned from where she'd been sitting on a stool in front of a mirror. Blushing deeply, she absently touched her blue-black hair, carefully sculpted and piled atop her head, then smoothed and adjusted the silver-embroidered dress. "Think it's too much?" she asked, a very girlish, hopeful look on her face.

"Not a bit."

Samantha turned as well, eyes flashing, fists on her shapely hips. *An' she looks even prettier than she did at our own weddin'*, Anson reflected. *'Specially mad.* "And just where have you been, you dreadful beast?" she demanded hotly. Remembering her manners, she sweetly welcomed Sira Periz, but then flared at her husband once more. "I haven't seen *you* for *days*, and I've sent messenger after messenger searching for you with no response at all. Your poor daughter began to fear you wouldn't be here for this!"

Anson gave his wife a stare that seemed to ask, "Really?" but then gestured vaguely behind him. "Been busy, my dear—an' you look truly fine yourself. But you know how it is, or you should. Might be that things're finally shakin' loose an' comin' to a head in the city. Maybe even due to this little sworay you arranged."

Samantha bit her lip, relenting slightly. "It was supposed to be just a small affair. I never dreamed it would become what it has."

Anson was nodding. "I'll wager it's got even bigger than when you last looked. Ever'body who thinks they're somebody is packin' theirselves in that room with the preachers. Might be for the best," he relented as well. "I got the impression comin' here—with Lewis," he assured his daughter, "that folks outside're choosin' sides." He shrugged. "Most seem behind

Lewis an' Don Hurac. Pretty firm, I'd say. Others look mighty glum, even angry. I sent Sal chasin' after one we think is actually General Gomez. Prob'ly still here to stir things up. Sal might miss the weddin', which is a shame"—he turned to look at Leonor—"but my 'poor daughter' never could'a doubted *I'd* be here. One way or another."

Leonor stood and raced into his arms.

"Now, now, leave off that snufflin'. You'll spoil all Samantha's hard work on yer face!"

Samantha hastened over with a kerchief and a brush in her hand. "Oh dear!" she exclaimed. "Izel, be a good girl and tell one of the guards to pass the word that we will be delayed a few moments more."

"*Mierda!*" Sal snapped, whipping off the wide, flat-brimmed straw hat he usually wore that might as well have had his name painted on it. The fact he was considerably taller than the average local and, other than the hat, wearing the same uniform as any other Ranger, made it especially difficult to blend in as he pursued the suspected Dom general. Passing a street merchant's stall with well-made cloaks for sale, he tossed his hat to an older, squat, but well-dressed woman with golden bangles on her arms before snatching up three of her cloaks and passing two to his companions. He gestured at them to remove their wheel hats as well. Before the old woman could explode with the fury building on her face—the soldiers in the city had been warned of dire punishments and simply didn't steal—Sal said in Spanya, "Take care of my hat, old mother. I'll be back for it—and to pay your askin' price for the cloaks."

The woman sat back with a satisfied nod, calculating what she could reasonably charge and how much she'd make off it.

"I don't see him anymore," advised Corporal T'shia, formerly one of Ki-sin's Holcano warriors. He was short and actually jumping to see over the swelling mass of people heading toward the vicinity of the wedding ceremony. That so many people were still gathering for it was starting to make Sal edgy.

"Quit hoppin' up and down, you idiot! *Jesu Christo!* Throw that cloak over your shoulders an' keep your feet on the ground." Sal used his higher vantage point to reacquire their quarry.

"I like that color better," T'shia said, snatching the rust-colored garment

Sal handed the other Ranger, an Uxmalo private, and replacing it with a yellow-tan-and-green-striped one. Sal rolled his eyes, still scanning and squinting. T'shia was a good Ranger and decent NCO, but he was a Holcano after all. Somewhat selfish, capricious, and extremely status conscious by nature. Sal caught a glimpse of a furtive return gaze at an angle across the packed avenue and pushed into the crowd. "There he is. Follow me!"

Not all those moving toward the wedding were only benignly curious. Some actually struck at Sal as he passed or menaced him with blades. He drew both his revolvers and that kept them back, clearing his path as well.

"Maybe we ought to send the boy with word there's bad men in the mob," T'shia suggested loudly, brandishing his own "Bowie sword" and keeping the younger Ranger between him and Sal. Sal shook his head. "One man alone in this press—he'd never get there alive. An' I expect the fellas back there're takin' due note."

They reached the place where Sal glimpsed Gomez, or the man they *thought* was him. He wasn't there, of course. "This way," Sal shouted, pushing against the stream of people again. "There's an alley ahead. I think he ducked in there."

Although they'd been incorporated into and were relied upon as part of the internal defense of the city, the extremely narrow alleys, not actual avenues and barely wide enough for a cart (or gun), were deemed the most dangerous places any wandering or exploring members of the occupation force could go. They were, in fact, where virtually every murdered soldier turned up. Sal and his comrades, even the trooper from Uxmalo, weren't drunk or naive young infantrymen, used to the support of their comrades around them whenever danger loomed. Like every man admitted into the Rangers, each was a combat veteran, or in the case of Ocelomeh or Holcanos, practiced woodland killers. Sal himself was one of the five or six deadliest men in the army. Anyone can be surprised, however, and they proceeded with care.

There was no danger at once. The alley was empty, every doorway blocked, and they quickly raced down it and exited onto another, slightly less congested street. After a moment's hesitation, Sal plunged into another alley. This one, about halfway down, was occupied. None of the dozen or so tough-looking men packed into it seemed to notice them at first, strangely focused almost entirely inward. That's when Sal noted that their quarry, also taller than average, was in the middle of the press.

Motioning his comrades to halt, his first impression was that the man who might be General Gomez, shouting loudly at those around him, was arguing with or haranguing some followers. He couldn't make out the words. Regardless, Sal couldn't have been more stunned when "Gomez" suddenly shrieked in agony.

"*No mames!*" Sal exclaimed, loud enough that some of the apparent killers heard and turned to face them. "Uh-oh," he added lowly before shouting in Spanya, "Stop! What are you doing to that man?"

A burly, bearded man with an ornate officer's pistol in his hand shoved his way into view. "This is no concern of *herejes invasores*," the big man spat. "We merely kill a *traidor a dios*. You should thank us."

"I want to talk to him. I have questions."

He had all the killers' attention now. More than one was armed with a pistol. All apparently carried blades, from knives to swords. The big man with a beard glanced over his shoulder, smirking. "You are too late. Even if he is still capable of speech, you will not like what he has to say."

A musket shot sounded, back the way they came, echoing loudly through the city as if it was fired in a canyon. More musketry followed in a rising clatter.

"That don't sound good," Corporal T'shia said.

Still holding both revolvers, but not raising them, Sal told the gang's apparent leader, "I'm afraid I must insist, Senor."

The big man shrugged as if unconcerned, then barked, "*Matarlos!*" He started to raise his pistol.

The weapon barely moved before his left eye geysered blood and viscous fluid. Sal had shot him there so fast that none of his accomplices had even begun to obey him. The relatively small .36 caliber ball the Paterson Colt boomed into his head didn't have tremendous energy, but at barely twenty feet, it still blew out the back of his skull and rained pieces of it and bloody gobbets of brains all over his companions. Stiff-legged, he fell straight back among them.

"At 'em!" Sal roared at his comrades, dropping two more men as quick as that. Corporal T'shia and the Uxmalo private leaped ahead, armed with single-shot pistols and Bowie swords. Sal stood back, firing until his first five-shot revolver was empty, then drew his own blade and charged as well.

It wasn't really even a fight. The closest ruffians were blocked from fleeing by those behind and died very quickly. The rest tried to run. Never one to allow enemies a chance to retreat if he could prevent it—anyone you didn't kill today might kill you tomorrow—Sal emptied his other pistol in the backs of sprinting men. Two dropped at once, and two others shrieked as they fled. The one who didn't react to being shot didn't make it to the avenue beyond. The Uxmalo dropped another with his more powerful, but less accurate weapon. T'shia didn't shoot, but slashed the last to flee deeply in the side. The man screamed piteously and stumbled away, blood fountaining from a severed kidney. He wouldn't get far.

"I think two got away unhurt," T'shia said breathlessly, looking at the fallen men for survivors. Finding one still alive, he knelt to slash his throat.

"Don't kill him yet. We might have questions." Sal didn't even seem to be looking. Instead, his gaze was fixed on the man they'd been chasing. "General Gomez, I presume?" he asked the squirming, hissing form that seemed to be trying to hold his guts in.

"Yes!" the man gasped. "I am he. Your 'great enemy' here," he managed to snort.

Vaguely intrigued by the sarcastic response, Sal knelt to see what he could do to help, or at least *seem* sympathetic. He affected a solicitous tone. "What do you mean? Why did those men try to kill you?"

"Try?" Gomez snorted again. "They have succeeded!"

Sal shook his head and tsked. "Perhaps not. We have excellent healers, skilled in the use of medicines that prevent infection. You may yet live," he lied. Even through the welling blood he could see (and smell) that the man's intestines had been cut. *Best to learn what I can, and quickly*, he thought. "Here," he said, handing over the cloak he hadn't yet paid for. "Press this against your wound to slow the bleeding. And before I take you to the healers, you must give me a reason. Answer a few simple questions."

"I may as well," Gomez replied, bundling the cloak over his belly, eyes clenched in pain. "In spite of what you did to my army, I have been working to *help* you since you arrived."

Sal's eyes widened with even more surprise. "How's that, General? Why?"

Rocking in pain, teeth clenched, Gomez took a moment to respond. Finally, he did. "The 'why' is simple enough; I've decided it's important that you win." Still gasping, he looked away. "I am just a soldier. All I have ever been. The . . . religious foundation of the Dominion has never been my driving force. It is the same for many of us from the west. But even that rather strictly interpreted foundation has been warped and perverted out of all reason by Tranquilo and his movement. He and it are the true power behind the old regime, and their brutal, bloody fervency now runs rampant." He hissed a sigh.

"Left in power, it is only a matter of time before any dissent, even in the west, will be exterminated. Tranquilo and his minions will cleanse the world of all but his own foul followers." He looked up at Sal. "They are quite mad, you know?" Sal only nodded, afraid to interrupt, and Gomez continued. "For my failure against your 'Coronel Cayce,' I was broken and commanded to remain in this place. To die, no doubt. But also to encourage resistance." He shook his head. "I couldn't do it, and have done my best to stop it."

He coughed hard and painfully, and blood suddenly spurted from his lips. "Oh dear," he murmured as the flow eased, voice weaker than before. "It seems I was right after all. Perhaps it is just as well." He reached up and grabbed Sal's sleeve. It was getting very dark in the alley, and the distant musketry had thinned the throng of people at each end. Many still out there were shouting and bearing torches now, occasionally illuminating Gomez's pale, sweaty face. His expression was intent. "I had to be subtle, counseling only that a rising should wait for the proper time. My arguments grew more vocal of necessity in recent days, however, and . . . others began to doubt my resolve." He gestured at himself. "This is the result."

Sal took Gomez's hand in his. "Who were these 'others'? How many do they lead?"

"Tranquilo's own pet Reaper is the worst. A hulking brute named Escorpion."

Sal pursed his lips. "I know him. I *thought* I saw him. So Escorpion truly is here?"

"Yes," Gomez whispered weakly, fading quickly from loss of blood. "He is a beast. He will let nothing deter him from performing any task Tranquilo has set him and commands many hundreds who wish you ill."

"Who else? Who else?" Sal insisted, gently shaking the man when he realized Gomez had closed his eyes. They fluttered open.

"I . . . suspect Armonia," he managed, barely audible. "You do as well, if you are wise. He is *not* what he seems," he added as emphatically as he could. "Yet I cannot be sure about him. He is an enigma. I strongly doubt he supports you, but I do not believe he is loyal to Tranquilo. Someone else, perhaps."

Those words were spoken so softly, Sal thought Gomez was finished. "Who?" he questioned, shaking the man harder.

"I do not know," Gomez rasped. "Don Hurac himself, perhaps, thinking he can control him. Or the Primer Patriarcha Sachihiro. I believe they are friends." He weakly coughed up a gobbet of congealing blood. "Or he may only be loyal to himself..."

A tight volley of musketry boomed loudly, and there was no question who fired that.

"Cap'n Hernandez," hissed Corporal T'shia, tilting his head toward the end of the alley they came in. Sal looked and saw a dense pack of men bearing torches moving their way. They didn't sound friendly, but weren't in a hurry either. The swathe of bodies on the cobblestones probably explained that.

"I think I'm the only one still loaded," T'shia reminded. "We better go," he added emphatically.

Sal stood. "Yeah," he said, but his voice remained calm and a little distant.

"We takin' him?" the Uxmalo Ranger asked, pointing at Gomez.

Sal shook his head, almost visibly refocusing. "No. He's gone, poor bastard. Would'a liked a longer talk with him."

"What about this one?" T'shia asked, prodding the other moaning survivor with his boot.

Sal shook his head. "Don't think we can. Leave him."

T'shia merely nodded and knelt, swiftly slashing the man's throat.

Well, Sal thought philosophically, *I didn't say, "Leave him alive."* "Let's go," he said, starting to lead his men away. "Colonel Cayce needs to hear what we learned, but I'm damned if I know the quickest—or safest—way back."

CHAPTER 20

Lewis was just as stunned by Leonor's beauty as her father had been when a still-sweating but freshly brushed Giles Anson brought her to him. And it wasn't just the magnificent dress or the light, expertly applied dusting of makeup she wore, it was the inner beauty he'd recognized for quite a while now that she'd finally revealed for all to see. He'd watched lovely women go to the altar of matrimony before, usually to be joined to a brother officer. He'd heard people describe them as "radiant," and he'd agreed, but never really saw it. Now he did. Leonor seemed to genuinely glow, the smile on her unveiled face revealing every internal emotion.

There was love, he thought, quite a lot, but it was mixed with various measures of other feelings, finally, deliberately, exposed. Lewis believed he saw a trace of triumph combined with humor, but there was also a heavy dose of fear and vulnerability. He doubted she feared *him*, any more than she might an enemy. But her feelings and concern for him left a gap in the armor she'd built around her heart and he understood it perfectly. His fear of losing her, for her safety, had surmounted every other concern. He knew it would grow even harder for him to suppress his instinct to protect her from herself. Perhaps she saw that recognition in his own expression, perceived that same mix of love and fear he saw in hers? Maybe that was why she seemed to radiate a kind of ethereal light that left everything around her rather dark and indistinct by comparison.

The fifers had resisted an attempt at the traditional wedding march, though a fiddler performed a lively rendition. The drummers merely tapped the rims of their instruments as she and Anson followed her mix of martial and extremely feminine bridesmaids through the gap in the throng, grown respectfully or curiously silent. Colonel Reed, standing by Lewis as his best man, stifled a chuckle and whispered, "My God, it isn't *really* a march to the scaffold." Lewis, Anson, and Leonor herself all had to stifle chuckles themselves. Awkwardly handing his daughter off to the groom, Anson stepped somewhat woodenly back, where Samantha deftly took charge of him.

Father Orno, Reverend Harkin, and even Don Hurac all made brief statements before Orno and Harkin began the ceremony, actually taking turns. Lewis was sure they spoke a great deal about the true nature of God as they knew Him, and His real purpose for marriage. He also caught pieces of a number of pointed references to God's admonitions to treat women well, which might've been poorly received by the locals, but he wasn't really listening. Throughout, he felt entirely enveloped by Leonor's glow, lost in the depths of her big, brown eyes, which gazed so intently into his. Colonel Reed actually had to prod him when it was time for the vows and he had to respond. He got through that in a kind of daze, fearful he'd merely mumbled, so wholly did he remain focused on the beautiful young woman beside him. He did note that she responded to Harkin's queries and repeated her vows in a crisp, confident tone, but as much as he wanted to enjoy, even savor, the proceedings, it was if Leonor had somehow enthralled him, sequestering him from every distraction.

Reed poked him again and grabbed his hand, putting something in it. "It's the ring, Lewis," he said with great amusement. "You're supposed to put it on her finger now."

Lewis nodded somberly. Regardless of his current curious state, he was a man of action. Given a task or duty to perform, anything besides just standing there, he'd manage it. He became aware that Varaa-Choon had passed a golden band to Leonor as well, and grasping the ring Reed gave him in a death grip so he wouldn't drop it, he grimly proceeded to put it on the appropriate finger of Leonor's hand. Heart pounding and a rushing sound in his ears, Lewis stood at stiff attention as Leonor did the same, murmuring through a chuckle, "Lord, Lewis, loosen up! You look like you're havin' a tooth pulled!"

Finally tearing his gaze from Leonor, he looked at a beaming Reverend Harkin, seeing the expression of amusement he wore, almost mirrored by Father Orno.

"There!" Harkin said. "It's done, and about time too!" He grinned benevolently all around. "Lets us pray!"

Lewis remembered now that he'd been told they'd recite the Lord's Prayer before the announcement of marriage. He knew it well and could certainly say the words. He was just wondering what the locals would think when a sudden commotion tore him from his reverie. He instantly recognized the sound of a struggle in the crowd just a few yards away. Instinctively, he gathered Leonor into his arms and dove at the altar, crashing into Harkin and Orno and driving them squawking to the floor.

A pistol exploded, shockingly close and loud. Looking up into the billowing smoke, he was surprised to watch Don Armonia ride Don Hurac down as well, even as Alcalde Estilio dropped to his knees, blood spreading swiftly across the ivory-white weskit under his golden coat. Pitching forward, he slammed down on his face.

One of Giles Anson's mighty Walker Colts roared almost at once, and the chamber was filled with screams of terror and outrage.

"Don't run, don't run!" Anson bellowed. "Anyone who wants to live, drop to the floor!" Some of the locals did as they were told, but Anson hadn't expected most to obey. He was right. The panic did help reveal more assassins, however, struggling to hold their positions and bring their own pistols to bear amid those dropping or fleeing. Third Pennsylvania guards were crashing toward them, muskets shoving people aside, bayonets fixed. Several more shots sounded simultaneously and Lewis saw a ball tear one of Don Armonia's sleeves where the man still lay atop Don Hurac. His and Leonor's friends were drawing sabers if they had them or rushing to protect Don Hurac as well.

"Get off me!" shouted Leonor. "I've got my pistols!" Lewis already knew that. One had painfully jabbed him in the ribs. On the other hand, he doubted anyone heard her over the screams and shouts and shooting but him.

"Stay put and leave them hidden, for now!" he shouted back, somehow almost certain it was better that no one knew she was armed. "Protect the parsons," he added. Jumping up, Lewis drew his own saber, joining Varaa with her backsword in hand.

The first thing he saw was the overall pandemonium, the vast majority of locals still fighting toward the exit. A few were actually struggling with armed men, keeping the swords or pistols pointed up or away from others. He thought he recognized some of the more cooperative hidalgos, men who knew their survival depended on the defenses they were helping prepare. He started to lunge to their aid, but heard Anson's big revolver roar again. Looking toward him, he saw his friend standing protectively over his wife, currently crouched by his leg, a wreath of smoke encircling them both. The look on Anson's face was utterly devoid of emotion as he slapped the Walker's loading lever back in place (the otherwise useful contraption tended to flop down under recoil), cock the piece, aim, and fire again. The second of two men advancing around to the right, trying to get past Lewis's saber-wielding wedding party, tumbled against the wall and slid to the floor. The first was already down, kicking spastically with most of his head blown off.

The rest of the assassins, perhaps a dozen men, apparently realizing their surprise had been spoiled and only a concerted effort might succeed, joined one another in a shout and charged. Few still wielded pistols; their weapons now empty, they'd drawn short swords and long knives. Lewis, Reed, Har-Kaaska, Itzam, and Agon charged to meet them, quickly joined by Varaa-Choon and Sira Periz.

Few of Lewis's senior officers were truly proficient with a blade. Coryon Burton was, but he wasn't present. Then again, Lewis could make do, his power and aggressiveness making up for a lot of formal training, and Itzam and Agon could handle themselves as well. Varaa and Har-Kaaska were better. To Lewis's surprise, so was the tiny Sira Periz. But they weren't fighting professionals either. A couple might've been Dom soldiers in disguise, possessing some training with a sword, but they led the attack and were quickly cut down, mostly by Varaa and Sira.

The clang of blades and bloodcurdling screams were punctuated by Anson's revolvers and in mere moments, the fighting seemed to be over. The former wedding attendants were left gasping in the smoke amid a carpet of bodies, hands on their knees. Even as Lewis examined his companions for wounds (Har-Kaaska and Agon both had slashed sleeves and bled from cuts to their arms), the noise outside suddenly swelled with the crackle of muskets.

"We have to get Don Hurac to safety," Lewis said. "He must've been the primary target. Damned assassins," he spat, looking around. Most of the "peaceful" locals had fled and others were finally rising and leaving. A few remained, at least outwardly angry and supportive. *But how do I know?* Lewis wondered. *How do I fight enemies who won't stand under a flag, or will turn a wedding into a battlefield? I have no experience with this.*

"Maybe not," Leonor countered, finally standing. Armonia and his personal guards were helping Don Hurac up as well. Vice Alcalde Don Amil was fluttering around him. "They could'a gone for Don Hurac a bunch'a times before. This was the first time so many of our leaders were so exposed, together."

Lewis shrugged. "Then they were after all of us. What difference does it make? We still need Don Hurac safe. Colonel Agon? Please observe the events outside and direct your troops as you see fit. Send word of the situation as soon as you can."

Don Hurac moved over, followed by his surviving entourage, as Colonel Agon and Colonel Itzam dashed away. In addition to Alcalde Don Estilio, one of "His Supreme Holiness's" guards had been killed.

"You don't seem injured," Lewis observed before bowing his head very slightly to Don Armonia. "Well done, sir. I saw what you did."

Armonia waved that away, almost irritably.

"I rejoice that *you* were not injured, nor was your bride," Don Hurac said, turning to Leonor as she and the clerics approached. "My most profound apologies that your ... interesting ceremony was interrupted."

"It was practic'ly over anyway," Corporal Willis said, poking his head out from behind Anson to speak. He had one of Lewis's pistols in hand, but it hadn't been fired. Leonor glared at him. "Not quite," she countered, raising a brow at Reverend Harkin.

"Indeed," the one-armed minister gravely agreed. "There remains a final detail."

A true volley sounded outside, fairly large, and the tumult in the street was rising.

"We must remove Don Hurac," Colonel Reed reminded, but Don Hurac shook his head. "Please, do not worry about me. I can get safely to the palace by myself—and the palace is surrounded by much of your army."

"How?" Lewis asked, remembering he'd wondered about that earlier.

"A tunnel," Don Amil provided.

"A tunnel?" Lewis repeated with surprise, supposing he must've subconsciously assumed such a thing couldn't exist. The flooding "dry" moat they built around the city and the perpetual damp of the "Holy Sanctum" under the great temple had reinforced that assumption. Of course, no one had told him different either.

"Yes," Don Hurac confessed a little defensively. "From there to here, and other places as well. Quite convenient, if often somewhat . . . sloshy, I'm told. The one in question is currently quite dry."

Lewis turned his gaze to Don Amil, who shrugged. "It should be quite safe. That's the way we came earlier."

"Who else knows about these tunnels?" Lewis asked.

Don Hurac glanced at Armonia and replied, "I'm informed that no one not present even knows they exist—except our abdicated enemy, of course."

Lewis hesitated because that enemy was clearly still represented in the city. After what just happened, combined with the growing sound of battle outside, Lewis finally knew for certain that all his preconceptions that taking an enemy's capital ended the war were no longer valid. At least against their current foe. Still, moving Don Hurac in the open seemed to invite disaster. A single sniper, even an archer, could throw all their efforts into chaos. "Very well," he said, looking back at Don Hurac. "Take all your guards, and these two"—he gestured at the two closest 3rd Pennsylvania troops—"as well as Father Orno, Reverend Harkin . . ." He glanced around. Several helpful civilians had remained. "Them too." His gaze swept to Leonor. "Please also take my wife and Mistress Samantha. I'd ask that you take Sira Periz, but she'll want to command those elements of her division she brought."

"I *knew* this was comin'," Leonor said aside to Samantha. "An' why send *me* off?" she demanded louder.

Lewis just smiled at her. "Didn't you just promise to obey me? I'm sure I heard that part right."

Varaa *kakked* a laugh and clapped her hands together.

Lewis smiled even broader. "Besides, you're not exactly dressed for combat."

Leonor looked down at herself, nodding reluctantly. "That's fair," she conceded. "But I don't have to 'obey' you as a wife yet, 'cause we ain't fully married." She pointed at Harkin. "He didn't finish *that* part."

"My goodness! She's right!" Harkin exclaimed. "That won't do at all. And who knows when we'll have another chance?"

"Hafta start all over from scratch." Corporal Willis chuckled and Leonor seared him with a scowl.

"No, no," Harkin objected. "Quickly, both of you, join hands!"

Leonor snatched Lewis's hand with both of hers and held it close, leaning against him.

Harkin smiled. "In the eyes and name of Almighty God and in the presence of these . . . diminished witnesses, I declare you to be husband and wife." Beaming, he began to say, "You may kiss the bride," but Leonor had already thrown her arms around Lewis's neck to kiss him hard on the lips.

"'Fraid you ain't gonna have much of a weddin' night, Lewis," Anson said wryly as he and his new son-in-law pushed out of the former town house, past the enclosing wall, and into the embattled street, followed closely by Varaa. The other officers had left earlier when Agon reported on the situation. Pitch-dark had replaced the evening light, but flaming torches provided illumination for them to view a dense semicircle of green-uniformed backs. Colonel Agon stalked up behind them, from where he'd been protecting the entrance to the villa. Beyond the troops was a scene of utter chaos among the surging humanity as townsfolk fought among themselves. After the initial attempt to break through that provoked Major Arevalo to fire on the most violent rioters, the bayonet-barbed cordon had served more as a boundary for civil war than anything else.

"You may be right," Lewis said, "but we have to get this sorted out. Decisively so."

Colonel Agon spoke. "Arevalo says the crowd was peaceful at first, apparently genuinely interested in the proceedings, but a number of Blood Priests appeared, openly wearing their red robes and leading gangs of armed ruffians. They fired first and struck some of my men. Troops around them returned fire, and things escalated after that. The volley seems to have dissuaded any more concerted attacks against us, but . . ." He waved. "As you can see, the whole city now seems to fight itself."

"Cap'n Hernandez, comin' in! Hold your fire there . . . an' point them stickers aside, damn you!" came a shout from the mob, and the ranks of green-coated soldiers bowed in a bit, passing through Sal and Corporal T'shia, who were supporting another limping Ranger between them. All three looked haggard and blood spattered, and Sal was missing his distinctive hat. Half a dozen equally rough-looking townsfolk came through the gap with them, eyes wide and panting. Agon's men tried to push them back.

"No, leave 'em be," Sal called out, gasping. "Those fellas—an' a couple they lost—saved our asses." Handing his wounded Ranger off to some troops helping Izel Tuin with the injured, Sal stepped over. "We caught Gen'ral Gomez," he told Anson. "It was him, all right. *Claimed* he'd been helpin' us by keepin' the *locos* under wraps."

"He *would* say that," Agon said skeptically.

Sal nodded. "If he thought it'd do him any good. I b'lieved him, though, since it was those same maniacs that done for him. We only caught his last words, as it were."

"He's dead?" Lewis asked.

"Gutted like a fish in an alley," Sal confirmed.

"Did he say anything else?" Anson asked.

"Only that there's plenty o' radical Doms in the city, which is obvious now, I guess, an' he kinda suspected Don Armonia o' bein' in cahoots with 'em. Didn't know that for sure," he hedged, noting that Lewis and Anson exchanged glances at that, "but he was sure of another fella. You remember that big bastard who shadowed Tranquilo? 'Escorpion'?"

Lewis nodded. So did Anson. Varaa swore under her breath.

"He's here," Sal confirmed. "Gomez figured he was the biggest wheel in the city, behind all o' this." He waved at the fighting again.

"Leonor, Samantha, an' Don Hurac are *with* Armonia," Anson urgently reminded Lewis.

"I know," Lewis practically snapped back, before turning to Agon. "Did anyone get through to the camp around the palace? I wonder if they're encircled there as well."

"I detached a company to escort Colonels Reed, Har-Kaaska, and Periz to headquarters. No encirclement will stop them, and I assume they will relieve us quite soon."

"We don't need relief," Anson objected, glaring at Lewis. "We *need* to get after Armonia in them tunnels."

Lewis rounded on him. "Don't you think I want that too? But which tunnel? Which turns do we take? Have you ever been down there? If Armonia means to make mischief, he'll have done it before we can stop him. We have to rely on the guards to protect Don Hurac—and I trust Leonor to protect Samantha. So should you. We have to focus on what we *can* do: getting rid of Escorpion, his Blood Priests, and all those rising up here. If the Gran Cruzada comes and catches us fighting in the city, we'll never be able to keep them out."

Anson seemed to accept that. "All right. What'll we do?"

Lewis looked at Agon. "We're going to press this crowd, hopefully with the help of those inclined to aid us. We'll ask them to fall back but try to hold a cordon to the sides. Then we'll push the rioters into the arms of our relief."

Agon was shaking his head. "You want civilians to do that? They'll never hold them all."

"I know. Nothing for it. They'll hold some, maybe most, and we'll crush them." His expression turned grim. "You may lose some men, but they'll offer no quarter to any who resist." He looked back at Anson. "You and your Rangers will get the rest over the next few days."

"How? . . . Wait. I *told* you we ain't police!"

"You won't be, any more than you've already been. Up till now, people have likely avoided helping us find the subversive elements out of fear of reprisal. You'll assure them that won't happen."

"How?" Anson repeated.

"Simple," Lewis said. "I'm turning you loose again. The populace will be more afraid of you than Blood Priests, more fearful of *not* telling you what you want to know than what the enemy will do to them."

Anson looked skeptical. "Never thought I'd hear you tell me to beat information out of folks."

Lewis was shaking his head. "That's not what I mean. You'll get their cooperation—and the attention of anyone even thinking of opposing us— by promising to *kill* every Blood Priest and traitor to Don Hurac they point out, then going right then and doing it." He turned to Agon, but Varaa was shaking her head.

"In that case, you must do more than turn Major Anson and his Rangers loose. They will do their part, no doubt, but you need the locals involved as more than just informers. Let the militia do most of the work." She waved around. "They have seen there is an element, maybe even a strong minority, that will fight just to give their maniacal former masters an opportunity to slaughter everyone here. We are not the only ones who will view that position as insane."

Agon was nodding in thoughtful agreement. "Many may fall victim to simple grudges," he cautioned, "and it would be better for us if we're not seen as the direct cause of that. I believe Warmaster Choon has outlined the proper approach."

Even Anson was nodding and Lewis spoke to Agon directly. "Very well. Colonel, if you please, address the crowd and try to tell our friends what we mean to do, with their help. Let's get on with this."

"This place gives me the creeps," Leonor told Samantha, who was clinging to her arm, stepping around the damp places on the stone floor, lit by the torches of the guards behind them. Don Hurac's personal guards led the way down the dank, subterranean avenue. Don Hurac, Don Amil, and Don Armonia walked side by side behind them, closely followed by other people Leonor didn't know. She and Samantha, along with the clerics, came next, just ahead of the infantrymen from the 3rd Pennsylvania.

"You have no idea, my dear," Samantha said in a long-suffering tone. "I've always hated tight, dark places, and it was all I could manage just to come down here. I feel more oppressed with each passing moment."

"S'like a rat warren," one of the infantrymen murmured worriedly behind them. "There'll *be* rats soon enough, I shouldn't wonder."

"Nonsense," Harkin proclaimed. "There may be other unpleasant things, but I doubt there are rats."

"Rats are possible," Father Orno disagreed in a conversational tone that sounded like he was trying to lighten the gloomy atmosphere at the expense of the nervous soldier. "Though rats can hardly cope with . . . those other things."

"Like what?" the other infantryman anxiously asked. "Worse than rats?"

Don Hurac's laugh drifted back. "Fear not. I'm reliably informed this passage is frequently cleared of such pests. All the tunnels under the city are kept remarkably clean."

"Who does the work?" Leonor probed. "Thought you tole Lewis only these fellas even knew about 'em. Your guards don't do all that."

Don Hurac hesitated.

Don Armonia seemed almost to jerk out of some silent reverie. "Slaves," he said dismissively. "Only slaves. They also wash out the sewers by some means, using the lakes to the north and south. The mechanism for that must be ingenious." He glanced at Don Amil. "Although, with the construction of the flooding 'dry moat,' the sewers may have flooded as well. With Alcalde Estilio's unfortunate demise, perhaps you can help me look into that."

"What slaves?" Leonor persisted. "All the slaves are s'posed to be freed. What're they doin' when they ain't flushin' sewers—an' who're they doin' it for?"

"The woman has posed a fair question," Don Amil conceded, looking at Armonia.

"What was it?" Armonia asked. "I rarely attend the gabble of females and fear I am . . . somewhat distracted by our ordeal, not to mention that . . . most bizarre ceremony."

Don Hurac nodded graciously. "It has been a distressing evening for us all, but I have every confidence our liberators will quickly restore order."

"Our liberators," Don Armonia said lowly, somewhat sarcastically. "Yes, they certainly saved us from those vile assassins."

Leonor was growing furious, but controlled herself, knowing her anger threatened to distract her from what she viewed as a very pertinent point. Armonia had remained an enigma, and everyone was suspicious of him. On the one hand, despite his demeanor, he'd become tight with Don Hurac and was virtually his constant companion. This despite the fact no one in the Holy City ever heard of a "Voz de El Gente," or "Voice of the People." Oddly, that alone meant nothing. Nearly every member of the Dom aristocracy had some sort of title in its bloated bureaucracy, whether they ever did anything or not. And a man in the position Armonia claimed would've likely been the very least heeded official in the city. In his defense, he had helped organize the civilian labor battalions and made sure they were equipped and fed.

On the other hand, though he acted as if he was devoted to Don Hurac and he believed Tranquilo and his Blood Priests were the true cause of the fall of the Holy City and the worst thing ever to happen to the Dominion, he made no secret of his preference for the "old ways." Don Hurac might now consider those pre–Blood Priest customs despicable and barbaric, but just as he hadn't converted overnight, it was probably too much to ask it of everyone else. The fact Armonia didn't automatically support all of Don Hurac's reforms probably made him more believable, not less.

Leonor knew her father didn't think that. Spying on him had been one reason he'd been absent so much of late. And she, like him, believed Armonia's organizational work could just as easily be applied to subversive as supportive elements. She began to watch him closely as they made their way down the long, arched tunnel. Another cross-passage was coming up; they'd passed four already, but Leonor noted that Armonia appeared to be looking intently at the next one.

"My daughter asked who these former 'slaves' might be, and who they might be in league with," Samantha stated, loudly and forcefully, voice echoing down the passage. Though Don Amil and Don Hurac both glanced back at them, Don Armonia did not.

"Somethin' ain't right," Leonor hissed aside to Samantha, slowing her step. Her highest duty to the cause might demand that she protect Don Hurac, but she felt a higher duty to her father's new wife.

"Why are you slowing, my dear?" Harkin asked, voice also practically booming down the corridor, finally causing Armonia to frown over his shoulder. "We must be nearly there. Are you all right?"

"Fine," Leonor assured, bending down, but watching ahead. "I got somethin' in one o' these stupid shoes Mistress Samantha made me wear."

"Stupid shoes indeed!" Samantha exclaimed indignantly, then hissed very low to Orno, Harkin, and the following soldiers, "Something is dreadfully wrong. Be prepared." She raised her voice again. "Have you any notion how difficult it was to have those shoes made? None of mine would fit her great, monstrous feet," she pretended to say aside to Father Orno with a fond smile. "Nor would they have been appropriate with her dress. I actually measured one of her bare feet in her sleep—they're not *truly* monstrous." She chuckled, then continued proudly, "And I commissioned a cobbler in Vera Cruz to make them!"

"As far back as that?" Father Orno politely inquired, though he now also focused on the group just ahead.

"Yes," Samantha proclaimed, tone triumphant. "Even then, I knew this day was inevitable." She frowned. "I never imagined it would end so . . . inconveniently, of course. The whole grand reception, shot! I had *so* looked forward to the dancing."

Still crouching, Leonor was grateful for Samantha's deliberate prattle, distracting attention as she fished under the folds of her rumpled dress for one of her Paterson Colts.

A roar sounded, and men erupted from the gloom of both side passages ahead, crashing into Don Hurac's guards. The roar was immediately mixed with echoing screams and curses and the sound of steel on steel.

"Shit," Leonor said. "I hate it when my bad feelin's come true." Drawing her revolver, she stood, keeping the weapon concealed in a fold of fabric. The group behind Don Hurac, Don Amil, and Don Armonia had absorbed the trio as they fell back and all began to retreat together. Several turned toward Leonor and her friends, however, suddenly brandishing blades. Others started stabbing the men right beside them. "Shit!" Leonor said again, more forcefully. The two infantrymen pushed past, Springfield muskets leveled.

"Damn," said one. "Can't shoot. We might hit Don Hurac!"

"It's the bayonet, then," the other said resignedly, voice wavering. Regardless, both men advanced briskly enough, meeting what could only be another pack of assassins with a shout. The infantrymen were both "original" members of the 3rd. That meant, in spite of their reluctance to face rats, they'd seen their share of battle and put that experience to use, aggressively joining the fight.

Whatever they fought for, none of the assassins was well prepared to face them, and two died very quickly, wicked, needle-sharp, triangular bayonets skewering them almost at once. More screams resounded in the passage, the dank smell of mildew overcome by the copper-iron tang of blood and stench of pierced bowels.

"That one, Bill, *that* one!" an infantryman shrilled, twisting to avoid the thrust of a short sword.

"Which I'm doin' me best, ain't I? This one's stuck on me blade!"

"Kick 'im off, then! Ah! There!" cried the first man, smashing the steel butt of his musket into a hairy face, the crackle of shattering bone and teeth amazingly loud in the confined space. The first soldier finally pulled his blade free with a sucking *pop!* and immediately lunged past his comrade to stab another.

The fighting between the first attackers and guards seemed to be in hand as well. Those men had largely been provided by Colonel Agon, veterans all, and again, despite the initial surprise and resultant casualties, the difference in experience and weaponry started to even the odds. A musket fired deafeningly when one of the infantrymen found a quick gap and shot an assassin about to slash one of those guards, and the target teetered back into the darkness and fell without a sound. A closer attacker stabbed the soldier in the upper leg. Hissing in pain, he bashed the man away with his musket and slammed his bayonet in his chest. With a cry, he fell to his knees when his leg suddenly failed him. His comrade quickly covered him.

It was then that Leonor saw Don Amil, eyes wide and arms slashed and bloodied, struggling with a man holding a long knife. All the torches had been dropped, throwing mad shadows on the walls and arched ceiling, and the smoke from the musket shot made it hard to tell who his attacker was from behind. But Don Hurac was just beyond, face suffused with shock and terror. That was all Leonor had to go on, her *sense* that Don Amil was protecting Don Hurac. That made the other man an enemy... probably. *Better not kill whoever it is, just in case*, she decided. Raising her revolver, she shot the man in the back, squarely through his right shoulder blade.

Whoever it was, he screamed and dropped the knife, then screamed again when Don Amil overcame the arm, slamming it into the wall of the tunnel. An instant's consideration convinced Leonor she'd chosen well because Don Amil still seemed more intent on holding the attacker back than turning on Don Hurac. Utterly expressionless now, Leonor strode forward, casually shooting the nearest assailants until only one round remained in her Paterson. Hiking up the heavy skirt of her dress, she drew the other one. Giving an astonished Don Hurac a curt nod as she passed him, she walked up behind his still-battling guards. Only two were left, standing against four assassins. "'Scuse me, fellas," she said, shoving the revolver past a guard's shoulder to shoot his opponent in the face. The man fell back, kicking. As quick as she could cock it, the Paterson barked again, catching its next target in the back of the neck as he turned to run, blowing out his throat. The last two enemies were only fleeing shadows by then. She considered throwing a shot after them anyway, but decided to save it. *This might not be over*, she thought.

"Keep your eyes peeled," she told the gasping guards, then turned to see what was what. There was a lot of blood and quite a few bodies. Nearly every one of Don Hurac's civilian followers was down, and there was no telling at a glance which had been treacherous or loyal. Some were only wounded and lay moaning in the blood, but aside from insuring none were still dangerous, she ignored them. Don Hurac was gazing at her with something like awe mixed with fear. Don Amil seemed somewhat dazed, but his expression was similar to his master's. Reverend Harkin, Father Orno, and Samantha were picking their way forward, joining the two Pennsylvania infantrymen, one limping heavily, but both grinning hugely.

"I swear," said the unwounded soldier. "And Colonel Cayce just *married* her!"

A grin cracked through Leonor's "battle face," and she nodded. "He sure did, but he knew what he was gettin'." Her eyes finally settled on the first man she shot, still leaning against the tunnel wall. "Well. I'll be derned. Don Armonia. I shouldn't be, but I'm surprised. Guess you were just too obviously a villain ta believe."

"I am killed," Armonia hissed and spat. "Killed by a *woman*."

"You ain't killed yet," Leonor scoffed. "I expect it hurts pretty fierce, though."

"Why?" Don Hurac asked softly, stepping closer. "Why save my life and then . . . this? Why . . . any of it?"

"Because you are *doomed*, you fool!" Armonia responded derisively. "Even though I have been numbered among the Blood Priests myself—of *course* I hold no such position as I claimed. Have 'the people' ever deserved a voice?" He sneered. "Still, I was tempted to give you a chance since you *are* the legitimate Supreme Holiness, and this put me at dangerous odds with . . . certain other factions with whom I was intended to coordinate." He shook his head. "But the changes you insist on cannot be condoned by God." He glared at Father Orno. "The *real* God." He looked back at Don Hurac. "So I helped plan the rising in the city to get you here, now, but was not consulted about the attack at that blasphemous wedding ceremony. It took me as much by surprise as you. Even then, I wasn't attempting to save *you*. We merely collided as I lunged to push Don Amil or Alcalde Emilio to the floor."

"Thinking we might be easier to manipulate!" Don Amil snapped furiously.

Armonia only nodded. "Granted, Estilio was my first choice." He gestured at Leonor and the clerics. "But I would have tried to save them as well, given the chance."

"What on earth for?" Harkin mused aloud. "You couldn't have thought to manipulate *us*."

"Why not?" Armonia demanded. "You would have believed whatever I said, at that point."

"But . . . why?" Harkin asked, just as mystified now as Don Hurac had been.

"It's terribly simple, actually, if not very obvious. Ultimately, I would have needed your help to replace Don Hurac." A grim, pained chuckle escaped him. "You see, I had long played the role of Supreme Holiness for the masses, during our various ceremonies, and found I rather liked it. And if I couldn't keep it, at least I might hold the place for another more deserving."

"Tranquilo?" Father Orno guessed.

Armonia rolled his eyes. "Of course not. He is truly mad. And Brother Escorpion, the man behind the attack on the wedding, is merely Tranquilo's tool. He would gladly kill *me* now, so I needed protection from him as well."

"Who, then?"

Armonia shook his head. "I shall not say."

"How could you think we'd help you after you had Don Hurac killed?" Reverend Harkin practically raged. "We were here! We would've *seen*!"

"Why not support me?" Armonia asked, genuinely surprised. "Someone would have to hold the people on your side against the Gran Cruzada. Never doubt it still comes."

Leonor shook her head and pointed at Armonia with her pistol, wagging it like a scolding finger. "You people are crazy. 'Sides, case you haven't noticed, most folks still in the city're already on our side. An' them that ain't, Escorpion or whoever, will prob'ly get sorted by my father"—she smiled—"an' new husband before the sun's up." She looked at Father Orno. "Now let's hurry an' see if we can get these hurt men some help"—she tilted her head at Armonia—"an' get him to a rope."

CHAPTER 21

It took longer than the darkness gave them to "sort" the rebellion in the city. The four militia regiments were mobilized, but they took more time to muster than expected. That was actually a good thing to know, and the leadership cadre would have to work on that. There were, understandably, a large number of absences, quite a few members already fighting on one side or the other. Under the "direction" of Itzam, Agon, Sira, and Anson (all but Anson being a "local" of a sort themselves), each regiment, backed by regiments of the regular army and a battery of guns on call, scoured a quarter of the city. A fire broke out in the northwest quarter, probably deliberate, but no one stopped their hunt for the enemy in their midst long enough to fight it, and it threatened to consume everything in its path. Har-Kaaska's 2nd Division was diverted from supporting the locals and tasked with fighting the blaze. The men and women in that quarter had mostly come from outside the city and needed no help killing traitors, but Har-Kaaska's veterans were hard-pressed to extinguish the flames before grain stores and some of the ammunition-packed armories in the area were threatened.

The hardest fighting was on the opposite side of the city, southeast of the great central temple, and it was brutal indeed. The "rebels" were surprisingly numerous and well armed there. On the other hand, Don Hurac's "loyalists" were just as thorough and bloodthirsty when it came to eradicating their own people who were not only busily slaughtering anyone who didn't believe as they did, but would've gladly helped leave them at the mercy of Blood Priests. That quarter was the only place Giles Anson and his Rangers, along with Dukane's battery of 12pdr howitzers, saw action. Sadly, it was virtually impossible that every single loyalist had fled that part of the city, nor could anyone reliably tell the difference in the heat of the moment. The one consolation was, by the time Anson and Dukane literally blasted their way down city streets in the early light of the following day, most would've gotten away. At least that's what they told themselves.

Anson had established his headquarters at the base of one of the lesser pyramidal temples, and that's where Lewis and Leonor found him under an overcast morning sky. No rain threatened, as the thick clouds were high and white, but it was uncomfortably humid. Both Lewis and Leonor had long since changed into their usual battle dress, but neither had slept. They hadn't enjoyed so much as a moment alone, for that matter, having to cope with the aftermath of the multiple assassination attempts while overseeing the suppression of rebels around the main temple. Then had come other complications . . .

"Are you all right, Father?" Leonor asked Anson as she stepped down from her horse. The Ranger looked uncharacteristically subdued.

"Carry on," he told a couple of Rangers and some locals in green coats, waving them away. He then turned to his visitors. "Been a rough night." He sighed, then looked more closely at Lewis and his daughter. "You two don't look so great either," he observed before adding, "These people are crazy." He had no way of knowing he was echoing a statement his daughter made earlier.

"It's been a long night—and morning—for everyone, I'm afraid," Lewis said cryptically. "How are the local troops holding up? How are they performing?" he asked.

"Not bad." Anson sounded surprised by that. "No complaints about their willingness to fight." He waved down one of the streets his Rangers and Dukane's battery were clearing. "An' they been . . . findin' plenty motivation," he appended bitterly. "They ain't really trained for this kind o' fightin', though. None of us are, for that matter. It's like Monterrey all over again. I finally put in some o' our boys 'cause they have more experience an' the locals were losin' too many." He sighed again. "Seen some terrible things. Locals rubbed out by locals. That sorta thing. Found where one o' 'our' hidalgos had been stayin'. Guess he ran home to protect his family when the fightin' broke out last night." He shook his head. "Poor bastard was crucified, still alive when we found him, but his wife—I guess it was his wife—an' six kids had been beheaded right where he could see. Stuff like that . . ."

"Jesus wept," Lewis said lowly.

Leonor's face clouded with fury. "How're we s'posed to fight that kinda crazy?" she demanded. "An' they did it just to horrify *us* too. I mean, even our supporters here would kinda expect it, I guess. But not us. How?" She looked at Lewis, eyes starting to swim. "How do they understand us so well, know what that'll do to us, but we don't understand them at all?"

"I don't know," Lewis replied quietly.

Anson cleared his throat, looking at his daughter. "They didn't just do it for us," he said, then changed the subject. "I heard what you an' Samantha went through. Word got around pretty fast." Glancing at Lewis, he asked, "Don Hurac's okay, then? What about Armonia?"

"Don Hurac's fine. He's with Zyan. That woman is a marvel, figuring out a way to be so important to a man in this society." Lewis's tone hardened. "Armonia is patched up for now. We have to keep him alive to hang." He hesitated. "Did you hear that Captain Beeryman's back?"

Anson's eyes widened, and he looked in the direction they came as if expecting to see him. "Boogerbear's here? No, first I've heard. Where is he?"

"Resting," Lewis replied. "I ordered his whole force to their tents. Hanny Cox's section as well. If anything, they're more worn-out than we are."

"But if he's here, personally . . ." Anson began, and Lewis nodded.

"Right. The Gran Cruzada's on its way. He's seen it. Even fought a few actions with its scouts. He believes the vanguard will arrive in about ten days. Maybe a couple weeks."

"Jesus, that was fast," Anson murmured. "Last we heard, he was scrappin' with some o' Tranquilo's guards close to some place called Teocaltiche, or somethin'." He snorted. "Had an 'understandin'' with 'em."

Lewis was nodding. "I gather his arrangement held up surprisingly well and it was his . . . acquaintance among the enemy who warned him of the main army's approach. He waited to see for himself, of course, and was apparently able to make close observations entirely due to his enemy 'friend.' I can't wait to hear more about that. Mr. Beeryman did confirm that it looked to him that the vanguard, roughly the first quarter, perhaps third of the enemy host, outnumbers our whole army by itself." Lewis paused. "And based on his description, it's at least as modern and professional as any Dom force we've faced."

"How did they look? The soldiers, I mean."

Lewis nodded, understanding the true meaning of the question. "That may be our biggest advantage. He said they look lean and scary, but hungry as well. They can't be supplied by sea anymore and, in his words, have 'plumb scoured the country they're movin' through of anything that can be ate.' His source advised him the enemy army will be relying on this city—and our supply train—to sustain it."

"So this 'General Xacolotl'—that's his name, right?"

Lewis nodded.

"He'll have to try to finish us quick."

"That's how I see it."

"An' the longer we hold him, the worse it'll be for him."

"Also true, most likely." Lewis pursed his lips and scratched the whiskers on his neck under his beard.

"What?" Anson asked. "Somethin' else is eatin' you," he stated.

Leonor frowned and said, "We also got a dispatch from Vera Cruz, right before Boogerbear came in." She paused. "It's bad."

Anson waved around and tilted his head toward the ongoing fighting. The thunderclap of one of Dukane's howitzers seemed to punctuate his meaning. "Today's the day for it," he grumbled.

Deciding to just spit it out, Leonor said, "Uxmal has fallen. Most o' the noncombatants got out, gone to Itzincab, but it's likely the rest, includin' Colonel De Russy, held out to the last. Like Travis at the Alamo, I guess," she added miserably, looking down.

"Captain Holland has been evacuating all our other outposts to Vera Cruz and Techolotla," said Lewis.

"He'll be hatin' that, wishin' for a big sea fight instead. Makes sense, though," Anson speculated absently, also looking down. "Poor ol' De Russy. Never wanted ta be a soldier. Now he'll always be remembered as one." He nodded at his daughter. "Like Travis, or Leonidas." He looked back at Lewis. "What about Sira Periz? She's gonna be in hell, what with her city fallin' while she's gone. She gonna want to take part o' the army to win it back?"

Lewis shook his head. "Varaa's with her. Took her the news." He inhaled deeply. "Sira can be impetuous, but she's no fool. She might blame me for not going to protect her city sooner..."

"That's a buncha crap," Leonor defended. "De Russy told us himself he could hold!"

"Regardless," Lewis continued, "she'll understand that now that Uxmal has actually fallen, we can only retake it with the whole army. And we can only do *that* with a secure supply base, which is now Vera Cruz."

"An' Vera Cruz only stays safe if we beat the Gran Cruzada," Anson finished. Another howitzer boomed, followed by a lot of carbine fire. "I swear, Lewis. To think you two got married last night an' all this started up. Ain't very lucky."

"Only the fightin' in the city started last night," Leonor scoffed. "Everything else had already happened."

"Still..." Anson gave Lewis a funny look. "You *knew* this would happen, didn't you? The fightin' here, anyway. That's why you finally agreed to the weddin' all of a sudden."

Lewis glanced uncomfortably at Leonor. "We all felt the tension festering, so the... timing may have been influenced by my hope we could sort things out before we were faced by an outside threat," he conceded. Watching Leonor's fury mount, he quickly added, "But the timing was the *only* thing. Not the intent, or sincerity of my feelings. I would've done it sooner, in fact, if I hadn't sensed the opportunity..."

"Oh, just shut up, Lewis!" Leonor snapped. "I know who you are. *What* you are. You're a soldier, through an' through. More than that, though, you're a strategist. No, I don't think you'd'a married me if you didn't love me, just to start a fight." She actually chuckled. "Fact is, even I can see that earlier after we got here wouldn't've kicked things off like this. The weddin' would'a just been folded in with all the other weird stuff goin' on. Waitin' awhile." She shrugged. "I guess I'd be a little disappointed if you hadn't used the weddin' the best way you could to help the cause!"

Lewis tentatively smiled at her. "You're not mad?"

Leonor shook her head. "Didn't say that. But I do understand, an' I guess I approve. Just wish we had a *little* time alone!"

Anson burst out laughing. When he began to recover, he waved them away. "Go," he said. "We're gettin' this straightened out well enough. Nobody needs either of you just now. Find a place, find some *peace* while you can. I know it helped me, an' I thank the good Lord for Samantha every day. Enjoy your weddin' . . . *day after* off." The humor faded from his face. "Seriously, Lewis. I know we just found out we're about outa time to get ready for the god damned Doms, but there ain't a thing you can personally do about it until we finish up here." He tilted his head down the street. "When we do, things'll get busy for everybody, an' God knows if you'll find any time after that."

With a glance at Leonor, Lewis reluctantly nodded. "Very well," he said gravely. "I do have orders for you, however. I want you to lead all our mounted troops out of the city within two days. Half the modern, flying artillery, and all the spare mounts as well. You'll use those to carry supplies and munitions at first, hiding it in caches. After that, you'll need more replacement animals out there"—he pointed generally toward one of the distant walls—"than we will in here."

"When do you want us back?"

"I don't. You'll take every opportunity to harass and slow the enemy—"

"Avoidin' decisive engagements, o' course," Anson pressed wryly.

"Of course," Lewis confirmed very seriously. "Personal reasons aside, I simply can't spare you, or any of our mounted regiments. Go do what you do best, as carefully as you can, but stop as soon as the enemy reaches the city."

"Stop? What for?"

Lewis finally smiled a little. "I want the Doms to think you've joined us inside. Again, at least for a time."

Anson grinned. "But I'll still be on the loose."

"In a sense. Continue to gather intelligence and watch for signals from us, but do your best to avoid contact." He smiled again. "Until I cut your leash again."

"Always a buncha damn restrictions," Anson grumbled.

Leonor laughed and hugged her father. "Go on, now," he said. "Go on an' do . . . whatever it is the oddest pair o' newlyweds I ever heard of can think up to do. Me an' Reed an' Agon an' Har-Kaaska can handle things for a damned *day*, by God." He chuckled. "I'll keep Varaa busy too, so she don't find you an' bug you."

Lewis nodded his thanks, looking at Leonor again. "There's one last thing I have to do first, and I'd appreciate your company, my dear."

Leonor nodded, raising a brow.

"I need to see Sira Periz. I can't deny the possibility she'll blame me for the loss of her city, but I believe she'll continue to do her duty. She must return to Texcoco and rejoin her division at once. When she arrives, I want her to start moving much of the stockpiled ammunition forward as quickly as she can, especially case shot and canister for the artillery. We must prepare for a complete circumvallation once the enemy appears, and I can't imagine they'll be foolish enough to permit our continued supply. At the same time, I doubt they'll split their force and move to surround Texcoco as quickly, and Sira *should* be able to replace whatever she sends."

Surprised, Leonor asked, "You ain't gonna have her bring her division up? She's *really* gonna want to fight, ya know."

"She'll have her chance," Lewis assured, "just not here," he added cryptically.

CHAPTER 22

MARCH 5, 1849

A rumble of horse hooves echoed dully off the trees bordering the grassy, dew-damp vale below. On either side of the road, morning sunlight glistened bright on high green stalks in the humid chill.

"They're comin'," murmured Major Giles Anson unnecessarily aside to Captains Barca and Meder as the Ranger hoisted himself on his horse, Colonel Fannin. Barca's whole battery of 6pdrs was on line in the dense trees about eighty yards off and parallel to the Camino de la Plata, each gun laid obliquely to cover the entrance to the long clearing. This was to prevent them from firing directly across the road and endangering Dukane's battery of howitzers, similarly deployed and aimed. Felix Meder silently shook Barca's hand and trotted off to the left, holding his saber tight against his side so it wouldn't rattle. There he joined half his riflemen, roughly two hundred strong, behind a low, hasty earthwork they'd prepared to support the guns. The rest of his riflemen were with Dukane.

"Stand ready," Barca softly called to his gunners as Anson urged his horse into the trees behind, disappearing as he also veered left, quickening Colonel Fannin's pace to pass beyond Meder's men.

"Let a little slack in that lanyard," Lieutenant Hanny Cox mildly scolded Tani Fik, the Number Four man on his Number Two gun.

"Aye, easy does it, lad," hissed Preacher Mac over his shoulder. He and

Hahessey were crouched low beside the wheel hubs. "Tight as yer strung, that monstrous beast Hahessy could set ye off wi' his tiniest, wee little fart!"

Almost instantly, a low, *frapp*ing rumble came from the big Irishman.

"Oh, ye vile, filthy—"

"Silence!" Hanny whispered harshly.

Horsemen suddenly burst into view, a large squad of blue-clad Rangers thundering straight down the road, led by Sal Hernandez. His distinctive hat trailed flapping behind his head, restrained by the braided cord around his neck. None of the fleeing troopers so much as glanced their direction as they galloped past, shouting apparently nervous encouragement to one another. Even as they drew farther away, the pounding of hooves grew louder, and less than a hundred and fifty paces behind the last Ranger, an impressively tight column of fours pounded into view.

Hanny hadn't seen any enemies dressed like these. Protected by less elaborate bronze helmets than Dom lancers, decorated with long, red feathers instead of plumes, they also wore bright yellow shell jackets in place of the lancers' shiny bronze cuirasses. Black leather saber belts, white breeches, and black knee boots completed their uniforms. Armed as they were with musketoons, pistols, sabers, and short stabbing or throwing spears instead of lances, they looked to Hanny like Dom dragoons, but Sal had called them "Jinetes," which he translated as "light cavalry." Whatever they were, there was a lot of them, perhaps seven to nine hundred already in view. They'd been told to expect a regiment-size force.

"Almost . . ." Hanny began. Just then, as what looked like the tail end of the enemy formation emerged, Coryon Burton's bugler sounded the call for the artillery to commence firing.

"Battery!" roared Captain Barca. "By the battery . . . *Fire!*"

Six guns roared as one, spewing swarms of canister wrapped in sheets of orange fire within a billowing wall of smoke. A heartbeat later, Dukane's 12pdr howitzers, perhaps even more lethal with canister at the range involved, belched their own spreading clouds of death. The smoke from both sides roiled out across the back third of the Dom column and hung there a moment, impenetrable, hiding the terrible carnage wrought there. The sounds of horror were clear, however. A chorus of hundreds of high-pitched shrieks, from men and horses both, was the first thing to assail the souls of the ambushers.

"Reload canister and hold!" Barca cried.

Felix Meder's riflemen opened up, firing at will at chosen targets, sweeping a respectable percentage of apparent officers and NCOs from their horses. They got off only a single shot each before Coryon Burton's four hundred dragoons spilled from the forest across the track with a spine-tingling bellow. Sabers raised, they crashed into the confused, milling, terrified Doms. A brief, brutal slaughter ensued, but the dragoons didn't linger among the still-more-numerous enemy. They simply crashed through the stalled, floundering formation, hacking as they went. Severed arms and even heads arced in the air amid sluicing blood spray, marking their passage, and more horses and men screamed in pain.

Hanny glimpsed Burton whirling his horse around, halting his men out in front of the guns, shouting for them to re-form. They quickly did so, and mere moments later, they surged into a charge back through the Doms. Shattered as they were as a unit, individual Doms had recovered themselves enough to meet the dragoons with spears, musketoons, or sabers. Coryon took losses of his own this time. Hanny saw blue-coated figures stabbed or shot from their saddles. Others slumped over or recoiled from injuries, but managed to stay on their horses. Still, Burton's dragoons mauled the enemy just as savagely as before and were soon re-forming in front of the far trees again. This time it took longer, and even from where he stood, Hanny heard the young dragoon officer shouting to control his men or order his wounded out of the fight.

Doms with authority, either moral or official, yelled at their own men to close up and face their tormentors. To their credit, most of them did, forming a ragged line on the corpse-cluttered road, feverishly preparing for the dragoons' next attack. Unfortunately for them, that's when Anson swept out of the trees on Hanny's side of the road and swarmed forward with five hundred Rangers. Wholly unexpected, they slammed into the enemy from behind, shooting and stabbing with ferocious abandon.

The Doms shattered.

The smoke that had choked the rear of the column had finally begun to clear, revealing a heaving mass of wounded men and animals. Panicking Dom troopers tried to flee back through them. Some already there who'd miraculously survived were already fleeing from whence they came. Lunging horses did their best to find a way through the remainder. Many crashed down, throwing and rolling over their riders. A few yellow-clad horsemen got back up, running or hobbling after their comrades, but neither the Rangers nor dragoons pursued.

A bugle sounded the same sharp call as before, and Barca yelled, "Fire!" before the last notes were heard. Cannon went off more raggedly this time, but it made no difference at all. Each of the staggered, thunderous reports sent another load of canister whistling and buzzing into the routing, clumping Doms, churning up the mass of broken, mangled flesh, living and dead. Another six rounds from the howitzers across the road utterly wrecked whatever lingering discipline and courage the ravaged cavalry clung to. Then the dragoons charged again, sweeping in behind the few hundred Doms still fighting Anson's Rangers—to escape, more than anything, it seemed—and the last Jinetes scattered, fleeing every which way, mounted or afoot.

There was still no effort to chase them, and mere moments after the proud light cavalry had galloped into view, two-thirds at least lay dead or dying amid the blood-streaming wreckage of their regiment. A diminishing flurry of shots and the thuds and cracks of sabers striking flesh and bone quickly gave way to the tumult of agony. At no time had Hanny felt threatened, and the scene he beheld was enough to make him gag.

Boogerbear galloped back over in front of Barca's battery, his unnaturally large "local" horse named "Dodger" still looking overburdened by the big Ranger. His long dark beard was splashed with blood as if he'd personally savaged the enemy with his teeth.

"Thank God those bloody Rangers're on our side," Preacher Mac murmured low.

"Aye," Hahessy agreed. "An' they do take best advantage when Colonel Cayce turns 'em loose. That they do."

"That's why the Doms are so scared of them. Call them 'Los Diablos,'" said Hanny's friend Kini Hau, stepping up from the limber behind.

"They call us all that," corrected Hoziki, the Number Three man. His tone was vaguely cheerful, unusual for him. Then again, Doms had killed his mother, and he hated them even worse than most.

"Aye," Preacher Mac agreed. "Shouldn't wonder they'll hae a even less flatterin' title fer Mr. Anson's Rangers."

"Sharp an' quick," Boogerbear called out to Barca as he pulled his horse to a halt. "By God, Ramon Lara an' his lancers would'a loved this shit. Well done, lads," he added louder for the benefit of the rest of the artillerymen and nearby riflemen. Felix Meder was trotting over to join Barca. "Major Anson's compliments," Boogerbear told the officers, "an' he wants all the artillery limbered up an' pulled out on the road by batteries right quick—just a bit over from the mess we just made, o' course."

"What about the rifles?" Meder asked.

"You'll stay in support o' the guns, an' help move 'em out, if ya please. Hafta get 'em past some deadfall on this side."

"Of course, sir."

Boogerbear rolled his eyes. "How many times I gotta tell you young fellers, I ain't no god . . . derned 'sir.' Even if I was, I'm just a cap'n, like you."

"Yes, sir," Meder automatically replied.

Hahessy laughed out loud. "Yer stuck with it, I reckon . . . sir," he added with a touch of sarcasm. "Any man monstrous enough ta pull *me* apart like a fly . . . *I'll* call 'im 'sir' with no complaint!"

Hardened as they all were, after what Barca's artillerymen and Meder's riflemen had just seen—and done—the laughter that followed was good for them all. Not least because Hahessy, once feared or reviled by most of the army, was now able to mock himself. Boogerbear nodded at the big Irishman with what looked like newfound respect.

"What next?" Barca asked. "More of the same?" he added a little dismally.

Boogerbear nodded. "Reckon so. Ask young Hanny; we already done this a couple times. Bastards just don't catch on. Too puffed up ta learn from us, I guess. Still, this little scuffle hurt 'em more than the others, an' I bet they'll put out some flankers, at least, er send smaller scouts out ahead of a big reaction force." He shrugged. "What I'd do, anyway. Devils're pretty full o' theirselves, but they ain't stupid. They'll learn, by an' by, an' we'll throw 'em another twist."

Barca cleared his throat. "What about our wounded?"

"You got any?" Boogerbear asked. Barca shook his head. "Well, there's bound ta be some, 'mongst the Rangers or dragoons," he speculated, looking out where that fighting had been. "Bound ta be," he repeated. "Haul 'em out on your caissons till we get back to the baggage train, if ye would."

"Of course," Barca agreed. "But what about enemy wounded and prisoners?"

"Ain't takin' none," Boogerbear answered simply. "What would we do with 'em?"

Glancing out at the aftermath of the fight, all could now see a number of Rangers catching and gathering loose horses. Others, however, mostly Ocelomeh and probably Holcanos, had dismounted and were wading through the downed Doms and animals, thrusting with sabers to dispatch any live ones they found with equal efficiency. "It's a mercy, y'know, for man an' beast," Boogerbear quietly assured them, guessing how they felt. "Doms won't try ta heal none o' them wounded, they'll just send 'em on, as painful as they can. Figger it's their duty." He scowled. "An' them are the lucky ones, compared to those that got away unhurt. Those'd be smarter ta just keep a'runnin'." He shook his head. "Prob'ly won't, though. Now let's get on with it. More Doms'll be close behind the bunch we beat on, an' they'll try ta catch us. Gotta get ready for 'em."

As if to punctuate his warning, one of the raucous Dom horns began to blare in the distance, quickly answered by another.

"What is the meaning of this?" General Xacolotl roared with some difficulty as he strode, puffing, rapidly and purposefully up the small rise in the center of the marching camp established by his army's vanguard. He was breathing hard, holding his golden sword scabbard as he walked, hand shaking with fury. He'd been several miles back with the main body of his army, but came at once when Teniente Juaris, a newcomer to his staff who'd commanded the mixed force that escorted His Supreme Holiness, Primer Patriarcha Sachihiro, and Holy Patriarcha Tranquilo out of the Holy City to meet the Gran Cruzada, informed him what was going on. He and his entourage had left their horses at the bottom of the slope, and many of the aides and staff members rushing to keep up with him wore somewhat nervous expressions. There were exceptions. One who stood out was Teniente Juaris himself, whose expression was bitter and angry.

What frightened the others was that Xacolotl was addressing a rather large gathering of Blood Priests in the company of Tranquilo, Sachihiro, and the Patriarcha de la Guerra, Don Thiago de Feliz Río. The rather pitiful figure of the Blood Cardinal Don Frutos del Gran Vale was there as well. Don Frutos had filled out amazingly since the ordeal of his humiliating defeats in the south and his long, arduous journey to join the army. With only the trappings of his former authority, however, a bright red robe with gaudy gold embroidery, he cut a pathetic figure that even the lowliest Blood Priest could ignore with impunity.

The always emaciated-looking Tranquilo, though draped in his own ragged, filthy red robe and hood, radiated all the authority in the world when he turned his malevolent, sunken-eyed gaze on the overall commander of the enormous army, who came to a stop before him. "I beg your pardon?" he squawked as if demanding an answer to a ludicrous question. "That should be obvious even to you, *General*," he added in a tone of supreme condescension, emphasizing the title as if it were equivalent to "slave." Raising his scrawny arms under the robe, he gestured around. The camp was huge, filling what had once been several large grain fields laboriously cleared of forest timber. Countless tents radiated geometrically away from this raised center, upon which a number of naked Blood Priests a few yards away gestured and capered and chanted in front of tens of thousands of watching soldiers.

Other Blood Priests, also naked except for the blood splashed upon them, waited while yellow-clad Jinetes were dragged forward, one after another, before being stripped and stretched across a heavy stone platform the Blood Priests took with them everywhere. There, the men screamed as their bellies were opened with green obsidian knives, their entrails pulled out, and priests practically crawled inside to reach under the ribs and cut out their beating hearts. The hearts were then held up and triumphantly displayed as they jetted the last blood inside them upon the priests, who danced under the crimson rain. Only then did a heavy blade descend to chop off the head of the victim.

The whole vanguard of the army was watching this spectacle, and now this confrontation. "This evening we not only make an example of those who cravenly fled the enemies of God, we provide Him with a feast of blood," Tranquilo's buzzard-like voice loudly proclaimed. "It might be the blood of cowards," he sneered, "but if even the blood of heretics can nourish God, so can that of these traitors who disgraced our holy endeavor. Perhaps God even prefers such blood!"

A roar surged up from the army around them, though it wasn't the same kind of sound one heard from city dwellers at a sacrifice of slaves. This didn't sound approving at all.

"You finally go too far!" Xacolotl shouted. "You there, hold! Release that man!" he bellowed as another pale, terrified trooper, his obviously badly wounded arm wrapped in a bloody, makeshift bandage, was brought to be stripped. The priests paused a moment, looking to Tranquilo. The hooded figure held up a gnarled hand, and the priests obeyed.

Xacolotl stood alone, in front of his cringing officers. Turning slightly, he too raised his voice to carry. "This army was built to serve God," he shouted. "To expel the heretics invading the Californias. Very well. Opposing heretics is the duty of every man. Then we were attacked by other heretics from the south and our mission changed. That also is appropriate. This new threat is greater and more immediate." His eyes drifted to Don Thiago, the "Patriarcha de la Guerra." "I was then told that His Supreme Holiness, who now travels with us, had decreed that none were to be left to bear witness to our army's change of mission and direction. No citizen of the Dominion, whom *all our efforts are designed to benefit*, could know our new purpose and live." He took a long breath. "Enforcing this command was... distasteful to many, but it came from God's own messenger. It was done."

His sad expression turned angry. "Now this!" he shouted, and the army roared again. As soon as he could be heard, he continued. "The Jinetes who were crushed and fled must be punished. It is the way." He faced Tranquilo again. "But this remains *my* army to punish and reward as has always been done, as is *expected*; one in ten survivors *should* have been beaten to death by their comrades. The rest split up and placed with other units." Glancing at the pile of gutted, headless corpses, he growled, "You are destroying them all!"

"Their cowardice already destroyed them," Tranquilo retorted.

"They escaped a carefully choreographed massacre!" Xacolotl shouted back, glare shifting to Don Frutos. "Not the first of which our forces have endured at the hands of the same opponent."

"All the more reason for this display," cried Don Thiago beside Tranquilo. The two couldn't have looked more different, one appearing wretched and seeming too thin and ancient to even be alive, the other bordering on obese and always dressed in his finest. Yet they'd been inseparable since they united. "There must be no repeat of what happened this morning as we draw closer to the devil's own nest."

"It *will* happen again," Xacolotl said as if stating a fact. "Will you eventually 'sacrifice' all my mounted troops? The only thing preventing similar catastrophes befalling our *infantry*? By all accounts, we do not enjoy overwhelming superiority over the enemy's mounted forces. Lancers are largely sons of *patricios* and even Jinetes are hidalgos, often men of property. Our greatest strength is our numbers of infantry, yet we need every mounted man. I cannot spare so many to . . ." His lip curled. "Exhibitions such as this." He shook his head. "No. One in ten, as is customary, is more than enough." He gazed again at the heap of bodies and scattered heads. "And I think that number has already been surpassed."

Don Thiago sputtered. "If you fear running short of horsemen, put infantry on the beasts. As you say, we have plenty of infantry, largely doing nothing but walking along through the countryside." Though the army, and Don Thiago and his priests, had slaughtered every human they came in contact with during their march back from the frontier, they had, of course, confiscated everything of value. Including horses.

Xacolotl ground his teeth. "Can you ride?" he snapped.

Don Thiago's eyes went wide. "Why . . . No, of course not! Why should I ever do such a thing?"

"Why indeed?" Xacolotl replied. "Perhaps this is the one thing you have in common with the majority of your flock—which includes our infantry. Horses are expensive, and I assure you very few of our soldiers have ever ridden one. Even if they have, it takes long training to do so as well as any of the men the enemy—and you—have slaughtered today. I will spare you no more of them. I cannot."

"You dare defy us? You dare defy *me*?" Tranquilo seethed, though not loud enough to be heard by the army.

"You? Yes. I know not what real authority has been invested in you." He glanced at Don Thiago. "Any of you. But *my* authority over this army remains absolute until His Supreme Holiness himself declares otherwise." Xacolotl's gaze finally fell upon Primer Patriarcha Sachihiro. The tall, thin young man with the brooding brow was dressed very differently from his companions, far more like a wealthy, high-status *patricio*. Yet it was understood he had been declared the official successor to His Supreme Holiness, the former Don Julio DeDivino Dicha. "Much has changed since I embarked on my original mission, but I understand *you* are His Holiness's chief representative."

Sachihiro looked surprised to be noticed, let alone recognized. After a look at Tranquilo and clearly searching for his voice, he finally nodded. "I am. As his successor, only I can speak for him."

"Has he expressed his desire that I be replaced?" Xacolotl quickly asked.

Sachihiro cleared his throat, expression revealing racing thoughts and calculations. Suddenly, apparently making a decision, he quickly stepped over to join the general. "He has not," he said more firmly. The glare that Tranquilo's skeletal face managed to spread across itself was enough to make the young man shudder.

Xacolotl simply nodded. "Then, unless there are further . . . bloodless rites required to bring it to a close, I declare this . . . assembly dissolved. The Blood Priests among us will kindly consult me before involving my army in anything like this again. Teniente Juaris," he barked, pointing at the bound survivors of the light cavalry regiment. Perhaps two hundred still lived. "Take charge of those men," he ordered. "Have their wounds tended and see them assigned to other regiments. Make sure you take some yourself. Your recent losses left your irregular regiment understrength as well, did they not?"

"Yes, General," Juaris replied with satisfaction in his voice. He didn't see the venomous glance Tranquilo threw at him.

General Xacolotl only nodded, turned on his heel, and marched away. Some of his officers quickly joined him. Others were more hesitant. Sachihiro followed as well, taking long steps to catch up with the general. Amazingly, so did Don Frutos. Xacolotl gazed at them both as he walked down the slope toward the horses. Everyone else hung back once again, stunned by this new development.

"Those men will kill us for this," Don Frutos said conversationally, surprising both of his companions. Neither had heard a word from him before.

"They may try," Xacolotl agreed.

"They *will*," stressed Sachihiro. "You must kill them first. I order it, in the name of His Supreme Holiness!"

Don Frutos chuckled. "Kill who exactly? Don Thiago and Tranquilo?"

"And all the Blood Priests." Sachihiro nodded. "When I supported them, I never dreamed they'd attempt to take over entirely. Yet that is clearly their aim. They are monsters!"

"The general might succeed in ridding us of those"—Don Frutos tilted his head back the way they came—"but we would still be murdered at once.

The army is full of their converts, even plants. Priests themselves, quite a few."

Sachihiro looked horrified. "I would have been better off staying with them!" he fearfully declared.

"Perhaps," Xacholotl conceded. "But Don Frutos is right. He has been with us longer than you and has apparently seen." He paused and raised a brow. "Though I had assumed he was one of them, now."

"Not hardly," Don Frutos snorted. "I was a terrible general, but an accomplished survivor. I acquiesced and kept silent, enduring Tranquilo's abuse until he decided I was no longer any concern. Despite the fact that, as a Blood Cardinal, I not only remain senior to him regardless of the titles he invents for himself, but represent the very traditional system he has set out to destroy. I suspect he only let me live for my title. The legitimacy he might one day have to force me to convey upon him."

"But now we're all out in the open against him," Sachihiro almost moaned.

"The army can protect us, I think," Xacolotl said, "and by confronting Tranquilo over the travesty he was engaged in, I will have strengthened the loyalty of most. But we cannot move directly against the Blood Priests or their leaders." He shrugged. "It should be enough that they know if we're murdered, *they* will surely die."

"A standoff, then," Sachihiro said dubiously.

"In effect." Xacolotl nodded. "For now. One way or another, our primary duty not only remains, but coincides with theirs: the destruction of the heretics infesting the Holy City. They cannot do it without me to lead the army, and I cannot do it if I'm dead. So things will likely remain much as they have been, only now with more open enmity. That in itself will be refreshing," he reflected.

CHAPTER 23

MARCH 14, 1849

There came a tentative knock on the door to the modest sleeping quarters Lewis and Leonor had taken upstairs of what had been a small eating establishment facing the main temple square. Other officers had finally taken similar rooms, often shared, and the block of buildings had been incorporated into the defenses around the plaza. Never a deep sleeper, Lewis awakened at once. For perhaps the first time in his life, however, he didn't immediately rise to a summons. The warm naked skin of the woman under the covers in the bed beside him was hard to break contact with. He longed to just stay where he was. "What is it?" he asked as low as he could, in case Leonor was still asleep. A groan of annoyance, muffled by a pillow, reminded him his new wife was a light sleeper as well. "If that's that damn Willis, I'll bash his stupid head in," came a muted grumble.

"Which it's Corporal Willis, sir," the knocker replied softly, "here on strict orders from Colonel Reed, sir. I never would'a woke either of you so early, orders or no," he added piously, "but this . . . it's one o' them things you *ordered* me to wake you for." Lewis had begun to realize that Willis's voice was uncharacteristically deferential about the time the door pushed forcefully open and Varaa stepped in without hesitation. Lewis quickly sat up, inadvertently pulling the covers off Leonor, exposing her small, firm breasts. Even as he realized what he'd done and tried to cover his angrily rising wife, he saw Willis in the lamp-lit hall behind Varaa, eyes bugging out as he squeaked and fled.

Varaa watched him and blinked. Turning back to her friends, she *kakked* softly, tail swishing, and shook her head.

"Varaa!" Leonor barked. "What the devil? We're both naked! That's what doors are for."

"Doors." Varaa chuffed. "The Ocelomeh have no doors. Most went naked half the time before you made them wear uniforms."

"What about where you came from originally?" Lewis asked, rubbing his eyes.

Varaa hesitated. Even after all this time, she still refused to speak much about the land of her birth. "There were doors," she finally admitted, "but what difference does it make? I've seen both of you naked." She nodded at Lewis. "Him when he was so sick, you remember." She shuddered. "All naked humans are hideous to me, like you have some dreadful disease that makes most of your fur fall out."

Lewis laughed; he couldn't help it, especially when Leonor glared at him. But even Varaa wouldn't disturb them for no reason, and his expression swiftly sobered. "They're here, aren't they?" he asked.

Varaa blinked and nodded. "They're here." She looked at the closed window shutters behind their bed that would've still leaked significant light if the sun were up. "As you can see, it is still dark, but a messenger came from Anson, and now our pickets on the western road are coming in." She paused. "They heard the approach of a large mounted force and fell back as ordered, but as they did so, they saw what they described as an 'endless river of torchlight' pouring down from the mountains to the west. You can see it from the western ramparts now."

Lewis felt a chill between his shoulder blades and shared a look with Leonor. They'd expected the enemy in a week and redoubled their efforts on the defenses. Some were quite ingenious, he thought, though he'd somewhat misled most everyone in regard to his own most diabolical contribution. That week had stretched to nearly two, largely due to Leonor's father's efforts, stinging the enemy advance at every opportunity. That stopped working, however, and became more costly as well. General Xacolotl ultimately prevented Anson's ambushes by simply pushing through them faster than they could be prepared. This torchlit night march was probably a good example. Xacolotl was ensuring his final rush forward would remain unopposed.

"All right, we're getting up," Lewis assured Varaa. "Just close the door, if you please."

"Which I got both yer breakfasts started," came Willis's shout, floating down the hall. "You'll need your strengths today," he added.

Varaa blinked amusement and started to turn, then paused. "Should I pass the word to alert the army?"

Lewis contemplated that. The "long roll" of drums calling the men to action was a traumatic way to wake up. "I don't know this General Xacolotl, but I can't imagine any competent commander, which we must assume he is, marching his army through the night—which it appears he has—straight into an assault on our walls. Even if he does, the troops already on duty can make sufficient noise to wake and alert the rest in plenty of time."

Varaa closed the door, and Lewis looked at Leonor, sitting up beside him in the returning gloom. Even in the darkness, the sight of her strong, slender, supple form and understated (perfect in his eyes) beauty quickened his heart. She'd become a part of him, filling that empty space he'd never acknowledged, even while staunchly defending it from hurt. He'd imagined it to be a vulnerability he must never reveal or expose, but now he knew it for the source of strength and happiness it truly was. She'd confessed to a similar revelation, even harder for her to recognize after what she'd endured. Both were amazed to find such joy and inner peace under the circumstances, and Lewis sensed an amused, triumphant hesitation on Leonor's part to say "I told you so," or "Samantha was right." She had been, after all. They'd been wise to seize this time together while they could. Although they'd been very busy preparing for the enemy by day, the passion they'd shared in their nights alone had given them both a deep sense of fulfillment neither had ever known and certainly fortified them for what was to come.

"They're here," Lewis said as stoically as he could, trying to hide how dismal he felt.

Leonor clasped him close, kissing him fiercely, before pushing him sternly away, forcing a grin. "Yeah. Get up, Colonel Cayce." Her grin turned impish. "Time to put yer soldier suit on over yer husband suit an' lead yer army ta glory."

Lewis chuckled and slid out of bed. "'Husband suit,' huh? Well, having been a soldier all my life, I never thought I'd so much prefer a different uniform." His own smile faded as he stood and retrieved his "soldier suit," draped over the back of a chair. "You're right, of course, though we both know there'll be little enough glory." He snorted, raising his battered, red-trimmed shell jacket. "And Corporal Willis will be scandalized that I don't let him brush this down."

"He'll just chase you with his brush, takin' a swipe whenever you stop long enough," Leonor said, pushing the light blanket aside and rising as well, distracting Lewis again when she stretched. "If I'm feelin' disposed, I might even hold you still for him. Depends on if he poisons me with breakfast," she added.

The sky behind them was gray in the east, silhouetting the distant, deep purple mountains, when Lewis and Leonor joined Varaa; Colonels Reed, Har-Kaaska, Itzam, and Agon; and Majors Arevalo and Olayne on the new parapet over the western gate. Others stood nearby, but were giving the senior officers space. The only enlisted personnel at hand were several first sergeants, Sergeant Major McNabb, and a dragoon corporal with a bugle. The wall all around them was lit with torches and the lunette down below was illuminated by lanterns. Forms were moving quickly down there, artillerymen preparing their guns and infantrymen moving into place between them.

The river of enemy torches was plain to see, flooding down toward them across a broad front, likely more than a hundred paces wide, significantly overlapping the primary road, the Camino de la Plata, that led directly to them. There was no end to the dense, lighted column either, and it seemed to go on to infinity.

"Our first hint the enemy was pressing forward through the night came somewhat earlier," Colonel Itzam explained. "We began to hear a great, thundering roar, mingled with considerable bugling and other frightening noises." He chuckled uneasily. "I confess, most of us were quite alarmed, and some even said you should be called."

"Word from the understandably unnerved pickets eventually revealed the ruckus was the result of a vast stampede of monstrous beasts," Colonel Reed expanded. "Few came this way to cross the canal, the vast majority flooding north along the west coast of Lake Texcoco. But it's obvious now what stirred them to flight." He gestured toward the tide of torches. "Even in the dark, this General Xacolotl knows how to make an entrance." He turned to Colonel Agon. "You said you've met him?"

Agon nodded. "Not formally, nor can I say I know him. Our sole encounter, that I recall, was years ago and placed us on opposite sides of a strategic argument our senior officers were engaged in. I know he has built a reputation since then," he conceded. "And I suppose he must have talent or he never would have been entrusted with something on the scale of the Gran Cruzada." He shrugged. "Even in the Dominion as it was, connections and sponsors could only accomplish so much."

"You told us General Gomez was good," Leonor reminded.

Agon shrugged again. "I thought he was. And perhaps he truly was competent—against bands of native *insurrectos* on the southwest frontier. That's where *his* reputation was built." Leonor saw him rub the angular goatee on his chin in the torchlight. "Of course," he continued, "I thought that I was good . . . before I met Colonel Cayce."

Lewis snorted dismissively. "You *were* good, and are," he countered. "Before, you were always constrained by idiots above you. That's the only reason we're all here now."

They could hear puffing on the ramp behind them and Father Orno and Reverend Harkin hurried to join them, gasping at the sight when they saw it. But the puffing came from Don Hurac. Since the recent attempt on his life, he went nowhere unless completely surrounded by a detail of Agon's best troops. He likely didn't really need them anymore, since losing a great deal of weight, but Zyan and Mistress Samantha each had one of his elbows, helping him mount the platform. He'd always had an eye for female beauty, however, often buying the comelier (and therefore more costly) young slave girls to serve in his household or row his personal barge. That wasn't always easy work, but he never molested them, and it saved them from sacrifice or a life as a brothel slave and earned their fierce loyalty. That was even before his "enlightenment," and had gone a long way toward convincing Lewis his conversion to the cause was sincere.

"Thank you, my dears," Don Hurac graciously told the ladies. "The two most beautiful women in the city, carrying me all about. Am I not the most fortunate man?" He frowned at the flaming spectacle far out beyond the wall. "Oh dear," he exclaimed.

"The glare of the torches makes them look more numerous," Colonel Itzam speculated.

Har-Kaaska shook his fur-maned head. "No. I doubt that more than one in three or four bears a torch. You see? As the day brightens, it becomes apparent many men fill the gaps between the lights."

No one else but Varaa and her similarly sharp Mi-Anakka vision could see that yet, but no one doubted him.

"They'll send their lancers around us to cut the road east," Lewis suddenly said. "We need to send word to Sira Periz at Texcoco."

"Already done, Lewis," Reed said.

Lewis nodded. "Then I'll want to talk to the messenger from Major Anson. Please send for him."

"Already done as well," Reed assured. "Poor devil was worn ragged, but I knew you'd have questions. I told him to get food, but hold off on sleep."

"We should destroy the bridge over the canal before the lancers cross it," Justinian Olayne pressed again, returning to a source of disagreement. He and others had wanted to place charges and blow the bridge when the enemy tried to cross. "It's in range of our guns," he continued, "and they'll have to repair it. We can play havoc with their engineers as well and keep them on the other side for days, if not weeks."

Lewis sighed and shook his head. "I confess, the idea's more tempting now that I see what's coming. My objections remain, however. Not only will the bridge serve as a funnel for your guns as they attempt to get their army across, but if we make it too difficult, they'll eventually just go around one of the great lakes—either north or south, it makes no difference—and approach us from the east. If they do that, they'll not only be in position to threaten Texcoco and other helpless cities with no part in this fight as yet—and I fear they'll go through such places like locusts," he said grimly—"but they'll block our only avenue of retreat." He glanced at Don Hurac. "If such a thing ever becomes absolutely necessary," he consoled. Then he reached up and touched his chin through his whiskers, expression clearly thoughtful in the gathering light. "Besides," he continued flatly, "it's too obvious."

He chuckled at the looks of surprise. "Think about it," he said. "Of *course* we should destroy the bridge. We should've already done it. No doubt the enemy expected us to and is prepared, their engineers ready to bridge the canal here, or more likely closer to the lakes where fewer of our fixed guns will range. Since we've left it, they'll try to use it, and that'll give Mr. Olayne's batteries a lovely target for a while. It will also—I hope—leave General Xacolotl unsure that we can, or will, destroy other bridges later..." He pointedly refocused on the scene before him without further elaboration.

As expected, large formations of lancers eventually gathered in front of the advancing infantry, the brightening day revealing them in all their flashing, colorful glory. Bronze helmets, wicked, red-ribboned lance points held high in a forest of vertical shafts, and polished cuirasses reflecting the very first rays of the sun. Horns droned behind them, and Dom infantry began to spread out, forming into what looked like regimental blocks that stacked ponderously out on either side of the column, widening the front. More rippling red standards stood over each block, and the brilliant yellow, black, and white uniforms the sun now bathed made them look like a spreading lake of gold coins.

"Impressive," Reed said, voicing a monumental understatement.

"There are so many," Don Hurac gasped.

"We can't even see a quarter of 'em yet," said Sergeant Major McNabb, tone grimly neutral.

"Dear God," Reverend Harkin said.

Lewis turned to Major Olayne. "The lancers will soon begin to cross the bridge. How many of your guns along the walls are fully manned?"

"A quarter of them at all times. And all those in the lunettes."

"More than sufficient, I think," Lewis said. "Have those that will bear fire on any lancers that come within five hundred yards of the dry moat." That was about how far the outer city once extended, and the range was clearly marked. All the ground within three hundred yards had been sewn with traps; entanglements; shallow, zigzagging trenches filled with sharpened stakes; then a wide field of caltrops, which were small, four-pointed iron spikes that would always leave one sharp tip pointed up when cast on the ground. Most of these had been made by blacksmiths from nails salvaged from ash heaps from the burnt wooden ruins of the outer city. "No sense showing the enemy how many guns we have all at once, or how far they can shoot. Solid roundshot only, for now," Lewis added.

Olayne nodded, slightly mystified, before giving instructions to the bugler.

Varaa clapped her hands together, grinning all around. "This promises to be *most* exciting," she said. Looking at Lewis and tilting her head toward the enemy lancers still forming perhaps half a mile distant, she continued, "The enemy has been kind enough to stage a morning pageant for us. To show us what they bring against us. Reveille has sounded, and word is swiftly spreading. I doubt anyone will be alarmed by an alert." She grinned. "Now might be time to stage our own demonstration that these formidable walls are backed by men just as determined to smash their pretty army."

Lewis managed a confident grin in response. Warmaster Varaa-Choon and he truly did "think alike," as she often claimed. And he suspected she knew even he was intimidated by the vast force before them. If he was unsettled, how could he expect his troops not to be? She'd suggested the best way to settle them all.

"I agree," he said, turning to Colonel Reed. "Sound the long roll, if you please. Have the army stand to." He paused. "And we'll have all the colors uncased as well," he added.

CHAPTER 24

Teniente Juaris had assembled his new, mixed regiment of *Jinete* scouts just behind the first two thousand lancers preparing to cross the dangerously inviting bridge over the canal. Shading his eyes to look at the Holy City in the distance beyond it, he could hardly believe this was the same place he'd left barely two months before. A lot had happened to him since. He'd faced the heretic enemy again, more than once, and even come to know them a little. They still frightened him (though he could never acknowledge that), and he was well aware of how lethally competent they were, even against overwhelming numbers. But though they'd surely kill him in battle, he no longer felt a threat to his soul. On the other hand, Tranquilo, whose vague approval he'd briefly enjoyed, advocated and required all sorts of things on God's behalf that didn't set well with him at all. Juaris was a child of the Dominion and knew that God could be quite demanding, in both obedience and blood, but could no longer imagine *any* God being as . . . wantonly cruel and wasteful as the one Tranquilo professed to represent.

Having faced the enemy Rangers and their wonderfully mobile artillery himself, he thought he knew exactly what had happened to the *Jinete* regiment they shattered. No one could have stood against that, and Tranquilo's effort to slaughter the survivors forced his open break with the powerful, deranged cleric. Only when he'd gone to the general to protest, fully expecting to be killed himself, did he discover he didn't stand alone. He'd won a powerful patron in General Xacolotl, who seemed to have his own strong faction of followers, but he knew he'd made a deadly enemy as well. Since then, he'd tried his best to do his duty and remain unnoticed.

His orders at present were to follow the lead lancers around the Holy City and disperse his scratch regiment into companies of scouts. Mounted troops were useless against fortifications—and that refocused his thoughts on all the changes that had occurred here as well.

The whole ramshackle outer city was simply gone, and the high walls of the inner city, already formidable to view, had obviously been reinforced and backed by fighting platforms. Extensive, sturdy-looking overhead protection had even been erected. This far away, he couldn't tell how many places had been pierced for artillery, but there seemed to be quite a few. Even as he watched, he heard the familiar tinny notes of the enemy's war horns and a feral rumble of countless drums. In mere moments, the sparsely manned tops of the walls begin to fill with hundreds and hundreds of troops, mostly wearing uniforms that matched the morning sky behind them, and colorful flags started unfurling to ripple in the morning breeze.

"It would seem they are ready for us, Teniente," whispered Senior Decurion Yulis, his horse edging close enough for him to be heard. Juaris nodded. He still got a sense from his subordinate that he didn't quite approve of his fraternization with the big Ranger with the unlikely name of "Boogerbear," but Yuris had clearly approved of Tranquilo's behavior even less. He'd strongly supported his attachment to Xacolotl's faction.

"So it would, Senior Decurion," Juaris replied. "And I believe we're about to discover *how* ready." He tilted his head forward as the lancers in front of them, formed into a column of fours—the widest formation the canal bridge would accommodate—began moving out.

"There are a lot of guns on those walls," Yulis pointed out.

"Thank you, Senior Decurion," he retorted wryly. "I had not noticed. Fall back to the rear and keep the men moving, no matter what."

Juaris thought he had a better idea of the enemy artillery's range than most and was surprised when the lancers, then his Jinetes, were allowed to gallop across the bridge without opposition. He had a bad moment when his own horse's hooves thundered on the stout wooden timbers, thinking the cannon had opened up after all, but that wasn't the case. He still cringed as they rode parallel to the west wall, peeling to the south under the mouths of all those guns and with so many blue-clad infantry watching just a few hundred paces away. Yet nothing happened.

Clear of the west wall, the lancers veered east, just beyond the obstacles emplaced to hinder an assault. Without any fire laid on them so far, the lancer officer must've grown cocky and decided to taunt the heretics by parading right past them at barely three hundred paces. *Stupid*, Juaris thought, when he saw the fiery white blossoms of smoke erupt along the wall before he heard or felt the blasts. He instantly pulled his horse hard right, his own men peeling out after him. The thunder roared, and he glanced forward and left just in time to see a rising cloud of ash and dust explode all around the leading lancers, mulching and smothering them in a blizzard from hell, while lesser plumes rose down their length.

Horses screamed and crashed as roundshot tore off their legs or spattered their bodies in half. Heads and torsos of men quite simply exploded in scarlet mists. A bright cuirass with a gaping hole through front and back fluttered away like a pair of leaves. More plumes of dust geysered skyward as roundshot struck both short and long, but those that hit home rarely felled just a single target. Most bounded up, destroying more men and horses in the thick column.

"Ride wide! Open the range as fast as you can!" Juaris shouted behind him, largely without need as he urged his horse into a sprint. All his own men had followed his lead, many lancers now veering to do so as well. A few more cannon fired, skating through and ravaging more lancers, but soon most of the horsemen were clear. "Or so those lancers will think," Juaris fumed aloud. He knew their enemies could shoot much farther. They'd only stopped now to fool those watching from behind. "I will get word to the general and hope he listens," he said to himself. The leading lancers were coming up beside him, and he saw that the highest-ranking officer left was a wide-eyed *teniente*, like himself. "Keep them wide," he shouted. "We're still not out of range, even here."

The other officer gaped back in shocked horror. Not only were they well past the ordinary range of their own guns, it dawned on Juaris then that this was the first taste the other man ever had of being on the receiving end of anything remotely like this. "Believe me," Juaris snapped, the dust in his throat making his voice harsh. Slowing his horse, he stood in his stirrups, gazing back. They were six or seven hundred paces out now, the once-cultivated field they rode on ominously cleared even farther, as if inviting them to camp right there. Back where they'd come under fire, half a dozen horses milled around, one or two squealing and limping badly. There was no telling how many men had fallen, either killed by roundshot or broken when their horses crashed. Some had surely been trampled to death. He guessed the toll at more than a score. "We'll re-form on the road to the east," he shouted at last. "But go no closer than I do," he warned. The lancer officer nodded quick agreement.

"Well done, Mr. Olayne," praised Colonel Reed. More lancers were streaming past the city, now charging full speed and swinging much wider as soon as they crossed the bridge. "Gave them respect for our defenses—but not *too* much." He bowed his head slightly to Lewis. "Better they learn that lesson more painfully later. Please pass my compliments to your gunners for their marksmanship, and their restraint in particular."

"Thank you, sir. I will."

"Those lancers will cut our communications with Sira Periz and Texcoco," Father Orno observed.

"Yes," Lewis agreed. "But we're well prepared for a siege and we believe the enemy isn't. General Xacolotl will attack us sooner rather than later if he doesn't want his army to starve. So . . . one way or another, our communications with Texcoco, Vera Cruz, and Techolotla shouldn't be interrupted for long."

"And we can signal Father," Leonor reminded, a hint of concern in her voice. "He's still out there, somewhere, and will have somebody watching. He can send messengers for us too."

As many as seven thousand lancers might've ultimately ridden past them, but Lewis showed little concern. Such a force could indeed go marauding through the countryside, but they'd find little to sustain them and would pose small threat to Sira Periz at Texcoco. They'd be no use at all in an assault on the Holy City. The enemy infantry and artillery were the principal threat in that respect, and Lewis and most of his army watched for most of the morning while that massive force tediously approached and deployed on the western plain below the mountains across the canal.

Much of the Dom army began building a vast camp, complete with emplacements for huge, 36pdr siege guns. Those could easily range to the city walls from the thousand or so yards they were being prepared at, but Major Olayne had expected them and reengineered the walls accordingly. A lengthy, concentrated bombardment might eventually force a breach, but there were two problems with that. First, of course, was the expectation that the enemy relied on a swift resolution. Second, even the very best Dom artillerymen had never shown the capacity to deliberately hit a target the size of a gun at such a distance, while all of Olayne's artillerymen, even with their much smaller guns, could do so quite frequently. The 36pdrs were the only Dom guns of any real concern and when the battle began, the enemy would quickly discover they'd better move them back out of their own effective range or lose them.

A large percentage of the first Dom infantry to arrive remained in their regimental formations, however, making no effort to build any camp.

"They'll soon start sending infantry across the bridge," Har-Kaaska surmised.

"Aye, sir, but they'll hate it when they do," McNabb said with a predatory gleam in his eye.

"Perhaps," Lewis hedged. "Though I wonder if they'll try to parley first." He smirked. "Never any point to it, but it seems to amuse them."

"We should send them a blizzard of case shot if they do," Olayne suggested. "Destroy their whole high command."

"Tempting," Lewis conceded. "On the other hand, it might be interesting to see who we face, and how they all feel about each other."

They'd taken the report of Anson's messenger shortly before, and his wasn't the first observation, supported by Boogerbear's "acquaintance" and the testimony of a few desperate deserters, of possible friction in the enemy leadership.

"You ain't goin' out ta meet any o' those devils, Lewis," Leonor said flatly. "Not again. Father says Don Frutos is with 'em, an' that damn Tranquilo too. They both tried to murder you at the first 'parley' we had."

"She is right," Don Hurac solemnly agreed. It was known by all that Tranquilo was with the enemy, but Armonia had confirmed—under some duress—that Don Frutos was supposed to have joined the army as well, though he'd been stripped of virtually all his power. This testimony came just before Armonia was quietly and privately hanged. He hadn't revealed the whereabouts of "Brother Escorpion," who hadn't been found during the mop-up of the rebellion, and no one else betrayed him either. In Armonia's case, at least, it was believed he simply hadn't known. Most suspected the hulking Reaper Monk escaped the city during the fighting. "We cannot spare you," Don Hurac stressed.

"Just a thought," Lewis said vaguely.

As it turned out, the enemy wasn't interested in a parley. Not yet anyway, since a series of horn blasts and indistinct shouts started the center front Dom regiment marching toward the bridge, flowing from its impressive rectangular formation back into a fat column, six men abreast.

"Shall we hold back this time, Colonel Cayce?" Olayne asked.

"No point," Lewis replied. "And this is the sort of thing we've been waiting for: tightly massed infantry. Case shot only, though," he chided with a grim smile. "Don't wreck my 'funnel' with solid shot. And any enemy troops that get across but move *beyond* the range of the bridge, about seven hundred yards, leave them alone. We'll continue to withhold a full education."

"No, sir. I mean, yes, sir," said Olayne. His face turned red and there were gentle chuckles while he spoke to messengers who quickly dispersed along the western wall, then the bugler, who sounded the appropriate calls. After that, they all waited and watched while the first regiment approached the bridge and another began to re-form into a column to follow. Aside from artillerymen in the widely spaced gun emplacements calling out to one another, an expectant hush fell when the bridge began to fill. The troops upon it suddenly began to run in ranks, and a delayed roar reached them.

"Fire!" shouted Olayne, his young voice breaking slightly. The nearest guns on the wall vomited smoky flame, and a rush of booming thunder followed as every other west-facing gun fired as well, including those in the lunette below. Dozens of case shot shrieked downrange, sputtering fuses trailing spiraling or tumbling smoke streamers. The shells started exploding roughly two and a half seconds later, flashes appearing amid ragged gray flags above and just this side of the bridge. As always, some went long or short, a few even plunking in the canal before blowing smoky spray in the air, but most sent jagged shell fragments, musket balls, and smoldering pitch scything down on the men on the bridge.

It was a slaughter. Scores were ripped and shredded by searing-hot metal and a wail of fear and agony mounted. Some Dom soldiers were already almost across, and these quickly sprinted to their right, but the passage grew increasingly difficult as the column was stalled by mounting mounds of dead and wounded. None of this stopped the attempt entirely. Following troops climbed over writhing bodies or threw them over the shell-splintered rails. Both living and dead casualties rained down in the water, and it soon became apparent to Lewis that the lakes and canal harbored swarms of deadly fish just as ravenous as their cousins lurking in the sea. The water around and under the bridge started roiling and frothing as the fish fed. Still, even as the gunners on the walls labored to keep their weapons loaded and firing, the Doms kept coming, the second regiment now pushing forward as well.

These regiments seemed to be organized in the old, "traditional" manner, each composed of about three thousand men. By the time the west wall of the city was entirely swathed in smoke, the morning breeze powerless to clear the choking air or cool the hot guns, maybe a thousand men had run or been carried to an area not yet under fire, but thousands more had clotted the bridge with blood-streaming bodies or glutted the churning water below it. The Doms were undeterred, and that second regiment, already somewhat mauled by long rounds, still climbed and burrowed forward.

"Damn them," seethed Reed. "That's damn good infantry down there. Highly disciplined at any rate. Yet they just keep thoughtlessly wasting them!"

"Could they hope to run us out of ammunition?" Olayne asked, horror growing in his voice. The enemy was quite literally offering themselves up for slaughter, and while the young artilleryman was proud of his gun's crews, no one watching such apparently pointless suffering could remain unaffected by the senselessness of it all.

"We are sitting on top of a major source of their regional munitions," Varaa said. "They can't be counting on us quickly running out, though not for the reason they think. We're not using very much of theirs, after all. Only the unmodified 8pdrs, if I'm not mistaken? But don't forget, they don't think like us. The 'true believers' will *envy* those dying on the bridge, certain they'll be carried straight to paradise for their pains."

"She's right," Agon growled sadly. "Even I once believed that way, that agony is the price of grace and salvation."

Don Hurac's eyes were filled with tears, and Zyan was supporting him again. "I think only now, from this perspective, do I truly see the hideous price that belief collects from the faithful themselves, not just their victims."

Clearing his throat, Lewis turned the subject back to the practical. "Well, they're trying the bridge, as I knew they would, but the effort has only undermined their attempt to overawe us with numbers, so they'll have to try something else," Lewis predicted. "Look there"—he pointed—"back among those other regiments drawn up behind where the first ones started." Huge carts drawn by tandem teams of the monstrous, armored "armabueys" were pushing through the formations.

"Your glass if you please, Mr. Olayne," Lewis said, extending his hand for the artilleryman's leather-wrapped brass telescope. "Thank you. I seem to have left mine behind this morning." Raising the glass, he quickly adjusted the focus. "Yes," he finally said. "Confirmation of another report, by Mr. Burton's dragoons this time." He handed the telescope back, and Olayne looked for himself.

"I see," he said. "Rather ingenious."

"Well, what the devil is it?" Reed asked, impatient.

"Barges," said Varaa. She didn't need a glass. "Each of those vehicles carries three each, perhaps stacked on another, supported by axles and wheels. If I had to guess, I'd say that together, deployed end to end, every one of those carts—I see almost twenty, so far—will make a bridge almost exactly the width of the canal."

"I concur," Lewis agreed. He turned to Olayne. "Slow your fire on the bridge to a more manageable rate."

"But . . ."

"Don't stop," Lewis told him, "but there's no need to exhaust your men and risk bursting an overheated gun. Once those barge bridges are deployed, you can fire on them as well. Even try to sink them with solid shot from time to time, but there'll soon be almost as many crossings as we have guns along this wall." He held his hands out at his sides. "They were always going to cross, and we wanted them to do it here."

"Can I have some of the better crews try for the beasts as they position the barges?" Olayne asked.

Lewis considered. "Yes, but only then. I still don't want you firing past the canal. Right now, they're emplacing their siege guns in range. When the time comes, I want them destroyed, not just moved."

"Yes, sir."

And thus, a considerable percentage of the massive Dom army mounted its main effort to cross the canal over the next several hours. The bridge remained under fire, but more and more of the enemy raced across, gathering with their lucky comrades. They'd all simply watched as the first barge bridge was erected, curious how it would go. To the surprise of many, the placid pair of armabueys plodded straight off in the water, snuffling, spraying noses pointing upward as their drivers urged them on and they either swam or just walked on the bottom. Clearly, their tough hides and armored shells were more than the voracious fish could cope with. A score of men with levers clinging to ropes around the sides of the barges had shoved the first one off the top with a splash when there was enough room for it, and other men secured it to shore. About halfway across, the second barge was launched, practically floating off the lowest one, which was unhitched and secured to the near side of the canal while the armabueys were led quickly away, off the southwest corner of the city, where those who'd successfully crossed were gathering. The center barge was cinched in between the end ones and all the cables securing them together made taut. By then, another regiment of Doms had already been waiting to cross.

"Well done," Olayne had conceded, impressed. "Can I fire on them now, sir?" he'd asked Lewis.

"By all means, as soon as the enemy starts crossing. And feel free to experiment on ways to disrupt the construction of the other bridges. Again, don't wear out your men and weapons. There'll be plenty of opportunities for that later."

"I'm curious, Colonel Cayce," Father Orno said, and Lewis raised his brows. "Why not keep savaging the enemy as they cross, while you can?" He'd waved a hand. "Yes, I understand you don't want to stress the men and guns on this wall and you want the enemy here instead of elsewhere, but ... well, perhaps you might bring more guns from other walls? It seems an opportunity is being lost."

Lewis had taken off his wheel hat and scratched his scalp, realizing he needed a drink. The thick, drifting smoke had irritated his eyes and throat. "I can see why you think that," he'd granted. "The one real advantage the Doms have over us is numbers—"

"Precisely!" Orno had interrupted. "Yet Major Olayne, with just a few great guns, has almost effortlessly gouged deeply into those numbers without the loss of a man. I am frankly mystified as to why you would not press that advantage."

Lewis had nodded and said, "They've seen our exploding case shot today. Perhaps it surprised them, but I doubt it. We've laid in quite a bit of it, but of all our munitions, we're shortest on that. But that's beside the point. To have any hope of success, the enemy has to mass against us, attack at least two walls at once to spread us out, and bring that superiority in numbers to bear. To actually beat them, we have to let them."

Varaa, Agon, Reed, Leonor, all the "professionals," had nodded at that, but Father Orno still didn't get it. Lewis had smiled patiently. "I fully expect Mr. Olayne to destroy several more thousands of the enemy before they accomplish what they set out to do today—make it more difficult for him to make every shot, within the constraints I've put on him, worthwhile. That's a fine thing, but compared to the varying but inarguably huge numbers we'll face, those thousands are practically nothing."

He'd paused. "The Doms use grapeshot, and it's unpleasantly effective at longer ranges. It simply can't compete with canister at close range, however. A single salvo of canister from all the guns of, say, two walls at once, will kill more Doms in an instant than Mr. Olayne can manage all day." He'd bowed his head to Olayne. "Under his current limitations, as I said."

The west wall guns had kept booming as they talked, the nearest aimed at an armabuey. Lewis paused to watch with interest as a solid shot flew straight at it. The shot cracked through the thick armored hide, and blood jetted several yards from its side. A surprising amount of time passed before the creature reacted, but when it did, it was spectacular. The thing suddenly sprinted forward, dragging the beast hitched just behind. That animal flailed its spiked tail in panic and smashed the following barge cart, scattering all the men on top. The first creature then crashed on its side in the canal and thrashed every appendage with astonishing power, throwing water up high in the air.

"In any event," Lewis had continued, "though I'm sure these Doms know about canister as well, I doubt many of them have faced it before. Canister, and rapid musket fire at close range, is what'll eventually break them." He'd paused. "If anything will."

Father Orno hadn't seemed quite satisfied with that strategy, and Lewis wasn't best pleased with it himself. Perhaps it showed? As the long bloody day wore on, a few of the guns on the wall were replaced, but only due to damage or for preventative maintenance. And the gun's crews were relieved more than once. No additional guns were brought up. Half the visible infantry was stood down as well, to continue their labor on internal defenses or supervise locals as they did so. All the while, the costly Dom crossing continued and the vast army started digging their own defenses south of the city. Supply wagons and Dom light artillery started coming across, drawing excited attention from Olayne's gunners, who competed to hit these high-value targets, but Lewis instructed Olayne to tell his gun's crews to keep focusing on enemy infantry. So, eventually, another Dom camp started rising in their defenses—staying outside that seven- or eight-hundred-yard mark—and the enemy kept filling it up. Lewis knew that effort would dramatically increase after the evening sun edged down past the mountains to the west. Firing after dark, at anything other than the as yet forbidden camp, truly would be a waste of ammunition. Lewis had no doubt much of the enemy army would be firmly in place around the city by dawn.

"I hope I'm doing right," he finally said lowly so only Leonor could hear. With no real threat of a direct attack on the city that day, most everyone else had taken to coming and going. Lewis remained and watched, taking refreshment from Corporal Willis, who brought food and drink to him and Leonor. She'd been standing by him all day. Varaa too, for that matter, who'd only occasionally briefly left. Colonels Reed, Itzam, Agon, and Har-Kaaska would stand watches with their divisions, and Major Olayne and First Sergeant McNabb had resolved to take turns supervising the artillery at night. Varaa was peering down over the wall and talking to McNabb at the moment.

"I keep thinking Father Orno might've been right," Lewis continued, before snorting. "And I've been 'overthinking' this whole thing all along." He waved around at the walls. Their tops, as well as those of the taller buildings and conical temples, were turning a kind of golden red, washed by red clouds up above. It suddenly seemed a quite appropriate color. "I've never fought a purely static battle, and a static defense at that."

Leonor leaned close, wrapping both arms around his left one and hugging it to herself. "No choice, is there? Not with those numbers." She nodded out over the wall.

"I don't know," he confessed. "I've heard you mention Colonel Travis often enough and can't help wondering if this is how he felt, gazing out at

General Santa Anna's army from the walls of the Alamo. He was a cavalryman, if I recall, but corked himself up in a fort anyway. Had to be frustrating. I'll always be a flying artilleryman at heart. I crave maneuver because movement is life—and death for the enemy. But here I am too."

Leonor shook her head. "But you've got close to thirty thousand veteran soldiers, not countin' Sira's division in Texcoco or the ten thousand–odd militia in here. Travis had less than two hundred men, few any better than our militia."

"He lost."

"Sure. Never had a chance. He was stupid to get 'corked up' in the first place. Should'a run when he had the chance."

"And we shouldn't have? It seems the percentage we're outnumbered by is actually somewhat similar."

"Not even close," Leonor denied. "Veteran soldiers, remember? On top o' that, you ain't stupid. You got real reasons for everything you're doin'. Lethal ones, for the Doms." She grinned in the growing gloom. "An' on top o' everything, you got my father out there, leadin' close to five thousand men, all told—includin' most'a your precious 'flyin' artillery,' who're gonna give fits to the Doms. Mr. Travis never had none o' that."

Lewis smiled at his wife. "Succinct and to the point. I love that about you. I tend to overthink everything, and Father Orno got me wondering if a simpler strategy might be better after all, just killing the enemy wherever and whenever they're in range."

Leonor waved that away. "You answered him well enough. He might not 'a liked it, but your *plan* makes plenty o' sense to the rest of us." She poked him playfully in the ribs. "Quit overthinkin' that you're overthinkin' things. Just do what you do: when the 'Gran Cruzada' does attack, tomorrow or a week from now, you'll wreck 'em like you been plannin' for since before we ever got here."

Lewis smiled back, a little uncomfortably, and acted as if he meant to speak. Finally, he just shook his head.

Varaa drifted away from the wall to join them. A pair of guns fired, the yellow-orange flashes now painfully bright. Varaa turned to watch a pair of case shot burst colorfully over a barge bridge choked with troops. Screams drifted back. Varaa grinned hugely at them and clapped her hands. "Don't tell me," she said. "Our great leader is wracked with his usual pre-battle doubts?"

Leonor nodded theatrically.

"What do you mean, 'usual'?" Lewis asked.

Varaa lowered her voice. "You can hide nothing from me," she declared. "Remember—"

"Yes, I know," Lewis interrupted. "We both think alike."

"Exactly."

"Does that mean you have 'pre-battle doubts' as well?" Lewis taunted.

Varaa blinked her bright blue eyes, which seemed almost lit from within. Lewis suspected it had something to do with their size and how they gathered and reflected light, enabling her to see so well in the dark. "Of course," she said airily, "how could I not? But my concern is only ever for you and my friends, all my adopted people." She *kakked*. "I don't even worry about surprises because if you haven't already decided what to do when they happen, you will." She grinned again. "So. While you lay awake and worry all night, I shall sleep like a youngling." She blinked meaningfully at Leonor. "The Doms can do nothing against us tonight, and there will be plenty watching them, regardless. Take Colonel Cayce to your quarters. Perhaps you can divert his ever-active mind. But make sure he gets a *little* sleep, so his mind is rested when we need it."

CHAPTER 25

MARCH 15, 1849

"Don't fool around, do they?" Leonor murmured, gazing out from atop the rampart over the gate at the teeming Dom position that had sprouted so dramatically overnight. She and Lewis and virtually all the army's commanders were gathered again, this time over the smaller, but still substantial, southern entrance to the city. This gate, like its twin piercing the northern wall, didn't open on the terminus of a major highway, but had arguably been even busier than those in the east and west because they catered to the passage of everyday commerce from the lakes and docks the now-erased outer city once encompassed. Don Hurac had explained that the trade from other towns, villages, and cities around the lakes, indeed even the huge quantities of fish that were such a big part of the city people's diet, only came in from the north and south because it was all strictly taxed and regulated. Therefore, in a sense, those two gates had been the main arteries supporting the very life of the Holy City. Now it seemed the enemy had chosen the one in the south as its primary avenue of destruction.

A huge part of the Gran Cruzada still brooded across the canal and menaced that approach while other significant forces, each boasting perhaps fifteen to twenty thousand men, were digging in to the north and east, landed by means of galley-like barges that rowed troops over the water. The defenders had attempted to deny the enemy that capability by seizing and burning every boat they could find, but the transports were just as simple and crude as the bridge barges and had likely been swiftly constructed of green lumber cut and shaped from the forests on the surrounding mountains. Now the Doms threatened every principal approach, but the largest force, possibly equal to the "reserve" still on the other side of the bridge, had focused on expanding and massing within the works they'd started to the south the evening before.

"No," Agon agreed. "Dominion armies do not . . . 'fool around' when competently led." He paused. "Or sufficiently motivated. And our—I mean *their*," he quickly corrected, "field engineers are as competent as those in this army. You've seen their works before," he reminded, gesturing around, "and they learn their trade on civil projects when not at war."

"We heard them at it all night," said Colonel Reed. "Saw their lights as well." He chuckled and looked at Lewis. "I doubt you need to ask how often I denied our artillerymen permission to fire." He frowned. "Their boats and all the work to the north and east came as a surprise, however."

Lewis grunted. "This General Xacolotl seems cleverer than most Dom generals we've faced." He smiled at Agon. "Present company excepted, of course. But he's demonstrated right off the mark that we can't take anything for granted, and we don't dare weaken any part of our defense to strengthen another."

"There is *no* way that any twenty thousand men can take the north wall from *my* men," Colonel Itzam stated with certainty.

Lewis nodded. "I'm sure of it," he agreed. "But just overnight, Xacolotl showed he has the capacity to move enough men to strike you with *forty* thousand, if he wants." He held up a hand with a smile. "Which I'm sure you'd repulse as well, but maybe not if you're understrength. So we can't send any of your men to reinforce anywhere else the enemy might try to convince us is more dangerously threatened."

Varaa cocked her head to the side and blinked at Lewis, tail whipping. "Last night I was concerned you might be feeling a little overwhelmed. Now you sound intrigued."

Lewis looked around. He knew Varaa would never even hint at his concern if she wasn't sure he'd soundly refute it.

"I was tired," he said. "I'd just spent the day watching all the Doms in the world descending on us, after all." Nervous chuckles sounded around him, and he nodded out at a hundred or so enemy troops that had ventured from their breastworks and were now busily erecting a large, brightly colored, rectangular fly about halfway between the enemy lines and the beginning of their own defensive entanglements. "Now I'm . . . intrigued, as you say." He pointed at the fly. "Partially because the enemy seems curious about us as well, and means to invite a visit. They probably just want to deliver the usual admonishment that resistance is pointless and we can avoid a measure of misery if we surrender ourselves to humane execution." He shook his head. "But regardless of the odds, that isn't the act of a perfectly confident enemy." He smiled. "And there's still *so much* unpleasantness we can drop on their heads that they haven't even seen."

"So you're really goin' out there to see 'em?" Leonor questioned, her tone flat.

Lewis grinned at her. "I wouldn't miss the chance. Don't worry," he added, catching a glimpse of his orderly slinking around the periphery of the gathered officers. "I'll take Corporal Willis again. He can save me like he did the last time Tranquilo and Don Frutos tried to murder me."

"Oh God," Willis moaned.

Ignoring the corporal, Lewis turned his gaze to Agon. "And you'll be with me this time, instead of with our enemy. I'm sure you'll quickly recognize any attempt at treachery."

Agon straightened. "I will be delighted." His expression turned predatory. "I too will be . . . intrigued to see General Xacolotl again, and I wouldn't miss the opportunity to confront the loathsome Tranquilo and Don Frutos as enemies."

"But, Colonel, what should we do if there *is* treachery?" asked Major Olayne, concerned. "What if they mount an attack while you're down there"—he gestured—"at their mercy?"

Lewis laughed. "They won't attack. That would defeat their objective for the meeting, the same as my going, in fact: to meet and measure the enemy. I expect they'll make *some* sort of demonstration, but I'm confident you'll respond appropriately." He glanced at Leonor. "And as for us being 'helpless,' I wouldn't worry about that. Be ready, though," he cautioned. "They might mount an assault as soon as the parley is over and their own participants are safe. If the circumstances warrant it, between Colonel Agon and myself, I'm practically certain we can provoke one."

A messenger was sent to have an escort scrounged up—there weren't many mounted troops in the city—and horses brought for those who'd go with Lewis. Willis grumbled as much about that as he had about going along. He hated horses. He'd been an artilleryman himself, most emphatically of the "foot" variety, and just as Lewis still wore his dark blue jacket with red trim, Willis stubbornly stuck with sky blue, trimmed in yellow. That combination probably prevailed in the defenses around Vera Cruz, but Willis was the only one wearing it here.

Once the erection of the pavilion was complete, two golden spears were stabbed in the ground in front of it. A lance was then hoisted and braced between them with a long, white, gold-edged streamer flowing in the morning breeze under a leather-wrapped point.

"I've learned that is how they summon a parley in the west," Agon supplied. Having now fought so many Doms from there, Lewis had heard it as well.

"Mighty civilized," Leonor observed sarcastically.

A short, double column of lancers in gleaming brass cuirasses and helmets, about twenty in all, filed out from behind the enemy works under their bloody red flags emblazoned with jagged gold crosses. A cluster of gaudily dressed officers and the apparently obligatory figures in red robes followed behind them. A clot of half a dozen Reaper Monks in brown tunics brought up the rear. Leonor snarled at the sight of them.

"That's our signal, I suppose," Lewis said cheerfully. "We may as well see what they have to say." Unhurriedly, he turned and headed for the switchback stair down from the gate top rampart. Leonor followed closely, joined by Colonels Agon and Itzam. Colonels Reed and Har-Kaaska both wanted to go, but Lewis refused. "If there *is* treachery, someone must remain to command," he'd told them. His own party was completed by Varaa and Sergeant Major McNabb.

Dragoon Lieutenant Buisine led their escort, an equal mix of a dozen dragoons and Rangers who'd been reserved as messengers. The lead Ranger was a Holcano, but he held up a four-by-four-foot version of the Stars and Stripes, while the lead dragoon behind Buisine carried the blue banner with stars and an eagle above the streamer with "Third Regt US Dragoons" painted on it. Lewis nodded at the standard bearers in approval, then smiled at Buisine. The young dragoon officer was only here because he'd been lightly wounded and sent back with a dispatch to get treated. He'd been caught by the enemy's arrival.

Lewis's own horse, Arete, stood saddled and waiting in front of the gate eating deep purple grapes from the hand of an "old" 1st US infantryman who might've been twenty. He grinned as Lewis stepped up. "She's a rare wonder, Colonel," said the young man. "Sweetest horse I ever saw. Beautiful teeth as well."

Lewis grinned back. "She likes you. I've seen her take fingers and whole hands off with those teeth. A few ears and big hunks of shoulders too."

The youngster jerked his hand away in horror, and Leonor laughed as she mounted her own horse, held by another infantryman. "Only the enemy's, soldier," she said. "She only bites, kicks, an' stomps the enemy. She's sweet as a lamb to her friends."

"Especially when they bring her grapes," Lewis agreed, swinging up on his Ringgold saddle. "Anything sweet, in fact."

Buisine rode up, saluting. "Good morning, sir."

"Good morning, Lieutenant," said Lewis, returning the salute. "I'm glad to have you with us. Stay on your guard for treachery." He smiled at the Rangers. "And keep these miscreants in hand, if you please."

The Rangers chuckled grimly, absently touching their weapons and looking to Leonor instead of Buisine. They might be attached to the young dragoon officer, but there was no doubt whose lead they'd follow.

"Open the gate!" Lewis called louder. Eight infantrymen under the gatehouse heaved up on the heavy wooden crossbar, raising it on top of their shoulders and stepping away. The great leaves of the gate quivered before being pulled inward by other troopers standing nearby. Without another word, Lewis touched his heels to Arete's flank, and the spirited warhorse pranced out into the lunette beyond. To Lewis's clear consternation, the infantry and artillerymen in that position cheered him as he passed among them, Leonor and his other companions quickly forming a column around and behind. Obstacles were shifted aside, and Arete's hooves thundered on the meager timber bridge, all that now spanned this section of the "dry" moat protecting the south wall of the city. Lewis looked down at the murky water they crossed.

"I'm told that seepage has filled it to five or six feet in places," Agon informed him, guessing what caught his attention.

Willis snorted. "An' the fellers've been throwing in fish from the lake, for good measure. Buggers'll be gettin' hungry by the time we start feedin' 'em Doms."

"If the Doms cooperate," inserted Colonel Itzam.

"Which they won't have a choice, will they, sir?" McNabb replied. "A dry moat might be better, less intimidatin' tae the enemy till they're trapped down in it, but all said an' done, a moat is a moat . . . is a moat."

"Let's just hope the enemy hasn't discovered it yet," Varaa said. "There was no such thing when they last viewed the ground, and our obstacles should've kept them too distant to inspect it. With luck, it will remain a surprise to disrupt their first grand assault, at least."

Leonor looked at Lewis again as their horses clopped along, carrying them out in the open between their defenses and the massive Dom army positioned, it thought, beyond the range of their guns. None of them had ever seen such a huge force assembled before and the one they approached, beyond the bright pavilion, barely constituted a quarter of the enemy host. All the same, no matter what he thought or felt, Lewis remained erect in his saddle, radiating calm and confidence as his eyes swept the enemy position. As an afterthought, it seemed, he finally focused on their destination and the enemies awaiting them there.

The lancers were still mounted, arrayed in a line, holding their flags and pennants high. Chairs had been arranged around a heavy, ornate table, but no one was seated. Several officers in gold-trimmed and embroidered sun-yellow coats over ivory knee breeches and weskits stood in one knot, along with one of the only men Leonor recognized at once: the slightly less scrawny Blood Cardinal Don Frutos. Though seemingly better fed, the red-and-gold-robed man under the wide-brimmed galero looked to have aged considerably. His once-jet-black mustache and goatee now more resembled the scales of a silvery fish.

A second knot was near, but noticeably separate from the first. All were surrounded by Reapers in brown tunics and stood in bloodred robes arranged around the man she knew as "Father Tranquilo." Despite his clear leadership of that other group, he was just as scruffy and malevolent as she remembered.

"Remain mounted with the escort," Lewis hissed at her, tone heavy with tension his expression concealed. "You can see better on your horse and I trust you to cope with any betrayal quicker than anyone else," he added in explanation. With that, he brought Arete to a stop and dropped casually down from her back. Varaa dismounted just as quickly, prompting growls of disapproval from the Blood Priests, but these were interrupted when

Agon, Itzam, and Sergeant Major McNabb quickly climbed down as well, handing their horses off to Lieutenant Buisine's dragoons. Willis reluctantly dismounted, but kept hold of his horse. Buisine remained mounted himself, eyeing a young Dom officer standing back behind his superiors.

"So," Lewis began with a grin, "based on past experience, I take it we're here to insult one another before the killing resumes?" He nodded at Don Frutos and then Tranquilo. "Either that, or you've devised some plot to try to murder us before the battle." He gestured behind him. "If that's the case, I'd advise you to abandon it."

Tranquilo sneered and began to form a retort, but one of the enemy officers, taller than the rest and dressed only slightly more richly, stepped forward, shaking his head. "There will be none of that, I assure you." He glanced at Tranquilo. "Not this time. After all, are we not colleagues—even partners of a sort—joined to initiate the greatest battle this world has ever seen?"

"That we know of," Agon qualified.

The officer bowed his head respectfully, acknowledging the possibility. "Indeed, General Agon. Yes, I do remember you, sir." He looked back at Lewis. "And it is in that spirit of partnership that I come to greet you now." He straightened. "You have been identified to me as Colonel Lewis Cayce, an officer in the Army of the United States, a nation on another world from which we must assume my own ancestors sprang. I confess that subject amazes me, but that is not why we have been brought together."

Lewis thought Reverend Harkin would disagree, but waited while the man hesitated. "Nor would I choose to name the tragic differences that place us in contention," he continued, gesturing vaguely at Tranquilo and the Blood Priests. "Those things are *their* concern, are they not? Instead, I prefer to adhere strictly to the things we have in common—things we might share as comrades under different circumstances."

The man cleared his throat. "My name is General Xacolotl, and I am honored to command the force arrayed against you." He raised a hand. "And though it is true that God commands and requires me to destroy you, I would first offer praise for your accomplishments thus far. You have my deepest admiration, sir," he continued with what sounded like total sincerity. "Never in the history of the Holy Dominion has anyone caused such a stir! First, you arrived much like our own revered founders, frightened, confused, and sorely depleted I shouldn't wonder, and were immediately faced with unimaginable challenges." He glanced at Itzam. "Beguiled into aiding frontier rebels, you molded them into an army capable of crushing our own local forces." He gifted Agon a patronizing smile, prompting a growl from the green-coated officer. "Knowing the magnitude of your enemy's resources and an isolated defense could only end in your doom, you mounted an offensive campaign of admirable scope—ultimately even capturing our holiest city of all. My congratulations."

Xacolotl frowned. "Sadly for you, you are now spent. Your base of operations at Uxmal has fallen." He paused as if expecting that news to surprise them, but continued, "And you are now isolated from your outpost at Vera Cruz. Be assured that our forces that cleansed and razed Uxmal will eventually move against Vera Cruz as well. You cannot expect further support."

Leonor wondered if his omission of Texcoco, Puebla, and Techolotla was significant.

"And what of *your* support?" spat Colonel Itzam, spurred to fury by the mention of Uxmal. "A mere trickle from the western provinces at best? We're aware of the desolation your army leaves behind it, eradicating competing mouths and eating its way across the landscape like *lagostas*, or an endless herd of great, grazing beasts!"

Xacolotl frowned at Tranquilo and his cluster of Blood Priests and Reapers, but turned back to see Lewis shrug, a small enigmatic smile on his face.

"Frightening, fascinating creatures, your messenger dragons," Lewis conceded. "I envy how quickly you communicate across vast distances. But we have our own means of doing so, and I expect our closer observations are better than yours."

"Regardless," Xacolotl said, "you sit upon all the supply we shall need. All we must do is take it."

"That's true," Lewis now agreed, adding with heavy irony. "That's *all* you have to do." He shook his head. "I'll admit you speak more respectfully than other Dom generals I've met—and crushed—but you're just as derisive and arrogant. You underestimate us just as badly. Don't make the mistake of presuming your grand plan will long survive contact with our own."

Xacolotl grinned, eyes sparkling. "There, you see? *That* is precisely why I desired this meeting—to make the acquaintance of another mind that thinks much like my own!"

Lewis sighed. "Well, I don't know whether to be flattered or insulted, but I'll choose to take your statement as a compliment to my army." He gestured at Tranquilo. "On the other hand, if the rest of our conversation follows the forms we've grown used to, we may as well just get on with our fight. We've often heard the part where you graciously offer to slaughter us mercifully in exchange for our surrender, threatening misery and torture if we refuse."

"No such offer shall be made this time!" Tranquilo snapped. "You had your chance, time and again." A terrible smile twisted the Blood Priest's face. "Every single soul behind those walls will earn more agonizing grace than they can possibly imagine!"

Xacolotl sighed. "I believe you may already know the Holy Patriarcha Tranquilo. And may I also present his... particular associate, the Patriarcha de la Guerra, Don Thiago de Feliz Río. We do not agree about everything," he plainly stated, "but I will not argue with them over your disposition." He quirked a brow. "Though the Blood Cardinal Don Frutos, who I understand is also known to you, and the Primer Patriarcha Sachihiro"—he bowed his head to another young man in his knot of leaders—"both directly represent His Supreme Holiness, the former Don Julio DeDivino Dicha, Tranquilo and Don Thiago somehow speak with his voice."

"Doesn't that strike you as strange?" Agon asked.

"Quite." Xacolotl's expression hardened. "Traitor," he added simply.

"How very amusing!" barked Varaa. "You call Colonel Agon a traitor when he and Colonel Cayce are here as the voice of your *real* Supreme Holiness, Don Hurac!"

"We cannot hear the words of demons!" cried Don Thiago, even as he almost comically covered his ears. Many of the Blood Priests did the same, oddly proving the lie.

"You heard her," Lewis said darkly. "And though I may not speak with his exact words, I'll tell you what he offers."

"Silence that man!" Tranquilo screamed at the lancers, whirling toward them, lunging for the closest trooper's pommel holsters. Even as the lancers shifted to grasp their weapons, Leonor drew both her revolvers, the dragoons presented their Hall carbines, and the Rangers raised musketoons. Everyone seemed to freeze in place.

"As I was saying," Lewis continued mildly, "Don Hurac declared *our* war over some time ago, and I've agreed to abide by his wishes. It is you,

General Xacolotl, and the factions you protect"—he glared at Tranquilo—"including those despicable Blood Priests, who are the true traitors in rebellion." He took a long breath. "Even so, Don Hurac has agreed to pardon you all. Most of you," he qualified with another significant glance at Tranquilo.

"In exchange for what?" Xacolotl ground out, incredulous.

"Nothing more than your honorable surrender, disarmament, and oath of allegiance. He—and we—will even ensure that you're fed."

Xacolotl gaped, taken entirely aback. He'd brought no mercy to this meeting. That just wasn't how things were done. He had to be thinking hard, however. A large percentage of his mighty army must secretly believe Don Hurac truly was their legitimate ruler. That could leave him weaker than his numbers implied. Even Sachihiro's worried expression seemed to turn hopeful. "What else?" Xacolotl asked, teeth clenched.

"Nothing else," Lewis said, then shrugged. "Just . . . peace."

Leonor's focus remained on Tranquilo, keeping her front sight centered on his head, but she managed a quick glance at Xacolotl. She couldn't read him at all, but had an instant's hope there might be a chance this all might end right here.

The moment quite literally came crashing to an end when the concussive thunder of distant, heavy guns suddenly swept across them. Even as the bone-shaking rumble continued, massive, shrieking roundshot tore at the sky, smashing hard into the west wall of the city, throwing great clouds of dust and debris. Tranquilo seized the distraction, drawing a long-barreled pistol from the lancer's saddle holster, fumbling with the cock as he raised the muzzle toward Lewis. "Kill them!" he screeched.

Leonor never made a conscious decision to shoot the vile Blood Priest. Danger to the man she loved, combined with a simple "they shot at us, we shoot at them" reflex, was all it took to tighten her finger on the curious folding trigger of the Paterson Colt in her right hand. The pistol barked, and Tranquilo's eyes rolled white in their sockets while dark blood sprayed out in a stream between them. In an instant, the chief Blood Priest, one of the very founders of the order, crashed to the ground like a sack of dry bones.

"Shit," Leonor murmured.

Lancers shouted and surged their horses forward but were immediately met by a volley of fire that shattered animals and spilled men from their backs. They still had the dragoons and Rangers outnumbered, however, and closed with lowering lances. Screams skirled in the rising cloud of dust. Varaa drew her sword and slashed a lancer as he passed, cutting his thigh to the bone.

"God damn it!" Lewis roared, even as he drew his saber. "Cease firing! Stop fighting!" It was no use. He climbed his spinning horse and glared at Xacolotl, pointing his saber at the man. "What's the matter with you? You *know* this is madness!"

"I gave no order," Xacolotl responded, a young officer behind him pulling him back toward his horse. "*I gave no order!*" he shouted adamantly, seeming as shocked as Lewis. It made no difference. In an instant, he was gone, and his officers fled to their mounts. The horse holders and Reapers armed themselves and charged. That's when Lewis caught a glimpse of Don Frutos standing over the young man introduced as "Sachihiro," the "Primer Patriarcha." Don Frutos was drawing an ornate dagger from the side of the dead man's neck. Looking up at Lewis, he actually grinned and bowed his head as he wiped his blade on the blood-spattered tunic.

"God damn you!" Lewis bellowed, urging Arete toward him.

Before his horse could take a step, Leonor intercepted her. Grasping both her revolvers in her left hand, she took Arete's bit at her mouth with her right. Anyone else might've drawn back a bloody stump, but Arete loved Leonor dearly. "We gotta *go*, Lewis!"

Two Reapers with short swords were coming, crouching low, trying to sneak past Leonor. Arete snarled like only a horse can and flicked a kick at one of them, effortlessly caving in his face. Leonor glanced down with a look of surprise and snapshot the other in the top of the head.

"Shit, shit, shit!" ranted Corporal Willis, trying to mount his own spinning horse while keeping it between him and another Reaper. "Hold still, you damned shaggy flea farm!"

Leonor shot the man threatening Willis as well, and he fell, clutching his chest. Willis gave her a long-suffering look and simply launched himself over his saddle. Looking at the enemy lines, Leonor saw more lancers already on the way, pouring through the gate from the enemy works. Varaa, Agon, Itzam, and McNabb were mounting, their escort still fighting the closest lancers, sabers ringing.

"Look!" Leonor shouted, pointing with her pistols. The surviving enemy embassy was being herded aside and away, an avenue opening to give the reinforcing lancers a rapid approach. "Sorry I killed that evil bastard just when I did, but I don't think it'd made any difference. Somebody planned this," Leonor insisted.

"Don Frutos," Lewis told her. "We'd become so focused on Tranquilo, we forgot all about him. Break off! Fall back to the city!" he shouted at Buisine. The dragoon had three mounted troopers left, perhaps as many Rangers, all fighting for their lives. The lancers had discarded their primary weapons, now slashing quite competently with sabers. Lewis believed his mounted troopers were generally more lethal, man for man, but not necessarily with sabers.

Willis was finally properly in his saddle, a pistol in his hand.

"After you, Colonel," Buisine yelled back, ducking down and parrying an overhand slash with his own rising cut. Deflecting the blow, he lunged with his blade and took his opponent through the throat, just above the cuirass. Leonor's revolver barked again and again, and Varaa spun her horse to aid the beleaguered guards, tail high, naked backsword in her hand.

"No, Varaa," Lewis yelled. "Let's go."

Reluctantly, Varaa obeyed, and they all raced back the direction they came. Finally gaining a very slight gap, Buisine pulled his remaining troopers away. The Stars and Stripes still streamed above them, but Buisine was clutching the blue banner of his dragoons himself, tight against his side.

Cannon fire rippled along the top of the western wall and smoking case shot swirled away toward the distant Dom batteries. They never saw the shells burst, but Lewis could imagine the sleeting shrapnel slaughtering the siege gun's crews. He'd half expected Xacolotl to open with those weapons while they spoke and had intended his decisive reply as another argument for peace. Now all that was dust. Don Frutos had outplanned them all, even Tranquilo, and battle was certain.

Pounding across the little bridge, which seemed to actually bounce underneath them, Lewis finally stopped and turned in front of the still-open gate. A few hundred lancers had chased them to the edge of the defensive entanglements and now guns on the wall above started booming, throwing case shot into their midst. Ragged flags of smoke snapped over them, dust kicking up on the ground as musket balls, sputtering pitch, and pieces of shell casings slashed down. Men and horses crashed amid unearthly squeals, but the lancers swiftly pulled back.

This time, the cannon followed, harrowing Dom riders all the way to their lines and beyond. An unnerving moan arose on the wind as exploding case shot fell deep in the infantry position, snapping brightly over blocks of forming infantry and setting tents and other combustibles alight. "We need to be up on the wall," Lewis said, trotting quickly through the gate. "Shut it," he called when Buisine's men came through. Infantrymen took their horses, and he and his companions sprinted up the switchback stair. The "long roll" was already sounding, echoing down the valleylike streets of the city, standing all the defenders to.

"That might've gone better," greeted Colonel Reed as Lewis and his party rejoined him.

Lewis shook his head. "No. I might've hoped, for a moment. I think we actually *had* their General Xacolotl." Agon nodded grim agreement, and Lewis continued, "But there was never any chance." He quickly explained what occurred. "And now they're coming," Lewis said, pointing. One great block of infantry, the closest to the canal bridge, had begun to move forward amid a roar of horns and pounding drums. He'd expected something like this, but couldn't see it from below. "Having met him, I doubt Xacolotl would be so rash, move so quickly to the attack with so little knowledge of what awaits him. I think he was just as surprised by events as we were. No, someone else has engineered things so we *have* to fight." He smiled at Leonor. "And instead of the enemy fearing to attack the legitimate 'Supreme Holiness,' now their God demands vengeance for the deaths of their chief Blood Priest and 'Primer Patriarcha.'"

"I didn't shoot that second fella," Leonor defended.

"Don Frutos killed him. I saw it," Lewis confirmed. "I think he's behind all this." He sighed. "So with battle already joined, Xacolotl will be handed a fait accompli—a contest he *has* to take charge of. I almost feel sorry for him."

"That fellow who pulled him away was Teniente Juaris, the same man we had an 'arrangement' with," said Lieutenant Buisine, just joining them. He was breathing hard and had an ugly saber slash down the side of his face from temple to jaw. "He hated Tranquilo, and I expect his general did as well. Juaris must admire Xacolotl to act as he did to save him. The point is, I suspect you're right and no one's given Don Frutos much thought for some time—which left him free to plot."

"We'll have to ask Don Hurac how this changes things," said Colonel

Reed, nodding out at the growing assault. Light artillery had opened in response to their own bombardment, but 8pdr roundshot would have little effect on the walls at this range. It might cause damage and inflict casualties in the city behind them, but couldn't much affect their defense. None of the Doms' siege guns had fired again, as yet. As if on parade, another block of infantry had begun to advance. Just like the first, it was clearly aimed straight ahead at the wall. "But now it seems we have a battle on our hands," Reed reminded.

Agon snorted. "Such as it will be. I don't see any bridging equipment, nothing to even throw in the moat to attempt to cross upon. Perhaps they really don't know it's there? I don't even see any ladders." Disgust had entered his voice. Not at the soldiers, but those who'd send them forward like this.

Lewis nodded. "Gentlemen," he said, addressing all the division commanders with him, "go join your commands. God be with you all." He hesitated. "*Wreck* them, do you hear? I got the impression Xacolotl knows what he's about and this impetuous assault will be the only time the enemy comes at us so predictably and ill-prepared. Make them regret it."

CHAPTER 26

"Old-style" Dom regiments were roughly three times the size of the ones Lewis had organized to oppose them, each composed of around three thousand men arrayed in three rigid ranks. Even Agon had agreed such formations were too big, too cumbersome, but now all the blocks of advancing enemy infantry had three full regiments stacked behind one another, bringing a total of about nine thousand men. Just those first two blocks already moving boasted more than half as many men as Lewis's entire defense, which was split to defend four long walls. Yet regardless of that, or even whether more Dom regiments joined the initial assault, it was more than likely that most of those enemy soldiers were doomed.

Artillery was booming all around the city now, literally shaking the air and lashing every enemy position with case shot. Confusion and terror heaped up on every hand as thick as the great columns of smoke. But the closing blocks of infantry, majestic and stately, remained unmolested. At roughly three hundred paces from the southwest wall, the first Doms entered the defensive obstacles and immediately began losing their intimidating alignment. The outermost obstacles, mostly thousands of sharpened stakes driven too deep in the ground to easily pull, along with countless iron caltrops strung all around, would've been more effective in the dark, but still slowed and fractured the enemy ranks as they were forced to avoid the stakes or caltrops stabbing through boots and feet. Screams accompanied the growing disarray.

"An attack is brewing to the north," called a messenger from his horse down below the rampart as Lewis, Leonor, and Varaa hurried along with Colonel Reed, dodging troops rushing to position themselves near what looked like the center of the assault in the south. Agon had taken his horse to join his men in the northwest. Most of the militia, now under his command as well, had been moved to defend the west gate. That was their strongest position, and it was hoped they'd hold firmer there.

"Colonel Itzam won't be there yet," Reed warned, huffing.

"His boys'll do fine until he is," Lewis said with conviction. "Ride back to Mr. Itzam," he called back to the messenger, who was avoiding hurrying civilians and pacing their progress. "I've no doubt he'll be there by the time you return. Extend my compliments and regards. He knows what to do and needs no reminder of his duty."

The messenger saluted and galloped away.

"It's going to be a bloody mess," Reed ventured, watching the now tentative enemy advance over the wall. "Our Ocelomeh and Holcanos might enjoy the slaughter, but killing helpless men won't sit well with our other lads."

"It must be done," Varaa insisted. "We can show no more mercy than the enemy would." She pointed. "And I'd venture that morale is even more important to them than us. Breaking up their formations as they attack, denying them the support of comrades on either shoulder, will have started to crack it already."

"I hope you're right," Lewis said.

"Of course I am!" Varaa snorted.

They finally reached a point about half the distance between the south gate and southwest corner of the city wall, deep within the section Reed's 1st Division defended. Like other such places, this had been prepared as a command post, flanked by guns and surrounded by roughly woven sacks full of earth. The enemy advance hadn't quite stalled, but the drum cadence had slowed considerably, allowing men to re-form as best they could.

"About a hundred and fifty paces, I think," Reed now estimated, stroking his chin whiskers. "They're about to reach the first trench."

"Time to discourage them further," Lewis said.

Reed nodded. "Bugler," he barked at a young man who'd been matching his stride all along. "Sound the call for the artillery to fire independently."

The sharp notes of the trooper's instrument rose over the tumult, echoed around the walls by others. Gunners had been expecting it, and those in close contact with the enemy finally called for their men to load canister. Infantry prepared as well, loading and priming their weapons. All but a few of Felix Meder's riflemen were off with the mounted forces and those still in the city were widely scattered, most attached to artillery units, as usual. Also as usual, they'd been tasked with picking off officers and NCOs. On the other hand, though a hundred and fifty paces was an impossible distance for accurate, individual, aimed fire with smoothbore muskets, they were more than sufficiently lethal and had a massed target impossible to miss.

Gunners held up their hands, fists clenched, demonstrating their readiness to section chiefs. NCOs paced behind the infantrymen, wiping rods in hand, shouting encouragement and admonishments or passing calm words of advice to younger, less experienced troops. There was no final, preparatory command, no grand signal to unleash the maelstrom. The men simply knew it was time. Dozens of cannon roared almost as one, spewing the curious yellowish smoke unique to canister. Hundreds of muskets fired as well, their own fogbank of white smoke billowing out, obscuring the enemy. Shrieks of pain and roars of terror and fury rose from within the roiling cloud.

The strengthening morning breeze quickly swept it away, revealing great, bloody swathes gouged out of enemy regiments and keening, mewling forms squirming on the ground. Return fire slashed back from the closest regiments below and a cascade of defenders tumbled back from the wall.

"Keep yer stupid, bloody 'eads down, can't ye?" roared a 1st US NCO. "That's what the bloody damned wall is for. Load yer arms under cover, damn ye!"

"Buck an' ball, lads! That's the style!" bellowed another. "Load faster, there!" Men tore musket cartridges with their teeth, pouring a touch of powder in their priming pans under the frizzens then dumping the rest down their barrels. Mashing the paper cartridge still holding the ball and three pieces of drop shot into a wad, they rammed it all down together. Shiny iron ramrods flashed in the sun.

"Reload! Reload canister!" came high-pitched cries from artillery section chiefs. Guns rumbled on their timber emplacements as they were heaved back into battery, Dom musket balls *spang*ing off muzzles or throwing stone dust and lead fragments at the crews.

"Fire!" shouted the closest gunner on their right, and his captured 8pdr spewed another whistling stack of 110 musket balls. Almost immediately, other guns fired, joined by the clatter of muskets. Soon, the roar of independent fire became continuous and just as deafening as that first salvo had been. More and more gaps were blown in the advancing block of men. Worse, just as the enemy seemed to realize they had to pick up the pace and move quicker, they reached the first trench, which was even more thickly staked with sharpened impediments, and were slowed under the merciless fire once more.

"My God, Lewis," Reed said as lowly as he might be heard over the thunder, "those devils have already lost a thousand men, at least."

"Closer to two thousand," Varaa judged cheerfully.

Reed shot her a disapproving glance. "Quite possibly. At this rate, with two more trenches, they'll never even reach the moat."

"All the better," Lewis said grimly, evaluating Reed's expression. "Your humanity is laudable, Colonel, but this isn't our doing. If they come, we must kill them." He pointed at the dead and wounded, most struck in the head, being carried down from the rampart. A Dom roundshot ricocheted off the top of the wall, raising cries as it sprayed the closest troops with painful shards of stone. "They're doing their best to slaughter us, after all."

"What have you done?" murmured General Xacolotl even as he watched a *third* block of infantry begin to advance into the churning, blood-streaming ground below the fire-breathing walls of the Holy City. "It *was* you, was it not?" he demanded, turning to face Don Frutos. Teniente Juaris put a restraining hand on his right bicep, and that might've been the only thing that kept Xacolotl from drawing his sword and killing Don Frutos there and then. *Perhaps not,* he slowly realized as his perception expanded. Surrounded as they were by a reinforced "guard" of Blood Priests and Reapers, Xacolotl and all his most trusted officers would've been killed at once if he tried. That the Blood Priests, even Don Thiago, clearly supported Don Frutos was as surprising as anything else.

The fortified camp was already a shambles, and flames and smoke leaped high all around, but shells no longer exploded there since the heretic artillery was now otherwise occupied. Don Frutos waved absently at the battle. "I gave the order," he confirmed. "Your plan would have taken too long," he added dismissively. "Mine will work faster."

"By what authority did you order my men forward? And I thought you had given up planning battles," Xacolotl said harshly.

Don Frutos blinked. "Oh, be assured that my authority is more than sufficient, though I do fully recognize that I am not very good at planning battles. I may still need you for that." He paused. "And this is essentially *your* plan, General, only significantly hastened."

At a loss, Xacolotl waved at the dreadful assault under way, quickly consuming so many men. "Then . . . But *why*?"

Don Frutos pursed his lips and affected an expression of remorse. "I had no choice but to order the advance. The men would not be stopped once word spread of the foul murder of the Holy Patriarcha Tranquilo and our poor Primer Patriarcha Sachihiro by the heretics during our parley. Even more devastating, it will soon be learned that our beloved Supreme Holiness, the former Don Julio, was called to join God by one of those beastly explosions the heretic artillery was throwing about. Due to your . . . temporary incapacitation, *only* I, as the next in line of succession, was able to unleash them to seek their vengeance." He smiled.

Xacolotl might've been shocked by the sudden violence and mind-pounding bombardment that followed the collapse of the parley, but the attack commenced immediately and he hadn't been "incapacitated" at any point. Faced with a quickly evolving new reality, he chose his words carefully. "Then . . . since you must have arranged to unleash my army before the parley even began, I must . . . congratulate you on your precognition. No doubt it was divinely inspired."

Don Frutos nodded enthusiastically. "Astonishing, is it not? I am overwhelmed."

Xacolotl looked at Don Thiago. "You and your Blood Priests agreed to this?" *This wasteful battle and treacherous assassination?* he added silently to himself.

Don Thiago nodded gravely. "His Holiness Don Frutos and I have agreed about a great number of things for some time, even before he was essentially banished to your army. Most obvious of these was something you must surely have been aware of yourself—that Father Tranquilo, God bless him, was entirely insane. He had served his purpose in this life, building the power of the Blood Priests and creating a path for them to become *patriarchas*, even Blood Cardinals. But his ambition had no limit. He would have *abolished* the Blood Cardinals and installed himself as Supreme Holiness. What would become of the rest of us? Anarchy! Chaos! Turmoil amongst ourselves! How could Blood Priests in their thousands choose only one among them to rise above the rest?"

He shook his head sadly. "Only Blood Cardinals hold God's mandate to rule the Dominion, and Don Frutos has long supported the chief reform my order desires: that Blood Priests be eligible for elevation to their ranks. Only by embracing tradition might a Blood Priest one day rise even farther without strife. Therefore . . . Father Tranquilo's task on this world was complete and it was time for him to go to God. What's more, the army will think the heretics sent him!"

"They *did*!" Don Frutos gleefully reminded and the two of them erupted with near-girlish giggles.

Xacolotl squeezed the bridge of his nose between closed eyes. "Very well," he said roughly, "but what has that to do with what passes now? Thousands of my men are dying. I . . . humbly ask again, why?"

Don Frutos cleared his throat. "If Father Tranquilo and I agreed on little else, we were both conscious of the fact that this army is too big to feed, even if we take the stores in the Holy City intact." He arched an eyebrow at Xacolotl. "In addition, and I hope you will forgive me saying so, your command over such a force left you with unlimited potential power of your own. Certainly more power than I am comfortable with."

He turned and watched a moment while the better part of twenty thousand troops struggled and suffered and died to cross the carefully prepared killing ground they had no hope of surviving. "Finally, God will drink deeply from the pious blood we send him this day—and the heretics will be lulled into thinking this is the way we shall continue to strike them."

Xacololotl sighed deeply, listening to the roar of battle. "That implies that you will, at some equally accelerated point, implement some of the subtler aspects of my plan? You need me to help organize that?" *Obviously,* Xacolotl thought, *or I would already be dead.*

Don Frutos turned to him with a smile. "Indeed, my dear general. At present, however, you need only focus on feeding your regiments to God—and bringing up more to replace them as if you mean to keep doing so indefinitely."

"That will certainly demolish the army," Xacolotl granted, tone sick, "but I doubt it will crack those walls. Do I at least have your blessing to let my men *try* a little more effectively?"

Don Frutos waved a hand. "Of course. The heretics will grow suspicious if you don't. And who knows? They might even succeed!" He chuckled. "But I think you can leave any 'cracking' of walls to me."

CHAPTER 27

The Battle for the Holy City raged throughout the day, with assaults eventually pressing every wall except the one in the west. There, the enemy artillery had redoubled its efforts to cover a continual crossing of troops to reinforce or replace regiments already shattered by attacks on other walls. Defending artillery was increasingly hard-pressed to counter that fire. The heavy Dom siege guns had finally been pulled back beyond the range of spherical case or reliable solid shot accuracy, but the city wall remained an almost unmissable target at any distance, and the Doms could finally sustain a nagging, bone-shaking fire. And the massive 36pdr balls that did miss generally fell in the city beyond. They weren't explosive, but they only had to smash a building with candles or lamps inside to start numerous fires that had to be fought.

The life expectancy of enemy gun's crews on their numerous, closer, field pieces remained quite short as gunners on the wall brought them under fire with exploding case, but unless the guns themselves were wrecked, new crews quickly returned them to service. All the while, artillerymen on the walls, whether engaged in counter battery fire or mulching enemy infantry, were wearing themselves ragged and already digging deeper into their ammunition reserve than anyone had expected. Especially when it came to canister. No one could have possibly imagined the Doms would just keep taking such appalling losses.

The "American" infantrymen were wearing out too, most having already fired more than twice their ordinary combat allotment of sixty rounds from their hard-kicking weapons. Quite a few had fired two or three hundred shots and as many as a quarter were off the line at a time, cleaning fouling-choked muskets, clearing misfires, and knapping or replacing flints, even attempting more significant repairs to hard-used weapons. Long-hoarded supplies of spare springs and screws, even ramrods to replace those that broke, bent, or were inadvertently fired away, were dwindling. Weapons that failed completely, with burst barrels or shattered wrists, were stripped of parts and replaced by those of the wounded or killed. There were more of those available all the time.

The Doms finally reached the moat in numerous places by midafternoon and, though stymied by this new obstacle for a time, they took to firing devastating massed volleys that felled more unwary defenders. Tired men move slow and make mistakes, and more and more, particularly artillerymen, were falling prey to pure accidents. In addition to enemy fire, infantrymen were wounded by their own worn or filthy muskets that fell off at half cock and fired while they were loading them. Artillerymen were injured by guns recoiling into them or smashing feet when they were rolled up to fire. Several of the more inexperienced crews had men who'd lost arms or been killed when they rammed charges down on lingering sparks. Lewis regretted all his losses but considered those due to accidents the most tragic of all.

"My God," exclaimed Reverend Harkin, peering over the rampart at the teeming enemy now deep within their trenches and entanglements amid a vast panorama of suffering and destruction. "How long can they endure this slaughter?!"

Harkin, Father Orno, and Don Hurac himself had come up to find Lewis shortly before. Harkin wore a dark blue uniform frock without rank, and Orno had his own black version of the mounted uniform. Don Hurac surprised them by appearing in ornate scale armor with a servant carrying a beautiful sword belt and helmet. He'd explained that he must "set a warrior's example" for his people.

"It's startin' to look like they can take it just as long as we can dish it up,"

Leonor answered grimly without looking up. She'd finally disassembled her Paterson Colt to wipe out the barrel and chambers and was currently reloading the rounds she'd expended that morning.

Risking another quick glance over the walls themselves, between volleys, Lewis and Varaa shared a meaningful look.

Varaa said to the others, "The south lunette is still smashing them, taking the attackers down the length of the wall on either side in the flank, but I fear it may be in danger."

Lewis nodded and continued the explanation. "The boys down there have been murdering them," he agreed, "and the Doms keep swarming them for that, but also because of the bridge and gate right behind the lunette." He frowned. "I think it's time to destroy the bridge and pull the men behind the wall. The Doms're finally bringing ladders up, and what look like big rafts they've bound together." His frown twisted into an expression of distaste. "They're bringing other things too."

"Surely rafts won't do them much good," Reed observed skeptically.

"They don't mean to use them like rafts, to ferry men across," Varaa said. "They're throwing the bodies of their dead in the water, dragging them up from all around. I think they'll use them as foundations for bridges the raft things will become."

"Good God!" Harkin breathed.

"And some of the ladders are big, long things that look like they'll reach the top of the wall even from the bottom of the moat," Lewis added. "They'll probably try to swim or wade across whether the 'bridges' work or not."

"Can they do that?" asked Father Orno.

Lewis paused, then nodded. "It'll cost them a lot of men, but it's already obvious that won't stop them." He looked at a group of young soldiers nearby, watching him and waiting. "Messenger," he called, and one stepped forward, saluting. Lewis returned the gesture. "Go to the south lunette on the double and tell the ranking officer to abandon the position at his convenience and retire through the gate. Once inside, he'll destroy the bridge." Unlike the west bridge, all the rest had been rigged to blow. Lewis continued, "We'll send reserves to cover his movement since I expect the enemy will sense an opportunity and redouble their efforts. If he can't bring his guns in with him, he'll make sure they're thoroughly destroyed. Is that clear? Good, now go."

Beckoning another messenger, he pointed the young man at Reed.

"Find Major Ulrich, Third Pennsylvania," Reed told him. "My compliments, of course, and briefly explain the situation. You do understand it?"

"Yes, Colonel," said the soldier, an Uxmalo by his accent.

"Very good. Tell the major I want him to send another company to thicken the defense over and around the south gate at once."

The second messenger raced off after the first. Infantrymen were firing over the wall where Lewis and Varaa just had their look and one of them cursed and fell back, hand pressed hard on a blood-streaming cheek. A comrade crouched to check him before glancing up at the officers. "Just a scratch. Damned lead splatter or rock chunk, I'm thinkin'," he said.

"Well, take 'im down tae the aid station an' git yerself back," called a corporal a short distance away. "No damned malingerin'!"

"Never, Corporal!" cried both soldiers.

"Aye," said the corporal to the wounded man, "an' soon as they patch that little leak, git yerself back here as well!"

Don Hurac edged closer to Lewis. "Your army tires, yet your troops remain keen."

"We're all tired, Your Excellency, but these men are veterans who fight for a cause."

"And they've never known defeat," Varaa supported.

"Yet . . ." Don Hurac paused before continuing somewhat nervously. "I know it's only the most meager part of your defense, but . . . did you account for losing the south lunette so soon? On the very first day of battle?"

Lewis looked at him. "I didn't, frankly couldn't, expect anything like the assault we're enduring. I don't think any sane commander could. Even Colonel Agon, a former Dominion general himself, never sustained such a wasteful attack so long. So no, I didn't think we'd lose the lunette this quickly." His voice had risen as he spoke, revealing a measure of the horror and frustration he felt. "Can even *you* now imagine, as one who once worshipped him, a God so craven and vile as to require such suffering from those so devoted to him?" He shook his head violently as if shaking a crawling insect off his neck. "If you can, you're on the wrong side in this fight and we never should've supported you." Raising his voice to carry to the nearby troops over the fighting, he shouted, "But I'll rely on the valor of my army to 'account' for *anything* those poor, damned, misguided devils try!"

A hoarse, feral cheer erupted around them, spreading as soldiers passed what he said. Even so, the fighting around the south gate quickly increased in volume and Lewis leaned close to Reed. "You have things here in hand. I'll go back and observe the situation around the lunette for myself."

Reed nodded. "Be careful," he cautioned, then smiled at Leonor. "Make sure he keeps his fool head down."

Her revolver reloaded and reassembled, Leonor slid it into its holster. "That's my only job right now," she assured him.

Varaa followed again, and this time they were joined by Father Orno, Reverend Harkin, and Don Hurac, as well as Don Hurac's guards and the usual entourage of messengers. Lewis walked quickly but stopped at intervals to offer words of encouragement to tired, powder-stained men as they fired over the wall. Occasionally, he knelt by a wounded soldier and gripped his hand or gave him a pat before ensuring he was being helped, or about to be, then moved along. More cheers marked his progress. He quickened his pace as he neared the wall behind the lunette, however. The fighting was fiercest there, and his soldiers needed no distractions.

Dom troops were surging through the water around the lunette, holding muskets and cartridge boxes over their heads. Quite a few could barely breathe, only their noses or faces above the dark, slimy water. Still, they fought their way through the mass of floating ladders and blood-streaming, bobbing bodies, with geysers of spume erupting around them. The roar of voices was filled with screams because many of those splashes were tinged with red, the musket balls causing them hitting flesh.

The gate stood open and men were staggering through. One group was heaving on a captured 8pdr, even as Dom musket balls took one man down and sent splinters flying from the carriage. Lewis doubted the other guns would be saved. Hurrying around them among too many fallen men were only half a dozen still on their feet. Two were crouching near the breech of one gun, a corporal hammering a hardened spike into the vent with a mallet. He spun and dropped with a shriek. After an instant's hesitation, the other snatched up the mallet and gave the spike another hard strike. Apparently satisfied it would go in no farther, he deftly struck the spike on the side, snapping it off. Grabbing his corporal by his shoulder straps, he pulled him over the trail of the gun, dragging him backward.

Doms were climbing out of the water alongside the lunette, and more crawled over the heap of bodies straining the bridge in front. Several infantrymen rushed out the gate, shooting at the enemy before lending a hand with the fallen man. The four who'd been working on the other gun were down to two as well. One fled while the other stretched his lanyard as far as he could and cringed as he crouched and pulled it. With a terrible crack, the gun (clearly much overloaded) violently exploded, throwing shards of itself at the enemy—and everywhere else. Probably stuffed halfway to the muzzle with canister, everything in front of it died. But something must've struck the brave artilleryman as well. Blown down by the blast, his torn jacket and trousers red with blood, he managed to rise onto his hands.

"Go!" he screamed to the other men, now hesitating under the smoky shadow of the gate arch. "Shut the gate an' blow the bloody bridge, damn you!" More Doms were climbing out of the water on both sides of the lunette, bellowing triumphant war cries.

Watching the drama unfolding below, Lewis felt Leonor squeeze his arm. He suspected she did it to anchor them both against their urge to run and help. Captain Cullin, in charge of the relieving company, must've been moved by the same imperative, roaring at infantrymen of the 3rd Pennsylvania clogging the gate to fire outward.

"Get back, you fools! The lunette's gone. Do you want to let the devils in?"

That finally did the trick, and the men gathered there joined in the effort to heave the great leaves together. When the massive crossbeam dropped in place, Cullin shouted at a sergeant, "Blow it!"

The sergeant rushed to one of two protected boxes by the gate, lifted the lid on one, and removed a short coil of sturdy rope. Grasping it with both hands, he jerked it as hard as he could. The rope ran through a small hole laboriously bored through the wide base of the wall and was lightly buried where it crossed the lunette and became invisible where it ran under the bridge. There it entered another box, half-full of gunpowder, where it was secured to the sear of a cocked Dom musket lock. That box was sealed in a cask of Dom gunpowder—secured under the bridge with four others. Two such ignition arrangements had been prepared in case one failed or its rope was severed or bound by something. It wasn't. In an instant, the entire bridge, much of the lunette, and hundreds of Doms, living and dead, were heaved into the sky by a titanic roar, a ball of fire, and a roiling tower of billowing smoke.

"Take cover!" someone shouted. Varra and Leonor dragged Lewis under the overhead protection constructed along numerous key sections of wall. Don Hurac's guards did the same for him and the others. Moments later, shattered timbers, earth, and parts of bodies thundered down amid a reddened mist from the moat. Almost at once, Lewis was back in the open, looking over the wall. The bridge was gone entirely, and nothing had survived in the water nearby, the overpressure killing anything the blast itself spared. Most of the lunette was gone as well, the remains of the guns tipped into the water. Of the wounded artilleryman, there was no sign.

"I've seen examples of your army's devotion to the cause before," Don Hurac said, stepping up beside Lewis along with the others, "but perhaps never quite so singular as what I just viewed."

Lewis was shaking his head, and Leonor spoke. "No, sir. The cause gives 'em heart an' a reason to stand, but they do what just happened for each other."

"Perhaps there is a measure of that among our enemy," Don Hurac granted. "Many of their smaller formations, equivalents to your 'companies,' I should think, are conscripted from the same towns and villages. They are . . . connected, as your men are. Ultimately, though, they keep coming like they do because it's preferable to suffer and die and go to their God in battle, among friends and family, than suffer far more and be damned for refusing."

The lull that followed the terrible blast was short. Dom officers immediately ordered more of their men into the steaming moat. Going for floating ladders or bringing up more, they were quickly met by growing musket fire and blasts of canister.

"It would be best to step back now," Varaa reminded, luminous blue eyes turning skyward as she did so. The sun, now nearing the high mountains in the west, was smeared by a growing haze, and the sky overhead was iron gray.

"Right," said Leonor. "S'posed to keep your fool head down, remember?"

"It's going to rain," Varaa announced.

Lewis looked up as all of them backed away from the wall. "Damn," he murmured. "Let's pray it doesn't."

"What?" asked Reverend Harkin. "Surely rain will help us. Those devils can't possibly keep this up in the rain!"

"Actually, I'd be surprised if they didn't," Lewis countered grimly.

"Think," he continued. "Rain won't much affect the artillery unless our men grow reckless. An occasional misfire, perhaps. But the infantry..." He shook his head.

"What?" Harkin repeated.

"More misfires than not, as the fouling in their muskets turns to black soup," Varaa warned.

"That's right," Lewis agreed. "Then it'll basically be their bayonets against ours as more and more of them reach the walls between the gun emplacements. They'll eventually start reaching the top." He took a long breath. "For all intents and purposes, it'll be down to spears. Positively medieval. And their numbers will finally start to matter."

A messenger came huffing up the switchback stair behind them, saluting when he stood before them. "Report," Lewis said.

"Colonel Agon begs to inform you that Major Anson risked a flashed message asking that a message *he* saw be repeated. The thing is, sir, we ain't *sent* any message."

Lewis and Varaa exchanged another meaningful look and Lewis said, "If we didn't do it, which I can't imagine why anyone would, then someone else did—and Major Anson wasn't the intended recipient."

"Pretty clear we didn't get all the Blood Priests or their supporters in the city," Leonor said, "an' at least one of 'em knows how to contact the ones outside."

Father Orno pursed his lips. "But how can they really hurt us, within the midst of a hostile army?"

Lewis looked at him a moment. "I don't know. And that's what worries me." He turned back to the messenger. "Go back to Colonel Agon, but alert the reserves to be on guard for further unauthorized communications—flashing light where it shouldn't be. If they've already seen that, put a stop to it. That said"—he glanced around—"Colonel Agon will signal Major Anson that it's time to begin massing his mobile force east of the city." He pointed at another messenger. "Make sure Colonel Reed is aware of these developments, if you please."

Leonor looked troubled. "You're signaling my father already?"

"Yes," said Don Hurac, tone objecting. "What is the meaning of that?"

"Just trying to be prepared," Lewis assured him. "The main problem with static, defensive battles is all you can really do is react to what the enemy does. Our only initiative lies in keeping the enemy guessing about the quality, depth, and determination of that defense." He paused, then added, "And staying ahead of the enemy's expectations should it ultimately fail."

"Ladders!" shouted a sergeant close to the nearest gun emplacement to their right. Lewis noted the trail of that weapon had been placed on one of Justinian Olayne's ramps, to lower its elevation. "Topple the ladders as soon as they touch. Don't let 'em start up 'em—they'll get too heavy to shift!" the sergeant kept shouting. Troopers retrieved long staffs with Y-shaped yokes on the end from behind them and started heaving ladders away from the walls. Others leaned out and fired muskets straight down. More and more of those started falling, however, as Doms across the moat shot back. The 8pdr to their right coughed canister at them, groaning and creaking as it rode up the ramp before sliding back down, almost into battery. Olayne's idea seemed to work well enough, but it would be hard on the gun carriages. It was growing quite dark much sooner than it should, and cannon and musket flashes glared bright. Lewis felt a patter on his hand and raised it to see and confirm his concern. "Damn," he said again. "Rain."

"Perhaps we should rejoin Colonel Reed?" Varaa suggested.

"Very well," Lewis agreed. "Soon enough, one place'll be much like another."

CHAPTER 28

WEST WALL

The rain came hard at first, lasting until nearly dark. It eased after that, but a cold drizzle lingered. Since heavy humidity alone can render flintlock muskets ineffective over time, especially without proper precautions, the drizzle practically stopped almost all small arms fire, from both sides. Percussion weapons like Hall carbines would've fared better, but most of those were off with Anson and his mounted troops. More and more Doms were making it on ladders and starting to threaten troops on the walls, and the sounds of battle had grown vaguely more dreadful. Screams and curses were louder, and the whole thing sounded more metallic as most of the fighting now involved the clash of bayonets and blades. Perhaps the only consolation was that the enemy artillery was practically silenced as well.

Some defending guns, particularly those most recently captured, experienced troublesome misfires when quill primers or smoldering linstocks got wet, but most of those stoppages were relatively short-lived. Many of the guns on the walls had already been converted to use the Hidden's patent percussion locks. These sent a hot jet of fire down the vent and were less susceptible to failures. A large number of the locks had been copied, even simplified, and cast from brass in Vera Cruz. Cannon couldn't do much about Doms who'd run their gauntlet and were now right up against the walls, but with no return fire, they could smash even more of the enemy as they closed. Rain and darkness or not, all the camps thrown up around the city still burned and provided sufficient lurid light for the artillerymen to continue their savage execution.

Still, even as the long battle seemed to rage everywhere else, there hadn't been a real effort against the westernmost wall. Doms were still surging over all the bridges across the canal between the lakes before rushing to reinforce assaults under way, and the guns on the west wall kept pounding them, but there'd been little work for the infantry there. Colonel Reed and Colonel Agon had cautiously pulled a few regiments from there through the day and sent them to counter greater threats.

Major Arevalo tilted his head forward, pouring water out the front fold of his black tricorn hat. He was in charge, under General Tun, of the far left of Agon's 4th Division, now standing with Major Olayne and Major Don Roderigo, whose 1st Vera Cruz was on the right of Reed's 1st Division. A lot of his men were acting as NCOs in a city militia regiment entrusted with securing the gate. After the recent rebellion, a large detachment of these troops was actually positioned to protect the gate from *inside*.

Each time a big gun fired, spitting a sputtering case shot to burst over distant Dom concentrations on the bridges, the drizzle turned to a brief, heavier shower, as if the concussion shook water from the sky. Arevalo tipped his hat again and said aside to Olayne, "It remains disconcertingly quiet here, compared to elsewhere." He grinned ruefully. "Aside from the thunder of your great guns, of course."

"With the rest of the army so busy, I feel somewhat guilty," commented Don Roderigo.

"Bored, you mean," Olayne prodded lightly. He liked the "hidalgo" from Vera Cruz who often complained that something always seemed to intervene to keep his regiment from the thick of the fighting. He was devoted to the cause and proud of his men, but they'd never really been tested in battle. He'd occasionally begun to wonder aloud whether he and his men were trusted. "Don't worry, Roderigo," Olayne went on. "You'll have plenty of business soon enough." He waved outward. "The lads are holding well everywhere else. Doms'll try us before long." He paused. "I can't get that 'message' Major Anson reported out of my mind. His signal came from the hills north of the enemy's grand reserve—"

"That they've been frittering away all day," Arevalo inserted.

"Just so," Olayne agreed. "But for Anson's men to see it, it had to be aimed at the enemy's largest and freshest remaining force, across from the only place we're not currently under assault. They'll come," he ended grimly.

"Perhaps," Don Roderigo admitted. "Still . . ."

Huge, bright muzzle flashes suddenly bloomed in the dark, and the only possible sources had to be the giant Dom siege guns, firing much closer than they'd been.

"Damn," Olayne said as all three of them instinctively crouched a little. Two massive 36pdr balls shivered the wall, quite close, and several more shrieked overhead with the sound of ripping canvas, crashing in the city behind them. An instant later, they heard the deep, booming reports like thunder down in a valley.

"I'll swear those roundshot were glowing!" Don Roderigo exclaimed.

"They were," Olayne confirmed. "They've heated them deliberately to start fires."

"Surely it's too wet for that," Arevalo objected.

"No," Olayne denied. "Not if they stop inside a building."

"How did they get them to fire?" asked Don Roderigo, now gazing behind at the city.

"Simple enough," Olayne told him. "They dried the guns out. Probably protected the vents and priming with something. They're not stupid. Our lads with captured guns have managed. So can they. They just lulled us into *thinking* they couldn't."

"Fire," Don Roderigo observed, pointing. "One of the grain storehouses," he added. There were several such buildings running parallel behind what was referred to as the "business district" surrounding the great central mall fronting the pyramidal temples. Olayne could see flames beginning to gush from the shattered roof of one. Another fire was growing not far from the villa serving as a dining hall for the officers. Shapes could already be seen running about, beginning to organize to fight the fires. Much of the rest of the city was blocked from their view by the mass of the biggest, main temple.

"Major Olayne!" came a warning shout from one of the closest gunners, and Olayne turned back toward the enemy. Every field piece the Doms had left must've fired. It wasn't a brisk salvo, just a long, booming ripple of fiery muzzle flashes. Dozens of roundshot started smashing into the wall at once.

Men were flayed by flying fragments of stone and one was hit squarely in the head, blood-fountaining body dropping beneath a reddish haze. A tremendous gong sound drew their attention to a gun, struck on the muzzle, that flipped up out of its carriage and crashed down on men already ravaged by fragments of the shattered shot.

"Medical orderlies!" Arevalo roared, gazing in horror at a section of the heavy, protective overhead timbers that had collapsed on a half dozen of his infantry.

"Target those guns!" Olayne shouted at his artillerymen.

"They've moved them, sir. It'll take a few rounds to find the range in the dark," the closest gunner warned.

Some of the enemy guns had already reloaded and were firing again, causing more havoc atop the wall. In the jetting light of vent flashes, Olayne thought he glimpsed canvas rain flies rigged over them. He also realized the gunner was right, but the enemy artillerymen hadn't just moved their weapons, they'd brought them much closer. The fury of the Dom bombardment increased rapidly, clearly focused on his own gun positions and slowing the rate of fire his men could maintain.

"Messenger," Olayne called aside. "Spread the word down the wall. The Doms have moved their guns right up to the other side of the canal. Gunners should only have to adjust their range and fuses by a couple hundred yards."

"I'm not sure you should change your targets just now," shouted Don Roderigo.

"Why is that?" Olayne cried back over the roar of cannon and crashing impacts.

"The flashing of your exploding shells over the bridges," he began, then coughed and wiped his eyes. He'd caught a large dose of rock dust in the face. He continued, "It shows me the Doms have stopped going 'round us and are massing to the front." He waved around. "All this they have saved back until now, and I suspect they *want* you to focus your great guns on theirs!"

Arevalo had stepped closer to the wall. "He is right!" he yelled back. "They are coming here."

"In what strength?" Olayne asked, hurrying to join him. "My God," he said. Despite the damp air, the cloud of stone dust and gunsmoke was thick, but a ripple of cracking case shot obliged him with a brief, spectacular view.

"All of them," he answered himself. Turning back to the nervous messenger, standing rigid in the maelstrom, he grabbed the young soldier by the arm. "Send two others to tell our gunners to keep firing on Dom infantry. Use canister at their discretion as the enemy nears. You and you"—he motioned two more messengers forward—"go to Colonel Reed and Colonel Agon. Inform them we're preparing to receive a major assault. We've lost several guns to the enemy bombardment and may require reinforcement directly."

The young men were nodding anxiously, waiting to be sent on their way, but something behind them, in the city, caught Olayne's attention. "My God," he said again, physically turning the messengers to see. Silhouetted by the spreading fires, hundreds of shapes were sprinting across the cleared ground behind the main western gate, the roar of their voices distinct from the cacophony of battle. All were armed with something, spears, swords, farm implements, a few muskets, even pieces of timber, and quite a few urging them on openly wore the red robes of Blood Priests. There were furious or panicked shouts from the militia inside the gate, and a sloppy musket volley clattered in the faces of the rebels, tearing at their ranks. There was little firing after that. Even if the muskets weren't wet, there was no time to reload before the rebel charge smashed home. Screams and roars intermingled with clashing weapons.

Olayne shook the messengers. "I fear we'll need those reinforcements more quickly than I thought. Go!"

"They're charging!" shouted Don Roderigo. Olayne shook his head. *Of course* . . . Then he realized the commander of the 1st Vera Cruz was still facing outward, and Olayne rushed back to his side. It looked like the whole Dom army was swarming forward through the obstacle-filled killing ground in front of the west gate. Hundreds were falling, lamed by caltrops, crashing down in trenches, even impaling themselves on sharpened stakes. Others were going down in bloody swathes as canister clawed at them. None of that even seemed to dent the mighty horde. Soon, thousands of Doms would be under the guns and into the moat, throwing up the vast numbers of ladders they carried and scaling the walls.

"The strange signal from earlier!" Olayne gasped. "*This* is what it meant—that our enemies within were prepared to strike in concert with those outside! Back to your men, Roderigo," Olayne added, clasping the major's shoulder. "Send some down to the gate if you can. I assure you, your lads'll be in the thick of it this time!"

Wide-eyed, Don Roderigo turned and stepped quickly back among his own men, shouting orders. Rushing out from under the overhead shelter where they'd been trying to keep their muskets dry, some of his men made for the switchback stairs to go and aid the militia. Others rushed to take places on the wall. Arevalo was calling loudly for much the same thing, sending men against the rebels, but most to join the handful who'd been up with the artillery all along. The closest Doms were already within two hundred yards and all cannon along the wall had switched to canister, sweeping great chunks out of the sprinting mob. Infantry started firing as well. Dom infantry was shooting too, often on the run, expending a carefully protected load that might be the only shot they'd fire. Most could then be seen inserting long-bladed plug bayonets in the muzzles of their muskets. The defenders had already affixed their own socket bayonets, long, triangular-bladed weapons now even available for use on captured muskets. And unlike the Doms, Colonel Cayce's troops could keep shooting with bayonets in place—if the weather let them.

Olayne cast his gaze to the sky. The humidity remained thick enough to swim in, but it was getting colder and the rain had stopped. He didn't know much about weather in general but remembered cold air was usually drier. "Lord," he said aloud to himself, "Your will be done, but if it's all the same to You, I'd be grateful if You hold the rain back awhile."

"I think that's been part of this battle," shouted Major Arevalo beside him. Olayne looked questioningly at him.

"The part between God and the Devil," Arevalo elaborated. "The devil who has ruled this land so long that we *thought* he was God."

"You think the devil made it rain?"

"Of course!"

"Then... why didn't God stop it?"

"You waited until now to ask Him," Arevalo joked, then grew serious. "God works in the open for all to see, but the devil is sneaky. He sent rain to spoil our defense, and it fell hard at first. *Very* hard—then only gently. Don't you think that was God fighting for us? Now the rain has stopped!"

"But... it may start again," cautioned Olayne. "And even if it doesn't, the damage may be done." A great roar went up as the Doms reached the wall and ladders fell against the top. Even then, the enemy artillery continued to fire, insensitive to the fact they'd kill their own men. Of course, that was true for the whole battle so far. Another roar rose as the struggle for the gate behind them intensified.

Arevalo shrugged. "The rain is over," he said confidently. "And though I am new to this . . . old faith your people resurrected in us, even I understand we cannot expect God to do everything for us! I have faith it is His will that we win—but what *is* winning? We may not yet even know."

"Well," said Olayne, confused by that, "winning for me, tonight, is living through this."

Infantrymen along the wall were shooting or stabbing downward now, with too many ladders rising too quickly to fend them all off. Just as alarming, a procession of armabueys was being led forward, each with a large box strapped atop its back, like a howdah on top of an elephant, only no one was riding in it. Men leading the beasts were dropping like flies, victims of musket fire and canister, but they were replaced and the animals plodded on, seemingly oblivious to the fire. Olayne didn't know what the things were carrying, but doubted he'd like it. That's when he saw the first Dom reach the top of the wall, frantically swinging his musket like a club to bash a path for himself. One of Arevalo's green-coated soldiers smacked the weapon aside with his own and another drove a bayonet in the enemy's chest, twisting professionally and pulling back. The Dom screamed and fell. But there were more. In moments, every infantryman atop the wall was fighting for his life. Arevalo drew the sword at his side, a fine, straight-bladed rapier. "Then we must fight," he said.

═══════════

Don Hurac and the two clerics had remained on the south wall, moving to join Colonel Reed, but Lewis, Leonor, and Varaa had taken to their horses. With the enemy seeming to hit nearly every wall at once, they'd found it easier to keep pace with events if they were mobile. None were naive enough to suppose their fight to suppress the insurrection in the city had been wholly successful, so in addition to a train of mounted messengers, they'd retained Lieutenant Buisine and the rest of their surviving escorts from earlier to resume their duty.

They'd been to the east wall where Har-Kaaska's 2nd Division was doing well enough. A sizable enemy force, perhaps twenty thousand, had been pressing there fairly briskly, but the Dom commander wasn't getting the inexhaustible reinforcement going to the main force this side of the canal, to the south. The attacks had been determined and costly to both sides, but, as Lewis predicted, appeared primarily intended to keep Har-Kaaska's division fixed in place. Har-Kaaska had recognized that himself and quietly sent a couple regiments to strengthen the south, where the fighting had been fiercest all day.

The torrential rain was just easing when Lewis's party neared the center of the city, the huge camp at the base of the great temple not much farther. There they encountered more activity than there'd been for most of the distance. Few civilians had been out and about, and most they'd seen had been organized into fire brigades, fighting the flames in buildings here and there. None of those fires seemed out of control. One thing to thank the rain for. They'd passed a few miserably sodden and frustrated soldiers manning obstacle "gateways" through internal defenses and been passed in turn by rushing ambulance wagons bearing wounded to the hospital section.

The rain had slowed to a spiteful drizzle by the time they passed the new army headquarters, relocated to the villa/dining hall. They didn't stop because no one of importance would be there at the moment and there was little activity around it. Lewis's goal was the headquarters tent that had become a small addition to the larger hospital tents now erected all around it. Dry bedding would be at a premium for the wounded, and Lewis was afraid the whole camp might be annexed by the surgeons' needs before this was done.

There were lots of civilians here, mostly women and children. Some merely sat shivering in tight, wet groups with haunted eyes, gazing around as if resigned to being trapped on a drowning island in a sea of flame. That wasn't a bad analogy since, with the exception of the fires, the whole city was dark, yet surrounded by strobing flashes of war. It reminded Lewis more of being in the bottom of a river valley he couldn't escape with a forest fire raging all around. He didn't like that notion either. Other civilians kept busy by helping the surgeons and nurses, carrying stretchers and sloshing buckets, boiling water and tending smoky fires to do so, or arranging the dead in lengthening lines. It was the wounded, similarly arranged (though generally under dripping cover), moaning, screaming, or lying stoically silent while they waited for treatment, that bothered Lewis most. He'd come to terms with the fact that on some strange level, he rather loved a battle.

He couldn't explain it and no longer really tried. But there was nothing about *this* aspect of battle that appealed to him at all. If anything, it only made him furious with whoever had provoked the fight in the first place and made him more determined to destroy them. He'd stopped trying to reconcile that contrast as well because it couldn't be done.

Irrationally, Lewis found himself wishing Dr. Newlin was here, instead of at Texcoco. Newlin would be the first to confess that, with a few exceptions he'd specialized in, the Uxmalo and Ocelomeh healers were better at this sort of thing than he. But here, just now, Lewis wanted to see a familiar face coping with the suffering he'd grimly decided to view for himself before making his next stop with Colonel Agon on the north wall. To his surprise, he quickly found one, or rather two, almost at once.

Even before he could dismount, he saw Samantha Anson step out of one of the tents that glowed yellow from the lanterns inside, a bloody white apron tied around her neck and waist. Pausing a moment under the misty drizzle, the Englishwoman put her hands on her hips, stretched her back, then closed her eyes and raised her face as if taking refreshment from the gentle moisture. A moment later, another young woman Lewis quickly recognized as Hannibal Cox's sweetheart, Izel Tuin, stepped out beside Samantha and spoke to her. Samantha opened her eyes and began to respond, but then saw Lewis. Pleased recognition rapidly gave way to annoyance and Samantha stalked over with Izel in tow.

"We need more ambulances!" she exclaimed without preamble. "The carts we have available simply aren't keeping up. They're dreadfully overloaded when they arrive, men stacked like lumber, which is only adding to their misery!"

"You have all we can spare," Lewis told her. "I wish there were more."

"Rubbish!" Samantha snapped, waving toward the center of the plaza, where new temporary corrals had been erected. "I can't even count how many beasts you have idling there, languishing uselessly and pointlessly hitched to every imaginable vehicle—limbers, wagons, what have you—and most fully loaded!"

Leonor doubted that. With Samantha so deeply involved in the army's logistics effort, she probably knew exactly how many vehicles and animals had been prepared and left in harness, and how each wagon was loaded. It was possible she believed Lewis had ordered it so the vehicles could be moved if threatened by fire, each provided with their full allotment of horses to keep them from scattering if the corral was damaged, but Leonor doubted it.

"I've repeatedly attempted to requisition some of the empty wagons, but am consistently refused. 'Colonel Cayce's orders,' I'm told." She said the last with her impression of the voice of a deeply stupid man.

"I'm sorry," Lewis said, looking around, noting an example of what Samantha spoke of: a wagon clattering up on the cobbles from the south wall, most likely. Wounded cried out with every jostle and bump. They weren't exactly stacked, but were uncomfortably crowded. He seemed to gaze at them in a calculating fashion, then took a deep breath. "Very well," he said sadly, reversing himself, which was something he rarely did. "You may use half the empty wagons, but no more. That should give you more than a dozen additional vehicles." His tone turned serious. "I'm relying on you to abide by that. Perhaps you've taken notice from time to time that I occasionally have reasons for what I do."

Izel smiled up at him, her tired, melancholy expression suddenly radiant, but Samantha only gave a sarcastic salute. "Of course, *Colonel*, as you say. No more than half—whether that's enough or not. Now do run along. You're missing your battle."

Leonor saw a flash of hurt on Lewis's face, quickly concealed, as he pulled Arete's head around and urged the warhorse northward. Buisine and their escort clopped after him. Leonor paused, frowning down at her new mother-in-law with a mix of annoyance and understanding, but mostly concern.

Samantha sighed deeply and held up a hand. "I know, that was mean and I am already sorry for it. No doubt he came to speak to some of his boys and now I've run him off. I'll make sure they know he was here. Soldiers can be so very strange," she said as though mystified. "I saw it as a girl with my father, in India, how they all take such heart from a word of encouragement—from the very man whose orders caused them pain." She wiped her damp face with a rag tucked in her apron. "And he did ease our transport concerns. It's just . . . well, I expect you know how I feel."

Leonor nodded at her, then smiled at Izel. "Y'all're fightin' your own part of our battle here," she agreed. "The hardest part, I reckon. I couldn't do it. I'll stick by Lewis to fight mine."

"She didn't mean it," she told Lewis when she joined him just beyond one of their innermost defensive lines, hooves clattering loudly on the cobbled, nearly deserted thoroughfare leading to the north gate. Another of the hastily constructed walls was ahead, its few current defenders silhouetted against Agon's flashing guns, dulled by a kind of misty fog that had replaced the rain.

"I know," he acknowledged. "She was venting her own fatigue, frustration, and sadness. I understand completely."

Leonor was sure he did.

Leaving their horses with Buisine and the escort at the base of the north wall, Lewis, Leonor, and Varaa climbed to the top. They were immediately swamped by the chaos of surprisingly fierce fighting. Mostly former Doms themselves, Agon's green-coated soldiers were fighting just as desperately against figures climbing ladders as any soldiers Lewis had seen. Perhaps even more so. Roaring faces twisted by fanatical hate that appeared at the top of the wall were bashed with buttplates or stabbed with bayonets and sent shrieking down to the moat. Squads of men heaved against poles with Y-shaped yokes to topple ladders. Bellowing triumphantly, a cluster of Doms suddenly spilled through a gun embrasure a little to the right, perhaps half the men who'd been stacked up on a ladder. Artillerymen fought them with their implements, smacking heads with rammer staffs or worms, but bayonets made short work of them. Leonor drew one of her revolvers and Varaa and Lewis both drew their blades, but green-coated infantrymen roared in against them. One managed to fire a carefully hoarded shot, blowing a Dom back over the wall. The rest were pinned against it. Something sputtered and smoked and Lewis realized an artilleryman had lit the fuse of a case shot with a torch before dropping it over the wall. There was a muffled *crack* and a rising cloud of smoke followed by shrill screams almost at once.

"*That's* enough to give me the shakes!" Lewis shouted, but his tone was approving. "Where's Colonel Agon?" he shouted at a harried-looking corporal who'd lost his hat and was bleeding from his uncovered scalp. The man sketched a salute and pointed west, but his words were lost as another gun, trail on a wedge, boomed and coughed canister down out of sight. Lewis got the idea and threaded his way through the fighting men, Leonor and Varaa behind him. It wasn't long before they found Agon, blade in hand, shouting back and forth with Colonel Tun. Tun was pointing west.

"Colonel Agon! Colonel Tun!" Lewis greeted with a shout. "The fighting here is brisker than I expected. What do you make of it?"

The former Doms saluted, and Lewis saw Leonor cringe. She didn't say anything, though. No enemy could see them do it here. Lewis saluted back.

"Colonel Cayce," Agon shouted back. "I'm pleased to see you well." He gestured around. "Yes. Hot work. The enemy didn't start with as many men here, but it's likely as many have been skirting around to us from the canal crossing as have been doing so to the south. No doubt my messengers have kept you informed."

Lewis nodded.

"More recently, there has been that." Tun pointed. Dozens of big barges seemed clotted together along the distant lakeshore on the water. Some were burning, smearing the rest—either abandoned or half-sunk and covered with bodies—with a guttering, hellish light. "They started that right after dark," Tun continued, "but once we set the first one alight, the rest were easier targets."

"We appear to have put a stop to their . . . maritime adventures, and this current push feels like a last, desperate effort," Agon said, but tilted his head at Tun. "Or diversion."

"Diversion?"

Tun pointed his sword west, almost slashing an artilleryman bringing another charge to his gun. "A messenger just arrived from Major Olayne, warning of a major assault over there. Some of the local *rebeldes* we missed are attacking from inside as well." Tun never smiled, but his expression was grimmer than ever. "That could be very dangerous."

Lieutenant Buisine found them, dragging another gasping dragoon. "Colonel Cayce," he yelled over another cannon shot, "this messenger is from the west wall. You need to hear him, sir."

"Thank God I found you," the messenger wheezed, trying to catch his breath, the gunsmoke making him cough after the sprint up from the horses. "There's a big attack on the west wall, focused on the gate. Inside and out at once. All the Doms in the world just charged across the killin' field, overran the lunette, an' hit the outside while Blood Priests in the city—real ones with red cloaks an' all—whipped a couple thousand locals at the gate before anybody even knew what was what. There weren't much more than militia there at first, on the inside, I mean, an' . . . well, the gate went pretty quick. Boys on the walls sent down what they could to keep the gate stoppered, but they're still fightin' the Doms on the *outside* too!"

"My God," Lewis breathed. "All coordinated, like this attack here, I expect. Probably elsewhere." He looked at the others. "I think the meaning of the mystery communication Major Anson reported is clear." His gaze focused on Agon. "Take everything you can spare, even what you can't, to relieve the west wall. I've no doubt Colonel Reed will be doing the same. If we can't close that gate before the enemy gets significant forces in the city..."

"I will go," Tun suggested, interrupting. "My men are closer, and there is less pressure on the northeast corner." He looked at Agon. "And you cannot hold here with much less."

Lewis gave a quick nod. "Very well, but bear in mind that if one wall falls, they all do. We'll have no choice but to retire to the inner defenses."

"Can we hold them there?" Varaa asked, tail snapping in agitation.

Lewis cleared his throat. "No. Those defenses were meant as a last resort, hopefully never needed. Certainly not until after many days or weeks of bleeding the enemy. *Never* after only a single day and night," he added in a bitter tone. Probably only Leonor, and maybe Varaa understood he was blaming himself for the growing crisis. He continued, "More due to the enemy's stupidity than our own preparations, we've bled them more than I ever expected this soon, but I don't think it'll be enough." He sighed. "Come, there's much to do, and we're wasting precious time."

Shod hooves skidding and clattering on damp cobbles again, Lewis and his companions raced back toward the central plaza, calling on the few men manning the inner defenses to be on guard for civilian insurrectionists as they passed. He'd never dreamed enough of those could remain to pose a serious threat, certainly not as many as the attack on the west gate implied. Knowing full well what would happen to them, anyone here still willing to aid the enemy had to be insane. And despite the apparently suicidal devotion displayed by enemy troops, he'd never thought a similar madness could be so widespread among civilians. People with families. His mind couldn't wrap around it. He *hoped* all the crazies were fighting in the western city, but there was no way to know, and they had to be careful.

They drew to a stop in front of the headquarters building, which seemed much busier now. A lot of frightened civilians milled about, but more soldiers too, mostly messengers being directed where to go. The sound of battle still rumbled all around, but was swelling to the west.

"Colonel Cayce!" cried Captain "Mal" Harris, pushing his way closer through the press. Lewis saw that most of his B Company of the 1st US was present. Many had wounds, and all were filthy, wet, and exhausted.

"Captain," Lewis acknowledged, returning the man's salute but hesitating to dismount.

"Colonel Reed knew you'd come here," Harris explained. "He's inside with Don Hurac and the clerical fellows. Pulled us off the line for a rest, and to redeploy at need. He replaced us with A Company, from the reserve. Captain Sime. Dark hair, ghastly scar on his face—you remember him."

"Of course," Lewis said impatiently. Sime wasn't a particularly memorable officer, aside from a disfigurement inflicted by what was essentially a giant toad, but Lewis knew each of his "old" soldiers.

"Yes, well, perhaps you might let Colonel Reed explain things," Harris suggested self-consciously.

"I will," Lewis said, stepping down and handing over Arete's reins. The captain seemed surprised. Even more so when Leonor and Varaa handed theirs to him as well. Lieutenant Buisine coughed to hide a chuckle as the trio disappeared through the door.

"Well," Harris huffed, awkwardly holding the animals as if he'd never done it before. "I don't know whether to be insulted or honored." Everyone knew how Colonel Cayce felt about his horse.

"Just go with 'honored,' Mal." Buisine laughed. "And besides, you were just standing there, doing nothing." The infantry captain's face reddened. "Damn you—and all horse soldiers," he growled. "We've been fighting all damned day. And what have all your mounted comrades been up to? Swanning around outside somewhere, away from the battle!"

Buisine held out a placating hand, sobering. "Simmer down, Mal. You've had a hard time. Everyone has. I was only fooling." He paused and lowered his voice. "But as for Major Anson and his mounted troops . . . if things turn out the way I figure Colonel Cayce fears they will, they could be the only thing that saves our precious asses."

CHAPTER 29

MARCH 16, 1849

Colonel Reed's expression was grim when he looked up from a rough drawing of the city laid out on a table. Don Hurac, Father Orno, and Reverend Harkin were with him, as were several 1st Division officers. The large room smelled of smoke and damp wool. Lewis noted the presence of Vice Alcalde Don Amil with some surprise. "You got the word?" Reed asked.

"Yes," Lewis said. "We were with Colonel Agon and have already sent Colonel Tun to reinforce the west wall."

Reed sighed. "And I just sent all the reserves from the south wall, including some chaps Har-Kaaska loaned me. God help us if they try anything like this at the other gates."

"They can't possibly . . . can they?" asked Don Hurac. "You have been *destroying* their army all around the city since"—he hesitated—"yesterday morning, now. Their only unravaged reserve of any size is to the west."

Reed looked at him. "Obviously, the condition of their troops makes no difference to them."

Rubbing his chin through his whiskers, Lewis considered the map. "It might be starting to," he murmured, then looked up. "I'm certain, and I think we all agree, General Xacolotl didn't start this fight. We don't even know if he's still alive. But Don Hurac's right. A lot of the army assaulting the walls must be on the verge of becoming combat ineffective. Whole regiments have been shattered, the initial ones virtually exterminated, along with large portions of those they've kept throwing across the canal. Agon thought so in the north. They simply won't have the organization and cohesion to keep this up everywhere much longer, without stopping to reorganize and refit. That's my current thinking, anyway.

"Whoever started the battle—Don Frutos, I'll bet—didn't care how wasteful it would be, and the whole thing has been aimed at preparing for this push against the west wall. If we can beat that back, there's still a chance we'll stabilize all the walls and force the enemy to take a breath. Don Frutos'll have shot his bolt, and maybe Xacolotl will take back over." He shook his head. "That might be just as dangerous in the long run, but I bet he'll be more careful with his troops and take his time." He frowned. "God knows he won't be as desperate for rations as he was and he'll have more time to take."

Reed straightened. "Perhaps. But first we have to stop them. I shall take all the troops here and any I can scrape up on the way to ensure we're secure from the west."

Lewis was shaking his head. "No, Colonel. You'll stay here. I'll go."

"Not acceptable!" Reed adamantly objected.

Lewis smiled and straightened from the table as well. "I don't believe you heard what you just said, my friend. I still command this army, and it's my duty to save it, if I can. On the other hand, you're a better organizer than I am—always have been—and I'm leaving it to you to prepare for the worst. All the things that have to be done to abandon the city."

"Abandon . . ." began Don Hurac, shocked by the very thought.

"Yes, Your Excellency. We already have . . . several plans for that possibility, but if it comes to it, one must be chosen and set into motion." He looked at Reed. "You're the man for that. It may even be wise to start loading the wagons with wounded now, as well as collecting guns on new carriages that the limbers can pull. Take them from places less pressed at the moment." He frowned. "The wounded will be the biggest problem. I released more wagons to transport them to the hospital section than originally planned. Until all can be gathered together again, walking wounded will . . . well, they'll have to walk."

"Most'll want to fight," Leonor predicted. She and Varaa were the only ones present other than Reed who'd discussed a possible evacuation in the middle of a fight with Lewis.

"Some might have to," Lewis said grimly.

Don Hurac was sputtering. "You can't... we can't... *I* shall *never* leave this place now that it's in our grasp!" he insisted.

"If the enemy takes it from us, you'll have no other choice," said Varaa.

"Never!" Don Hurac snapped emphatically.

"You shall!" asserted Zyan, surprising everyone when she shed her usual placid voice and expression, replacing them with a stark, fierce passion. Now she stepped forward from where she'd been resting on a hassock in the middle of some other tired, rattled-looking ladies. All wore bloodstained tunics from helping the healers. "You told me all along it was the *people* you cared for, not the Dominion that ruled them," she insisted. "I believed you because you sacrificed your place in the Dominion for *me*. A mere *woman*! Then you swore—to them and me—to defend those who came to you from the wickedness of that old, terrible God. No *place* was part of that oath! If the walls around this city can no longer guarantee their safety, you *shall* lead your people wherever you must to find it!" She took a ragged breath. "You swore to *God*—the real one, not the vile beast whose stink yet lingers here. Are the people no longer as important as the place?"

"Well said, Mistress Zyan," Reverend Harkin said.

"Indeed," agreed Father Orno.

Just as shocked as the rest of them, Don Hurac had physically recoiled from this very different Zyan from the one he'd always known. Now he looked around, expression lost. "It is just..."

"I know, Your Excellency," Lewis said softly, then more firmly, "Let's just make sure it doesn't come to that. But we *must* prepare." He hesitated, looking at Reed. "If it does, we'll have to implement some of the... general contingencies we've considered."

"Don't worry about that," Reed stated grimly. "If any Doms get past the walls, I've made provisions for some of those duties to be performed without further orders."

"Good," Lewis said. He'd left a few orders to that effect as well. "Please make sure the healers are evacuated quickly. No heroics from them, especially Mistress Samantha. Have her carried away if you have to." He smiled.

"The same goes for you. Don't make me detail keepers to carry you off as well."

Reed held up a hand. "Don't worry. In that event, this army will be such a disorganized mess—someone will have to sort it out."

Lewis nodded, then looked at Leonor and Varaa. "Let's collect our horses—and Captain Harris. He and his men looked at loose ends."

Company B of the 1st US was already tired, but it fell in quickly enough and followed behind Lewis's mounted party at a rapid pace, muskets high on their shoulders. Harris and his lieutenant had their own horses, and both assured Lewis their men had cleaned and dried their weapons. "The cooler air has helped," Harris said. "Barring more rain, they'll fire." Lewis shouted back at the messengers and other men behind for his bugler, Corporal Hannity, to move up and ride by him.

Stone shards sheeted down nearby, skittering close on the cobbles as they went around the great temple, the result of a strike on the sacred structure by a 36pdr.

"Blood Priests'll make somebody hang theirself or swallow hot coals for hittin' that," Leonor quipped and Varaa *kakked* a laugh. Harris chuckled uneasily. They returned to the main thoroughfare leading to the western gate, and their view of it was now unobstructed.

"God above, look at that," murmured Buisine.

More troops were already on the road ahead, streaming in from the alleyways running north and south, their hobnailed shoes raising a thunder like hooves as they ran, mostly in step. What drew the dragoon's exclamation, however, was the scene atop the distant wall. It practically seethed with desperately struggling figures, lit by the flash of guns. Worse, glaring torches and burning structures revealed a dark mass of men fighting at its base.

"Rejoin us ahead if you please, Mr. Harris," Lewis said, tapping Arete into a canter.

"Sir," Mal acknowledged. Once again, Leonor, Varaa, and Buisine and his men urged their horses to follow.

"Who's in front of me?" Lewis shouted as he neared the rear of the column ahead.

"Most'a the First Ocelomeh, sir!" came a strongly accented reply.

"Well done, lads," Lewis called, clattering past them. "Who commands?"

"I do, sir," came a self-conscious voice. Lewis pulled Arete up, looking down at a Mi-Anakka, one of only three in the army, saluting him. "Only of necessity, I assure you."

Varaa stopped her horse and leaned over in the saddle. "Koaar-Taak, former consul," she said neutrally. "Broken to the ranks for . . . misbehavior in the face of the enemy," she continued more darkly. Koaar looked at her. "Yes," he confirmed. "Deservedly so. But even you said the time may come for me to redeem myself—and my race." He straightened. "Major Ixtla was wounded on the wall and his second was killed. The men themselves chose me to replace them."

Lewis crisply returned the salute. "Very well. I've no doubt you earned their esteem. You're brevetted major. Position your regiment on this side of the secondary defense line. Who's that up ahead?"

"Thank you, Colonel. You will not regret it. I believe the Second Uxmal preceded us. Colonel Tun and part of Fourth Division are already engaged with the enemy near the gate."

Lewis peered forward. "Captain Harris and his company of the First US are behind us. Hold them here for the present."

"I—"

A blinding flash of orange-yellow fire seemed to consume the whole area around the west gate of the city, almost instantly followed by a second searing glare, just before a momentous double blast buffeted Lewis and everyone around him, knocking men flat and sending horses capering. He caught an instant's glimpse of small and large debris, scores, maybe hundreds of men, even cannon, rocketing or tumbling into the sky. The smoke from the bombs, for that's what they must've been, billowed up and out like an enormous fogbank, the point of origin glowing through.

Even Arete, used to just about anything a battle could offer, flinched and danced, but hadn't started jumping about like Leonor's and even Varaa's horses. Both females quickly got their animals under control, and Lewis patted Arete's neck affectionately. Buisine and Hannity settled their horses as well, but Buisine's men and the messengers weren't as lucky. One of the latter even lost his seat and fell hard on the cobbles. NCOs bellowed and infantrymen stood, even while debris rained down. Some of it fell on troops to their front, and there were screams and cries of alarm.

"Stand fast and prepare to face the enemy, Major Koaar," Lewis said loudly. "I fear they've breached the gate."

"Bombs that big would've blown a wide gap," Varaa advised. "And we might've just lost hundreds of men. The Doms as well."

"We've seen nothing to make us think the prospect of casualties gives the enemy pause." Lewis urged Arete forward. "Let's see what we have to cope with now."

There was an eerie near silence in the smoke-fogged gloom that Lewis and his party picked their way through, scattered bodies sprawled all around. Dazed and staggering troops they met were sent back to join Ko-aar, but others, largely in the green uniforms of Agon's men and many possibly deafened, still knew they were needed forward and coalesced around Lewis as he advanced. "Coronel Cayce!" cried several men in a small group, and Lewis veered toward them, only to see them supporting the badly injured form of Major Arevalo. He seemed to have at least one broken leg, and his uniform and exposed skin were badly scorched.

"Coronel," Arevalo said through cracked and bloody lips.

"Take this man back to the hospital section at once!" Lewis ordered.

"A moment, sir, if you please," Arevalo managed. "I was on the wall when it exploded."

"We found him over there," said one of the soldiers, gesturing behind him with his head. "Landed on the roof of a building an' slid off it, like."

Lewis's eyes went wide. "Then I must congratulate you for your astonishing survival," he said.

Arevalo shook his head. "They brought the bombs to the gate with armabueys," he related. "It was already open, and our men were trying to seal it, but they just led the beasts up through the arch and detonated them. With fuses, I suppose." He looked down. "Major Olayne was fighting beside me. I doubt he was as fortunate as I."

"Coronel Tun is dead as well," supplied one of the soldiers, shouting over his deafness. "A great timber crashed down upon him."

"Don Roderigo was to the left of us," Arevalo supplied. "He may have survived." He tried to straighten on what might be a good leg and winced. "Losses on both sides will have been horrific, inside and outside the gate, but the Doms will recover and exploit the breach."

He was right. The roar of fighting was already mounting again.

"Then we'll have to stop them, won't we? You men, do as I said. Be careful with him." He looked down at Arevalo. "I pray you'll recover. We can't spare you."

Arevalo caught Leonor's eye and grinned. "The irony of that statement overwhelms me. You do remember that *she shot* me, the first time we met."

Lewis grinned back. "I do, but that was a different time. Go."

He looked up. "The rest of you," he called loudly, "form a line behind us as we advance. You men on the flanks, summon all you see who're able to join us!" That was already happening to an extent, but even as troops began to gather and stand, just as many, panicked or disoriented by the terrible blast, were streaming or limping to the rear. After the trauma of the long fight, topped by this latest terror, some might've been entirely lost. A few would keep running until they reached a physical barrier or simply dropped from shock or exhaustion. Lewis had seen that before and knew it wasn't even always about courage. Regardless of their personal bravery, most men had a breaking point that could unleash anything from abject terror to suicidal fury. He'd personally been afflicted with the latter during the Battle of Monterrey. But most who were teetering on the edge just needed instruction. A purpose to focus on.

"Bugler," Lewis shouted behind. "Sound the rally, and keep it up! Varaa!" he cried as the bugle began to blare. "Ride amongst the troops; tell them to dry their muskets. We'll have to deliver some sharp volleys."

The bugle call came none too soon, because the hellish aspect of the vicinity only increased. A great number of buildings on either side of the thoroughfare and alarmingly deep into the city had been set afire by flaming debris. Despite the earlier rain, those fires were starting to catch and spread. Dark, steamy smoke was piling high atop the flames in the night. The street-level gunsmoke was finally starting to clear, however, and Lewis caught his first glimpse of the broad, gaping swathe of carnage and destruction where the west gate had once stood.

That passage had been about twenty feet wide, protected by a lunette and blocked by a gate that had been sufficiently reinforced with iron to take the point-blank fire of a battery of 6pdrs. The gate was now gone entirely, and so—more or less—was the whole wall itself for more than forty paces. Nothing lived or moved atop the wall for that distance again in both directions. Past that, dazed or addled troops were starting to fight again, desperate figures clashing on the parapet, but friend or foe, their battle had become superfluous. With a deep, moaning roar of war horns, movement in the haze within the gap presaged the appearance of a tide of fresh Doms, yelling as they came.

Turning his horse to view the gathering force at his disposal, Lewis frowned. Some men were still furiously drying their weapons, drawing soppy, blackened wads of tow from their barrels with ramrods, or wiping flints and priming pans with shirttails and picking their vents. Others were already tearing and ramming cartridges down their barrels. NCOs strode behind them, bellowing at men and shoving them into a crescent-shaped line, three deep in places, but generally only two. *Not enough*, he told himself. *Not nearly.* It would have to do for now.

"Lewis!" Leonor snapped sharply. "If you wanna fight here, you'll do it behind the line." To her surprise, he didn't argue, urging Arete back through the troops. "Make way," Varaa cried. "Let the colonel through."

Men shifted and made a path, many calling out in Leonor's support. "You can see just as good behind us, sir. We'll keep the rascals off ya," shouted an artilleryman armed with a musket.

"I know you will, boys," Lewis responded loudly. "And you needn't hold them long by yourselves. Help is on the way."

"Huzza for Colonel Cayce!" bellowed one of Agon's former Dom troops. "Huzza! Huzza! Huzza!" came the growing, strengthening reply. Someone raised a four-by-four-foot standard—the Stars and Stripes—and Lewis felt a lump in his chest. "I'm proud of you boys!" he shouted. "Hold the line, and protect the standard!"

"No officers but us," reported Varaa, rejoining them. "Their own must all be dead."

"They have you, Warmaster Choon," Lewis told her. "The remnants of perhaps three regiments. Your brigade, for now."

Eyes blinking, Varaa dipped her chin, then raised her voice in that curious way Mi-Anakka had of making their words carry. "Front rank, make ready!"

Roughly two-thirds of those men, possibly as many as four hundred, had cleared and loaded their weapons. Peering to the front at the swelling mass of Doms, waiting only heartbeats as the leading edge of the horde drew closer, she shouted, "Make them count! . . . *Fire!*"

Most of the weapons actually discharged, and the booming volley was the first such sound in quite a while. Screaming figures tumbled in the smoke like a wave crashing on a beach. "Front rank, reload. Second rank, take aim . . ." Bayonet-tipped musket barrels came down and steadied over the shoulders of the front rank, where men hastily loaded their weapons. "Fire!" More screams replied from the smoke. "Rear rank, take aim! Fire!"

Lewis was surprised that the third volley seemed louder than the first and saw when he looked that its numbers had swelled to match the others. *We might have a chance after all*, he mused.

"Front rank," Varaa called, and Lewis hoped they'd had time to reload. "Take aim! Fire!" *Crash!* So they had, it seemed, and the strength of that volley had increased as well, as more men made their muskets ready. "Second rank, take aim! Fire!"

With the enemy so tightly packed, each volley had been devastating, but the bodies of those in front had protected others surging behind. Stomping or stumbling over the wounded and dead, they just kept coming, bristling bayonets forward. With a terrible roar and crash of steel and wood, the noise of muskets smacking muskets and those probing, thrusting bayonets, the whole line bowed back and the front two ranks were suddenly too busy to reload their weapons again. Still, they'd trained for this kind of fighting, the front rank taking advantage of opportunities to stab their foes when they could, but working hardest to block or divert their efforts while the second rank took advantage.

The Doms likely hadn't trained quite as much. This was the very first real battle for the Gran Cruzada, after all. What they may have lacked in expertise and technique, they made up for with numbers and ferocity. As defenders in the front rank were stabbed or beaten down, others stepped up from the second to take their place. The rear rank kept firing independently for a while, or dragged wounded and dead from underfoot. Most eventually had to step into the second rank, then the first.

"Colonel Cayce!" cried a messenger, and Lewis turned. The man didn't salute and Leonor nodded approval. Not that it made any difference. As Lewis was still mounted, it was obvious he was an officer. The only reason he hadn't been shot was because all the Doms had stopped up their muskets with plug bayonets. "Major Koaar's respects, sir," the messenger continued urgently. "He's established a strong position on the defensive line to your rear. In addition, Major Beck has arrived with the remainder of the First US, and Colonel Agon himself has brought two regiments of the Fourth Division from the north wall and assumed command."

Lewis looked at Leonor. "Sounds like too much," he said worriedly, "but there's no longer any point in standing here. Start them pulling back," he shouted at Varaa. She blinked understanding.

"You go first," she yelled back, then cried even louder, "Prepare to retire by ranks!"

"Let's go," Leonor urged. "We're just in Varaa's way."

Lewis nodded and turned Arete before urging her back toward the low wall where they'd left Harris and Koaar. There they were met by a rising cheer from the troops behind the wall, as well as Agon and Marvin Beck.

Lewis exhaled and said lowly to Agon, "I wish they wouldn't do that. I don't feel like being cheered."

Agon shook his head. "*They* feel like doing it. If you hadn't rallied the men from the wall, the enemy would have carried this position before we could stop them. There are times when your modesty means nothing compared to the morale of your men."

"Well said," murmured Lieutenant Buisine, just loud enough to be heard. Lewis arched an eyebrow at him, and the young dragoon shrugged.

Looking back at Agon, Lewis asked, "But how can we afford so many men from the walls? You were barely hanging on."

"The enemy eased their attacks," Agon said simply. "I believe that either by signal, messenger, or prearranged understanding, the forces attacking all the walls—except those closest to the south gate, I've heard—understood that many of them were to immediately surge around to the west gate"—he nodded forward—"*here*, to take advantage of the breach."

"A breach they knew would happen, one way or another," Lewis said, comprehension dawning.

"Your man, Arevalo, said it was walkin' bombs," supplied Leonor. "Them giant armadillos carryin' 'em."

Agon frowned. "Yes. I spoke to him. Thank you for sending him to the rear, by the way." He sighed. "He told me that Colonel Tun is dead. He and I were never friends, but we knew each other for many years, and there was mutual respect."

"He'll be missed," Lewis consoled, but returned to his immediate concern. "How many Doms abandoned the attack where you were?"

Agon seemed to concentrate. "It's difficult to be certain in the darkness. About half, I should think. Perhaps more."

"Still leaving enough to get over the wall if it's too weakly defended."

"Possibly," Agon conceded reluctantly, "but I didn't bring *everything*."

"How many guns?" Lewis asked, watching several captured Dom cannon being heaved up behind the wall by their crews.

"Only a battery—six," Agon assured.

"I've got a battery coming too, sir," said Marvin Beck. "Should be here directly. Damned Dom guns're hard to move. I wish we had some of our own."

"Those are with Major Anson for a reason," Lewis said absently, watching Varaa's fighting withdrawal, almost cringing as her men were whittled away while the mass of enemies grew. Leonor knew him well enough to see a profound decision being made behind his impassive features. He turned back to Agon and Beck. "You'll have to hold them here as long as you can."

"We'll hold 'em forever with enough men," Beck said with confidence.

"You won't be getting many more," Lewis said flatly, and Beck and Agon both blinked as if they hadn't heard him right. Lewis quickly explained. "General Xacolotl didn't strike me as a maniac, so I kept thinking this couldn't be *his* battle plan. It began as if on a whim, without proper development, and it's far too wasteful. I can't imagine any general being so negligent with the lives of his men and assumed Don Frutos or some mad Blood Priest just threw it together and attacked, regardless of cost. Upon reflection, however, there *has* been a plan—a fairly good one, in fact. Consider the barges on the lake and across the canal. The circumvallation and initial positioning of the siege guns, the deliberate efforts to focus our attention—and draw it from where it's needed. Then the bombs, of course. All that took careful planning and preparation. A good, *dangerous* plan, only rushed beyond reason."

"Which doesn't mean it will not still work," Agon agreed, eyes widening. "The pressure is relieved from the walls just when we must weaken them to counter this." He waved forward. "But we can't *stop* the enemy here without doing exactly that! Regardless of the terrible casualties we've inflicted, there are simply too many..."

"And when we weaken the walls further, they come over and get behind us," Beck said just loud enough for them to hear. He shook his head. "With everything happening so fast, probably faster than Xacolotl planned, it might've even worked *better*, if you hadn't figured it out," he added miserably. He took a long breath and looked squarely at Lewis. "So what do we do?"

Lewis gathered them all in his gaze. "*You'll* give Varaa and those men out there a place to fall back to, then hold. As long as you can. We should be able to spare *some* reinforcements, and certainly more guns"—he looked at Agon—"because we're going to evacuate *everyone* off the north and south walls west of this line. They'll connect the wall to these defenses," he continued, "before they fold back to our inner works." He paused. "But while that's happening, they'll torch everything behind them, and I mean *everything* in the city that'll burn."

"What good will that do?" asked Captain Harris. "We'll be trapped in an inferno."

Lewis ground his teeth. "No," he said. "We won't."

CHAPTER 30

"Now!" Varaa bellowed, backsword raised high. "Make a run for it!" Her "brigade" had pulled back within fifty paces of the fortified wall, reaping a terrible harvest, but her men weren't the only reapers, and the force had shrunk to roughly a regiment in size. *Maybe a thousand left*, she thought. Counting all the troops on the wall, no more of whom could possibly escape, the majority of the militia and Tun's reinforcements, then the count her "brigade" once swelled to, she suspected the army had lost seven or eight thousand men.

After standing heroically in the face of an avalanche, her troops broke and ran at the sound of her voice. A few lingered dutifully close, but she spun her horse and kicked its flanks. A Dom lunged with his bayonet, the blade passing between her and the horse's neck. She swung her sword and opened the man's throat, geysering blood splashing her face as she passed. Another Dom had stabbed a man in the back, just ahead, and she drove the tip of her blade in the back of his neck, twisting and tearing it out. Her horse squealed as more bayonets stabbed at its haunches. It kicked as it ran, pulping a face, and was still gaining speed when it leaped the low wall and some fearfully crouching soldiers. Reining the horse in with difficulty, she finally got it stopped long enough to jump down and hand it off to a green-coated soldier before running back toward the wall.

"Warmaster!" Agon called, and Varaa veered to meet him, but her eyes were searching to see how many of "her" men remained beyond the barrier. She saw a few of them die. Most were obviously wounded and went down under stabbing bayonets and bashing musket butts as they were overrun, but it seemed the vast majority of the survivors had reached the relative safety of their comrades. Just as well, because the defenders here couldn't hold their fire any longer. Muskets were already firing, in fact, and their crackle swiftly swelled to a continuous roar. A pair of cannon fired to her left, smashing deep bloody gouges in the teeming mob of Doms. Another section of guns spewed canister, double loads by the sound and recoil, and the musketry continued to increase. Whole layers of the leading edge of the enemy were peeling away, and the surf-like power and inevitability of the horde began to slow and scatter like a wave on a rocky shore.

"You won't break them," Varaa shouted at Agon, and he gave her a quick glance that seemed to say, "Don't you think I know that?" *Of course he knows*, Varaa thought ruefully. *He was one of them once. And these Doms have already shown they're not like the ones we fought at Texcoco.*

"No," he agreed. "Those men are here to die. Better against us than if they fail. But now they face a wall again and more fire than you could deliver. That will give them pause once the pressure from behind them eases. They may even draw back a short distance for a while, to reorganize their ranks and perhaps drive out their bayonets so they can return our fire." Regardless of the damp, the cold air was much drier now. That had been a blessing when only the defenders seemed to realize it, but it would be obvious to all, by now.

Varaa nodded. Screaming Doms were actually mashed against the wall in many places as other men pushed them forward. Their expressions showed a kaleidoscopic jumble of terror, agony, frustration, and rage. Worse for them, few could even wield their weapons and could do nothing as they were bayonetted or shot. The dead remained like empty hand puppets, reeling and flopping lifelessly, unable to fall.

"It's the worst thing I've ever seen," Varaa confessed.

"The same for me," said Agon.

Varaa looked at him. *Indeed*, she thought, *and even crueler for him. These are, after all, his people.*

Cannon were firing steadily now, as fast as they could be loaded. The enemy was being savaged and, for the moment, could do little in return. A few men were falling back from the wall, stabbed by bayonets, but most being injured were actually victims of their comrades, painfully blasted in the face by the vent jet of their neighbor's musket. Those men would fight on, of course, cursing loudly and adjusting their high collars or hat brims. The bloody patterns on their cheeks or in their ears would heal into gunpowder tattoos.

"Coronel Cayce has rushed to headquarters to consult with Coronel Reed," said Agon. "He left word for you to join him at your convenience."

"He took a lot for granted, didn't he?" Varaa grumbled back. "What about you?"

"We hold. Until summoned to withdraw."

"Withdraw where?"

Agon looked at her as if wondering how much she already knew of Lewis Cayce's contingency plans. "I was hoping you might tell me."

Varaa blinked. With a few others, she'd speculated with Lewis on how they'd evacuate if they had to, even made suggestions regarding preparations. But they'd never imagined *these* circumstances. At least she hadn't. Now that she had to, she thought she began to envision Lewis's plan. She jokingly proclaimed it all the time, but she actually did think a lot like him. "If I had to guess," she finally confessed, "I'd say we shall have to abandon the city and make for Texcoco."

Varaa's horse was starting to limp by the time she reached the central plaza. She regretted pushing the poor beast, knowing it was in pain. She'd have to find another if she could, but wasn't sure that would be possible when she saw the scene at the foot of the great temple and was struck by the stark contrasts there, amazed that such chaos and apparent order could coexist in the same time and place. Surrounded by the roar of battle and glare of spreading flames, flocks of wailing civilians, mostly women and children, rushed and gaggled about like gallinas being chased by ravening wolf-lizards. Men were attempting to calm or control them, both walking wounded soldiers and what were probably respected hidalgos, but they didn't seem to be having great success. Varaa thought angrily that the civilian men might've been more effective if many hadn't still wondered why they should try. "Mere" women were largely former slaves and their unclaimed children had even less value. There'd been limited progress countering thinking like that in the short time they'd been here.

At the same time, the tent city of the army camp was rapidly collapsing as tents were taken down, mostly by walking wounded as well. Wagonloads of wounded were still coming in, drivers cursing obstructions. Their gloomy cargoes were still being treated as quickly as possible at the hospital tents, but other hurt soldiers were being loaded back in those wagons or others that then moved into a queue on the avenue to the east. She wondered briefly how many—if any—wagons would be left for the tents. As far as she could see, most hitched limbers and caissons had already gone elsewhere, and supply wagons were lining up as well. A regiment of tired, battered-looking troops, a few wearing bandages, had formed along the road in front of the shops. An officer took his place at their front, NCOs shouted, and the troops set off up the street.

"Lewis may not have wanted this, or even expected it, but thank the maker he planned for it," she muttered aloud to herself. "As usual," she added with a snort.

Dismounting, she led her hurt horse to a picket line where several others stood, heads hanging low. *Messenger horses*, she guessed. *Riders are probably wounded or dead.* After a quick inspection, she chose one that was still or already saddled and took it. Swinging up on its back, she realized she'd have to shorten the stirrups, but that would wait until she spoke to Lewis. Urging the horse past the hospital tents, she saw Samantha again. The Englishwoman looked exhausted, but was directing some of the female nurses or orderlies, showing which crates of surgical implements and supplies to load into yet another wagon. Catching her eye, Varaa moved closer when Samatha beckoned.

"We've been told we must evacuate the city," she said somewhat incredulously. She gestured toward where the harnessed animals, limbers, caissons, and wagons had waited. "Obviously, having helped prepare for whatever 'just in case' scenario Lewis imagined, I knew it might be needed." She took a breath. "I just never *believed* it would. Now, I can't imagine how." She seemed almost desperate, and Varaa knew she was worried about the wounded. "You just returned from the breach, did you not? How bad is it?"

"There was . . . a setback," Varaa confessed. That was no secret. Clearly, word had spread that the west wall was open. "But things are not yet desperate. Colonel Agon was holding well when I left. But things could go wrong very quickly and I urge you to delay nothing." She paused. "Save *nothing* for the last minute," she stressed, "particularly your *own* departure!"

Samantha pursed her lips, but nodded. Varaa started to move on, but Samantha stopped her, calling, "Wait!" Varaa looked back, but Samantha hesitated before asking, "How will we do it? We're entirely surrounded, are we not? How on earth does Lewis expect us all to break through to safety?"

Varaa *kakked* a bitter laugh. "Not *all* of us will. No one could expect that." She blinked her huge blue eyes very quickly. "Our own 'grand crusade' to free this land of the Dominion shall end in defeat, I fear, and defeat is something Lewis has never known. I am not sure how he will cope with it, but my *faith* in him is secure. We will lose here," she said bluntly, "and in retrospect, I suppose that was always inevitable. Perhaps Lewis has known all along. Yet my faith in him drives my suspicion that even as this battle ends in defeat, he will still somehow win the war for the driving 'cause' we've fought for."

"And what's that?" Samantha demanded, waving angrily toward the hospital tents. "Our God over the enemy's?" she said almost mockingly. "That's what many of those poor boys fought for, in a nutshell. What will they have suffered so much to achieve if we lose?"

Varaa shrugged again. "If the enemy is wrecked, even in victory, the 'cause' will survive. What is it you ask? Freedom, for one thing. Somewhere," she added. "That's essential for some to live a better, more secure life. And yes, even worship a better, more benevolent God. For Lewis, I think, the 'cause' has always been the survival of his army—and *his* greatest sacrifice, more than his life, will be losing so much of it to save the rest."

Brusquely nodding at Samantha, Varaa kicked her new horse into motion, heading through the swirling, chaotic, still strangely orderly motion toward the headquarters building. More horses were tied to a long, low, sawhorse-like arrangement of heavy timbers outside, and she added her own to the group, noting with interest that Har-Kaaska's large, duck-faced, bipedal mount was also standing nearby. It alone wasn't tied, and it watched her with apparent recognition as she stepped inside. More officers were gathered than before and a fug of smoke had made a dense haze. Though she still preferred her pipe, she accepted a dry cigar from an orderly passing them around and commenced to add to the fog as she puffed the thing to life and caught her first words from the hastily assembled "conference."

"... Yes, I understand, sir, but that will be incredibly dangerous," Colonel Itzam, commanding 3rd Division, darkly advised. "It will almost immediately draw all the devils in on us, all along every wall."

"That's what we *have* to do," Lewis said earnestly. He and Colonel Reed were leaning over the map again, fingers pressing on different parts, looking at the grim faces around them. Seeing Varaa, Lewis asked, "Agon is holding?"

"He was when I left, though it seemed every Dom from across the canal was pouring in on him."

"They are," Major Manley of the 1st Uxmal confirmed. Varaa suspected he'd been called to represent the forces still on the south wall. "We could see that pretty well," he continued to Lewis. "All the barge bridges are packed with troops an' nobody's firing on them anymore. In addition," he continued, looking around as well, "the assaults against us, even near the south gate, have tapered off, as elsewhere, and a lot of the enemy in front of us is shifting to the west."

"Agon *must* be reinforced," said Colonel Reed.

"Yes," said Lewis, "but carefully. I hope to replace him entirely with a fresher rear guard as our movements progress." He looked back at Itzam. "But before that can happen, we need the secondary defenses properly manned and *all* the Doms drawn into the city. Even better if we can lure those to the east in as well, over the north and south walls. Only the east wall will stay fully manned." He bared his teeth at Colonel Har-Kaaska. "Make it as hot as you can for the bastards there. Make them *want* to go climb easier walls!"

Har-Kaaska bared his teeth as well, his Mi-Anakka canines much more pronounced and intimidating. "We slaughter them virtually without resistance as it is. I'm sure most would happily go elsewhere, if allowed. Perhaps they will, if their officers hear other walls are easily scaled."

Lewis looked at the others. "Then that's what they have to hear."

The 2nd Uxmal's Major George Wagley was standing by Har-Kaaska, shaking his head. "But stopping them at the secondary line . . ." he said skeptically.

"*Holding* them," Lewis stressed, "just long enough for us to contract our defense to the *third* line. Where the streets and buildings of the city can disrupt and funnel their attacks. They'll come at many places in small, disorganized groups, and even where they mass, we'll slaughter them. By then, Har-Kaaska will have sallied Fourth Division, broken through the enemy remnants, and secured the flanks of our evacuation."

"With practically all the enemy inside the city, their communication and coordination will be nonexistent," Varaa put in with approval. "No commanders remaining outside can rally a meaningful response to oppose us."

"I've already arranged for other things to begin complicating that as well," Lewis cryptically agreed.

The only sound in the large chamber for a long moment was the muted tumult outside. Don Hurac stepped slowly forward and stopped beside the table. "So it truly comes to this," he said lowly, tone full of sorrow. "No more plans or ideas for defense, no more effort at all to save the city."

Lewis cleared his throat. "I fear, Your Excellency, that will only cost us precious time and lives. The only thing that remains for any of us now, yourself included, is to save what we can. As many as we can." His gaze became hard. "While we turn this place into a grave for the enemy."

Another silence stretched until Reed coughed and spoke gravely. "Yes, well. Whatever happens, even if everything goes perfectly—which it won't—it will be a ... painful endeavor."

Lewis could only nod, accepting every consequence of Reed's overwhelming understatement.

"I know."

CHAPTER 31

"Move it, boys. Down you get. Move your lazy arses!" First Sergeant Visser bellowed the last at some straggling members of his 3rd Platoon, Company B, 3rd Pennsylvania, as they poured off the wall into the open area behind it. Lieutenant Aiken was in front and Visser was bringing up the rear. Glancing behind, he couldn't see any Doms climbing over the top just yet, though they'd made such a show of abandoning the position, the enemy would surely come. He paused a moment before following his men, waiting for that. Sure enough, a bayonet glinted in the light of the flames spreading through the western part of the city as it tentatively probed upward. Then there were more, followed by black tricorn hats. Eyes started peering over the wall.

"Ay, you filthy bastard," he called to one of the men who met his eye. "C'mon an' get me, damn you. I'll be waitin'." With a rude, taunting gesture, he shifted his musket in his hand and pounded down the stairs. A distant whoosh of flame spit at the sky, bright enough to leave an afterimage. A large store of oil, most likely. The city was full of the stuff: corn oil and something like flaxseed oil for cooking, lubrication, paint base, and waterproofing, among countless other things. Whatever its purpose, it burned, and Colonel Cayce had been having it all gathered up since they got here. *The fire's startin' to get frightening*, Visser confessed to himself. As wet as it was, he never would've thought the whole city could burn, but it looked very much like it would. Of course, a lot of the buildings away from the city center were wood, at least framed with it, and covered with something like lath and stucco. *Besides, the fire's getting plenty of help*, he conceded. Other platoons in the 3rd Pennsylvania and additional regiments, no doubt, had been detailed to feed it, section by section, with oil and torches. *Good thing there isn't much wind.*

He found two of his men awaiting him at the bottom of the stair. "Private Rayley, Private Garca, didn't I tell you to go?" he growled.

"I—*we* thought we should wait," Rayley said earnestly. "What if you tripped an' fell, or lost your way or somethin'? Couldn't just leave you for the Doms, Sergeant."

Visser snorted angrily, though he was secretly pleased. Young as he was, Rayley was one of his old-world veterans and actually reminded him of Hanny Cox. Garca was an Itzincabo, about the same age and also a veteran now. Both thin as reeds and gangly as storks, they were good boys and thick as thieves. He couldn't reveal his appreciation, though. "An' what were the two of you, the scrawniest crows in the company, gonna do in the horrifyin', ridiculous event I actually needed your help? Carry me? You? Bah! Can't hardly carry your ownselves, most days."

"We would have tried, Sergeant," Garca said gamely.

Visser sighed. "Aye, an' got yourselves killed. Now let's get moving, damn you." He tilted his head back up the stairs. "The Doms are coming." Triumphant shouts were rising from the top of the rampart as more and more Doms found it void of defenders. "Scamper, lads," Visser urged, and all three took off across the empty space between the wall and the remaining buildings, canteens and the contents of their haversacks clanking against their weapons. A couple of musket shots chased them, smashing cobbles and spattering lead around their feet. Garca was leading, and Visser shouted, "*That* way, fool. The alley to the left. An' you worried *I'd* get lost. Shit," he gruffed.

Garca veered into the indicated gap in the buildings while Visser and Rayley caught up. The light from the flames barely reached them there, and considerable debris had been deliberately scattered about. "Shit," Visser repeated, tripping and almost falling over a timber before a lantern brightened the street at the end of the alley ahead. Lieutenant Aiken and a couple of troops had stopped to wait for them.

"All good, Sergeant?" Aiken asked.

"Sir," Visser replied with a shrug, "if it's *ever* good to see the enemy climbin' over our defenses after us. Nobody left behind but those poor dead fellows from A Company, killed by roundshot." Despite heavy fighting, the 3rd Pennsylvania had suffered few immediately fatal casualties, and nowhere that they defended had the enemy even reached the top of the wall. Until now.

"Nothing for it, Sergeant. Well done. And yes. Apparently, the new plan is to let the fiends think they're winning."

"They aren't?" Visser prodded.

"Major Ulrich says no, but Captain Cullin believes it'll be a matter of perspective," Aiken wryly replied. "Either way, we've still got our work cut out. Let's go. The regiment is forming behind the wall on the next street back."

The noise of hard shoes running, lots of them, perhaps even studded with hobnails, came from behind. "We're with you, Lieutenant," Visser prompted.

They raced across the street into another alley, quickly picking through more obstacles with the aid of the lantern. The next broad street came into view, a low rock wall about shoulder high on the far side. Most of the regiment was already in place, peering at them as they approached. Visser got a momentary lift when he saw the damp regimental standard hanging limply nearby.

"I believe we're the last," Aiken called out as they passed through a gap, and someone shouted to "Close the gate!" More than a dozen men rushed to do so. It wasn't a proper gate, of course, just a framework of heavy timbers festooned with long, sharp stakes on the side facing the enemy. Once heaved into position, it was braced by more timbers. It would have to suffice. "I must see Captain Cullin," said Aiken, "but we'll pass by your platoon, Sergeant." The six of them trotted to the west behind other troops settling in to wait behind the wall. Soldiers festooned with what looked like leather gunners' haversacks were moving along distributing paper cartridges while others carried buckets of water. Despite the cool night air and earlier rain, fighting was always thirsty work.

Visser had spent considerable time helping erect this very position. He'd largely supervised his men and many locals as they did most of the work, mixing mortar and stacking heavy stones. Harder than that in many ways had been tearing down more buildings to clear another space behind it. Those built of stone had contributed directly to the wall, but no wood had been used in its construction (except for the various gates), nor was any salvaged timber left nearby. All had been moved elsewhere for use in other projects such as the "bombproof" shelters on the outer walls. Only now, with the flames to the west inching closer, was Visser grateful for the extra effort.

"I'll be damned," he suddenly blurted as they slowed to a walk.

"Almost certainly," joked Lieutenant Aiken.

"Excuse me, sir, but it just hit me. All this." He waved at the wall running east and west, now backed by thousands of troops—and guns, Visser now noted. "Somebody *knew* we'd be here at some point in the fight. *Knew* there'd be fire, even had us scour the city for oil to spread it."

Aiken seemed to contemplate that. "Did they know we'd need the oil because they knew it would rain?" he asked. "Don't you think it equally likely these works are merely the result of good contingency planning?"

"If you say so, sir," Visser replied, but he wasn't convinced and it showed.

Aiken pursed his lips, but shook his head. For the first time, Visser saw how tired he looked. "Here is your platoon, Sergeant." He paused. "If it makes you feel better to imagine that this, and everything we've endured, is part of some grand scheme, by all means, don't let me dissuade you."

Roaring voices echoed down the alleyways they'd so recently used. "Be careful, Sergeant," Aiken then said before raising his voice. "God be with all you lads!" With that, he was gone.

"Do you really think this is part of the plan?" Garca asked anxiously. Dom soldiers were pouring from the alley, spreading out to the sides. Other alleys were disgorging the enemy as well. A few muskets fired at them, but officers and NCOs roared their displeasure.

"Make ready, boys, but hold your fire," Visser shouted before checking the priming powder in the pan of his musket. Here in the open, the fire in the west gave plenty of light to see that it looked a tad damp, but hadn't turned into soup. His weapon would likely hang fire, but would probably shoot. He'd just have to aim through it. He finally looked at Garca and huffed. "I don't know, son. And I guess it doesn't much matter."

Enemy officers were shouting, waving swords, and Dom NCOs were kicking and shoving their own gasping troops into a battle line. The crack of a rifleman's weapon somewhere to the left near a gun dropped one of the Dom officers right on his face, boots kicking spastically. A small, ragged cheer was heard.

"Wish we had more of those riflemen," Rayley lamented. "And they get to shoot whenever they want, close or far."

"That's because they have to take their targets when they can," Visser said. "And they're a hell of a lot more likely to hit one than you, Private Rayley. At any distance." Some of the men around them chuckled. Rayley wasn't renowned as a marksman. *But neither was Hanny Cox*, Visser reflected. *Now they say he can hit a man at five hundred paces with a 6pdr ball! I wish he and his big gun were with us.*

"That said," Visser continued aloud, "them Doms are formin' not fifty paces away. Each of you, even Rayley, can strike a man that far—an' you'll have your chance any moment if I'm any judge. Our officers're just waitin' for the devils to bunch up better. Might kill more than one with each shot, if you're lucky." For the first time he realized most of the enemy weapons didn't have bayonets driven into their muzzles. A few still did, but their owners were whacking on the cross guards trying to drive them out. That could only mean they intended to trade volleys, at least for a while, before they charged. Even protected as they were by the wall, so many thousands of musket balls in the air at once were bound to hit some of his men. His boys. He forced a fierce grin onto his face as he bellowed, "Big ones line up, little ones bunch up, an' we'll stack 'em up in heaps!"

A cannon fired, near where Visser imagined Major Ulrich probably was. That was the signal for all the guns on this line to open up, slashing the enemy with canister for as far as he could see in either direction. Most fired too close together for Visser to count them, but there must've been a dozen, at least. *We didn't have that many in reserve*, he realized as squalling, agonized cries erupted to his front through the smoke. More cannon thundered all around the city, sounding different than they had on the outer walls. *The whole battle's down on this inner wall now, an' somebody ordered those guns pulled back from the outer one before we even started leavin' it.*

Drums rattled loudly in the confined space, almost a canyon running through the city. "Battalion!" came a distant cry. "B Company!" came Captain Cullin's voice. Dom officers were bellowing what must be similar preparatory commands.

"Take aim!" Visser heard—probably Lieutenant Aiken. Hundreds of muskets, bayonets bristling, had risen to point at the enemy. Some swayed wildly, nervously, while others were as steady as death.

"*Apunten!*" came many Dom voices.

"*Fuego!*" and "Fire!" were both heard in the same instant.

"Kill them! Smash them!" roared Colonel Har-Kaaska as he crashed through the Doms at the very head of the 2nd Uxmal. The regiment had cleared the east gate at a run and formed into a flying wedge. It wasn't pretty; no one had ever even practiced such a maneuver, but it came together well enough to get the job done. For once, the speculation had been right on target. Less than three or four thousand Doms had remained "on guard" to the east, most already directed to reinforce efforts against other walls, or even march around and enter the city from the west. As the defenders fell back from the wall and the Doms swarmed over in pursuit, all but this remnant Har-Kaaska was attacking had marched away, regiment by regiment, to try their luck where the going was easier.

Commanders would've been lured by the prospect of glory—a few words of praise for their actions to God was all the "glory" they sought—and none would be earned where they were. Truth be known, most of their common soldiers only hoped to live through the battle, but some would be tempted by loot. Enough of it might set them up for life, even make them hidalgos. A whole city—the greatest and richest in the world, they believed—would soon lie dead at their feet, and looting was always encouraged.

No soldier could keep more plunder than he could carry with ease (though private arrangements among supply wagon teamsters weren't unknown), and attempting to keep more could be considered diminishing one's usefulness as a soldier of God or actual *theft* from God (the priests). Punishment for that, as for any crime, was severe and permanent. Yet even common soldiers who found and surrendered great riches might earn some meager praise for themselves, perhaps a small percentage as well. Such was rumored to have occurred on occasion. The vast majority of Dominion soldiers were mere *hombres libres* conscripts, and even the most remote possibility of a better station in life was a strong incentive to glean what they could for God.

In any event, troops left out of the bulk of the fighting thus far, seeing an opportunity for gain of whatever sort, were happy to seize it. That left only the vastly diminished force Har-Kaaska was gleefully slashing through, his huge, strange mount stomping men down or kicking them aside. With him came the lopsided wedge of the 2nd Uxmal, stabbing, shooting, and bashing a growing gap in the enemy line. The field beyond the eastern gate was quickly cleared, and the 2nd Ocelomeh roared through the lunette, across the moat bridge, adding mass to the breakthrough. The Doms fought back desperately, their still-superior numbers collapsing in from the sides and taking a terrible toll, particularly on the Uxmalos, but now the rest of 2nd Division, minus the 1st Itzincab, flowed out in a line to either side, preventing their comrades from being encircled while they smashed the disorganized enemy flanks and started rolling them up.

By the time the first elements of Colonel Itzam's 3rd Division, the 1st Pidra Blanca, burst through the gate, the struggle in front of the city's east wall was essentially done. Thousands had fallen in what might've been the most brutal fighting thus far. The bombing of the west gate killed more in an instant, on both sides, but this hadn't taken much longer—less than half an hour. Barely more time than it took all the men to flood through the gate.

Though the gallant 1st Uxmal had virtually ceased to exist, Har-Kaaska himself somehow survived. Colonel Itzam was frankly astonished to see him riding slowly back on his bizarre mount as men spread out, NCOs shouting to establish their perimeter and "make sure" of wounded Doms as they went. Other men were dragging hurt comrades toward the road. Itzam evaluated the Mi-Anakka Colonel, once "king" of all the Ocelomeh. He and his mount were both haggard and bloody, the strange duck-faced animal practically riddled with streaming wounds. It had drawn the most fire, no doubt, but as bad as it looked, its thick hide would've prevented the soft, wildly aimed musket balls from penetrating deep enough to kill it. But Har-Kaaska would've been a tempting target as well—the "demon" controlling the monster.

"How much of that blood is yours, Colonel?" Itzam asked when Har-Kaaska drew near.

Har-Kaaska managed a grin, feral teeth gleaming. "Some, I suspect. I hurt all over and can't really tell." He waved his long, bloody sword. "All my limbs are still working, at least."

Itzam frowned. "Well, the ambulances will come as soon as half of my division clears the gate. I suggest you let a healer have a look at you."

Har-Kaaska waved that aside. "No time. The Doms will eventually figure out what we're up to. I doubt they'll all even *fit* in the city—nor will they want to enter it once the fires spread wider. We must both prepare our divisions to screen the evacuation."

Itzam grunted. "And how will you help with that when you topple from that beast due to a leak that might have been patched?"

Har-Kaaska blinked something like frustrated annoyance, then jerked a nod. "Very well. You make your point. Now tell me—I had to leave the conference early to prepare my division for its role—what is to be the order of march? More specifically, when will Lewis evacuate the civilians?"

Both knew, even more than the baggage train, the civilians would pose the greatest challenge to their successful withdrawal. The column could only move as fast as they did, and coming through the gate in their panicked thousands, they might stall it entirely.

"After the ambulances will come half the mobile artillery. It will deploy in our support. Next will be the walking wounded and essential baggage—food, ammunition, and medical supplies. Only then will women and children be allowed out. Don Hurac is doing his best to organize that, and the local men are quite scandalized. Colonel Reed was haranguing them as 'preposterous brutes' who must earn our protection by taking up arms. There are plenty to go around, just now." His expression of distaste turned to one of satisfaction. "I heard Reed proclaim that their *men* would withdraw alongside ours."

"A fine fellow, Mr. Reed," Har-Kaaska observed, watching the flood of troops continue.

"Yes." Itzam sighed. "After that, I expect things will turn murky as the inner defenses in the city shrink back." He gestured at the nearby gate. "Ultimately, to here. Lewis wants the remnant of Agon's Fourth Division to follow whatever other baggage and guns can be saved. He means to remain with First Division and the other half of my Third until the last, ideally contracted until only a tithe of the Doms can actually come against him." He shrugged.

"It must be hard to leave so much of your division under the command of another," Har-Kaaska mused.

"I brevetted Raul Uo to major. He is a good man." Itzam chuckled. "For a landlocked Itzincabo. And I couldn't be two places at once. We might be quite busy out here."

Har-Kaaska huffed loudly. "I don't think Lewis should linger inside. Knowing him, he will try to be the last man out. That should be Reed or—no offense—you. It's too dangerous."

"I agree entirely," Itzam confessed. "Although I do not think he is mad enough to be the *very* last man out. He understands his responsibility."

Har-Kaaska grunted. "Have you *seen* him in battle? He gets . . . distracted."

"Unlike you," Itzam commented ironically, but then his brows came together. "I don't know what his new grand strategy is, or even if it *is* new, quite honestly, but after his initial surprise at the, well, *pace* of this battle, he seems strangely confident."

Har-Kaaska blinked, his blood-matted tail popping behind him. "Lewis *always* seems confident . . . damn him." He looked at Itzam. "Lewis Cayce is the greatest warmaster I have ever known, but I never thought this would work. Then we accomplished so much, came so far, won every battle . . . and I gradually came to believe. Now that my original expectations are proving correct, I have difficulty believing *that*."

Itzam watched the first ambulance clatter past, its driver snapping the reins, urging his horses into a trot. It wouldn't be a comfortable ride for his cargo, but it beat being left for the Doms. "I know how you feel," he said at last as another ambulance hurried by. "But did it ever occur to you, as it just has me, that perhaps he agreed with your earlier assessment himself, all along—and yet he truly does remain as confident as he seems? I hope that is the case. I just wish I knew why."

"Spike that gun an' fall back this instant!" roared Sergeant Major McNabb, rushing up behind the last gun's crew on the inner north wall. It was the final fixed position on that side of the fallback defenses. With Major Olayne missing and presumed killed, McNabb had inherited the responsibility, if not the rank, of Chief of Artillery. Like elsewhere in the city, the Doms had been stopped and were fighting a dismally traditional linear battle of crashing volleys. The American line was holding, firing independently (and more effectively), but that could only last until the enemy gathered their full strength and sorted themselves out. They were taking horrendous casualties and could've piled their own yellow-clad dead into a macabre breastwork at this point, but there were always more men rushing forward through the alleyways to take the places of the fallen. It was like trying to stop the advance of paint spilled from a pot by smacking it with a hammer. And the exchange wasn't nearly as one-sided as before, on the outer wall. Men in blue lay sprawled in death everywhere McNabb looked.

"Which we just loaded the beauty, didn't we?" shouted the gunner in reply, flinching from a spray of lead spattering back from the muzzle. His young face with red stubble was already bleeding from cuts caused by similar strikes.

"Then fire it an' spike it, damn you! We're about tae fall back on the gate!"

Musketry crashing all around, the gunner finally glanced back at McNabb. His eyes were so red they looked bloody. "Oh, I hate ta spike her, Sergeant Major. She's a lovely, sweet gun, she is!"

"Then die with her, if ye like," McNabb snapped back. "But there's another, just as fine, back behind us. An' she'll nae do a blessed thing wi'out yer dead crew tae serve her!"

"*Another* gun ye say? We won't go back ta the infantry, at all?"

"Me sacred word. We've more bloody guns than crews for the now."

The gunner jerked a nod. "Ye heard 'im, lads," he cried to his surviving crew. "Off wi' ye. I'll do the necessary me'self." Pricking the charge and pooling loose powder on top of the vent, he snatched the linstock from his Number Four man before giving him a shove. One of the captured guns not yet fitted for a new carriage or lock, this one had to be fired by slow match. Stepping outside the left wheel, he arced his arm over it until the smoldering slow match inserted in the linstock touched the priming powder. A bright jet of fire lanced up from the vent and the gun rolled back from the smoky, yellow-white blast.

"God a'mighty!" cried the gunner, dropping the linstock and falling to a knee.

McNabb rushed over and crouched beside him, protected for the moment by the wall. "Yer hit, lad!" he exclaimed, feeling hot blood on the man's back when he tried to keep him upright. The red eyes found his. "Aye" was all the gunner said before blood poured from his mouth. With a final effort, he handed over a large nail that might've been salvaged from one of the buildings they'd torn down. It was slightly bigger around than the vent of his gun. With that, he sagged lifelessly in McNabb's arms, and the grizzled artilleryman gently laid him down.

"Such a damned, rotten shame. At least ye took a pack o' the devils off wi' ye. I'll spike yer gun for ye, lad." Searching around for something to drive the nail into the vent, there was nothing very suitable at hand. He finally settled on a fist-size rock broken off the wall. That would do, yet he hesitated, suddenly loath to disable the gun himself. Losing a gun to the enemy was anathema to any artilleryman, as bad or worse than losing their colors. *It isnae like they'll be takin' one o' our guns, now is it?* he rationalized. *Just gotta keep 'em from usin' this piece on us.* He'd already ordered and watched a lot of other guns spiked, but actually setting his own hands to the task didn't sit well at all. It was then he finally felt, one way or another, this fight was lost.

"We're pulling back to the gate, Sergeant Major. Colonel Agon is already gone, and we have to fill the gap," came a cry from behind him. One of Raul Uo's lieutenants.

"Aye," McNabb shouted back, then sighed. "Right with ye."

CHAPTER 32

It didn't show on his face, but Leonor knew Lewis Cayce's heart was breaking as he watched so much of his army, particularly those brave men who'd followed him from the start, wither like a moth's wings too close to a flame. And to linger much longer might very well—quite literally—burn the whole moth. He'd ordered (likely condemned) numerous squads and companies to hide from the Doms throughout the city to spread fire around and behind them as they massed around the shrinking perimeter of defenders. From where he and his entourage, now including Don Hurac, Reverend Harkin, Father Orno, and a filthy and bloodied Colonel Agon now watched from astride their horses—they were the only ones mounted near the east gate—it looked as though those men might've been a little too successful.

Flames were leaping high in the sky in every direction they looked, making a firestorm wall that would finally prevent more Doms from entering the city—if any were left to come—but also scorched and prodded their fighting men forward with ever-growing desperation. And Lewis's troops were fighting just as hard to keep them back. It was a wholly hellish, surrealistic scene. The singularly vicious battle was dreadful enough to hear and view, but the maelstrom of flames and smoke and firework-like explosions of collapsing buildings that swirled around the towering temples lent the whole thing a warped, otherworldly aspect.

"This is hell," said Reverend Harkin. He'd been repeating that over and over. "We are in hell."

Leonor glanced over her shoulder to the east. The city wall blocked her view of the distant, mountainous horizon, but the sky above was starting to glow pink beyond wispy, fish-flesh clouds. *"Dawn* in hell," she pointed out.

Lewis stirred himself and cleared his throat. "Where we won't remain much longer. The women and children are out, and the survivors of Fourth Division are going out now, along with the last artillery we'll take." He'd finally ordered that only fully converted pieces be saved, and they hadn't even collected and staged half of those. The rest, likely still on the walls, were probably burning by now. "Messenger," he barked.

"Which I guess I'm the last one left for that," griped Corporal Willis, awkwardly urging his recalcitrant horse forward. Man and animal clearly hated each other. *Probably too much alike,* Leonor mused. "Hafta send yer precious, useless dragoons next," Willis added, sneering at the men with Buisine.

Lewis looked surprised. "Corporal Willis! Where have you been? I thought we'd lost you."

Willis glared back. "Nearly did, to Mistress Samantha, who had me fetchin' an' carryin' like a damned boo-ro. She's finally outa the city, by the way. Shoved her out the gate myself," he added piously.

"Well done," Lewis said. "Now go and have the rest of the wagons emptied of tents and such and have them prepared to carry our last wounded out."

"Your tent too?" Willis complained.

"Especially mine. It takes up half a wagon by itself."

"Which mine's in there *with* it, an' the rain flys, the cots, my favorite blanket . . ." Willis grumbled. A spent musket ball warbled by and he flinched. "Jeez!"

"Just do it," Lewis said. "Mr. Buisine?"

"Sir?"

"Detail one of your men to find Colonel Reed. Compliments, of course, and tell him to start pulling his center force back as quickly as he deems practicable. Have other messengers instruct the north and south lines to shift toward the gate as appropriate—while maintaining contact with Reed—and start exiting the city as their lines compress. Is that clear?"

Buisine looked at his last dragoons, who nodded, but only after sending slightly resentful glances at the remaining Rangers. Those men simply wouldn't leave Lewis without a direct order from him. Certainly not with Leonor watching. "Very well, hurry along," Buisine told the dragoons, "but get back here as quickly as you can." Touching their hat brims, the three men spurred their horses into motion and clattered away.

"Not much left for us to do. Not in here," Leonor hinted at Lewis. "Maybe it's time we got out too." By "we," she meant "he," and everyone knew it.

"You should leave," he said, without any expectation she would. "You all should," he said louder, addressing Don Hurac and the clerics. "There's one final thing for me to do, however." He took a deep breath. "I must share this last act of the tragedy that I brought my men here to perform."

Leonor shook her head, irritation growing. "That's pretty damn stupid," she accused. "The 'last act' is gonna be leadin' your army ta safety. Them outside might already be in danger an' they need you too." A bright flash lit the city not far from the abandoned main temple area and a thunderous boom, louder than the guns, rolled over them. Leonor doubted it was one of their ammunition stores. Plenty of those had already gone up and the sound wasn't right. *Probably a big grain warehouse*, she thought. Those had been carefully targeted, and the dust could violently explode. *Doms ain't gonna find much left to eat*, she imagined with satisfaction. *Not much'a anything at all*, she mused. The only part of the city not violently burning was ravaged by battle. The heat and smoke were bad even here, and some of the Doms were surely burning already. She waved around. "No matter how many Doms we kill—or roast—we're still gonna be outnumbered. The retreat'll be a nightmare too. Your men'll need you for that."

"Is that truly what all of this was?" asked Father Orno, with a glance at a miserable Don Hurac. "This whole thing, all we accomplished, nothing but a tragic play?"

Lewis didn't answer. Reverend Harkin coughed and said, "It would seem to have turned out that way." He stared at Lewis. "Yet I simply refuse to believe it. Surely, sir, at some point, you must have thought we could win?"

Lewis stirred and met his eye. "Yes." He cleared his own throat. The smoke from the flames and battle was quickly getting worse. "And believe it or not, I still think victory of a sort is possible."

"But not here," Don Hurac submitted. That was increasingly obvious, as was the fact that any victor here will have won nothing but ruins.

Lewis shook his head. "No, Your Excellency. Not since it became clear your elevation had no meaning to our enemy. I'd entrusted considerable hope in that possibility." He held up his hand to take the sting away. "It's not your fault, sir. It might still have worked if not for the nature of our enemy. And the Gran Cruzada, of course. We never had a chance of defeating such a force in open battle. So"—he managed a bitter smile—"'hope' never being a plan, I proceeded to make others. Unfortunately for you and this remarkable city, you and it were the only bait that would draw the whole enemy army to a place of our choosing, that we'd fully prepared to inflict the most harm upon it. To even the odds to a degree. I'd hoped to do more," he confessed, then snorted. "There's that ridiculous word again: 'hope.' It does too often color what we do, especially when the enemy breaks the rules we think they'll use. Fortunately, at least for your people here," he stressed to Don Hurac, "the 'evacuation in the middle of battle' plan, for lack of something more elegant to call it, was sufficiently elastic to serve."

Lewis bowed his head to Leonor. "What now remains of *this* act of the tragedy is to discover if the effort, the suffering and bloodshed, was worth it. We'll only know that when the remnants of First and Third Divisions still fighting here are successfully evacuated as well."

"There's likely to be a fight outside," Leonor reminded. "How are we gonna break contact? Or will we?" She shook her head. "Damn it, Lewis, now I'm just as confused as anybody. It ain't that I don't trust you. Of course I do. I *married* you! But even if all the Dom infantry out there are wiped out an' the Doms can't shift any more before we're loose, somewhere out there, there's *thousands* of Dom lancers! Just about *all* of 'em. That we haven't seen much of 'em since they got here doesn't mean they're gone. Our column's gonna be a mess: wore-out men, civilians, wagons, walkin' wounded, all strung out . . . Ain't you worried them lancers'll swoop down an' tear it apart?"

For the first time, certainly that morning, a genuine smile lit Lewis's face. "No," he said. "Not in the least."

Poom! Poom! Poom! roared the guns to the right of First Sergeant Visser, and the leading edge of the mob of Doms was virtually smeared away. He could barely breathe in the growing heat and smoke, and the mental similarity of the scene to strawberry jam spread on a biscuit nearly made him gag. And the enemy army *had* degenerated into a gigantic mob. Faced by the staggering fire of the mixed but contracting and deepening ranks of the 1st US, 3rd Pennsylvania, and the meager remnants of the militia, even some of Agon's men, they were also being lashed forward by the raging, relentless advance of the flaming holocaust behind. Regardless how dedicated to their God or fearful of their leaders, even the most rabid among them might've broken by now if they could. But escape was now impossible through the burning city, and that only left the east gate—blocked by the retreating enemy.

Sergeant Major McNabb bellowed at the closest artillerymen, "Right, lads, back wi' ye now. Another thirty paces!" That would take them within a hundred paces of the gate where other guns were already gathering.

"First rank, fire!" yelled Captain Cullin, voice rough and cracking as he paced behind the survivors of his company. A volley exploded in the face of the Doms, now pressing desperately hard, spilling more screaming men to the cobbles. Another company, 1st US men, spat a near-simultaneous volley just beyond the heavy section of cannon, pulling back. Musket balls clattered against the guns or thumped into flesh, dropping defenders almost constantly. The Doms could only fire independently now, and the bashing force of controlled, repeated volleys, was the only thing holding them back.

As soon as Cullin's 3rd Pennsylvanians had fired, First Sergeant Visser shouted for the front line to retreat through the ranks. "Fall in on the guns an' reload. You know the drill by now!"

"Second rank, fire!" grated Cullin.

Crash!

Visser repeated his previous command and added, "Well done! Fine execution. Bloodied the bastards good with that one. Third rank, make ready!"

"Third rank, fire!" Cullin rasped.

Crash!

A Dom musket ball snatched Visser's hat off his head and he thought his scalp was on fire. Reaching up, he gingerly explored a furrow in the skin and his fingers came away bloody. "Bastards," he grunted. "Hair's already thinnin' on top. Didn't need that."

"You're lucky, Sergeant," said Private Rayley, passing on his way to the rear. The youngster looked terrible, powder-blackened face streaked with sweat, blood, and tears.

"Fourth rank, fire!"

Crash!

"Private Garca?" Visser asked.

Rayley pursed his lips. "Gone. Took one in about the same place as you, just a little lower. Back at the wall." He gestured toward their first fallback position, now beyond the enemy and the flames. It had still been dark then. Now the sun was fully up and they'd been fighting without pause.

"I'm sorry, lad. I know you were close. Now get yourself back with your mates." He raised his voice. "Fifth rank, make ready!"

"Don't have any left, Sergeant," Rayley said mournfully. "I think I'm the last in your platoon."

That may be, Visser realized. He'd seen Corporal Cirano fall, shot through the chest, and heard that Lieutenant Aiken was wounded. As a matter of fact, Captain Cullin's was the only officer's voice he still heard—and his had been the only sergeant's. No platoon had kept its integrity, and A and B Companies were all mixed up. He made a decision. "You're actin' corporal now, Rayley. When you get back on the line behind us, look for our lads. Pull 'em together. In fact, get any sergeants you see to start sortin' the companies as well. Men always fight better among friends, not to mention organized."

"Nobody's gonna do what I say," Rayley objected.

"They will," Visser insisted. "Most'll be more than happy to have an order ta follow. You'll see. An' the order's from me, anyway. Any who don't like it'll have me to deal with. Now go!"

"Fifth rank! Fire!"

Crash!

"Well done, lads. Fall back on the guns." A man dropped at his feet as he turned. Another dropped his musket and clutched his arm, screaming. Visser saw a man pull him to the rear, seizing the loose musket as he went. Turning farther, he saw only two ranks remained and Rayley was gone. "We'll all be joinin' you soon, boys," he called. "Doms'll be hot on our heels so be ready to give 'em a slap! Sixth rank, make ready!"

Dom officers were shouting, voices desperate, and Visser finally realized that as many screams seemed to be floating toward them from the rear of the enemy as the front. He'd learned to speak Spanya as well as most, but the only word that reached him from the roaring voices was *"Bayonetas!"*

Oh Lord, he thought. *They're gonna charge us.*

"Sixth rank, fire!" Captain Cullin practically croaked.

Crash!

"Sixth rank, stand fast," Cullin quickly added. "Sixth and seventh ranks, fix bayonets! Prepare to retire in contact!"

Visser had never heard that command before, but its meaning was self-evident and easily understood. Looking to the far right, he saw the 1st US making the same preparations.

"Oh Lord," he repeated, barely aloud. "This is it."

Horns blared from within the mass of Doms, building in volume as more and more joined in. Few Dom horn calls had more than a couple notes, and none were very complicated. The sheer size of their regiments made it difficult for them to respond to complex commands. That was irrelevant now, and all the defenders recognized this call as the signal to charge. With a thunderous roar that drowned all the firing, not to mention the seething groans and shrieks of a dying city, the Doms surged forward. The crash of contact was almost immediate, the clash of weapons, war cries, shrieks, bellows of agony and rage rippling across the front.

The American line recoiled alarmingly as men were heaved back by the irresistible mass. First Sergeant Visser found himself stumbling backward, hands clutching his musket almost entirely numb from the blow he'd instinctively blocked. A giant of a man in Dominion yellow and black had brought the point of his bayonet down, preparing to run him through, when Visser tripped over a body and fell, the bayonet lunging past overhead—right where his chest would've been. It mattered little. Lying on his back, he was a dead man, and a shrill sense of terror clenched his heart. A glittering red triangular bayonet suddenly snaked through from the side and drove deep through the ribs under the giant's overextended right arm. His eyes went wide, and he coughed a spray of blood as the bayonet twisted and withdrew. Visser had to scramble to keep from being pinned by the falling man.

"Up ye git, Sergeant! No malingerin', now!" yelled a voice he recognized. One of his own, after all, whom he'd scolded with similar words more than once. Other hands helped pull him up, and he realized at least one of the ranks that already fell back had returned to bolster the line, firing loaded muskets into the faces of their foes.

"Thanks, lads," he shouted, unable to identify any of his other helpers. They were already busy, stabbing and bashing. Hands sore but working again, he used his own musket to knock an enemy's aside and drive his bayonet through the man's throat. Blood sprayed high as the figure tumbled back, knocking others over. The panic Visser had felt quickly transformed into burning rage, and he fought like a fiend, roaring and swearing, pausing only to wipe clammy sweat and blood from his eyes, the latter seeping down from the furrow in his scalp.

The enemy didn't pause—they couldn't. Continuously blaring horns and the searing heat behind pressed them on, relentlessly shrinking the American defense. As that defense contracted, however, pushed back and diminished by attrition, it also grew tighter, stronger, better able to resist the fewer numbers that could actually get at it, even as it neared the final, bristling, defensive line.

Exhausted, but utterly focused on the fight, Visser jerked his bayonet from a squalling Dom's belly with a savage twist, but slammed into something hard and immobile behind him. Risking a quick glance, he realized he'd backed into the muzzle of a captured Dom 8pdr and men were shouting at him to clear the front.

"We're at the gun line, lads!" he yelled as loud as his wrecked voice allowed. "Smash the devils back an' flow through it. You'll have a rest in a moment."

Twisting to let a bayonet slide past him, the sharp edge of the blade deflected by his leather cartridge box strap, he savagely stabbed the Dom behind it before ducking down and crawling under the axle of the gun. Clawing hands dragged him out from beneath it and practically threw him aside. Other men were already staggering through the massed infantry between the guns and into the strange, relative peace behind them. Visser was blinking and coughing when Captain Cullin found him, grabbing his arm and pointing at the gate with his bloody sword. A number of mounted figures were gathered there. Oddly, it looked like most of the 1st and 3rd's musicians were there as well.

"Well done, Sergeant. Well done indeed." Cullin's voice was like a dry wagon axle, and his dark blue frock coat had several wet holes in it. None of the wounds seemed debilitating, and Visser hoped they were shallow, but his white sword belt was stained almost black. "Major Ulrich is over there with Colonel Cayce, waiting to lead the men out. Help gather those you were fighting with and take them through the gate. We'll all be backing through soon enough."

"Yes, sir. Thank you, sir. What about Colonel Reed? Is he over there?"

"Yes, he made it. A little the worse for wear, but still in one piece." He paused. "I'm afraid Major Beck hasn't been seen, so Major Ulrich will command the First US as well as our regiment. At least for now." He passed a sleeve across his face. "We may not both make a full regiment together, after this," he added bitterly, then he tilted his head thoughtfully. "Listen!" he said. The drums by the gate were thundering now, a dozen or so, and the fifes joined in after the flourish. The "Old 1812" was immediately recognizable, drowning the enemy horns, and a great cheer went up from the battling troops. The gun that Visser just crawled under boomed and belched a cloud of smoke and canister, followed at once by nine more.

Mangled bodies tumbled back under the smoke and spray of blood. "That's the style, you devils!" Cullin roared, voice practically shattering. "We may be in hell, but we've made it our playground. Come to us and die, you filthy, godless, buggering bastards!" He whirled to face Visser. "Go!" he croaked. "Get the lads out and don't tarry in the gateway. We've only a short time left to save all the fellows we can."

Visser hesitated, watching the gunners feverishly reloading over the gory heap of flesh they just made and infantry slashing out irresistible volleys by ranks once more. "What'll happen, sir?"

Cullin nodded toward the mounted officers. "What Colonel Cayce planned from the start, is my guess. As soon as we bash them back enough, we'll all make a run for it. Then everything this side of the gate will drop straight into hell for real."

Visser didn't know what that meant, but seeing Corporal Rayley rushing up with seven or eight men, he trotted over to them. "You found some of our boys, I see," he said with satisfaction. "There was another . . ." He looked around. "*Was*, at least. Either way, we need to get everyone who just came through the line out the gate at once."

Varaa and Leonor had been watching tired, bloody troops streaming through the gate, Reverend Harkin and Father Orno joining them at last, gently helping pile wounded men on some of the last of the wagons. Orno was wearing a brittle smile, murmuring a version of the Lord's Prayer while Harkin repeated, "He heals the brokenhearted and binds up their wounds. He will wipe every tear from their eyes . . ."

"I know He will, Parson," called a pained voice from the wagon over the seething roar of battle and the nearby musicians, "but a taste of opium—or whatever it is them healer women use—wouldn't go amiss."

"Soon, lad," Harkin assured as he followed the wagon through the gate. "Soon."

Varaa's gaze was drawn to the parapet above the gate and behind the stairs leading up. Here, along the eastern wall, was the only place all the stairways made straight ramps without the switchbacks used elsewhere. She finally realized why when she saw the men, a mix of troops and militia, making preparations. She got Leonor's attention and indicated what she saw, then turned back to Lewis. "We need to go," she urged again, but Lewis shook his head.

"Just a little longer. I won't leave any of our men to what's going to happen, nor condemn another man's soul to bear the responsibility for it."

"They're Doms!" Leonor snarled. "They deserve it."

Lewis glared at her. "Their leaders do," he angrily agreed. "Not the poor bastards they've pushed into this. And I doubt any of their real leaders are here. But there'll be more than enough of the enemy after us as it is and I won't leave them any of this city as a prize." He waited through the staccato booming of guns, shredding another deep layer of Doms. John Ulrich had moved over there, still mounted, braving the sporadic but still considerable enemy fire. Leaning over to speak to Captain Cullin, he passed his own final orders before turning and galloping back. Leonor's heart was in her throat the whole time the able and popular officer, a former NCO, was so exposed. Somehow, he made it to the gate. They were all still in lethal range of Dom muskets, of course, but few—if any—of the enemy could see them over the fighting right in front of them. Ulrich stopped in front of Lewis. "The next salvo of the guns will signal the fallback. Mr. Cullin will determine how many ranks to send at once. Can't have all of them simply break and run. Not yet."

"Very good, Major. The time has come for you, Colonel Reed, and Colonel Agon to exit the city. Har-Kaaska and Itzam can't handle the whole army by themselves." He looked at Don Hurac, with Don Amil still by him. "You must go as well, Your Excellency. Your people will need you badly."

Don Hurac sighed deeply, glancing above the gate, expression tortured. Turning to view the inferno engulfing the Holy City beyond the fighting, he sank even lower in his saddle. "There truly will be nothing left, will there? The greatest city in the world."

"Thousands of your people will remain, sir," Colonel Reed pointed out. "We tried," he added gravely, clearly sad as well, but more for his men than the city. "And it was worth the effort." He seemed to be trying to assure himself of that. "But Mistress Zyan was correct. It is the people that matter, not the place." Nodding at Lewis, he gestured for all the other officers and officials to precede him through the gate. His expression made it clear he'd push them if he had to. Threading their way through the still-constant stream of battered troops, in moments they were gone. Lewis, Leonor, and Varaa were alone with their diminished escort once more. Only one of Buisine's dragoons had returned, and Corporal Willis was back, grumbling loudly and impertinently enough to draw a glare from the dragoon lieutenant. Lewis ignored him, as usual.

"All right, lads," he called to the musicians. "Out you go. You've accompanied this dance long enough. Move as quickly as you can up the road, but stay together and urge the other fellows along. Strike up a tune with a lively beat. That may help."

The guns drowned the musketry again, and Lewis saw the rear two ranks peel away from the line. They didn't break and run, but Cullin had clearly told them to hurry. In moments, the space just inside the gate was flooded by roughly two hundred men. Lewis was surprised to see First Sergeant Visser and several of his platoon fight their way back in against the flow, doing their best to organize it. He'd seen Visser leave some time ago and assumed he'd simply left. Now he guessed the first sergeant and his men had been helping keep things sorted, directing men back to their companies and regiments as they re-formed outside the wall. Now, while his men kept working, Visser pushed his way through the crowd until he stood by Lewis. He didn't salute.

"Colonel Cayce, sir, Colonel Reed sent us to help tidy the rush, as it were, like we been doin' outside."

"I thought that was your purpose. Well done, First Sergeant."

"Yes, sir. Thank you, sir, but he also wanted you to know the enemy's finally startin' to take notice of things. No real opposition yet, not much left close by outside the walls to do it with. But a squad of Ranger scouts—don't know where they came from, there's just half a dozen or so—rode up an' reported that the Blood Priests on the other side of the canal are floggin' up what amounts to a whole other army to cross. Point is, he suggested you hurry things along, if you can."

Lewis nodded. "Thank you, First Sergeant. We will." He gauged the fighting as more and more musket balls *vipp*ed and warbled past. Arete was stomping her hooves, anxious to join the fight or flee. Everything, including the guns, had pulled back into a tighter perimeter, the infantry probably re-forming their lines on the hubs of the guns as they recoiled. The heat and smoke of the burning city, combined with gunpowder smoke, was becoming unbearable, and the musketry on both sides was reaching a frenzied crescendo. "I believe things are coming to a head. Keep hurrying the men in the gateway along." He saw one of the last wagons being loaded with wounded. "We'll have to abandon those wagons. Have details carry the wounded out. Release the animals and lead or ride them through."

"The horses, sir?"

"Yes. We'll need them. And the enemy won't," he added cryptically. "Go, quickly now!"

The Doms in the city hadn't been fighting to win for some time, only to get out through the gate themselves. What was left of the 1st US, 3rd Pennsylvania, and whatever miscellaneous troops and militia were still with them were fighting to keep it clear for themselves. Lewis had never seen anything like the desperation and ferocity on display. His heart was breaking, yet his pride in the men under his command—that they could keep holding so long against so much—threatened to spill the tears in his eyes.

"Damned smoke," he muttered, wiping his face with his sleeve. Suddenly, the roar of battle somehow redoubled when the line finally started cracking near the center left. Only about half the guns fired, reaping another red, shredded crop and sending the Doms across from them reeling back, but the center was failing, stabbed and trampled down.

"Sound the retreat, Corporal Hannity!" Lewis barked. The gate was just now starting to clear as men literally dragged their comrades through.

"Hannity's hit, sir!"

Lewis looked at the bugler, crouched over in the saddle. "Can you blow the retreat, son?" he asked. Hannity nodded and straightened slightly, bringing the bugle to his lips, but then teetered and nearly fell from his horse. One of the Rangers steadied him. Lewis didn't hesitate, kicking Arete, and the powerful warhorse surged forward. "Get them out, Varaa! Everyone!" he called over his shoulder. "Take Leonor, Lieutenant Buisine, forcefully and across your saddle if you must!"

Torn, Buisine stifled a protest and moved to obey, only to be met by

Leonor's stone-cold expression—and one of her revolvers pointed at his eye. "Get out," she snapped, and charged after Lewis.

"Shit!" Buisine shouted in frustration, starting to follow.

"No point," cried Varaa, jumping down from her horse. "Follow me."

"Where?" asked the dragoon, sliding from his saddle as well.

"Take the bugler and our horses out," Varaa called to a spluttering Willis and the few others with him, then looked at Buisine and pointed at the rampart. "Up there. Only one thing left we can do."

"What's that?" the dragoon asked, chasing her toward the stairs and scaling the first of the long, steep steps.

"Don't you pay any attention?" Varaa shouted back. "Lewis's 'last job' he didn't want anyone else to do."

"He told you what it was?" Buisine asked, huffing, and gently batting Varaa's tail out of his face.

Varaa blinked and shook her head as she reached the top of the wall. "No, but I saw men up here preparing, saw what they were doing." She shrugged. "*I* knew what he intended at once. Lewis and I think alike, remember?"

SLASHING HIS SABER at Doms pouring through the cracked center, Lewis roared out, "Fall back! Everyone back to the gate." Arete reared slightly and kicked a Dom in the face. Bones crunched and he went down, screaming and streaming blood. "Re-form at the gate!" Lewis continued, slashing down at another Dom, hacking deep between neck and shoulder. "Re-form with your bayonets out, long enough for your comrades to get clear." He spun Arete, the horse kicking and flailing as he caught sight of a gun's crew trying to spike their weapon. "Forget that," he bellowed at the men. "There's no time—no point. Pull back!"

Lewis felt a musket ball snatch his sleeve and saw another clip Arete's mane just behind her ears. A cluster of Doms had encircled them. Arete screeched and sidestepped when a Dom bayonet stabbed her shoulder. Another sliced the top of Lewis's thigh. Fending off another bayonet thrust with his saber, he drew one of his rarely used .54 caliber M1836 pistols from its saddle holster, thumbed back the cock and shot a man who'd grabbed his other leg, trying to pull him down. He glimpsed some of his men trying to fight through to him, but doubted he'd last long enough. Suddenly, two of his attackers fell in quick succession and Leonor appeared beside him, revolvers in both hands and smoke wreathing her head. Dashing around in front of him, she shot two more Doms and took an instant to glare at him. "Get back *yourself*, you fool!" she shouted, blasting the hole she'd come through back open with her revolvers. It wasn't clear if she hit anyone, but the seemingly endless shots the mad, terrifying woman fired were enough to force many back. "*C'mon!*" she screamed. "Your men're already doin' what you told 'em, now you do it too!"

Turning Arete, Lewis followed his wife while menacing another Dom soldier with his saber. That one, and others, now seemed more intent on avoiding the lethal pair than attacking. "'Fool,' is it?" he shouted over the tumult. "Not a very respectful way to address your commanding officer."

"Appropriate for my damned fool of a husband, though," Leonor snapped back. A dense hedge of bayonets was starting to bristle at the gate just a dozen paces away, and it briefly parted to let them pass. The swarming Doms continued forward through the suddenly vacated space, but hesitated to close on the small, deadly remnant of the fiends they'd been fighting for over twenty-four hours. Like a pack of starving wolves considering a porcupine, none seemed anxious to be the first to throw themselves upon it.

Lewis looked at the crowded gate, men squeezing through as quick as they could. He saw First Sergeant Visser pulling others from the inner shell of the defense and shoving them at the exit. Dom officers were shouting at their men to clear their muskets, to drive their bayonets out of their muzzles.

"Lewis!" came a shout from above, and Lewis saw Varaa leaning over the parapet above. "They're getting ready to shoot their way through."

"Why am I not surprised to see you up there?" Lewis called back. "I know," he added. "Is everything ready?"

"Yes," Varaa replied, her tone sounding vaguely uncomfortable.

"You know what's required?" he pressed.

"I do."

"Of course she does," Lewis murmured, then raised his voice again. "Do it."

Varaa disappeared from view.

The clatter of musketry began to resume, from the Doms as well as defenders right behind the line of bayonet men. Projectiles cracked and spattered on the stone arch or *whumped* into the sloping earthen ramp beneath the ramparts. Then, a loud, clunking rumble was heard from the long stair to the right and a large, heavy cask, almost as big around as it was tall and barely fitting between the wooden handrails, came rolling down, picking up speed. Doms had already started up the stair, now outside the convex perimeter, but the cask bowled through them, raising terrible screams as it crushed or smashed them aside. Bounding up at the bottom, it landed hard on the cobbles with a crackle of wooden staves. Viscous liquid sprayed from the cask as it careened wildly into the mass of Doms, driving deep in among them. More casks were already rumbling down behind it, on every nearby stair accessing the wall.

The casks alone made fine, deadly projectiles, crashing and leaping wetly through Doms with irresistible force like giant roundshot, each killing or maiming with their size, weight, and inertia alone, but few came to rest in one piece, most flying apart and disgorging their contents. Those that did stop were promptly demolished by others—soaking the ground and men all around in oil. The enemy clearly knew the meaning of this and terrified cries rose up. Most stopped shooting at once, the front of the mass recoiling back. They couldn't go far against the press behind them, however, and the panic surged.

"Out, out, out!" Lewis roared. Visser didn't know what was happening, but redoubled his efforts. The bayonet-bristling hedge shrank quickly as men behind it flowed through the gate. Lewis's gaze was drawn to the flames beyond the Doms, roaring and licking closer. It might be a while before they ignited the oil. In spite of the heat, its vapors weren't particularly flammable as far as he knew, but he wasn't relying on that. Something he'd seen earlier had given him the answer.

Barrels of oil had initially been a central part of Lewis's defensive plan, placed on all the walls to pour down and ignite on attackers in an effective—if troubling—medieval way. But none had yet been used for that, and Lewis ordered they not be as soon as the west wall went. He'd known then that the oil, in addition to other accumulated stores, would be needed to fire the city—and for this last-ditch effort to break contact here. Now, the last cask of oil on the eastern battlements had been tipped down the stairs, forming a thick, somewhat tacky lake around and among the Dom horde. It even smelled vaguely sweet.

With a far-carrying shout from Varaa, specific troops still on the walls quickly lit some remaining case shot with their fuses left uncut from torches or braziers and hurled them as far as they could out into the enemy. Several seconds passed before the first one exploded with a muffled crack, slashing men with jagged fragments and spewing sputtering, smoky pitch. Flames gushed up immediately, searing screeching flesh and lighting oil-soaked uniforms. *Crack, crack, crack, crack!* went other exploding case, and more flames roiled up amid dark, swirling smoke, spreading exponentially more swiftly and greedily the farther they raced. The screams were otherworldly, utterly nightmarish. Lewis clenched his teeth and tried his best to harden his heart as thousands of men started to burn, surging back at first, then heaving desperately from side to side, squealing human torches lighting their comrades. All movement near the gate ground to a horrified halt for an instant, men craning their necks to look back behind them.

"Clear the gate, damn you all," Leonor belted out, holding her hand over her face to shield it from the searing heat. "You wanna burn up too? Move!"

Needing no further encouragement, the exodus took on a frantic life of its own, actually sweeping First Sergeant Visser along with the rush. A solid wall of flame had spread between the rear guard and the Doms, and the troops standing there, sweat steaming from their uniforms, turned and started to shout for their comrades to hurry as well.

"See you outside," Varaa yelled down from above. Lewis looked up and nodded at his friend. He knew the people left up there would slide down the outside of the wall with ropes.

"You've had your way, Lewis," Leonor snapped sharply, still holding her hand over her eyes, her wild-eyed horse prancing in place. "Last one out, like you planned." The rear guard had contracted to barely a score of men, pleading for their fellows to hurry.

"That wasn't as important to me as seeing what I did. Hearing it. Feeling it," he added. "I suppose this makes me as much a monster as the enemy," he mused over the shrieks.

"Horseshit," Leonor spat. "But you *are* a fool," she stated flatly, "tryin' to fight a 'civilized' war against monsters. Sure, it's too damn bad for the innocents, but war's always hard on them. You've done what you could for those you could"—she waved toward the roaring flames—"but there's nothin' you can do for the poor bastards the *real* enemy sends ta kill us. An' that's the main difference," she continued more softly. "You've done all this to *save* people. Your own, first an' foremost," she conceded, "but that's only natural—an' none o' this would'a happened if *they* hadn't come here to kill." She urged him toward the gate, where just a few men still lingered.

"Honestly, I'm glad you've finally decided to start swingin' with both fists an' do whatever it takes, no matter what."

Lewis looked at her. Leonor had a soft, sensitive side, but he was probably the only one who'd ever seen it. She'd grown much more affable and approachable, even humorous and openly happy of late, but her harsh, pragmatic, cold-blooded nature always prevailed in a fight. The very idea of following any kind of "rules" in war was nonsensical to her.

Nodding, he had to agree with her now. He'd turned her father "loose" on the enemy at times, aware the Ranger would do unpleasant things, and was suddenly as appalled by his hypocrisy as he was horrified by what he'd just done. At the same time, he knew it had been necessary, and it was far past time he turned *himself* "loose."

"Yes," he said grimly. "I have—and I will." Looking behind at the hell he'd opened one final time, he urged Arete forward and followed the last of his men and his wife through the gate.

CHAPTER 33

There was a cold breeze out of the north, enough that Lewis's sweat-soaked uniform gave him a chill once he was outside the wall. The shock to his lungs was equally abrupt when he tried to take a cleansing breath. It ended in a chest-wrenching coughing fit that doubled him over in the saddle. Leonor was still beside him, eyes red, coughing too. Everyone around was similarly stricken, gasping infantrymen trying to run with streaming eyes and noses to join the column on the road while wounded were lifted or helped atop wagons and caissons. Lewis finally managed a full, deep breath without falling into a fit, and it came as a glorious relief. The towering column of smoke from the city was leaning hard to the south, and the only smell of it, at the moment, came from his clothes. He was surprised how much dusty gray ash clung to the wool. Ash was everywhere, in fact, and that struck him as symbolic of his whole effort to take the war to the enemy and have their fight here. It was certainly symbolic of the end of his fight for the Holy City. Now would come the battle to save his army and escape. To survive.

"Are you the last?" called Major Ulrich, riding closer with a cobbled-up staff, eyes straying to the city turned inferno behind them, the walls now like the rim around a great caldera spewing volcanic fire. Har-Kaaska and

Colonel Itzam were with him, as were Willis and a Ranger, still leading Varaa's and Lieutenant Buisine's horses.

Lewis nodded, turning. "The last," he replied, "except for those on the wall." A score or more blue-clad forms were snaking down lines, coughing and running from the heat and the scene they'd been the last to observe. "There won't be anyone else out the gate," he added. "I hope more of our people, perhaps trapped on other walls, managed to make it here."

"A few," Ulrich said sadly. "A very few. I fear most of the brave fellows who fired the city behind the enemy were caught by them or the flames."

Lewis nodded woodenly. He'd expected that. "And the situation here? Where's Colonel Reed? Don Hurac?"

"Colonel Reed went forward, toward the front of the column, with Colonel Agon flogging it along as quickly as possible. Don Hurac will have stopped with his people, no doubt. They're gaggling along with the baggage." He shook his head. "I don't mean that the way it sounds. The civilians are trying their best, many helping with the wounded and driving wagons. More even armed themselves and went forward to join Agon's men." He gestured to the north and south. "Parts of Colonel Itzam's and Colonel Har-Kaaska's divisions are deployed on the flanks, eyeing the enemy buildup there—mostly to the south at the moment. All infantry, so far," he added meaningfully, "and doing nothing threatening at present."

Varaa-Choon and Lieutenant Buisine jogged up, surrounded by clouds of ash that lifted off them in the breeze like smoke. Buisine was still gasping from his own coughing spell, but Varaa appeared unflappable as usual as she retrieved her borrowed mount from Willis. "That's probably all they had orders to do," Varaa opined with a slight grin. "'Go see what's happening to the east.' And now they await further orders." She regarded Lewis with her large, blue eyes. "We may have lost the city, but they didn't take it. This has been at least as great a disaster for them as us. Worse. Whoever commanded the enemy was obviously prepared to sacrifice a large percentage of their army, but I doubt they were willing to lose as much as they did. We will see no initiative on the flanks." She *kakked* a bitter laugh. "Just imagine being one of their officers there, convinced they'll be impaled if they exceed their orders, but equally worried they'll suffer for not 'doing the obvious.' How dreadful."

"Colonel Itzam and I can handle what is there at the moment in any event," assured Har-Kaaska.

Lewis was wiping at the sweaty grit in his eyes with one hand while patting Arete with the other. He leaned forward to inspect the wound on her shoulder. Like his own thigh wound, it had stopped bleeding, but needed stitches. "Fine," he said, "but we're leaving now, before the enemy receives orders to pursue or force another fight." He peered up at Har-Kaaska. The Mi-Anakka looked terrible, and so did his strange mount. "I expect your division's in little better shape than you?"

Har-Kaaska snorted, blinking, but nodded. "Part of it. Those regiments that spearheaded our breakout are already with the column. The same as Colonel Itzam's roughly handled men." He grinned. "Did you know that Koaar-Taak commands the First Ocelomeh again?"

Lewis gestured at Varaa and Leonor. "We saw him in the fighting after he assumed that responsibility. We didn't know if he made it."

Har-Kaaska's grin faded. "He did, and his regiment stayed with Colonel Agon until they pulled back. They are our vanguard now. Badly mauled, I fear."

Lewis was nodding. "We'll have to get them some help." He stretched his back and groaned. "I want to pull your flanking forces back to the column. Third Division and half our artillery will be our rear guard," he told Itzam, "backed by the Second and then what's left of the First. If the Doms want to chase us, they'll have to do it in column as well, right up behind us on the road. It's too muddy to advance in a combat formation, especially when we reach cultivated ground. And no matter how slow we move, we'll still be faster than their armabuey-drawn artillery. There'll be nothing but infantry, and we'll bloody their noses for them."

Brows furrowing, Ulrich said, "You don't sound very worried about pursuit."

"Not true. They *will* come after us, and we'll have to kick them off our backs, but we should have time to reorganize the column before the threat from behind is too great. God send we might even be able to rest the men a bit. But right now, I'm most worried about the vanguard. Somewhere out there are a hell of a lot of Dom lancers, and we need to be ready for them."

"Well done, Your Holiness," said General Xacolotl to Don Frutos, his tone searing with bitter sarcasm. "Congratulations are in order. The Holy City is yours."

Don Frutos, now Supreme Holiness in fact, if not officially, rounded on his general from where they observed the fiery holocaust, still to the south of the city. The smoke carried over them, for the most part, but the smell of death and burning flesh was nauseating. And even with most of the horrors they'd unleashed hidden behind the walls, there were plenty in view even here to cause the gorge to rise. Yellow-clad bodies were strewn, almost uninterrupted, from just a short distance from where they stood all the way to the moat. There, the corpses were mingled with the wreckage of ladders and bridging barges. Most disconcerting, many seemed to move. Xacolotl was positive a great many wounded languished there, but he'd been forbidden to retrieve them. Don Frutos reasoned that any who might be usefully returned to duty would find their own way back for treatment. Those who couldn't would nourish God with their blood and go to Him drenched in the grace of misery.

Of course, all sorts of carrion eaters were already swarming to the feast; lizardbirds in their multitudes made a constant cawing, shrieking roar, fighting one another or their flightless cousins for the choicest morsels. Xacolotl hoped they were the source of most of the movement he noted. They would be soon enough, regardless, since a number of dangerous predators had boldly appeared as well. Nothing much bigger than a man as yet, but just as dangerous, made brazen by the unprecedented feast. And high overhead, avoiding the smoke, large flying monsters—wild versions of messenger dragons—patiently circling and swirling on erratic winds.

Xacolotl stood alone, in effect, among the preening Blood Priests in their garish red robes. He hadn't wanted any of his diminished staff present where they might fall foul of Don Frutos's mercurial temper. He'd even sent Teniente Juaris away, ostensibly to lead his men to find the lancers and pass his instructions, but just as much to save him from some painful whim that might strike Don Frutos. Especially when, sickened as he was by the cost of the Blood Cardinal's "victory," he might almost welcome his own separation from the madman's service, regardless of how unpleasant it would be. The Blood Priests murmured angrily at his tone.

"Have a care how you speak, especially in front of others," he added lower. "And some of this is your responsibility. I used your plan, after all."

"It was no part of my plan to move so quickly—and wastefully," Xacolotl denied.

"God has no patience for the plodding pace you envisioned," Don Frutos retorted airily, "and none of the blood spilled for Him is wasted." As quick as that, a benevolent smile replaced the scowl on his face. "Take heart, General: whether you initiated it or not, your plan worked magnificently! God is pleased. *I* am pleased, and so should you be. It is . . . unfortunate the city has been destroyed, but we already knew it would be necessary to replace its inhabitants. Their loss is inconsequential."

"Is it equally inconsequential that *half* my army has been lost as well?" asked Xacolotl, more careful of his tone.

Don Frutos dipped his bearded chin. "Yes. More especially now that we won't have the stores of the city to feed them all. I already told you your force would have to be . . . somewhat reduced. But the heretics have been diminished as well, by at least the same percentage, I should think, so the overall advantage remains with you as you pursue their battered remnants. You see," he continued, somewhat condescendingly, "I have done you a favor! Had *you* lost so much of your army assaulting those terrible walls, I would have been forced to make an example of you. And regardless of the care you would have taken, you cannot know that your ultimate losses would have been significantly less. Now the heretics have no walls to hide behind and you shall be free to maneuver your army—something I could never do—and destroy them in the open, with honor. Like a soldier should!"

Xacolotl took a long breath, stifling another bitter retort. Finally he nodded, but paused, thinking quickly. "If it pleases Your Holiness, I will send fresh regiments after them directly, as soon as they can be organized on this side of the canal. It will take somewhat longer to reconstitute the infantry that was already here, in contact. There's little hope for any of the thousands within the walls, but even those close by outside were dreadfully mauled. On the other hand, I have already directed that some other infantry I dispatched earlier and all the lancers should combine to prevent the enemy's escape. That may take a day or more as well," he warned. "The infantry was sent across the lake and must locate the lancers, some of whom had been dispatched to explore as far as Texcoco. The rest should not be far, engaged in searching for the enemy's elusive mounted forces. I never believed that all of them were in the city, and now it seems almost none of them were. Few riders were seen to depart. In any event, I hope to prevent their rapid retreat and hold them on this side of the escarpment, at the Río de Purification, until our full force can catch them against it."

Don Frutos waved that away. "Trivialities best left to a military mind. I have every confidence you will manage quite well." He assumed an expression of regret. "I need not describe the consequences of failure, I am sure."

"No, Your Holiness. I understand completely. By your leave, I'll begin . . . rebuilding my army."

Don Frutos shooed him away.

"It's time to stop, Lewis," Leonor said, doing her best to stifle a jaw-wracking yawn. They were riding near the middle of the column among the wagons full of wounded. Lights glowed within them as surgeons and healers did what they could while the vehicles creaked along, only the smooth surface of the Camino Sagrado making that possible at all. It still had to be incredibly uncomfortable for the badly hurt, packed tightly on the wagon beds. Moaning and crying were constant and there were occasional shrieks, likely caused by the actions or movements of the healers themselves. The wagons, some still dedicated to supplies, seemed to go on forever in both directions, trundling along side by side, and weary troops trudged through the mud in the ditches alongside the road. It wasn't that long after nightfall, but virtually everyone had been up and fighting, then marching hard for the better part of two whole days. Few had eaten anything either, other than a little dried meat or fish and the hard tortillas that seemed always available.

In addition to her concern for the army, Leonor was worried about Lewis. Worried and increasingly annoyed. He'd participated in reorganizing and rearranging the column, but hadn't much spoken otherwise. She suspected his mind was churning with schemes, as usual, but that never stopped him from talking before. She knew he blamed himself for the loss of so many of his precious troops, not to mention the city, and feared his stoic silence was a sign of remorse and self-doubt. That possibility was beginning to stir her anger. Lewis—her *husband* now—wasn't the sort to mope, and defeat or not, the loss of the Holy City truly should turn out more disastrous to the enemy than them, and he'd obviously laid many layers of careful plans to ensure that. They'd likely destroyed at least half of an army eight or ten times the size of their own, and she was beginning to understand that was precisely the outcome he'd planned and prepared for from the start. He'd even practically admitted as much. But it wasn't what he'd *hoped* would happen. Perhaps he was merely sad for the losses and disappointed his "best-case" scenario had failed. He might even feel guilty over the barbarous way they'd exited the city. Lewis was a man of honor and an old-fashioned soldier who'd continue to defend his honor no matter how despicable their enemies were. *That must be it*, she thought. *He's pushin' the army more like he's runnin' from the scene of a crime than from the enemy. That won't do.* She cleared her throat and continued.

"The army's exhausted—understandably," she pressed. "Too many wounded we took at the end haven't had any care at all, to speak of, an' men are startin' ta straggle. Can't help it. Be a hell of a thing if they took the worst the Doms could throw at 'em just ta drop dead from fatigue. Or get took pris'ner," she added darkly.

"She's right, Lewis," Varaa said. "I know you want to cross the Río de Coatepec before making camp, to put it between us and pursuit, but it is easily crossed even without the bridge and will pose no real obstacle to the enemy. The Río de Purification gorge is where we will break contact."

"And that's where all our scouts are telling us the enemy lancers are headed," Lewis countered. "If they occupy it before we get there—"

"Let 'em try," Leonor interrupted defiantly. "Besides, not only is there little chance we'll get that far first, them tryin' ta beat us'll be good for us in the short term. It'll give the front of our column a break. Every outfit up there has been hammered. I'm still not sure why you had Colonel Reed move First Division up through the day. *Half* of 'em are gone, an' they were the last ones out of the city, for cryin' out loud."

"The last of our oldest comrades here are in the First," Lewis said. "Maybe a quick march while they could still manage it was the best way to get them as far as I could from the Doms behind us."

"I don't believe that," Leonor retorted. "But they're prob'ly safer for now. An' whether they get there first or not, the Doms ain't *takin'* the crossin' over the Purification River. My father's out there, remember? He's got almost all our mounted troops, the flyin' artillery, an' he knows what he's doin'. Trust him."

Lewis reached over and put his hand on her shoulder. She wasn't as far as usual since he was riding a short, narrow, "local" horse while Arete rested. Leonor, also riding a fresher mount, had stitched the wound in Arete's shoulder herself, after Varaa brought ointment from the harried healers.

"If there's one man I trust to do what he sets out to above anyone else in the army, it's Giles Anson," he assured before taking a long breath and letting it out. "Very well," he said, beckoning to a messenger. He'd been rejoined by those who survived the retreat from the city, and others had been appointed to him. "Go forward and inform Colonel Reed and Colonel Agon we shall be stopping for the night. Obviously, no marching camp is practical, so the First and Fourth Divisions will deploy across the road and to either side in battle formations, pickets to the front and plenty of men on watch." He gestured around. "Same here, and we'll need even more pickets on the flanks to protect the wounded from predators drawn to the smell of blood. We'll have a few guns unlimbered to stand watch as well. The farther we get from the city, the larger those predators are likely to be," he reminded, then added, "No tents. The lads'll just have to sleep on their arms." He looked around. "Corporal Willis?"

"Which I'm still here with you, sir," the man grumbled piously, "sittin' on blisters heaped up on piles 'tween my arse an' this iron-hard saddle, crosst the back o' this vicious beast."

"Good," said Leonor lightly. "You've conjured yer very own padding, then."

Willis glared at Lewis's wife.

Almost desperate for such humor, Lewis nearly barked a laugh, but managed to restrain himself. "Well done," he said simply instead. "Stay here with the supply wagons, and when they're settled, use who and what you need to get some hot food cooking. A lot of food. Beans, if nothing else. But you'll be in charge of making sure it gets distributed."

"That could take all night!" Willis complained. "Sir," he amended.

"It might, but you can't cook and distribute it all yourself. I'm sure you'll catch some sleep." Lewis gestured to the rear. "Now we'll go speak to Colonel Har-Kaaska and Colonel Itzam and contemplate how to arrange the rear guard."

By the time they collected Har-Kaaska and reached Colonel Itzam at the very rear of the column, Lewis almost changed his mind because the first regiments of the enemy could be seen, bearing torches and looking like a fiery serpent once again, just a few miles away. Unlike when they swept down on the city, this serpent wasn't endless, but it wouldn't be all the Dom army either. From the fact they'd delayed at all, Lewis predicted General Xacolotl was back in charge and brought only the freshest troops with him. More would come as they reassembled.

"It's a shame our men are so spent," Itzam said with regret.

Lewis nodded. "It is. I doubt that force is much larger than ours, and if we could hit them in column, on the march . . ." He sighed. "That won't happen, of course. As soon as our column contracts into its final position, we'll deploy Second and Third Divisions and all the rear-guard artillery into battle formations. No tents," he said again, "but we'd better have a trench and mound. Plenty of fires as well. Send parties to collect firewood and whatever you can for breastworks from the closest stand of timber. Do it quickly, before the enemy gets much closer. By the time they do, I want it to look like all four of our divisions are waiting for them."

"They'll be tired as well," Har-Kaaska said, nodding. "I doubt they will seek battle tonight."

"I'm not expecting it either," Lewis agreed. "But if Xacolotl is over there, we'll have a whole different fight on our hands."

"What do you think he'll do?" asked Varaa.

Lewis snorted. "No telling. If it was me, though, I wouldn't mount a full attack at all until my whole force was up and the enemy was trapped against the Purification River gorge." He looked at Leonor and smiled. "That's where our fight'll be, but *we* aren't going to be trapped."

They stood and watched the enemy approach for a considerable time. Eventually a number of musket flashes stabbed at the darkness when Dom scouts met 3rd Division's most distant pickets. A brief but fierce firefight resulted, but eventually the spreading campfires made it clear the enemy was stopping for the night as well.

Lewis cleared his throat after the long silence. "Get some rest," he told the rear-guard commanders. "We'll be moving again before first light. Once we're across it, we'll blow the bridge over the Río de Coatepec. I know it won't stop those people, but anything we do to inconvenience them is worth the effort."

"You need rest too," Leonor said. "C'mon. Maybe we can find a gun tarp to crawl under."

CHAPTER 34

MARCH 17, 1849

"An' why're we settin' up *here*, sir—if ye please?" asked Private Hahessy as Captain Barca sat on his horse in front of Hanny Cox's Number Two gun. Company after company of Rangers and dragoons, and other batteries of flying artillery, were streaming past on the Camino Sagrado and disappearing into the forest behind the unlimbering guns. Other dragoons and mounted riflemen were spreading out in the trees behind the clearing as if finding nearby camps for themselves.

Barca glanced back at the big Irishman. "Because Major Anson told me to place my battery here," he answered irritably, "and I told Lieutenant Cox, who told you to do it. That's why. That's how it works, Private."

Hahessy tilted his hat and scratched his forehead while "his" gun was unhitched and the horses pulled the limber back. "But why *here*," he persisted, "an' not across the bloody great chasm back behind us an' up on them cliffs where a buncha other big guns—which ain't even ours—are bein' emplaced, I hear? An' diggin' in they are, as well. While we're plunked down here, in the open." He waved to the sides, where the rest of Barca's guns, as well as Elijah Hudgens's battery, were making a long line in the tall grass growing up around platter-shaped stones. Even at this higher elevation, the sun that rose that morning with a strong south wind stood hot and bright above them and the horses and limbers were moving into the shade of that middling dense forest. It would've been a beautiful spot, high and scenic and sporadically wooded with a view of the glittering Lake Texcoco and brooding purple mountains far to the west, if it weren't so unseasonably warm and still rather uncomfortably humid.

Captain Barca turned his horse and sighed, tilting his own hat slightly back to expose the short, tight black curls over his dark forehead. He was reluctant to encourage Hahessy's impertinence, but the man's behavior was so improved from his previous, possibly murderous contempt for others that he'd rather cultivate a little familiarity than leave him feeling looked down upon. With recruits from everywhere, and especially those from around Gran Lago filling this "New American" army—as nearly everyone called it now—with troops of every shade, skin color caused less division than the branch trim they wore on their uniforms. But as one of very few old-world Black men in the army, and an officer now as well (there were more in Captain Holland's little navy), Barca remembered well the resentment prejudice could fuel. Besides, young Hanny had truly done wonders with the big, bitter Irishman, and he'd feel the first effects of a relapse. When he spoke again, he did so much louder, as if explaining the situation to all the crews of both batteries, more than a hundred men all told.

"We've been a little busy, dodging Dom lancers, and as far as we know they have no idea of the size of our mounted force or even where it is. They, on the other hand, thunder around like a shiny-brass-and-yellow herd of those giant, long-necked *serpientosas* and couldn't hide from our Ranger scouts if they tried. We've knocked off a few, nearly wiped out their damned Reaper Monk scouts, I'm told. But Major Anson has been hunting a place for a suitable reception for all or most of the rest at once." He paused. "Unfortunately, as you've all no doubt heard by now, the capital city of the Dominion fell to the enemy the night before last and our army has been forced to withdraw with the whole Dom army on its heels."

He managed a grin, hoping it didn't look as insincere as it felt. "That means all the Dom lancers will gather together and try to secure the Purification River bridge, to trap our army on this side. Sooo . . . we're setting up our little reception in a place we *know* the enemy will come. That makes it easier."

He smiled at Hanny, who'd been talking with Sergeant Dodd about something to do with the Number One gun. Then, with a glance at Hahessy, he continued. "We'll have support. The dragoons and riflemen who escorted us here if nothing else. But it's been pointed out to me that a number of guns are digging in on the cliffs on the other side of the river, which is *not* just over our shoulders, but about two miles back. That force includes most of Colonel Sira Periz's Fifth Division, which Colonel Cayce summoned forward from Texcoco some days back—as if he *knew* all this would happen." Barca shook his head. "You can think what you care to about that. But the Doms wouldn't ever just charge up at Fifth Division, especially with no way at it but a narrow stone bridge, so we're going to lead them to it by the nose and when we're finished with them, there won't be a Dom lancer left. Nothing'll stop Colonel Cayce from marching his whole army to safety." He nodded and urged his horse on. "Now . . . back to work."

Hanny hurried over to the Number Two gun, and Apo Tuin advanced from the limber as well. "My God, Hahessy," Hanny hissed. "It's one thing when it's just me and our section, but how many times have I told you not to pester the captain?"

"He's a good 'un, he is. An' sees the right o' tellin' the lads what's what, when reminded."

"Aye, but it ain't up tae *yew* tae do the remindin', now is it?" Preacher Mac groused. "Ye'll git us all on a punishment detail."

"Not with a fight a'comin'," denied Private Hoziki. Hanny looked at the often stoic "local" recruit with amusement. His English had acquired an accent that mixed Mac's and Hahessy's at times.

"That may be," retorted Apo, "but it might still get us a shitty detail *after* the fight."

"Mark me words," Hahessy declared. "The fight'll be shitty enough."

Preacher Mac nodded. "Aye, an' high-soundin' aims, like thrashin' Dom lancers, can't hide our true purpose o' clearin' the way an' holdin' it fer the army tae cross."

Hanny pursed his lips. "And the wounded," he added softly, with a glance at Apo. Both knew that Apo's sister Izel—Hanny's sweetheart—would never leave the wagons full of injured men. Their mutual concern that she might not have made it out of the city at all went unsaid.

Thundering hooves on the hard-paved road erupted from a copse of trees a few hundred yards to the front, heralding another long, thick column of Rangers, dragoons, and riflemen. Riders with nine-foot lances held upright were even visible still emerging from the trees when the column drew up at the gun line.

A bugler near the front sounded officer's call, and Barca and Captain Hudgens rode to meet it, near enough in front of Hanny's section, just to the right of the road, that he merely took a few steps closer. The other section chiefs came trotting up. No salutes were exchanged, but Hanny recognized the entire mounted command: Major Anson, Captain "Boogerbear" Beeryman, and Captain Felix Meder. He was surprised when Captains Sal Hernandez and Ramon Lara, the latter commanding their own lancers, came cantering up from farther down the column, accompanied by the big Holcano warrior Kisin, who'd been attached to Sira Periz. Even less expected was a pale, frail-looking Hans Joffrion, the dragoon officer who'd actually been captured and crucified by the Doms. He'd been barely alive when rescued, and Hanny never imagined he'd see him in the field again. Perhaps he couldn't walk very well or swing a saber with feet and hands that had been nailed to a cross, but he appeared to ride well enough.

"Good afternoon, gentlemen," Anson greeted the artillery officers with a smile. He gestured at the gun line. "Mighty intimidatin', clearin' the woods ta see a dozen guns pointin' down my throat." He nodded to the east. "A scree-covered slope goin' up on that side, an' another goin' down to the west. No place close by ta get around, so the Doms'll have to come right at you." He pointed at Hudgens's guns. "And you've got our lovely twelve pounders too."

"Bloody damned lancers won't like it at all when they get here, sir," Hudgens said, his British accent still strong. He smiled at Felix Meder. The two had been friends since they first came to this world, both of them privates back then. "You an' your riflemen'll all be stayin' with us, I trust?"

"Nearly all," confirmed Meder. "And a good many more dragoons."

"All very welcome," Barca said, then added a little hesitantly, "I understand there may be as many as seven thousand of the devils."

"Thereabouts," Anson confirmed. "But don't let that give you the squirts. We don't expect you to stop 'em cold," he added, as if reminding him. "Just chop 'em up an' whittle 'em down, but most important, *break* 'em up an' get 'em to chase you all mixed up in them trees." He waved toward the woods. "Our boys should be cuttin' trails for you to pull back on, an' we expect the Doms'll be as keen ta take your guns as you are ta save 'em." He leaned forward in his saddle. "Bring 'em to the river bridge in a mob, if you can, an' we'll smash 'em there."

The burly Holcano, wearing little more than a breechcloth and dragoon jacket, barked an unnerving laugh. "Finally, a proper fight for my warriors." He grinned and added cryptically, "And our friends."

Anson looked at him. "Your 'friends' are already in place? I ain't seen hide nor hair of 'em."

"They are ready," Kisin assured.

"Good."

Hudgens cleared his throat. "Who'll command here? I mean, obviously, Captain Barca and I will command our batteries, but who'll control the fight? Tell us when to pull back—and where to go?"

"I will," Anson said with finality.

Boogerbear was shaking his head. "Nope," he said, matter-of-factly. "You got more important shit to do." He nodded at Lara. "He's got his lancers, an' the dragoons at the bridge'll need Hans." He glanced at Joffrion, then looked back at Anson. He didn't need to say that anyone here might wind up afoot. "You an' Sal can handle all the Rangers yerselfs," he continued, "an' you'll be the one ta signal Sira Periz an' lead the attack ta save us." He crossed his arms over his massive chest. "That leaves me an' Felix."

"That leaves *me*, you big fool." Meder snorted.

"Nope," said Boogerbear again. "There needs to be two of us used to fightin' with artillery an' their support together, for when we get back in them woods. One man can't keep track o' *two* strung-out batteries an' the men fightin' ta cover 'em." He looked at Hudgens and Barca. "No offense, but you two'll be plenty busy just with yer guns."

Anson frowned, but nodded. Boogerbear had been his Ranger sergeant for so many years it was sometimes difficult to remember what a talented and successful officer he'd become. One of their best for this sort of thing. His "proper" military terminology might be limited, but so was Anson's. "Professional" Rangers and deadly fighters or not, neither had ever been regular army. "Damned if you don't make sense from time to time—no matter how nonsensical you sound," he finally said. "Just don't get your fool self killed." He arched a brow at Meder. "You either, son."

"How long do we have, sir?" Barca asked. "To prepare," he added.

Anson looked over his shoulder, a thoughtful expression on his face. "They may be an hour behind us. Maybe less, but not much more. I'd get somethin' ta eat if I was you." Spurring his horse, Colonel Fannin, forward, he waved to the artillerymen. "Good luck, boys. Give 'em hell an' we'll see you all at the bridge."

Hanny glanced at his friends on the gun. "I hope so," he said lowly. "I sure do hope so."

The column began to move, but Sal Hernandez, Ramon Lara, and even Kisin stayed a moment, moving closer to Boogerbear. Sal stuck out his hand. "Be careful, Oso Monstruo," he said with a grin.

Boogerbear grinned back and shook Sal's hand. "No fun in that, amigo," he said, in his usual low, mild voice.

"Nevertheless, do not waste yourself. We will need you," said the Mexican lancer and former enemy as he shook hands as well.

Kisin leaned forward to clasp forearms. "Pay no attention to them, my friend. Enjoy your fight!"

With that, they turned and rejoined the column. Lighting a cigar, Boogerbear looked back at the artillerymen. "Go hit the shade. Eat somethin' if ya want. Make sure yer familiar with the trails the dragoons're cuttin' back behind ya. Don't worry, Doms're off the road right now, to the west. We'll see 'em as they cross that low spot yonder, movin' up to it. An' Major Anson's right; they'll have to get on it to come at us. We'll have plenty o' warnin'."

It was somewhat less than an hour before they saw the first sign of the enemy and, as Boogerbear predicted, the long column approached the road before it disappeared behind the trees. And then there were the scouts, a squad of lancers that showed up in the road cut, several milling there while others bolted back to warn their comrades.

"Let's get the fellas ready," Boogerbear said. Most of the men had retired to the shade under the trees to the rear, but Felix Meder's bugler called them back. Gun's crews, already carrying implements, took their posts, and Meder's riflemen and dragoons fell in between the guns.

"What is that, Felix? 'Bout three hundred yards?" Boogerbear called.

"About that," Felix agreed.

"Any o' your boys make that shot?"

Felix snorted, then called out the names of four men while he drew the ramrod from under the barrel of his M1817 rifle and sat on the ground, using his rammer to hold the rifle steady as he aimed. Five mounted lancers were waiting in the road cut. "Call out your targets," Meder told his chosen men.

"Far left," said one. "Far right," said another.

"Second from the left."

"Second from the right."

"That leaves the middle one for me," Felix gently groused. "You fellas could've left me an easier one—he's half-blocked by the horse on his left." There were chuckles at that. "Somebody count it off." Felix's tone had changed to a soft, serious monotone as he concentrated on his rifle's sights and the target. One of his sergeants slowly counted to three. On the heartbeat when he would've said four, all five rifles cracked loudly, white smoke blossoming out to obscure the targets for several moments before the moist, sluggish breeze dragged it away. Two riderless horses were circling nervously while the rest were trotting off to the side. Only one of those had a rider, and he was slumped low in the saddle.

"Good shootin', Felix," said Boogerbear as the riflemen stood. "Too bad we don't have a few hundred more o' yer men."

"Thanks, but most men could do it, with practice." He held up his rifle. "What we need is about a thousand more of these."

Boogerbear nodded. "Yeah, well, we ain't gonna get 'em. Not till we have time ta improve the quality an' quantity of our manufacturin'. All them that might do that're either with the army or slavin' away convertin' an' improvin' captured Dom muskets. We'll get it done someday. Gotta win *this* fight, first."

Felix frowned. "I hate to break it to you, but I think we're in the middle of *losing* this one."

Boogerbear shook his head. "I don't know Colonel Cayce as well as some, but I wouldn't be so sure o' that."

"Permission to commence firing?" called Elijah Hudgens. He was senior to Barca and technically commanded all the artillery here.

Boogerbear blinked. "What at? All the Doms're off in them trees. Can't see 'em yet."

Hudgens smiled. "But we know they're on the road in the trees, and we know how deep the woods are. We have a fair amount of exploding case that won't be much good to us once the enemy emerges, but can make their time on that road in the forest a living hell."

Boogerbear's face lit up. "Well, sure, then. They already know we're here, I reckon, so let 'em have it." He glanced at Felix. "I hadn't thought o' that.

"Battalion, action front!" roared Hudgens, addressing both batteries. "Load case with fuses cut for four to seven hundred yards and target the tops of those trees accordingly! Lay them in above where you imagine the road should lie."

"Battery!" Barca yelled, then repeated Hudgens's order. The section chiefs of both batteries, including Hanny, did the same for the two guns under their direct command. The "dance of death" proceeded at the double as each individual gun's crew performed their elaborate preparations to load and fire their weapons, consciously or unconsciously racing the crews to either side.

"The good Lord says tae 'give tae them that ask ye,' an' them devils're just beggin' fer this—but they're gonna *hate* our little giftie when they get it!" Preacher Mac said as he placed a fixed round in the muzzle.

"Aye, Preacher," said Hahessy in a satisfied tone, ramming the load down the barrel. "Amen ta that." Finished, they stepped outside the wheels and took their places by the axle hubs. Neither man wore a saber, which all "flying" artillerymen were entitled to and plenty of which had been captured from lancers in the past. Instead, they and many other crew members that started as infantrymen had their "borrowed" muskets slung tightly across their backs. Even Hanny and Apo eschewed sabers—they had no training in their use—and wore muskets the same way. Barca allowed it since they'd never used them to the detriment of serving their guns. And besides, they'd needed them before.

"First section is ready!" Hanny cried, raising a fist—instead of the saber he didn't have. As usual, likely due to its greater experience, Hanny's section was prepared to fire somewhat faster than the rest. Moments later, however, the entire battalion was ready.

"Battalion!" Hudgens bellowed. "By the battalion . . . *Fire!*"

Twelve guns erupted as one, the roar of 12pdrs noticeably louder than 6pdrs, the shriek of shot bucking damp air unusually fierce. Moments later, the shells started crackling over the distant trees, the reports drifting back over several seconds, depending how their fuses were cut. Gratifyingly, the claps of bursting shells were accompanied by muffled screams and squeals of men and horses.

"Battalion," Hudgens shouted while his artillerymen serviced their pieces and heaved them back to the line they'd recoiled from, "reload and commence firing at discretion!" The first section—Hanny's—was quickly ready to fire again, and his two guns did so before any others, but then the thunder became almost continuous as all the artillerymen plied their grisly trade with a will.

"How much case shot do you have?" Boogerbear shouted at Hudgens.

"My battery has about five rounds for each gun in their limbers. More in the caissons, of course. I suspect Captain Barca is similarly supplied. Due to the nature of the combat we've faced here and unlike the 'old days back home,' the rest of our ready ammunition is roughly split between solid shot and canister."

"Figgered so," Boogerbear said, nodding forward through a momentary clear patch in the smoke that revealed Dom lancers pouring rapidly from the road cut and spreading out to either side. "'Bout time to switch to canister, I guess. It's good out to three hundred yards, right?"

"Roughly," Hudgens confirmed before turning to shout at his gunners. "Enemy in line in the open to the front! Load canister as convenient and commence rapid fire. Correct your ranges as appropriate."

The barrage of already loaded case shot quickly dwindled, the final flags of darker, pitch-fueled smoke over the forest replaced by the deeper boom and yellowish smoke that accompanied the swarming beehives of musket balls each gun began to spit. The few glimpses they got of the result were horrifying, even heartbreaking. Swathes of men and horses crashing and tumbling as they deployed, not yet even charging. And the loudest screams came from innocent animals that meant them no harm at all. Regardless of their losses, the Doms kept positioning themselves at the gallop, streaming out into thickening and lengthening lines, red pennants fluttering atop a growing crop of uplifted lances. A horn blast sounded, one they all now recognized as a preparatory call, and they knew this first formation, possibly the better part of one of the enemy's heavy regiments, would soon sweep forward. They'd have to. They were losing hundreds of men every moment they waited.

"Get ready, boys," Boogerbear shouted. "Don't neglect the flanks. Their line's longer than ours, an' they'll try ta swarm 'round us."

"Lieutenant Priddy, take your troop of dragoons to the right," ordered Meder. The Dom line was longer on that side, and all Priddy's men had Hall carbines.

"Sir," replied Priddy. "You heard the man, Sergeant. At the double!"

"Load and hold!" Hudgens bellowed at his artillerymen, and Boogerbear nodded approval. They were slaughtering the enemy, but it was impossible to tell how many were preparing to charge. Boogerbear estimated between eighteen and twenty-five hundred. Aside from the cannoneers, he had about seven hundred dismounted dragoons and riflemen to face them. And charge they would, almost at once, hoping to smash through his line. If they succeeded, all his men would die. It was possible some would survive the first assault. They might even destroy it in the melee that followed, but they'd be in no position to repel the second strike—which would be forming behind the first one, preparing to come at once.

Elijah Hudgens obviously understood that. His artillery might not directly kill quite as many by holding its fire, but by waiting until the enemy was coming at speed, the hammer blow of a dozen guns firing simultaneously could break the lancers' momentum and might shatter the charge entirely.

The gun line fell silent, except for the shouts of artillerymen urging one another to hurry. Barca and Hudgens were both yelling instructions at their section chiefs, whose gunners (including Hanny) might have to keep adjusting their elevation until just *before* the exact, right instant. If it came to that, they'd have to move swiftly to escape the deadly recoil of their pieces.

The enemy horns sounded again, the call to advance, and the first line of Dom lancers stepped off at a trot. As soon as the proper interval was achieved, the second rank followed, then the third. When all the enemy horsemen were moving under their fluttering pennants and ribbons, polished brass cuirasses and helmets and lance heads glittering under the afternoon sun, their formation almost geometrically rigid despite their losses, the horns sounded the charge. It was a stirring, terrifying display. Without hesitation and with the precision of some kind of terrible machine, all the long lances dropped down to the horizontal, seemingly aimed directly at whoever was watching, and the entire long block of horsemen surged forward.

"Hold!" bellowed Boogerbear, a reminder to everyone. Few things on any earth, even the huge, predatory beasts on this one, can be as intimidating as a remorseless line of dazzling lance heads backed by tons of thundering equine power. The urge to fire at once, almost uselessly in the case of those armed only with musketoons, was immense. There was, however, quite a flurry of audible farts, perhaps even other things. The nervous chuckles and half-hearted derision of comrades probably gave men heart.

Hudgens was gauging the speed of the enemy approach and shouted,

"Your range will be one hundred and fifty yards. Set your elevation and stand clear!"

"Thank God," Hanny said aloud, twisting his elevation screw about half a turn counterclockwise and scrambling out from behind the Number Two gun. The enemy would reach that distance in seconds. "Hurry up, Sergeant Dodd," he yelled at the gunner on the 6pdr to his right. He was hard to see over the riflemen and dragoons crouched on one knee between them.

"I'm clear, Lieutenant Cox!"

Hanny raised his fist. "First section is ready!"

Captain Hudgens peered hard to the front, then glanced at Boogerbear. "Time," he said urgently. Boogerbear nodded. "Battalion," Hudgens roared, voice cracking slightly, "*by* the battalion . . . Fire!"

Twelve guns bellowed with ear-pounding, face-slapping, gut-churning force, gushing smoke and jumping back, jangling and rumbling. The angry screech of hundreds of musket balls swept downrange, thumping and clattering as they struck flesh and armor. And here on this field, many projectiles grazed up off the flat rocks in the tall grass, still hitting targets on the bounce. Though the result was audible to everyone, only a few on the flanks actually saw what seemed like nearly every horse in the front Dom rank go down. They did so in a screaming tangle of breaking legs and necks, some quite literally cartwheeling as they crashed. Lances splintered, and men, often already riddled with bloody holes, were smashed or sent flying through the air. More bodies were smeared against the stones as horses rolled and slid over them. It was as if the Doms had run up on the teeth of God's iron comb, dropped from the sky, and very few managed to miss it.

Worse in a way was yet to come when the second rank crashed into the first. Some of those in it, and even in the third rank, had been struck by balls that missed the first, so there'd been some chaos already. More experienced or quicker-thinking men simply tossed their lances and immediately focused on controlling their mounts. A few were even successful. More of them tried to press on, to leap or avoid the calamity to their front. Most of these failed and added their bodies or their squealing, crippled mounts to the growing, dreadful barrier of flesh and bone. The third rank, however, pulled up mostly intact, milling momentarily as they sought cohesion and direction.

"Commence firing at discretion!" Hudgens called.

"Riflemen, dragoons . . . open fire," shouted Felix Meder. None of the cannon were reloaded yet, but the dragoons and riflemen instantly started shooting.

"They'll try ta flank us now," Boogerbear rumbled at Hudgens. "Start pullin' your guns back by sections."

Hudgens, thrilled by the obvious destruction and chaos he'd wrought, was confused by the order. "We smashed them, sir. I think we can hold!"

Boogerbear shook his head. "Nope. They dipped a toe in the river, an' we bit it off, but it was just a toe, son. We'll start back while we can, before they stomp us with both feet."

The guns had started barking again, joining the dismounted horse soldiers in decimating the third rank of lancers. Frowning, Hudgens called to Barca. "We'll have all the limbers back out of the woods, prepared to withdraw the guns by prolonge. Bugler? Sound the call."

Barca nodded. Retiring by prolonge was an unusual tactic whereby a gun was essentially roped to the limber instead of hitched directly to it so it might continue to be loaded and fired even while being drawn to the rear. Every crew practiced it, but Hanny's section might've been the only ones who'd done it in action before. "Limbers forward" had been sounded, and the horses and vehicles were thundering back to the line.

"You mean to use the prolonge on *all* the guns, sir?" Barca asked.

Hudgens blinked. "Of course. Why not?"

Boogerbear growled. "If you fellas're gonna *debate* this, you better hurry," he said, pointing beyond the wreckage of the first Dom lancer regiment. The second one was filling out swiftly, taking a few casualties of its own, but it was deploying considerably farther to the right. There wouldn't be much space between the defenders and the treacherous slope over there, but they *would* get around them if they didn't move quickly.

"You make my point, sir," Barca said, also gesturing at the lancers as he turned back to Hudgens. "The enemy will come at *my* side of the road. With respect, sir, I think it would be better if you simply withdraw. At least your twelve pounders. They might be our best weapons for this sort of thing—they throw twice as much canister—but they're also very heavy; their crews have never used the prolonge in action, let alone through a forest; and frankly I think they're too valuable to risk to capture. Join your six pounders to mine if you must, but hitch the bigger guns normally and send them straight back up the road. They can unlimber there and deny the easier path to the enemy. Once the Doms give up on that, the twelve pounders can proceed to the crossing." He paused, thinking fast. "They might be a godsend, covering us from there as we emerge from the forest."

"Well reasoned, Captain Barca," Hudgens reluctantly conceded. "We'll do as you suggest. But I'll stay by you with my six pounders."

Decision made, the two battery commanders separated to speak to their section chiefs. Even before the horses pulled the limbers near, gun's crews had unwound the prolonge ropes from carriage trails, threaded them through the lunettes, and were waiting to secure them to the limber pintles. Captain Meder was dispatching more dragoons to the right as the Dom lancers started that way, their ranks forming a column. They didn't have much time.

Boogerbear was the sole mounted officer at the moment and had the best view of the battlefield. He watched as the 12pdrs were limbered up and their crews climbed atop the lead horses and limber chests. Their section chief and several other crew members hopped on horses that two of their number led up from the rear. With a shout, the big guns lurched and were drawn groaning and clattering from the field, iron tires exploding flat rocks beneath them. Looking to the front, Boogerbear saw the death throes of the first lancer regiment. Wounded men and animals still staggered about, and mounds of screaming flesh continued to heave and roll while the crackle of rifles and Hall carbines picked off milling survivors. Heading to the right, the flanking regiment was picking up speed in spite of already taking fire from Barca's battery.

"Time ta go. Ever'body back," he shouted, wondering what the call for "retire by prolonge" might be. Either there wasn't one or the bugler didn't know it either, simply sounding the retreat. The men knew what to expect, however. As each gun fired, the chief of the piece shouted for the men on the lead horses to "drive on." Prolonge ropes stretched taut, briefly jerking the gun trails off the ground before the heavy weapons started to move. The rest of the crews followed on foot, ready to load again as soon as their guns came to rest. Neither crew in Hanny's section waited that long.

Even while moving, more loads of canister were taken from ammunition chests and carried to their respective Number Two men. With the gun rolling away from them, and the Number Ones, those men were able to insert and ram charges in relative safety—as long as the Three men risked life and limb trotting between the gun and limber to maintain pressure on the vents with their thumbstalls. This should prevent any lingering sparks from previous shots flaring and detonating the load being rammed, but if a Three man fell, he'd likely be crushed by a wheel. Boogerbear shook his head and said to himself, "Ballsy. But if we weren't in such a fix, I'd call that stupid as hell." He noted that Meder had all the riflemen and dragoons pulling back and he and the bugler and several messengers were briefly alone to the front while an increasing number of dismounted lancers behind the wall of corpses took it upon themselves to start shooting at them with musketoons. Balls began whizzing around them or kicking up grass clippings, gravel dust, and stone shards. "You look like yer sittin' on a anthill, Private," he told the bugler with a smile. After another glance at the flanking column, he added, "Reckon it's time we took ourselfs back ta the trees. How's that?"

"I'm willin' . . . if you insist, Cap'n," the bugler nervously replied. Barking a laugh and pulling his horse, Dodger, around, Boogerbear led them to the rear. At the woods, he called to some of the reserve dragoons, "You boys that's been cuttin' trails, make sure them artillerymen know where they are when they get here." He paused, looking around. "Not as many of ya as I expected."

A dragoon sergeant stepped up. "Most'a the lads're still at it, sir. Woods're pretty thick an' deep. Others are takin' ever'body's horses, seein' as how we'll be fightin' on foot." A predatory grin crossed his face. "Which them lancers'll have to do as well, an' they ain't gonna like it. Not as good at it as we are, sir."

"No," Boogerbear agreed, standing in his stirrups. Yet another heavy regiment of lancers was deploying out of the road cut in the distance. "But there's gonna be a lot of 'em."

CHAPTER 35

"Thumb that vent, god damn you!" Hahessy practically screamed at Hoziki as he rammed another charge down the bobbing, clanking barrel. "I heard it hiss, like a great fat snake! My oath, if me arm gets blown off at the shoulder, I'll beat ye ta death with it!" They'd already stopped once to fire and Hanny hadn't even stepped in to aim. The flanking Doms weren't charging, exactly, doubtless to avoid the disaster that consumed their comrades, but they were closing with haste. Hoziki could point the gun well enough with the handspike.

"Which I'm *tryin'*, damn you back!" the young "local" snapped. "I tripped. Nearly fell."

"Well, I hope I step in yer useless smushed guts if I hear that vent hiss again," Hahessy snarled.

"Leave off 'im, ye monstrous heathen," chastised Preacher Mac. "An' like as not, that vent's hot enou' tae cook 'is flesh through the thumbstall!"

"As long as I'm riskin' me precious parts ta his negligence, he can stop the vent wi' his bleedin' *tongue*, if he must," Hahessy groused. "Aye, an' we can trade places whenever ya like."

Mac shook his head. "I'll nae take the only task ye ever learned tae manage as well any goat."

"*Goats* now, is it?" Hahessy growled menacingly.

Mac nodded cheerfully. "Great, fat, awkward goats, tew, wi' backward, twisty horns, an' smellin' o'—"

"Section, halt!" cried Hanny, interrupting the banter. The mounted artillerymen pulled up the horses. "Wait till those fellows on the right are clear, then shift the trail left." That would point the gun right, where the Dom lancers were massing to drive between them and the woods like a wedge.

"Front's clear," shouted Hoziki, echoed quickly by Sergeant Dodd on the gun to their right.

"Shift them and prime!" Hanny yelled over a burst of carbine and rifle fire. Captain Barca's farthest-right section must've started loading in motion as well because they fired before Hanny's was ready. He watched, impatient, as Hoziki stood clear and Tani Fik tightened the lanyard. "Fire!"

Poom! Poom!

More Dom horses and riders went down. Captain Barca ran up behind them, hand on his saber scabbard. "Take your section all the way back to the trees this time," he said, pointing. "A party of dragoons will be waiting to show the way through. But linger long enough to give the Doms another good dose."

"Will our horses make it?" Hanny asked nervously. He had no desire to withdraw his section by hand.

"If you stay strictly on the trail the dragoons are clearing. They took their own horses that way."

"*Are* clearing or *have* cleared?" called Apo from where he stood by the limber.

"They'll finish by the time you reach those still working on it," Barca replied in a confident tone his expression didn't support.

"Yes, sir," Hanny said, then shouted back at Apo. "Reload canister and drive on—to the trees."

Once there, every gun managed at least two more "good doses," foiling the desperate flanking wedge, before they finally pulled back under the shade of the forest. The whole fight changed after that.

At first, it was almost quiet and the shooting all but stopped. The only direction in which the artillerymen could see more than thirty yards or so was straight back the way they came, and no targets appeared at once. Dragoons and riflemen, crashing through the woods off the trail between the guns in a ragged skirmish order, could see even less. Hanny didn't know whether Boogerbear or Meder was in charge of their detachment, even if it mattered, but somebody directed the dragoon and rifle NCOs to shift the bulk of their men closer to the guns so they could pop out on the trail in support if needed, leaving only a few of their number strung out to keep visual contact with the men supporting the next section over. That was the only way they could keep any semblance of a line on the twisty main path and avoid firing into friends.

The Doms apparently only paused long enough to dismount and secure their horses, perhaps regroup or reinforce. It wasn't long before they came after them, churning up the very trails the guns retreated by, even crashing through the thicker trees the dragoons attempted at first. Wild firing erupted as dragoons and riflemen engaged the larger groups from the flanks, and sharp, odd-sounding roars came from cannon now lost to Hanny's view. There was a constant crackle, separate from the gunfire, from projectiles smacking trees. The forest started filling with smoke.

"Gun Number Two, halt!" Hanny cried. The trail was rarely wide enough for both his guns to move or stop side by side, and as Number Two's gunner, he'd stay with it. He wished Captain Barca had joined them, but he'd gone with the "center" section of the battery. "Prime it, Hoziki!" he shouted, observing that the blackened muzzle of the gun was pointed near the center of a pack of Doms, yelling and shooting musketoons as they charged on foot. Lead balls were zipping around, cracking when they hit the gun carriage.

"Ready!" Hoziki squawked, stepping out from behind the wheels.

"Fire!"

Instantly, the mass of Doms vanished behind the belch of smoke and maelstrom of dead leaves and small branches the concussion blew into the air. Shrieks and cries accompanied the fading report.

"Drive on!" Hanny screamed. "Past the Number One gun, if you can. We'll leapfrog back."

"A moment!" cried Apo Tuin. "One of the horses is down. We're cutting him out of the traces!"

"Hurry!" Hanny shouted. "Load!" he added to his crew. Something wet sprayed across his face, blurring his vision red, and the Number Four man, Tani Fik, clutched his chest and dropped bonelessly to the ground. "No," murmured Hanny, starting to kneel.

"Nay," warned Mac, "ye'll do the puir, wee lad nae good. An' we'll nae avenge 'im if we're all cut doon as well."

Billy Randall had arrived with the next round of canister in his big leather haversack. He stared down at his dead friend while Mac came around the wheel and took the charge from him.

"You'll have to take his place," Hanny told Billy. Just then, the gun started moving, the trail digging into the soft, moist earth. For an instant, Hanny feared one of the wheels would crush the fallen youngster, but it rolled past without inflicting further injury on the corpse. Then the gun started rolling faster, and Mac and Hahessy were hard-pressed to load it.

"Thumb that vent!" Hahessy roared at Hoziki.

"I am!" the local cried. He was actually riding the carriage trail as he pressed down on the vent. Hanny was trotting now. They came up alongside Dodd's gun, barely clearing the axle hubs, and Dodd gave Hanny a grave nod. The two had never been friends, and Dodd, a professional artilleryman, had understandably resented being under the command of a "boy" from the infantry, but they worked well together, and there was respect. *Maybe if we both survive this . . .* Hanny began in his mind, but then shook his head. *No sense wondering about that.* Hardly an instant after Hanny's gun cleared Dodd's, the other weapon halted and blasted its own cloud of canister down the trail. It was met by another loud chorus of screams.

Hanny looked ahead. There was no place to switch back at once, he realized, and doing so too frequently was pointless anyway, as fast as both crews were loading. They'd trade places again when they could, more to share exposure to harm than to rest their crews. Dragoons were still in the woods to their sides, firing as fast as they could. *I just hope their fellows have finished the trail,* he thought. *We're slowing the pursuit, but we won't last two minutes if the road runs out.*

It didn't, and they were eventually met by filthy, sweating, exhausted dragoons who downed tools, retrieved weapons, and fell in with their fellows as they began emerging from the forest. They took cover together as best they could, still defending the guns as they clawed their way clear. A couple came out in pretty good shape, retaining most of their animals and crews. Two that emerged somewhat to the left were barely moving, each down to a single pair of straining animals with bloody men draped over them, the limber, even the gun. Hanny's section was between those extremes. Four horses remained hitched to his Number Two gun, but only three still pulled Number One. Both had only about half the crews and replacements they'd started with, but they could still fight. Sadly, Hanny would never know if he and Dodd could've been friends. The other gunner fell during a determined Dom rush that had Hanny's crew resorting to their small arms just as the end of the trees came in sight.

It was perhaps a miracle that any of them made it this far, but the most astonishing survivors of all might be Preacher Mac and Daniel Hahessy. They'd served their gun in the most exposed positions throughout the fight. Both were wounded and bloody, but so was nearly everyone else, and they still walked briskly by the gun. Hanny sighed deeply, feeling the ache in his side where a ball burned his flesh just under his ribs on the left. He shifted the musket, now slung on his shoulder, that was pressing on his wound. Raising his gaze, he looked around.

He recognized this place. Even more scenic in its way than the clearing where they first met the lancers, this was a broader, rockier plain, layered with thin, flat stones ranging in size from gravel to tabletop. Most were about the size of plates. Unlike their previous position, little grass had found its way up through the rocks. The same forest they'd passed through seemed to resume atop the high escarpment cliffs beyond the dizzying chasm a few hundred yards away, but only small clumps of strange, stunted trees thrived close around them.

Hanny had been awestruck the first time he viewed the Río de Purificación and the gorge it had slashed deep in the earth at the base of the escarpment over the eons. He didn't know how far below the river raced, sluicing out of the surrounding mountains to eventually pour into Lake Texcoco, but there was no crossing but the ancient stone bridge for a great distance in any direction. And the rearing cliffs, perhaps a hundred feet higher than the ground they now crossed, made it look like this side of the world had snapped off and dropped below them. Squinting sweat-gummy eyes, he saw horses and caissons crossing the bridge spanning the great crack in the earth about four hundred yards to his right front. More horses and both the 12pdrs had stopped near the small, rough-looking structure squatting to the side of the road on the near side, where the forest grew closer to the span.

His reverie was fractured by a resurgence of carbine fire directed into the woods. A gun fired into them as well. Captain Barca approached unsteadily on the teetering stones. "More horses and men are coming to aid the nearly disabled guns," he said somewhat breathlessly, pointing toward the bridge. "Direct your section to position itself to defend the crossing, if you please."

"Of course, sir. I have to report we're getting low on ammunition," Hanny warned, "and the caissons—"

"The caissons have already off-loaded men and ammunition," Barca assured. He paused. "It's possible we lost a couple of guns in the woods and Captain Hudgens hasn't emerged. I count only eight guns present, aside from the twelve pounders, of course." He frowned. "If Captain Hudgens is lost, you'll have to assume command of our battery while I try to get his back in action."

Hanny was shocked and began to protest. The other two section chiefs were senior. He quickly looked around and didn't see them right away. "Me, sir?" he asked.

"You, sir," Barca stressed. He glanced at the hardest-hit crews. "Mr. Hudgens's people have suffered the most, but there should be sufficient replacements. Now hurry along, Lieutenant. You've worked independently often enough. You know what to do, whether I'm with you or not." Without another word, he hurried toward the wreckage of Hudgens's battery.

Hanny took a deep breath and turned to Apo, who was offering his canteen. Hanny took a grateful gulp then said, "You're in charge of our section. Get it moving up to the bridge. I see Captain Beeryman there, still on his horse. He'll give you further instructions, no doubt."

Apo must've overheard at least part of the conversation with Barca. He blinked but nodded. "Where are you going, Hanny?"

The skinny young officer shifted the musket again and tilted his head toward the other four guns in their battery. Their crews were doing their best to sort themselves out, but many of the men were shocked and hurt, and even the most intact crew was having trouble getting organized. "To get them moving. Now go!"

Replacement artillerymen, many riding fresh horses, quickly gathered around, going to work at once. In some cases they actually roped fresh horses into mangled traces where others had been cut out of them. It was a near-run thing. No sooner had Hanny prodded and berated the rest of Barca's battery into motion across the rocks toward the bridge, and Barca finally got the most ravaged section with the worst-hurt crew moving as well, did the last dragoons and riflemen start pelting out of the woods like the hordes of Satan were chasing them. As far as those hurt and exhausted troopers were concerned, they were.

Hoarse-voiced NCOs shouted for them to fall in with their comrades and pull back in skirmish order, yet little order of any kind could be salvaged in the face of growing, withering fire from the denser throng of dismounted lancers emerging behind them. Once more the sunlight glared on burnished armor and bright yellow uniforms along a tree line, but this time they came with the flashing fire and smoke of their short-barreled musketoons. Worse, though they'd been effectively delayed in the forest, that allowed all of their regiments to join them. Now they poured out in their thousands.

Twin booming roars resounded from the 12pdrs by the bridge and a pair of case shot hissed overhead to explode above the enemy, scything down dozens, but Hanny noted little effect on the rest. Dom lancers were the pride of the enemy army, high-status sons of *patricios* who'd been mauled by Anson's mounted troops throughout their advance on the Holy City, and that day in particular. Now they thought their enemy was at bay, their own personal, mortal enemy: the American Rangers, dragoons, riflemen, and dreaded flying artillery. All seemed trapped before them, and they swarmed ahead with triumphant roars.

Riding one of the horses pulling 3rd Section's Number Five gun, Hanny caught sight of Captain Felix Meder shouting for his dragoons and riflemen to retreat. Even as his men turned and fled, Meder calmly raised his rifle, aimed, and took a deliberate shot. Nodding satisfaction, he started to turn as well.

"Captain Meder!" Hanny shouted. "Climb up behind me!"

Meder flashed a quick grin, gauging the speed of the four horses, limber, and gun. Each of the animals had at least one rider, and five men were on the limber, three on the chest and two on the footboards. "Don't mind if I do." Slinging his rifle over his shoulder, he grabbed Hanny's arm as the younger officer leaned over and offered it. Jumping and grabbing the back of the saddle with his other hand, he hauled himself up.

"That was exciting!" he exclaimed close to Hanny's left ear.

"More than I expected," Hanny confessed. "You nearly pulled me off!"

Meder laughed.

"You find this amusing?" Hanny shouted, incredulous.

"I do. Here come the Doms, swarming after my 'panicking' fellows to pounce upon our diminished, beleaguered remnants, baying for revenge while we clog the bridge in terror..."

"That's funny?" Hanny snarled.

"It will be... satisfying," Meder smugly replied. After a pause, he asked, "Where's Captain Hudgens? Those other guns are his, aren't they?"

Hanny waited while the horses clambered over a particularly noisy patch of stone, silently praying none would be injured by the uncertain ground. "He never came out of the woods," he finally replied, and Meder's grin vanished.

"Damn," he said softly, barely heard. "He wouldn't have wanted to miss this next bit," he added with anger mixed with sorrow.

Boogerbear was rapidly organizing a desperate, semicircular defense of the bridge, roughly two hundred yards wide by one hundred deep, with nothing but the bridge and the terrifying chasm at its back. Hanny directed the gun and crew he'd taken charge of through a gap awaiting them on the right, and Captain Barca brought the remnants of the other mauled battery clattering through, directing the crews to unlimber their pieces and place them in the space they'd just used. Riflemen and dragoons were still coming, gasping as they ran and diving in behind comrades already shooting at their pursuers.

"Take charge of our battery!" Barca cried at Hanny. "Over there," he added, pointing at the other side of the line, the right side of the defense. "As soon as our front is as clear as it can be of friends, start giving the enemy double loads of canister! That should cool their enthusiasm."

Hanny rushed over to "his" guns, dodging men dashing back and forth between limbers or loose ammunition chests. Other men were assisting wounded toward the bridge even while incoming fire, wild as it was at the moment, added to their number and the chaos. All the while, riflemen and dragoons, hopelessly intermixed, fired back at the shouting, raging Doms.

"Where the divil did Fifth Division go?" Hahessy's incensed voice met him as he neared the Number Two gun. "Thought it was diggin' in on the heights yonder, I did," he added, gesturing at the top of the wooded cliff roughly two hundred yards behind them, across the gorge.

"They're hidin', ye fool, fer the now," Mac guessed, but his tone was confident.

Hahessy turned to stare. "Hidin', are they? I don't see 'em. An' why should they do such a thing?"

"You're *not* that stupid, Hahessy," Hanny snapped impatiently, then proceeded to ignore the big Irishman. "Battery! Load double canister!" he roared.

Number Five and Seven men rushed from limbers or dismounted ammunition chests carrying their heavier loads in leather haversacks. The one serving the Number Five gun, just a boy really, cried out and sprawled on his face. Shot through the chest, he was dead before he hit the ground. The gunner pulled the haversack off him and held it open while the Number Two pulled the fixed charge and canister out, inserted it in the muzzle, then did the same with the second canister full of musket balls that the Number Six had cut loose from its powder bag. The replacement Number One man on what had been Dodd's gun crashed back in a spray of blood and fell over the axle, dropping his staff. Snatching it up, the Number Two rammed the load and stepped back to crouch by the wheel hub.

Grinding his teeth in the growing tension, waiting for all the guns to make ready, Hanny himself felt the increasing fire when the buttstock of the musket hanging by his side jerked violently back and a ball gouged off a spray of wood splinters.

"Number One is ready!" cried the gunner there.

"All guns ready," Apo urged, just as the pair of 12pdrs bellowed to the left again and canister seethed through the mob. The front ranks of the enemy charge were barely fifty paces away, the crackle and thump of small arms on both sides now a constant roar. Both the dismounted Doms and dragoons were dropping with a frightful regularity. Hanny could see the faces of the enemy, twisted with hate and terror, mouths wide, gasping for air or bawling curses. In moments, they'd be upon them.

"Battery, by the battery . . . Fire!" he almost shrieked, voice cracking. All six of his guns fired together with a deeper boom and more violent recoil that sent them rolling and clattering back over the stony ground. The sprays of projectiles they spat didn't have the usual range, but remained plenty lethal at this shorter distance, and there were twice as many of them. The whole leading edge of the enemy advance collapsed in a writhing, mangled, mewling heap, especially when Barca's scratch crews on what was left of Hudgens's guns joined the slaughter.

Yet it wasn't enough. Now that they could see them all on this side of the trees, it looked like there were more than the seven thousand lancers they'd anticipated. Worse, and utterly unexpected, a dense column of Dom infantry came double-timing up the road.

"Where the divil did *they* come from?" Hahessy shouted indignantly.

"Does it matter?" Mac replied.

"Aye, ta me it does. An' why didn't our Rangers an' dragoonies tell us about 'em, then?"

"We've heard the Doms ferried infantry across the water against the city," Apo speculated. "They must've carried more over here to join their mounted troops. But it *doesn't* matter. We still have to hold this crossing."

Hanny knew it was true, but he was less and less sure they could. *And speaking of Anson's Rangers . . . they couldn't have already crossed to safety . . . could they?* "Silence on the guns," he snapped, mostly at Hahessy, then raised his voice. "Reload double canister and fire at discretion! Keep it up as long as you can!" He doubted that would be long at all. The mindless Dom charges were tapering off, and the brutalized lancers were starting to use the macabre barricade of bodies for cover while the infantry—a heavy regiment, it appeared—began to deploy behind them. They'd add overwhelming mass to a final push. And in the meantime, the lancers were taking the opportunity to fire more carefully, taking an increasing toll from the gun's crews and the dragoons and riflemen screening them. The latter, in particular, were quickly dwindling.

"Let 'em have it, lads," called Felix Meder pacing behind the line. He'd slung his precious rifle and acquired a Hall carbine from a fallen trooper in favor of its higher rate of fire. Even as he stepped behind Hanny, he jacked the lever on the bottom of the weapon down, tilting the front of the breechblock up, before biting open a paper cartridge and pouring the powder and squeezing the ball into the exposed chamber. Pulling the lever firmly back in place, he cocked the hammer and fished a percussion cap out of one of the small front pockets of his jacket and fitted it on the nipple. Raising the weapon to his shoulder, he quickly fired before moving on, casually reloading again.

Gun Number Two belched more canister, quickly followed by Number Four. Soon, all ten remaining guns in the two batteries were smashing flesh together. Frustratingly, much of that "flesh" was already out of the fight. Hanny started to order his gunners to aim higher, to rain canister down beyond the horrific breastworks, but realized they already had. Still, since the defenders' wounded, and even dead, were being helped or dragged away by what looked like "local" civilian volunteers—*and where did they come from? 5th Division?*—they didn't even have bodies for cover.

"We have to pull back," Apo shouted at Hanny, standing right beside him. "We'll lose the guns if we don't."

"I know," Hanny yelled back, guts churning at the thought. Hanny feared losing his gun—*all* his guns, now that he was responsible for the whole battery—even more than dying. His Number Two gun would always be special, however. Just as much as joining the tight-knit crew that served it and gradually becoming a member of that odd, highly specialized and professional family had made a new man out of Hahessy, it had made Hanny the man he was as well. He felt like the better part of his personal identity was symbolized by that heavy, dangerous, demanding weapon he'd grown so good at employing, and it was unthinkable that the enemy might lay their filthy hands on it.

"We'll withdraw by recoil," he suddenly decided, "contracting the perimeter as we do. That'll help fill gaps in our supporting troopers as well." He raised his voice to a shout. "Don't push your guns back into battery after they fire. Shift them as necessary to maintain the line—adjust off the muzzles of your neighbors—but let your guns withdraw themselves!"

Captain Barca must've given a similar order because the whole defensive crescent began to tighten around the near side of the bridge. With their ever-dwindling numbers, there was nothing for it, really. That Hanny's superiors agreed with his assessment and the solution was quickly confirmed.

"Captain Barca's compliments," cried a ragged, blood-spattered messenger arriving on foot, left arm bound in a red-soaked sling. "Says we need to start gettin' the guns out," the messenger continued. "Outermost ones first, the others as they near the drop-off, an' as they can."

"My respects to Captain Barca," Hanny acknowledged, voice full of exhaustion. "We will comply." After the messenger left, Hanny turned to Apo. "I'm starting to wonder if Hahessy wasn't right. Where are Major Anson and the rest of our mounted troops? And I don't think it was just a rumor that Fifth Division is on the heights across the gorge. Why aren't they supporting us?"

"We remain a lure?" Apo suggested.

"Must be," Hanny agreed. "But how long? How many of us will they sacrifice for some scheme we don't even know about?" he added bitterly.

"I'm sure, whatever it is, it will be worth it," Apo defended loyally.

Hanny regarded him askance. "I hope so. I hope to God you're right."

The casualties they suffered began to diminish, the farther they withdrew from contact. Musketoons, particularly those carried by Dom lancers, were notoriously inaccurate, and only the sheer concentration of fire ensured that they continued to kill or wound any of the blocking force at all. The damage had already been done, however. Even as guns on the flanks began to be withdrawn toward the bridge by hand, men pulling them backward by the trail handles while others heaved on the spokes, barely enough men were left to crew guns still on the line. And these "crews" increasingly included dragoons and riflemen who could no longer employ their small arms.

"Dom infantry's movin' up, Lieutenant Hanny!" roared Preacher Mac, pointing to the front before taking another charge to insert in the gun.

Hanny squinted through the smoke. It was hard to tell at first since the yellowish tinge of the canister smoke was strikingly similar to the color of Dom uniforms. But the black facings and cuffs defined the human forms, and it looked like Mac was right. Long, serried ranks with upright Dom flags were indeed approaching with admirable discipline. Hanny heard a galloping horse skid to a clattering stop nearby and turned to see the hulking, bearded form of Captain Beeryman looming over him. One hand held a revolver as well as his reins, and the other was pressed hard against his side, blood soaking the wool around it. Even his horse had more than one bleeding hole in its coat. "That's it, boys," he said. "Yer a buncha famous heroes, but now it's time to spike yer guns an' run."

Hanny bridled. "I'll hear that from Captain Barca first," he objected, then, after a glance at his men, he shook his head firmly. "No, it doesn't matter. We're *not* leaving our guns!"

"Hear him, by God!" shouted Hahessy, voice strangely strained.

Boogerbear paused and stared at Hanny, oblivious to the musket balls *vipp*ing past. "Cap'n Barca's wounded. Pretty bad. He went back on one o' the twelve-pounder limbers. Had to practic'ly tie the spunky kid on it." He raised his gaze at the enemy. Fire from the Dom lancers was diminishing as they started to stir in preparation for being joined by the infantry. "Hell with it," he said. "I can't order that. Won't, anyway." He glared back at Hanny. "I *will* order you back, though, to the bridge. How you do it's up to you." He looked around. "Where's Cap'n Meder?"

"Here," said Felix, holding up the borrowed Hall carbine. He looked at Hanny. "Figure we'll keep doing what we can for these poor, misguided red stripes."

Boogerbear nodded. "Thought you might." With a respectful nod at Hanny and Felix, he turned his horse and urged it to the rear. Hanny gave the rifleman an appreciative smile, then raised his voice. "Battery! Loaded or not, it's time to go. Secure implements and prepare to move by hand to the rear!" He waited while men quickly positioned themselves, a few dragoons and riflemen still shooting, but most joining the gun's crews lifting the trails or hoisting heavy ammunition chests. With another glance at Felix, Hanny bellowed, "At the double time, march!"

Those who endured the next dreadful moments, the nightmare sprint across rough, loose, uneven stones while shooting at an overwhelming enemy or straining to heave or pull the remaining trio of one-ton cannon, would be haunted by the experience for the rest of their days. Those who survived it would. As soon as they made their break, the rest of the perimeter collapsed on itself, racing for the bridge that suddenly became hopelessly congested. And at that instant, the Doms were after them, roaring, cursing, wildly shooting. Hanny's guns, having inflicted the utmost horror and casualties upon the Dom lancers, weren't just hated above all other things at that moment, they were the closest and slowest. The lancers, reduced to a mob, focused their pursuit on them and came on like a ravening pack of wolf-lizards. First, they had to clear the heap of dead, however; a more difficult feat than they might've supposed. Arms and legs and entrails entangled them, shifting bodies brought them down, and wounded grabbed them, begging for assistance or the mercy of death. That brief delay was all that gave anyone the slightest chance.

Still, men who were fleeing or still fighting with Hanny fell with every heartbeat, it seemed, screaming or silent. The only words uttered by the survivors were breathless gasps of encouragement or panting curses when the numerous protruding irons on the guns or ammunition chests bruised thighs, calves, elbows, or knuckles as they wrestled with their burdens. Hanny had seized the left-side trail handle of "his" Number Two gun himself when Billy Randall's head erupted like an exploding melon and he dropped beneath the left wheel. Mac and those helping with the spokes had no choice but to roll the wheel right over the corpse. It was obvious they couldn't hurt him. But that left only Apo supporting the heavy trail until

Hanny joined him. The problem was, Hanny was a good bit taller than Apo, and he took more of the weight until Felix Meder replaced Apo, shifting his carbine to his left hand, grabbing the handle with his right.

"Now . . . I know . . . things are desperate," Hanny attempted to joke between gusts of breath.

"Shut up . . . Mr. Cox," Felix gasped back. "Just a bit . . . farther. We're . . . not going to lose this damned gun now!"

There were two 6pdrs in the battery ahead of them, holding their fire, and a tight knot of kneeling riflemen and dragoons who weren't. Other guns were beginning to fire, however, up on the ridge across the chasm. Some of 5th Division's artillery had finally been heaved forward to support them. Apparently afraid to risk hitting their own with canister, they were blasting solid shot into the mass of Doms, shredding great bloody trenches through tightly packed bodies. Glancing back as he labored, Hanny saw Preacher Mac fall, his leg simply dropping from under him.

"Someone . . ." he managed to shout before he was struck as well, just under the right collarbone.

"Shit!" Felix cursed as Hanny spun to the ground, leaving him with a wrenched back and suddenly supporting the trail on his own. "You fellows get Mr. Cox—and someone give me a hand!"

"I'm fine," Hanny croaked, scrabbling awkwardly to the side. He wasn't, of course, but something had loosed a fresh surge of strength within him, and he practically bounced to his feet. He noted with surprise that his whole right arm was virtually useless, but the terrible pain he expected was absent. Remembering Mac, he started to shout for someone to help him when he saw the tall Scotsman bellowing objections as he was hoisted and carried like a flour sack over the shoulder of the even bigger Hahessy. Turning, he observed the Number Two gun drawing even with the pair already in place, the other two passing around to the left. "Trail down, right there!" he shouted at Felix. "That gun is already loaded!"

"Then get your stupid self out from in front of it!" Apo screeched at him.

Hahessy was struggling past him with the groaning, grousing Mac amid the whir and warble of musket balls when Hanny heard a meaty *thwock* similar to the one that struck him a few moments before. Hahessy grunted and staggered, but churned determinedly forward, hobnailed shoes crunching the scree under his and Mac's considerable weight. Hanny joined Hahessy and they passed between the guns, all three of which then fired at once. The howling mob converging on the shrunken defense crashed to a shattered, mutilated halt, a bright red haze and flying debris composed of everything from gravel to wrecked weapons to body parts spraying skyward from the triple trip-hammer blows. Hanny worked his jaw, trying to clear the pressure in his ears as he turned to the front. "Reload!" he rasped, but then had to suppress an overwhelming urge to retch.

He'd seen a great many horrifying scenes in his short military life and probably caused the worst ones himself, but nothing he'd yet witnessed could equal the sheer awfulness of that point-blank discharge of a mere three guns with double loads of canister. Most of the Dom soldiers who'd made it less than a dozen paces distant weren't even recognizable as men anymore. All that remained was a smoky, quivering mound of what revoltingly resembled strawberry preserves festooned with shredded, bright yellow scraps of cloth. He heard others vomiting now, though whether it was due to the sight they beheld or their recent exertion, he didn't know.

And the dying wasn't finished. Even as scratch crews rushed to reload the guns and rifle and carbine fire resumed, the inertia of the charge behind that dreadful, mangled crescent trampled and crushed more victims still. It wouldn't matter in the end, not to Hanny and his friends. He was getting dizzy, starting to drift, even as he briefly wondered how many of his crew, his section, were left. Not many, he knew. Soon, there wouldn't be any. The bridge was still clogged with men and guns, and regardless of the growing support from across the river gorge and the bloody breakwater they'd built around the dwindling clot of defenders on this side, the enemy would eventually sweep the blockage away with sheer numbers and overwhelm them. Hanny's thoughts went to Izel. He hoped she was well and wished at least Apo could remain for her.

"Snap out of it, Hanny," shouted Felix, right in his face, tearing his shell jacket open and sending brass buttons flying. He quickly ripped Hanny's blood-soaked shirt as well, mashing a wadded-up part of his own torn shirt against the suddenly painful place on Hanny's upper right chest. "Captain Beeryman's down," Felix continued. "Or his horse is. I don't know. But we might be the last officers left over here. We *have* to hold a bit longer!"

Hanny blinked. "Why?" he murmured, barely audible over the tumult.

Felix shook him, a grin splitting his filthy, blood-spattered face. "After all we've been through, you don't want to miss the *fun* part, do you? It's *happening*, you fool. Can't you hear?"

"Fun part?" Hanny shook his head incredulously and worked his jaw again. "Hear what?" He did hear it, though, it just hadn't penetrated the gunsmoke around his mind. "Is that a bugle?"

"Yes! An honest bugle! Not one of those ridiculous, mooing Dom horns. And drums too! I didn't expect the drums. But you know what that means?"

Hanny coughed and winced. The pain was surging fast. "Infantry. *Our* infantry." His eyes widened. "My God! Colonel Cayce is here!"

"The guns are ready, Hanny!" Apo shouted, and Hanny turned to him. "It's your section, Apo. Carry on."

The short Uxmalo returned a single grim nod before bellowing at the top of his lungs, "Section! *By* the section . . . Fire!"

CHAPTER 36

The tinny notes of a bugle call blaring to the west preceded a growing thunder of hooves and a chorus of wild, feral cries rising from hundreds of throats.

"They waited long enough!" Leonor groused, standing in her stirrups to see beyond the Doms, hoping to glimpse the dwindling defense at the bridge. It couldn't be done. All they really had to tell them it remained active at all were the booming guns and billowing clouds of smoke.

"Coordinating this maneuver has been somewhat complicated," Varaa defended, blinking at Lewis. He sat stony-faced beside the road cut atop Arete once more while infantry streamed past in column at the double. Remnants of the 1st Uxmal were first, followed by the decimated 1st US and 3rd Pennsylvania under Major Ulrich, and an equally diminished pair of regiments under Agon's personal command.

Despite the rapid, weary march they'd endured to get here, the drums had commenced the long roll, and men poured swiftly into the open with bright muskets high on their shoulders with fixed bayonets. The daylight made them look like a glittering blue torrent, rushing in behind the rear ranks of the Dom infantry, the Stars and Stripes and regimental flags bravely streaming. The river of men turned green as Agon's troops brought up the rear, quickly dressing their lines. The presence of these hard-used formations had been the luck of the draw. Having been shifted to the front of the retreating column to relieve them from proximity to the pursuing Dom army, these veterans had been the only choice to take advantage of this situation. Leonor hated that they'd be exposed to further danger so soon, but couldn't have preferred anyone else.

"And we had to give those unexpected Dom foot soldiers time to deploy so we could come up behind them," Varaa continued.

"I know," Leonor snapped. "It's just . . . Boogerbear an' those poor fellas up there've had to hold a lot longer than we wanted. I'm sick o' us losin' good, brave men."

Varaa tilted her head at Lewis. "No more than he, I assure you."

"I know that too," Leonor exclaimed in frustration.

The thunder to the left gave way to a flurry of firing just before there was a tremendous crash, punctuated by the screams of men and horses. Varaa pointed. "They shouldn't have to hold much longer. Your father has struck!" Leonor could see it: Giles Anson's Rangers and dragoons, sabers slashing, musketoons blasting, followed Lara's lancers in carving their way deep into the left enemy flank.

Lewis suddenly jerked in the saddle as if shaken from a trance and urged Arete forward into a trot to parallel the deploying infantry. With a glance at each other, Leonor and Varaa followed, pursued by Lewis's staff and messengers. Lewis veered into a gap between the 3rd Pennsylvania and Agon's men and paused beside Major Ulrich's and Colonel Agon's mounts, looking first to one side then the other. These bloodied remains of five regiments might be roughly equal in numbers to the single Dom infantry regiment they were about to face. Combined with the dismounted lancers, the enemy would have a strong advantage if they weren't already disorganized by their current fight, assailed by surprise from the left, or had any expectation of being attacked from the rear. And yet another fearsome shock was about to strike.

Anson's bugle call, still sounding even now, was suddenly echoed by another from within the woods to the east, on the right. The forest crept closer to the bridge there than elsewhere and a great, decidedly unnerving roar accompanied the latter signal with a hair-raising noise that hadn't been heard on a battlefield for quite some time. Lewis's somber expression finally changed to a relieved, almost gleeful grin.

"There it is!" he exclaimed. "By God, I never thought I'd be relieved to hear that dreadful war cry again!" A messenger had come from Anson detailing his plan to detach "Captain" Kisin and all his former Holcanos in the Rangers to join with the elusive Grik "general" Soor and his semireptilian warriors. Soor hadn't retained many loyal Grik after so many were killed in battle, and those still with him had avoided associating too closely with the army that destroyed them. (They found army proscriptions against eating their enemies particularly tedious.) They'd continued to provide scouting intelligence to Kisin, but most never saw them, and they'd been virtually forgotten. Apparently, however, Soor's war band had grown somewhat, joined by local Grik who hated the Doms. Kisin had reported that Soor now had almost five hundred warriors who'd join the fight—as long as Lewis wasn't picky about their diet.

At that moment, loping right along with Kisin's mounted Holcanos, a horde of terrifying Grik, bristling with savage teeth and claws in addition to the weapons they carried, exploded into the Dom right flank, sweeping into the lancers who'd advanced almost to the very edge of the gorge. Wailing Doms were slashed or trampled, some even plummeting over the precipice as they recoiled from the apparent demons in horror. Kisin's troopers yipped and howled as they fired into faces and chests from mere feet or inches, and, shrieking and roaring, Soor's warriors hacked their way toward the survivors at the bridge.

"The artillery on the bluff has ceased firing, sir," Ulrich informed Lewis.

"Very well," Lewis replied. "We will advance."

NCOs and officers among the Dom infantry had heard the rumbling drums behind them, and now the change of beat and skirling fifes that signaled their enemy toward them. They shouted and shoved at their soldiers to turn their backs on the other unexpected calamities. It was a difficult chore. The Doms had been confident of victory, their meager foe trapped, the infantry unneeded and only advancing to crush any lingering hope. Now they were assailed from every direction at once, somehow surrounded by unknown numbers that fought with savage abandon. The flank attacks by themselves would've eventually spent themselves and been forced to retire or engage in a costly slugging match. The same would've happened to Lewis's infantry, most likely. Combined just so as they were, the moment that Boogerbear and Meder's force had sacrificed so much and so long for had come. At a range of about one hundred paces, with rushed and panicked musket fire starting to be directed at them, John Ulrich turned to Lewis. "With your permission, sir."

Leonor urged her horse alongside Arete and reached to grab Lewis's hand and squeeze. With a small smile at his wife, Lewis gestured at the former Dom officer and said, "With Colonel Reed commanding the column behind us, Colonel Agon is your direct superior."

"By all means, Major Ulrich," Agon said with a slight nod.

"Thank you, sir." Ulrich faced the front and bellowed, "Brigade, halt!" The command was echoed by officers and NCOs, and the drums went silent. The roar of battle swelled ahead as the long ranks of troops jostled to dress their formations at roughly sixty paces from the enemy. More sporadic fire came at them, and men began to scream and fall, but barely half the enemy had even turned to face them yet, their officers screaming to alert them to their peril. "Brigade!" Ulrich bellowed again. "I can't say to do this for your homes, for they are likely lost, but many of your wives and sweethearts are with the army or at Vera Cruz. The fiends to our front would either block their passage or stand between us and them. I call on you all to take up the torch our many lost comrades have passed, to open the way to preserve our people and the dream of liberty we've struggled to spread in this land. That ideal may have suffered a setback, but as long as we fight, as long as this army exists, the cause will never die." He paused. "Give them hell, boys, and let none of the whoresons escape!"

A huge, roaring cheer erupted, followed by more shouts of officers and NCOs. The first volley, unsurprisingly, came from the front rank of the 1st US, but it was followed almost instantly by Agon's regiments and the 3rd Pennsylvania and 1st Uxmal. The billowing white smoke hid the enemy entirely, but was already clearing by the time the second rank of each regiment added their fire. In moments, the crashing volleys were continuous.

"Look, Lewis," Varaa shouted in her friend's ear. He turned to glance behind them in time to see a constant stream of agitated horses pushing through the woods and being collected by clots of Ramon Lara's men. "Dom horses. Hundreds of them," Varaa continued. Lewis nodded. Sergeant Major McNabb had been given the task of capturing all the lancers' mounts on the other side of the forest. Apparently, they'd been successful.

"I hope they didn't miss a single one," Leonor said. "We'll always have an advantage as long as we're mounted an' the Doms ain't." Lewis looked back to the front. The smoke was so thick there was little to see, though despite the wall of moans and screams that swept back across him, there was also an increasing number of muzzle flashes. Hard as it had to be for them, the Doms were still fighting.

"We can only give them a few moments more," Lewis advised Agon. "Our flank attacks will be struggling by now."

Agon bowed his head. "You're right, of course." Raising his own voice, he shouted, "The Brigade will prepare to charge!"

The drums began thundering again, and the fifers took up the "Old 1812."

"Charge bayonets!" Ulrich roared, and another great, feral cheer resounded as the ranks of men surged forward, bayonet-tipped muskets leveled.

Lewis twisted his reins around his left hand and drew his saber with his right. Leonor grabbed his arm near the elbow. "Why?" she demanded. Never shy about joining a fight herself, when necessary, she simply didn't see it now. Especially when any officer on horseback in an infantry fight would draw a lot of attention. Still, she wasn't angry, just concerned about Lewis's current motivation.

Lewis began to reply, then shut his mouth.

"Because we must end this quickly, if we can," Varaa said impatiently, drawing her own sword. "*He* must," she added. "This whole campaign to win victory with defeat has scarred him deeply—that is *exactly* what it has been, you know—and he'd not be the man you came to love if he didn't finish it now."

"That makes no sense," Leonor objected. "An' how do we win by losin'? As for 'finishin'' it—"

Varaa cut her off, pointing her sword at the backs of the charging infantry. "All that aside, Lewis is a leader—a true 'warmaster,' like me—and the battle is there, not here. He can no longer influence its outcome from behind."

Ulrich looked disapproving, but drew his own sword. Agon did as well, with more relish. The whole entourage followed suit, with varying degrees of enthusiasm. Only Corporal Willis voiced his dissent with a single, dismal word: "Shit."

"Thank you, gentlemen," Lewis said. "There are close to thirty of us, combined. We'll hit them like a splitting maul and smash them in two." He nodded forward. "I'll see you all at the bridge." A thunderous crash and shrill of screams in the dense smoke heralded the impact of their infantry. With their own defiant shout, Lewis and his officers thundered into battle.

At first, they passed only the dead or dying, bloody forms on the rocky ground either frozen in death or writhing in misery. Next came the green backs of Agon's troops, who, heeding the shouts of their sergeants, battered open a gap for the horses. Then there was only the kaleidoscopic frenzy of desperate faces, stabbing and flashing blades, the orange flowers of muzzle blasts from musket or pistol, and the frantic toss of surging horse heads, teeth bared in fury, pain, or fear.

Arete killed more men than Lewis, almost joyfully smashing them to the ground as she bashed through the press, tramping on bodies with heavy, sharp hooves, striking out to break heads and chests. *Her* teeth were bared to tear flesh and crunch bones. Leonor's horse did its share, gamely riding men down as she shot others alongside her with her revolvers. But Leonor's animal, like others around it, was unnerved and confused by what it was doing and, like crossing a soft-bottom stream, labored onward only to get through with it. Arete was entirely different, enjoying herself immensely while she did what her nature demanded, like a warhorse out of myth.

And Lewis was the same, in a way. He'd finally unleashed himself, venting all the tension, loss, frustration, and fury he'd been stoically bearing over the last dreadful days, possibly weeks . . . *maybe even since the damned campaign started,* Leonor conceded Varaa's point. She watched as he parried a bayonet thrust with his saber, immediately turning the blade and slashing downward to split a man's head with a kind of *bok* sound. Wrenching the blade free, he combined the movement with a swipe across the side of another Dom's neck that resulted in a bright red fountain. Arete suddenly sidestepped to knock down a threat to the left with her hindquarter before casually stomping the soldier to death, midgallop, and Leonor didn't know whether Lewis directed the move or Arete did it on her own.

"Ain't she grand!" she breathed in admiration before shooting another Dom who was trying to reach Lewis from the left. The man's head jerked back when his eye exploded and he dropped out of sight. Her first revolver now empty, she drew the second. Varaa caught her attention then, lunging forward to her right and swinging her sword with a loud and disconcertingly cheerful keening sound. Varaa's blade was long and straight and perfect for stabbing, but also heavy and sharp enough to slash. The last third or so of the spine toward the tip was razor-sharp as well, just as lethal in a backswing. She knew how to use it too. Great sprays of blood seemed to rise around her in a cloud.

Major Ulrich was having trouble. Though always an aggressive infantryman, he'd never been a swordsman, and he and his horse had both taken wounds. At the moment, two Dom soldiers had ahold of him, trying to pull him down. Ironically, being on either side of him, they were largely canceling each other's efforts and even protecting him from the blows of others they barged through with their own flailing bodies. Ulrich was roaring like a bear and savagely bashing one on the head with the guard of his weapon. Just as the skull finally cracked and blood and brains arced up, Colonel Agon skewered the soldier on the opposite side. Ulrich gave him a grim, thankful nod and charged on.

And that's the way it went for what seemed an age but couldn't have been more than moments. Leonor had drawn her bowie sword and slashed with it when she could in order to reserve her final shots. Lewis even had one of his pistols in hand, using it as a club or to parry strikes. If he'd actually fired it, she never saw. It became increasingly difficult to know how many of their party remained. She'd seen some of them fall, but didn't know who, and the smoke was thickening again as they smashed through the shattered enemy infantry ahead of their own and entered the confusion of the dismounted lancers. Lancers still had their musketoons, easier to load in the press.

Agon's beautiful black horse screamed shrilly when a ball blasted deep in its barrel, but Ulrich urged his own bleeding mount to its side, and Agon jumped across as his animal reared and fell. Leonor felt a painful blow near the top of her shoulder, and the shoulder strap button gouged her cheek as it flew away. She even moaned when an officer caught her left leg with his saber, the edge slicing through her knee-high boot and cutting her calf. She expended a precious shot on him, firing down through his ornately decorated hat into the top of his head.

"Stop shootin', damn you. They're ours!" came a shout to the front. Leonor thought it was Boogerbear. Another familiar-voiced scream rose behind her, however, and she spun her terrified horse. Corporal Willis was right there, having doubtless kept close from the start. Even as she watched him flail wildly around at jabbing sabers and grasping hands with a borrowed saber of his own, his horse was going down. She didn't know if he'd screamed in pain or fear.

"Hold on, you fool," she bellowed, charging the half-dozen lancers trying to drag him from the saddle. Her own poor animal responded well, trampling men and tossing others aside until a musket ball slapped into its neck and smashed its spine. It exhaled a shriek and dropped straight down, allowing her to leap from its back before it rolled on its side. A Dom was on her at once, trying to keep her off-balance with an inverted musketoon while he drew his blade back to swing. His face was contorted by a rictus of rage. She barged directly at him, crashing painfully into his cuirass with her right elbow while driving her bowie sword up under his jaw. Blood flooded down her arm and across her face before he fell away, but her revolver dropped from her numbed right hand. Something struck her in the side of the head, sending her hat flying, and a saber slash seared across her back. Head spinning, vision reduced to a pair of small circles in a growing, blurry blackness, she gasped and staggered to a knee. She barely saw the blur of blue motion as Corporal Willis hurled himself at her attacker with another wild screech. Shots exploded around her, seemingly from all directions, and she expected to feel the fatal blow any instant. Instead, she heard her name. Looking up, she blinked away the gritty tears of pain filling her eyes, and her improved vision caught Lewis leaning down from Arete's back, hand extended. Her father, Sal Hernandez, and half a dozen Rangers had smashed a perimeter around her, firing outward with pistols and musketoons, the harsh barking of her father's massive Walker Colt revolvers dominating the reports.

"Take my hand, my love," Lewis shouted urgently. A bloodied Corporal Willis was being dragged aboard a saddle across the lap of one of the Rangers. Looking quickly around, Leonor saw her bloody Paterson lying on the rocks half under a body. Seizing the weapon, she reached for Lewis, and his strong hand wrapped her wrist and she felt herself hauled up on Arete's back behind his Ringgold saddle. "Hold on to me," Lewis said as he turned the big mare toward the bridge. In mere heartbeats, they'd broken into the bedraggled perimeter still guarding this end of the crossing, and she saw it was little more than a trio of silent guns where some of her father's Rangers and a few Holcanos and Grik had gathered to reinforce a handful of wounded artillerymen, dragoons, and riflemen, now using the guns as a breastwork of sorts. The frightening Grik gave her a start, as they always did, their teeth, claws, and weapons bloody, but many of them were wounded as well and they'd clearly been fighting as friends. Lewis turned Arete again and pointed at the battle.

"We've cracked them in two," he said with satisfaction, watching the infantry fill the space their charge had torn through the Doms. Now, men in green, for the most part, joined by the 1st Uxmal, were stabbing and shooting into this new central "flank," starting to drive the Doms west toward where the bulk of Kisin's force had drawn back and established a line in the trees. Ulrich was directing the rest of his detachment of 1st Division in a similar effort to push the rest of the force to the east—all while both kept their men churning toward the bridge.

"They're startin' ta break," Boogerbear mildly observed, moving to join them. "Thowin' their weapons away an' runnin'. How 'bout that?"

Lewis watched a few moments longer. There was no more fire directed at them, and the front was quickly clearing. Except for the bodies, of course. He finally nodded. "I think you're right, Mr. Beeryman." He pursed his lips at the big Ranger, still tightly holding his side. "Perhaps now you'll take a moment to let someone inspect your wound?"

Boogerbear nodded at Leonor. "Her too. Big cut across her back."

Lewis dismounted and helped his wife down. "I know, I saw," he said, expression flaring. His anger quickly fled, however. He hated everything the enemy stood for, but it was pointless to rage at an enemy, likely dead, who caused a wound in battle. He started to escort his wife to some healers who were tending many wounded. The bridge was largely clear of guns and caissons, etc., and that made room for one of 5th Division's fresh regiments and its personnel to cross. The infantry was just starting across, mostly men from Vera Cruz and Techolotla, looking very sharp and fresh and fine. The healers had clearly come first.

"You stay here," Boogerbear suggested, dismounting himself. The horse actually seemed to groan with relief. "There's still a battle on, Colonel. I'll take her."

Lewis hesitated, searching Leonor's face. She pushed him. "I'm fine anyway," she said. "Just a scratch, ain't it? Gettin' it looked at'll give me a chance to reload my pistols. Finish the fight, Lewis."

He nodded reluctantly before climbing back on his horse. "One of these days," he began, but she waved him away.

"I know. Now go."

By the time Lewis rejoined Anson and Sal and a very pale Hans Joffrion, the battle was indeed practically over. Clots of fierce fighting remained, particularly where Doms were in contact with Soor's Grik warriors, but hundreds had simply thrown down their weapons and stopped fighting, many sitting down on the ground. Some of these were killed as well, the battle madness raging in their foes. The infantry restrained themselves most rapidly and even the Rangers, rarely accustomed to taking prisoners, managed to control themselves more quickly than one might expect. Lewis had to send a messenger to stop the Holcanos, and another to insist they stop taking heads. He learned later that some of the Grik dragged a number of bodies away, but Soor's warriors had fought extra hard and suffered serious losses to be first to relieve Meder's and Boogerbear's few survivors. He chose not to make an issue of it.

Otherwise, about all that remained for him to do was detail what he discovered was the 4th Vera Cruz to take over the perimeter, take charge of prisoners, and get them and the American wounded back across the bridge. The rest of the army would arrive shortly, and they had to clear the crossing.

"C'mon, Preacher," Hanny Cox said to his Scottish friend. He gestured at Apo and Hoziki, the only other surviving members of his section not yet evacuated. "We'll help you up. Gotta get you across to Fifth Division's hospital section and get that ball out of your leg."

Preacher Mac was sitting against the wide stone entrance wall arranged like a funnel that narrowed onto the bridge where the wall became a low rail. Hahessy was sitting by him, chin on his chest like he was resting. The big Irishman wasn't resting, though. After carrying him to safety, he'd dropped Mac to the ground and arranged him as comfortably as he could. When Mac tried grudgingly to thank him, Hahessy waved it away and spoke his final words. "Ain't like it was a effort, ya damned eejit Scot. Best time o' me life, it was. Bein' a real artilleryman, part o' a fine gun's crew." He then sat down himself and quietly died from at least three mortal wounds through his chest that Mac hadn't noticed until he was gone.

Mac sighed and looked up, his filthy face streaked with dry tears. A harried healer had cut away his blood-crusted trouser leg and roughly bound his wound. "I hate tae leave 'im," he said softly.

"We've left enough of our boys already," Hanny sadly agreed, "but I know what you mean. I'll try to make sure they all get collected. I promise."

To everyone's surprise, Hoziki had tears in his eyes. "He was a good man," he murmured.

Apo looked at him. "No, he wasn't, not really. He was trying, though."

"And that's all that matters," Hanny added, his own voice turning rough. "He was trying to be a better man, a good artilleryman, maybe even a friend. I think he managed all three at the end."

"Aye," Mac agreed.

A short silence ensued, broken only by the moans of other wounded, the clatter of hooves on the rocky ground, and a last flurry of musket fire in the woods to the west. Finally, Apo cleared his throat, eyeing Hanny. "Well, Mac isn't the only one with a hole in him. Izel will kill me if you die."

"What about our gun?" Hoziki asked. "An' these other two? We can't leave them unattended." The wooden carriages of all the weapons were so riddled and splintered that it looked like they might collapse under the weight of the tubes.

"You got one limber left here, an' I already sent back for your others," said Boogerbear, striding over with Leonor beside him, as well as a battered-looking squad of infantrymen. Hanny focused on the Rangers at first. Both wore bandages around their torsos, but only Leonor had bothered to put her uniform jacket back on. The dark hair covering every inch of Boogerbear's skin, not to mention his great, bushy, blood-clotted beard, made him look more like a beast than a man. He dipped his head at Mac and Hanny. "Best you two ride 'em back with the guns."

"We'll make sure you get there," said one of the infantrymen with stripes on his sleeves.

Hanny stared for a moment before recognizing the face under the filth and blood spatter. "My God. First Sergeant Visser!" he exclaimed.

"Aye," said an equally bedraggled soldier beside him.

"Is that Private Rayley?" Mac managed as his friends helped him up.

"Corporal Rayley, now," the man corrected.

Hanny turned back to Visser. "I'm glad you made it, First Sergeant."

Visser took a long breath. "You as well. All of you. I told you once that you and your lads were still 'my boys,' regardless, and your guns would never be overrun as long as my company supported you." He waved around. "Well, we weren't here with you, but we came as fast as we could, right up the middle, after Colonel Cayce and his officers. Nearly didn't make it in time." He glanced at Hahessy. "Didn't for some, but I kept my word, by God."

Hanny clasped his hand and shook it. "Yes, you did, First Sergeant. You did."

"Aye, the First Sergeant's our very own *fée marraine*, he is," grunted Preacher Mac as the horses in front of the first limber approached and they started to move him aside.

Visser just blinked at him.

"It's French," Boogerbear, of all people, explained with a grin. "Means 'fairy godmother,' or some such."

CHAPTER 37

Another regiment of 5th Division, led by Sira Periz herself, came across to recover as many more wounded and dead as they could and build several great pyres to cremate the slain. There was simply no way to bury them all before the scavengers made it too dangerous to even try. Flames leaped high over the massive wooden platforms covered with bodies that had been constructed from deadfall and trees that were felled in the forest. The rest of the army began to arrive about an hour before dark, marching past the melancholy infernos close enough to feel the heat and smell cooking flesh. Many of the troops grimly saluted, but others were overwhelmed with emotion, so soon after their own desperate escape from the burning city. A few of these broke down in sorrow and delayed shock, comforted by their close companions. Others smoldered anew with a vengeful fury they hoped to vent quite shortly. Lewis Cayce's army had been cruelly diminished, but it certainly wasn't beaten.

Eventually, as night fell and the army continued past, the flames glared on lurid shapes slouching and scampering furtively among the corpses of Doms that had been moved some distance from the road by their own captured comrades. Fifth Division soldiers maintained a nervous guard against larger, more dangerous monsters, but aside from a few curious visits by flapping lizardbirds that drew a few ineffectual shots and irate bellowing by

NCOs, little else seemed inclined to meddle with the giant noisy serpent tramping along the road when there was plenty of carrion for all. The blood-dripping ambulances and wagons full of wounded had attracted bolder predators all along, hoping to snatch a morsel or two, but none of these were much larger than a man, and since a number of wounded remained armed, all such attempts that made it through the pickets and now the Fifth's security met a volley of musket fire in the face. Two such creatures were killed outright, and the rest were driven away.

It took several more hours for the whole battered army to pass the dwindling flames of the pyres and cross the ancient bridge. Scouts frequently reported that the pursuing Dom army was coming up close behind. Its commander must know by now that his blocking force had failed to trap them against the gorge, but aside from the near-continuous skirmishing, his vanguard made no effort to meaningfully engage.

"He knows he would lose whatever he rushed to deploy," Har-Kaaska said with assurance. He was giving his big, weird, wounded mount a rest, and this was the first time Leonor ever saw him on a horse. He'd hurried ahead to join a gathering of officers lingering by the road as the rear-guard regiments finally reached the bridge. Lewis was there (with Leonor, of course), as well as Colonel Reed, Sira Periz, Anson, Agon, Ulrich, Itzam, Joffrion, McNabb, Lara, and Sal Hernandez. Father Orno and Reverend Harkin had joined them, as had a disheveled Mistress Samantha, who sat her own horse beside Anson. A company of mounted Rangers stood by, as did Felix Meder and a handful of mounted riflemen. Don Hurac and his entourage were seeing to the needs of the refugees in his care. "It has been a hard march," Har-Kaaska allowed, "but my division is well recovered from our breakout fight."

"I am sure they are," Varaa commented, though her tone and blinking betrayed skepticism similar to Leonor's. She didn't doubt they'd fight, even make a fine account of themselves, but they weren't yet ready to. Of course, the enemy's vanguard would be just as tired. Kisin and a couple of his Holcano Rangers confirmed it when they galloped up.

"The Doms are stopping, making camp." He pointed at the trees behind. "Beyond that stretch of forest and the one beyond. We saw tents going up and campfires spreading." He grinned evilly. "They've halted just short of the carpet of dead we left for them to see and will have their own issues with feasting monsters in the night." Leonor looked around, but Meder and his men were probably the only ones present who'd actually killed some of those lancers. They'd lost more than half their dragoons and riflemen and nearly all of their two finest batteries that day, before the decisive part of the battle even began. At least the two guns lost in the woods had been retrieved, along with practically all the lancers' horses. She'd taken that news to Captain Barca herself and he'd been briefly cheered to hear it. Briefly. He blamed himself for all the men he'd lost, which was nonsense, but it was likely he'd end up losing an arm as well.

"So there won't be another fight. Tonight, at least," Reed said. He sounded relieved. And exhausted.

"No," Varaa agreed. "There will be no more fighting here at all unless the enemy general is a fool."

Agon looked at her curiously and Lewis explained, "We'll all be across the bridge tomorrow, our men who've seen hard fighting already on their way to Texcoco." He bowed his head at Sira Periz. "Fifth Division is well placed. It can easily hold the enemy back and prevent them from crossing the bridge if they try. A few days, at least. Using armabueys, it'll take them that long to bring up artillery, and that's the only way they can hurt us."

"Either way, they'll never get the bridge," Anson said with satisfaction. No one asked why they didn't just destroy the bridge now. All understood that it would remain as bait for as long as seemed practical.

Reverend Harkin yawned hugely, stifling it as best he could, then spoke. "In that case, since there appears to be no imminent action, I suggest we all get some much-needed rest."

"Perhaps a prayer is in order," said Father Orno, his tone very soft. "It might seem odd after the last few days, and particularly here on this bloodsoaked ground, but I believe we should give thanks for our salvation."

Harkin nodded a little uncomfortably. "Of course," he said with a glance at Lewis, as if expecting an objection. Lewis seemed to shake himself, emerging from inner thoughts, then nodded encouragingly at the one-armed parson.

"By all means," he said. "Most appropriate." He then added somewhat grimly, cryptically, "I think, all considered, that things have turned out better than we ever had any reason to expect."

"You think it is *over*, then?" Itzam asked incredulously.

Lewis shook his head. "No. I doubt it'll *ever* be over. Not in our lifetimes. But I also doubt we'll see fighting tomorrow." He nodded down the road toward the enemy. Clouds had moved in after dark, and their bottoms were lit by the fires of a mighty camp. "The enemy has pursued us with caution, perhaps even fear. Certainly respect. I expect we finally face a competent general. Perhaps even their General Xacolotl. Regardless how poorly and wastefully it was executed, whoever contrived the plan that ran us out of the Holy City—which it would have eventually, regardless—won't attack a fortified bluff across a deep gorge on a narrow bridge first thing in the morning."

"What do you think he'll do?" asked Leonor.

Lewis gazed at her fondly, thankfully. Then he smiled. "I expect he'll want to talk." He turned to Father Orno. "Now, I'd dearly love to have that prayer, if you please."

Lewis had been right about the enemy desiring a parley, although there was a strange battle of sorts before that could happen. Shortly after the morning drums, as the rising sun began to brighten the cold, clear, highland morning, a couple of Dom regiments, about six thousand men, marched into view, flags flying, and deployed at the edge of the far forest. The great pyre had burned down to blowing ashes but the battlefield of the day before still worked with carrion eaters of all shapes and sizes, raucously feeding on the thousands of enemy dead. After a long, deliberate pause to make it clear what they were doing, the enemy ranks began firing volleys far out of range of the defenders, advancing through the smoke with parade ground precision.

"Should I have my artillery commence firing?" Sira Periz inquired of Lewis. The battle-worn divisions and baggage and ambulance trains were already preparing to depart, but all their commanders had assembled to view the unfolding events of the morning, largely the same group that gathered the evening before, with a few additions.

Lewis held up a hand. "Not yet," he said, tone vaguely amused. "I don't think they're targeting us at the moment." That was fairly obvious. Swarms of lizardbirds exploded into the air, and other screeching monsters fell under the massed fire or scattered in terror. Even a couple of disconcertingly large predators, the sort that looked like huge walking mouths with long tails and often required artillery to kill or discourage, were sufficiently intimidated or discomforted by the mass of projectiles to roar indignantly and pace off the nightmare field. By the time the Dom infantry had advanced about half the distance to the bridge, all they shared the previous day's battleground with were the shredded remains of other Dom soldiers, many already stripped to white, gleaming bones.

"Jesus," Anson exclaimed. "*Those* are disciplined men. Standin' there 'mongst the skeletons o' their own comrades. The stink alone'd have half our boys pukin' out their guts."

"Someone is showing off, I think," agreed Colonel Reed.

Lewis nodded. "Making a point, certainly, but with at least one secondary motive." He pointed at a lone lancer cantering forward up the road beyond the infantry. He'd pierced a white cloth with his saber, and it fluttered in the sunlight as he held it aloft.

"Think I know that fella. Name's Teniente Juaris," Boogerbear said, drawing looks of surprise. He seemed much recovered, though with what was probably the only blue jacket big enough for him shot to pieces and soaked with blood, he was back to wearing a sky-blue vest and blousy red shirt. He chuckled at the expressions he saw. "Hell, there used to be *Comanches an' Mex'kin bandits* I knew well enough to talk to." He tilted his head at Anson, Leonor, and Sal. "We didn't always kill *ever-body* we met."

"Do you feel up to riding down and having a word with your acquaintance?" Lewis asked.

"Sure. C'mon, boy," Boogerbear said to Dodger, aiming his horse at a path that led down to the deeply sunken road cut. "Easy does it," he added mildly. "Reckon we're both a touch sore today." Lewis and the rest lost sight of him for a moment until he reappeared, confidently trotting his horse across the bridge. After what seemed like an amiable exchange with the Dom officer, Boogerbear returned.

"It was Juaris, sure enough," he reported to Lewis. "Their general, Xacolotl, kindly requests the 'honor' of a word or two with you, Colonel. Says he'll pull his troops back now the battlefield's as clear as he can make it, an' bring no more than eight fellas with him. Just officers, no guards. Plus Juaris again. Explicitly swore there'd be no Blood Priests this time. I got the impression the others're his division commanders or their deputies. Either way, a total o' ten. Asks that you limit yer party to that number."

"Interesting," Agon commented.

Lewis nodded and looked around as if choosing who should go.

"You can't seriously mean to accept," Don Hurac objected. He'd been among the first to join the gathering officers that morning, anxious to discover what the day would bring.

"He's got a point," Reed nodded. "Your last meeting didn't go very well," he added dryly.

"That's why *you* won't be going. Again." Lewis smiled. His gaze went to Don Hurac. "I *had* hoped the rightful Supreme Holiness of the Dominion would be willing."

Don Hurac seemed taken aback, but then straightened in his saddle. "Why... yes. Perhaps I shall."

Even Lewis was surprised by that quick reversal, but only dipped his bearded chin in acknowledgment.

"Who else?" Leonor pressed, tone somewhat menacing. She hadn't improved as much as Boogerbear. Even if she wore an entirely new uniform, it was plain that her back was in agony. Still, Lewis smiled at her. "You, of course. And your father."

"You can't go without me," Varaa proclaimed.

"Or me," insisted Sira Periz. "I have lost my home, my people's home, to those monsters and have not yet even properly confronted them."

"Of course," Lewis agreed, looking apologetically at Har-Kaaska, clearly anxious to go. "But the only other division commander I'll risk is Colonel Agon." He smiled at the former enemy who'd become a friend of sorts. "Not because he's expendable, but for the same reason I want Don Hurac. I hope to make them think." His eyes quested around. "Otherwise, we'll represent our other force branches with Sergeant Major McNabb and Hans Joffrion."

McNabb frowned. "Thank you, sir, but I'd recommend Captain Barca for the honor. He's damn sure earned it."

Lewis pursed his lips. "He absolutely has. Unfortunately, the healers were forced to remove his arm below the elbow last night. The bone was utterly smashed."

"What about Lieutenant Cox?"

A fond smile touched Lewis's lips. "*Brevet Captain* Cox was also wounded and is enjoying the jealous attention of a lovely young lady healer who's adamant he not exert himself."

"Or fight," Varaa supplemented. "If it comes to that," she added, noting Don Hurac's look of alarm.

Hans Joffrion cleared his throat. "For that reason alone, I must decline. Without a dedicated guard, you need as many as possible present who can defend you." He raised his gnarled hands, barely able to grasp his reins. "I would only be a liability."

Lewis smiled again. "Never, Hans. And I want you there."

LEWIS, LEONOR, VARAA, Anson, Don Hurac, Colonel Agon, Colonel Alcaldesa Sira Periz, Sergeant Major McNabb, Major Hans Joffrion, and Father Orno, who'd won a coin toss with Reverend Harkin, rode forward to meet General Xacolotl and his entourage, who, by then, were already waiting near the center of the ancient stone bridge. They were all dressed in their best, even the one Boogerbear identified as Teniente Juaris, in yellow-and-black uniforms embroidered with gold and silver and dripping lace, glistening black boots, and decorative black tricorns. Saber scabbards and hilts glistened brightly, and most had likely never been separated in anger.

All stood in stark contrast to the comparatively drab field uniforms Lewis and his companions wore. The wool had been brushed, brass buttons polished, and saber belts freshly whitened, but wheel hats had largely lost their shape, branch trim was faded and stained, and boots were scuffed and wrinkled beyond the ability of polish to hide. Sira's and Leonor's were the only uniforms that didn't show hard use, but both women's faces reflected the long campaign. Even the animals they rode were quite different. The Doms were all mounted on shiny black chargers with glittering tack that matched their riders. A few of Lewis's comrades rode the same, captured from the enemy, but most were atop the shorter, hardier "local" beasts with black and brown stripes. Some of those were veterans as well, crisscrossed with stitched, healing cuts. Lewis's big chestnut, Arete, probably wore the most of these, but she held her head high, and her eyes seemed to mirror the determination and contained violence that shone on Lewis's face.

Leonor's gaze drifted across the field of bones beyond the bridge to the Dom infantry that had, indeed, pulled back, then away to the east, where the snowy mountaintops towered high in the sky and the forest-rimmed gorge plunged down to the distant river, still lost in darkness. The bridge they all occupied seemed as insubstantial as a plank laid over a crack in the earth. It was a breathtaking sight.

General Xacolotl finally cleared his throat and broke the silence that had extended for some time. "We meet again, Colonel Cayce, and again you have impressed me with your accomplishments." He paused as if expecting

Lewis to return the compliment. When he didn't, he continued, quickly, almost perfunctorily, naming his officers. Lewis finally spoke to introduce those with him, merely reminding Xacolotl he'd already met Leonor and Varaa—he didn't care if the other Doms had—then proceeded to the others. "First, I'd like to present Colonel Sira Periz, commanding our Fifth Division. I'll enlighten you on the significance of that directly. She's also the Alcaldesa of Uxmal in the Yucatán. I'm sure you're aware of events down there and can understand she's highly motivated to destroy you. And this is Major Hans Joffrion of the 3rd Dragoons. He had the misfortune of being taken prisoner by your forces and was *crucified* before we could rescue him." He took a meaningful breath before continuing. "You may have heard of Colonel, formerly General Agon, who once commanded your 'Army of God in the South.' It was he who stalled your breakthrough at the west gate of the city." His voice took on a tone of satisfaction. "Beyond him is Sergeant Major James McNabb, acting chief of the artillery that has so . . . painfully inconvenienced you." He paused only slightly before adding, "And speaking of inconvenience, I'd like to present Major Giles Anson, chief of our mounted forces." He feigned a concerned expression. "I understand that his Rangers, riflemen, lancers, and flying artillerymen, along with Major Joffrion's dragoons, have caused you considerable grief." Noting a whispered "Los Diablos," and the bitter expressions that formed on some of the enemy, he gave his father-in-law a fond smile. "That's something he's excelled at since this war started."

Lastly, he waved Father Orno and Don Hurac forward. "These two men aren't soldiers, but could likely both destroy your army with just a few words. The first is Father Orno, who knows the whole story of the faith your own priests twist and pervert. The second, of course, is His Excellency Don Hurac, who even you must all regard as the rightful 'Supreme Holiness' of your Dominion."

There was a longer, clearly uncomfortable silence after that. Xacolotl broke it again, appearing to ignore everyone but Lewis. "Yes. Well. I hope you know that I was not responsible for the treachery that spoiled our last meeting, nor was I in command of my army during its foolish and costly assault on the Holy City." Lewis only nodded slightly in confirmation. "I am glad," Xacolotl said in apparent relief. "I would not have an opponent such as you, who could destroy half my army even in defeat, think I was that . . . incompetent."

Lewis let Arete take a step forward. "I never thought you were incompetent," Lewis said. "Your plan—I suspect it *was* yours, only accelerated by others—was sound. But whether you were in command or not, *assuming* that my army was defeated at the Holy City betrays a continuing lack of perceptiveness on your part."

Xacolotl blinked and leaned back in his saddle.

"Indeed," Lewis continued, gesturing at Don Hurac, "though we did bring the rightful Supreme Holiness there, in hopes your people and army would throw off the blight of the Blood Priests." He gestured then to Colonel Agon. "And I commanded *free men* who once shared your faith, yet fought as hard or harder against you than any others, to show you a better way. A way that makes better and more faithful soldiers unafraid of the bestial faith ruling yours..."

Lewis sighed. "If those things had worked, a lot of bloodshed could've been avoided. At least between us. And I was prepared to try them for that reason. But your belief that *we* were defeated reveals your greatest false assumption of all: that *I* ever marched on the Holy City to do anything other than draw your Gran Cruzada with certainty to a place of *my* choosing to wreck it, and leave it the crippled, demoralized husk it is now."

There were gasps, not all from the Doms.

"That's why you were always prepared to escape," Sira murmured.

"Never even *meant* to hold it," added McNabb.

"You never..." began Don Hurac and Father Orno at once.

"He *hoped*," Varaa told them in a scolding tone. "By the *Maker* he hoped."

"But 'hope' ain't a plan," Anson ground out.

"No," agreed Leonor, gazing at Lewis. Though Varaa and she had discussed this and she knew that others suspected, now was the first time Lewis openly admitted it and she felt her heart go out to him. No one had a stronger sense of honor, and she knew how devastating it must've been for him to mislead so many—with a mere hope that he surely must've shared—only to have it dashed. All that would remain in his heart now was that he'd deluded people he cared for, who trusted him, and he couldn't even apologize to so many. No doubt he'd dwell deeply on that as well. At present, however, his expression was firm.

Xacolotl managed a smile. "You also lost at least half of *your* army. What have you now? Perhaps fifteen thousand? A formidable force to be sure, but I now pursue you with ten times that number."

"*Thirty* thousand," snapped Sira Periz, which wasn't quite right, but close. "My fresh division is behind us, dug in on the bluffs above. Not one of your soldiers will cross this bridge alive."

Xacolotl paused again, contemplative, before gazing over his shoulder at the troops near the trees. At roughly four hundred paces, they were far enough back that it was difficult to make out individuals. He sighed and looked back at Lewis. "It would seem you believe you are prepared for anything, then. But perhaps I may yet provide one singular surprise." He glanced aside at Juaris. "I suppose this is as good a time as any."

Juaris nodded back. "No shoot!" he shouted in English at Anson, directly across from him, even as he whipped out his saber and spun in his saddle. Anson and Leonor both drew revolvers, cocking them as they rose. Lewis, Sira, McNabb, and Agon had their own sabers half out of their scabbards. No one charged or fired, however, because Lewis just managed to shout, "Hold!" when Juaris's blade slammed down at the junction of neck and shoulder on the officer just behind him. Blood sprayed like a fountain. Even more astonishing and just as sudden, three other of Xacolotl's officers turned on two more and they went down helplessly under the hacking blades and geysering blood.

Xacolotl never even turned to watch the slaughter. He merely controlled his jittery horse and calmly faced the leveled blades and muzzles of Lewis's party. When Juaris edged back up beside him, wiping his saber blade with a rag, Xacolotl glanced down and flecked at a drop of blood that somehow landed on his coat cuff. "My apologies," he said. "But you came to the point rather quicker than I anticipated and the time had come for absolute clarity between us. To achieve that, it was necessary to break with the expectations *those* officers cherished. They were not Blood Priests precisely, but were certainly in league with them. Don Frutos would never have allowed me an independent command without the supervision of such creatures. Not now." He grimaced. "I was sure of them because they were not known to me, yet were appointed by Don Frutos himself to replace some of my own handpicked division commanders who contrived to fall in the battle they didn't participate in." A strange expression crossed his face. "Now, tell me true, Colonel Cayce. I *did* finally surprise you, did I not?"

Lewis snorted. "You did. I never expected that."

"You promised 'no treachery' too, though," Anson said with a cautious grin, lowering the hammer on his monstrous revolver.

Xacolotl smiled rather vaguely. "Perhaps I should have specified that there would be no treachery directed at *you*. Regardless, now we can continue our visit more amiably. Certainly more candidly."

"I am *quite* confused," Don Hurac exclaimed, exhaling a breath he'd probably been holding.

Xacolotl bowed low in his saddle. "Then let me explain, Your Supreme Holiness."

"I think he just did," Leonor said aside to Lewis.

"Perhaps so," Xacolotl confessed, surprising them all again merely by responding to a woman. "I hope you will take this action as evidence that I consider *our* conflict at an end. Let me be clear, however; I do not mean to join you, nor will I lead an insurrection against Don Frutos. At least not overtly and not at once. The army behind me is all I will ever have, and I can only count on roughly half of it to support me at present." He glanced at Don Hurac. "Support *you*. An open break with Don Frutos right now might only result in that half and the other slaughtering each other. Moreover, in the long term, Don Frutos can still draw on forces from the west." He looked at Lewis. "I must, therefore, continue to *appear* to oppose you."

"But . . ." Don Hurac blurted, pleading, "Let *me* speak to your army! We can all turn around and retake the Holy City! All can still be made right!"

Xacolotl shook his head. "The Holy City is lost forever, to any of us. What's more, so is the country around it, all the way to the Californias. Tranquilo and then Don Frutos and his minions have seen to that. The land is laid waste, depopulated. Dead. Further fighting over it is gratuitous and pointless. Worse, from my perspective, *my* army is already dead to Don Frutos. He can't even *feed* it for long, nor does he plan to. He wants it to destroy you, of course, but is perfectly content for you to destroy it—and me— as well."

Don Hurac was almost spluttering now. "But . . . but . . . if Don Frutos has ravaged the country and has no intention of saving it, even for himself, what could his aim possibly be? What will he *rule*? *Where* will he do it?"

"His aim is quite simple: Complete, perfect power, not even subject to God because *he* will be the ultimate agent of God's will. He uses the Blood

Priests to gain it, but even they will have to scramble for whatever crumbs he drops. As to what and where, he cannot let any not fully devoted to him who have felt or witnessed this war survive. That would sow doubt in his... semidivinity. Only a small step beyond the norm in the Dominion," he reminded Don Hurac, who had to nod in agreement. "That essentially leaves only the western coastal cities that can be preserved, but a degree of conservatism might resist his 'reforms' even there. He will have nothing if he scours those places, so I suspect he will simply use them and leave them. The future of the Dominion has always been in the south, around and beyond the Pass of Fire. Don Frutos will shape his new empire there."

He sighed, looking at Agon. "I understand that your first campaign against Colonel Cayce was directed—poorly—by Don Frutos. You knew him, so I cannot speak for you, but I fear the rest of us all rather badly underestimated him."

Agon was nodding, thoughtfully, grimly.

"I certainly did," Don Hurac confessed. "I knew him. Well, I thought. I knew he was ruthless and ambitious, but believed him incompetent."

"As did I," said Agon.

"I as well, when Tranquilo sent him to me," said Xacolotl. "Though he well concealed his ruthlessness. I considered him a fool. And he obviously deluded Tranquilo." He shuddered. "Of course, Tranquilo was quite insane."

"*He* started all this in motion, long ago, and Don Frutos has stolen the outcome," Father Orno murmured gravely.

Anson was glaring at Xacolotl. "And you won't join us to stop it," he said levelly.

Xacolotl shook his head. "You do not understand. It *cannot* be stopped! Even if my army survived the inevitable internal strife, can *you* support *both* our armies in a monstrous civil war in the west, against the most populous region of the Dominion? On the other side of the *continent*?"

Don Hurac and Father Orno both looked down.

"Logistics alone would be impossible," Varaa said dismally.

"So... we all just quit and go home?" snapped Sira Periz. "*I* cannot go home." She glared at Xacolotl. "Uxmal has been taken."

The Dom general actually looked somewhat apologetic. "I am sorry for that. The only consolation I can offer is that there can be little further support for our forces in the Yucatán either. They will have to consolidate their gains and perhaps even take a defensive stance for a while. Ultimately, however, if I am right about Don Frutos's plans, the Yucatán will eventually endure constant war until it is pacified."

"Knowledge of wars like ours cannot be allowed," Agon said bitterly, sarcastically, "but wars of conquest for the glory of God are encouraged."

Xacolotl nodded.

Frowning, Lewis nodded as well. "So, what do you suggest?" he asked, gesturing at the bodies. "You say our fight is over, so I'll make an assumption now that you have a plan."

Xacolotl straightened. "I do. Part of one. I am sure we will need to confer again, at some point. But for the present, we will soon part as if our meeting has ended in violence. Teniente Juaris will accompany you. He helped formulate my plan and can answer any immediate questions you are bound to have. I shall sadly be forced to inform his strikingly devoted mounted force—the last I have, it seems—that he was struck down in the same, ah, confrontation that claimed these other ... gentlemen." He waved a hand distastefully at the corpses. "In summary, once we are all quite clear, you will detonate the charges I am sure your engineers have emplaced to thoroughly destroy this bridge."

Varaa actually *kakked* a chuckle and nudged Lewis in the ribs. Leonor smirked. Lewis just shrugged. "I never really thought you'd fall for it," he defended to Xacolotl. "And the bridge has to go, regardless."

"Of course," Xacolotl agreed, eyes straying. "A pity, actually. Like many great structures throughout this land, this bridge was ancient long before there was such a thing as the Dominion." He looked back at Lewis. "With no way across, a battle here is pointless and I will be forced to make the long, rough march down to Lake Texcoco and cross the river on barges. They will first have to be floated over from around the city or constructed anew. That will take many tedious days. Not enough for you to fall all the way back to Vera Cruz, but you will have a good start. Well beyond Puebla, I am sure. I shall pursue you relentlessly," he added loftily.

"What then?" Lewis asked, keeping a noncommittal, skeptical tone.

"Then you abandon Vera Cruz by sea, more or less at your leisure, while I lay siege to it. I say 'at your leisure,' but that is assuming I am supplied. If not, we will have to make some covert arrangements." His expression hardened, and he looked Lewis in the eye. "My 'cause' is now similar to yours, I suspect. The survival of my army. I won't let it starve."

"Why should we surrender Vera Cruz?" Varaa asked. "More fresh troops await us there, and the works are impressive." She blinked at Xacolotl. "You can't take it from us."

Though some of his officers grumbled, the Dom general surprised them yet again by speaking directly to Varaa rather than pretending he couldn't hear the voice of a demon animal.

"I will concede that is possible, yet it is but a single city. You couldn't possibly hold Techolotla as well. Not for long. And eventually, every *single* other coastal city that might be touched by your corrosive presence will be ravaged as well. Don Frutos could never let you rest there, making a nuisance of yourselves. He *would* reinforce me then, and harry you from the sea as well. You could not grow crops and certainly could not trade. You would live with endless war under constant siege."

Lewis grunted, and Leonor looked at him. "Avoidin' that was our whole reason for takin' the war to the Doms in the first place," she said.

"We might as well have just stayed home and defended my city in the Yucatán," Sira agreed with her.

"You're asking that I accept defeat after all," Lewis accused. "I won't. Not while any chance remains. Too many people, civilians, have placed their trust in this army to save them, and too many men have died to do it. I won't stand here and calmly concede we've lost."

Xacolotl actually chuckled. "Why should you? In a way, you've actually won. But if saving your people and your army truly is your primary objective, you have to leave Vera Cruz to complete your victory."

"Where would you have us go, then?" asked Hans. "Where there won't be 'perpetual warfare.'"

"North," Xacolotl promptly replied. "The far north. You might even 'liberate' some of our more distant outposts near the Great River. You know of it?"

Lewis and Anson exchanged glances. "If you mean the Rio Grande, yeah, we know it," Anson said. "We know Comanches too, which we've heard are up there on this world too."

"They are," Xacolotl conceded, "the very reason no Dominion troops will ever chase you past it. The land is vast and fertile, but far. Even farther from the direction Don Frutos means to advance the Dominion. And unlike the Imperials in the Californias that the Gran Cruzada was built to eject, more as a matter of religious principle than for the land, the Comanches cannot be driven out." He glanced at Anson. "They are too much like you and we have never had a peaceful meeting with them."

"Us neither, most often," Anson mused. "But maybe it'll make a difference *when* they came here—an' that we don't get along with Doms."

"That was my thinking, and I hope it is so," said Xacolotl. "I have no doubt that you could ultimately defeat them." He frowned. "At least make them *respect* you like they never have our lancers. You might even make peace because both of you would have a strong incentive. Our few expeditions simply left them with it." He took a deep breath and sighed, looking back at Lewis. "If that is what you choose to attempt, I wish you the best of fortune because whatever haven you manage to establish there may be the only place I and others may ultimately escape ourselves."

Shortly after the two parties split, whooping and hollering and shooting as they galloped away from each other, the great bridge over the river chasm vomited fire and smoke and shattered shards of stone. The roar of the blast echoed repeatedly off the mountains, close and far, and seemed to rumble down the crack in the earth all the way to the distant, shimmering lake. The crash of falling stones echoed down in the gorge as well, and the sound went on for a surprising length of time. When the smoke and rock dust finally cleared, all that remained of the bridge were the massive foundations for the arches that were anchored in the living rock itself. Scouts from both sides inspected the ruined crossing, and they exchanged a few hopeless shots. Convinced the bridge was utterly destroyed, Xacolotl's army turned around and marched back toward its camp. Sira Periz's 5th Division started striking tents, limbering guns, hitching wagons, and before midday, it was on the march.

Varaa was strangely excited, almost prattling about the prospects of a new adventure in an unknown land and the possibility of establishing the republic Lewis craved without the trouble of repairing the Dominion first. Leonor was less enthusiastic, contemplating Comanches, but when her father, now rejoined by Samantha as they rode with Sira and various other senior officers, seemed somewhat philosophical about it, commenting, "Boogerbear and Sal speak their lingo pretty well, an' if I can make friends with Ramon Lara, Colonel Agon, even that weird Holcano, Kisin, who knows what'll happen," she started wondering if it was possible herself. Warlike as they were, Comanches were certainly more rational than Holcanos, and the ones she remembered never ate anybody.

Dr. Newlin, who'd come up with Sira, joined Samantha in contemplating the logistics of such a move, discussing possible places to go and how to move their army and all their thousands of civilians who'd want to go, not to mention as much of their industrial base they'd established at Vera Cruz as they could. Almost everyone was talking about embarking on a real future, some rather darkly, but most with actual eagerness, as if the decision to enact Xacolotl's plan had already been made. Even the army had seemed to catch the mood, breaking into cheerful song as the drums rattled and the fifes squeaked loudly. It was then that she noticed Lewis's unhappy expression and that Sira Periz, Don Hurac, and Father Orno looked particularly grim as they spoke softly with Reverend Harkin and Colonel Itzam. Leonor soon discovered that her guess regarding the reason for their distress was only partially correct when Sira cleared her throat and spoke to Lewis.

"You know it is the best solution," she told him. "The only one that offers the possibility of sufficient seclusion from the Dominion to promise a chance for peace. A chance to grow a new nation that may one day pose a realistic threat to it."

"I know," Lewis said, then hesitated. "But you won't be coming."

"No," Sira said. "Many of my people and other Yucatános will share that chance with you, but too many remain trapped by the Doms, at Itzincab and elsewhere. They will not surrender, and I must help them resist the invader."

"We'll help you," Lewis told her, and Sira smiled at him.

"I know. After the great exodus from Vera Cruz, which I am sure will take many trips by all of Captain Holland's ships, he will carry me and a volunteer force down to the Yucatán. We will organize further evacuations, help those who wish to continue fighting, and *you* will keep us supplied with weapons and ammunition." She was still smiling, but it wasn't a request. Lewis knew it and simply replied, "Of course. I'm thinking of joining you, in fact."

"Whoa," said Anson, "that won't work." He tossed a glance at Samantha. "I'm kinda thinkin' the same myself, only goin' down by land. Just me an' Lara, maybe that devil Kisin, an' a couple o' companies of Ocelomeh an' Holcano Rangers. You'll need Sal an' Boogerbear or I'd take them. Go a'rangerin' again one more time, like the old days." He grinned and looked again at his wife, who seemed ready to explode. "Just for a while," he assured.

"To see how things shake out." He shrugged. "We'll *need* to know." He turned a glare at Lewis. "But you gotta hold things together an' *keep workin' ta make a safe place for my wife an' daughter, damn you.* Even if Boogerbear can make friends with Comanches, we don't know what's past 'em. You might have to fight somebody else a war up there."

Sira and Father Orno were frowning and nodding, Reverend Harkin grumbling. "Don't be absurd, Colonel Cayce," he said. "The effort in the north will need you more, and if it does not succeed, Alcaldesa Periz's quest must also fail."

Leonor had been scowling at her father, as much for implying she needed protection as anything, but he was right about their need for intelligence. Who knew how long such a trek would take him, though.

"You must go without me, Major Anson," said Kisin. He'd been riding alongside them in the shade of the overhead trees near the edge of the road. "I must now think of my people as well. General Soor has already left us with what remains of his. I expect he means to hide them. As much from the Doms as other tribes. You will remember that his talent for making them cooperate is rare." He looked at Varaa and Har-Kaaska, the latter now riding his strange bipedal mount once more. In their capacity as leaders of the Ocelomeh, they'd been his bitterest enemies for most of his life. Now they were comrades, if not friends. Finally, he looked at Lewis. "My people were once as insular as Soor's, the different tribes just as contentious. That is how you crushed us." He shook his head. "I would not see that again. This time we have spent as part of your army, as 'Ameri-cans,' has made me want to stay one, be part of a tribe than can disagree yet continue to work together. We will even take more than one name, like you Ameri-cans have!" His tone was growing enthusiastic. "I have discussed this with others, and we would be proud to take the names of men you have lost, take their strength into us—without even eating them! Their names will carry on!"

Lewis couldn't help but chuckle at Kisin's earnestness, but his humor was short-lived. Harkin nodded, his expression quite serious. "You need not have two names to be an American, but I think the men we've lost might be pleased by the honor your people propose."

Leonor smiled in agreement, then pursed her lips at the troubled look returning to Lewis's face. "You can't go to the Yucatán either," she said gently. "Father's right about that."

Lewis considered that before forcing a smile. "Perhaps. It's just . . . well,

I'm sure that everyone has guessed by now that my ultimate intention was to smash Xacolotl in front of Vera Cruz. We would do it, and he knows it," he added with certainty. He blew out a breath. "But *he* was right as well, about the aftermath. Even such a victory would be costly, and there'd be little point to it in the long run."

"But it is not in you to leave a fight unfinished," Varaa guessed.

Lewis glanced at her and nodded.

Leonor rolled her eyes in frustration. "Who said anything about that? *Course* it ain't finished, but we won't ever 'leave' it either. We'll help Sira any way we can, an' as long as the Yucatán's pokin' at the Doms, we can *keep on* doin' it without 'em worryin' much about what we're up to in the north. The only real difference for you would be that you wouldn't be leadin' big armies in the field, chargin' back an' forth on Arete an' wavin' yer damn saber." Her tone darkened, turned bitter. "You keep doin' that, yer *gonna* get yer fool head shot off someday. Won't be any use to anybody then, an' you'll leave *everything* you wanted to accomplish 'unfinished.'"

Lewis reached over and grasped Leonor's hand in his. She resisted at first until she saw his genuine smile and he softly said, "It seems everybody but me is right about what we should do today. Even our enemy." They rode on like that, holding hands in silence as they'd come to do from time to time, while the others looked on, waiting while his expression slowly changed to a neutral one that most who knew him recognized as supreme determination. "That's what we'll do," he said lowly. "Evacuate this land and build a new nation, a 'New United States' in the north." He glanced at Sira Periz. "While giving you all the support we can. I swear we'll never abandon your people." Raising his voice loud enough for everyone around them to hear, he spoke once again. "And we'll come back in force, one day. If it takes a hundred years, we *will* be back to scour the scourge of the Dominion away, once and for all."

And they did exactly that. War between the Dominion and what became the "New United States," or NUS, never really ended, nor did the fledgling republic's support for resistance against Dominion occupation of the Yucatán and elsewhere. The following generations saw no large-scale land battles since the enemy "south of the border" never posed a threat from that quarter, even in early days while all the displaced "Americans" occupied a pair of the northeasternmost outposts of the Dominion as General Xacolotl had suggested. Still, the army remained intact and vigilant while the first new settlement, called "De Russyville," was built near where Brownsville, Texas, would have been.

That's where Major Giles Anson finally rejoined them slightly less than two years later. He was met by a thriving community, even a small shipyard, as well as an irate wife and a toddling son. He described what had been the central Dominion as a "murdered wasteland," and it's said he remained troubled for the rest of his days by what he witnessed of the horrors that consumed it in the aftermath of the army's evacuation following the campaign for the Holy City.

Keeping an uncharacteristically low profile while passing back through after his foray to the south (making a nuisance of himself alongside Sira Periz, riding with Colonel Itzam for several months), he found Gran Lago and then Vera Cruz being reinhabited by "colonists" from the west. Those people knew nothing about any war and were merely "reclaiming important port cities after a virulent outbreak of El Vomito Rojo wiped them out. Bad luck for the previous inhabitants, but God was satisfied with their sacrifice and the sickness would never return." There was no word or sign of General Xacolotl at Vera Cruz, and the place was under the administration of a Blood Priest Patriarcha. There was also a new "order" of professional soldiers called "Blood Drinkers," who, it was rumored, ritualistically drank human blood to bind themselves directly to God's service.

Anson and his men audaciously mingled for a time and learned a great deal before deciding to search for Xacolotl in hopes of finding him and some of his men on their way north. Instead of following the Camino Militar, however, they took the path of their previous campaign in order to inspect Puebla, Texcoco, and the Holy City, and possibly the nearby cities of Guadalupe and

Chalco that shared the Great Valley of Mexico. That's where they found Xacolotl, or what was left of him.

The populations of Puebla and Texcoco had largely accompanied Lewis's retreat, but no one who stayed was spared, and both cities had been burned and the rubble leveled. It was worse in the Holy City. All that remained were the walls, still scorched and shattered by battle and fire, but even the ruins inside had been cleared away, except for the relatively undamaged temples—and approximately thirty thousand T-shaped, flame-scorched crosses.

Even after what must've been months, the stench was appalling. The entrances had been blocked so walking carrion eaters had been somewhat frustrated. And there were so many bodies that the flying sort hadn't been able to eat them all before they grew less palatable. Thousands of seared, sundried, and nibbled-on corpses still hung from the crosses or lay in crumpled heaps below them. Xacolotl himself was found, impaled, presumably where he could watch what was happening to a portion of his army. He was identified by the shredded scraps of the uniform scattered around his fragmented remains. No one would ever know exactly what happened. Perhaps he hadn't cleaned house well or quickly enough and the part of his army he'd been concerned about got the jump on the rest.

Guadalupe and Chalco hadn't been razed, but the awfulness of what they found in both quite innocent cities was just as devastating. At least the populations had apparently been comparatively humanely "sacrificed" by beheading, the corpses and heads heaped in numerous separate piles. There was no telling how many died since the scavengers had cleaned things up better, but the ornate golden cauldrons emplaced near dozens of stained stone altars to catch the blood of the murdered still remained. Giles Anson was sure they'd discovered the place where the first "Blood Drinkers" were initiated and is said to have remarked, "My God, boys. I think all our hard fightin' accomplished was to make the bastards worse."

He led his men north after that, confirming the interior had indeed been laid waste. There were multiple reasons for that, but by then the enemy was likely aware of where Cayce and his people had gone, and the primary purpose may have become to create a deep, wild buffer between the Dominion and what they came to consider "Los Diablos del Norte." The only, somewhat meager, bright spot in all this occurred after Anson's party traversed hundreds of miles of rough country—one of his men wrote a stirring account of *their adventures—and shortly before they got "home." Barely forty miles shy of the Rio Grande River, they came upon a ragged turmae of thirty-three half-starved lancers led by Senior Decurion Yuris, who'd been second-in-command to Teniente Juaris. Juaris had told him where to go if things in the army turned unpleasant. Fortunately or unfortunately, depending on how one looked at it, Yuris had been patrolling north toward Techolotla (this was near the end of Xacolotl's "siege" of Vera Cruz) when whatever happened occurred and could shed few further insights into the events that led to the murder of so much of the army. Perhaps it was enough that Xacolotl, who couldn't have overwhelmed the defenses at Vera Cruz regardless, had allowed the enemy to escape.*

In any event, with its southern border relatively secure and the Comanches they met surprisingly eager to ally with people strong enough to keep the hated Dominion away while they fought tribes of marauding Grik in what would've been Oklahoma, Kansas, and Colorado, Lewis Cayce's army necessarily dwindled in size. There was too much for his men to do, especially those more experienced in civilian pursuits, just to re-create the industrial and agricultural capabilities they'd already established more than once on this world.

Over the next few years, the roughly 180,000 "New Americans," including those the army evacuated and a growing stream of refugees smuggled out of the Yucatán, established more towns and outposts, spreading generally northeastward along the coast, but venturing north as well. (The NUS would eventually encompass what its people would once again call Texas, Louisiana, Alabama, Mississippi, and much of Florida.) Its population would also quickly double in numbers, then increase exponentially despite many losses to the countless, often entirely unknown monsters in the new land. There were other dangers too, other people on occasion, always mysterious and frequently dangerous. Colonel (by then) Buisine took a regiment of dragoons and Captain Hannibal Cox's flying battery to aid their Comanche friends against a particularly large tribe of Grik. Together, they utterly crushed it and a tradition of true cooperation was born.

A new constitution was ratified by an elected congress; the only real difference from the one it was virtually copied from was that slavery of any sort (other than labor punishment for convicted criminals) was explicitly outlawed. That was partly why no effort was made to contact the Imperials it was presumed still dwelled in the Californias. Not only did they keep women as slaves, Juaris had told them the empire had basically sold them out to the Doms. There was also the fact that they were half a continent away, of course.

Though still considered young for the job—a small way in which the constitutions differed—the hero rifleman Felix Meder was elected as the first president of the republic with the slogan, "He'll always shoot straight with you." The retired Colonel Ixtla, formerly of the 1st Ocelomeh, was vice president. Lewis Cayce and (in absentia) both Colonel Itzam and Sira Periz declined to be considered for nomination. Lewis was, to no one's surprise, the first secretary of war. He ensured that a small but strong core of professional soldiers, "regulars," would always be maintained, along with an especially robust train of flying artillery. No one doubted that without their superior artillery everyone would've been doomed. Besides, artillery remained useful for other things, like controlling the depredations of monstrous beasts. Nearly every new settlement rushed to raise its own section of artillery militia.

The NUS continued to modestly prosper as its founders eventually pursued new lives or dropped from the pages of history. Just as Reverend Harkin spread his Presbyterian version of the Christian faith, Don Hurac became a priest in the tradition of Father Orno, eventually more amused than anything that he was the rightful "Supreme Holiness" of the evil Dominion. He and Zyan, "properly" married in a somewhat bizarre Uxmal Orthodox ceremony presided over by Harkin, had three more children to replace those they'd lost. Giles and Samantha Anson had three children of their own, and Samantha went into the mercantile trade with Dr. Newlin. Though Samantha remained a prominent figure in the NUS, little is known about her Ranger husband after that. Some sources indicate he returned to the Yucatán with Sal Hernandez and Bandy Beeryman to kill Doms, but not before the first copies of his Walker Colts were made. "King" Har-Kaaska went back to the Yucatán as well, with some of his Ocelomeh and a number of Holcanos who still had family there. Kisin became an envoy to the Comanches, whom he came to deeply respect. He even occasionally interceded between them and some less ferocious tribes of Grik since he spoke a version of their language. As we have learned, nearly all "Grik" tongues share a basic similarity.

In the fall of 1859, Admiral Eric Holland—still hale at somewhat past the age of ninety, most guessed—was lost at sea when his beloved *Tiger* was wrecked in a dreadful storm near the eastern mouth of the Pass of Fire. She'd been in company with the new screw frigate *Essex* (named by him and unencumbered by anything resembling a carronade) on one of his frequent forays against Dom shipping attempting to supply enemy troops in the Yucatán. *Essex*, under Captain Sessions, performed a daring rescue and saved everyone but Holland before *Tiger* sank. Most suspected the ancient mariner rode his ship down by choice. Still, the necessarily small yet increasingly high-quality navy Eric Holland fathered was a constant annoyance to the Doms in the Caribbean and was eventually instrumental in the capture of Cuba and a number of other islands.

Varaa-Choon grew bored with peace and, missing the children no one ever knew she had (they would've been long grown by then), concocted a scheme with Captain Stanley Jenks and some of his crew to "go home" aboard *Nemesis*. Unwilling to attempt the Pass of Fire again, Jenks understood he could never return to the Empire, but was entranced by what Varaa must have revealed to him of what we now know was the "Republic of Real People" in southern Africa, not only inhabited by her strange race, but humans and others as well. Though most now believe she did eventually tell Lewis a bit more about where she came from, Jenks was not assured that, once he visited the Republic, he would be allowed to leave. There's evidence he was, however, as there are accounts that Varaa herself returned to the growing NUS more than once. But the secret of her homeland was never widely known until our own Captain Garret rediscovered it nearly a century later.

Lewis Cayce remained a soldier all his life. He did ultimately serve three terms as president, largely at the urging of Agon, who was his vice president for two. When Agon died in office at the beginning of the third, his faithful old friend Arevalo took his place and followed Lewis into the presidency. Leonor Cayce, with whom Lewis had five children, often joked to Arevalo, "Good thing I didn't shoot you better back when we met." She was known to wear those same Paterson Colt revolvers under her dress even then. When she wore a dress. After her children were grown and her husband retired from all public service but the army, the two of them often rode the length and breadth of the new country they were winning, visiting forts and the most remote military posts and settlements.

Lewis never personally engaged Dominion forces again, but ninety-seven years after he swore his people would finish the fight, the NUS and their Comanche allies joined the Grand Alliance led by Matthew Reddy consisting of the United Homes, the "American Navy Clan," the Republic of Real People, and—ironically—the Empire of the New Britain Isles. In the great war against *the Grik Empire, the League of Tripoli, and the Holy Dominion, it was the NUS that provided the bulk of the ground forces against the Doms. It may have taken almost a century, as Lewis once predicted, but they did go back, and they won decisively.*

Sadly, as of this writing, it is suspected that a spark of the Dominion yet smolders in the trackless wilds of South America. All the Grand Alliance is quite understandably war-weary, and most hope that ember, if it truly exists, will stifle there. I must confess a fear that it will flare again, at least as a fanatical tool of the confounded League, and we'll all regret not vigorously stomping those coals before they spread and erupt into a raging inferno that burns our children.

Excerpt from the afterword to Courtney Bradford's
Lands and Peoples—Destiny of the Damned, Vol. I,
Library of Alex-aandra Press, 1959

ACKNOWLEDGMENTS

As always, I must thank my great agent, Russell Galen, and my wonderful editor, Anne Sowards. They are the best. I also feel compelled, as I did for the Destroyermen series, to acknowledge the efforts of the copy editors condemned to cope with my somewhat unconventional prose, particularly all the weird speech patterns and accents—many made-up and quite a few that are unique to specific characters. I can just imagine them reading along and suddenly crying "Ack!" when they see every grammatical rule they cherish suddenly cast aside. I suspect they now simply murmur, "Oh. Damn. Dialogue. I'm just skipping over that."

Most of all, I wish to thank all the fine people out there who enjoy my yarns and inspire me to keep writing them. I love hearing from you on my author Facebook page and website. If you take the time to contact me, I *will* respond!

Finally, for those who haven't heard, I'm excited to announce that my next project will revisit a few old Destroyermen friends who've been called on to embark on an exciting, deadly adventure across unknown seas! I can't wait to share it with you. In fact, here's a short excerpt:

"Eat! Goddamn!"